The Song of Songs and the Ancient Egyptian Love Songs

The unabashedly sensual *Song of Songs* and the Egyptian love songs represent the two bodies of love poetry which have survived from the ancient Near East. In this study, Michael V. Fox offers the first comprehensive, comparative literary-philological examination of the poems—one that includes complete translations, individual commentary, discussions of literary techniques, themes, and concepts of love, as well as a new hieroglyphic transcription of the Egyptian texts. The result of this exhaustive scholarship is a fresh understanding of the *Song of Songs*, seen in its context as an ancient Near Eastern love song, and the largely neglected Egyptian lyrics, many of them interpreted here for the first time. Egyptologists, Bible scholars, and anyone interested in ancient or comparative literature will find this an invaluable resource.

Michael V. Fox is Professor of Hebrew and Semitic Studies at the University of Wisconsin–Madison and currently chairman of the department. His essays on ancient Egyptian and biblical literature have appeared in a variety of scholarly journals.

The Song of Songs and the Ancient Egyptian Love Songs

Michael V. Fox

THE UNIVERSITY OF WISCONSIN PRESS

Published by
The University of Wisconsin Press
114 North Murray Street
Madison, Wisconsin 53715

3 Henrietta Street
London WC2E 8LU, England

5 4 3 2

Printed in the United States of America

Publication of this book was made possible in part
by grants from the Andrew W. Mellon Foundation
and the Wisconsin Society for Jewish Learning, Inc.

Library of Congress Cataloging in Publication Data
Fox, Michael V., 1940–
The Song of Songs and the ancient Egyptian love songs.
Bibliography: pp. 409–426.
Includes index.
1. Bible. O. T. Song of Solomon—Criticism, interpretation, etc.
2. Love poetry, Egyptian. 3. Egyptian literature—
Relation to the Old Testament. I. Title.
BS1485.2.F69 1985 223'.9066 84-40494
ISBN 0-299-10090-1

Contents

Preface

I am indebted to the people who read and commented on the manuscript of this book or parts of it: Gilead Morahg, John Hobbins, Stanley Stein, Kelvin Friebel, Barbara Granick, Warren Dean (who copied my hieroglyphic transcription in a hand that the Egyptian scribes would have approved of), Eugene Cruz-Uribe (some of whose interpretations of the Egyptian texts are included in my commentary, indicated by the abbreviation ECU), and Lowell Ferris (many of whose felicitous renderings I have used in the translations). I thank several scholars who helped me on specific questions: Peter Shore, Klaus Baer, Edward F. Wente, Irene Grumach-Shirun, and Virginia Lee Davis, and Donald Lowle. Above all I am grateful to my wife, Jane, who edited the manuscript, influenced the analysis, and showed me that sexist language can be avoided without clumsy circumlocutions. The ability to do so is especially important when writing about works in which more than half of the chief characters are female and whose authors may well have been women (songstresses of the sort frequently depicted in Egyptian paintings and mentioned in the Bible).

I am grateful to the Graduate School of the University of Wisconsin-Madison for research and travel grants, to the University's Institute for Research in the Humanities, which gave me a semester in which to devote myself to writing, and especially to the Wisconsin Society for Jewish Learning, a group of Wisconsinites dedicated to the support and encouragement of Jewish scholarship in Wisconsin.

This book and the labor that went into writing it I dedicate to the memory of my father, Leonard W. Fox.

Madison, Wisconsin — March, 1984

Editorial Notes

Transliteration

Semiticists should note that Egyptology uses a system of transliteration different from that for Hebrew, and that some of the letters used (*i*, *ḏ*, *ṯ*) do not represent what they do in transliterations of Semitic languages; see Gardiner, *Grammar* (p. 27) for an explanation of the Egyptian system. In rendering Egyptian words, I generally use the transliteration indicated in Erman-Grapow's *Wörterbuch*.

Reference to hieroglyphic signs follows the category-item numeration in the sign list in Gardiner's *Grammar*, e.g., A 1 = seated man, N 11 = moon.

For Hebrew I use a relatively broad transliteration, not indicating vowel length but distinguishing *shewas* and compound *shewas* by raised letters. I use *y* to mark the *mater lectionis yod* after *ṣere*, though not after *ḥiriq*, because this method seems more helpful in word recognition. The so-called medial *shewa* is not indicated.

Sigla Used in Translations

( ) addition for clarity of the translation
[ ] restoration (in cases where I do not specify the Egyptian words being restored, the reconstruction should be understood as an attempt to suggest the general sense of what stood in the lacuna).
⟨ ⟩ emendation
. . . lacuna or illegible text
—— text obscure though legible

I will remove most of these encumbrances when quoting in Part Two the verses translated in Part One, leaving the brackets only when the restoration or emendation is major.

Egyptian songs are identified by number. Nos. 1–54 are love songs; nos. i-vi are texts in Appendix A.

Unless otherwise indicated, all translations are my own.

Some Terms

1. I usually refer to the lovers in the love poems as "the boy" and "the girl." These couples are commonly referred to as "man" and "woman," but this may give a somewhat misleading picture of the pair and of their relationship. While some of the Egyptian lovers may be mature, the Shulammite is clearly still in her family's domain, as most of her Egyptian counterparts seem to be (see especially nos. 10, 32, 36). In no poem is there the slightest evidence that the lovers are married, and in many they clearly are not. Until quite recently marriage usually took place in the early or middle teens. Data on the typical age of marriage in Ramesside Egypt are lacking, but an Egyptian wisdom book of the Ptolemaic period advises boys to marry at 20 (ʿOnchsheshonqy 11,7), which age is probably meant as a maximum. We can deduce from documents of the Ptolemaic period that one woman married at 14, another at 18 (Pestman, 1961:5). Müller (1899:3) calculated the marriageable age in Egypt to be about 12 for girls, 15 for boys. Data about the age of marriage in Israel are sparse. According to the chronologies in II Kings, Josiah and Amon married at 14, Jehoiakin at 16. Jewish law allows boys to marry at 13, girls at 12. *Pirqey Avot* (5:24) advises males to marry at 18. It would be reasonable to picture the girls in the love songs as between 13 and 16—approximately the age of Juliet—and the boys as not much older. While adolescence must have been much shorter than it is today, the young people portrayed in these songs are for the most part still very much adolescents, emotionally as well as chronologically—almost, but not quite, "men" and "women." In Hebrew, they would be called *ʿelem* and *ʿalmah*. In some poems, to be sure, the designations "man" and "woman" do seem more appropriate—for example, nos. 38–40—but on the whole the impression given is of youthfulness, and I have not tried to draw finer age distinctions.

2. I use the term "to make love" (and "lovemaking") not as a euphemism for sexual intercourse, as it is now commonly used, but in the older sense, which includes a broad range of activities expressing sexual love, from caresses to coitus. The term is vague about the details of the activities, as indeed are most of the poems. Nor is "sexual love" a euphemism for coitus; it refers to a love between the sexes in which one of the bonds is sexual desire.

3. I refer to the national background of the Song of Songs as "Israelite." Since I think the book was composed in postexilic Jerusalem, I might more precisely call it Judean or Jewish. But because I am not certain of this dating and do not want to prejudice the issue, and because I often need a more general designation, I usually choose the broader term "Israelite," which I understand as referring to the Jews after the Babylonian exile no less than to their ancestors.

4. "Brother" and "sister" in the Egyptian songs, and "sister" in the Song

of Songs, are used by the lovers as terms of endearment and do not imply a sibling relationship.

5. I follow traditional usage in using "the Shulammite" as a convenient designation for the girl in the Song of Songs, although I think it likely that *haššulammit* is a common noun meaning "the perfect one" rather than a personal name or a gentilic derived from a place name; see commentary to 7:1.

6. I use the term "stich" (which has sometimes been applied to the couplet and sometimes to its two constituents) to refer to the "members" or "lines" of a verse; "A" and "B" of a couplet are both stichs. Two and three stichs bound in parallelism or syntactic subordination constitute couplets and triplets. The format of my translations gives a separate line to each stich and indicates couplets and triplets by levels of indentation.

7. The Song of Songs is also known as Canticles and the Song.

Abbreviations

AASOR	Annual of the American Schools of Oriental Research
AcOr	*Acta orientalia*
AEO	Gardiner, *Ancient Egyptian Onomastica*
AHW	W. von Soden, *Akkadisches Handwörterbuch*
AJSL	*American Journal of Semitic Languages and Literature*
AOS	American Oriental Series
B	Papyrus Chester Beatty I
BASOR	*Bulletin of the American Schools of Oriental Research*
BASP	*Bulletin of the American Society of Papyrologists*
BDB	Brown, Driver, and Briggs, *Hebrew and English Lexicon of the Old Testament*
BHK	*Biblia hebraica*, 3rd ed. (ed. Kittel)
BHS	*Biblia hebraica stuttgartensia*
BIE	*Bulletin de l'Institut d'Égypte*
BIFAO	*Bulletin de l'Institut Français d'Archéologie Orientale*
BJRL	*Bulletin of the John Rylands Library*
BKAT	Biblischer Kommentar: Altes Testament
BO	*Bibliotheca orientalis*
BZAW	Beihefte zur *Zeitschrift für die alttestamentliche Wissenschaft*
C	Cairo Love Songs
CAD	*Chicago Assyrian Dictionary*
CBQ	*Catholic Biblical Quarterly*
CdE	*Chronique d'Égypte*
CDME	Faulkner, *A Concise Dictionary of Middle Egyptian*
CED	Černý, *Coptic Etymological Dictionary*
DLE	Lesko, *A Dictionary of Late Egyptian*
DM	Deir el-Medineh (ostraca)

ECU	Eugene Cruz-Uribe, private communications
EEF	Egypt Exploration Fund
ET	*Expository Times*
FIFAO	*Fouilles de l'Institut Français d'Archéologie Orientale*
GKC	*Gesenius' Hebrew Grammar* (ed. Kautzsch-Cowley)
Gram.	Gardiner, *Egyptian Grammar*
H	Papyrus Harris 500
HAL	Baumgartner, *Hebräisches und aramäisches Lexikon*
HAT	Handbuch zum Alten Testament
HO	Černý-Gardiner, *Hieratic Ostraca*
HPBM	*Hieratic Papyri in the British Museum* (ed. Budge)
HTR	*Harvard Theological Review*
HUCA	*Hebrew Union College Annual*
IFAO	*L'Institut Français d'Archéologie Orientale*
Int	*Interpretation*
JAOS	*Journal of the American Oriental Society*
JARCE	*Journal of the American Research Center in Egypt*
JBL	*Journal of Biblical Literature*
JCS	*Journal of Cuneiform Studies*
JEA	*Journal of Egyptian Archaeology*
JNES	*Journal of Near Eastern Studies*
JSOT	*Journal for the Study of the Old Testament*
JSS	*Journal of Semitic Studies*
JTS	*Journal of Theological Studies*
KAR	*Keilschrifttexte aus Assur religiösen Inhalts*
KAT	Kommentar zum Alten Testament
KHWB	Westendorf, *Koptisches Handwörterbuch*
KRI	Kitchen's Ramesside Inscriptions
LÄ	*Lexikon der Ägyptologie*
LE	Late Egyptian
LEG	Černý-Groll, *A Late Egyptian Grammar*
LEM	*Late-Egyptian Miscellanies* (text: Gardiner; transl. and com.: Caminos; unless otherwise specified, LEM refers to text)
LES	Gardiner, *Late-Egyptian Stories*
LFHS	Caminos, *Literary Fragments in the Hieratic Script*
LRL	*Late Ramesside Letters* (text: Černý; transl. and com.: Wente; unless otherwise specified, LRL refers to text)
LTNK	Gardiner, *Literary Texts of the New Kingdom*
MÄS	Münchner ägyptologische Studien
MDAIK	*Mitteilungen des deutschen archäologischen Instituts, Abteilung Kairo*
ME	Middle Egyptian

MGWJ	*Monatsschrift für Geschichte und Wissenschaft des Judentums*
MIFAO	Mémoires publiés par les membres de l'Institut français d'archéologie orientale du Caire
NÄG	Erman, *Neuägyptische Grammatik*
NJPS	The new Jewish Publication Society translation of the Bible
OMRO	*Oudheidkundige Mededelingen uit het Rijksmuseum van Oudheden te Leiden*
PEQ	*Palestine Exploration Quarterly*
PN	Personal name
Pyr.	Pyramid texts
RA	*Reallexikon der Assyriologie*
RAD	Gardiner, *Ramesside Administrative Documents*
RB	*Revue biblique*
RSV	Revised Standard Version
RT	*Recueil de travaux*
SAOC	Studies in Ancient Oriental Civilization
SPAW	Sitzungsberichte der preussischen Akademie der Wissenschaften (phil.-hist. Klasse)
T	Papyrus Turin 1966
TQ	*Theologische Quartalschrift*
TT	Theban tomb (by number)
Urk.	*Urkunden des ägyptischen Altertums*, 1903 ff.
UT	C. H. Gordon, *Ugaritic Textbook*
VT	*Vetus Testamentum*
WAD	Von Deines-Grapow, *Wörterbuch der ägyptischen Drogennamen*
Wb.	Erman-Grapow, *Wörterbuch der ägyptischen Sprache*
WMT	Westendorf-von Deines, *Wörterbuch der medizinischen Texte*
ZÄS	*Zeitschrift für ägyptische Sprache und Altertumskunde*
ZAW	*Zeitschrift für die alttestamentliche Wissenschaft*

Introduction

Intimately, across millennia, the ancient Egyptian love songs and the Song of Songs speak to us, saying things we can understand well about matters we care about deeply. They sing about pleasures, joys, desires, drives, confusions, pains, and hopes that we ourselves have known or can easily imagine. We enjoy vicariously the pleasures of the young lovers and smile at their frustrations with the knowing sympathy of shared experience. We can read the ancient love songs with the special pleasure of recognition that comes from finding our own most private feelings expressed in the poetry of far-off times and places. Evanescent emotions are made immortal in art.

Yet though poets can talk to us across eras and cultures about love, we must appreciate the variety no less than the commonality of human experience. Cultures, and for that matter individuals, differ in their perceptions of love as well as in their modes of expression.

While we cannot know that the views the ancient Egyptian and Israelite songs express are *the* Egyptian view of love or *the* Israelite view of love, they certainly do show *some* Egyptian and *some* Israelite views of love, and therein lies their importance for cultural history. For by transmitting, inscribing, and preserving these love songs, the ancient Egyptians and Israelites showed that they valued these views. These songs were transmitted and valued even though they do not speak of great issues of myth and religion, of questions of state or events of national history, of birth or death, of sin or salvation. They tell rather of individual feelings and private concerns, showing us how some sensitive observers with the gift of poetic expression saw sexual love and the behavior of adolescent lovers, matters that may not seem to bear on national history and religion but that were surely of profound importance in the lives of individuals in the cultures that gave rise to these love poems.

Like Jane Austen's novels, the Egyptian love songs and the Song of Songs are delicate vignettes, painted on a "little bit (two inches wide) of ivory" with a fine brush. The songs are about young lovers—no more than that, but that is a lot. The love songs unapologetically limit their scope to the human heart, the hearts of anonymous, young, "unimportant" figures. But precisely because the vista of these songs never goes beyond individual experience, they can reach deep into that experience to explore and reveal that most precious and peculiar complex of emotions: sexual love.

My goal in this book is to lead to a richer understanding of the literary treatment of love in Egypt and Israel: what the Egyptian love songs and the Song of Songs say about love and lovers and how they say it. I begin by translating and interpreting the various poems (Part One), for literary comparison and investigation of a genre should proceed from interpretation of individual works. The interpretation of these difficult poems involves the interpreter in many philological problems that must be addressed, even if many of the difficulties cannot be resolved.

In interpreting the Egyptian songs I am largely on my own, for there is as yet no comprehensive commentary on them, but only the brief notes in Müller's *Liebespoesie der Alten Ägypter* (1899), the notes to White's translation (1978), and comments scattered thoughout the scholarly literature.[1] In interpreting the Song of Songs, on the other hand, I am aided (and burdened) by the mass of commentary that has built up around the Song for two thousand years. Inasmuch as the Song is complex, beautiful, and difficult, it always repays renewed investigation. I am able to offer new insights because I have earlier commentary to start from and because studying the Egyptian songs gives rise to new ideas about what to look for in ancient Near Eastern love poetry.[2]

In interpreting these love songs I strive to look at each song in its entirety. I argue that several of what are commonly regarded as collections of songs among the Egyptian texts are really unities, single songs compounded of several stanzas, and further that the Song of Songs too, though often considered a loose collection of short songs, is in fact an artistic unity. Appreciation and understanding of these ancient love songs, particularly the Egyptian ones, have been hampered by an atomistic reading that fails to relate the parts of the poems to one another and thus quite misses the shape and sense of the whole.

1. The most valuable are Gardiner's notes to his translation of P. Chester Beatty I (1931: 31–38), Iversen's comments on the "Nakhtsobek Songs" in P. Beatty I (1979), and Derchain's remarks on the Cairo Love Songs and parts of P. Harris 500 (1975).

2. Landy's *Paradoxes of Paradise* (1983) appeared too late for me to take account of his intriguing conclusions and interpretations. Many of his arguments strengthen some of the conclusions I have arrived at, in particular with regard to the unity of the Song. His insights often heighten one's sensitivity to the literary texture of the Song. But although I can follow his analysis in many details, I find his main conclusions farfetched, a considerable overreading of the Song's symbolism.

A holistic approach alone can lead to an adequate understanding of the artistry and meaning of these poems.

In Part Two I inquire into the literary treatment of love in ancient Egypt and Israel, discussing the following issues:

1. Language, date, and historical setting of authorship, and possible channels of literary transmission from Egypt to Israel.
2. Composition and structure: what are the boundaries of the songs and what are the thematic and structural relations among the units that they comprise?
3. Function and setting: why and where were the love songs sung?
4. Mode of presentation: whose are the voices that speak within the poems, and how do the speakers communicate with other persons in their world?
5. Themes: what do the poems talk about, and how does the Song of Songs differ from the Egyptian songs in its handling of those themes it has in common with them?
6. Love and lovers: Here I draw together and build on the conclusions of the earlier discussion for an overview of the types of love and lovers shown in the love songs. How do the poets perceive the nature and behavior of lovers and what ideas of love do they present? How do they think lovers interact with society and with each other, what do they perceive to be the emotions love comprehends, and what effect do they believe love has on the way lovers see the world? The literary treatment of lovers' perceptions, implying a particular understanding of the relation between love and the world, leads finally to what we might call the metaphysics of love.

At the end of the book are appendices with some other Egyptian texts of relevance to the discussion, a concordance to the Egyptian texts, and a hieroglyphic transcription of them.

The broader literary discussions in Part Two grow out of the exegesis of the individual poems in Part One and are often dependent on arguments made there, but the book need not be read in sequence. I suggest that you first read the Egyptian love songs, referring to the notes at this stage only insofar as necessary for a general understanding of the poems. I offer my interpretation in a single literary comment after the notes to each poem. Become familiar with the Egyptian poems, and, above all, enjoy them. Then look over my interpretation of the Song of Songs. You can get an idea of my approach to the Song by reading the introductory remarks to each unit. Then proceed to Part Two, referring back to the commentaries as necessary. Chapter 8 can also be read alone, for although it builds on conclusions reached earlier, it should be comprehensible on its own.

In this book, literary comparison is not an end in itself, but rather a means to achieving greater understanding of the love poetry of two ancient cultures. I discuss the Song and the Egyptian love songs together because they throw light on each other. In particular, the purposes, techniques, and ideas of the Song are illuminated through comparison with its Egyptian predecessors, though sometimes the later work will cast light backward onto the earlier poetry.

Reading always requires models: we understand a text or an oral discourse by comparing it with other texts or discourses. When we come to a text for the first time, we ask ourselves what *kind* of text we are reading. We answer with a broad, "heuristic" genre concept, which we progressively narrow and refine as our understanding increases.[3] An audience always has expectations about the type of discourse it is about to hear. Writers build on these expectations about the type of characters speaking, their setting, what they are supposed to be doing, what attitude we are supposed to take toward their actions, and so on. Genre-built expectations make possible the delight and insight of surprise, for there can be surprise only when there are expectations to be violated. The Egyptian love songs give us an idea of what an ancient Israelite audience would have expected in a love song, thus helping fill out the generic context lacking in extant Hebrew literature.

We must use the Egyptian songs for this purpose with caution, of course, for they are separated from the Song of Songs by time, language, and culture. But the Song and the Egyptian love poetry are appropriately read together because their similarities, which I will try to establish in the course of this study, run deep. Some of these we may summarize at the outset.

The Song of Songs and the Egyptian love songs explore the same subject—sexual love between human beings. They are, moreover, the only secular love songs to have reached us from the ancient Near East.[4] They are alike in the use of dramatic presentation; that is to say, they show *personae*, whose words alone create the world of the poem (see chapter 6). The center of their

3. On the meaning of genre and the role of genre-expectations in understanding a text see in particular Hirsch, Jr., *Validity in Interpretation* (1967), chap. 3. Genres, like sets, may be defined broadly or narrowly. For my purposes it is adequate to define the love-poetry genre as those poems that express or speak about sexual love. Within this broad genre there are numerous narrower genres that may be variously defined, such as the Praise Song or the Wish Song (see chapter 7). I will call the narrower genres "types."

4. I argue for their secularity in chapter 5. There are Mesopotamian texts that border on secular love poetry, as well as a fragmentary text that may be part of a secular love poem; see pp. 247f. Psalm 45 can hardly be called a love song. It lauds the righteous glory and martial prowess of the king, then officiously admonishes the Tyrian bride to forget her homeland and obey her new husband and master, enticing her to do so by promising that the king will take pleasure in her beauty and that she will receive gifts and her sons be given high offices. Ps. 45 shows us just how different wedding songs, at least royal wedding songs, could be from the sort of love song studied in this book.

interest is always the characters' feelings, personalities, and experiences rather than those of the poet. The personae they create are young lovers, not yet married. The eroticism in both the Egyptian and the Israelite songs is lush but delicate. Egyptian and Israelite poets alike seem to accept premarital sex with no hesitation. They are fascinated by love and delight in its intensity and variety. Both create worlds that are bright and happy, with few pains and shadows; the only pain recognized is that which comes from not having one's beloved present, and even that grief is never portrayed too gravely. The lovers are all intent on the present experience, giving no thought to the past and little to the future. The songs do not touch upon the great issues of sexuality and marriage that could so easily color any talk of love. Procreation, family ties, future well-being, social stability, and national prosperity—these poems ignore them all. In addition, the Song and the Egyptian love songs have several particular themes in common, though they treat them differently (chapter 7). There are also many minor motifs and usages common to the Egyptian songs and Canticles, which I will point out in the commentary on the latter.

It is not, however, the discovery of similarities alone that justifies literary comparison. Differences are no less important. Often the value of literary comparison is to offer a contrast, showing us where the work at hand diverges from similar works. In fact, as Richmond has shown in *The School of Love* (a study of Western love poetry traditions that has influenced and aided my understanding of the poetry I am examining), the significant character of related poems is defined neither by their similarities nor by their differences, but by the differences between them at their points of maximum resemblance (1964:280). In other words, the often-remarked similarity of the Praise Songs in Canticles to their Egyptian counterparts (chapter 7) is what makes the difference in their use of imagery especially significant for understanding the Song's view of love (chapter 8). Discovery of sources and parallels is, therefore, not the end of comparative criticism but an aid to deeper interpretation, for we can best understand the individuality of a text by discovering where it diverges from the works it most resembles. This is so even when we compare texts where there can be no question of influence of the one on the other.

There is additional value to comparison when we are reading texts connected genetically—that is to say, where there is an unbroken chain of influence linking two texts—the earlier work being heard or read by later authors who incorporated its ideas, attitudes, themes, or forms into their own work, which in its turn influenced later authors, and so on until we arrive at the second work being compared. When there is such a genetic link we can examine not only differences and similarities but historical development as well. In such cases we see poets building on their predecessors' perceptions and modes of expression, often surpassing them in breadth of vision, depth of understanding, and power of expression. Evolution of this sort has characterized the long and continuous history of Western love poetry, as Richmond (1964) has shown. In Western love poetry we can trace how poets continually took themes, ideas, and literary conventions from their predecessors and used them with greater psychological nuancing and increased self-awareness. We can show how in time a new understanding of love developed, one not negating earlier views but going beyond them, as, for example, the Stuart poets came to recognize that the modes and conditions of perception largely govern what is seen. When ample materials for literary history are available, one can follow developments spanning centuries. It can be shown, for example, that the similarities between the way Catullus treats the theme of the fleeing doe and the way the Stuart poets handle it are not due to spontaneous generation, nor are the differences due to a sudden and erratic jump, but rather the degree and type of divergence are the result of a continuous accumulation and reshaping of poetic resources (Richmond, 1964:251–59). This is the type of evolution that I believe connects Canticles to the Egyptian songs.

In my opinion the similarities justify a hypothesis of at least indirect dependence, that is to say, the supposition that the Song is a late offshoot of an ancient and continuous literary tradition, one whose roots we find, in part at least, in the Egyptian love poetry. I do not assume that the author of the Song necessarily knew Egyptian or borrowed directly from Egyptian originals (though that is by no means impossible). It is more likely that Egyptian love poetry was sung in Palestine, where it became incorporated into the local literature and developed there in new ways. In chapter 3 ("Channels of Literary Transmission") I discuss when and how this could have happened.

At the same time we must recognize that a genetic link between the Egyptian love songs and the Song of Songs cannot be proved. It is almost impossible to prove literary dependence in cases where we lack positive evidence of the author's acquaintance with the earlier works or with other works that were themselves shaped under their influence, and such evidence is lacking here. We can only argue for the likelihood of dependence by pointing out the possible channels of transmission and by observing the similarities between the works, as I will do throughout this book. We cannot add up the similarities and subtract the differences to arrive at a positive or negative answer to the question of dependence. Therefore the decision for or against the hypothesis of dependence is finally a subjective—and uncertain—one. If this book provides a basis on which to make that decision, it will prove of value, even if the decision is negative. I believe that most of my observations and interpretations can stand independently of the hypothesis of dependence. If you are not persuaded that there is a genetic connection, you can use the parallels for their heuristic value.

While fundamental similarities and probable genetic linkage make the Egyptian love songs and the Song of Songs suitable for comparison, there is a certain unwieldiness in this comparison because we are comparing one poem with a group of poems. The main corrective for the imbalance is to keep it in mind. The comparison is possible because Egyptian love poetry is sufficiently uniform to allow generalizations that apply to most of the poems and adequately characterize the extant poetic tradition as a whole. Isolated exceptions do not invalidate such generalizations, though these exceptions must be noted and evaluated. (Statements I make about *all* Egyptian love songs have to be understood, of course, as applying to the ones we have. Future discoveries might invalidate some generalizations.)

A lopsided comparison of this sort requires us also to remain aware both of the individuality of the various Egyptian songs and of the accidental uniqueness of the Song of Songs. The Egyptian songs do not speak with a single voice in all matters. At the least they present different types of lovers, not a single stereotyped couple. Nor should we assume that Israelite love poets spoke with one voice. Canticles is a representative of Israelite love poetry, the only love song the culture preserved and raised to a special status of holiness. But since we do not know to what degree it was typical of Israelite love songs, we would not be justified in generalizing from it to the Israelite view of love. Our conclusions are for this song alone.[5]

Another comparative approach one could take would be to look at the Song in the light of other biblical passages that speak of relations between the sexes, in particular the Garden of Eden story, Genesis 2–3. Trible (1978) has done just that, both carefully and sensitively. Trible interprets the Song of Songs as telling of the *redemption* of the love story that went awry in Eden. In the Song, man and woman are again in mutuality, harmony, and equality in a garden. While I am not persuaded by many of the parallels she draws between the two texts nor by certain elements of her reading of the Garden of Eden story, I find that the comparative route I have chosen has led to some similar conclusions about the concept of love and sexuality in the Song. In the private paradise of the lovers in the Song, as in Eden, there is no male dominance, no female subordination, no stereotyping of either sex (Trible, 1978:161). In the Song, pre-Fall harmony and oneness are relived in a private paradise. While the Song, in my view, does not respond to the Garden of Eden story or deliberately build on its themes, a comparison of the two can highlight the attitudes underlying both texts. I do not, however, think that it is *redemption* we see in the Song, but rather a love unconscious of any Fall, with never a hint that sexuality might be under a curse that would require redemption. I do not follow this path of comparison further, but leave it to the reader to weigh the results the two perspectives lead to.

In general, literary comparisons may give us ideas and add the weight

5. Other love songs too were certainly known in Israel. Ezek 33:32 refers to them and Isa 5:1ff. implies their existence, see "Love Poetry as Entertainment" in chapter 5.

of analogy to particular interpretations, but they cannot prove the validity of those interpretations. Even when the two works or groups of works being compared are demonstrably linked by a chain of influence, literary comparisons do not prove particular interpretations, because a certain literary usage may fulfill a function in the later work that is entirely different from its function in the earlier one. Rather, the comparison of structurally or thematically related works (whether or not the observed similarities are due to the influence of one work on the other) offers us *models*—of attitudes, concepts, forms of expression, literary devices, and so on—which help us fine-tune our reading of the texts. That is why I have chosen to study the Egyptian love songs and the Song of Songs together.

For reasons I will explain in chapter 5, I do not see a significant connection or a fundamental resemblance between the Song and the Mesopotamian Sacred Marriage liturgies. Nevertheless, my discussion of the Song does not require rejecting the hypothesis that the Sacred Marriage Songs—and others—left a mark on love poetry in Israel.[6] While I do not claim that Egyptian poetry alone constitutes the background of the Song, I do claim that of all the extant works, Egyptian love poetry is the closest in character to the Song and thus the most valuable for its interpretation. As evidence I offer the results of this study.

While my goal is twofold—richer interpretations of both the Egyptian love songs and the Song of Songs—my emphasis will generally be on the latter, partly because earlier works usually illuminate later ones more than the other way around, and partly because of a critical judgment that in artistry and insight the Song is a more significant object for interpretation.

6. On the other hand, I find Rabin's hypothesis of Tamil influence on the Song (1975) most unpersuasive. Rabin surmises that the Song was written by someone who became acquainted with Indian love poetry during a visit to the Indus Valley during First Temple times, perhaps as early as the time of Solomon, when there were extensive mercantile contacts between Judah and India. But it is not necessary to turn to India to find parallels to the qualities in the Song that Rabin considers to be derived from Tamil love poetry. These are:

(1) The woman as chief speaker. By Rabin's reckoning, 56 verses in the Song are spoken by the woman, 36 by the man (omitting debatable verses). Among the 42 units of Egyptian love poetry (see p. 6 for a definition of "unit") in which either the female or the male can be identified as the speaker, the female speaks in 28 while the male speaks in 26.

(2) A woman's yearning for an absent or unobtainable beloved. This is less frequent in the Song than Rabin thinks, but in any case there are strong parallels in Egyptian poetry—e.g., nos. 12, 15, 32, 34, 36, 38–40 (note especially the latter).

(3) Aesthetic descriptions of nature as symbols of lovers' emotions. These are indeed more prominent in the Song than in the Egyptian love poetry, but they are found in the latter too; see nos. 3, 5, 17, 18, 20D, 21E, 31, 54.

Furthermore, as Brenner (1983) has shown, the mention of spices originating in East Asia is not (contrary to Rabin) evidence for Indian influence, even if some of the spices were imported from there. The names of two of the spices (*nerd* and *karkom*) were probably borrowed through the medium of Persian.

The Egyptian songs are delightful. I have read them for several years with unflagging pleasure. I feel I have come to know intimately the young people depicted in them, for the poems are delicate portraits, drawn with simple strokes that yet suggest a world of detail. But the Song far surpasses them—in the sensuousness of its language, the richness of its imagery, and the ardor of the love it depicts. The Song, in its perception of love as communion and as a way of seeing the world, goes beyond the Egyptian vision of love. Yet it can only enhance our appreciation of the achievement of the Egyptian love poets to see what the genre they founded developed into. Nor do we detract from the creative genius of the Song's author in recognizing that she or he was heir to the resources of a long tradition, shaped for centuries by unknown singers of lost songs, until it had evolved from its auspicious Egyptian beginnings into the masterwork of love songs, *šir hašširim*, the Sublime Song.

PART ONE

Translation and Commentary

CHAPTER I

The Egyptian Love Songs

Introduction

The Egyptian love songs present special difficulties to the translator. Literary Late Egyptian has not received comprehensive analysis. This dialect is quite distinct from non-literary LE, which was the spoken language of the Rameside period and was used in letters, oracles, business records, economic and legal documents, and the like. The grammar of non-literary LE received comprehensive treatment in Černý-Groll, LEG (1978). The verb system of literary LE (surveyed by Groll, 1975–76) combines elements from ME (regarded as the classical literary language in the New Kingdom), forms and usages from non-literary LE, and forms found only in the literary dialect. In the present state of knowledge, the tenses of verbs are often uncertain. Some ambiguity is due to the verb system's being an amalgam of forms from different sources. This uncertainty sometimes makes it difficult to determine the precise course of events related in a song (thus especially in "The Stroll," nos. 31–37).

In addition to linguistic difficulties, many textual problems face the interpreter of the love songs, including orthographic errors, blurred and damaged words, and lacunae in the manuscripts. At times I have attempted to restore the gaps, but all such restorations must be regarded with caution. A case in point is the first edition of the Cairo Love Songs (nos. 20A–20G, 21A–21G), where Spiegelberg (1897) restored 41 signs. These were all sensible restorations, but only five were verified by fragments later to appear. Still, restorations are part of the interpreter's task, and I often take my chances. Restorations given only in English are attempts to indicate the general sense required by the context rather than to specify the exact words lost.

The love songs characteristically use rare and exotic words and phrases whose exact meaning is uncertain, sometimes unknown. We are, however, aided in our guesswork by the presence of *determinatives* (= dets.), signs at the end of words that indicate the class of thing to which the words belong—for example, 𓀀 = man, 𓆰 = plants, 𓈗 = water and other liquids, 𓀁 = speech, emotion, or eating. Thus we may know that a certain word is the name of a plant without knowing just which plant is meant.

Translation often requires some flexibility in rendering tenses. For example, context occasionally gives the present-tense *tw.i ḥr stp* a hypothetical or future connotation (see no. 21A, n. a; no. 47, n. h). It is often awkward to render the initial prospective *stp.f*, though basically an optative, as "may I choose." Since a wish may come close to resolution, the initial prospective *stp.f* often indicates asseveration (as shown by its use in oaths: e.g., P. Turin 1966, 1,15), rather than merely hope. Inasmuch as the English future tense can express determination as well as fact, I have often rendered the initial prospective *stp.f* "I'll choose," etc. (examples in no. 20C).

The main problem in the translation and explication of the love songs lies in the nature of the songs themselves. Love songs abound in allusions and ambiguities, particularly in erotic matters. A fondness for ambiguities is characteristic of Egyptian literature in general, but it is most prominent in the love songs because of their erotic content and their basic purpose—entertainment. The audience would have derived pleasure from deciphering hints and allusions, which are often a sort of riddle. This allusiveness necessarily makes the interpreter's task more difficult and the results less certain, for it is impossible to know whether a supposed hidden meaning the interpreter thinks to have revealed is the product of the poet's heated imagination or of the interpreter's.

It is possible that all or some of the songs were accompanied by mimetic dance (see pp. 256f.). Such a visual presentation would have greatly aided the audience in grasping the events implied in the songs and would thus have allowed the songs to be even more allusive and enigmatic. The task of the reader is then all the more difficult in the absence of these visual aids.

The following commentary is directed to two groups of readers: readers who know Egyptian and have a background in Egyptology, and readers (in particular Bible scholars) who do not. Some remarks will thus inevitably seem too elementary for the first group, while others will be of no interest to the second. A similar problem will arise in the commentary to Canticles.

A general literary comment follows the last note to each poem, but at times literary matters, being inextricable from philological questions, are treated in the notes. I have tried to formulate such comments in a way comprehensible to the non-Egyptologist. My philological comments are intended only to justify and explain the translations, so for the most part I do not discuss matters (such as details of orthography) that do not bear directly on translation.

NUMERATION OF THE EGYPTIAN SONGS

Rather than multiply systems of numeration, I have used the reference system set out by Hermann (1959:4–8). This will facilitate reference to Hermann's study and to other works that use this numeration. I have had, however, to make some changes in this system. My numeration does not include songs that I do not consider love songs. (Texts related to the love songs in various ways are in Appendix A marked by lower-case roman numerals, i-vi.) I have also had to change the numeration of the Cairo Love Songs because the new edition of this text (Posener, 1972) includes seven units not in the edition to which Hermann had access, and furthermore the stanza division in the old edition is incorrect. The Cairo Love Songs are now numbered 20A–20G and 21A–21G (for Hermann's 20–27), so that there are now no poems numbered 22–27. I have also added nos. 19A and 19B after 19 to indicate two songs of which fragments remain at the end of P. Harris 500.[1]

Hermann's Numeration	My Numeration
1–19, 28–53	same
lacking	19A, 19B
20–27	20A–20G, 21A–21G
54	App. A: iii
55	App. A: v
lacking	App. A: i, ii, iv, vi; 54

In some cases I have marked poetic units within stanzas by capital letters in parentheses—for example, no. 8(A)—for ease of reference. This subdivision marks units of content and is not dependent on any metrical or structural theory, although quantitative symmetries will often be made apparent by the subdivisions. In particular I have noticed that stichs frequently form quatrains, and that songs often conclude with a couplet. Also noteworthy is the appearance of isolated stichs at the beginning of songs to set the scene, see for example nos. 3, 7, 12, 13, 14. I have not, however, found any principle that can demarcate strophes without forcing presuppositions on the text.

Hermann considers the 55 units he lists to be separate songs, and this idea has been generally, perhaps universally, accepted by scholars. But as I try to show in the course of the commentary and in chapter 4, many of these units are only stanzas of larger songs. For example, "songs" 31–37 in Hermann's

1. A 6th dynasty text from the mastaba of Mereruka at Saqqara is identified by Drioton (1961:140) as a love song and numbered 56 by Hermann. This text is, however, only the title of a dance and a brief description of a dancer's skill (see Wreszinski, 1914:III, 29; 2nd register). The text is illegible in places and very obscure, but it is certainly not a love song, nor does it have any particular connection with the love songs.

listing are not seven songs of one cycle but seven stanzas of a single song ("The Stroll"). In other cases, as in the first and second groups in P. Harris 500, the units that Hermann lists are indeed independent songs. I therefore refer to the units in this numeration neutrally, using the abbreviation "no.," both when the units are independent songs and when they are stanzas in a longer song. "Unit" when used with regard to the Egyptian songs refers to the sections marked off by the pause-mark (the arm). "Group" refers to a cluster of these units whether it is a collection of songs or a single song.

STICH DIVISION

In some texts stichs or verses are marked off by red dots (the format of my translation reflects their placement). These were inserted after the manuscript was written in order to facilitate oral reading (Erman, 1925:9f.). Since they are used in prose as well as in poetry, they are not, strictly speaking, "verse-points." Rather they mark places at which the scribe felt the reader should pause. There is considerable flexibility in their use (just as there has been in the use of the comma in English over the last few centuries), so that it is hard to deduce from the manuscripts clear rules for their placement. They are usually at the end of a clause or sentence. Generally they mark off *stichs*, the compositional "lines" that combine in parallelism or that complement each other as main clause and subordinate (circumstantial or purpose) clauses. When the verse-points are not present, stich division is often uncertain. In general, as Lichtheim (1972:107) points out, stichs (she calls them "metrical lines") consist of complete sentences or complete dependent clauses (circumstantial, participial, or relative). Sometimes, however, the verse-points bracket two short dependent clauses in one "verse" or stich.

Basically I agree with Foster's description of the "thought-couplet" as the elementary unit in Egyptian poetry (1977), and I have used his approach in the arrangement of my translation. The triplet is, however, more frequent in this poetry than in the work Foster examines (the ME Instruction of Ptahhotep), and his rules are of course not entirely applicable to LE grammar.

TITLES

The red headings found on some groups are not usually distinctive enough to distinguish different songs, and so I give the major songs titles suggestive of their content.

UNTRANSLATED SONGS

In addition to the songs translated here, there are a number of ostraca that have been identified as love songs by their editors (the identification is sometimes quite uncertain) but that are too fragmentary to translate even for the purpose of identifying motifs:

From Posener, 1977–80 (FIFAO XX, iii): DM 1635 + O. Turin 6625; DM 1646, 1647, 1650, 1651, 1652, 1653.

From Černý-Gardiner, HO I: O. Nash 12 (HO I, 40,6); O. Leipzig 6 (HO I, 7,4).

Source I: P. Harris 500

This 19th dynasty papyrus (BM 10060: Budge, HPBM, Ser. II, pls. XLI–XLVI) is said to have been discovered in a casket in the Ramesseum at Thebes. This MS is a sort of literary anthology. The verso contains two stories, "The Doomed Prince" (transl. Lichtheim, 1976:200–203) and "The Capture of Joppa" (Wente, 1972:81–84). The writing is generally clear, but the papyrus is damaged in many places. This manuscript makes rather promiscuous use of the man sign (A 1), both as a substitute for the woman sign (B 1) and as a space-filler. I disregard the man sign or treat it as a woman sign as need be without further comment.

The love songs on the recto are divided into units by the pause-mark (the arm). There are three groups of units and two fragmentary songs, all but the first group marked by titles written in red. The beginning of the papyrus is lost, but the first group probably had a title written in red like the second two groups and the two short songs at the end (nos. 19A, 19B). Groups A (nos. 1–8) and B (nos. 9–16) are collections of independent songs, eight in each. Group C (nos. 17–19) is a single song of three stanzas. The separation of the first sixteen units into two groups (by the heading before no. 9) apparently has nothing to do with content, because the units in both groups appear themselves to be independent songs with few thematic connections among them. This separation is best explained on the hypothesis that each group was formed and transmitted independently before copying. After no. 16 comes "The song which is from the tomb of King Antef" (App. A, no. ii), which is not a love song but a *carpe diem* originating in the traditions of mortuary poetry.

GROUP A: NOS. 1–8 (RECTO 1,1–4,1)

1. (Girl)

(A) . . . [a] Am I not here with [you]?[b]
Where have you set your heart (upon going)?[c]
Should [you] not embrace [me]?[d]
Has my deed come back [upon me]?[e]
. . . the amusement.
If you seek to caress my thighs[f]
. . .

(B) Is it because you have thought of eating that you would go forth?
Is it because you are a slave to your belly?[g]
Is it because you [care about] clothes?[h]
I have a bedsheet![i]
Is it because you are hungry that you would leave?[j] . . .
(Then) take my breasts
that their gift[k] may flow forth to you.

(C) Better a day in the embrace [of] my [brother][l] . . .[m]
than a thousand myriads while———.

a. The beginnings of all lines in col. 1 (nos. 1–3) are missing.

b. Emend to *ḥnᶜ.k*.

c. Lit., "Whither do you set your heart?"

d. *Bn ḥpt.[k]*: the negation of the initial *stp.f* (as in 3,4: *bn grw.i*), combining ME and LE forms.

e. Reading *sp.i spr* (1,2) [*r.i*], see CDME, p. 223, for the phrase. The first, third, and fourth stichs have no formal sign of the interrogative.

f. . . . *msdt.i m pȝy.i mn[ty]*, with the dual *mnty* treated as masc. sg. (*Gram.* §511, 1a). Lit., "the upper parts of my legs, namely, my thighs."

g. Lit., "a man of his belly."

h. Reading *in[-iw ḥr.k] ḥr ḥbsw*.

i. *Ifd*, "linen cloth," with bed det. (only here?), showing that the reference is to a bedsheet.

j. Here, as often in this MS, the suffix *-k* is written *-kwi*, under the influence of the writing of the stative.

k. Lit., "their property, content" (*ẖt.sn*). Omit *t* after *ẖt.sn*.

l. "Brother" and "sister" are frequent terms of affection and intimacy in the Egyptian love songs. The usage probably arose because siblings are the closest blood relations; only the closeness of that relationship is implied by the epithets. The usage does not derive from the supposed custom of sibling marriage (see Hermann, 1959: 75–78).

m. About two words missing.

The girl chides her lover for his eagerness to leave her bed "the morning after."

2. *(Girl)*

(A) Your love is mixed in my body,
like . . . ,
[like honey(?)] mixed with water,
like mandragoras[a] in which gum is mixed,
like the blending of dough with . . .[b].

(B) Hasten[c] to see your sister,
like a horse (dashing) [onto a battle]field,
like a . . .
. . . its plants,

(C) while heaven gives her[d] love,
like the coming of a soldier(?),[e]
like . . .

a. The *rrmt*, a kind of fruit, is a recurring motif in the love songs. The fruit clearly had erotic significance. Keimer (1951:351) identifies the *rrmt* with the aphrodisiac mandragora, and I have followed that rendering, although the identification is not certain. In fig. 3, the two women in the center are holding mandragoras.

b. We find mention in the medical texts of all these ingredients, except for the mixture of gum resin with the mandragora, as multipurpose medicines. Love "mixed" in the body of the girl affects her like a strong drug. The three parallel similes do not have the same syntactic structure.

c. The first two visible signs in H 1,8—*sḫ* (no det.)—do not seem to be the end of a word. Rather, *sḫ3s* is a writing of *sḥs* (cf. H 5,12) contaminated by the synonymous *3s*.

d. Sc. "your sister's," i.e., "my (love)." Also possible: "its," sc. "heaven's."

e. Müller (1899:46) reads *ʿḥ3*, translating "(. . . wie das Einherziehen) eines Kriegsheeres." *W3w n* ("coming of"?) is difficult. The translation is a guess based on context.

The girl expresses her desire by metaphors of inseparable, pleasant mixtures; compare no. 20B.

3. (Boy)

(A) The vegetation(?)[a] of the marsh(?)[b] is bewildering.[c]
[The mouth of] my sister is a[d] lotus,
her breasts[e] are[fd] mandragoras,
[her] arms are [branches(?)],
[her] ——— are ——— ,[g]
her head is the trap of "love-wood,"[h]
and I—the goose!

(B) The cord(?)[i] is my . . . ,
[her ha]ir[j] is the bait[k]
in the trap[l] to ensnare (me)(?).[m]

a. *Smw* (or *smwy*) + the determinative for emotions and speech (A 2). *Smw* with the plant determinative refers to plants in general, while *smyt* (according to Wb. IV, 119–20) is a specific plant used as medicine. "Plants" best fits the present context, since the parts of the girl's body are being compared to specific plants. The written form here may be due to confusion with a homophone in dictation, though it may also be an orthographic pun on *smy*, "be happy"; according to Wb. IV, 121, however, the latter word is not attested before the Ptolemaic period. A word *sm* with the hand-to-mouth determinative (A 2) is attested in ME (Wb. IV, 121, 1), but the meanings suggested (CDME: "help, succour, deed, event, affair, pastime") do not fit this context.

b. *Ḥny*: probably the same word as *ḥnt*, "swampy lake" (CDME, p. 171 = *ḥnw*,

AEO I, 7*: "lake," "marshy area"). *Ḥny* may be a pun on *ḥnwt.i*, "my mistress" (ECU).

c. *Tḫḫ*: emend to *tḫtḫ*, "to disorder," "confuse"; see Wb. V, 328, 8, although the determinatives here are not among those indicated in the Wb. For *tḫtḫ* see Caminos, LEM, p. 173, with references.

d. *Wᶜwt*, a writing of *wᶜ*.

e. *Mndt*, a writing of the dual; see Stricker, 1937, and cf. the writing of *g3b* in the next stich.

f. *N*, for the *m* of predication, as often.

g. *Mtn*, "inscribe," +*wg3*(?), "feeble," "woe," +*hnt*(?). I cannot make sense of these words.

h. *Mry*-wood, a pun on *mrwt*, "love." On the unidentified *mry*-"wood" see Caminos, LEM, p. 122, with references.

i. *Krṯ* (H 2,1) (if correct; the *k* is very uncertain): a semiticism of uncertain meaning (Helck, 1971:523, no. 262; see Caminos, LEM, p. 216).

j. *Šnw* = "hair" and "net."

k. Lit., "worms."

l. On *pḫ3* see Caminos, LEM, p. 184. For pictures of traps and a discussion of traps and fowling in ancient Egypt, see Grdseloff, 1938, and Schäfer, 1918/19.

m. The last word is obscure, but the determinative associates it with trapping.

The girl in this conceit is a marsh whose charms constitute a delightful tangle of plants. The youth draws closer, disoriented by their profusion, until like a bird he snatches at the bait—her hair—and is trapped. The theme of the "love trap" appears in no. 10 as well.

4. (Girl)

(A) My heart is not yet done[a] with your lovemaking,[b]
my (little) wolf cub![c]
Your liquor is (your) lovemaking.[d]
(B) I ⟨will not⟩[e] abandon it
until blows drive (me) away[f]
to spend my days in the marshes,
(C) (until blows banish me)
to the land of Syria with sticks and rods,
to the land of Nubia with palms,
to the highlands with switches,
to the lowlands[g] with cudgels.
I will not listen[h] to their advice
to abandon the one I desire.

a. *Bw nᶜ ib.i n* [=*m*]: lit., "my heart is not yet lenient, mild"; that is, she is not yet willing to ease up on him and call it quits. *Bw stp.f* is the literary LE equivalent of non-literary *bw iri.t.f stp.f*, which expresses "not yet" (LEG §20.8.2).

b. *P3y.k mr.t(i)* (= *mrt*, infinitive, masc.); for the spelling of the infinitive cf.

f3y.t(i) in H 3,4, *rḫ.t(i)* in H 2,11, *mrw.ti* in O. Gardiner 304, no. 5, *sfḫ.t(i)* in H 4,8, etc. The infinitive of *mri*, found here, probably refers to the sex act rather than to the emotion of love. Compare *iri.s mr(t)* in O. Cairo 25227, vso. 4–5 (Daressy, 1901), a phrase synonymous with *nk*, "fornicate."

c. *Wnš* can mean "wolf" or "jackal." The *wnš* represents a lusty lover in no. 49 too. If *wnš* here means "jackal," we may compare the little foxes or jackals (*šuᶜalim*) in Cant 2:15. In Theocritus, *Odes* I, 48–50, and V, 112, foxes or jackals (*alōpekes*) represent lascivious young men and women, as a scholium to Ode V explains (Wendel, 1914:179).

d. *Dd*, determined by the phallus sign; a semiticism (corresponding to Hebrew *dodim*) meaning sexual lovemaking. "Your liquor [lit., "beer"] is love"; i.e., the intoxicant you offer is lovemaking, you ply me with the liquor of love. *P3y.k tḫ*, being more defined than *dd*, is the subject. *Dd* is an emphasized predicate, see NÄG §455.

e. Emend to *b⟨n⟩ [i]w.i r ḫ3ᶜ.f* (H 2,2–3).

f. *Št* = *šd*, "take away, remove," cf. *ᶜ3 n št*, Wb. IV, 550, 12–13. On the spelling see n. b.

g. *Nḫbw* (with the city det. taken from *Nḫb*, El Kab): a type of terrain, tentatively identified by Gardiner as "fresh land" (P. Wilbour II, 28f., 178ff., 198).

h. *Nn iw(.i) r sḏm*, cf. H 5,7: a literary construction (NÄG §503), alongside LE *bn iw.i r stp*.

The poet uses five words, most of them rare, for different types of rods, as if deliberately demonstrating verbal virtuosity. The massing of synonyms here emphasizes the girl's determination not to abandon her lover. *Šbd* and *ᶜwn* ("sticks and rods") are products of Syria, while palm staves are associated with Nubia—and Nubian policemen (Derchain, 1975:79). The exact meaning of most of the terms for rods used here is unknown, but perhaps they are all appropriate to the places they are associated with in the poem.

Derchain (1975:79f.) interprets this poem as the girl's rejection of her parents' plan to marry her off to a "little wolf," supposedly an insulting epithet implying excessive lasciviousness, this being the quality that displeases the girl. It seems quite clear, however, that the girl is saying the exact opposite—that she will not yield to pressure to leave her "little wolf," a term of endearment, as the use of "my" in itself suggests. However lustful this youth may be, he has not yet satisfied the young lady's desires.

5. (Boy)

(A) I am sailing north with the current(?),[a]
    to the oar-strokes(?)[b] of the captain,[c]
my bundle[d] of reeds on my shoulder:
    I'm headed for Ankh-Towy.[e]
I'll say to Ptah, the Lord of Truth:[f]
    "Give me (my) sister tonight!"[g]

(B) The river—it is wine,
its reeds are Ptah,
the leaves of its lotus-buds are Sekhmet,
its lotus-buds are Yadit,
its lotus-blossoms are Nefertem,[h]
. . . joy.
The earth has grown light[i] through her[j] beauty.
(C) Memphis is a jar of mandragoras
set before the Gracious One.[k]

a. *Mẖnmt*, with water dets. (thus transcribe, rather than *ẖnwt* with Müller): a type of water; probably to be emended to the better-attested *ẖnmt* (Wb. III, 383, 2). Derchain (1975:80) explains *ẖnwt* as "coche d'eau," supplying a boat det. (P 1), but that reading does not fit the traces.

b. *Sẖ3* + man-with-stick det. (A 24), otherwise unknown (Wb. IV, 268,1).

c. *Sḥn*, "commander" (Wb. IV, 218, 1). Derchain (1975:81) explains it as "contract of hire"; cf. Demotic *sḥn*, "lease," LE *sḥnw*, "commission" (Wb. IV, 217).

d. *Mrw*, "bundle," another play on *mrwt*, "love." The bundle of reeds may be a pallet to sleep on during the long voyage (Derchain, 1975:81).

e. The necropolis of Memphis, a major cult center of Ptah (LÄ I, 266f.).

f. "Lord of Truth" is Ptah's epithet as judge of the dead; see Altenmüller, 1975:70.

g. Derchain (1975:80, 82) translates "donne-moi une fille cette nuit!" and interprets the prayer as cynical: the little wolf, rejected by a local girl (no. 4), has taken hire as a sailor on a ferry and gone off to the big city to find someone to sate his lust. This interpretation is, however, very unlikely, for "sister" is used only of one's own beloved, never of "girl" in general. The first-person suffix, lacking here, is often omitted. "Une fille," on the other hand, where the indefiniteness was to be emphasized, would certainly require *wᶜ*.

h. Ptah is the chief god of Memphis, Sekhmet is the goddess of war and disease, and Nefertem is their son, the lotus god who gives life through his fragrance and light when he opens in the morning. *I3dt* ("Dew"?) is an otherwise unknown goddess, but the Amduat records a deity called *i(3)dt-t3*, "Dew of the Earth" (Hornung, 1963: no. 411).

i. Lit., "it is through her beauty that the earth has grown light," a ME emphatic construction occurring in literary LE; see Groll, 1975–76:244f.

j. A fem. noun must be supplied as an antecedent for *nfr.s*, probably "my sister" or "Hathor," although the *p* in the lacuna in 2,8, if correct, makes restoration difficult. The traces do not seem compatible with a name of a god.

k. That is, Ptah. On *nfr-ḥr* see Spiegelberg, 1917:115.

This song tells of a youth's voyage to Ankh-Towy, presumably for a festival, where he will meet his beloved. He sails downstream, and as he thinks of her, he perceives the divinity in nature.

The last image views the city of Memphis not in terms of its physical appearance but rather from the perspective of its god Ptah. The city is like a bowl of love-fruit (see no. 2, n. a) set before him. Thus the reader senses the affection the god feels for his city and his pleasure in it. The god's sensual pleasure in his city is reminiscent of the affection for Thebes expressed by a letter writer who says, "May Amon bring you back prosperous that you may fill your embrace with Thebes" (LRL 44/9). Love for one's city is the subject of a short essay in P. Anastasi IV, 4, 11–5, 5 (LEM, p. 39).

The lotus, which is especially charged with divinity in the boy's eyes, is a rich symbol in Egyptian religion. It represents creation and regeneration and is the womb from which the sun is born daily. When the lotus opens in the morning, the world is filled with light (LÄ III, 1091–96; see below, no. 20C, n. a).

6. (Boy)

I will lie down inside,
    and then I will feign illness.[a]
Then my neighbors will enter to see,
    and then (my) sister[b] will come with them.[c]
She'll put the doctors to shame[d]
    (for she) will understand[e] my illness.

a. *K3 mr(.i) n ʿḏ3*: lit., "then I will be sick in deceit."

b. *T3 snt*: lit., "the sister," as often. Since the literal translation is rather awkward, I will translate this phrase "my sister" throughout when the boy is speaking, "your sister" when he is being addressed.

c. The series of sentences starting with "then" or "so" (*k3*) shows the boy carefully working out the steps in his scheme.

d. *Bḥnr* = *bḥl*, a loanword, apparently cognate to Hebrew BḤL, "be disgusted," although a less harsh nuance is required here.

e. *Ḫr iw.s rḫ*: since *ḫr* + dependent *iw* introduces a concessive or adversative sentence ("although"), this *iw* must be the *iw* of the third future (LEG 9.2.5). The writing of the infinitive here (*rḫ.ti*) is influenced by the common writing of the infinitive with pronominal suffixes (see no. 4, n. b).

The boy plans a stratagem to get the girl he desires to visit him: he will pretend he is ill, and she will be among the visitors. Yet perhaps the illness he feigns is more real than he realizes, for the last line speaks of his illness as a real one that cannot be diagnosed by the physicians, but only by his beloved. He is suffering from love-sickness. Compare the motif of love-sickness in nos. 12 and 37 and in Cant 2:5, 5:8. *Mr*, "sickness," may be a pun on *mrwt*, "love."

7. (Boy)

(A) The mansion[a] of (my) sister:
Her entry is in the middle of her house,
her double-doors are open,
her latch-bolt(?)[b] drawn back,
and (my) sister incensed!
(B) If only I were appointed doorkeeper,
I'd get her angry at me!
Then I'd hear her voice when she was incensed—
(as) a child in fear of her!

a. *Bḫn* means "mansion" or "castle." The word implies that the girl belongs to the nobility, at least in the eyes of the lovestruck youth.

b. *Ḳf3w* (H 2,12); not in Wb. Perhaps emend to *ḳr3t* = *ḳ3rt* (Müller, 1899:19). *Pri* ("drawn back"?), however, is awkward as the predicate of "bolt."

In this humorous song the youth envies the young lady's doorkeeper, who left the door open and is now the object of her anger. Better to bear her anger than to be ignored! Fecht (1963:76) explains "double-doors" as an allusion to the vagina. The repetition of the possessive "her" with the words "house," "bolt," "double-doors," and especially "entry" (*r*, lit., "opening") suggests that the poem bears a hidden meaning that tells just what the boy wants to do when he gets inside the house. The hidden meaning, it should be stressed, in no way obscures the interesting little portrait of a frustrated lover standing outside a girl's literal house.

8. (Girl)

(A) I am sailing northward
on the [Canal] of [the Ru]ler.
I've entered that of Pre.[a]
My heart's set on going
⟨to⟩[b] the preparation of the booths
at the entrance of the Ity Canal.[c]
(B) I'll set out to hurry,[d]
and shall not pause,
since my heart has thought of Pre.[e]
Then I will see my brother's entry—
he's heading[f] toward the Houses of ———.[g]
(C) I am standing with you
at the entrance of the Ity Canal,
for you've [brought] my heart to Heliopolis.[h]

(D) (Now) I've withdrawn with you to the trees of the Houses
of ——— (?),
that I might gather the fronds[i] of the Houses of ——— (?),
that I might take (them) for[j] my fan.[k]
I'll see what it(?) does![l]
(E) I am headed to the "Love Garden,"[m]
my bosom full of persea (branches),[n]
my hair laden with balm.
I am a [noblewoman],
I am the Mistress of the Two Lands,[o]
when I am [with you].

a. Pre is the sun god. The Canal of Pre is the eastern branch of the Nile, irrigating the region of Heliopolis (Derchain, 1975:83; AEO II, 155*). The movement from the present-continuous *tw.i m ḫd* to the present-perfect *ʿḳ.k(wi)* shows that the speaker is relating events as they happen.

b. Reading ⟨*r*⟩ *t3 ḥr n3 n imw*. *Ḥr* is used of setting up booths or tents in Urk. IV, 325.

c. The Ity Canal (AEO II, 174*) connected Heliopolis with the Nile. Derchain (1975:83f.) says that the occasion described here is the opening of the canal at high-water, a time of public celebrations.

d. Cf. *iw.s ḥr f3y.s r sḫsḫ* in P. d'Orbiney 10,6 (LES 20/6).

e. *Sḫ3 ḥ3ty.i*, a circumstantial *stp.f* indicating the relative past tense, a form characteristic of literary LE; see Groll, 1975–76:240f.

f. Or, "I am heading"; text unclear (H 3,6).

g. Some structure in the environs of the sanctuary. Neither the reading of the name nor its meaning is clear.

h. That is to say, it was love for you that drew me to Heliopolis. Iwn-Re (AEO II, 144*, no. 400) = Heliopolis.

i. Lit., "trees" (*šnw*).

j. *M* for *n* (NÄG §599); but *m*, "as," is possible too.

k. A number of different renderings of the verses in section (D) are possible, depending on whether the *stp.f* forms are taken as circumstantial with relative past meaning, initial prospective, non-initial prospective, or emphatic.

l. The antecedent of *irt.f* must be "fan." But what will it do that is of special interest?

m. The lovers go to a *dd* (fem.), which in P. Anastasi III ro. 2,5 and 3,7 (LEM, pp. 22f.) refers to a type of garden (it is written with the tree and house determinatives). Elsewhere *dd* designates sexual love and can mean "copulate" (Caminos, LEM, p. 425; see no. 4, n. d). So *dd* here may mean "love garden." Even if the words are not to be associated etymologically, *dd* here is probably a pun on *dd* "love-making."

n. Or fruit. The fruit of the persea comes to maturity at the time of the Nile's rise and is naturally associated with the fecundity the waters bring. The girl's carrying a bosomful of persea is a promise of her own fertility (Derchain, 1975:85). P. Anastasi

III, 3,3–4 (LEM 23/3–4) refers to youths at the festival of Khoiakh whose arms are "bent down" with "foliage" (*dbyt*), "greenery" (*w3ḏt*), and flax (*mḥ*). P. Sallier IV, verso 4,3 (LEM, 91/9f.) speaks of "noble ladies," also apparently at a festival in Memphis, whose arms are full of the same vegetation.

o. That is, queen of Egypt.

This song, like no. 5, describes a lover's journey to a cult center, here seen from a girl's perspective. The two songs do not, however, tell of the same couple, for the speakers are headed for different places. The events of this song progress as the girl speaks. In (A) she is thinking of the meeting with her lover as she sails to Heliopolis. As she speaks she turns from the Canal of the Ruler into the Canal of Pre, then into the Ity Canal. In (B) she has landed and is now heading to the meeting place. In (C) she is standing with her lover, and in (D) the two of them move into a wooded area where the Houses of ——— stand, where she picks branches. In (E) she goes to the "love garden," carrying the branches she has gathered, and expresses her feelings of exaltation in her lover's presence.

GROUP B: NOS. 9–16 (RECTO 4,1–6,2)

The Beginning of the Entertainment Song[a]

a. The heading calls this group a "song" in the singular, although its units are clearly separate songs. The use of singular and plural in headings to various love song groups is not decisive in determining whether the group is a song or a collection of songs. The heading preceding the "Antef Song" designates its contents as *ḥs* ("song"), adding the plural strokes even though this song is clearly a unity (plural strokes can also be used for abstract nouns). The heading to "The Stroll" (nos. 31–37) refers to the contents as *rw* (plural) *nw* (plural), sc. "utterances of," perhaps with reference to the plurality of stanzas. The singular *ḥs* ("song") is used in the heading to "The Flower Song" (nos. 17–19), which, I believe, is indeed a single song, but the "Nakhtsobek Songs" (nos. 41–47), which most clearly do not constitute a single poem, are labeled *ṯs* ("saying") in the singular.

9. (Girl)

(A) The beauty of your sister,
  the beloved of your heart,
    when she has come back from the meadow![a]

(B) My brother, my beloved,
  my heart longs for your love,
    all that you created (?)![b]

To you I say,
  See what happened:

(C) I came prepared for (bird) trapping,
my snare in my (one) hand,
my cage[c] in the other,
together with my ṃat(?).[d]
(D) All the birds of (the land) of Punt[e]—
they have descended on Egypt,
anointed with myrrh.
The first to come
takes my bait.[f]
(E) His fragrance is brought from Punt;
his claws are full of balm.[g]
My heart desires you.
Let us release it[h] together.
(F) I am with you, I alone,
to let you hear the sound of my call[i]
for my lovely myrrh-anointed one.
You are here with me,
as I set the snare.[j]
(G) Going to the field is pleasant (indeed)
for him who loves it.[k]

a. The words *nfrw n snt.k mryt ib.k ii.ti m š3w* (section (A) in the translation) have been taken by most translators to be part of the heading, even though they are not written in red as is the title proper ("The Beginning of the Entertainment Song") and are not appropriate to the title. They are rather a one-membral sentence that sets the scene (as in the opening of no. 7). Section (A) could be the poet's introduction, spoken to the boy, but it is more likely that the girl is speaking of herself here in the third person than that the poet addresses the youth in this verse alone.

b. H 4,2 reads *tw*(?) *ḳm3.n.k nb*, a crux. Delete *tw* as an extension of *mrwt.k*. *Ḳm3*, "create," may be used of producing conditions and emotions (Wb. V, 35, 15–19). I take "all that you created" as modifying "your love."

c. Emend to *ṯb*, "bird crate" (Wb. V, 360, 12). *Db* (Wb. V, 434, 9) is probably a phantom word.

d. Müller (1899) transcribes this obscure hieratic group (H 4,3) as *s(3)ḳ(3)yḳ(3)*, an unknown word with what seems to be an inappropriate determinative (irrigated land, N 23). The above translation (a guess) identifies *sḳ3ḳ3* with *s3ḳ* (Wb. IV, 26, 14–16), with reduplication, meaning perhaps a woven mat (ECU).

e. Punt, a place in the East Sudan bordering on Ethiopia, was noted for its spices and beauties. It acquired semilegendary qualities for the Egyptians, as shown by the record of Hatshepsut's expedition at Deir el-Bahri. See Herzog, 1968, and Kitchen, 1971.

f. Lit., "worm"; cf. no. 3.

g. Or, "his claws are caught by the balm": *mḥ* "full" and *mḥ* "caught" are homophones, but the written form favors "full." Again, we may have a pun: the bird's claws may be viewed as either filled with *or* held by balm because he has taken the bait. The image is taken from a technique of bird trapping: the branches of a tree were smeared with pitch and the birds that landed on them were trapped. *This* bird, however, is trapped by balm (*ḳmi*: lit., "gum," "resin"). The motif of the "love trap" is alluded to here rather transparently. Egyptian women would smear their hair with balms and perfumes (cf. no. 8, end), and, according to no. 3, the girl's "bait" lures the youth to her "net," i.e., her hair.

h. The antecedent of "it" (*st*, fem.) is *t3 wʿwy*, "the worm," i.e., the bait (fem.), rather than "bird" (masc.).

i. *Wʿ.kwi (r) dit*: for a similar construction see no. 36 (B c4,2): *tw.i wʿ.kwi r nhm*, lit., "I was alone to rejoice." *(R) dit sḏm.k ḫrw.i (ḥr) sgb*: *sgb* is a loud cry, not necessarily a lament. The girl is alluding to the fowling practice of imitating bird cries to lure the bird to the trap (Grdseloff, 1938:54; Jéquier, 1922:168f.). After the lovers detach the worm that has lured the bird (see n. h), the girl will call to the bird in its own language.

j. The determinative of *pḫ3* (see note to H 4,6 in App. C) apparently represents a trap; see Schäfer, 1918/19:184 and figs. 89, 90, which show traps in this shape. Note that only now does the girl set the (literal) bird trap.

k. The last clause is obscure: *n p3 nty (ḥr) mrrt.f* (for *mrt.f*), "of/for/to him who loves it (masc.)/him" (on the construction see LEG 53.9). It is not clear what the antecedent of "(loves) it (masc.)/him" is, but no emendation that adds clarity presents itself (the antecedent is not, in any case, "field," which is feminine). I take the antecedent to be *p3 šm*, "the going" (sc. to the field), although that makes the sentence tautologous. Perhaps the reference is intentionally vague: "it" = bird trapping? lovemaking?

This song describes a pleasant day spent in bird trapping. The bird that is trapped is exotic and fragrant, an adumbration of the quality of that day. A figurative meaning soon presents itself: the trapped bird is a boy, caught in the "love trap": among all the birds (= youths), one—the most fragrant—lands, takes the girl's bait, and is caught. We are cued in to the figurative sense in a number of ways. First of all, the birds are fantastic—anointed with myrrh. Then, immediately after mentioning the bird that separates itself from the flock, the girl says, "My heart desires you," suggesting that the bird and the boy are one. This bird is clearly not just a bird; he is her "lovely myrrh-anointed one." But the identification of bird with boy is not carried through as a conceit, for the maiden speaks of the bird as distinct from her lover when inviting him to let the bird go. There seems to be an intentional blurring of the edges of the metaphor: a figure is set up, but the audience is not allowed to "solve" the riddle and rest easy. We are not allowed to say finally that the bird *is* the boy and only that. It is a bird that at the same time represents the boy. Compare the blurring of the boundary between figurative and literal meaning in the use of the garden image in no. 18. In the present song, the sentence "You are here with me as I set the snare" implies that although the girl in this song has caught a bird, she has not yet set the (actual) snare. The same paradox caps off no. 10 and points the reader toward the figurative meaning of this bird trap.

10. (Girl)

(A) The voice of the goose cries out,
as he's trapped by the bait.[a]
Your love restrains me,
so that I can't release it.[b]

(B) I'll take my nets,[c]
but what shall I say to Mother,
to whom I go every day
laden down with birds?

(C) I set no trap today—
your love captured ⟨me⟩.[d]

a. Lit., "his [sc. the goose's] worm," i.e., the worm that traps him; cf. no. 9, nn. f and h.

b. *Bw rḫ(.i) sfḫ.ti st*: there is an ambiguity here, perhaps deliberate. "It" (fem.) may refer to the bait/worm, which is feminine, like the direct object of "release" ("goose" is masc.), or it may refer to "your love." The first meaning fits into the literal interpretation of the song, while the second meaning conforms to the figurative interpretation. The end of the song shows that (in the figurative meaning) the girl is indeed caught by his love and cannot release herself. *Sfḫ.ti*: *.ti* is a writing of the infinitival ending; see no. 4, n. b.

c. *Šnw* is written with a superfluous *iniw*.

d. Transpose *w* and man-with-stick, reading *iṯi wi*, a circumstantial *stp.f*, here functioning as a motive clause; lit., "since your love [= "my love for you"] captured ⟨me⟩." A girl uses almost the same words in no. 32 in explaining her agitation: *iṯi wi mrwt.f*, "love of him has captured me" (B c2,2). Similarly in no. 36 (B c4,1) a girl declares: *mrwt.f ḥr iṯt ib n ḫnd nb ḥr w3t*, "Love of him captures the heart of all who stride upon the way." *Iṯi* also means "take," "ravish" (sexually), as in Gauthier, 1931:140.

This song parallels the previous one and also no. 3. In no. 3 the youth said that he is the goose that snatches at the bait in the "net," meaning the hair (*šnw*) of the girl he loves.

This song presents a riddle. At the end of the song we learn that the girl did not set her trap today, but at the start we are told that the goose was trapped in a net. How so? To solve a riddle one must look for levels of meaning beyond the obvious, and indeed this song may be understood in two ways.

The literal level describes a simple episode and presents a pleasant and gentle picture of a girl so confused by love that she cannot carry out her usual tasks. She tells this to her lover as a way of expressing her love. There is some unclarity about her actions. Apparently she would be expected as a rule to remove the worm, in this way releasing the bird from the trap so that she could take her catch home, leaving the trap behind but carrying the nets.

At the same time the event represents the couple's falling in love. The end of the song tells us to reread the beginning. If she did not set a trap today, how could she have caught a goose? Answer: the goose is the boy, ensnared in the same way as the girl—by the love trap. Overwhelmed by love, she is unable to release the "bird"—or herself, for she too is caught in the love trap. So she will take her nets (*šnw*) and go home, but not with the usual catch of birds.

11. (Girl)

(A) The goose soars and alights:
while the ordinary birds[a] circle,
he has disturbed[b] the garden.[c]

(B) But I . . .
I am excited by (?)[d] your love[e] alone.[f]
My heart is in balance with your heart.[g]
May I never be far from your beauty!

a. *3pdw ꜥš3*: see Caminos, LEM, p. 130 (P. Anastasi I, 1b, 11) and p. 513. The "ordinary birds" are the other boys.

b. *T3ḥ.n.f*, a ME emphatic form, with "while . . . circle" as the emphasized adverbial adjunct. The meaning of the word is uncertain. It is probably the etymon of Coptic *tôh* (CED 203/2), "to disturb." This bird lands in the garden in a flurry of wings.

c. *Šnw* = "garden" (with the house det., as here), "hair," and "net"; see no. 3, n. j and no. 10, n. c.

d. If the restoration *msbb* (H 4,10) is correct (*ms* is fairly clear, and Müller apparently saw traces of a *b*), it may mean "rejoice in," "turn toward" (in affection), or the like. On the other hand, the traces at the beginning of H 4,11 do not quite conform with the usual form of the hand-to-mouth sign, the determinative required for emotion. *Msbb* does not elsewhere govern *ẖr*, so far as I can determine. Its apparent use with regard to disarray of hair (Faulkner, 1936:138) suggests that the verb means something like "be excited," "confused." This line may be explaining in what sense the "goose" has disturbed the "garden."

e. On the word "love": "my love" here refers to the beloved youth. The word *mrwt*, "love," has several uses in the love songs. It is generally used of the emotion love. At times it is used in a concrete sense to denote a beloved person, meaning "beloved"; i.e., "your love" = you, my beloved, "the love of my sister" = my beloved sister, etc. Two places where the concrete meaning is the most likely are: "I've drawn near you to see your love [= "you"]" (no. 17) and "I would see her love [= "her"] each and every day" (no. 21C, where *mrwt* is determined by the woman sign, which favors the concrete meaning); see further no. 20D, first line. In no. 34 the sentence at the start of the stanza, "when I think of your love," is reformulated at the end of the stanza, "whenever you [sc. my heart] think of him," showing that "love" can interchange with the pronoun. Frequently it is difficult to decide if the word is being used in an abstract sense (love) or in a concrete one (beloved person). Compare Cant 7:7.

"Your love" can also mean "my love for you" and so on, see no. 13, n. c. At still other times it seems that the word alludes to sexual relations, a meaning demonstrated most clearly in the Ramesside pornographic papyrus, in which a woman demands of an ithyphallic man: "Come behind me with your love; your penis belongs to me" (*m-di.i*) (Omlin, 1973:67), and the picture leaves no doubt as to the meaning of "come behind me." It is also possible that "love" there refers to the phallus. All these various meanings of "love" should be kept in mind while reading the Egyptian songs, for word-play allows more than one sense to be applicable in a single occurrence. For this reason I do not usually resolve the ambiguity, but translate "your love," etc., even when I interpret the phrase to mean primarily "my love for you."

f. On this use of *wᶜ.kwi* see NÄG §345.

g. That is, we feel the same way (*mḫ3* = "balance" and "resemble"); see nos. 17, 20A.

This poem is a variation on the central motif of no. 9, the lone bird leaving the flock and landing; compare no. 3. The girl in this poem sits alone and meditates on love. The image of the goose soaring, swooping, and alighting in a flutter embodies the excitement of the girl's emotions. The goose landing in a garden (= net, hair, and perhaps the girl herself) represents the boy falling in love with the girl.

12. (Girl)

(A) I have departed [from my brother].
[Now when I think of] your love,
my heart stands still within me.

(B) When I behold sw[eet] cakes,
[they seem like] salt.[a]
Pomegranate wine,[b] (once) sweet in my mouth—
it is (now) like the gall of birds.
The scent of your nose[c] alone
is what revives my heart.

(C) I have obtained forever and ever
what Amon has granted me.[d]

a. The space would allow a restoration such as *st mi ptr* (or *nw*), lit., "it is like the seeing of."

b. *Šdḥ p3 nḏm*: On *šdḥ*, a drink of uncertain identity, see Caminos, LEM, p. 157, LÄ II, 586. Lit., "pomegranate(?) wine—that which is sweet."

c. Thus lit. Compare "the scent of your nose" in Cant 7:9. The nose kiss, in which the couple rub noses and smell each other's face, was a common gesture of affection in ancient Egypt. In fact, the word for "kiss" was written with the nose det. from earliest times. See further Meissner, 1934.

d. The sense of the last sentence is: I have now attained what the god Amon has determined to be my lot, namely, your love. *Gm*, lit., "find," can indicate attainment or possession; see NÄG §313 Anm. for examples.

This song, like nos. 34 and 37, describes the "illness" caused by the loved one's absence: the girl's heart stands still, paralyzed, unable to function properly. Wine and cakes have become distasteful. Only the scent of her lover's nose can revive her ailing heart (*sꜥnḫ*, "revive," also means "nourish").

13. (Girl)

(A) The (most) beautiful thing has come to pass![a]
My heart [desires] . . .
your property (?)
as the mistress of your house,
while your arm rests on my arm,[b]
for my[c] love has surrounded you.

(B) I say to my heart within ⟨me⟩[d] in prayer:[e]
["Give me][f] my prince tonight,
(or) I am like one who (lies) in her grave!"[g]

(C) For are you not health and life (itself)?
The approach [of your face
will give (me) j]oy[h] for your health,
(for) my heart seeks you.

a. *P3 nfr ḫpr*: Simpson (1972:304) translates similarly. *P3 nfr* is implicitly superlative: *the* beautiful thing.

b. *Ḳ3bt.i* (with the arm det. and the flesh det.): *ḳ3bt* means "breast," but the arm determinative shows that here the word is either an aural error for *g3b.i*, "my arm" (*g* and *ḳ* begin to coalesce in Ramesside Egyptian, see LEG 7), or a deliberate pun whose second meaning is "your hand rests on my breast."

c. Lit., "your love." Occasionally the possessive pronoun of *mrwt* is an "objective genitive"; that is, "your love" = my love for you, "his love" = my love for him; e.g.: no. 2 (H 1,6), no. 10 (H 4,7,9), no. 32 (B c2,1), no. 36 (B c4,1), and possibly B c3,8.

d. Text has "within you"—assimilation of pronoun to "your love" and "you" in the preceding verse. For other cases of assimilation of pronouns see Gardiner, 1931:34, n. 1, and LES, p. 16a.

e. Lit., "in the prayers."

f. *Imi n.i*, "give me," would fit the small space available for restoration. Compare no. 5, "I'll say to Ptah, the Lord of Truth: give me (*imi n.i*) my sister tonight."

g. Lit., "my grave." A reed (*i*) has been lost before *is*, "grave."
h. Restoring *n ḥr.k di.f ršwt* (or the like).

The girl declares the joy love gives her. This is one of the few Egyptian love songs (see also no. 17) in which love is seen not only as sensual erotic attraction, but also as a partnership, a shared life in which the girl will be the "mistress" of her husband's house.

14. (Girl)

(A) The voice of the dove speaks. It says:
"Day has dawned—
  when are you going (home)?"[a]
(B) Stop it, bird!
  You're teasing (?)[b] me.
I found my brother in his bedroom,
  and my heart was exceedingly joyful.
(C) We say (to each other):[c]
  "I will never[d] be far away.
(My) hand will be with (your) hand,[e]
  as I stroll about,
I with (you),
  in every pleasant place."
(D) He regards ⟨me⟩ as the best of the beautiful,[f]
  and has not wounded my heart.

a. Lit., "what is your way?," taking the man det. (A 1, used in this text for the female det.) as the 2nd fem. sg. suffix (*w3.ṯ*). The dove reminds the girl that dawn has come and she must get up and go home.

b. *Ḏyḏy*, possibly to be transcribed *ḏtḏt*, is probably related to *ṯtṯt* / *ṯyṯy*), "quarrel"; cf. HO I, 49, 3, ro. 5: *iw.f ḥr ṯtṯt.f*, "he is accusing [or "scolding"] him."

c. The words that the lovers say to each other are formulated as the boy's promise to the girl.

d. *Nn iw.i* for LE *bn iw.i (r w3i)*.

e. *Iw drt m drt*: lit., "hand being in hand."

f. Lit., "He sets ⟨me⟩ as the foremost of the beautiful (girls)." This is not to imply that he has a harem, but only that this girl is his favorite. The *stp.f* in this stich and the *bw stp.f* in the next indicate habitual present tense (Groll, 1975–76:242f.).

The girl chides the dove for heralding the dawn that disturbs the sweet night of love. She implies that she went looking for her lover and found him in his bed, and then quotes their declaration of mutual and everlasting love.

15. (Girl)

(A) To the outer door
I set my face:
my brother is coming to me!
My eyes are turned to the road,
and my ears listen
for the ———[a] of the neglectful one (?).[b]

(B) I have set the love of my brother
as my sole[c] concern,
because ⟨ ⟩[d] him,
and my heart is not silent.

(C) It[e] has sent (me) a messenger,
fleet of foot in coming and[f] going,
to tell me he has wronged me.

(D) So in other words:[g]
he has found[h] someone else,
and she is gazing at his face.
(Well), what is it (to me)[i]
that another's nasty heart
makes me into a stranger(?)?[j]

a. *Šdšd* (finger + hand-with-stick det.): an unknown word referring to some action, perhaps cracking a whip.

b. *P3 mh3* + obscure det.: not to be connected with the "King Mehi" (*mḥy*) mentioned in other love songs (see "Excursus: Mehi and His Followers"). Nor is it a proper name, contrary to most translations, which take this to be the name of her lover. Lovers are never given names elsewhere in the love songs. Lichtheim (1976:191) translates *n p3 mh3* as "for him who neglects me." This translation requires emending the determinative (probably to a bad-bird [G 37] + seated man), but it accords with the context, for the girl certainly feels neglected. Müller (1899:25, and in a note to his transcription of H 5,9) emends to *p3 msḳ*, "the leather," which is not too unlike the current text in hieratic. Whatever the meaning of this sentence, it is fairly clear that the girl is listening for the sounds that will herald the approach of her lover.

c. Cf. no. 11, n. f.

d. A verb has apparently been omitted after *ḥr-nty* (= *ḥr-ntt*).

e. Sc. my heart. See comment below.

f. *M ʿḳ ḥr prt*: for the use of *ḥr* in coordination, see NÄG §193.

g. Gardiner (1938:243f.) has shown that *k3* = *ky* and that its proper translation is "in other words," "in short." That sense fits here and in no. 21A (C 18) as well.

h. Read *gm.f* or *gm.n.f*. The *-k* is a dittograph.

i. Taking *rf* as the enclitic particle (*Gram.* §252b); then "to me" is understood. Also possible: "What is it to him (*r.f*)?"

j. *Ḫppw*, otherwise unknown, here tentatively associated with *ḫpp*, "odd," "strange" (Wb. III, 259). Another possibility is that *ḫppw* is a geminating form of *ḫpi* ("to die") meaning "to kill" (ECU).

This song contains a number of obscure sentences, especially in the last section.

A girl relates her thoughts as she sits alone watching the door for her lover's approach. As time drags on, she receives a message that her lover may not be coming. This—she decides—means that he has found someone else. By the end of the song (D) she has convinced herself of this, and her eager anticipation has turned to petulance. A humorous view of lovers' anger is shown in nos. 1 and 7 as well.

Who sends her the message? (*H3b.f* can mean "he sends" or "it sends.") It could be her lover, although he is not mentioned in the immediate context, or it could be her heart. I think the latter is more likely, because "heart" is the closest antecedent for the pronoun, and because the preceding sentence, "my heart is not silent," suggests that her heart is about to say something. The point is that while waiting for her lover to appear, she convinces herself that something has gone awry: her lover has found another girl!

16. (Girl)

(A) My heart thought of your love,[a]
while (only) half my side-locks were done up.
(B) I have come hastily to seek you,
the back of my hairdo [loose].[b]
(C) My clothes and my tresses
have been ready all the while.

a. That is to say, you; see no. 11, n. e.

b. *Wḥ*ᶜ, "to loosen," seems required by the traces at the end of the lacuna and by the following ᶜ, but the hand-to-mouth det. (A 2) is peculiar. The last sentence must be translated as present-perfect or past tense (LEG 19.8.1), not future. The girl insists that her present disarray has not been her usual condition.

This song may be a sequel to the preceding: the beloved youth, for whom the girl was anxiously waiting, has finally arrived. In her excitement she runs out to meet him, leaving her hair and clothing in a mess. Her disarray testifies to her excitement and confusion, and she is embarrassed about her dishabille.

(At this place the papyrus has the "Antef Song"; see Appendix A, no. ii.)

GROUP C: NOS. 17–19 (RECTO 7,3–8,3)

The Flower Song

The Beginning of the Song of Entertainment

17. (Girl)

(A) *Mḫmḫ*-flowers:
my heart[a] is in balance[b] with yours.[c]
For you I'll do what it[d] wills,
when I am in your embrace.
(B) My prayer it is (?) that paints my eyes.[e]
Seeing you has brightened my eyes.[f]
I've drawn near you to see your love,[g]
O prince of my heart!
(C) How lovely is my hour (with you)!
(This) hour flows forth for me forever—
it began when I lay with you.[h]
(D) In sorrow and in joy,[i]
you have exalted my heart.
Do not [leave][j] me.

18. (Girl)

(A) In it are *sʿ3m*-trees;
before them one is exalted:[a]
I am your favorite sister.
(B) I am yours like the field[b]
planted with flowers
and with all sorts of fragrant plants.
(C) Pleasant is the canal[c] within it,
which your hand scooped out,
while we cooled ourselves in the north wind:
a lovely place for strolling about,
with your hand upon mine!
(D) My body is satisfied,
and my heart rejoices
in our walking about together.
(E) To hear[d] your voice is pomegranate wine (to me):
I draw life[e] from hearing it.
Could I see ⟨you⟩[f] with every glance,
it would be better for me
than to eat or to drink.

19. (Girl)

In it are *ṯ3yt*-flowers:
I took[a] your wreaths,[b]
when you came back drunk
and were asleep in your bedroom;
and I rubbed your feet,
while the children [in] your . . .[c]
[I(?)] rejoice in the morning . . .
Health and life within you!

No. 17

a. Read *ib.i*. The suffix may be merged with the eye sign.

b. *Mḫ3* ("balance"): a play on *mḫmḫ*-flowers, sc. "purslane" (see CED 99/7).

c. Lit., "balanced with you," or "resembles you." For their hearts to be balanced means that they are alike in disposition and feeling. Since our hearts are in balance, she implies, "I will do for you what it [my heart] wills." Cf. nos. 11, 20A.

d. Sc. my heart.

e. *T3y.i nḥt [nty] (ḥr) sḏm irty.i*: the restoration *nty* seems to impose itself after *nḥt* in H 7,4, for it fits both the lacuna and the signs under it perfectly (cf. 7,3, end); this restoration, however, produces an incomplete sentence, lit., "My prayer, which paints my eyes." *Iri* (participle) would fit the syntax, and there is room for the eye sign in the lacuna, but the signs below do not accord with the way *iri* is written elsewhere in this manuscript. Perhaps emend to *p3 [nty]*, assuming a scribal error. The parallelism, as well as the requirements of context, makes it most likely that the stich said something to the effect that it is her prayer that paints her eyes. "My prayer" = the object of my prayer, i.e., you; cf. the transferred use of the orthographic variant *nḥbt* in LRL 71/14, "Indeed you are (the object of) my prayer" (Wente, LRL, p. 83).

f. Lit., "My seeing you." In other words, my wish (namely, that we spend our lives together) and the sight of your face make my eyes brighter and more lovely than can any eye-makeup (which Egyptian women used lavishly).

g. Meaning: to experience your lovemaking? See no. 11, n. e. *N m33*, lit., "for (the purpose) of seeing."

h. *Bss . . . ḥnᶜ.k*, a ME emphatic form with the following clause as the emphasized adverbial. "It began when" renders the emphasized *ḏr* etc.

i. *Wnf* (Wb. I, 319, 20), "joy" (det. lacking). *Ṯsi.n.k ib.i iw g3s iw wnf*: a ME emphatic *stp.n.f* with parallel circumstantial clauses following as the emphasized adverbial adjunct. I take the point to be that he has fortified her heart for all time, whether they be in joy or in sorrow.

j. The last word is mostly illegible, but something like "leave" is expected.

No. 18

a. *Sᶜ3* ("exalted"): a play on *sᶜ3m*-flowers. Feeling "exalted," she declares that she is his favorite girl.

b. "Field": lit., "*khato*-land," on which see Gardiner, 1948b:II, 161ff., esp. 165–67 (Wilbour Pap.). Presumably the point of comparison is the richness and fruitfulness of the field. Woman is likened to a field in the Instruction of Ptahhotep, §21: "She is a fertile field for her lord . . . What she asks about is he who makes for her a canal." "Making a canal" alludes to sexual intercourse, whereby the "field" is "irrigated" and made fruitful (see below, n. c). We could call the "field" in this song a garden, since it contains a variety of cultivated flowers. These may represent the perfumes the girl wears.

c. The word written *ʿtt* is probably to be identified with *ʿ* (with water det.; Wb. I, 159) = "blocked canal." "Digging out" the blocked canal suggests defloration. Alternatively we can read *ḥ3t* (a body of water, Wb. III, 24, 15; P. Anastasi IV, 15, 8) for *ʿtt*, which is similar in hieratic.

d. Lit., "my hearing. . . ." Compare Cant 2:14 and no. 20A.

e. Or, "am nourished."

f. Emending *ptr.tw.i*, "I am seen," to *ptr.i tw*.

No. 19

a. *Ṯ3y* ("take"): a play on *ṯ3yt*-flowers. Alternative translation: "When you had come back drunk, I took your wreaths."

b. The expression "take wreaths" is used in the story of Horus and Seth (P. Beatty I, 16,6–7) when the gods celebrate the vindication of Horus, who is adorned with wreaths of justification.

c. Only the beginnings of the lines in col. 8 remain.

"The Flower Song": Each stanza in this song opens with a name of a flower and a similar sounding word, as if each flower the girl picks gives rise to a thought about love.

In stanza 1 (no. 17) the girl declares that her hour of pleasure in the garden with her lover is a fountain from which joy will flow to fill their lives. Their lovemaking is not the culmination of their love but the start of a shared lifetime, which may include both sorrows (an unusual note for an Egyptian love song) and joys.

Stanza 2 (no. 18) is divided into two main parts. The first part ((A)-(C)) describes the garden, the second ((D)-(E)) the girl's feelings. She first compares herself to the field (garden) in which she and her lover are walking and in which she has planted flowers, thus hinting that she is open to her lover like a fruitful field. The image of the garden begins as a simile but quickly slides into a description of the actual garden in which they are walking. Not all the details of the description can be applied to the girl, but the image of the pleasant garden tends to merge with her image. In this way the poet shows the harmony between external nature and the girl. In similar fashion the "garden" in which the youth in the Song of Songs "grazes" is both an actual garden and the girl herself, see in particular Cant 4:12–5:1. The speaker in "The Flower Song" says that seeing and hearing her lover keeps her happy and healthy; compare no. 2 and the sentence "For are you not health and life (itself)?" in no. 13.

I would surmise the import of the fragmentary stanza III to be that the girl is describing how her lover got drunk the preceding night and she took care of him. She rejoices in having him near her in the morning. The lines translated in this stanza show the Egyptian attitude toward drunkenness. There is no shame in drunkenness in its proper place. Rather it is surrounded by a romantic nimbus. This attitude is displayed most clearly in the depictions of banquets in tomb murals, in which the servants urge the guests to drink to excess while the excesses themselves are shown with good humor.

GROUP C: NOS. 19A–19B (RECTO 8,4–12)

19A. (Girl)
[Entertainment song (?)][a]

Come . . .
what is done to the . . .
love . . .
together in the meadow . . .
me in your beauty.
Come to me,
for my heart . . .
My weariness . . .

a. The beginnings of six lines of this song remain. The two signs written in red show that a title was lost in the lacuna. These signs, hand-to-mouth (A 2) + plural, suggest that the title ended in the word *sḫmḫ-ib*, "entertainment," as in the heading to no. 17.

19B. (Girl)

. . . two waterfowl.[a]
. . .
He puts ⟨me⟩ in his embrace in the day . . .

a. The last word of a title in red ink. The beginnings of three lines remain.

Source II: The Cairo Love Songs

The text of the Cairo Love Songs (Deir el-Medineh 1266 + Cairo Cat. 25218) dates from the 19th or 20th dynasty. The songs were written on a vase 36.5 cm. high and 43.0 cm. in diameter, inscribed over an effaced copy of the Wisdom of Amenemhet. Three fragments were published by Spiegelberg (1897) in hieroglyphic. Müller (1899) provided a copy of the hieratic text of those fragments. Posener's edition (1972) includes 28 fragments found at Deir el-Medineh in the 1950s. The 31 fragments recovered so far make up the greater part of the vase, but there are still major lacunae that make translation difficult, and since the exact contours of the vase are not specified in the publication, it is unclear just how much is missing at the end of most of the lines.

There are two songs, clearly distinguished from each other in form and content. The text as now restored has 13 units demarcated by the pause-mark (bent arm). It is, however, likely that we have here the remains of 14 units (stanzas), with a pause-mark lost in one of the lacunae of what is now the thirteenth demarcated unit, probably in l. 26. Originally, then, there would have been two songs of seven units (stanzas) each. Two other groups of Egyptian love songs are composed of seven units each, "The Stroll" (nos. 31–37) and the "Nakhtsobek Songs" (nos. 41–47). Furthermore, the first seven units of this text clearly form a group set off against the remaining units, and the seven-part division seems deliberate. The seventh stanza of the first song (no. 20G) is composed of two parts that are joined into a single stanza even though the first part is distinct from the second part in content and is both parallel to stanzas 5 (no. 20E) and 6 (no. 20F) and of the same length. The inclusion of the two parts of no. 20G in one unit shows a concern for composing the first song in seven units and increases the likelihood that the author has structured the second song similarly. Moreover, the last unit of the second song (no. 21G) as it now stands contains twice as many lines as any other stanza in that song, so it is reasonable to divide it into two stanzas.

The two songs in this source have enough in common to make it likely that one poet wrote both. They share the following motifs: the boy gazing upon the naked girl (nos. 20C and 21A; in the former he would see her through a wet diaphanous garment); the seal-ring on a finger as an image of close contact (nos. 20B and 21C—the restoration in the former is very likely); holding mandragoras (nos. 20B and 21A); being strengthened or made strong (*rwḏ*) by love or by something associated with the beloved (nos. 20A, 20D, 21B); and eternal unification of the lovers (no. 20B: "We will be together even when there come to pass the days of peace of old age"; no. 21F: "May he grant me my lady every day! May she never be separated from me!"). I do not see any narrative continuity between the poems.

The following translation and commentary differ in many details from my earlier treatment (Fox, 1980), particularly with respect to no. 21G. See Davis, 1980, for a response to my earlier interpretation of these songs.

GROUP A: NOS. 20A–20G (LINES 1–18)

The Crossing

20A. (Girl)

(A) . . .
[I dwell on] your love
through day and night,
the hours I am lying down,
and when I have awakened at dawn.
(B) . . .
Your form revives[a] hearts.[b]
Desire . . . your voice,
which makes [my] body strong, . . .
". . . he is weary(?),"
thus may I say whenever . . .[c]
(C) [There is no other][d]
in balance with his heart—[e]
only I alone.

20B. (Girl)

(A) Your love is as desirable . . .
[as] . . .
as oil with honey,[a]
[as fine linen] to the bodies of noblemen,
as garments to the bodies of gods,
as incense to the nose of [the king(?)].
. . . it enters into
. . .
[as a little seal-ring] to a finger,[b]
as . . .
It is like a mandragora[c]
in a man's hand.
It is like dates
he mixes in beer.
It is like . . .
[that he adds] to bread.[d]
(B) We will . . .
We will be together
even[e] when there come to pass
the days of peace of old age.[f]
I will be with you every day,
setting [food before you
like a maidservant] before her master.

20C. (Girl)

(A) My god, my lotus . . .[a]
  The north wind [blows] . . .
Pleasant it is to go to reach [the river].
  . . . breath . . .
    . . . flower . . .
(B) My heart desires to go down
  to bathe myself before you,
that I may show you my beauty
  in a tunic of the finest royal linen,
which is drenched in *tišps*-oil,
  [my hair plaited][b] in reeds.
(C) I'll go down to the water with you,
  and come out to you carrying a red fish,[c]
    which is just right[d] in my fingers.
I'll set it before you,
  while lo[oking upon your beauty.
(D) O my he]ro, my brother,[e]
  come, look upon me!

20D. (Boy)

(A) (My) sister's love[a]
  is over there, on the other side.
The river is about my body.[b]
  The flood waters[c] are powerful in (their) season,
    and a crocodile[d] waits on the sandbank.
(B) (Yet) I have gone down to the water
  that I may wade across the flood waters,
    my heart brave in the channel.
(C) I found the crocodile[e] (to be) like a mouse,
  and the face of the waters[f] like dry land to my feet.
It is her love
  that makes me strong.
    She'll cast a water spell for me![g]
(D) I see my heart's beloved
    standing right before my face!

20E. (Boy)

(A) (My) sister has come,
  my heart rejoices,
    my arms are open to embrace her.
My heart is as happy in its place[a]
  as a fish within its pond.[b]

(B) O night, you are mine forever,[c]
since (my) lady came to me!

20F. (Boy)

(A) I'll embrace her:
her arms are opened—
and I ⟨am⟩[a] like a man in (the land of) Punt.[b]
(B) It's[c] like the *misy*-plant,
which has become[d] a mixture.
Her scent is (that of) the *ibr*-balm.

20G. (Boy)

(A) I'll[a] kiss[b] her,
her lips are parted—
I am happy without beer.
How[c] the void has been filled![d]
(Divine) Menqet is adorned there,[e]
while conducting (me [?]) with . . .
[he]r bedroom.
(B) Come here
so I may speak to you![f]
Put fine linen between her legs,[g]
while spreading (her bed) with royal linen.
Take care[h] for the white linens of adornment.
(C) As for the ———[i] of [her] limbs,
the . . . of her limbs seems[j] like a thing
drenched in *tišps*-oil.

No. 20A

a. Or, "sustains," "nourishes"; cf. the phrase in no. 12.

b. The speaker believes that her lover affects others the way he affects her; cf. Nos. 31 and 36 and Cant 1:2–4.

c. ". . . he is . . . whenever": from the unplaced fragment (Posener, 1972: pl. 75) which probably belongs in the large lacuna after ll. 2–4 but does not connect directly with the words preceding the break on the left.

d. Restoring *nn wn kt iw.s*, although it is not certain that there was enough space at this point to contain this restoration in addition to the fragment. For the phrase see H 4,11 and 7,3 (nos. 11, 17).

e. Compare no. 11, n. g, and no. 17, n. c.

No. 20B

a. The words "as oil [lit., "fat"] with honey": from the unplaced fragment, pl. 75. A mixture of fat and honey (with other ingredients) is frequently prescribed in the medical texts, e.g., P. Ebers 313, 323, 533, 608. These ingredients are included in medicines for easing coughs, softening flesh, healing wounds, and the like. So the image here is probably of a soothing medicinal mixture rather than of a food delicacy.

b. ". . . to . . . as": from the fragment, pl. 75.

c. The mandragora's fruit resembles breasts, see no. 2, n. a, and no. 3, and see plate VIII. The image of the mandragora in a man's hand thus has erotic overtones.

d. Imagery of mixtures is used here, as in no. 2, to describe the relation of love to lover, but the specific images are different.

e. The particle *ꜣ* (mentioned in *Gram.* §245) bears a nuance of slight surprise, pointing to a fact that is contrary to expectation. It appears in LE mainly with *mk*, but it can occur independently; see Gardiner, 1948a:12f. An example is P. Anastasi III, 3,13: *ḫpr ꜣ msḏr n ꜥḏd ḥr ꜣt.f*, "The ear of a boy is indeed upon his back," where too it follows *ḫpr*. See also Vogelsang, 1913:170.

f. That is to say, death. Old age is never romanticized as peaceful in Egyptian literature (the healthy condition of the ancient Djedi in P. Westcar 7,15ff. is described in admiration, as something unexpected). "Old man" (*iꜣw*) is used of dead men; see, e.g., James, 1961:pls. III, 3, VIII, 2, XVIII, 1. "Old age" = death in Tylor-Griffith, 1895:pl. IX, 5; see Hodges, 1971:311–12. *Ḥtp* is used of the peace and rest of death; see, e.g., H 6,4 ("Antef Song"; see App. A, no. ii) and the Book of the Dead, spell 29. Egyptian couples could hope to stay together after death. The widow of a priest of Amon says: "We want to repose together. God cannot separate us" (Schott, 1950:154).

No. 20C

a. Although nowhere else in the love songs do lovers call each other gods, the usage here is no more extreme than the girl's calling herself the Mistress of the Two Lands in no. 8. The lotus is associated in mythology with creation and rebirth. Derchain (1975:71f.) says that "my god, my lotus" recalls the emergence of the sun god Re from the primeval ocean, Nun. That moment may be evoked again in the next stanza, where the youth emerges from the flood (Nun). The lotus also has erotic connotations, for the birth of the sun represents the regeneration of life. Compare the importance of the lotus in no. 5. The north wind also represents the power of revitalization and vigor.

b. Restoring *[šny.i nb]d*, although the hair det. is missing from *nbd* (suggested by V. L. Davis, private communication).

c. The "red fish" (*wḏ dšr*) is specifically the Tilapia (LÄ II, 224; Camios, LEM, pp. 77f.). I doubt that the girl means she is going to offer a real fish, for that would not be relevant to the context and the fish would, in any case, immediately slip out of her hands. Derchain (1975:74f.) says that *dšr* means "reddish brown" and that this phrase implies that the girl is offering *herself*. But the metaphor of offering oneself on one's fingers is obscure. At this point in the song the meaning of the phrase is a riddle; its answer comes in no. 20E, where the fish is identified with the boy's heart. The girl "captures his heart" as one captures a fish. The Tilapia was commonly used as an amulet and had sexual overtones, which it would not lose even when symbolizing the boy's heart.

d. *Mnḫ* = "appropriate," "right"; cf. P. Boulaq IV, 9,4: *tꜣ st mnḫt*, "the right place," i.e., "where it belongs." Other possible translations: "powerful," "effective," "active."

e. Compare the double vocative in the first line of the stanza.

No. 20D

a. I.e., my beloved sister; see no. 11, n. e.

b. *Itrw imy(tw) ʿwt.i*: lit., "the river is between my limbs." Derchain (1975:67): "Le fleuve pourrait engloutir [*wnm*] mon corps." But *itrw wnm ʿwt.i* could not designate future tense. Furthermore, *wnm* (if we read thus) lacks the required hand-to-mouth det. (A 2). I take the sentence to mean that he has now stepped into the river.

c. The term *nw* (or *nwn*)—the Nile at its height—evokes the immensity of the primeval flood (Derchain, 1975:68).

d. *Dpy*, "the devourer."

e. *Ḫnty*, "the one who stands before." Derchain (ibid.) observes that the first name for crocodile (*dpy*) is more suggestive of threat than the second, in accordance with the fact that the crocodile seems more threatening before the danger has been faced and overcome than afterward.

f. *Nt*: perhaps specifically "surface of water"; see Hornung, 1963:II, 170, n. 7. Earlier the water was called Nun, the primeval flood, again a more threatening image.

g. *Ḥsy* + water det. The magical papyrus Harris 501 (1,1) contains a water spell entitled "The fine sayings, to be sung, which fend off the swimmer" ("the swimmer" [*p3 mḥ*] is a euphemism for crocodile; Lange, 1927:12).

No. 20E

a. The heart has a "place" (*mkt*) of its own, from which it "jumps" or "flees" when agitated (cf. no. 34), but where it sits happily when its owner is at peace.

b. *Mš3*, whose precise meaning is unknown, appears in LFHS, pls. 3, 6, 10, pp. 18f., where it seems to indicate a pond where fish are kept after being caught. The youth's heart is the "red fish" the girl wanted to catch (no. 20C). Now it is caught—and happy to be so.

c. He addresses the night and declares that it, the time of lovemaking, now belongs to him as a successful lover. The night is similarly addressed in HO I, XL, 6,1. The phrase "the beauties [i.e., pleasures] of the night" (no. 21G) shows a similar delight in the night, as do the songs that complain of separation at daybreak (nos. 1, 14). In no. 46 the youth complains that the girl he desires refuses to listen to him "in *my* night," that is, the night that should be his. The night belongs to lovers.

No. 20F

a. Read *ḥr tw.i* for *ḥr.i*. Alternatively add *iw.i* after *ḥr.i* and translate "Her arms open unto me and I am like, etc."

b. Punt is a place in Africa that took on qualities of a half-legendary paradise; see no. 9.

c. The suffix of *iw.f*, which lacks an antecedent (*nty m Pwnt* is not appropriate), is probably indefinite, referring to the situation described; compare James, 1962:28, n. 72; Caminos, 1977:45 (P. Pushkin 127, 3,13).

d. *Pri m* = "come out as," "emerge as," used of drug preparation; see WMT 271. *Dmḏt* = "drug mixture"; ibid., 980. The context strongly suggests that the boy is referring to the preparation of an intoxicating drug, but the identity of the *misy*-plant is still unknown.

No. 20G

a. Read masc. for fem. suffix. The male is speaking.

b. The reed (M 17) before *snn.i* is otiose.

c. See Wb. III, 238,13. *Ḥ̱y* is usually followed by a determined noun (NÄG §688 Anm.); the syntax of this clause is unclear.

d. Equating *nhꜣy* with *nhi*, "lack" (Wb. II, 280, 11–12); lit., "how the lack has been completed!" This sentence apparently speaks of the fulfillment of the youth's wishes, the "lack" referring to the girl's absence.

e. Menqet is the goddess of beer, mentioned in the Book of the Dead, spell 101, and in various Ptolemaic inscriptions (e.g., Edfu I, 151, II, 42, 124, where there is reference to "the beer that Menqet brewed"). The significance of the statement "Menqet is adorned there [or "thereby"]" is unclear (*sꜥb* is sometimes used to denote decoration of statues of gods). Prof. Peter Shore has suggested to me that this sentence may refer to the custom of adorning jars with wreaths at festivities (see fig. 9). The boy may be saying that beer has been prepared for their private festivities.

f. Here the youth seems to address a servant, who was perhaps mentioned in the lacuna in l. 16.

g. Lit., "between her limbs." But see no. 20D, n. b.

h. *Sꜣw* + direct object is an antonym of *ꜥm ib*, "neglect"; see James, 1962:110. *Sꜣw* seems to mean "pay heed," "attend to" in P. Boulaq IV, 6,5 (Wisdom of Ani).

i. *Nḫꜥ*, with *-w* and plural strokes following the determinative (for examples of this order, see Wente, LRL, p. 64). The determinative is apparently the hoof (F 25), which Posener (1972: pl. 77) suggests is a substitute for the finger (D 51). This may be the same word as *nḫꜥ* + finger + man-with-stick (D 51, A 24), which appears in HPBM III, pl. 70, C2, a magico-medical text, where it is likewise obscure.

j. Lit., "is [are?] found to be like," "reckoned as." Emend to ⟨*s*⟩*w gmw*.

"The Crossing": In the first three stanzas (nos. 20A–20C) the girl tells her absent lover that she thinks only of his love, that his form and voice vitalize her, and that his love is deeply pleasurable to her. She declares her desire to go down to the water to bathe in his presence. From this we learn that she is on the river bank. The boy's words begin (no. 20D) by indicating that his beloved is indeed on the river bank, but on the other side, and strong currents and a crocodile separate them. Yet her love gives him courage and strength—it is as if her love had cast a spell on the water—and he crosses. As the tenses indicate (*hꜣ.kwi*, *gm.n.i*), he completes the crossing within the stanza and at the end of it he is standing with his beloved, perhaps in the shallows, for he says that she has come to meet him. His heart, he says, is as happy as a fish in its pond. We thus learn that the red fish that the girl said she would catch is in fact his heart, which now delights in being caught. He embraces her and rejoices (no. 20E), and then describes the heady effect of her embrace and kiss. He is now ready to bring the lovemaking to its culmination and orders someone, apparently a servant, to prepare a bed. She and her bed are to be clothed in fragrant luxury.

The crossing of the river clearly represents a psychological reality, the overcoming of hesitations and fears in order to attain one's desire. Perhaps the crossing was only in the boy's imagination. As Derchain observes (1975:69), the author plays with the opposition of imagination and reality and does not resolve the uncertainty. Derchain says that the motif of crossing Nun, past the crocodile, aided by a magical spell, is strongly reminiscent of the dead crossing to eternal life. The boy too finds a paradise awaiting him.

See further "Excursus: The Cairo Love Songs" below. For the structure of this poem see pp. 197f.

GROUP B: NOS. 21A–21G (LINES 18–28)

Seven Wishes

21A. (Boy)

(A) If only[a] I were her Nubian maid,
her attendant in secret!
(B) She brings ⟨her⟩ [a bowl of] mandragoras[b] . . .
It is in her[c] hand,
while she gives pleasure.[d]
(C) In other words:[e]
she would grant me
the hue of her whole body.[f]

21B. (Boy)

(A) If only I were the laundryman
of my sister's linen garment[a]
(even) for one month!
(B) I would be strengthened
by grasping[b] [the clothes]
that touch her body.
(C) For it would be I who washed out the moringa oils
that are in her kerchief.[c]
Then I'd rub my body
with her cast-off garments,
and she . . .
(D) [Oh I would be in] joy and delight,
my [bo]dy vigorous!

21C. (Boy)

(A) If only I were her little seal-ring,
  the keeper of her finger!
(B) I would see her love[a]
  each and every day,
. . .
  [while it would be I] who stole her heart.

21D. (Boy)

(A) If only I had a morning of seeing[a]
  like one who spends her lifetime (?)![b]
(B) Lovely is the land of Isy.[c]
  Blessed[d] is its service.[e]
Joyful is her mirror,[f]
  [into] which she gazes.
——— . . .

21E. (Boy)

(A) If only my sister were mine every day,
  like the greenery[a] of a wreath! . . .
(B) The reeds are dried,
  the safflower[b] has blossomed,
    the *mrbb*-flowers are (in) a cluster(?).
The lapis-lazuli plants and the mandragoras have come forth.
. . .
[The blo]ssoms from Hatti have ripened,[c]
  the *bsbs*-tree[d] bloss[omed], . . .
    the willow tree greened.
(C) She would be with me every day,
  like (the) greenery of a wreath.
All the blossoms are flourishing in the meadow,
  . . . entirely.[e]

21F. (Boy)

(A) If only she would come
  that [I might] see [her]! . . .
(B) I would hold festival to god,
  who makes her[a] be not distant (again).[b]
(C) May he grant me (my) lady every day!
  May she [ne]ver be separated from [me]!
If I spend a moment without seeing her,
  [I] get sick to my stomach.[c]
[So] I [shall hurry] to respond.[d]

21G. (Boy)

(A) [If only] . . .
. . . his soul.[a]
(B) I shall honor[b] him
with the beauties of the night,
and offer a fe[ast to him].
(C) May my heart settle down to [its] place![c]
. . . it,
every ill from [my] body.
. . . which seeks the sister,
whose body I cannot approach.
She'll banish [my illness(?)]![d]

No. 21A

a. The first six stanzas (nos. 21A–21F) begin with *ḥnr* [= *ḥl*] *n.i*, which was probably originally present at the start of the seventh stanza (no. 21G) too. On this particle see von Bissing and Blok, 1926:91f. The *n.i* can indicate possession, as in nos. 21D and 21E, but in nos. 21A, 21B, and 21C the wish is clearly to *be* something, not to have something, so *n.i* may be an ethical dative (ibid.; cf. P. Anastasi I, 2,7 and 25,1, LTNK 36/7). In C 24 (no. 21F), *ḥnr n.i* is followed by *iwt.s*, in Beatty I, g1,1 (no. 38), by *iw.k* ("come"), and in Beatty I, g1,1 (no. 39) and g2,1 (no. 40) by *iw.n.k*. In these cases the verb is a nominal form, so these sentences too are actually possessive (lit., "Would that I had your coming/having come").

The wish-particle requires the adjunct verbs to be translated in the hypothetical mood, even though they are formally present tense or present-perfect: e.g., *sw ini n.i* (ll. 18f.; no. 21A), "she brings" = "she would bring"; *iw.i rwḏ.kwi* (l. 19; no. 21B), "I am strengthened" = "I would be strengthened." The use of the first present is a vivid way of expressing a wish, allowing the speaker to describe a desired state as if it already existed.

b. Reading this line *sw (ḥr) int ⟨n⟩.s [g3y n] rrmt*. The line describes the maid's service that the youth would like to perform.

c. Sc. the beloved's.

d. *Ḫnm*, "give (sexual) pleasure" (*ḫnmt* = "harlot"; see Caminos, LEM, p. 187, with references). "She" in this sentence refers to the beloved girl. It is of course to the boy that she would give pleasure in his imagined state, not to the maid.

e. On *k3 ḏd* see no. 15, n. g. Here the youth sums up his wish by stating explicitly just how the girl would give him pleasure were he her maid.

f. *Sw ini n.i inw*: lit., "she brings me the hue." This idiom appears in Beatty I, ro. 17,5–6 (no. 45). It apparently means to show one's naked body. *Ini* may be understood in the sense of bringing a gift. Compare P. Anastasi I, 25,4–5: *di.s n.k iwn n ḳni.s*, "she would give you the hue of her bosom."

No. 21B

a. Lit., "piece of linen."

b. Or, "I would be strengthened as a male" (V. L. Davis, private communication). The determinative of *ṯ3y* is lost. *Ṯ3w* is also used of donning a garment (CDME, p. 302). Could that be the idea here?

c. Janssen (1975:282) identifies the *idg* as a kerchief. It is a relatively expensive garment.

No. 21C

a. "Her love" = "her"; see no. 11, n. e.

No. 21D

a. "A morning of seeing": a morning in which I see her and she sees me—a deliberately enigmatic phrase.

b. *Mi i-iri* [with female-det. + plural strokes] *ʿḥʿ.s*: an obscure phrase. The point may be: if only I were like a mirror that spends its lifetime in the beloved girl's presence. Omit the plural strokes of *i-iri*.

c. Tribute from Isy included copper (Helck, 1971:283f.). The speaker is saying that the land of Isy is fortunate in being privileged to supply the copper for the girl's mirror (which is here determined by the copper sign). The *b* (leg, D 58) in *isy* appears by mistaken association with *sb*. The walking-legs sign (D 54) is the correct reading, it is a pseudo-determinative from *is*, "go."

d. *Sbḳ*, "blessed," "fortunate," "precious" (?); see Caminos, LEM, p. 84, with references.

e. *Ḥnwt*: see Wb. III, 102, 1–2, and cf. 8. Or, "craft," "product" (CDME, p. 171).

f. *Wn(t)-ḥr* (+ copper det., N 34), "mirror." Wb. I, 313,7 gives this word only with the mirror determinative and says that it is first attested in the Saite period.

No. 21E

a. *W3ḏw3ḏ* here (l. 22) and below (l. 24) is written with the papyrus-roll determinative (Y 1, for abstract concepts) rather than with the plant determinative (M 2). Perhaps the idea is "like the greenness (or freshness) of a wreath," although that seems too abstract a comparison. It seems the speaker is wishing the girl to be as close to him as greenery woven into a wreath.

b. *K3ṯ3* (*kṯ*), also written *k3ḏ3*: identified as safflower by Keimer (1924:127). Helck (1971:522), following Burchardt, takes this word as a semiticism, corresponding to Hebrew *qoṣ*, "thornbush." But since the reference here is to a type of flower or fruit, a more likely equivalent is Hebrew *qṣ* (Gezer Calendar), later *qayiṣ* (Amos 8:1–2; II Sam 16:1, 2; Jer 40:10, 12; 48:32; Mic 7:1), "summer fruit." Safflower blooms in the summer. This semitic word was apparently given a more restricted meaning in Egyptian.

c. *Pfs* cannot mean "cooked" in this context. The meaning "ripe" may be suggested for this passage. *Pfs* is a variant of *psi*, which in Coptic (*pise*) also means "ripen" (KHWB 532). The semantic range of *pfs* is thus similar to that of Hebrew BŠL, which means both "cook" and "ripen."

d. *Bsbs* = Myristica? (Keimer, 1924:150).

e. The lacunae in this stanza and our ignorance of most of the botanical terminology used make translation especially difficult. Furthermore, the obscure syntax of this stanza can be construed in several ways. In particular, several verbs here taken as statives predicated of the preceding nouns could be *stp.f* forms—simple present or perfect.

No. 21F

a. Omit *s* of *i-di.s* (written with the bolt, O 34; not the usual form of the fem. pronoun in this text).

b. The force of *gr*, "also," "again" (Korostovtsev, 1973:§189, II), is not clear in this context.

c. Lit., "I turn over inside my stomach." We might say: my stomach does flip-flops. For other references to love-sickness, see nos. 6, 34, 37.

d. Posener's restoration in the last line, [*k3 ḥnw*].*i r ḏd wšbt*, is very probable in view of the remaining signs, although the meaning of the restored line in context is unclear.

No. 21G

a. Probably, "[If only god would give me my sister—I would praise] his soul!" or something similar. "His soul" (*k3*) is written with the god-determinative.

b. *Sšw3* for *sw3š*, with which it is often confused in LE.

c. That is, May I feel better; see no. 20E, n. a.

d. Placing the *-s* after the unusual det. (man with two sticks) and the papyrus roll. The sentence, "I hug her—and she drives illness from me" (*sḥr.s ḏwt ḥr.i*) appears in no. 37, which describes love-sickness. References to "every ill" in the lover's body in the present stanza and to the symptoms of love-sickness in the preceding one suggest that the present stanza too speaks of that illness.

"Seven Wishes": This song is spoken by quite a different person from the hero of "The Crossing." This lover only wishes and pines for the girl he desires. Each stanza begins with the wish-particle (assuming that it was originally present before no. 21G), and each stanza except for the last continues with an extended simile by which the youth expresses his desire for the constant presence of his beloved.

His wishing takes many forms. He wishes he were her maidservant, attending upon her constantly and seeing her naked body (no. 21A). He wishes he were her laundryman, touching the oils of her clothes and rubbing himself with her garments (no. 21B). He wishes he were her seal-ring, always near her (no. 21C).

He then wishes that he had a "morning of seeing" (no. 21D). He defines this wish obliquely and hyperbolically by praising the land that supplies copper (from which mirrors were made) and then declaring the good fortune of her mirror. Although he does not explicitly wish to be her mirror, that desire is implied. We see him imagining himself spending every morning throughout her lifetime (this may be the sense of the second verse) as her mirror. He would gaze upon her as she unwittingly gazed upon him.

In the fifth stanza (no. 21E) he wishes that she were with him constantly, bound to him like flowers woven into a wreath. This stanza begins with a list of the types of plants in the wreath. The speaker then apparently departs from the metaphor to describe a field in bloom, rich in varieties of flowers. This description does not seem to continue the original simile; instead, the imagery is now developed for its own sake rather than for the sake of comparison. Finally, however, the speaker restates his original wish and simile. The striking characteristic of this stanza, broken as it is, is the profusion of plants and flowers that fill the boy's fantasy-world.

In stanza 6 (no. 21F) he wishes that she would come to him, vowing to hold festival to the god who would bring this about (compare the references to prayers to Hathor in nos. 35 and 36 and particularly the promise to hold festival to her in no. 35). He complains of the misery of separation, a frequent theme in the Egyptian love songs. The final stanza (no. 21G) is unclear, but it seems to be a continuation of the same theme: he will give offerings to the god who grants him his beloved, who for her part would then banish his illness.

Thus the first four stanzas formulate the youth's wish as a desire to be near the girl: he would be one of the commonplaces of her daily life. In the next two stanzas he wishes for her to be near him: she should be to him like flowers woven into a wreath, she should come to him, she should be given to him. In nos. 21A–21D she is stationary; in nos. 21E–21G he is stationary, entirely passive as she comes to him or is given to him by a benevolent deity.

For the structure of this song see further chapter 4, pp. 197ff.

EXCURSUS: THE CAIRO LOVE SONGS

The Cairo Love Songs are sensitive and perceptive portrayals of two kinds of love.

The boy's love in "Seven Wishes" is introverted. While obsessed with the girl, he in fact speaks only of his own longings, interested less in the girl than in the experience of desiring her presence. The girl seems but an appendage to his fantasies, and his fantasies constitute the world of the poem. She remains an undelineated, amorphous figure, the contours of her personality never drawn, even vaguely. Her thoughts, desires, and even charms are not mentioned. Only in no. 21F does the speaker imagine himself relating to her as a man interacting with a woman, and even there the interaction is pale and abstract, not going beyond the statement that she should come to him. Furthermore, while he desires to serve her, he is in fact entirely passive, taking no action to achieve his goal but only longing and praying to get what he wants. Contrast his wish, "If only she would come, that I might see her" (no. 21F), with the determination of the youth in "The Crossing" to go forth to meet his beloved (no. 20D).

In the first four stanzas of "Seven Wishes," the speaker wishes to serve the girl and envies the "servants" in her life for being able to do so. The service he envisions has limited and one-sided erotic rewards: a stolen vision of nakedness, physical contact with her finger, fetishistic taction with her garments, and a vision of her face. In all these cases the girl remains unaware of him as a person, as he hides in the impersonal background of her daily existence.

By contrast, in "The Crossing" two individuals are acting upon each other and for each other. The girl speaks of the effect of the boy's love upon her—how it vitalizes her (no. 20A) and how it is mixed in her and joined to her as one thing to another with which it by nature belongs (no. 20B). In the similes in no. 20B, she describes not only the pleasantness of physical contact, but, more fundamentally, the harmony of mutually complementary things.

The mutuality of their love resounds also in the echoing of the girl's words in the boy's. The girl says that her lover's voice makes her body strong (*rwḏ*, no. 20A; l. 2), and he says that her love makes him strong (*rwḏ*, no. 20D; l. 13). She says that she will catch a red fish that will be "just right" in her fingers (no. 20C; l. 10), and when he arrives he says that his heart—certainly the same "red fish"—is as happy as a fish in its pond, where it belongs (no. 20E; l. 14). She mentions her thoughts at going to sleep and awakening (no. 20A; l. 1), and he speaks at length of her bed (no. 20G; ll. 17–18). She states her desire to go down to the river "to bathe myself before you, that I may show you my beauty in a tunic of the finest royal linen, which is drenched in *tišps*-oil" (no. 20C; l. 9). This wish is apparently fulfilled in stanza IV (no. 20D). But it is more than fulfilled in the final stanza (no. 20G), where we hear the boy describe the girl's bed in terms echoing her own words: "Put fine linen between her legs, while spreading (her bed) with royal linen. Take care for the white linens of adornment. . . . the . . . of her limbs seems like a thing drenched in *tišps*-oil." This echoing brackets the experience, showing how the girl's desire meshes with her lover's. In the Egyptian idiom, her heart balances his heart. And the echoing brings forth the central theme of the song: the earned fulfillment of mutual desires.

The outward orientation of the two partners and the mutuality of their feelings are embodied in the central image of the song in the fourth stanza, the middle of the song and its high point, where the boy crosses the river to meet the girl as she goes down to the water to join him. Even as he crosses he does not feel isolated in his struggle. Sensing her participation, he feels as if her love is magically subduing the hostile waters.

In contrast to the speaker in "Seven Wishes," who has only desire, the youth in "The Crossing" has will as well, the will to overcome obstacles, external and internal. The river becomes emblematic of the inner obstacles on the way to love, as the youth, emboldened by his girl's love, triumphs over his hesitations and can therefore exult, not only in her but in himself.

Because of the difficulties overcome on the way, and because both partners go forth to meet each other, the exquisitely depicted moment of their embrace reaches an erotic intensity far exceeding that of even the most sexually explicit love songs. The poet's delicacy and restraint heighten the intensity of the eroticism. For after the embrace and kiss, the poet does not describe the delights to follow, but only suggests them through the youth's order to a servant to prepare the girl's bed. The youth speaks not of the sensuousness of the act but of the sensuousness of her bed, where (we are to assume) the couple will make love. The youth speaks of the sheet tucked between his girl's legs, of her plush linen bed-clothes, and of the fragrance of her body. We are led to picture her there, wrapped in silky, scented luxury as she awaits her lover. The poem stops here. The imagination does not.

Source III: The Turin Love Song (Turin Cat. 1966; Scamuzzi, 1964:pl. LXXXIX Nos. 28–30)

The Turin Love Song appears in an early 20th dynasty papyrus, damaged many places, especially at the beginning of the lines in col. 1 (nos. 28–29). Its two columns contain a song of three stanzas. There is no pause-mark (bent arm) at stanza divisions, but the beginning of each stanza is clearly identified by sentences written in red, which introduce the speakers, three trees. Stich divisions are marked by red "verse-points."

The two lines immediately following the end of the song, written in a smaller script, are a short business memorandum.

The Orchard

28. *(Poet, quoting tree, then girl [?])*[a]

[The persea tree[b] moves his mouth and s]ays:

(A) "My pits[c] resemble her teeth,
my fruit[d] resembles her breasts.
[I am the foremost of the trees] of the orchard.

(B) I remain through every season,
which the sister spends with her brother.
. . .[e]
while drunk with wine of grape and pomegranate,
and bathed in moringa oil and balm.

(C) All [the trees]—except for me—
have passed away from the meadow.
I abide twelve[f] months in the gar[den].
I have endured:[g] ⟨I⟩'ve[h] cast off a blossom,
(but) next year's[i] is (already) within me.
[Of my] fellows I am foremost,
(yet) ⟨I am seen⟩[j] as second (rate).
(D) If this happens again,
I won't be silent for them—
. . .[k] for her friend.
(E) Then shall the misdeed be seen,
and the beloved (sister) disciplined,
so that she won't [spend the day again
with][l] their staves[m] and with lotuses,
blossoms of . . . and with lotus-buds,
ointments [and unguents of] fine oils
of all kinds.[n]
(F)[o] May she (rather) make you spend the day merrily,
in[p] a hut of reeds, in a guarded place."[q]
(G)[r] "Look, he goes forth in truth (?).[s]
Come, let's flatter him.
Make him spend the entire day
[with us in] his shelter."[t]

29. *(Poet, quoting the tree)*
The fig-sycamore moves his mouth,[a] and his foliage comes to speak.[b]
(A) "[See what I] will do:
[I will co]me to the lady.
(B) Is there anyone[c] as noble as me?
(And yet), if there are no servants,
I'll be the servant
[brought from Syria][d]
as booty for the beloved (girl).
(C) She had (me) put in her orchard,
(but) did not pour (a libation) for me,
[on the d]ay of drinking,
and did not fill my belly,
with the water of the waterskins.
(D) (I) was found useful (just) for[e] amusement,
[and was left] not drinking.
As my soul lives, O beloved one,
you'll be paid back for this!"[f]

30. (Poet, then tree)[a]

(A) The little sycamore,[b] which she planted with her own hands, opens
her [mouth][c] to speak.

(B) The drops (?)[d] in her mouth—
they're bees' honey.[e]
She is beautiful, her leaves [lovely],
[She is (?)] verdant and (?) flourishing (?).[f]
She is laden with fruit, unripe and ripe.[g]
She is redder than red jasper.
Her leaves are like malachite,
her ———[h] is like faience,
her wood is like the color of green feldspar,
and (her) ———[i] is like the *bsbs*-tree's.
She attracts those not beneath her,
(for) her shadow cools the air.
She [puts] a note[j] into the hand of a little girl,
the daughter of her chief gardener,
speeding her to the beloved (sister), (saying):

(C) "Come, spend time where the young people are:
the meadow celebrates its day.
Under me are a festival booth and a hut,
and my rulers[k] are happy and rejoice[l] at seeing you.[m]
Have your servants sent before you,
fitted out with their vessels.
One grows intoxicated just hurrying to me,
even before having taken a drink!

(D) Your attendants have come
bearing their supplies.
They've brought beer of all sorts,
and bread of all types,
plants[n] aplenty from yesterday and today,
and fruits of all kinds for delight.
Come spend the day in pleasure,
(one) morning, then another—two days,[o]
sitting in (my) shade."

(E)[p] "Her friend is at her right,
as [she] gets him intoxicated
and does whatever he says.
The beer hut[q] is disarrayed from drink,
but she has remained with her brother.

(F) The [cloths] are spread out beneath me,
while the sister 'strolls about.'[r]
But my lips are sealed[s]
so as not to tell[t] I've seen the[ir] 'words.'"[u]

No. 28

a. The poet does not stay hidden entirely behind the characters in this poem but rather quotes them, while sometimes speaking in the authorial voice. On the identity of the speakers in this stanza, see below, nn. o and t.

b. I suggest that the first tree to speak, whose name is now lost, is the persea (*Mimusops schimperi*). The persea's fruits can be said to resemble breasts, and the persea is almost always in bloom, as the tree in this stanza boasts of being. Theophrastus (*Enquiry into Plants* IV, ii, 5) describes the persea as follows:

> . . . in Egypt, there is another tree called the persea which in appearance is large and fair, and it most resembles the pear in leaves, flowers, branches, and general form, but it is evergreen, while the other is deciduous. It bears abundant fruit and at every season, for the new fruit always overtakes that of last year. It ripens its fruit at the season of the etesian winds; the other fruit they gather somewhat unripe and store it. In size it is as large as a pear, but in shape it is oblong, almond-shaped, and its colour is grass-green. It has inside a stone like the plum, but much smaller and softer; the flesh is sweet and luscious and easily digested; for it does not hurt if one eats it in quantity. [Transl. A. Hort, Loeb Classical Library ed.]

See also Pliny, *Natural History* XIII, 60f.; XVII, 60–62.

c. Possibly "berries": *npy* (Wb. II, 248,5) = *npry* (Wb. II, 249,5), usually meaning "grains." The pit of the persea has a yellowish-white kernel, which may be the part intended here.

d. Lit., "my form" (*ḳꜣy*). The fruit is the only part of a tree's form that could be said to resemble breasts.

e. Perhaps: "They sit in my shade." "My" is visible.

f. A verse-point is mistakenly placed here.

g. *ʿḥʿ* = "remain alive, endure" (Wente, LRL, 36, n. n, with reference to HO I, 80, vso. 15).

h. Read *ḫʿꜣ.i prḫ*.

i. *Pn snf* for *pꜣ n snf*, "the one of next year" (thus Wb. IV, 162,14).

j. For the confused existing writing (*ptr.tw.n*?; T 1,6) read *ptr.tw.i* or *ptr.w wi*.

k. There is room for two or three words in the lacuna before 1,7.

l. *Irt pꜣ hrw m*, written in compressed form, would fit here (1,8).

m. As Müller (1899:38) observes, *šbd*, "staff," must have an unusual meaning in this context. It would seem to refer to some item woven from flowers, or to staves about which flowers are braided.

n. It is difficult to connect these words ("their staves . . . kinds") with one another and with their context. They seem to describe accoutrements of the couple's merrymaking.

o. Addressed to a male (2nd masc. sg.), but to the boy and not to the tree, since the tree could not pass the day in a "hut of reeds, in a guarded place." Apparently the tree is now telling the boy to make sure that he and his girl do not lose the benefit of his, the tree's, shelter.

p. Supply *m* before *pr* in 1,9.

q. Guarded, presumably, by the tree, if he can be persuaded to keep quiet. The hut is a bower under his boughs, see no. 30(C).

r. This section is apparently spoken by the girl, urging her lover to join her in cajoling the tree into preserving their secret and letting them continue in his shelter.

s. *Pr.f m m3ʿt*: lit., "goes forth in truth," or "truly goes forth," an unclear idiom open to a variety of interpretations: he (the tree) is speaking the truth (cf. Žába, 1956:143); is serious; is really going off (to tell people); is truly blossoming. If the last interpretation is correct, the speaker now praises the tree. The speaker either is impressed by the tree's argument that beauty such as his deserves more attention or else is worried by the tree's threats to reveal what he has seen.

t. The concluding lines of no. 28 are difficult. In (F) there seems to be an abrupt change of implied auditor, as the tree apparently speaks to the boy (2nd masc. sg.), referring to the girl in the third person. In (G) there appears to be an even more abrupt change, as the speaker is now one of the couple, using the 1st plur. and referring to the tree in the 3rd masc. sg.

No. 29

a. Lit., "sends forth its mouth." Note the distinctively ME construction with the independent *iw stp.f* present tense. The tree in this stanza (*nh3 dbw*) has the man determinative (A 1) and is depicted as a male, even though it is treated grammatically as feminine.

b. The expressions "moves [lit., "sends forth"] its mouth" and "its foliage comes to speak" are figures for the "speech" of the tree heard in the rustling of its branches and leaves in the wind. The verbs of motion, "sends forth" and "comes," suggest the swaying motion of the branches.

c. "Noble" has a fem. determinative (B 1).

d. Restoration suggested by Maspero (1883:12), based on a phrase used in the annals of Thutmosis II. Only the determinative for foreign lands remains.

e. *Iw gm.tw.(i) r*: cf. LRL 10/5 and Caminos, LEM, p. 240 (P. Anastasi V, 12,6) and p. 84 (P. Anastasi III, 3,11), with reference to HPBM I, 47, n. 1.

f. *In.tw m b3ḥ.ṯ*: lit., "it will be brought back to [or "before"] you."

No. 30

a. Parts (A) and (B) are spoken by the poet, (C) through (F) by the tree.

b. The little sycamore, in contrast to the preceding two trees, is represented as a female, perhaps by association with the goddess of the sycamore; see literary comment.

c. . . . *(ḥr) wḏ [r].s*: lit., "sends her mouth"; see no. 29, n. a.

d. A plural noun: *ḏXḏ* + hand-to-mouth det. (A 2). The remnant of the middle sign most resembles the tail of a *ḏ* (I 10) (compare the forms of *ḏ* in 1,11 and 2,8), but *ḏḏḏ* is an unlikely formation (though it could conceivably be onomatopoetic for "murmur"). The middle sign might also be the tail of a spaciously written *f* (I 9); compare the form of *f* in *sfḫ* and *nfr* in 2,10. If the word is indeed *ḏfḏ*, we can associate it with *ḏfḏ* "drops" (Wb. V, 572,9). The word is not determined here by the expected three grains of sand (N 33), but there may be an orthographic word play in the hand-to-mouth determinative: since the tree has, as it were, a mouth (its leaves?), the drops of moisture or sap on it are in a sense its utterances. Theophrastus, *Enquiry*, IV, ii, 1, notes that the Egyptian sycamore puts forth abundant sap. Drops of sap could reasonably be compared to bees' honey.

e. A one-membral nominal sentence, on which see LEG 57.10.

f. The determinative for *rwd* is fairly clear. The two following signs are obscure, but are possibly to be read *.ti* (stative). Statives ending in *.ti* are used, though rarely, for 3rd fem. sg. (LEG 12.3.2c).

g. For *k3y* and *nḳw* (= *nḳʿw*) see WAD, p. 318.

h. *Iwnt*, with the finger + hand-with-stick dets. (D 51, D 40), as if indicating an action, unknown; perhaps for *inw* or *inwt*. *Inw* with pellet det. + plural strokes appears in P. Anastasi III, 3,6 (LEM 23/7), where it refers to something whose sweetness "surpasses" honey (see Caminos, LEM, p. 81). WAD, p. 36 suggests that *inyt* is the pit of the date and the seeds of flax. *Bit n in* (finger + hand-with-stick dets.) refers to a type of honey in P. Anastasi IV, 14,11 (Caminos, LEM, p. 208). Possibly, however, *inw* as written here is just a poor writing of *inw* "color."

i. *Nny* (Wb. II, 276,6), meaning unknown. *Nny* and *bsbs* are determined by the pellet sign (N 33), suggesting that the reference is to sap or berries.

j. *Wstn*: Wb. I, 367,6 gives only this occurrence. NÄG §135 takes it as a diminutive of *wst*. Perhaps we should simply emend to *wst*.

k. "Rulers" = gardeners?

l. The determinatives that *[ʿḏ]ʿḏ* ("rejoice") has here, namely child (A 17) + bad-bird (G 37), have apparently arisen through confusion with *ʿḏdw*, "youngsters."

m. *N p3 m33.ṯ*: see NÄG §409.

n. *R(n)pt*: Wb. II 435, 6–7; used of edible vegetables in Leyden 348, verso 7,5 (LEM 134/12), etc.

o. Lit., "morning after morning, to two days."

p. As Müller (1899:40) notes, from here on the little sycamore does not address the girl, but discreetly whispers its observations to the side.

q. The "beer hut" is apparently the booth in which the festivities take place. These have now come to an end, and the couple is left alone.

r. Lit., "And the sister is in her goings-about." The exact activity in view is uncertain, but it is clearly something best not revealed, for the tree promises to keep it secret.

s. Lit., "I am secret of belly."

t. *R tm ḏd*: shows the consequence of being "secret of belly." Erman (NÄG §795), however, says that the phrase has lost its final indication here.

u. *Ḏd mdw* (*r* is written before the phrase by habitual association with *ḏd mdw*; see NÄG §795) seems to be used as a noun meaning "words," "things," here coyly alluding to the couple's lovemaking.

The identity of the speaking voice is not always clear in this stanza. Part (B) consists of the poet's words describing the tree. Though this stanza opens, as do the others, with a *verbum dicendi*, the actual quotation of the tree's words does not begin until (C), where the tree sends an invitation to a young lady. In (D) the sycamore informs the girl that servants have brought food and drink for the picnic. The lovers' meeting is therefore not a secret tryst but a recognized part of the celebrations. What they *do* under the tree, however, may be considered less proper. The little sycamore promises not to tell.

"The Orchard": In contrast to the other love songs, the main characters in this poem are trees, while the lovers remain colorless and incidental to the poem's real concern, which is the virtue of selflessness rather than the experience of love. "The Orchard" further differs from the other Egyptian love songs (except for nos. 41–42) in giving prominence to an authorial voice rather than allowing the personae alone to speak.

It is probably a different couple under each tree, since the couple of no. 30 have not yet arrived as the third tree begins speaking.

The motif of the speaking, sheltering tree may originate in mythology. A painting from the tomb of Sebekhotep (TT 63, ca. 1415) shows a sycamore goddess offering Sebekhotep and his wife food and drink (see plate IX). The inscription on the left side of the pool says, "The sycamore of the west side of his pool, (the sycamore) whose name is 'The Nourisher of her Master,' says: 'You seal-bearer Sebekhotep, blessed one, "Hail to you," says (Re?) . . . At mealtime he feeds you with all good and pure things that are in . . .'" The inscription on the right says, "The sycamore on the east side of his pool, whose name is 'The Protection of her Master,' says: '"Sebekhotep, hail to you," says Re, "I shield you, O seal-bearer Sebekhotep!"'" As in no. 30 a notched sycamore (fem.) speaks in this inscription, there offering food, drink, and shade to the loving couple.

The first two trees demand attention from the lovers, who are (we may assume) too engrossed in each other to give the trees the attention they feel they deserve and to make them part of the festivities.

In no. 28 the persea(?) first (A) boasts of his resemblance to the girl (thus indirectly praising her). I am as pretty as she is—he implies—so why am *I* not receiving attention? He boasts in particular that he alone of the trees is in blossom the whole year (B), (C). He is indignant that he is not receiving the attention due his magnificence (D). Then he threatens that if he is neglected again, he will reveal what he has seen and the girl will be punished and kept from similar merrymaking in the future (E). He then turns to the boy and urges him to try to get his beloved to do what is necessary to ensure future use of the tree's shelter (F). The girl, it seems, then urges her lover to help her flatter the tree and soothe its bruised (and immense) ego (G).

The fig-sycamore likewise (no. 29) complains of lack of attention. The lovers did not let him participate in their festivities (i.e., did not give him libations), although, in spite of his nobility, he was even willing to serve as the girl's servant. He ends by intimating darkly, "you'll be paid back for this" (lit., "it will be brought back to you"). Judging from the threat of the first tree not to remain silent about what he saw and the promise of the third tree to provide safe concealment, it appears that the second tree is implying that he will reveal what he sees going on under his branches. His willingness to serve may be a better claim to attention than the first tree's vaingloriousness, but neither can compare with the unselfishness of the third tree, the little sycamore, who neither praises herself nor demands attention, but only invites the young lovers to enjoy the shade of her branches. She promises—without demanding anything in return—to keep their secrets. This is clearly the tree the poet favors. This tree alone is praised in the poet's own voice.

Despite the boasting of the first two trees and the praise given the third, this song is not a contest fable of the sort known from Sumer, for the trees are not arguing against one another. The poet does not, strictly speaking, judge among them, for instead of waiting until all three have had their say and then proclaiming one the victor, the poet praises the third tree *before* she has shown her virtues. The poet is showing three types, letting us know the excellence of the preferred tree even before she speaks, to avoid diminishing her modesty.

Source IV: P. Chester Beatty I

P. Chester Beatty I (Gardiner, 1931:pls. XVI–XVII, XXII–XXVI, XXIX–XXX) is a 20th dynasty papyrus from Thebes. This long papyrus contains the story "Strivings of Horus and Seth" (Lichtheim, 1976:214–23), three groups of love songs (whose text, remarkably, has been completely preserved), an encomium of Ramses V, a part of another hymn (probably to the same king), and a number of short business documents. There is no literary connection between the "Nakhtsobek Songs" (group C) and the two other groups. The "Nakhtsobek Songs" were inscribed somewhat later than the other two groups and by a different copyist. Units are separated by the pause-mark (the bent arm). Verse divisions are marked by red dots in "The Stroll" and the "Nakhtsobek Songs." My translation will conform to this punctuation except in a few cases where the copyist (who was not necessarily the author) clearly made errors in their placement, such as putting a dot in the middle of a clause.

Group A (nos. 31–37), which I call "The Stroll" because of the event that gives rise to the thoughts uttered in the song, is a unified poem of seven stanzas. A boy and a girl speak in alternate stanzas.

Group B (nos. 38–40), "Three Wishes," is a single song of three stanzas expressing one wish in three ways.

Group C (nos. 41–47), the "Nakhtsobek Songs," is a loose collection of independent poems. Nos. 41 and 42, however, may form a single song.

GROUP A: NOS. 31–37 (C1,1–C5,2)

The Stroll

The Beginning of the Sayings of the Great Entertainer[a]

31. (Boy)[a]

(A) One alone is (my) sister, having no peer:
more gracious than all other women.[b]
(B) Behold her, like Sothis[c] rising
at the beginning of a good year:
shining, precious, white of skin,
lovely of eyes when gazing.
(C) Sweet her lips[d] ⟨when⟩ speaking:
she has no excess of words.[e]
Long of neck, white of breast,
her hair true lapis lazuli.
(D) Her arms surpass gold,
her fingers are like lotuses.
Full(?) (her) derrière, narrow(?) (her) waist,[f]
her thighs carry on[g] her beauties.
Lovely of ⟨walk⟩ when she strides on the ground,
she has captured my heart in her embrace.
(E) She makes the heads[h] of all (the) men
turn about[i] when seeing her.
Fortunate is whoever embraces her—
he is like the foremost of lovers.[j]
(F) Her coming forth appears
like (that of) her (yonder)—the (Unique) One.[k]

32. (Girl)

Second Stanza
(A) My brother roils[a] my heart with his voice,
making me take ill.[b]
Though he is among the neighbors of my mother's house,
I cannot go to him.
(B) Mother is good in commanding me thus:
"Avoid seeing ⟨him⟩!"[c]
(Yet) my heart is vexed when he comes to mind,
for love of him has captured me.
(C) He is senseless of heart[d]—
and I am just like him!
He does not know my desires[e] to embrace him,
or he would send (word) to my mother.

(D) O brother, I am decreed for you[f]
by the Golden One.[g]
Come to me that I may see your beauty!
May father and mother be glad!
(E) May all people rejoice in you together,
rejoice in you, my brother![h]

33. (Boy)
Third Stanza
(A) My heart intended to see her beauty
while sitting in her abode.[a]
On the way I found Mehi[b] in his chariot,[c]
together with the "lovers."[d]
I cannot take myself away from him.[e]
(B) I should pass freely by him.
But see—the Nile is like a road,
and I don't even know where to put my feet:[f]
my heart is foolish indeed!
Why would you stride freely by Mehi?
(C) Look, if I pass before him,
I will tell him my swervings:[g]
"I belong to you"—I'll tell him—
and he will boast of my name
and assign me to the chief (band of the) ensnared(?)[h]
who accompany him.[i]

34. (Girl)
Fourth Stanza
(A) My heart quickly scurries away[a]
when I think of your love.[b]
(B) It[c] does not let me act like a (normal) person[d]—
it has leapt ⟨out⟩ of[e] its place.
It does not let me don a tunic;
I cannot put on my cloak.[f]
I cannot apply paint to my eyes;
I cannot anoint myself at all!
(C) "Don't stop until you get inside";
thus it[g] says to me, whenever (I) think of him.
(D) O my heart, don't make me foolish![h]
Why do you act crazy?
Sit still, cool down, until the brother comes to you,[i]
when I shall do many such things (?).[j]
Don't let people say about me:[k]
"This[l] woman has collapsed[m] out of love."

(E) Stand firm whenever you think of him,
my heart, and scurry not away.[n]

35. (Boy)

Fifth Stanza

(A) I shall laud the Golden One,[a]
extol her Majesty.
I shall exalt the Mistress of Heaven,
give homage to Hathor,
thanks to (my) Lady.[b]
I shall call to her that she may hear my supplications
and decree for me (my) lady.[c]

(B) She[c] came of her own accord to see me.
How great is what happened to me!
I became happy and glad and powerful,
when (I) said, "Ah! Here she is!"
No sooner had she come than the "lovers" bowed down,
because of the greatness of her love.[d]

(C) So I'll pray[e] to my goddess,
that she might give me (my) sister as a gift.[f]

(D) Three full days[g] (have passed)
since I made supplication[h] in her name,
but these five days she has been gone from me.[i]

36. (Girl)

Sixth Stanza

(A) ⟨I⟩[a] passed close by his house,
and found his door ajar.
My brother was standing beside his mother,
and with him all his kin.[b]

(B) Love of him captures the heart[c]
of all who stride upon the way—
a precious youth without peer!
A brother excellent of character!

(C) He gazed at me when I passed by,[d]
(but) I exult by myself.[e]
How joyful (my) heart in rejoicing,
my brother, since I (first) beheld (you)!

(D) If only mother knew my heart—
she would go inside[f] for a while.
O Golden One, put that in her heart!
Then I could hurry to (my) brother
and kiss him[g] before his company,
and not be ashamed[h] because of anyone.
I would be happy to have them see
that you know me,
and I'd hold festival to my goddess.
(E) My heart leaps up to go forth
to make me gaze on (my) brother tonight.
How lovely it is to pass by![i]

37. (Boy)
Seventh Stanza
(A) Seven whole days I have not seen (my) sister.
Illness has invaded me,
my limbs have grown heavy,[a]
and I barely sense my own body.[b]
(B) Should the master physicians come to me,
their medicines could not ease my heart.
The lector-priests have no (good) method,
because my illness cannot be diagnosed.
(C) Telling me, "Here she is!"—that's what will revive me.
Her name—that's what will get me up.
The coming and going of her messengers—
that's what will revive my heart.
More potent than any medicine is my ⟨sister⟩[c] for me;
she is more powerful for me than The Compendium.[d]
Her coming in from outside is my amulet.[e]
(D) (I) see her—then (I) become healthy.
She opens her eyes[f]—my limbs grow young.
She speaks—then I become strong.
(E) I hug her[g]—and she drives illness from me.
But she has left me for seven days.[h]

Title

a. *T3 sḫmḫt-ib* ʿ*3* is usually translated "the great entertainment" rather than "the Great Entertainer" (fem.), because the woman determinative is lacking. Yet "entertainment" (*sḫmḫ-ib*) is elsewhere masc., whereas *t3 sḫmḫt* is a fem. participle. Furthermore, the definite article is more appropriate if the reference is to a specific woman entertainer rather than to entertainment in general. "The Great Entertainer" is apparently the poetess (thus Schott, 1950: 10), and the verses are her "sayings." We hear in various places of songstresses of Hathor, goddess of love. It is quite likely that these women composed songs as well as sang them. Even though the meaning of the title is not quite certain, I will refer to the writer of this and the next song as a woman, as a reminder that there is no reason to assume that poetic composition was the exclusive province of men in the ancient Near East. The scribes of the manuscripts were probably men—all professional scribes were—but the authors may well have been women. The first poet of love known to us by name was a woman, Sappho of Lesbos. In fact, the first poet in history whose name is known was a woman, the princess Enhuduanna of Akkad.

No. 31

a. Since the boy and the girl speak alternately throughout the song, this stanza should be assigned to the boy (Hermann, 1959:106). Observe further that "she has captured my heart in her embrace" is more appropriately spoken by the boy than by the poet. Furthermore, in no. 35 the youth says that he saw the girl pass by his house, leaving little doubt that in this stanza we hear his thoughts as he watches her stroll by.

b. Emending *r nfr ḥr nbwt* to *nfr ḥr r nbwt*, an emendation presupposed by Gardiner's "comelier than all mankind" (1931:30). Another possible translation is "more (unique) than any gracious woman" (or "mistress") (suggested by ECU). The latter translation probably requires the addition of a feminine determinative (B 1) to *nfr ḥr* and the elimination of the plural strokes after *nbt*. On *nfr-ḥr* see Spiegelberg, 1917.

c. Sothis is the star Sirius, whose rising was supposed to occur in conjunction with the rise of the Nile and to bring fertility to the land.

d. "Lips": for the writing see no. 3, n. d. Supply *m* before *mdt*.

e. *Ḫnw*, written with the legs det. (D 54), by confusion with *ḫni*, "alight."

f. *Bdš pḥ.ty mrt ḥry-ib*, lit., "loose of buttocks, bound of middle." This phrase is puzzling because loose buttocks do not seem to have been regarded as beautiful in Egypt, judging from paintings of women. *Mr*, "bound" = firm? girdled? Brunner-Traut (1978:82) translates: "Lang gestreckt die Lenden unter gegürteter Mitte"; Lichtheim (1976:182): "Heavy thighs, narrow waist."

g. Thus Blackman (1933:203), translating *ḏ3 mnty.s nfrw.s*.

h. Lit., "necks."

i. *Msḥn*, apparently a variant of *msnḥ* (Wb. II, 146, 3–8), on which see Federn, 1966:55.

j. *Mryw*, with the phallus det., emphasizing the sexual nature of their love. In nos. 33 and 35, the "lovers" are a group of males who accompany a figure called Mehi. Here the term seems to include any male in love, such as the young man speaking here. See "Excursus: Mehi and His Followers" below.

k. That is, Sothis, who "goes forth" every year. Every stanza in this song, except for the first, is preceded by the number of the stanza, and every stanza, including the first, opens and closes with a word that plays on the stanza number. Here the key word is *wᶜ*, "one," "unique." A similar device is used in a hymn to Amon from the same period (Gardiner, 1905).

No. 32

a. *St3ḫ*: not in Wb.; causative of *t3ḫ*, "be stirred up" (of waters) (Gardiner, 1931:31). Perhaps *st3ḫ ib* is equivalent to *sḏḫy ib* (P. Sallier I, 5,8; Caminos, LEM, p. 314) (ECU).

b. *Di.f ṯ3y n.i ḫ3yt*: apparently *ṯ3y* is a passive *stp.f*, lit., "while he causes illness to be taken to me," referring to love sickness.

c. Text has "her." According to the present text of this stich, the girl's mother ordered the youth not to see her daughter again. If that reading is correct, we must emend "me" to "him" in the preceding stich. There is, however, no sign that the mother or anyone else is aware of the emotions of the youth, so it is best to read "him" in this stich; see no. 13, n. d.

d. *Iwty ib.f*: lit., "one who has no heart," in other words, who is confused or foolish. On *iwty ḥ3ty/ib* see Caminos, LEM, p. 13, with references. Note especially P. Anastasi II, 10,7–11,1, "I am one who knows not his own self. I am a senseless man (*iwty ib.f*) and spend the whole time following after my (own) dictates like an ox after grass." The girl in our song says that the boy she loves is "senseless of heart" (lit., "lacking heart"; no. 32), insofar as he is ignorant of her desire. At the same time she says she is "just like him"—confused and foolish, as she describes herself again in no. 34. Her words are more apt than she knows, for the boy has just said, "She has captured my heart in her embrace" (no. 31).

e. "My desires": the plural shows that her desire is ongoing.

f. Lit., "I am commanded to you," with *ḫr* instead of *n.k*, sc. "for you"; cf. Coptic *ša-*.

g. Hathor, goddess of love.

h. *Sn* = "two" and "brother."

No. 33

a. *Ḫnw*: an unusual usage. Perhaps we should take the house sign (O 1) as an ideogram (rather than as the det. of *ḫnw*), and translate "within her house."

b. "Mehi" (*mḥy*) is written here as if it meant "flax." Mehi is not the young lover but a third figure who mysteriously enters into the picture in this stanza; see the following excursus.

c. Lit., "on horse," meaning to ride in a chariot; see Gardiner, 1931:32.

d. Lit., "his lovers" (*n3y.f mryw*) see no. 31, n. j. As I understand their identity, they are "his" lovers not because they love him but because they are lovers and they belong to him.

e. *Iṯi.i m b3ḥ.f*: perhaps, "get control of myself in his presence."

f. Lit., "See, the Nile is like a road, while I don't know the place of my feet"—an idiom denoting confusion; see Hermann, 1959:106. Perhaps the idea is that in a state of confusion or desperation (cf. no. 40), one might run into the Nile thinking it a road. Compare also LRL 48/1, *iw bw rḫ.n st rdwy.n*, "not knowing the place of our feet."

g. *Pḫrw*, lit., "turnings." Probably elliptical for "turnings of the heart"; see Neskhons IV (Gunn, 1955:89, with references), meaning "change the mind." It seems that the youth is referring to the flip-flops of heart that love causes in him as it does in the girl (no. 34). The "turnings" may refer more specifically to the youth's indecisiveness, which is apparently reflected in this stanza, where he decides to stride boldy past Mehi (B), but then is unable to do so and changes his mind (C). In this stanza the boy relates his debate with his heart, while in the next the girl relates her debate with hers.

h. The *kpwy* (collective noun, fem. sg.) who accompany Mehi have not been identified. This may be another term for the "lovers," the group of males who are also said to accompany Mehi. Suys (1934:455) associated *kpwy* with *k3pw*, "bird-trappers," although the expected det. is lacking. Gardiner (1931:32) suggests a connection with *k3p*, "harem," although a different writing would be expected. Since bird trapping is a frequent motif in the love songs, one associated with the Love Trap theme (nos. 3, 9, 10), the connection Suys suggests is preferable, though since the "trapper" is elsewhere the girl, it is more likely that *kpwy* is a passive participle meaning "the group of those who are ensnared": in other words, youths caught in the snare of love.

i. "Accompany" = *imy ẖt*, "intended" = *ẖm*, and "third" = *mḥ-ẖmt*. The assonance is slight. *Nty imy ẖt.f* for *nty m ẖt.f* (NÄG §231).

No. 34

a. *Ifd sw ib.i 3s*: participle in adjectival predication, modified adverbially by *3s*. Lit., "My heart is a quickly-fleeing-sort."

b. "Your love" = "you," resumed by pronoun in last couplet; see no. 11, n. e.

c. Sc. my heart.

d. Lit., "go as human beings (go)."

e. *M* lost by haplography. "Jumped," or "departed": *tfy*, as in P. Anastasi IV, 2,5; 11,4; see Caminos, LEM, p. 133.

f. *Bhn* is an overgarment; see CED 30/4 (Coptic *bohn*). Gardiner (1931:32) translates "fan"; thus too Blackman (1933:202).

g. Sc. my heart. The seated-female det. (B 1) is used for the 2nd fem. sg. suffix. The meaning of the heart's demand seems to be that the girl should rush to the boy's home without pause (Lichtheim, 1976:186).

h. Lit., "don't make folly for me." Since *wẖ3* is separated from *iri*, the former is the latter's direct object; hence "make folly" rather than "act foolish."

i. "You" is masculine. The girl is talking to her heart.

j. An obscure sentence. I surmise that the girl is assuring her heart that when her beloved comes to her she too will do "many such things," behaving in actuality just as her heart is behaving now in imagination. Caminos (LEM, p. 234) takes the eye sign here as an abbreviated writing of *ptr* and translates "I have seen many likewise," which rendering, however, does not fit the present context.

k. There is no red dot here, although a break seems required by the length of the stich.

l. The demonstrative *tw* is an archaism.

m. "Has collapsed": *h3.tw* (= *h3.ti*), lit., "has gone down," "fallen."

n. "Four" = *fdwt*; "scurry," "flee" = *ifd*. The girl is pleading with her heart not to flee from her, not to scurry away from her on all fours like an animal. To be united with one's heart is to be calm and collected (cf. Amenemope 1,9). The heart (whether called *ḥ3ty* or *ib*) is a "second self," identical with the Ka. The heart dwells in the body but may leave it during moments of strong emotion. This concept receives graphic as well as literary expression (Spiegelberg, 1930:35–37). When the heart goes forth or "flees" to the object of its longing, its owner becomes confused and flustered. This concept is demonstrated most clearly by an essay in P. Anastasi IV, 4,11–5,5: "Behold my heart has gone forth furtively and hastens to a place that it knows. It has gone downstream that it may see He-ka-Ptah [Memphis]. However, if only I could sit (at ease) and wait for my heart that it may tell me the condition of Memphis. No task can I accomplish as my heart is sundered [or "jumps," *tfy*] from its place" (Caminos, LEM, p. 150, cf. P. Anastasi I, 4,11–5,2). The writer goes on to describe the illness and confusion his heart's "departure" has caused him.

The girl feels that her heart is a separate entity, possessing its own will. Her heart wants to go forth to the boy, but another part of her soul struggles with the heart and restrains it. This other part she identifies as "I," and the translation "ego" is suitable (if the Freudian terminology is not taken too rigorously). The Egyptians conceived of the heart as a separate entity that its owner does not completely control. The heart is liable, for example, to testify against its owner in the post-mortem court, so Egyptians want their hearts to remain with them, to be at one with them. The heart is not only the conscience; it is also the center of desire and impulse. Thus, for example, the common counsel to "follow your heart" means to act in accordance with your desires, to enjoy life. For the girl in this song, the heart is not the restraining element but the impulsive force, the id. And indeed she perceives her heart as an "id"—an "it," an other. In Egyptian psychology the heart embodies both id and superego, for both are perceived as somehow distinct from the essential self, the ego.

No. 35

a. The "Golden One" is Hathor, goddess of love. There is no verse-point here in the manuscript.

b. The "Lady" here is Hathor (written with the goddess det.).

c. The "lady" here is the girl he loves (written with the female det.).

d. "Her love" probably means "their love for her"; see no. 13, n. c, and compare B c4,1, "Love of him (*mrwt.f*) takes the heart of all who walk upon the way" (no. 36). Alternatively, "her love" may mean "her lovemaking," in which case the boy is attributing his sexual fantasies to the "lovers" as well.

e. *Smꜣ*ᶜ: written with a sail (P 5), by confusion with *mꜣ*ᶜ, "wind."

f. Egyptians prayed to Hathor for success in love. Such prayers are implied by declarations on statues at her temple at Deir el-Bahri: for example, "I am the priest of Hathor, (she) who hears the requests of all maidens who weep," and ". . . you inhabitants of Thebes . . . to tell your requests to the Cow of Gold [Hathor], the lady of happy life, the mistress of . . ." (Naville, 1913:III, pl. 9 A.c, B).

g. Lit., "three days to yesterday"; similarly in no. 37.

h. A verse-point appears here, probably by mistake; the syntax does not seem to call for a division. Yet it is possible that the poet (or scribe) wished to produce a four-verse conclusion.

i. "Five" = *diw*, "laud" = *dwꜣ*. The tenses of many of the verbs in section (A) are ambiguous.

No. 36

a. Text has "he passed." The 3rd masc. sg. suffix has appeared by assimilation to the suffix of "his house"; see no. 13, n. d.

b. "Kin": lit., "siblings"—*sn* + male, female, and plural determinatives.

c. No verse-point appears here, but without a division the stich would be unusually long.

d. *Gmḥ.f r.i m-ḏr snny.n.i*: a perfect-active *stp.f* followed by a preposition and nominal ("emphatic") *stp.n.f*, a mixture of LE and ME.

e. See no. 9, n. i.

f. "Inside": that is, into the boy's house, cf. *ẖnw* in no. 34(C).

g. Note the alliteration: *n sn.i snny.i sw*.

h. That is, I would not be embarrassed to kiss him in public; cf. Cant 8:1. Gardiner (1931:pl. XXV) takes *ṯm* to be a writing of *rmi*, contrary to Wb. V, 367, which gives *ṯm* as a separate entry, "ashamed," distinct from *rmi*, "weep"; see "Horus and Seth" 6,14; 7,2; Amenemope 5,6; 22,6; P. Anastasi I, 16,2. See also the discussion in Caminos, 1977:63f.

i. "Six" = *siswt*, "pass" = *sw3*. *Nfr.wsy m sw3*: lit., "how lovely it is, namely the passing." On the syntax see LEG 7.1.1.b.viii. Other possible translations are: "How lovely it is in passing," and "How lovely she is in passing." The last translation is the usual one, but since the authorial voice does not speak elsewhere in this song, I have preferred the translation that makes the verse the girl's own comment. Furthermore, assuming no. 35 to precede this stanza chronologically, the girl is not now "passing"; consequently it seems more natural for her to be thinking of the moment of passing in retrospect than for the poet to be remarking on her beauty as observed during an event that took place six days previously.

No. 37

a. *ʿḳʿḳ n.i ḫ3yt im.i ḫpr.kwi ḥʿwt.i wdnw*: although the syntax is obscure, the general intent of this sentence is clear—he has become ill and sluggish. It seems to me that this sentence is a conflation of two sets of alternatives: (1) *ʿḳʿḳ n.i ḫ3yt* with *ʿḳʿḳ ḫ3yt im.i*, and (2) *ḫpr.kwi wdnw* with *ḥʿwt.i wdnw*.

b. Lit., "I have forgotten (*smḫ*) my own body." He has become paralyzed and has lost control of his body. Compare the phrase "I am one who knows not his own self" (*ḏt.f*; P. Anastasi II, 10,7–11,1; see no. 32, n. d). Fecht (1963:83) says that *ḏt* is a euphemism for phallus; but that interpretation does not fit this context, which describes weakness and paralysis.

c. Emend *sn.i* to *snt.i*.

d. A medical text.

e. Or, "my well-being," written with the *wḏ3*-eye.

f. "Opens her eyes": that is, looks at me, pays attention to me. "Eyes": for this writing of the dual see no. 3, n. e.

g. *Iw.i ḥpt st*: present tense (as in ME). The boy experiences in imagination the events he desires.

h. This stanza is not bracketed by a word-play like the others but only repeats the word "seven" (*sfḫ*). The first line, however, contains the assonance *sfḫ / sf*.

"The Stroll" presents two characters speaking about a single event in their lives from their different points of view. While the story-line does not unfold chronologically, a simple plot holds the parts of the song together. I will summarize this plot and point to some of the threads connecting the various stanzas.

No. 31: A youth looks at a girl walking in the street, praises her in thought, and exclaims upon the powerful influence she has on all who see her.

No. 32: Just as the girl has "captured the heart" of the boy, so does love of him "capture" her. He is near her mother's house, she says, but her mother prevents her from going to him. Apparently her mother is aware of her interest in the staring youth. The girl admits (half-heartedly) that her mother did well in forbidding her to go to him, but she is nevertheless upset. If only he knew the intensity of her desire, he would send to her mother to request the girl as his wife; thereupon her mother, her father, indeed everyone, would join in her happiness. (The audience now knows that this love is mutual, but the lovers themselves do not know this.)

No. 33: The boy relates what happened to him one day when he set out for the girl's house. Both the event and the characters are obscure, and the meaning of several phrases in this stanza is likewise unclear. It seems, however, that the youth decided to go to the house of the girl he saw passing by (three days earlier?), but on the way he met a mysterious figure called Mehi passing by on chariot followed by a group of "lovers." The youth became confused and was seized by doubts. He was afraid that if he were to stride boldly by Mehi he would turn himself over to him and be put into the group called the *kpwy*. The meaning of this event is unclear, but the continuation of the song shows that his hesitations won out and he never reached the girl's house.

No. 34: In her previous statement (no. 32), the girl said that her beloved lacked heart and that she would become like him. And so it was: in no. 33 the youth spoke of his confusion and the folly of his heart. In this stanza the girl reports that she has indeed become "heart-less," so to speak, her heart fleeing from her (see no. 34, n. n). Thus the words of the boy and the girl mirror each other, even though neither is aware of what the other is experiencing. The expression "senseless of heart" (lit., "lacking heart"), which appears in no. 32, thus becomes the leitmotiv of this stanza, as the girl's heart "scurries away" from her and she pleads with it to return to its place, to calm down, not to make her into a fool.

No. 35: The youth declares that he will praise Hathor and will pray to receive the girl's love (A). He reports that the girl came to see him, speaking of the event as if it were *planned* by the girl, and thereby betraying the projection of his desires (B). He tells further of her influence upon him and also upon the (male) "lovers." Finally, he expresses his intention to pray once again to Hathor, but he also complains that he has not seen the girl since she passed by ((C)–(D)). Now the plot becomes clearer. We learn that four days previously ("three full days have passed") the boy had prayed to Hathor. This may refer to the prayer spoken of in (A), in which case this section is in effect a quotation of what he said four days earlier, or it may refer to an unquoted prayer. At any rate, five full days have passed since the girl walked by his house.

No. 36: This stanza parallels the first and fills in our picture of the circumstances in which the introductory stanza was spoken.

The girl's words echo the boy's: "Love of him captures the heart of all who stride upon the way" (no. 36) parallels "Lovely of walk when she strides on the ground, she has captured my heart in her embrace" (no. 31); "a precious youth without peer" (no. 36) parallels "One alone is my sister, having no peer" (no. 31); "He gazed at me when I passed by" (no. 36) parallels "She makes the heads of all the men turn about when seeing her" (no. 31). Thus the sixth stanza describes the same events as the fifth, but now from the girl's perspective.

The girl's mother had forbidden her to go to the boy. Nevertheless she believes that if her mother only knew the power of her desire she would agree to visit the boy's family herself and, presumably, would take her daughter along. Then (the girl imagines) she would dare to kiss him and make their love public.

No. 37: As the girl's absence draws on into the eighth day, the boy's desire turns to illness, until he must lie down, paralyzed by yearning. The same illness he caused her (no. 32(A)) she now causes him; such is the strange reciprocity of love. Only her presence, he believes, could cure him. But as the song comes to an end, a full week after the fateful stroll, the meeting so keenly desired by both youngsters has not yet come to pass.

The plot of this song is not revealed in a direct and simple manner. Certain events spoken of at the beginning of the song are clarified only later on, in retrospect. Complications like these may hamper our understanding of the sequence of events, but at the same time they increase the dramatic tension and draw us into the feelings of the characters.

Just what do the lovers know about each other's feelings? They have at least an inkling that the other is in love as well. The girl's mother has forbidden her to go to the boy (no. 32), so there was some external indication of her interest prior to the event narrated, or at least the mother had reason to think that such an interest could arise. The girl has reason to hope that the boy will come to her ("Sit still, cool down," she tells her heart in no. 34, "until the brother comes to you"), and indeed it has occurred to the boy to come to her (no. 33). The boy says that the girl is "lovely of eyes when gazing" (no. 31), so when in no. 36 she says, "He gazed at me when I passed by," we may surmise that their eyes had locked long enough to convey a hint of reciprocated love.

Yet their awareness of each other's love is certainly inchoate. The girl feels (correctly) that the boy is unaware of the intensity of her love ("He does not know my desires to embrace him"; no. 32). So far they seem to have done no more than to exchange glances. The boy expects her to come to pay a call if he is ill, but he thinks she will do this not on her own but along with other visitors. Clearly they are not yet acknowledged lovers. It seems that at the moment when the girl walked by the boy and their eyes met, something new passed between them, something that awoke in each an overwhelming flush of desire. Each wonders whether the other got the same message.

This song shows us the isolation of two youngsters in the throes of adolescence. Obstacles internal and external prevent them from breaking out of their isolation. The boy starts out for the girl's house, but for reasons that are unclear he gives in to hesitations. He goes on yearning for the girl and praying for her return, yet he is no longer able to take initiative. His inactivity and inhibition express themselves in physical paralysis. Now he is entirely passive as he waits for the girl's initiative. He feels that only a visit from her—a sympathy call—will restore his health. The song ends without his wish being fulfilled.

Alongside the boy's experience we learn of the girl's. Her thoughts match his. Whereas in "The Crossing" the echoing of one lover's words in the words of the other gave expression to the mutuality of love and to the harmony between the lovers' souls, in "The Stroll" the lovers' thoughts run in parallel tracks and never meet, with the result that the echoing only heightens the irony. Though the girl, at least, is aware of the boy's interest in her ("He gazed at me when I passed by"; no. 36), the two are not aware just how similar their souls are, and this similarity, this shared hesitancy, no less than the mother's orders, keeps them apart.

The girl's internal struggle parallels the boy's. Her heart "jumps" to go forth to him, but she struggles with it to keep it within her, and she apparently wins. But this is a sad victory indeed, for now she will stay home and wait for the boy, while the internal struggle that he undergoes ends in a similar victory for hesitation and fear, and he stays home and waits for her. The two lovers, each locked in a private world, do not know how similar their feelings are. Only the audience, privy to the innermost thoughts of the two, can sense the irony of the situation.

"The Stroll" shows one type of love. It is hardly an ideal love. But since the hesitancy and inhibitions of the two characters lead to frustration, we may say that the song "teaches" an ideal, though indirectly: lovers should be bold, open, and active. This, in fact, is also the "moral" of "The Crossing" and of the popular saying that urged: "Follow your heart."

The psychological observations and the hidden teaching in this song do not interfere with its value as entertainment or even with its humor. The frustration in which the song ends is not tragic. The poet takes the personae seriously but not excessively so. The boy and the girl are quite young, still bound to their families, and are perplexed by the stirring of desires still strange to them. One gets the impression that this is the first time they have run into these feelings, and that the end of the song is not the end of their story. Even while making the audience share the lovers' feelings, the poet preserves a certain distance between audience and personae by means of humor and irony. In this way the "Great Entertainer" invites her listeners to smile gently and knowingly at the exaggerated but easily recognizable reactions of the young lovers.

EXCURSUS: MEHI AND HIS FOLLOWERS

A mysterious figure called Mehi (*mḥy*) appears in three difficult Egyptian texts: no. 33, 52, and 53. Since he is introduced with no explanation, we may assume that the Egyptian audience was acquainted with him and his function. We can only note his characteristics and deeds as they appear in these three texts, assuming that the same figure is spoken of in all of them.

1. In the two ostraca (nos. 52, 53) his name appears in a cartouche, determined by a god sign, as if he were a king. In no. 33 the name has no marks of royalty, but there too he appears as an exalted, or at least noble, figure, for he rides in a chariot and has a group of followers with him.

2. According to no. 53 Mehi has a "fortress" (*ṯr*).

3. In the two ostraca, the two lovers, who are spending the day in drinking and lovemaking, "place" (*wꜣḥ*) before Mehi. *Wꜣḥ* is frequently used of making offerings, and since the name Mehi in this text has the god determinative, *wꜣḥ* probably has that meaning here.

4. The name Mehi has a number of homonyms that allow for puns (DLE, p. 234). The three most relevant within the context of love are:

(a) "Flax." In no. 33, the name is written with the dets. appropriate to flax, with no person determinative (A 1), although Mehi is clearly pictured there as a person. Perhaps we are to associate Mehi/"flax" with flaxen "ropes"[2] of love that can entangle and ensnare lovers.

(b) "To seize, trap." *Mḥ* is used to indicate the trapping of the goose (i.e., the youth) in the love trap in no. 10 (H 4,7).

(c) "Garlands" (DLE, p. 233). Garlands were worn on festive occasions.

5. According to no. 33, whoever approaches Mehi is liable to become confused and caught. The young man feels he is likely to give himself to Mehi

2. On the use of flax in rope-making, see Lucas, 1962:134–36.

and to declare, "I belong to you." Then Mehi will "assign" him to his followers, a group called the *kpwy* (possibly "the trapped ones"; see no. 33, n. h). In no. 53 the speaker declares, "I am upon your Ka" (*iw.i ḥr k3.k*), which seems to mean: I will do what you desire. Since Mehi is mentioned in the next line, and since the suffix of "Ka" is masculine, it appears that the speaker is addressing Mehi.

6. Mehi is accompanied by "lovers" (*mryw*, with the phallus determinative). The "lovers" are known only from "The Stroll," where they are called "his [sc. Mehi's] lovers" (no. 33). In no. 31 it is said that whoever embraces the girl described there is "like the foremost of lovers." Thus the "lovers" are experienced in matters of love. When the girl approached the boy, "the 'lovers' bowed down, because of the greatness of her love" (this probably refers to the love they feel for her; see no. 35, n. d); that is, they paid him honor as their chief. *Mryw* plays on *mr*, "to bind." Perhaps the "lovers" are youths who were trapped and bound in love and now accompany Mehi. *Mr* also plays on "ill," a word used of love-sickness in no. 6.

The "lovers'" bowing down should probably not be taken literally. We are hardly to picture a group of men bowing down in the street, for the rest of the poem presumes that the youth's falling in love remains unknown to others, and that would hardly be consonant with a strange public display. The youth is expressing an imagined reality, his feeling that all males, whomever they may otherwise love, must be overwhelmed by his maiden's charms.

Mehi is not known from another source. Mehi (if we take *mḥy* as spelled in these texts as a variant of *mḥ*) is a common name (see Ranke, 1935:I, 163), a shortened form of the name Amenemḥeb. Schott (1950:35) suggests identifying Mehi with one of the princes of the 18th dynasty, perhaps Amenophis II (1438–1412), who was known for his manly prowess and athletic interests, though that is an insufficient reason to identify the Mehi in the love songs with this king who lived over two hundred years before the songs were written. Smither (1948:116) and Schott (1950:35) think Mehi is the male lover, but Hermann is certainly right in saying that Mehi is a "Zwischenfigur," a sort of *arbiter amoris* (1959:106–7).

Perhaps Mehi is to be identified with one of the gods who are called Mehi (Wb. II, 127): Thoth (with the ibis head), the Sacred Steer of Athribis, and a minor deity with the form of a serpent (Book of the Dead, spell 168 A d; Edfu I, 332). The Mehi who appears in the love songs does not have animal form, but according to the Egyptian conception, gods can take on human form and walk about on earth. This happens in "Cheops and the Magicians" (P. Westcar) and (probably) in "Two Brothers" (P. d'Orbiney). It is therefore possible that Mehi in the love songs is a divinity or a fictional character who can sometimes be considered divine, but there is nothing to connect him with a particular god.

The following description of Mehi's character and function fits the information we have but is necessarily very tentative. He is a Cupid-figure who embodies the power of love. He wanders about the earth and holds young people captive in the bonds of love. Whoever turns himself over to love becomes one of Mehi's followers, one of the *kpwy* ("trapped ones"?), who are apparently none other than the group of males called the "lovers."

GROUP B: NOS. 38–40 (G1,1–G2,5)

Three Wishes

38. (Girl)[a]

(A) If only you would come to (your) sister swiftly,[b]
like a swift[c] royal messenger,
whose master's heart seeks the news,
for his heart is eager to hear it.
(B) All the (steeds of) the stables are harnessed for him,
while he has horses (waiting) at the rest stations.
A chariot is harnessed in its place—
no respite for him on the way!
(C) (Only) when he has reached the house of the sister,
will his heart rejoice.[d]

39. (Girl)

(A) If only you would come ⟨to your sister swiftly,⟩[a]
like a royal horse,
the choicest of a thousand among all the steeds,
the foremost of the stables.
(B) As his provender so his ⟨stride⟩[b]—
for his master knows his pace.[c]
If he hears the sound of the whip[d]
he cannot ⟨be restrained⟩.[e]
There is no captain among the foreign troops(?)[f]
who can overtake him.
(C) How the heart of the sister knows
that he is not far from the sister!

40. (Girl)

(A) If only you would come to (your) sister swiftly,
like a gazelle bounding[a] over the desert,
whose legs are shaky,[b] whose body is weary,
for fear has entered his body.

(B) A hunter,[c] dog with him, pursues him,
but they can't even see his dust.
He regards a resting place as a trap(?)[d]
and takes[e] to the river as a road(?).[f]
(C) (Then) ere (you) kiss your hand four times,
you will arrive at her "cave."[g]
You pursue the love of (your) sister,
for the Golden One it is who decrees her for you, my friend.

No. 38

a. The girl refers to herself in the third person, as happens not infrequently in the Egyptian songs: e.g., "Hasten to see your sister, like . . ." in song no. 2, which begins in the first person.

b. *3s.ti* and *3s.tw* (Beatty G2,1): 2nd masc. sg. statives; lit., " . . . to the sister, you being swift."

c. . . . *n 3s*: the genitive serves as an adjective. Alternatively *3s* may be taken as an (emphatic) *stp.f* serving as a genitive (*Gram.* §191), to be translated as a relative clause: " . . . the heart of whose master is impatient for [lit., "swift after"] the news."

d. In section (C) the lover becomes identified with the messenger to whom he was compared.

No. 39

a. The phrase "to your sister swiftly" should probably be supplied here on the basis of the opening lines in nos. 38 and 40 (thus Gardiner, 1931:35).

b. *Sw stnw* (bent-leg det., D 56, + walking legs, D 54): *stnw*, as a non-conclusive verb, cannot take the stative form (LEG 12.4). Emend to *sw (ḥr) wstnw* (haplography of *w*), in accordance with the dets.: lit., "he strides."

c. Lit., "feet." Since this horse's master knows what the animal is capable of and he gives it the best provender, and his swift gallop reflects this care.

d. *Isbr*: "whip"; see Caminos, LEM, p. 216, with references.

e. *Inwtw*: emend to *inty*, "drive back, restrain" (Wb. I, 102); thus Gardiner, 1931:35.

f. *Thr*: "foreign troops" (Schulman, 1964:21f.; but uncertain). The idea is that this horse can escape any danger. The theme of fleeing from danger becomes prominent in the next stanza.

No. 40

a. *Ḫ3p*: perhaps a variant of *š3p*, "to bounce," "bound"; see Caminos, LEM, p. 187; Blackman, 1933:202.

b. *Š3m* (*šm*): "reel" or the like; see Gardiner, 1931:36, and Caminos, LEM, pp. 182f., with references.

c. The text apparently reads plural + male and female dets., though in an unusual and unclear form. But according to the possessive suffix of "with him," we must read the singular here.

d. Illegible word. "Trap" is Lichtheim's guess from context (1976:187).

e. *In.n.f*: lit., "took"/"has taken," if the *stp.n.f* bears its ME tense-indication.

f. An idiom for confusion, see no. 33, n. f. "Road" is uncertain. The two strokes after "road"(?) can hardly represent the numeral "two."

g. *Rwrwt*, "cave," "den," with female det. The word is used elsewhere of a lion's den (Wb. II, 409,2). It appears in no. 49 (with the house det.) and in a variant form, *rwr* (with the female det.), in no. 41. It is quite likely a euphemism for vagina (Hermann, 1959:152; White, 1978:101).

"Three Wishes": Each of the three stanzas of this song is organized into three strophes. The three stanzas all have the same structure and express a single wish, that the youth hurry to his beloved. The components of each stanza are: (A) a wish, addressed to the youth, urging him to hurry to his "sister," with a comparison between the speed required of him and the speed of something that excels in swiftness—a royal messenger, a horse belonging to the king, and a gazelle; (B) an extension of the comparison, describing the image further; (C) a conclusion referring back to the lover and reinforcing the wish.

The character of the woman in this song is suggested indirectly, in the way she wishes for the speedy coming of her beloved. The images describing the desired speed progress in intensity and become rather grating: a messenger whose royal master presses him to hurry, a horse whipped to a gallop in escaping from an enemy, and a gazelle pursued across the desert by a hunter and his dog. The last comparison in particular is harsh and in fact does not seem to serve the point of the comparison, for the gazelle is not running *to* something but is fleeing *from* something, and his weariness, thirst, and panic can only hinder his flight. But the choice of images is not random. The imagery expresses well the wild and unrestrained force of lust, suggesting the intensity of the sexual desire of the youth rushing to his beloved's "cave" and of the girl waiting for him.

The poet shows us love in a perspective unusual in the Egyptian love songs, even though "The Stroll" depicts the confusions and fears that may accompany love. Similarly two contemporary narratives, "Two Brothers" (Lichtheim, 1976:203ff.; see summary in "Historical-Cultural Setting" in chapter 3) and the Demotic tale "Setne I" (Lichtheim, 1980:127ff.), portray the turbulent and even violent elements in sexuality.

GROUP C: NOS. 41–47—"NAKHTSOBEK SONGS" (RECTO 16,9–17,13)

The beginning of the sweet saying, which was found in a book container, and which the scribe Nakhtsobek from the necropolis wrote.[a]

a. On the title see Luft, 1973. The words, "which the scribe . . . wrote" are written over an erasure. On the basis of similar introductory formulas, Luft suggests that the original heading may have read: "The beginning of the writing with the sweet saying, found on a papyrus scroll from the time of King NN, may he live, prosper, and be healthy" or (less likely) " . . . found in the library of the god NN, may he live, prosper, and be healthy" (p. 112). The original heading would have indicated the time or place of origin rather than identifying the author. Above the crocodile sign in Nakhtsobek's name, Luft (p. 116) detects a *wsr* sign (F 12), which would fit a Ramesside royal name. By the usurpation, Nakhtsobek claimed authorship (implied by *ir.n*) of the scroll.

Ṯ3y drf, "while carrying a scroll," does not make much sense. Iversen (1979:78) explains the phrase to mean a box for written documents, assuming that the current determinatives of *ṯ3y*—(finger + hand-with-stick)—are erroneous.

Much in these songs remains obscure. Their interpretation is impeded by the presence of many obscure words and the frequent use of pronouns without proper antecedents, as well as a number of allusions that may be deliberately veiled.

41. (Poet)

(A) When you bring it[a] to the house of (your) sister
and blow(?)[b] into her cave,[c]
her gate(?)[d] will be raised up(?)[e]
that her house-mistress may slaughter[f] it.[g]

(B) Supply her with song and dance[h]
and wine and ale, which she set aside,[i]
that you may intoxicate her senses(?),[j]
and complete her[k] in her night.

(C) And she'll say to you: "Take me in your embrace,
and when dawn breaks that's how ⟨we⟩[l] will be.

a. The referent of "it" is unclear. Gardiner (1931:36) understands "it" as an "obscene" allusion. Hermann (1959:153), following Schott (1950:62), refers the first "it" to the collection itself, which should be brought to the girl's house to serve as a sort of magical formula. Schott regards nos. 41 and 42 as an introduction to the collection (nos. 41–47), giving instructions on the recitation of the songs and on the use of their magical power. But the first two songs do not in fact give instructions for recitation or magical acts, nor do the contents of the other songs seem intended to effect anything magically. Iversen (1979:78f.) translates "When you proceed to . . . ," emending *sw* to *swt* (similarly Luft, 1977:295), but this expedient does not solve the problem of the missing object of "slaughter." I suggest that the implied direct object of "bring" and "slaughter" is the animal brought for the feast (as payment?) and that the poet omitted the antecedent through carelessness. Compare "Our ox will be slaughtered inside" in no. 47.

b. *Ṯ3w* + water det.: Gardiner (1931:36) translates tentatively, "storm into," transferring the figurative sense of English "storm into" to the Egyptian word for "blow." Although the use of *ṯ3w* as a verb meaning "blow into" is otherwise unattested, the above translation requires fewer presuppositions than Luft's interpretation (1977:294), which takes both signs as ideograms (although there are no vertical strokes or dets.) and reads *ṯ3w-mw* (with the sail, P 5, substituting for the nestling, G

47). This combination he explains as a newly formed verb and translates "entfalte du den Feuchtigkeitszauber," a reference to the male's activity in sex.

c. See no. 40, n. g. The female det. reinforces the interpretation of "cave" as vagina rather than as a building or room. Luft (1977:297) translates "ihr Liquides" (though the liquid det. is lacking), but he does not succeed in showing that *rwr* ever had that meaning in Egyptian.

d. *Ḫrᶜ* + house det. (O 1): Luft (1977:298) takes this word as (an unprecedented) three-part composite word meaning "Schutz-des-grossen-Tores," the "door" being the vagina. The obscurity is hardly reduced by this expedient. Iversen (1979:80) equates *ḫrᶜ* with semitic *šrᶜ/šᶜr*, "gate." Blackman (1933:203) compares *šrᶜ*, "gateway," "keep" (see Peet, 1930:51, n. 20). The resulting translation is admittedly not very clear, even as a euphemism.

e. Luft (1977:295, 297) translates "Sie [sc. the maiden] wird geändert." The above translation follows Iversen's translation, "raised up," but the mummy sign (A 53) is clear in the hieratic and cannot be read as the man-with-stick sign (A 24) (contrary to Iversen), but rather must be regarded as a false det. occasioned by aural association with the *-ḳi* of *sḳi* (i.e., *sḳ3*, Wb. IV, 302–303).

f. *Stf* (or *stf*) = *sft*, "slaughter" (Wb. III, 443). The function of the second det., whether brick (O 39) or house (O 1), is unclear. Luft (1977:294, 298): "Ihre Laube [*nbt*] fliesst nun über [*stf*, with false dets.]." It is, however, doubtful that *stf* can mean "overflow" (said of the receptacle, not the liquid), and in any case the resulting translation is obscure.

g. See n. a above.

h. Thus Suys (1935:16f.), in a note to Ani (Cairo Boulaq IV) 3,7, where *ḫᶜb* is clearly determined by the dancing-man sign (A 32). Suys explains the peculiar det. in our text as an acrobatic woman dancer with her hair hanging down (see plate IX). He takes *ḫᶜb* as a variant of *ḫbi*, which sometimes has the hieroglyphic equivalent of the det. used here (see further Green, 1983:30, who observes that the acrobatic dancer det. is unique to *ḫbi* and nouns derived from it).

i. Thus Iversen (1979:80) for *ḫwi*, which is somewhat less unclear than Gardiner's "for her protection" (1931:36) or Luft's "sind ihr Schatten [*šwt.s*]" (1977:294).

j. *Šrgḥ*, an unknown word. Luft (1977:299) takes it as a composite: *š3* (for *š3ᶜ*) + *r* + *g(3)ḥ*, a noun supposedly meaning "Bis-zum-matt-sein," but the construction is dubious and in any case would not make an appropriate direct object for *tḥtḥ*.

k. Or, "end it"—unclear. *Mnḳ* (*ᶜḥᶜ*) in the Bakenkhonsu inscription means "to end (a lifetime)" (Iversen, 1979:81), and see no. 42, n. j. Here it seems to allude to sexual satisfaction.

l. Emended from *iw.w*, "they."

No. 41 offers advice on preparing a feast preceding a night of love-making, when the couple will lie in each other's embrace until morning. Nos. 41 and 42 may constitute a single song. In any case, they describe the same type of activity, on which see the comment following no. 42.

42. (Poet)

(A) When you bring it[a] ⟨to⟩ the hall of (your) sister,
while you are alone, without another,
you may do your desire in her snare,[b]
and the halls(?)[c] will blow lightly(?).[d]

(B) The heavens will descend in a breeze,[e]
(yet) ⟨will not⟩[f] blow it[g] away.
It (only) brings you her fragrance:
an inundating aroma that intoxicates
those who are[h] present.

(C) The Golden One it is who sends[i] her to you as a gift,
to make you fulfill your days.[j]

a. See no. 41, n. a. Supply *r* after *sw*.

b. Luft (1977:300f.) renders "Festplatz" on the basis of the occurrence of a *ḥg3w* on the Roman obelisk of Barbarino, where, however, the meaning is quite uncertain. The above translation follows Murnane, 1978:364. *Ḥgi* in Demotic (= Coptic *hasi* [Sahidic], *hači* [Bohairic]) refers to nets or snares for catching birds. Iversen uses the same etymology in translating (less appropriately) "its door latch" (1979:81). The symbolism of "snare" is hardly opaque.

c. Iversen (1979:81) explains *wnrḫ* (i.e., *wlḫ*) as *wl*, "cover" (Coptic *ôl*) + *ḫr*, "gate." Luft (1977:301) also takes it as a composite, which he translates (obscurely): "Ruderbänk-des-Kindeshauses." It is less far-fetched to connect the word with Demotic *wrḫ*, "hall," or the like (Erichsen, *Glossar*, p. 94; ECU).

d. *Ḫyḫy* = *ḫ3ḫ3*, "to winnow" (Wb. III, 233, 17; Caminos, LEM, p. 357), here perhaps used metaphorically of sexual activity. This word has several Coptic correspondences: *šôš* "to scatter," *šôš* "to make level, to balance out," and *šoeiš*, "dust"; see further CED 259f., KHWB 307. E. Cruz-Uribe, who pointed out the above correspondences to me, suggests that *ḫyḫy* in the present passage means something like "be undisturbed." That is to say, a light wind of the sort used for winnowing will blow without disturbing "it"—"it" (or "her") referring, with deliberate ambiguity, to both the girl and the perfume.

e. "The heavens will descend in a breeze" means that a breeze will come out of the sky; compare *rdi.n.sn iwt pt m ḏ' ḥr ḥy*, "They made the sky come in a storm with rain," or, as we would put it, they made a rainstorm come from the sky (Westcar 11,14).

f. Emend *n nfy.f* to *nn nfy.f*. The subject of *nfy.f* must be *ṯ3w* (masc.), "breeze."

g. Or, "her." The antecedent of *sw* is uncertain. The pronoun probably anticipates "fragrance" (Iversen, 1979:81). The "wind" (whatever that stands for) that "comes down" when the lover "blows" into the girl's house (no. 41; meaning uncertain) will not blow away the fragrance of her perfume.

h. *Nty-iw* (= *nty*) is a phonetic writing equivalent to Coptic *ete* (cf. LEG, ex. 1119).

i. *Wḏ(i)* with legs det., playing on *wḏ*, "to decree," "command"; cf. Beatty I, c2,3; 3,6 (nos. 32, 35) and g2,5 (no. 40) (M 13; Wb. I, 394).

j. Lit., "to make you complete your lifetime," that is to say, to make you live the entire lifespan allotted to you. "To complete one's lifespan" (*ʿḥʿw*) is a positive concept and does not merely mean to die. See no. 41, n. k. *Mnḳ.k st* (no. 41) and *mnḳ.k ʿḥʿw.k* (no. 42) appear to be a play on words, but the import is clear.

Nos. 41 and 42 seem to be two stanzas of one song. Each consists of ten stichs (marked off by verse-points) and falls into two strophes of four stichs plus one strophe of two stichs. Both no. 41 and no. 42 offer advice on how to get one's will of a lady. Certain allusions in no. 41 become more explicit in no. 42.

Who is the girl's "house-mistress"? It is doubtful that the girl's mother would be called that or would play the role envisioned here. (The expression "Mistress of the house" (*nbt pr*) is used of one's wife but not of one's mother.) It seems rather that she is mistress of a house of prostitution such as is portrayed in the Turin pornographic papyrus (Omlin, 1973) and described in P. Anastasi IV, 12,3–5, where a father chastises a young scribe for dissolute behavior in a brothel: "Now you are (still) seated in the house [*iwy.t*] and the harlots [*ḥnmwt*] surround you; now you are standing and bouncing. . . . Now you are seated in front of the wench, soaked in anointing-oil, your wreath of *ištpn* at your neck, and you drum upon your belly. Now you stumble and fall over upon your belly, anointed with dirt" (Caminos, LEM, p. 182). Although the father (or teacher) speaking in P. Anastasi IV takes a more jaundiced view of such goings-on than does the poet of nos. 41–42, they basically agree on what the "house" has to offer: sex, feasting (implied in P. Anastasi IV by the references to oil and wreaths), and plenty of strong drink. Observe too that in no. 42 the phrase "those present" implies group activities such as are mentioned in P. Anastasi IV and depicted in the Turin papyrus.

Compare further Prov 7:5–23, where a prostitute invites a youth to come to her house and says, "I have weal-offerings [at my place]; today I paid my vows" (v. 14). Commentators are divided on the meaning of these sacrifices, but the passage does indicate a connection between prostitution and animal sacrifices—perhaps just that sacrifices made meat available for feasting. Other motifs in nos. 41–42 are recalled by the words of the prostitute in Prov 7: "I have spread covers on my bed, cloths of Egyptian linen. I have sprinkled my bed with myrrh, aloes, and cinnamon. Come, let's imbibe love [*dodim*] until morning, let us revel in lovemaking [*ʾᵒhabim*]" (7:16–18). In particular, the last sentence resembles the invitation of the Egyptian girl quoted at the end of no. 41: "Take me in your embrace, and when dawn breaks that's how we will be."

Though it may seem strange if not repulsive that songs on the pleasures of prostitution should be included in a collection of love songs, we should note that some of the loveliest love poems in classical Greece and Rome and in Elizabethan England were dedicated to courtesans, and that the "love" spoken of in those songs often meant little more than raw lust leavened by self-pity.

43. (Boy)

(A) How skilled is she—(my) sister—at casting the lasso,[a]
yet she'll ⟨draw in⟩ no cattle![b]
(B) With her hair[c] she lassos me,
with her eye she pulls (me) in,
with her thighs[d] she binds,[e]
with her seal she sets the brand.

a. Iversen (1979:82) connects *iwnr* (i.e., *iwl*) with Demotic *ꜣl*, Coptic *alô*, *elô*, which translates *brochos*. CED 4/6 relates *alô* to *wꜣrt* (Wb. I, 252, 3–5).

b. *Nn ms.s* (child det., A 17) *irw* (cattle det., E 1): obscure. Possibly: "yet she shall not bring [i.e., pay] the cattle tax" (cf. Simpson, 1972:324), that is to say, because she does not actually catch cattle she does not have to pay the cattle tax. Alternatively, *ms*, in spite of the writing, may be taken as an enclitic particle (*Gram.* §251) and *irw* (or *ir kꜣw*) may mean "cattle herder" (although this is not attested elsewhere); thus: "but obviously she is not a cattle herder" (ECU). The simplest expedient is to take the writing of *ms* "child" as an aural error for *ms* "bring." *Irw* is then a variant writing of *iryt* (Wb. I, 114,18), "cow." The *nn stp.f* can express an asseverative future negation or a generalizing present; see NÄG §753.

c. Cf. no. 3. A girl's hair (*šnw*) is a "net" (*šnw*) that ensnares a young man.

d. Gardiner (1931:37) reads the pellet det. (N 33), guessing the meaning of *mny* to be "ruddle," which, however, would not be an appropriate means of "subjugating" (*ḳnb*). *Mny* + pellet det. does occur elsewhere (Caminos, LFHS, pl. 12,2), but *mnty* "thighs" is more appropriate here; see note to text, B 17,3, in App. C.

e. As in Demotic, *ḳnb* means "to fetter" (Iversen, 1979:82).

This poem is a carefully constructed conceit. Part (A) presents a riddle: how can it be that the young lady is skilled in casting the lasso yet does not catch cattle? The answer: it is not cattle, but *me*, that she (1) catches (with her hair), (2) pulls in (with her eye), (3) subjugates or binds (with her thighs), and (4) brands (with her seal), making me hers forever. Since the first three devices the girl employs to catch "cattle" turn out to be parts of her body, we may suspect that her "seal," applied after she binds the boy with her thighs, is part of her anatomy too.

Part (B) answers a riddle implicit in part (A). The undoubted emphatic formations of "she brings" and "she fetters," and the probably emphatic forms of "she casts" and "she brands," show that part (B) answers the question "*How* does she do her cattle catching?" rather than "*What* does she do?"

44. (Girl)

While you (yet) argued with[a] your heart—
"After her![b] Embrace her!"—
as Amon lives, it was I who came to you,
my tunic on my shoulder.[c]

a. *Ir m-di* (for *m-ḏr*, LEG ex. 1134) *ḏd.k*: *Ir m-ḏr stp.f* has a past-tense indication (LEG 32.2, 32.3).

b. Omit the superfluous *n.i* after *m-s3.s*.

c. A sign of haste; compare the similar motif in no. 16.

A girl scolds her boyfriend for delaying in carrying out his decision to come to her (a motif handled differently in no. 33). His delay forced her to take the initiative.

45. (Girl)

My brother is at the watercourse,[a]
his foot planted on the riverbank.[b]
He prepares a festival altar for spending the day
with the choicest(?)[c] of the beers.
He "grants (me) the hue"[d] of ⟨his⟩[e] loins.
It is longer than broad.

a. Lit., "is found" (passive *stp.f*); alternatively: *gm(.i)*, "I found" (perfect-active *stp.f*). *Ḫnini* + water det. appears in AEO I, no. 31, p. *7f., with references. Iversen (1979:84) explains *ḫnnini* [*sic*] as a diminutive of *ḫnw*, "river" (Wb. III, 173,5–8).

b. *Itrw*. Thus Iversen (1979:84), who compares Coptic *ḫaior*, "bank."

c. *Stnw*: taken as equivalent to *sṯnw*, "distinguished" (passive), thus "choice," although the expected dets. are lacking; very uncertain.

d. An idiom for showing them in their nakedness, see no. 21A, n. f.

e. Emend "my (?) [A 1] loins" to "his loins," because the girl is looking at her lover and describing him.

I surmise that the girl is saying—in a suggestive, "naughty" fashion—that as her boyfriend bends over while making preparations for their private festivities, she sees his nakedness under his loincloth. "It" in the last line probably alludes to his phallus (Gardiner, 1931:37, suspects it is "an obscene reference"), not to the plural "loins."

46. (Boy)

As for what she—(my) sister—did to me,
    should I keep silent to her?
She left me standing[a] at the door of her house
    while she went inside,
and did not say to me "Welcome!"[b]
    but blocked[c] her ears in *my* night.[d]

a. *P3 dit ꜥḥꜥ.i m r n pr.s*: lit., "(namely) the causing me to stand"—a nominal clause in apposition with "what she did to me."

b. *Wḥꜥ.k* with the legs det. (D 54) means "to return home," in particular in the evening (Wb. I, 349,10). Gardiner reads two dets., legs over phallus (D 53), and suggests that the word refers to sexual "release," a hapax legomenon in this sense (1931:38). Iversen (1979:85) correctly reads *.k* under the legs (see note to 17,7 in my transcription). The construction is probably *wḥꜥ.k (m) nfr*, lit., "May you come home in pleasantness"—in other words, "Welcome home!" Compare the sense of *m nfr* in no. 28 (1,9).

c. Reading *dni idn*. The ear sign is accompanied by a stroke and seems to be an ideogram; *dni* then lacks a det. Possibly, however, the ear sign is a det., as in Turin Strike Papyrus, ro. 3,5 (RAD 56,7).

d. That is, the night that by rights was mine; cf. no. 20E, n. c.

A youth stands outside the door of the girl he longs for and bewails his exclusion.

47. (Boy)

(A) ⟨I⟩[a] passed by her house in a daze.[b]
    I knocked, but it was not opened to me.
A fine night for our doorkeeper![c]
(B) Bolt, I will open (you)!
    Door,[d] you are my fate![e]
You[f] are my (very) spirit.[g]
    Our ox will be slaughtered inside.[h]
(C) O Door, exert not your strength,[i]
    so that oxen may be sacrificed to (your) bolt,
        fatlings to (your) threshold,[j]
a stout goose[k] to (your) jambs,
    and an oriole[l] to (your) lintel(?).
(D) But every choice piece of our ox
    will be[m] (saved) for the carpenter lad,[n]
that he may fashion us a bolt of reeds,
    a door of grass(?).[o]

(E) (Then) at any time the brother can come
and find her house open,
and find a bed spread with fine linen,
and a pretty little maidservant too.[p]

(F) The little maid will say to me,[q]
" . . . to the mayor."[r]

a. Read *snn.i* for *snn.k*: assimilation of suffix to the *.k* of *wḫ3.k(wi)*; see no. 13, n. d.

b. *Wḫ.k(wi)*: see WMT 207. In P. Ebers §855w, *wḫ(3) ib dp ib* is glossed as restriction of the heart, darkness in the belly, unconsciousness (*ʿm ib*). While *wḫ3* here cannot mean "unconscious," it may mean something like "befogged" or "in a daze," a condition perhaps due to excessive preoccupation with desire.

c. A fine night for him and not for me, for he is doing his job all too successfully.

d. Gardiner (1931:38) connects *ṯr* with *tri* in P. Harris I, 4,1, both of which may be loanwords from semitic *dl(t)*, "door."

e. A complaint directed at the door: you are the death of me. *Š3y* is determined here by Z 6, a sign indicating death. "Fate" = the type of death for which one is destined, as in "The Doomed Prince" (Lichtheim, 1976:200–203); cf. especially the words of the crocodile to the prince: "I am your fate, who has been following you" (P. Harris 500, vso. 8,11).

f. Omit *n* before *(m)ntk*. Possibly, however, *n* is for the interrogative *in*.

g. *3ḫ* + seated-man-with-flagellum det. (A 51): "Akh," a word generally meaning one's effective spirit after death. "Akh" does not seem to bear its usual meaning of beneficial spirit in this context. It occasionally designates evil or inimical spirits, as in the Bentresh stela, where a woman who has fallen ill is said to be "in the condition of one under the Akhs" (Žabkar, 1968:88f.). The boy may be accusing the door of being an Akh of this sort.

h. The simple present of *tw.tw (ḥr) sft* (LEG 19.4.1–2) is difficult in this context. This sentence is apparently a virtual apodosis of the preceding one: i.e., if you are my beneficial spirit, then our ox will be slaughtered inside. The construction would gain a future connotation by context: "is slaughtered" = "is as good as slaughtered." Compare the first present in wishes: e.g., no. 21A, n. a, and NÄG §482.

i. *B3w* = "strength" or "wrath," in particular the angry, punitive power of a god (Caminos, 1964:76f., with references; idem., 1977:66, with references).

j. *Pnʿt (pnʿyt)*, probably "threshold"; see CED 126/5 and KHWB 149, no. 1. The word appears in Amenemope 3,14.

k. Move the verse-point from here back to *pnʿt*, "threshold."

l. *Gnw* + *sp 2*: Most likely *gnw* is a type of bird (Wb. V, 174,2), and *sp 2* is a copyist's error for the alighting-duck sign (G 41), which is used as the det. of *sr* earlier in the line. The hieratic for *sp 2* and the alighting duck are similar enough to explain such an error. Possibly the copyist's eye was attracted to the *sp 2* closely following upon this word. For *gnw* (a bee-eater) see Blackman, 1915:III, pl. VI, 14, and Griffith, 1898:100. Van de Walle, 1978:46, identifies *gnw* as the oriole. Iversen (1979:87) takes *g(3)nw* as a writing of *ḳnw*, "many," but there is no reason to assume an otherwise unknown and very idiosyncratic writing of *ḳnw*—without the usual dets.—when that word is used in its normal form frequently in this papyrus.

m. Read third pl. for first pl., the latter being impossible in this context.

n. The term *ms ḥmww*, "carpenter lad" (Blackman, 1933:203) hides a second meaning, for it is a common epithet of Ptah, "the one who creates the arts," Wb. III, 86,12–14 (ECU). The youth will give the choicest pieces of his offering to Ptah, who as god of reeds (see no. 5) will make a door of reeds.

o. Reading unclear, but the word has a plant det. (M 2). Wb. V, 520 lists a plant called *ḏꜣys*, to which the current text may be emended.

p. Lit., "with them," apparently meaning with the girl and the bed, unless *ḥꜥty* (with plural strokes) is grammatically plural, "beds," in which case the maid is with the "beds." However, *ḥꜥty* (Wb. III, 43)/ *ḥty* may have plural strokes in the singular, as in *pꜣ 2 ḥty*, RAD 65,11; 66,6.

q. Emend the fem. suffix to masc.

r. The last two lines are obscure. Iversen (1979:87f.) takes the last line as a colophon and translates (with emendations): "She who sang to me was Tashere from the music hall of the children of the city-prefect." He emends *tnw* (*rnw*?) to *ḫnw*, "music," although it lacks the appropriate dets. His translation does not accord with the reading in Gardiner's corrigenda (1931:46), and in any case produces an unparalleled sort of colophon.

In this song the youth promises to let the door, with all its parts, participate in the couple's festivities if it will let him pass. Compare the motif of the trees' participation in lovers' trysts in "The Orchard" (nos. 28–30). The youth in no. 47 further promises a rich reward to the carpenter's apprentice (and/or Ptah; see n. n) if he will make him a door of grass that cannot keep him out. In the Book of the Dead, spell 125 c, §7 (Naville, 1886:II Schl. 27ff.), the personified parts of the gate of the Hall of Two Truths refuse entry to the dead man unless he can declare their names. The doorkeeper and the *bnš* ("jambs"), *ḳr* ("bolt" or "hinge"), and *pnꜥt* ("threshold") are mentioned. For example: " 'We will not let you enter past us,' say the jambs of this gate, 'unless you tell our name.' Accurate Plumb Bob is your name." (The meanings of the names of the door parts are largely guesses.)

Source V: Miscellanea

These 19th and 20th dynasty texts include some fragmentary ostraca from Deir el-Medineh that can be translated only in an experimental and partial fashion (nos. 49–53). The rendering of nos. 49–53 is intended only to show the motifs that appear in them. Other possible love song ostraca, which I do not attempt to translate, are listed above (see p.7).

48. A fragment written on the verso of P. Anastasi II (LEM 19).
(Girl)

If the wind comes, it is headed to the sycamore.
    If you come, [you are headed to me].[a]

a. Thus Erman (1901 : 147). This snippet may merely be a greeting like the other words on the verso of this papyrus instead of a love song.

49. DM 1038 verso.
(Girl)

. . . ———[a] behind me.
He is this love-wolf.[b]
. . . eating(?)[c] (in the?) cave[d]
that is within . . .
stones,[e] under the moringa-[tree].[f]
. . . eating of bread.
. . . offering to the gods . . .

a. *Idn*: "serve as deputy," "represent," "govern."

b. *P3 wnš dd*, determined by the phallus sign. Compare the affectionate epithet *p3y.i ṯ3 n wnš*, "my (little) wolf (or jackal) cub," which is followed by *dd p3y.k tḫ*, "(your) liquor is lovemaking" (no. 4).

c. *Ḳnḳn* (Wb. V, 56, 15), lacking a det. Cf. also Wb. V, 56, 12, which indicates that *ḳnḳn* is a food item appearing in later offering lists. Sacrifices and eating are referred to just below in this text.

d. *Rwrw*: compare the "cave" (of the girl) in nos. 40 (n. g) and 41.

e. *ʿrr*: Wb. I, 208, 11 gives "pebble." The det. here (brick, O 39) suggests "block of stone"; see RAD 57/11.

f. "Under the moringa-tree" is usually a divine epithet (Wb. I, 423, 10–13).

The combination of the cave, eating, and sacrifice motifs is reminiscent of no. 41. Noteworthy too is the conjunction of a sexual reference with cultic motifs.

50. DM 1040
(Girl)

Let me turn over.[a]
    Watch your body yourself!
Direct your face inside
    and you deprive[b] your heart
        of that pleasantness of body.

a. Or, "turn over," or "I've turned over," or "turn me over."

b. *Gbi m*: see Caminos, LEM, p. 57.

Although this ostracon offers four complete lines—perhaps the complete text—I cannot figure out what it means. It may not really be a love song.

51. DM 1078, recto.
(Boy)

I spend the day
imploring [my lady]: . . .
"Don't do (that) to me,
my lady, don't!
Don't leave me waiting!"[a]
(I) will take
my horse
before the wind[b]
in her love.
. . .
lead.
I lay me down[c]
. . . the water of the . . .
message.

a. *Ḫꜣꜥ* sometimes means "divorce," "repudiate" (Pestman, 1961:60). If we read *m (ir) isḳ.i* after it, we can translate "Don't repudiate me!" (ECU).

b. Meaning "hurry"? Perhaps the horse (not distinguished from "mare" in LE orthography) represents the girl (cf. Cant 1:9). If so, the expression has sexual implications. Compare the obscure role of the "wind" in no. 42.

c. Or, "clothe (the bed)." *Nmꜥ* can imply helplessness, as in Med. Habu 82, 14a, cf. "Horus and Seth," Beatty I, 3,11. Helplessness seems appropriate to this context, since the speaker sounds downhearted. The det. for being high, rejoicing, and mourning (A 28) appears after the lacuna.

A lover quotes his entreaty to his lady. The translation is divided according to the existing verse-points, which are placed at exceptionally short intervals.

52. DM 1078 verso.
(Boy)

The lady sails north while [drinking][a] beer.
An island is before him . . .
. . . sail.[b]
Cool . . .
. . . pure gold.
We will cast the heel[c] . . .
. . .
We will place (gifts) before
(King) Mehi,
saying:
. . . love.
Spend the day.

a. A word is missing, with only the det. for eating, drinking, and emotions (A 2) remaining. Perhaps [*m swri*] *n tḫ*: "in the drinking of beer."

b. Perhaps *ḥḏꜣy* = *ḥtꜣ*, "sail," which sense fits the sail det. (ECU).

c. An obscure phrase, determined (if the reading is correct) by an upside-down man. This det. fits the imagery of drunkenness and disorder.

The above translation is divided according to the existing punctuation (red dots), which hardly indicates *verses* (or stichs) in this text. This text is important for its association of love with King Mehi, on whom see "Excursus: Mehi and His Followers" above.

53. DM 1079
(Boy?)[a]

. . .
Beer is sweet,
when I am at his side
[and my] hands have not been far away.
The wind blows
as I say in my heart,
"______[b] . . . with sweet wine.
I am given to you[c]
by the powers of [love(?)]."
. . .[d]
My voice is hoarse[e] from saying,
"(King) Mehi! Life, prosperity, health!"
He is in his fortress.[f]
. . . ______ . . .

a. The sign for first person is masc. If the speaker is a male, then "his side" refers to Mehi, and "I am given to you" (masc.) is addressed to him.

b. An imperative. Perhaps "Get drunk!"

c. Lit., "I am upon your spirit" (*k3*), perhaps meaning that he is consecrated to him (*k3* often merely holds the pronoun). Compare no. 33, " 'I belong to you' [sc. to Mehi]—I'll tell him—and he will boast of my name." There too love brings the youth into Mehi's presence, though the lover hesitates to "give himself" to him.

d. Only the det. for house, room, etc. (O 1) remains. Perhaps the reference is to Mehi's fortress, mentioned further on.

e. *Ḫnr*, "hot," "hoarse," is predicated of "voice" in P. Berlin 10456, 14, where a medicine is prescribed for hoarseness; see Westendorf, 1974.

f. *Ṯr* = *ṯ3rt*, Wb. V, 356, 1.

54. O. Gardiner 304 recto (HO I, 38). Ramses III (ca. 1182–1151). (Boy)

My sister's love[a] is in the . . .
. . . body.
Her necklace is of flowers;
her bones are reeds.[b]
Her little seal-ring[c] is [on her finger],
her lotus in her hand.
I kiss [her] before everyone,[d]
that they may see my love.[e]
Indeed it is she who captures my heart,
when[f] she looks at me,
(I) am refreshed.

a. Probably = my beloved sister, see no. 11, n. e.

b. That is, slender and delicate.

c. The same expression occurs in no. 21C. The present stich is neither description nor praise. Its point may be: I—her seal-ring—am forever bound to her. Is he also her "lotus" (cf. no. 20C)? Only one or two signs are missing here, according to the editors, so that there does not seem to be space for a comparison. Even the above restoration may be too long.

d. *Wn bw nb*: the *wn* is superfluous.

e. *P3y.i mrwt* (spelled *mrwti*): the infinitive indicating physical lovemaking (see no. 4, n. b).

f. *R m–ḏr* for *ir m–ḏr*.

A short Praise Song. Compare no. 36, in which the girl declares her desire to kiss her beloved before the eyes of his friends and family (*iryw*); compare too Cant 8:1.

CHAPTER 2

The Song of Songs

Translation

(1:1) The Song of Songs, which is by Solomon.

(Girl)

(2) Oh that he'd kiss me with the kisses of his mouth—
for your caresses are better than wine!
(3) As for scent, your oils are good:
"Oil of Turaq" is your name.
That's why maidens love you.
(4) Take me with you, let us hasten!
The king has brought me to his chambers.
We will be glad and rejoice in you;
we will praise your caresses.
More than smooth wine do they love you.

(Girl)

(5) Black I am—but lovely—
O girls of Jerusalem,
like tents of Kedar,
curtains of Salmah.
(6) Pay no mind that I am swarthy,
that the sun has gazed upon me.
My mother's sons were mean to me,
made me keeper of the vineyards.
My vineyard I could not keep.

(7) Tell me, my soul's beloved:
where do you graze,
where do you rest your flocks at noon?—
lest I be like "one who wraps herself up"
by your companions' flocks!

(Boy)

(8) If you don't know,
most beautiful of women,
go on out in the tracks of the flock,
and graze your kids
by the shepherds' camps.

(Boy)

(9) To a mare in Pharaoh's chariotry
I compare you, my darling:
(10) lovely are your cheeks in bangles,
your neck in strings of beads.
(11) Bangles of gold we will make for you,
with spangles of silver.

(Girl)

(12) While the king is on his couch,
my spikenard gives forth its fragrance.
(13) To me my beloved is a sachet of myrrh—
between my breasts he'll spend the night.
(14) To me my beloved is a spray of henna—
in the vineyards of Ein Gedi.

(Boy)

(15) How beautiful you are, my darling,
how beautiful!
Your eyes are doves.

(Girl)

(16) How beautiful you are, my beloved, indeed delightful!
Indeed, our bed is verdant.
(17) The rafters of our house are cedars;
our beams are cypresses.

(Girl)

(2:1) I'm just a crocus of Sharon,
a valley-lily.

(Boy)

(2) Like a lily among brambles,
so is my darling among girls.

(Girl)

(3) Like an apricot tree among trees of the thicket,
so is my beloved among boys:
I delight to sit in his shade,
and his fruit is sweet to my palate.
(4) He brought me to the house of wine,
and his intent toward me was love.
(5) Put me to bed among fruit clusters,
spread me my bed among apricots,
for I am sick with love.
(6) His left hand is under my head,
and his right hand embraces me.
(7) I ask you to promise, girls of Jerusalem,
by the gazelles or the hinds of the wild:
do not disturb, do not bestir love,
before it wishes.

(Girl)

(8) Listen! My beloved—
he's coming now!
Bounding over the mountains,
leaping over the hills.
(9) My beloved is like a gazelle
or a young roe.
Now he stands behind our wall,
peering in through the windows,
glancing in through the lattice.
(10) My beloved spoke and said to me:

(Boy)

"Arise, my darling, my beautiful,
and come away.
(11) For see, the winter has departed,
the rain has passed and gone its way.
(12) The blossoms have appeared in the land,
the time of song has arrived,
and the voice of the turtledove is heard in our land.

(13) The fig tree sweetens its young fruit,
      and the vine is in bud, giving off fragrance.
Arise, my darling, my beautiful,
      and come away.
(14) My dove in the clefts of the rock,
      in the covert of the cliff—
let me see your form,
      let me hear your voice,
for your voice is sweet,
      your form is lovely."

(Girl?)

(15) Catch us foxes,
      little foxes
that spoil vineyards,
      for our vineyards are in bud.

(Girl)

(16) My beloved is mine and I am his:
      he grazes among the lilies.
(17) Before the day blows softly in,
      and the shadows flee,
turn, my beloved, and be as a gazelle,
      or as a young roe,
            on the mountains of Bether.

(Girl)

(3:1) On my bed night after night
      I often sought my soul's beloved;
            I sought him, but did not find him.
(2) I shall get up and roam the city,
      through the streets and squares.
I shall seek my soul's beloved.
      I sought him but did not find him.
(3) The watchmen who roam the city found me.
      "My soul's beloved—have you seen him?"
(4) Scarcely had I left them
      when I found my soul's beloved.
I seized him—now I won't let him go
      till I've brought him to my mother's house,
            to the room of her who conceived me.

(5) I ask you to promise, girls of Jerusalem,
    by the gazelles or the hinds of the wild:
do not disturb, do not bestir love,
    before it wishes.

(Girls of Jerusalem?)

(6) Look who's coming up from the wilderness
    in columns of smoke,
perfumed with myrrh and frankincense,
    all sorts of merchant's powder!

(Girl)

(7) Look! Solomon's own couch!
    Around it threescore warriors,
        from the warriors of Israel,
(8) all of them swordsmen,
    skilled in warfare,
each with his sword along his thigh,
    because of nocturnal fear.
(9) King Solomon made himself a canopied bed
    of the trees of the Lebanon.
(10) Its pillars he made of silver,
    its carpets of gold,
its cushions of purple,
    its interior inlaid with stones.

Girls of Jerusalem, (11) go forth,
    and behold, girls of Zion,
Solomon the king
    in the crown his mother set upon him
on the day of his wedding,
    on the day of his heart's joy!

(Boy)

(4:1) How beautiful you are, my darling,
    how beautiful!
Your eyes are doves
    seen through your veil.
Your hair is like a flock of goats
    streaming down Mount Gilead.

(2) Your teeth are like a flock of shorn sheep,
come up from the wash,
all of whom bear twins,
none of whom miscarries.
(3) Like a thread of scarlet are your lips,
and your mouth is lovely.
Like a slice of pomegranate is your cheek,
seen through your veil.
(4) Your neck is like the Tower of David,
built in courses.
A thousand shields are hung upon it,
all sorts of warriors' bucklers.
(5) Your two breasts are like two fawns,
twins of a gazelle,
which graze among the lilies.
(6) Before the day blows softly in,
and the shadows flee,
I'll make my way to the mountain of myrrh,
to the hill of frankincense.
(7) Wholly beautiful you are, my darling:
no blemish in you!

(Boy)
(8) Come from Lebanon, my bride,
come, from Lebanon draw near.
Come forth from the peak of Amana,
from the peak of Senir and Hermon,
from the dens of lions,
from the lairs of leopards.
(9) You have captured my heart, my sister, my bride,
you have captured my heart with one of your eyes,
with a single strand of your necklace.
(10) Your caresses—how beautiful, my sister, my bride!
Your caresses—how better than wine,
the scent of your oils than all spices!
(11) Your lips, my bride, drip honeycomb,
honey and milk are under your tongue,
and the scent of your garments is like the scent of Lebanon.
(12) A garden locked is my sister, my bride,
a garden locked, a spring sealed.

(13) Your watered fields are an orchard:
pomegranates with luscious fruits,
henna with spikenards,
(14) spikenard and saffron, cane and cinnamon,
with frankincense trees of all kinds,
myrrh and aloes,
with all the best spices.
(15) A garden spring,
a well of living water,
liquids from Lebanon.

(Girl)
(16) Awake, O north wind, and come, O south!
Blow on my garden that its spices may flow.
Let my beloved come into his garden,
and eat of its luscious fruit.

(Boy)
(5:1) I come into my garden, my sister, my bride,
I taste my myrrh with my spice,
I eat my nectar with my honey,
I drink my wine with my milk.

(Girls of Jerusalem?)
Eat well, O friends,
drink yourselves drunk on caresses!

(Girl)
(2) I slumbered, but my heart was alert.
Listen! My beloved is entreating:

(Boy)
"Open to me, my sister, my darling,
my dove, my perfect one,
for my head is drenched with dew,
my locks with the mist of the night."

(Girl)
(3) "I have slipped off my robe.
How can I put it on?
I have bathed my feet.
How can I get them soiled?"

(4) My beloved stretched his hand in through the hole,
and my insides moaned for him.
(5) I arose to open to my beloved,
and my hands dripped myrrh,
my fingers—liquid myrrh,
on the handles of the lock.
(6) I opened to my beloved,
but my beloved had turned away and gone.
Because of him my soul went forth:
I sought him but did not find him,
I called him but he did not answer me.
(7) The watchmen who roam the city found me—
they beat me and bruised me,
took my shawl away from me—
those who watch the walls.
(8) I ask you to promise, girls of Jerusalem:
if you find my beloved
do not tell him
that I am sick with love.

(Girls of Jerusalem)
(9) Your beloved—how is he better than any other,
O most beautiful of women?
Your beloved—how is he better than any other
that you make us promise this?

(Girl)
(10) My beloved is bright and ruddy,
preeminent among a myriad.
(11) His head is finest gold,
his locks fronds of a palm,
black as a raven.
(12) His eyes are like doves
by water channels,
bathing in milk,
sitting by a brimming pool.
(13) His cheeks are like beds of spices,
towers of perfumes.
His lips are lilies—
they drip liquid myrrh.

(14) His arms are cylinders of gold,
inlaid with jasper.
His belly is an ivory bar,
adorned with lapis lazuli.
(15) His thighs are marble pillars,
set on pedestals of gold.
His form is like the Lebanon,
distinguished as the cedars.
(16) His palate is sweet drink;
he is wholly a delight.
This is my beloved, this is my darling,
O girls of Jerusalem!

(Girls of Jerusalem)
(6:1) Which way did your beloved go,
O most beautiful of women?
Which way did your beloved turn,
that we may seek him with you?

(Girl)
(2) My beloved has gone down to his garden,
to the beds of spices,
to graze in the gardens,
and to gather lilies.
(3) I am my beloved's and my beloved is mine:
he grazes among the lilies.

(Boy)
(4) You are as beautiful, my darling, as Tirzah,
as lovely as Jerusalem,
as awesome as the most eminent.
(5) Turn your eyes away from me,
for they make me tremble.
Your hair is like a flock of goats
streaming down Gilead.
(6) Your teeth are like a flock of ewes
come up from the wash,
all of whom bear twins,
none of whom miscarries.
(7) ⟨Like a thread of scarlet are your lips,
and your mouth is lovely.⟩
Like a slice of pomegranate is your cheek,
seen through your veil.

(8) Threescore queens there are,
and fourscore concubines,
and maidens without number.
(9) But one alone is she—my dove, my perfect one—
one alone is she to her mother,
pure is she to her who bore her.
Girls beheld her and called her fortunate,
queens and concubines, and they praised her:
(10) "Look who's gazing down like the morning star,
beautiful as the moon,
pure as the sun,
as awesome as the most eminent!"

(Girl?)

(11) I've come down to the nut garden,
to see the fruits of the valley—
to see if the vine has blossomed,
the pomegranates bloomed.
(12) I do not know myself—
you've placed me in a chariot with a nobleman!

(Girls of Jerusalem?)

(7:1a) Come back, come back, O perfect one,
come back, come back, that we may gaze at you!

(Boy)

(1b) Why would you gaze at the perfect one
as if she were a camp-dancer?!
(2) How lovely are your feet in sandals,
O noblewoman!
The curves of your thighs are like jewelry,
work of an artist's hands.
(3) Your navel is a rounded bowl—
may it never lack mixed wine!
Your belly is a heap of wheat,
hedged about with lilies.
(4) Your two breasts are like two fawns,
twins of a gazelle.
(5) Your neck is like an ivory tower.

Your eyes are pools in Heshbon
by the gate of Bath Rabbim.
Your nose is like the tower of Lebanon,
looking toward Damascus.

(6) Your head sits upon you like Carmel,
  and the thrums of your head are like purple:
    a king is captured by the locks!
(7) How beautiful you are, how pleasant,
  O love, delightful girl!

(Boy)
(8) Thus your stature: it resembles a palm,
  and your breasts are like clusters.
(9) I said to myself, I shall climb the palm
  and lay hold of its branches.
Let your breasts be like clusters on a vine,
  the scent of your nose like apricots,
(10aα) and your palate like the best wine—

(Girl)
(10aβ) flowing smoothly to my beloved,
(10b) dripping on scarlet lips.
(11) I am my beloved's and his passion is for me.

(12) Come, my beloved, let's go to the field.
  We'll pass the night in the countryside;
(13) we'll go early to the vineyards.
We'll see if the vine has blossomed,
  the bud opened,
    the pomegranates bloomed.
There I will give you my love.
(14) The mandragoras give off fragrance,
  and at our doors are all sorts of luscious fruits,
    fruits both new and old:
my caresses, which I've saved for you.

(Girl)
(8:1) If only you were like a brother to me,
  one who nursed at my mother's breasts!
When I met you in the street I would kiss you,
  and no one would mock me.
(2) I would take and lead you to my mother's house,
  to the room of her who bore me.
I would give you spiced wine to drink,
  the juice of my pomegranate.

(3) His left hand is under my head,
and his right hand embraces me.
(4) I ask you to promise, girls of Jerusalem:
do not disturb, do not bestir love,
before it wishes.

(Girls of Jerusalem)

(5a) Look who's coming up from the wilderness,
leaning on her beloved!

(Girl)

(5b) Under the apricot tree I woke you—
there your mother conceived you,
there she conceived you, she who bore you.
(6) Place me as a seal upon your heart,
as a seal upon your arm,
for love is as strong as death,
jealousy as hard as Sheol.
Its darts are darts of fire—
lightning itself!
(7) Mighty waters cannot extinguish love,
nor rivers wash it away.
Should one offer all his estate for love,
it would be utterly scorned.

(Brothers)

(8) We have a sister, a little one,
who has no breasts.
What shall we do for our sister
when she is spoken for?
(9) Is she a wall?
We'll build on it a silver turret.
Is she a door?
We'll panel it with a cedar board.

(Girl)

(10) I am a wall,
but my breasts are like towers!
So now I've become in your eyes
one who finds good will.

(Boy)

(11) Solomon had a vineyard in Baal Hamon.
        He gave the vineyard to keepers;
    each would bring in for his fruit
        a thousand pieces of silver.
(12) But *my* vineyard is before me.
        You can have the thousand, Solomon,
            but two hundred go to those who keep its fruit.

(Boy)

(13) O you who dwell in gardens—
        my companions attend—
            let me hear your voice!

(Girl)

(14) Bolt away, my beloved, and be as a gazelle
        or as a young roe
            on the mountains of spices.

Commentary

I will not attempt to summarize the vast body of commentary devoted to this short poem or to discuss all the interpretations suggested for the various verses. I mention particular commentators not because they were first to suggest an interpretation—it is in any case often impossible to know who was first—but rather to refer you to sources where an idea is explained in context more fully than it is here. Full references to commentators cited here appear in the Bibliography. Pope's commentary (1977) provides a comprehensive summary of the history of interpretation and a broad selection of the interpretations offered for each verse. Ginsburg's commentary (1857; reprinted 1970) includes an extensive survey of the history of interpretation up to 1856, which is updated to 1970 in Blank's prolegomenon.

I discuss the composition and structure of the book in chapter 4. For the convenience of exegesis I subdivide the Song into units and these into sections. Since I doubt the existence of a comprehensive schema that would determine the division of the Song, I describe the segmentation as I proceed, attempting to determine units and sections in accordance with the natural continuities of dialogue and event. I point out pauses and breaks in the poem's movement, discussing as units passages where there is significant continuity of story or dialogue.

The format of the translation identifies couplets by indenting the B-stich, which may be parallel to its corresponding A-stich or grammatically subordinate to it. Couplets are the basic unit of composition in parallel verse (Geller, 1979:6). Triplets are sequences of interlocking couplets, with at least two parallel stichs: A B B′, A A′ B, or A A′ A″ (ibid., p. 14). Triplets are marked by a further indentation. This format also helps identify other structural relationships among the stichs, such as quatrains.

Units:

Title

1:1 The Song of Songs, which is by Solomon.

This opening verse, a title, attributes authorship of the book to Solomon. Though the title uses the older relative adjective *ʾᵃšer* (only *še-* is used in the body of the book), it is a later addition. Solomon is not the speaker, the subject, or the center of interest in this poem, nor is there anything in the Song itself imputing authorship to him. Solomon is mentioned only incidentally, as an example or byword (for 1:4,12 and 3:7, 9, 11, see ad loc.), or even the object of mockery (8:11–12). The title is the first known step in the appropriation of the book to religion, for it associates the poem with an ancient wiseman who was believed to have written other works in the Holy Spirit. Yet the title is not in itself evidence for an allegorical interpretation or even for an understanding of the Song as wisdom. Solomon was the logical candidate for the authorship of this book because his name is mentioned in it and because he was famous both for the number of his wives and for his songs.

The headings of two Egyptian song groups seem to attribute authorship to individuals: nos. 31–37, a song attributed to the "Great Entertainer" (fem.) and nos. 41–47, a group of short songs into whose heading Nakhtsobek inserted his own name. In both cases, it should be stressed, the precise meaning of these headings is uncertain and we cannot be sure that the headings (at least before Nakhtsobek's usurpation) were intended to indicate authorship.

The title of Canticles identifies the book as a "song" in the singular. Unlike the singular "song" or "saying" in the headings of some Egyptian texts (see p. 16), the singular is unambiguous in Hebrew. Whoever added the title to Canticles saw it as a single song. And unlike its attribution to Solomon, the view of the Song's unity is unlikely to have been biased by religious needs or traditional presuppositions, for while there are understandable reasons to give the book a halo of Solomonic authorship, there are none, as far as I can see, to call a recognized collection a single song. It would not have diminished the book's status to call it "Songs of Solomon," just as the Book of Proverbs was named "Proverbs of Solomon."

Most commentators agree that *šir hašširim* is a superlative (GKC §133i). Some of the examples commonly brought to demonstrate this type of superlative construction are admittedly not quite appropriate, because they involve nouns that imply hierarchies in which the superlative is what stands at the top (or bottom) of the hierarchy: thus *šᵉmey haššamayim* (I Kgs 8:27) are the heavens above other heavens, *melek mᵉlakim* (Ezek 26:7) is a king who rules over other kings, *ʿebed ʿᵃbadim* (Gen 9:25) is a slave subjugated to other slaves. The word "song" does not imply such a ranking. Better analogies are nouns that imply qualities, such as *ʿᵃdi ʿᵃdayyim*, the most ornamental ornament (Ezek 16:7); *ṣᵉbi ṣibʾot goyim* (Jer 3:19), the most glorious of the glories of the nations; *hᵃbel hᵃbalim* (Qoh 1:2, etc.), the most absurd of absurdities; *qodeš haqqᵒdašim* (Exod 26:33, etc.), the holiest of the holy places. The quality implied by "song" is musicality. *Šir hašširim* means something like "the most musical of songs," "the most harmonious of songs." In this sense it is "the sublime song."

ʾᵃšer lišlomoh modifies the preceding bound structure as a whole (cf. Ruth 4:3; II Sam 2:8; Gen 41:43), not the *nomen rectum* (*hašširim*); for the construction see König, 1897:§282d.

1:2–4

(Girl)

(2) Oh that he'd kiss me with the kisses of his mouth—
for your caresses are better than wine!
(3) As for scent, your oils are good:
"Oil of Turaq" is your name.
That's why maidens love you.
(4) Take me with you, let us hasten!
The king has brought me to his chambers.
We will be glad and rejoice in you;
we will praise your caresses.
More than smooth ⟨wine⟩* do they love you.

*1:4 *miyyeyn* (MT *miyyayin*)

1:2–4 The girl expresses her desire. Her love is already in full force at the start of the song. The structure of this unit is symmetrical: both vv. 2–3 and v. 4 have two couplets plus a concluding solitary stich.

In her enthusiasm, the Shulammite projects her love for the youth onto other girls (1:3b and 4bβγ). She emphasizes the "objective" nature of his excellence by including the presumed actions of other girls in her paean through the use of the first-person plural: "We will be glad and rejoice in you; we will praise your caresses." In similar fashion the boy in the "The Stroll" praises a girl's beauty by declaring the effect she has on the general male public: "She makes the heads of all the men turn about when seeing her" (no. 31). (Nowhere, however, do the speakers in the Egyptian songs include themselves in the broader group of admirers by the use of the first-person plural.) The Shulammite shows a complete lack of jealousy toward other girls, thus revealing her confidence in the boy's love.

The third-person forms in v. 2a ("Oh that he'd kiss me with the kisses of his mouth") and v. 4bα ("The king brought me to his chambers") are seemingly intrusive, but they should not be eliminated by changing the verbs to imperatives and making all the possessive suffixes into second-singulars (thus Budde, BHK). The lovers often address each other in the third person, sometimes switching back and forth rapidly from third to second person (e.g., 1:12; 2:1–3; 4:6; 6:9; 7:11). Third-person address carries a special tone of respect; see "Grammatical Person" in chapter 6.

(1:2) *Oh that he'd kiss me*: There is a pun hidden here, *yiššaqeni*, "Oh that he'd kiss me," suggesting *yašqeni*, "Oh that he'd let me drink." *Yiššaqeni* ties in with *n*ᵉ*šiqot*, "kisses," *yašqeni* with "wine." The same word play, but this time with both words made explicit, is found in 8:1–2.

with the kisses of his mouth: This phrase is not pleonastic, for not all kisses are with the mouth. A gesture of affection frequent in the ancient East (including the Far East) was the nose kiss, in which the couple would rub faces together and smell each other's nose (Meissner, 1934:915ff.). But the most intimate and sensual kiss was the mouth kiss, and this is what the Shulammite calls for. *Minn*ᵉ*šiqot* is literally, "some of (*min*) the kisses"; *mi(n)* here is partitive, not instrumental.

caresses: I render *dodim* as "caresses" because "lovemaking," which is more precise, often seems awkward in the translation. *Dodim* always refers to sex acts. (These acts may even be devoid of love, like the *dodim* the harlot tempts a youth to enjoy [Prov 7:18], or the harlotrous couching—*miškab dodim*—of which unfaithful Jerusalem is accused [Ezek 23:17].) But *dodim* includes more than sexual intercourse. When the Shulammite praises her lover's *dodim* in 1:2, she is elaborating on the sweetness of his kisses. When she says, "We will praise your *dodim*" in 1:4, she is declaring that she will tell of his kisses and caresses, as she in fact does.

LXX mistranslates *ddym* in this verse and 1:4; 4:10; and 7:13 as "breasts". Peshitta translates thus at 4:10 and 7:13.

better: *Ṭob* in reference to wine means "sweet" (Pope). I translate by the more general term "good" ("better") to bring out the way *ṭob* is repeated with different subjects.

(1:3) *As for scent, your oils are good*: The *lamed* of *l*ᵉ*reaḥ* means "with regard to," "as for"; see GKC §143e. *Lamed* introduces a *casus pendens* here as in Num 18:8 and Ps 119:91. This is not the emphatic *lamed*, for that would appear before the predicate, and moreover the non-coordination that would result between the singular *reaḥ* and the plural *ṭobim*, while possible, would be awkward. 6QCant reads *šmnym ṭwbym*, which does not provide satisfactory syntax.

"*Oil of Turaq" is your name*: *Turaq* is apparently a type of oil, perhaps named after a place (thus TaMaKh). This word is often emended to *muraq*, "poured" (which is how LXX and Aquila understood the word), but the oil's being poured would not enhance the praiseworthiness of the boy's name. For *šmn* 6QCant reads *mr-* before a lacuna, restored by the editors as *mrqḥt* (Baillet,1962:113).

(1:4a) *The king brought me to his chambers*: an enigmatic phrase, if taken literally. Why does the king suddenly appear and take the girl away to his chambers? Is she still there? The commentators, especially those favoring the drama theory (see "Drama" in chapter 6, and chapter 4, n. 8), usually assume that King Solomon brought the maiden to his palace. This assumption requires the creation of a complex story-line around the supposed event (Delitzsch, Ginsburg, and Harper, for example, do this). But subsequently in the Song there is no allusion to such an event, which, had it occurred, would be in the center of the drama. Commentators who regard the Song or this unit as a wedding song identify the king as the bridegroom, on the rather shaky parallel of 19th century Syrian wedding songs, where the bride and groom were (according to Wetzstein) called king and queen (appendix to Delitzsch, 1885:165). Nor does the statement in Pirqey de R. Eliezer §16, "a bridegroom resembles a king," show that it was customary to *call* a bridegroom "king."

"The king" indeed refers to the youth, but not because "king" is an epithet for a bridegroom; the couple are not at their wedding. Rather, "king" is simply a term of affection. In a similar vein, the Egyptian girl in no. 13 calls her lover "my prince" and the girl in no. 17 calls hers "prince of my heart." Similarly the girl in no. 8 says, "I am the Mistress of the Two Lands [i.e., the queen of Egypt] when I am with you." The lovers are called kings, princes, and queens because of the way love makes them feel about each other and about themselves.

brought me: Peshitta and Symmachus render "bring me" (imperative), apparently seeking to smooth out the second/third-person enallage, but see comment on 1:2 and "Grammatical Person" in chapter 6.

(1:4b) *We will be glad . . . smooth wine*: *Nazkirah dodeyka miyyayin, meyšarim ᵓᵃhebuka* is generally translated along the lines of RSV: "We will exult and rejoice in you; we will extol your love more than wine; rightly do they love you." But the noun *meyšarim* is problematic. It is generally taken as functioning adverbially in the sense of "rightly," "correctly." Now, *meyšarim* may mean physical evenness or levelness (as in Isa 26:7) or, more frequently, ethical righteousness (e.g., Prov 2:9; 8:6). But it does not mean morally neutral correctness or justifiability, the sense required by the usual translation of these verses. Ibn Ezra, however, explains *meyšarim* as "an epithet of wine" (*toʾar yayin*) and regards the comparative *mem* of *miyyayin* as applying to *meyšarim* as well. He is, I believe, basically right, except that his explanation requires understanding *meyšarim* in itself as a name for a type of wine, whereas the other occurrences of *meyšarim* in conjunction with wine (Prov 23:31; Cant 7:10) do not show the word functioning in this way. Gaster (1961) emended the word to *mimmeyraš*, "new wine," presumably cognate to Ugaritic *mrṯ* and Aramaic *meyrat*, and changed *ʾ^{a}hebuka* to *ʾ^{a}hab^{e}ka*, "your love," producing: "(We will extol . . .) more than new wine your caresses." But this proposal requires making two emendations, creating a hapax legomenon in the process, and assuming the existence of a noun form that does not occur elsewhere in the singular. Other proposals, such as Tur-Sinai's interpretation of *meyšarim* as sexual potency and Dahood's translation of *meyšarim* as "gullet" (Dahood, 1966:300), assume unattested meanings and produce texts that are hardly more meaningful than the MT. 6QCant reads *myšrym ʾhwbym*, which is not a satisfactory text either, since *myšrym* is not an adjective, nor is it something that might be modified by "beloved."

The word *meyšarim* is associated with wine in two other passages: Cant 7:10, *w^{e}ḥikkek k^{e}yeyn haṭṭob—holek l^{e}dodi l^{e}meyšarim*, " 'And your palate is like the best wine'—'flowing smoothly to my beloved,' " and Prov 23:31, *ʾal tereʾ yayin ki yitʾaddam, ki yitten bakkos ʿeyno, yithallek b^{e}meyšarim*, "Do not look at wine when it gleams red, when it gives forth its sparkle in the cup, flowing smoothly." The only translation of *l^{e}meyšarim* and *b^{e}meyšarim* that fits both these verses well is "smoothly." This usage is quite clear in Prov 23:31, where the next verse defines the word by contrast as it describes the after-effects of wine: it bites like a serpent's venom. The adverbs formed from *meyšarim*, namely *b^{e}meyšarim* and *l^{e}meyšarim*, show that *meyšarim* by itself means "smoothness" and may be used in particular of the smoothness of wine. This sense accords with the root-meaning[1] of the word (YŠR = "straight").

With this in mind I would divide our verse after *dodeyka* and point *yayin* as *yeyn*. I read: *nagilah w^{e}niśm^{e}ḥah bak, nazkirah dodeyka, miyyeyn mey-*

1. I use this term while aware of Barr's strictures against the "root fallacy" (1961:100–106). I understand the important heuristic concept "root-meaning" as a lexical abstraction. The assumption is that if most words with the same consonantal skeletons have a certain notion or referent in common, it is probable—though by no means certain—that another word with the same root will share that notion or referent. We can take a "root-meaning" as a starting point, asking to what extent it fits the context under discussion. Lexical extrapolation of this sort makes no assumptions about the ontological status of roots.

šarim ʾ^{a}hebuka. "We will be glad and rejoice in you; we will praise your caresses. More than smooth wine do they love you." *Yeyn meyšarim*, lit., "wine of smoothness," is equivalent to English "smooth wine." *Nazkirah*, lit., "we shall mention," here implies "praise," as in *ḥasdey ʾ^{a}donay ʾazkir*, "I will praise the mercies of God" (Isa 63:7), *ʾazkirah šimka b^{e}kol dor wador*, "I shall praise your name in every generation" (Ps 45:18), and more.

1:5–8

(Girl)

(5) Black I am—but lovely—
O girls of Jerusalem,
like tents of Kedar,
curtains of ⟨Salmah⟩.*
(6) Pay no mind that I am swarthy,
that the sun has gazed upon me.
My mother's sons were mean to me,
made me keeper of the vineyards.
My vineyard I could not keep.
(7) Tell me, my soul's beloved:
where do you graze,
where do you rest (your flocks) at noon?—
lest I be like "one who wraps herself up"
by your companions' flocks!

(Boy)

(8) If you don't know,
most beautiful of women,
go on out in the tracks of the flock,
and graze your kids
by the shepherds' camps.

*1:5 *śalmah* (MT *š^{e}lomoh*)

In this dialogue, the Shulammite first presents her problem to the girls of Jerusalem. Like many a girl before and after her, she saw herself ripe for romance before her family did. Her brothers placed upon her tasks that have resulted in some loss of beauty and restricted her to the confines of the family, not allowing her to develop independently as a woman. But that is in the past. Now she is determined to tend her own vineyard, and so she immediately turns to her lover and asks him where he can be found—where he "grazes" (sc. his sheep) and "rests" (them) (lit., "causes to lie down") during the noontime rest when she can visit him. At present, at the time of this dialogue, they are together. She asks him about his everyday practices so that she will always be able to find him. Otherwise she will have to wander among his fellow shepherds, exhibiting behavior that will make her look like a harlot, and does he want that? She is genuinely concerned with how people will view her, but her request also has in it a note of pique. The boy teases her back: If you don't know the answer to that question, then, very well, go visit the shepherds, for (he implies) *you* should know where I "graze" (R'H) and "cause to lie down." The youth is playing with the sexual connotations of "graze" and "cause to lie down," words the girl used in her question. She herself made this deliberate and playful misunderstanding possible by not supplying objects for the verbs "graze" and "cause to lie down" in v. 7. She, too, it would seem, is playing with words, for she knows the answer to her own question. Later she will declare, "My beloved is mine and I am his: he grazes (R'H) among the lilies" (2:16).

Lovers' pique is treated in a humorous vein in several Egyptian songs as well: nos. 1, 15, 46(?), and 47. Similarly, songs nos. 6, 7, 10, and "The Stroll" (nos. 31–37) take a humorous view of some other emotions occasioned by love.

(1:5) Black I am—but lovely: There would be no point in the Shulammite's complaint if black were the desired color, nor would she need to explain her swarthy complexion by telling what her brothers did to her (see Pope for a detailed discussion of the "black but beautiful" versus the "black and beautiful" interpretations). This blackness, of course, has nothing to do with race. The darkness caused by the sun was associated with a lower social status, for only those who could afford not to work outdoors could retain a fair complexion. She suspects that the other girls might look upon her with disdain because she has had to work in the fields. Such scorn would originate in social, not racial, prejudices. This declaration is not a refusal to be judged by the onlookers' standards, which tend to set blackness and loveliness as opposites. That is, she is not implying, "I am black *and* I am beautiful" (contrary to M. Falk, 1982:110). An emphatic "*and*" such as this interpretation assumes would require *w^{e}gam* or *w^{e}ʾap* rather than the simple conjunctive/adversative *waw*. Furthermore, if the Shulammite wished to defend blackness, she would not need to explain what happened to make her black. Rather, the tone of her words is defiance of the resulting attitudes of her comrades, who do not think as highly of her or take her as seriously as she thinks they should.

Girls of Jerusalem: 6QCant reads *bnty* for *bnwt*, probably a dittography of *yod* and not (contrary to Baillet, 1962:113) an archaizing form.

Kedar: QDR means "dark" and plays on "black" in the preceding phrase.

curtains: a metonymy for tents; see II Sam 7:2 (sing.) = I Chr 17:1

(plur.) and the parallelism between "tent" and "curtains" in Jer 4:20, 10:20, 49:29, and Isa 54:2 (Ginsburg, Pope).

śalmah: Point *śalmah* for MT *šᵉlomoh*, "Solomon"; thus Pope, Würthwein, Gerleman, et al.). Salmah is an Arab tribe. (The Targumim translate Kenite as *śalmaʾi* or *śalmaʾah*, Num 24:21; Judg 4:17; etc.). The tents of these tribes serve as an image for blackness, not loveliness. The phrase "but lovely" is parenthetical. The next verse shows that she is now concerned mainly with her swarthiness, and the comparisons in v. 5b are meant to make that point clear.

(1:6) *Pay no mind that I am swarthy*: *ʾal tirʾuni še-* is frontal extraposition of the subject of the subordinate clause (thus Ehrlich, comparing Gen 1:4; the construction occurs here with *še-* in place of *ki*).

that the sun has gazed upon me: The sun is spoken of as having eyes and having "gazed" (ŠZP) on her. The translation "that the sun has gazed upon me" (so most) is preferable to "for the sun, etc." (a causal clause), because the cause of her swarthiness does not need further explanation; it could only be a suntan. She is asking them to pay no heed to the fact "that the sun has gazed upon" her and tanned her. The alliteration of *šin* is striking; a similar alliteration appears in 1:2–3.

were mean to me: *Niḥᵃru* means "rebuke," "be angry against," or the like (Isa 41:11; 45:24). There is a play on *niḥᵃru* (ḤRH) "be hot," which brings to mind the sun's hot gaze. Her brothers "grew hot" against her, and the sun too scorched her.

My vineyard: "Vineyard" is meant literally in 1:6b, 7:13, and 8:11. Elsewhere it alludes to the girl. Here "vineyards" means actual vineyards, while "my vineyard" (with the emphasized possessive) must be interpreted figuratively, for we are hardly to suppose that the girl owned her own vineyard or that she would complain in this context about a financial loss that her brothers caused her. Rather, we are to understand that she has not been able to tend to her own needs as a woman, but has been forced to stay within the confines of her family. Pope understands "vineyard" as a designation of the maiden's body, specifically to her sexual parts. It is more likely that "vineyard," like "garden," does not stand for genitals, but rather for the young woman as a whole. Taking "vineyard" as a reference to genitals foists upon the girl a genital focus foreign to this song and absent from the Egyptian songs as well. Canticles and the Egyptian songs are concerned with the total experience of the lovers and the nature of their love.

I could not keep (loʾ naṭarti): NṬR not in the sense of preventing entry, as if the girl were confessing promiscuity, but in the sense of tending and cultivating, like the synonymous root ŠMR in Gen 2:15, which Onkelos translates with NṬR.

(1:7) *my soul's beloved (šeʾahᵃbah napši)*: *Napši* as a subject of a verb focuses on the speaker more than ʾ^{a}*ni* does. Pope's translation, "my true love," also reflects this extra intensity.

graze (tirʿeh): Or "feed." Three homophonic roots are fused in *RʿH*: (1) desire and will (from Aramaic RʿY); (2) friendship and companionship, as in *raʿyah*, "darling, companion," and *reʿim*, "companions, lovers" (a by-form of Rʿʿ); and (3) feeding, both as a transitive verb in the sense of pasturing flocks and as an intransitive verb meaning "to eat." Our poet makes frequent use of words from this "root" and plays with it in various ways. The youth is a shepherd (*roʿeh*) who "grazes" or "feeds" (*roʿeh*) among the lilies (lips?) of his companion (*raʿyah*). She desires him and he her, and he "eats"—enjoys sexual pleasures—with her. (The sexual connotation of "eating" is clear in 5:1; see also Prov 30:20. The sexual connotation is clear too in the phrase *roʿeh zonot*, "consort with harlots," Prov 29:3.)

rest (your flocks): lit., "cause to lie down," without an object.

lest (šallamah): a calque of Aramaic *dilmah*.

like "one who wraps herself up" (ʿoṭ^{e}*yah)*: Not to be emended to *ṭoʿ*^{a}*yah* (or *ṭoʿiyyah*), "one who goes astray" (BHK, Gordis, and many modern commentators), even though Targum, Symmachus, Peshitta, and Vulgate understood the word in that sense. The emendation only blunts the thorn in the girl's words. Harlots who carried out their business among the shepherds would wrap themselves in veils (Gen 38:14–15; observe that Tamar's having covered her face is given as the reason for Judah's thinking her a harlot, not as the reason for his failing to recognize her; see Pope and Tur-Sinai on Cant 1:7). Of course veiling was not in itself the mark of a prostitute. The Shulammite herself wears a veil (4:1; 6:7—although a different word, *ṣammah*, is used). But prostitutes might identify themselves as such by putting on veils in certain situations (such as in places frequented by shepherds) or in certain ways: observe that Tamar not only "covers" herself (KSH; Rebeccah does this too, Gen 24:65); she also "wraps herself up" (*wattitʿallap*, Gen 38:14). The Shulammite for her part threatens to be like one who "wraps herself up." (ʿṬH, usually used of covering oneself with a mantle or other large garment, is a near-synonym of ʿLP.) The Shulammite here warns her lover that if he does not tell where he "grazes" and "causes to lie down" (*tarbiṣ*), she will have to go searching for him and will seem like a loose woman.

(1:8) *If you don't know (ʾim loʾ ted*^{e}*ʿi lak)*: The ethical dative, which lays emphasis on the will of the actor rather than on the act (cf. Job 5:27), suggests here a willful element in her ignorance: *ʾim loʾ ted*^{e}*ʿi* means "If you don't know" (for whatever reason), while *ʾim loʾ ted*^{e}*ʿi lak* means "If you *won't* know"—though you could and should.

go on out in the tracks of the flock, and graze your kids by the shepherds' camps: spoken in a mock pouting tone: if you really don't know what the sole object of my desire is, where I "graze" (*roʿeh* with its threefold sense), then, very well, go after the sheep; me you will not find, but only the other shepherds. *Reʿi ʾet gediyyotayik* may indeed have a sexual connotation (as Pope, following Delitzsch, suggests), but this is hardly proved by Judah's payment of a goat kid to Tamar in Gen 38:17. Perhaps *gedi* is an idiom for breasts. In 1:14 "Ein Gedi" ("the spring of the kid") is in synonymous parallelism with "my breasts." The sentence "and graze your kids by the shepherds' camps" seems to be an idiom that more or less paraphrases "lest I be like 'one who wraps herself up' by your companions' flocks!" (v. 7b), but I know of no similar usage elsewhere.

1:9–17

(Boy)

(9) To a mare in Pharaoh's chariotry
I compare you, my darling:
(10) lovely are your cheeks in bangles,
your neck in strings of beads.
(11) Bangles of gold we will make for you,
with spangles of silver.

(Girl)

(12) While the king is on his couch,
my spikenard gives forth its fragrance.
(13) To me my beloved is a sachet of myrrh—
between my breasts he'll spend the night.
(14) To me my beloved is a spray of henna—
in the vineyards of Ein Gedi.

(Boy)

(15) How beautiful you are, my darling,
how beautiful!
Your eyes are doves.

(Girl)

(16) How beautiful you are, my beloved, indeed delightful!
Indeed, our bed is verdant.
(17) The rafters of our house are cedars;
our beams are cypresses.

The lovers express mutual admiration as they lie under the trees in a bower that the girl views as a house of royal luxury. He praises her (vv. 9–11, six stichs) and she him (vv. 12–14, six stichs). Then his words of praise

(v. 15) are echoed in hers, as she praises both him (v. 16a) and their "house" (v. 16b–17) in a dialogue of six stichs.

(1:9) *To a mare*: *Susati* is the feminine absolute with an archaizing suffix. Pope suggests that the comparison alludes to the practice of setting loose a mare in heat among the war-horses to cause havoc in battle, as happened at the battle of Kadesh in the time of Thutmosis III. But such an allusion is unlikely here. Even given Pope's explanation that cavalry customarily used stallions and not mares, *rekeb* does not necessarily refer to war chariotry; see I Kgs 1:5; II Kgs 5:9; Jer 22:4; and Isa 66:20; in all of which (and perhaps in Gen 50:9 too) the chariots are, as BDB says, "for dignity and display." One Egyptian text, which Pope himself quotes, tells about the fondness of a prince (later to become Amenhotep II) for a pretty mare of Pharaoh's stables. Such mares could be included in the term "Pharaoh's chariotry." Egyptian horses were famous for their excellence, and the best were naturally reserved for the royal stables. Song no. 39 uses "a royal horse" as an epitome of speed. Furthermore, the youth in Canticles immediately specifies the basis of the comparison, namely the girl's ornamented beauty, not her sexually arousing effect on males.

I compare you (dimmitik): present tense; the comparison follows.

(1:10) *lovely are your cheeks in bangles . . .* : She is as lovely in her jewelry as the royal horses of Egypt are in their decorated bridles and harnesses. The exact meaning of *tor*, "bangle" (so Pope), is uncertain, but the Targum uses *tora*ʾ to translate *śapah*, the "lip" or collar of the priestly ephod (Exod 39:23). It is thus likely that *tor* is a circular or semicircular ornament (so Ginsburg, who derives it from TWR, "to go round"). The Egyptians wore ornaments that partially encompassed the cheeks and hung down over them; see fig. 9.

(1:11) *Bangles of gold we will make . . .* : Since her cheeks are lovely in bangles, we will make her especially precious ornaments from gold and silver. By saying "we" the youth seems to invite others to share in his admiration of his beloved, just as she included others when praising him (1:3–4, and cf. the youth in nos. 31 and 35).

(1:12) *While the king is on his couch (mᵉsibbo)*: *Meseb* = "couch," as in mishnaic Hebrew. Such a couch could serve for feasting and for sex (b. Shab. 62b, 63a). *ʿad še-* is also a mishnaic usage. As elsewhere "king" is an affectionate epithet of the youth (TaMaKh); see on 1:4. His couch is the bed of boughs mentioned in v. 16.

my spikenard gives forth its fragrance: A simple boast about her spices would have little point. Her "spikenard" is her lover (thus Ibn Ezra, Murphy [1981], and Ginsburg). He is her spikenard just as he is the "sachet of myrrh" and the "spray of henna" lying between her breasts. All the while she is on his couch and lying close to him, she enjoys his fragrance.

Origen observes that spikenard emits its scent only when rubbed. Spikenard is the *Valeriana jatamansi*, a very expensive spice (Mark 14:3–6). Rubbing or squeezing the hairy stems produces the fragrant spice. Thus "my spikenard gives forth its fragrance" may have an additional erotic implication.

(1:13) *between my breasts he'll spend the night*: *Yalin*, it should be noted, means to spend the night. (LYN can mean to abide for a longer period [usually said of abstract qualities; see, e.g., Isa 1:21; Job 19:4; 41:14], but it never means to spend a *shorter* period of time.) The sentence can also be translated: "To me my beloved is a sachet of myrrh, which spends the night between my breasts."

(1:14) *in the vineyards of Ein Gedi*: adverbial modifier of "he'll spend the night." "In the vineyards of Ein Gedi" is a metaphorical restatement of "between my breasts." Ein Gedi is a luxurious oasis nestled in a ravine.

(1:15) *Your eyes are doves*: " . . . that is to say, her eyes seduce and powerfully incite love in the heart of those who desire her, like doves, which are the most enticing of all animals in matters of desire" (TaMaKh). The common denominator of eyes and doves is their softness and gentleness, and perhaps also the oval shape of both. See further on 4:1.

(1:16) *our bed (ʿarśenu)*: Like *meseb* and *miṭṭah*, *ʿereś* designates a couch that could be used for feasting; see Amos 6:4.

(1:17) *The rafters of our house*: *qorot batteynu*, with the *nomen rectum* in the plural, as in mishnaic Hebrew (Ehrlich).

2:1–7

(Girl)

(1) I'm (just) a crocus of Sharon,
    a valley-lily.

(Boy)

(2) Like a lily among brambles,
    so is my darling among girls.

(Girl)

(3) Like an apricot tree among trees of the thicket,
    so is my beloved among boys:
I delight to sit in his shade,
    and his fruit is sweet to my palate.
(4) He brought me to the house of wine,
    and his intent toward me was love.
(5) Put me to bed among fruit clusters,
    spread me (my bed) among apricots,
        for I am sick with love.

(6) His left hand is under my head,
and his right hand embraces me.
(7) I ask you to promise, girls of Jerusalem,
by the gazelles or the hinds of the wild:
do not disturb, do not bestir love,
before it wishes.

This unit recapitulates the motifs of 1:9–17 as follows:

Exchange of praise	1:9–11, 15–16a	2:1–3
Reclining together	1:12–14, 16b–17	2:4–7
on the couch	1:12, 16b	2:5a
in the "house"	1:17	2:4a
in each other's embrace	1:13–14	2:6

Vv. 1:9–17 and 2:1–7 belong to the same scene. The scene comes to its conclusion in the adjuration in 2:7, where the girl asks her comrades not to disturb her lovemaking. The adjuration is a sort of fade-out here and at 3:5 and 8:4 (though the latter two verses are not the last verses in their respective units), leaving what follows to the reader's imagination. Compare the ending of "The Crossing" (no. 20G), where too a sensuous description of the lovers' bed implies future pleasures in it.

(2:1) *I'm (just) a crocus of Sharon*: This is not self-praise. Self-praise would not be in character for the girl or the poem. (The self-praise in 1:5 is defensive and balanced by mention of her swarthiness.) If "I'm (just) a crocus of Sharon" were a boast of beauty, it would be discordant. Rather it is an expression of modesty (thus Ginsburg, Tur-Sinai), though perhaps the maiden is also fishing for a compliment. She says: I'm just a little flower, hardly noticeable among the thousands of flowers that cover the valley.

a valley-lily (šošannat ha^{ca}maqim): The use of the plural *^{ca}maqim* indicates that the phrase is generic, "a valley-lily" rather than "a lily of the valleys," for a single lily could only be in one valley. Similarly the parallel *ḥ^{a}buṣṣelet haššaron* is more strictly translated "a Sharon-crocus." The Shulammite does not live in the Sharon, but is likening herself to one of the crocuses that grow there.

(2:2) *Like a lily among brambles*: The boy turns the modest self-appraisal to highest praise: you surpass all the other girls as the lily surpasses the brambles.

(2:3) *Like an apricot tree . . .*: As in 1:16, the girl here models her praise of her lover upon his praise of her. *Tappuaḥ* here, as the parallelism shows, refers to the tree and not to the fruit. The *tappuaḥ* is not the apple, for cultivated apples are a relatively recent development, while the wild apple, which is not indigenous to Palestine anyway, is scarcely edible. *Tappuaḥ* is probably the apricot (Moldenke, 1952:184–88).

I delight to sit in his shade: lit., "I delight and I sit," the first verb virtually governing the second (Ginsburg, Gordis). Past tense is possible, but she seems to be speaking of present experience in this unit (see especially 2:4–5). This sentence explains the comparison between the boy and the apricot tree: the Shulammite delights in sitting in his shade alone and in tasting his fruit. Apricot trees offer these pleasures; brambles do not. To taste sweet fruit is to enjoy kisses of the mouth; see 5:16 and 7:10. For "his shade" and "his fruit" we could as well translate "its shade" and "its fruit."

The images the Shulammite uses to describe their relative positions are balanced in an egalitarian fashion. In 1:13 he is a sachet of myrrh nestled between her breasts, an image that pictures her as the dominant and sheltering party, whereas in 2:3b he is the tree in whose shade she sits, so that he is now the dominant and sheltering member of the pair. The boy is not a "sturdy chestnut tree" nor she his "clinging vine."

(2:4) *He brought me to the house of wine*: The "house of wine" is commonly identified as a tavern or banquet hall, the banquet being presumably for a wedding or for some sacral celebration, depending on one's interpretation of the Song's overall function. But this is not their wedding, nor is there the slightest suggestion of ritual feasting. And neither a tavern nor a public banquet is an appropriate setting for the lovemaking of the couple in this song, a major theme of which is separation from the city (see "Love in the Garden" in chapter 7).

Beyt hayyayin is simply any building or structure where wine is drunk. In this case it is the structure described in 1:16b–17: "Indeed our bed is verdant. The rafters of our house are cedars; our beams are cypresses." Their house, the "house of wine," is a bower under the trees in the field or orchard. It is, in a sense, a banquet house, but it is a very modest one. In 1:4 this structure is called the king's chambers. (*Ḥeder* [1:4] and *bayit* occur in synonymous parallelism [3:4, etc.] and can function as interchangeable members of the same image [Exum, 1973:55].) Such booths for lovers' trysts are mentioned in the Egyptian love songs; see "Love in the Garden" in chapter 7.

his intent toward me was love: In other words, he intended to make love to me. *Degel* is cognate to Akkadian *diglu*, "glance," "intent," "wish" (from *daglu*, "to look"); see Pope. *ʾahᵃbah* here means the act of lovemaking, as in Prov 5:19 and Jer 2:33, rather than the emotion of love, for that emotion is already alive in both lovers and does not need to be the object of *intention*.

(2:5) *Put me to bed . . . spread me (my bed) . . .*: Since she is "sick," albeit "love-sick," she must lie down. SMK (here in piel, as occasionally in mishnaic Hebrew; see Jastrow, *Dict.*) indicates putting to bed or preparation of a bed (Ps 3:6); this is the root of *śᵉmika*, "rug," "blanket" (Judg 4:18). RPD, whose root-meaning is "to spread," likewise indicates preparation of a bed (thus Tur-Sinai; see also Job 17:13), and *byt hrpd* means "sleeping house," in Lachish Letter IV, 5. RPD is probably a by-form of RBD; cf. Prov 7:16. It was customary to lie on spread rugs for sleeping, but the Shulammite wishes to lie among fruit clusters and apricots (*b^e*- meaning "among," as in 2:3a). Following close upon the comparison of the youth to an apricot tree, mention of the fruits naturally makes one think of the youth's caresses. The girl wants to be surrounded by the sweet fragrance of his lovemaking. Certainly she is not calling for aphrodisiacs (contrary to Pope). This love-sick girl hardly needs artificial stimulants.

ʾᵃšišot does not necessarily refer to raisin cakes. G. R. Driver (1950:144) explains *ʾᵃšišah*, on the basis of the Arabic cognate, to mean "inflorescence," first with reference to the inflorescence of the palm, then specifically with reference to raisin cakes. But there is no reason to restrict the word to palms or raisins. On the contrary, *ʾᵃšišey ʿᵃnabim* in Hos 3:1 suggests that *ʾᵃšišot* requires further definition if it is to specify raisin cakes. Here it may be defined by the parallel *tappuḥim* and refer to the apricot in blossom.

Egyptian love songs nos. 6, 12, and 37 describe the symptoms of love-sickness, in particular weakness and loss of control over the body (nos. 6, 37). There (as in 5:8) the love-sickness is caused by the beloved's absence. Here his presence causes much the same symptoms.

The imperatives, ostensibly directed to the girls of Jerusalem, are a sort of rhetorical imperative, a strong way of expressing a wish for what is already the case, as if to say: may I be snugly bedded among my beloved's caresses. V. 6 makes this image explicit: she is held in his embrace.

(2:7) *I ask you to promise* . . . : lit., "I adjure you . . ." This adjuration recurs in 3:5 and 8:4, each time immediately following a statement that the couple is embracing or is about to embrace. Pope interprets the adjuration as a request to the girls not to stir up sexual desire by means of aphrodisiacs before the proper time, which time has now arrived. In other words, by this adjuration she is now actually *requesting* stimulants. But there would be no point in such a request. The Shulammite's desire is already well aroused, and she has no need of aphrodisiacs, now or later. In any case, there is no point to a repeated request not to excite love until it is *willing*, when the request is from the mouth of a girl who (as Pope says) is never averse to love anyway.

What does she want the girls of Jerusalem to do? The only thing they *could* do that they should *not* do is disturb the couple, and this is indeed what the Shulammite is charging them not to do. "Love" here refers to the act of lovemaking, as in 2:4b, Prov 5:19, and (most unambiguously) Jer 2:33; see also no. 11, n. e.

by the gazelles or the hinds of the wild: Mesopotamian magical spells mention the gazelle as the epitome of sexual potency: for example, "By the love (power) of the gazelle, seven times . . . copulate with me" (e.g., Biggs, 1967:26). But it is difficult to see this signification here, especially since the gazelles mentioned in the spells are male. The best explanation is that of Gordis (1961:26–28), who argues that *ṣᵉbaʾot* and *ʾaylot haśśadeh* are circumlocutions for titles of God, the first for (*ʾᵉlohey*) *ṣᵉbaʾot*, (God of) hosts, the second for *ʾel šadday*, El Shadday. (The first term is more likely a circumlocution for *YHWH ṣᵉbaʾot*, which Tsevat, 1965, has explained as a phrase compounded of two nouns in apposition, "Yahweh, [is] Armies." *Ṣebaʾot* can therefore imply a name of God.) The author uses these animal names to avoid divine titles in a secular context. We see here the first sign of a tendency, which became important in the Talmudic period, to substitute for divine names and titles in oaths various words, sometimes meaningless words such as *baḥerem* ("by the fish net") and *bᵉḥayyey haqqayiṣ* ("by the life of summerfruit"), see the discussion in Lieberman, 1942:125–27. Gazelles and hinds are thus mentioned because of the sound of their names, but their beauty too makes them appropriate to the context, as in Prov 5:19, "a hind of love and a roe of grace" (Ginsburg).

Śadeh, usually translated "field," in conjunction with animals means the wild, uncultivated countryside (Gen 2:19, 20; Exod 23:11, 29; etc.)

disturb, bestir: *Taʿiru* and *tᵉʿorᵉru* signify disturbance of some sort (thus Gordis and many others), not excitement or arousal of desire. There is no case where ʿWR is clearly used of sexual arousal. It is often used of waking or arousing a sleeper. *Taʿiru* and *teʿorᵉru* are chosen for this verse because the way one disturbs lovemaking is to wake the couple in the morning; compare the girl's complaint against the dove in no. 14 for disturbing her and her lover.

before it wishes: elliptical for "until it wishes to be disturbed, woken up." The point is not that the girls of Jerusalem *should* wake the couple at the proper time, but that (at least) they should not disturb them before then. As Pope points out, "love" is implicitly personified by the use of the verb ḤPṢ here.

This unit (2:1–7) at once recapitulates the motifs of the preceding one (1:9–17) and goes beyond it. After the exchange of endearments between the lovers in 2:1–3a, the Shulammite tells her comrades: I delight in my beloved's caresses, so he brought me to this little "house of wine" intent on making love. Now I am love-sick, overwhelmed by desire, and wish to lie down surrounded by the fruits of love. He is now embracing me, so please leave us to ourselves and do not disturb our lovemaking.

The girls of Jerusalem serve primarily as a sounding board for the Shulammite. Their main function is to be present to be spoken *to* (see chapter 8). But now they are to leave. Their presence is reminiscent of that of the "young people" in "The Orchard." The little sycamore invites the girl: "Come, spend time where the young people are: the meadow celebrates its day. Under me are a festival booth and a hut . . ." Other young people are present at first, but at some point they leave and the lovers remain alone: "The beerhut is disarrayed from drink, but she has remained with her brother. . . . But my lips are sealed . . ." (no. 30). The poet of Canticles, who is also discreet, delicately closes the scene here, as at 3:5 and 8:4, with only a suggestion of what is to follow.

2:8–17

(Girl)

(8) Listen! My beloved—
he's coming now!
Bounding over the mountains,
leaping over the hills.
(9) My beloved is like a gazelle
or a young roe.
Now he stands behind our wall,
peering in through the windows,
glancing in through the lattice.
(10) My beloved spoke and said to me:

(Boy)

"Arise, my darling, my beautiful,
and come away.
(11) For see, the winter has departed,
the rain has passed and gone its way.
(12) The blossoms have appeared in the land,
the time of song has arrived,
and the voice of the turtledove is heard in our land.
(13) The fig tree sweetens its young fruit,
and the vine is in bud, giving off fragrance.
Arise, my darling, my beautiful,
and come away.
(14) My dove in the clefts of the rock,
in the covert of the cliff—
let me see your form,
let me hear your voice,
for your voice is sweet,
your form is lovely."

(Girl?)

(15) Catch us foxes,
little foxes
that spoil vineyards,
for our vineyards are in bud.

(Girl)

(16) My beloved is mine and I am his:
he grazes among the lilies.
(17) Before the day blows softly in,
and the shadows flee,
turn, my beloved, and be as a gazelle,
or as a young roe,
on the mountains of Bether.

The Shulammite is in her house just before dawn when her lover comes from afar and secretly invites her to go out with him to the fields. The meaning of her response is not quite clear, but she appears to urge him to flee quickly before sunrise. V. 17 points back to v. 9 and closes off the unit.

The maiden speaks of the events as if they were happening in the present, at the time she is speaking (*hinneh zeh* in vv. 8 and 9 is a clear indicator of the immediate present tense). In this way she conveys immediacy and excitement. Nevertheless the events she relates occurred in the past, as is shown by the quoting phrase, "my beloved spoke (*ʿanah*) and said to me," where the perfect *ʿanah* breaks the series of seven participles. She is narrating the events to listeners (probably the girls of Jerusalem), just as she does in the parallel unit, 5:2–6:3 (Delitzsch). All the youth's words are a quotation encompassed in her narration.

(2:8) *Listen!*: *Qol* is often best taken as a virtual imperative, "hark" (Gordis), or perhaps as elliptical for "I hear a sound" (Luzzatto on Isa 40:3).

My beloved—he's coming now (*dodi hinneh zeh baʾ*): *Zeh* reinforces *hinneh* (Delitzsch, Ehrlich, GKC §136d). It may emphasize proximity in time or place, or both together. Compare Isa 21:9, "Look, here comes a chariot," and also I Kgs 19:5.

(2:9) *My beloved is like a gazelle or a young roe*: He resembles it in speed, and perhaps also in the power of its sexual desire. In the spring gazelle bucks wander the mountain seeking mates (Feliks, 1964:59). "Three Wishes" (no. 40), too, uses the gazelle as a figure for a youth speeding to his beloved, but with a vastly different tone: here the emphasis is on serene grace, as the lover comes of his own will, there it is on panicky haste, as the gazelle is pursued by a hunter.

After v. 9b, LXX adds "on the mountains of Bethel [*Baithēl*]," an addition presumably based on 2:17b (on *beter* understood as Bethel, see below on v. 17). But since *beter* is there rendered "ravines," the addition in v. 9b suggests the possibility that *koilōmatōn* in v. 17 is an exegetical revision.

peering in through . . . glancing in through: *Min* is used from the speaker's point of view. The youth is looking from the outside inward.

(2:10b–13) A magnificent description of earth's awakening in spring.

(2:10) *my beautiful*: LXX adds "my dove" here and in 2:13. In v. 10, Vulgate has "my dove" after *ra*ᶜ*yati*. "My dove" was probably a scribal elaboration in different Hebrew texts. LXX lacks *ul^{e}ki lak* in v. 10.

(2:11) *the winter has departed*: The "winter" (*s^{e}tayw*) in Palestine is the rainy season, which usually ends in mid-April. The time envisaged is May or June, when the figs and vines begin to ripen, the vines blossom, and the migrant birds appear.

(2:12) *the time of song (zamir)*: or, "the time of pruning." This stich is in "Janus parallelism" with the A-stich and the C-stich of this verse (Gordon, 1978:59); that is, it is deliberately ambiguous and faces two directions. *ᶜet hazzamir* means (1) "the pruning season," which according to the Gezer Calendar is the two months between "the month of harvest and measuring" and the "month of summer fruit";[2] and (2) "the time of the song" (of birds). The first meaning looks back to the preceding description of the change of seasons; the second looks forward to the mention of the song of the turtledove.

in our land: The possessive pronoun conveys with amazing conciseness powerful feelings of ties to the land. These ties are not the national bond of a people to its territory, but rather the bond of the individual to the earth, which is to say, the bond of the individual spirit to nature.

(2:13) *The fig tree sweetens its young fruit*: *Ḥan^{e}ṭah*, correctly explained by Ibn Ezra and Ginsburg as meaning "to sweeten," is the same verb as ḤNṬ "embalm" (Gen 50:2, 3, 26). Embalming was done by infusion of aromatic mixtures. Here the fig tree is pictured as sending its fragrant fluids to its unripe fruits, in a way reminiscent of the vines' and the mandragoras' giving forth their fragrances (2:13; 7:14). The personification suggested in this phrasing implies that the springtime blossoming is not something that happens to nature but something that nature does.

and the vine is in bud: *S^{e}madar* refers to the bud of the vine. V. 13, "We'll see if . . . the *s^{e}madar* has opened," shows that the *s^{e}madar* is the bud, which may or may not have opened. The season envisioned in this passage is thus early spring, that is, April or May. In *w^{e}hagg^{e}panim s^{e}madar* the predicate noun is used adjectivally; cf. Exod 9:31; Ezra 10:13 (Ginsburg).

(2:14) *My dove in the clefts of the rock . . .*: "Dove" is a term of affection. Used in this context the epithet suggests a point of comparison: he is unable to see through the lattices or to reach her (Ibn Ezra), while she for her part is hesitant, like a reticent dove, to go forth from her covert.

your form (*mr*ʾ*yk*): Point *mar*ʾ*eyk*, a *plenę* writing of the singular, like *midbareyk* in 4:3.

2. Lemaire (1975:15–18) argues that *zamir* means "vintage" and that the setting is the grape harvest in June–July. The description of the blossoming of the land, however, pertains more to April–May.

(2:15) *Catch us foxes . . .*: an enigmatic verse, whose literal meaning has no relation to the context. But if the verse is meant figuratively, what is it a figure for? And who is speaking? There are many ways of explaining this verse—all of them more or less guesses. Of the common explanations, these are the least forced:

1. The verse is a wish (spoken by either lover) that nothing be allowed to harm the girl's blossom of feminine charm. The foxes stand for any harmful force; cf. the apparently proverbial use in Neh 3:35 (Budde).
2. The verse is a wish that nothing be allowed to harm blossoming love (Delitzsch).
3. The "vineyards" represent nubile girls (1:6; 8:12), and little foxes represent lustful youths (Rudolph, Gordis).

I tend toward the third interpretation. The jackal or wolf cub represents a lusty lover in Egyptian songs nos. 4 and 49. In no. 4 the girl calls her lover "my (little) wolf cub." (Egyptian *wnš* means "jackal" or "wolf," and Hebrew *šuᶜal* means "jackal" or "fox," so the correct translation for both might be "jackal.") In Theocritus, too, foxes symbolize lascivious young men and women (Ode I, 48–50, and Ode V, 112), and the theft of grapes represents sexual intercourse, as a scholium to Ode V explains (Wendel, 1914:179). The plurals "foxes" and "vineyards" do not exactly fit the situation in Canticles, but perhaps the verse is a saying or a snippet of an earlier song (thus Murphy, 1981:112). "Vineyards," however, may be a "plural of composition" referring to one girl's body; for other examples see GKC §124b. The girl calls her bosom "the vineyards of Ein Gedi" in 1:14, and in 6:2 *gannim* apparently alludes to the same thing as *ganno*, i.e., the girl's body. "Foxes," on the other hand, must be a true plural.

According to my tentative interpretation of this verse, the Shulammite's reply—requested in v. 14—begins here. (There are examples of women speaking of themselves in the 1st pl. in amatory contexts in Mesopotamian literature; see chap. 5, n. 23.) Her reply is coquettish (Murphy, 1981:112). She is gently teasing her lover, "tending" or "guarding" the vineyards as she was ordered to do. She is saying: watch out for the little fox out there—his intentions are clear enough! The term *ʾeḥᵉzu* is used playfully, for it can mean "trap" (in order to get rid of) or "hold on to" (so that he cannot get away), as in 3:4 (cf. Würthwein). The banter in 2:15, by this interpretation, is erotically suggestive as well as affectionate and gentle. In any case, *ʾeḥᵉzu* is a rhetorical imperative, an emphatic wish addressed to no one in particular. LXX and Vulgate have "foxes" only once, but the repetition (as in MT) seems preferable for stichometric balance.

(2:16) *My beloved is mine and I am his*: The girl declares their mutual love, as in 6:3, where the order of the clauses is reversed.

he grazes among the lilies: lit., "who grazes . . ." This is an expression of delicate and luxurious pleasures. He grazes or feeds (*roᶜeh*) not in the pasture but among the most delicate and lovely of flowers. "He grazes/feeds" is ambiguous as to the implicit object—himself or his sheep—but in context the phrase certainly alludes to lovemaking, explaining the preceding sentence by specifying in what way the lovers belong to each other. The phrase may allude in particular to kissing, for lips are compared to lilies in 5:13. The phrase may refer to lovemaking more generally, the lilies being the girl's charms in her "garden," where the boy "eats" (see 4:16–5:1). (On the various connotations of *roᶜeh* see commentary to 1:7.)

(2:17) *Before the day blows softly in, and the shadows flee*: Opinions are divided as to whether v. 17a refers to the coming of evening or morning. *ᶜad šeyyapuaḥ hayyom* is a phrase without clear parallel and might mean either. But the logic of the context points to the morning. The shadows of day do not "flee" as the sun sets, but stretch out, *niṭṭim* (Jer 6:4; Ps 102:12), and linger until they cover the earth. When the sun rises, the shadows of night may be said to flee. Furthermore, the events described here fit the end of the night better than the evening. The girl is in her house and hesitates to go out. The boy speaks to her in secret, something that would be difficult to do in the late afternoon, when her family would be on their way home or at home and awake. And if we suppose that the meeting occurred during the day, what would be the point in her urging her lover to flee before nightfall, when the danger of being caught would be less? Or what would be the point in urging him to come *to* her (if that is the intention) before nightfall? If she is calling him to her, we would expect her to tell him to come after dark. We should therefore picture the scene as taking place just before dawn.

Opinions are also divided on whether she is urging her lover to flee or to come to her to spend the rest of the night. While I consider it fairly certain that the time to which she is referring is the morning, I am not sure whether she is calling him to her or sending him away, and I am not sure that we are supposed to be sure. But even a double entendre has a primary meaning, a meaning you are supposed to hear before you catch the hidden meaning. The primary meaning here is that he should flee. *Yapuaḥ* may then refer to the morning breeze. As day approaches, the Shulammite urges her lover to flee the way he came. *Sob*, "turn," indicates turning *from* her and departing, not turning *to* her, which would require "to me." Whenever SBB indicates physical turning and lacks an adverb specifying the goal, it means either going around and encompassing something, pivoting, or turning *away* from something. Thus the imperative *sob* in I Sam 22:17, 18 means "turn from me [Saul] to something else," and *wattissob* in I Kgs 2:15 means "[the kingdom] turned away [*from* me] and went to my brother." (SBB probably could indicate turning *to* the speaker if it were accompanied by *ʾelay*, though there are no examples of this in the Bible.) Furthermore, there would be no point in the Shulammite's calling her lover to turn *to* her at a time when he was already facing her and speaking to her. So she is probably telling him to depart.

on the mountains of Bether: Many identifications have been suggested for *harey beter*, including the following:

1. The *mons veneris*, which has both "spices" (as in 8:14?) and a cleft, in Hebrew a *beter* (thus Haupt 1902a:233; but can *beter*, whose root-meaning is "to divide, cut in two," really mean "cleft" in the sense of *rima mulieris*? And why "mountains," in the plural, if *mons veneris* is meant?).
2. Breasts, which are "mountains" separated from one another (Lys). (But again, *beter* is probably not the appropriate word for that sort of division.)
3. Mountains that divide, or will divide, the lovers from each other (Ginsburg).
4. Mountains of spices, on the assumption that *beter* is a type of spice synonymous with *b*[e]*śamim* in 8:14 (Peshitta translates "spices").
5. Mountains of the ravines, hollows (LXX *orē koilōmatōn*).
6. Mountains in a place called Bether (Vulgate, Aquila, Symmachus).

The last explanation is the most likely, at least as the primary meaning of the word. Carroll (1923/24:79) identified this Bether with modern Bittîr, Bar Kochba's Beitar, a village 11 km. southwest of Jerusalem, occupied in the First and Second Temple periods. The town's name is variously spelled. In a verse following Josh 15:59 in LXX A, *baithēr* is mentioned. In LXX B this is spelled *thethēr*, undoubtedly a corruption of *bethēr*. Jerome quotes this verse in his commentary on Micah 5:2 and spells the name *Baether*. In his commentary on Zech 8:19, he writes *Bethel*, for *Bether*. In I Chr 6:44 LXX A, *baiththēr* is mentioned instead of Beth Shemesh. In III Esdras 5:17 LXX B, a *baitēr* appears. *Beitar* is usually spelled *bytr* in the Talmud, but in the Jerusalem Talmud *byttr* appears, as does *btr* (j. Ber. I, 3:4). (The geminated *-t-* seems to be original, but some of the above spellings suggest secondary aspirantization of the *taw*). There is no phonological obstacle to identifying Canticles' *btr* (original pronunciation uncertain, but probably with a geminated *-t-*) with Beitar/Bittîr. The mountains of Beitar are mentioned here because of their proximity to Jerusalem, the locale of the Song. Even today you can see gazelles running on the hills west of Jerusalem, a vision of extraordinary grace. The Shulammite is urging her lover to return like a gazelle on the mountains over which he came to her like a gazelle.

3:1–6

(Girl)

(1) On my bed night after night
I often sought my soul's beloved;
I sought him, but did not find him.
(2) I shall get up and roam the city,
through the streets and squares.
I shall seek my soul's beloved.
I sought him but did not find him.
(3) The watchmen who roam the city found me.
"My soul's beloved—have you seen him?"
(4) Scarcely had I left them
when I found my soul's beloved.
I seized him—now I won't let him go
till I've brought him to my mother's house,
to the room of her who conceived me.
(5) I ask you to promise, girls of Jerusalem,
by the gazelles or the hinds of the wild:
do not disturb, do not bestir love,
before it wishes.

(Girls of Jerusalem?)

(6) Look who's coming up from the wilderness
⟨in⟩* columns of smoke,
perfumed with myrrh and frankincense,
all sorts of merchant's powder!

*3:6 *b^e^timrot* (MT *k^e^timrot*)

This unit shares with the preceding one the theme of the nighttime search. This time it is the girl who goes forth to seek her lover. Each lover is willing to face the dangers of the night to seek the other. The girl asks the watchmen where her lover is and gets silence for an answer; they neither help nor hinder her. But soon she finds him, embraces him, and declares she is going to take him back home. The adjuration again hints that she and her lover are about to make love.

There are those who see this unit as a narration of a dream (Delitzsch, Budde, Würthwein, Gordis), for the story begins in bed and continues with some very strange behavior on the girl's part—she goes out and wanders the streets at night. But while the events do have a dreamlike quality, there is no sign that the girl is asleep. As for the strange behavior, we may compare no. 34, where love makes a girl "crazy" and "collapsed" (or "lost"). That girl managed to control her desires rather than follow her heart in pursuit of the boy, but as a consequence of her restraint those lovers never did get together. The Shulammite, on the other hand, who follows her desire and behaves strangely, finally does attain her wish.

(3:1) *night after night*: lit., "in the nights," the plural showing a repeated action, thus: "I have often sought." *(Bal)leylot* means "by night," "nightly" in Ps 16:7; 92:3; and 134:1 (the events referred to in those passages occur repeatedly). It is never a plural of composition meaning one specific night. In other words, the Shulammite has often lain in bed seeking her lover in her heart, yearning for him. This night she decides to get up and go out to look for him in the city streets.

sought: that is, sought him in my heart. BQŠ means "to desire" in Exod 10:11 and I Chr 21:3 (and elsewhere, but not as clearly). Egyptian *wḫ3*, "seek," is likewise used in the sense of desire: e.g., "If you seek (*wḫ3*) to caress my thighs" (no. 1), and "my heart seeks you" (no. 13).

I sought him but did not find him: After her declaration that she will seek her lover, the repetition of this phrase suggests a sigh. LXX adds: "I called him but he did not answer me," as at 5:6.

(3:3–4) The absence of an answer or reaction on the part of the watchmen suggests steely indifference. We imagine the lone, scantily clad girl standing before the armed watchmen in the dark and empty streets, asking if they have seen "my soul's beloved" (as if they could know or might care who it is her soul loves). She does not say that they did not answer; her silence seems to reinforce theirs. She immediately leaves them to continue her search: she must find her beloved by her efforts alone. She soon finds him and swears she will not let him go until she has brought him home.

The tenses in these verses are ambiguous. We might translate, "I seized him, and I would not let him go, till I had brought him . . . ," but the imperfect *ʾarpennu* seems to signal a change in time perspective: she took hold of him in the recent past and is now holding on to him, but she has not yet brought him home. In v. 4b she moves from narration to statement of the present situation, as she does in very similar circumstances in 5:7–8.

It is unclear whether she intends to bring him to her mother's house right then and there, or is resolving not to lose sight of him until she brings him home and makes their love public sometime in the future. In 8:1–2 we get the impression that bringing him to her mother's house is something she cannot do quite yet, for in that passage she wishes that she and her lover had a recognized relationship that would allow her to kiss him in public and bring him home. Thus I am inclined to take 3:4b as an expression of intention. As for now, she and her lover are together, and she asks the girls of Jerusalem not to disturb their lovemaking.

my mother's house: Compare 8:2. An unmarried girl's home is elsewhere called her "mother's house"; thus Gen 24:28; Ruth 1:8. The girl in "The Stroll" (no. 32) too identifies her home as "my mother's house."

to the room of her who conceived me: "House" and "room" frequently appear in synonymous parallelism. "Room" here is a poetic automatism, in which a near-synonym is used for the sake of completing the parallelism without changing the denotative meaning of the sentence (on the phenomenon see Haran, 1972).

(3:5) *I ask you to promise . . .* : See comment on 2:7. Having found her beloved and taken hold of him, the Shulammite once again asks the girls of Jerusalem not to disturb them. As in 2:7 and 8:4, the adjuration not to disturb love follows upon a reference to embracing. This time, however, the adjuration is not preceded by the statement "His left hand is under my head . . . ," for the couple are not yet lying together.

(3:6) *Look who's coming up from the wilderness*: lit., "Who is this coming up from the wilderness?" This is not a real question, nor is v. 7a its answer. The combination of adjuration and question in 8:4–5 shows us that the question does not begin a unit but rather responds to the adjuration. In 2:7 the adjuration ends a unit, but here and at 8:4–5 it produces a response. The response is a rhetorical question expressing surprise and admiration. The same question, with a different continuation, appears in 8:5, where there is clearly no answer. A similarly structured question in 6:10—lit., "Who is this gazing down like the morning star . . . ?"—is also a clearly rhetorical question expressing admiration. The implicit and obvious answer to all these questions is—the beloved girl. Certainly the sentence "Look! Solomon's own couch!" (v. 7a) does not answer "Who is this . . . ?" (the parallels in 8:5 and 6:10 show that *mi* means "who," not "what," and that *zo'̓t* refers to the girl, not to an object).

We cannot be certain who the speaker is. While it could be the Shulammite expressing surprise at her own good fortune, she does not speak of herself in the third person elsewhere. It might be the boy speaking in admiration—though it would not be quite appropriate for him to express surprise such as this question implies. The speaker is probably the girls of Jerusalem, who are addressed in the preceding adjuration. The similar exclamation in 6:10 is put into the mouths of noble women. It is an exclamation most appropriate to onlookers, such as the noble women or the girls of Jerusalem. The girls of Jerusalem have not expected their friend to be "coming up from the wilderness," just as the noble women have not expected the swarthy commoner to shine forth like the dawn star.

TaMaKh caught the intent of this verse: "Having concluded the words of the beloved girl, [the poet] goes back and says that when the beloved girl entered, all who saw her extolled her and remarked in surprise and amazement on her perfection: 'Who is this coming up from the wilderness!'"

The phrase "coming up from the wilderness" is obscure. Neither here nor in 8:4–5 would it make sense for the Shulammite to charge her comrades not to bother her and her lover, and then to appear from the wilderness redolent with perfumes (3:6b) or clinging to her beloved (8:5b), especially since the couple is nowhere said to have gone down to the wilderness. The theory that a wedding procession is described in 3:6–11 does not help explain the phrase, for why would the wedding start in the wilderness?

Gordis (1961:20) thinks that the passage describes the approach of a Phoenician princess, with her retinue, across the wilderness lying to the east and southwest of Palestine, but that is not a logical approach from Phoenicia. Elsewhere (p. 56) Gordis thinks of an *Egyptian* princess, but an Egyptian too would be more likely to follow the coast road and approach from the west. In either case, the princess would not arrive from the desert on the wedding day itself (v. 11). Nor does Gordis explain why the couple is coming up from the wilderness in 8:5.

Gerleman thinks that the wilderness is the Theban desert, the occasion an Egyptian festival. Aside from the inherent dubiousness of the theory (see below on 3:7ff.), a procession described as returning from the Theban necropolis would be said to *come down* from the desert.

I do not think the phrase should be taken literally. It is probably an idiom, and as such its meaning is not the sum of its parts. The logic of an idiom lies beneath the surface of its words. The phrase "coming up from the wilderness" may imply a majestic appearance from afar and thus be used of the Shulammite's "dazzling" emergence as a woman in love.

in columns of smoke: MT reads: "like columns of smoke," but there is little point to the comparison as it stands, for how can columns of (incense) smoke be "coming up from the wilderness"? A very minor emendation (*kaph* to *bet*) produces "in columns of smoke," a phrase explained in the following stich: she is encompassed in columns of smoke of incense.

all sorts: See GKC §127b.

3:7–11

(Girl)

(7) Look! Solomon's own couch!
  Around it threescore warriors,
    from the warriors of Israel,
(8) all of them swordsmen,
  skilled in warfare,
each with his sword along his thigh,
  because of nocturnal fear.
(9) King Solomon made himself a canopied bed
  of the trees of the Lebanon.

(10) Its pillars he made of silver,
    its carpets of gold,
its cushions of purple,
    its interior inlaid with ⟨stones⟩.*

⟨Girls⟩* of Jerusalem, (11) go forth,
    and behold, girls of Zion,
Solomon the king
    in the crown his mother set upon him
on the day of his wedding,
    on the day of his heart's joy!

*3:10 *ʾ^{a}banim*, (MT *ʾah^{a}bah*); *b^{e}not* (MT *mibb^{e}not*)

This unit (which all other commentators begin at 3:6) describes Solomon's wedding chamber and bed. Most take the unit as a description of Solomon's wedding. If it is only that, it is the only passage in the Song that has nothing to do with the young lovers who speak throughout and with whom alone the poem is otherwise concerned. Solomon, for his part, plays no role in the events elsewhere in Canticles. He is mentioned only for the sake of comparison in 8:11–12. Why should a little song from his wedding pop up here? It is, to be sure, possible that this is indeed an epithalamium composed for Solomon's wedding (thus Gordis) and passed down through the ages, picking up two distinctively mishnaic constructions along the way (*miṭṭato šellišlomoh* and *ʾ^{a}ḥuze ḥereb*; see ad loc., below), and one Greek loanword (*ʾappiryon*, perhaps received by way of Aramaic). Mere mention of Solomon is flimsy evidence for Solomonic origin. But even should we assume that this unit originated as a Solomonic epithalamium, we must still ask how this unit functions in its present context and how it relates to the lovers who speak elsewhere in the Song. I think that its purpose in Canticles is in fact no more to describe Solomon's wedding and his bed than the purpose of 8:11–12 is to record leasing arrangements in royal viniculture during the United Monarchy.

Other commentators, recognizing that Solomon's wedding is in itself irrelevant in Canticles even if the book is taken as a loose anthology, have hypothesized that it was customary in ancient Israel to call a groom "king" and "Solomon" and to carry the couple in a wedding procession. This interpretation recognizes, rightly I believe, that many of the details of this passage must be interpreted as metaphors and hyperboles, and that the historical Solomon really has no direct connection with it. Certainly this passage describes wedding festivities—this is explicit in v. 11. On the other hand, if the Song was put together (whether by author or redactor) with any thought given to the placement of the parts, the couple has not yet reached the wedding day.

Gerleman suggests that 3:6–8 (which he sunders from vv. 9–11) is based on descriptions of the procession of an Egyptian festival, in particular the Lovely Festival of Opet and the related Lovely Festival of the Valley, which included processions to and from the Theban necropolis. Gerleman says that a redactor joined 3:6–8 to vv. 9–11 in order to use the description of the Egyptian procession to heighten the splendor of the king in his throne room, which vv. 9–11 describe. This theory is very dubious. The question "Who is this coming up from the wilderness?" would make even less sense as a query about a cultic procession than one about a wedding. The similarities between 3:6–8 and the Egyptian festivals are too vague to justify the connection. Almost any stately occasion, mobile or not, would involve an honor guard and the burning of incense. In any case it is the girl, not the bed, that is perfumed with incense, as the question "*Who* is this . . . perfumed with myrrh . . . ?" shows. And once the description of the Egyptian festival was adjusted to Israelite circumstances, as the reference to Solomon shows it was, there would be no point in mentioning the wilderness. The latest evidence for the Lovely Festival of the Valley—which is the festival that included a procession to the desert and a return at night—comes from the 18th dynasty, before the time of the Egyptian love songs. Though it is likely that the festival was celebrated in some form in the following Ramesside period, a snippet of a song based on that festival would hardly show up in Israel some centuries later.

The difficulties in understanding this unit have resulted first of all from the assumption that v. 7 is an answer to v. 6, which assumption gave rise to the conclusion that 3:6–11 describes a procession coming up out of the desert. However, as argued earlier, v. 6 is a rhetorical question, and v. 7 certainly does not answer it, for "coming up" must refer to the girl, not to the couch. The word used here for "couch" is *miṭṭah*, an object that can be either portable (I Sam 19:15) or stationary (Amos 6:4; Est 1:6). Nothing in 3:7–11 suggests that this bed is moving.

King Solomon is not one of the characters of the Song. Mentioned only as the archetypal rich monarch with many wives, he is a foil for the boy, in the same way that the queens and concubines are foils for the girl in 6:8.

As Ibn Ezra perceives, Solomon is only a *mashal* in 3:7–11. Ibn Ezra's interpretation is unusual and worth quoting. As he sees it, 3:6–4:1 are the words of the youth. When he sees his beloved running toward him in the morning after she has spent the night seeking him, he exclaims in wonder (in Ibn Ezra's paraphrase):

> Who is this coming up from the desert? . . . Even King Solomon had need of many warriors to guard his bed so that robbers would not seize it because of its beauty, so how did this girl come up from the desert by herself? And furthermore, whenever King

Solomon took a woman he desired, he had to build her a magnificent *ʾappiryon*, and he would be inside the *ʾappiryon* . . . . "*Raṣup ʾahᵃbah*": that is to say, when he was "hot" [*śarup*, lit., "burnt"] for one of the girls of Jerusalem, he would put a crown on his head [to enhance his attractiveness]. All this Solomon would do; only then would he see his desire. "You are more beautiful, etc."—but you are more beautiful than the woman Solomon desired, and I can see you without having to make a magnificent building [*ʾappiryon*].[3]

Ibn Ezra thus sees that there is no procession here and further that Solomon is mentioned only to provide a contrast to the young lover. Gebhardt too (1931:28) stresses that Solomon's function is strictly to serve as a type-figure. He interprets 3:6–11 as *mocking* the excessive splendor of Solomon's wedding, which was the antithesis of the simple wedding celebration of the young lovers. The problem with the interpretations suggested by Gebhardt and Ibn Ezra (they are basically the same, except that Ibn Ezra does not see the lovers as getting married just yet) is that if they were correct, the passage would be describing at length what is scorned (the luxury of Solomon's wedding) while not mentioning what is affirmed (the simple circumstances of the young lovers). What this interpretation correctly sees as the real purpose of the contrast—to praise the simplicity and gratuitousness of the lovers' relationship—would be lost by the imbalance. In the contrasts drawn in 6:8–10 and 8:11–12, on the other hand, it is the positive side that is prominent.

What Gerleman says about 3:9–11 I would apply to 3:7–8 as well: this passage alludes to the young lover, who here and elsewhere is referred to as king in a "royal disguise" (see "The Nobility of Lovers" in chapter 7). More precisely, his beloved puts him in that role. Thus 3:7–11 does not contrast the youth and Solomon, but implicitly likens them. The youth is praised indirectly through an enthusiastic and extravagant description of his leafy bed in a garden booth. The Shulammite, who is probably the speaker here, has previously called that booth the royal chambers (1:4), praised its construction (1:17), and called it a "house of wine," a place for feasting (2:4). She has lauded the bed (*ʿereś*) that is in it (1:16) and has spoken of the bed as a royal couch (1:12). Now she elaborates on these motifs, describing her lover's bed as a majestic couch in a splendid pavilion—Solomon's couch, as it were, and on no less an occasion than the royal wedding. Her beloved's presence makes their surroundings royal. Thus the lovers have no need of actual royal luxuries: they luxuriate in love. This is the message of 8:7b, 11–12 as well.

The ostensible setting of this description is the king's wedding day, per-

3. This is from Ibn Ezra's second interpretation of 3:1–4:3 (the first glosses words, the second explains the story, and the third gives the allegorical meaning). It is extraordinary both for its literal approach and for recognizing that Solomon is outside the framework of the story. Moreover, from the way he has the boy speak about Solomon, it seems that Ibn Ezra recognizes that Solomon is not the author of the Song.

haps at a point in the wedding feast when the king rests on his couch surrounded by the splendiferous trappings of royalty. But this does not mean that the youth whose situation is being indirectly described is himself celebrating his wedding, but only that his girl regards his surroundings as equally magnificent. Beyond that, since it is a young couple lying together in the bower, their situation and hopes naturally give rise to thoughts of the day of their wedding, which in their fantasy is a royal one.

It is not clear who is speaking in 3:7–11. It might be the youth, using a depiction of Solomon's wedding festivities to embody his own feelings of elation. Or 3:7–8 alone may be spoken by the boy, who points to his bed in the bower and says: This is none other than the bed of Solomon!—to which the girl replies by amplifying the description of the royal chamber (vv. 9–11). We might also imagine the girls of Jerusalem describing the couple's bower in wonder and hyperbole, perhaps slightly jocular hyperbole, a tone we can hear in v. 6 as well. In that case, vv. 10bβ–11 is the Shulammite's rejoinder: Yes, the bed is indeed royal, and my lover's wreath is a crown. I think, however, that it is the Shulammite speaking here, describing her "king" to the girls of Jerusalem (who are addressed in 10bβ–11), for it is she who is involved in most, if not all, of the give-and-take with them, and they seem to take part in the festivities in the garden (see on 2:7). The Shulammite is boasting to them of the majesty of the leafy bower.

(3:7) *threescore warriors*: a typical number, as in 6:8, meaning "many." Sixty warriors are mentioned here mainly to complete the picture of the royal setting, but this detail also expresses the sense of security the girl feels when lying with her beloved in the countryside. Krauss (1936b) argued that the warriors are actually groomsmen who guard the bridal chamber on the wedding night against nocturnal demons. There is some evidence for this practice in Pirqey de-rabbi Eliezer §12, where the ministering angels are compared to "groomsmen who guard the bridal chambers." Whether the sixty warriors represent bridesmen or are simply the royal bodyguard, they are standing around the couch (they may be pictured as outside the bridal chamber) and not moving in a procession.

(3:8) *all of them swordsmen*: The passive participle *ʾ^{a}ḥuzey* is used (as in mishnaic Hebrew) instead of the active participle to show a characteristic or habitual action. From the parallel with *m^{e}lumm^{e}dey milḥamah*, lit., "learned of warfare," it appears that ʾḤZ here means "learn," "be skilled," like Akkadian *aḫāzu*, "learn" (Perles, 1922:52f.). Greenfield (1964:532f.) pointed to a similar usage in Ugaritic: *ʾḫd ḥrṯh*, "skilled in plowing."

because of nocturnal fear: to ward off fear such as comes at night. The widespread fear of supernatural dangers on the wedding night is well documented by Krauss (1936b) and Pope. But any night presents dangers, and a king would always have a bodyguard.

(3:9) *canopied bed* (*ʾappiryon*): Widengren (see HAL) derived this word from "Iranian" *upari-yana*, "litter," but no such Iranian word exists (Rundgren, 1962:70f.). Some scholars derive *ʾappiryon* from Sanskrit *par-yanka*, "litter" (see BDB). Gordis, who wishes to date 3:6–11 to Solomon's time, prefers this etymology also. But the *-k-* in the Sanskrit word, as well as the distance of India from Israel, militates against that derivation. Hebrew did adopt words of Indian origin for some objects acquired from there by trade, but sedan chairs would hardly be imported from afar when they could be built from local materials (as this one is; note "trees of the Lebanon"). In any case languages closer at hand have words similar to *ʾappiryon*, and only an interpreter's determination to date the passage closer to Solomon's time could produce a Sanskrit etymology like this.

Some translations and commentators find the description of the *ʾappiryon* more suitable to a permanent structure. The Peshitta translates *mgdlʾ*, "tower," in spite of the resemblance of *ʾappiryon* to Syriac *pwrywn*, "bed," "litter," and in spite of LXX's precedent, *phoreion*, "litter." (One Peshitta MS translates *kwrsyʾ*, "throne," which is an independent interpretation, while another does use *pwrywn*; see the Leiden edition. *Mgdlʾ* is less obvious and thus probably older than the latter translation, while *pwrywn* looks like an "improvement" dependent on LXX.) Ibn Ezra glosses *ʾappiryon* as "magnificent building" (*binyan nikbad*) on the basis of context. Gerleman suggests an Egyptian etymology, *pr*, "house," with a preformative *aleph* and an afformative *-ywn*. (Actually the Egyptian word probably ended in a *-y* or a vowel, so that the afformative could be the familiar diminutive *-on*.) The *ʾappiryon*, he suggests, is the throne room.

Most commentators regard LXX's *phoreion* as the etymon of *ʾappiryon*, and this seems most likely, since the phonetic differences are easily explained (Rundgren, 1962). But the borrowing need not have been direct. A word similar to *ʾappiryon* appears in various forms in Aramaic and Syriac. To ascertain the semantic range of *ʾappiryon* we should consider its uses in Aramaic, which may be the intermediary in the borrowing, although the available sources are later than the composition of Canticles. Related words in Targumic and Talmudic Aramaic are *pwrywmʾ*, *prywn*, *pwryynʾ*, *pwryʾ*, *pwryh*. These words seem to have the same meaning. The *pwryʾ* (to use the most frequent form) is a bed. It may be used as a litter for a bride (Cant. Rab. iv 22), but it is not strictly a palanquin for a procession. In b. Ket. 10b we are told that a *pwryh* is called this because people "are fruitful (*parin*) and multiply on it." In b. Shab. 118a the furnishings proper to the lodging of the poor are a *pwryʾ wby-sdyh*, "a bed and a pillow." *Pwryʾ* refers to beds that are not carried or used in processions in b. Bab. Bat. 9a, b. Shab. 121a-b, and Yalqut, Gen. §70 (see *Aruch Completum* and Jastrow, *Dict.*). Syriac *prwtʾ* has a similar range of meaning and can also signify a cradle (see Delitzsch, 1885:

65). In Tar. Jer. II on Deut 32:50, *pwryyn*ʾ refers to a bridal bed with a canopy (*gnn*ʾ). We can conclude that even if *ʾappiryon*, *pwry*ʾ, *pwryyn*ʾ, etc., did ultimately derive from Greek *phoreion*, they acquired a broader range of meaning than the Greek word, which means only "sedan chair." In Aramaic it means any bed, or more likely (as the range of ascertainable uses seems to indicate), any covered bed. The word *ʾappiryon* in Cant 3:9, even if ultimately derived from *phoreion*, does not in itself imply a bridal procession. What seems to be described is more than just a bed, for it has columns, an "inside," and (probably) a paved floor; see below.

(3:10) *Its pillars*: These are the pillars holding up the canopy of the chamber. *ʿammud* refers to a vertical pillar (and, by extension, to a pillar of fire or smoke).

of silver: overlaid with silver, like the pillars of the Tabernacle (Exod 27:17 etc.); cf. the "pillars of bronze" before the Temple (which would not have held up the roof if they were pure bronze; I Kgs 7:15 etc.).

its carpets: or, "upholstery." *R*ᵉ*pidah* is a cloth one spreads (RPD; see comment on 2:5); thus Peshitta *tšwyth*, "its carpets, blankets" (used for sleeping on). This *r*ᵉ*pidah* is made "of gold," i.e., has gold threads woven into it.

its cushions: *Merkab* is a collective term for cushions or bolsters that one sits on; see Lev 15:9–10, where *merkab* is defined as *kol* ʾᵃ*šer yihyeh taḥtayw*, "whatever is under him" (Ehrlich). (*Merkab* in Lev 15:9 refers to these same items as "every item [*miškab*] upon which the man with a discharge sits" in v. 4 and *k*ᵉ*li*, "item," "implement," in v. 6.)

its interior inlaid with stones: "Inlaid with love" (MT) is a pointless metaphor. G. R. Driver (1950:135) explains *ʾah*ᵃ*bah* here and in Hos 11:4 as meaning leather, cognate with Arabic *ʾihab*, "skin," "raw leather." However, RṢP in the Bible always applies to floors, where leather would not be used, and not to the overlay of walls. We should move the pause forward to this word and emend it either to *hobnim*, "ebony" (Graetz), or to ʾᵃ*banim*, "(precious) stones" (Gerleman), the *-m* coming from the following word, MT *mbnwt*. The reading ʾᵃ*banim* is preferable, for floors in royal dwellings might well be paved with valuable stones, as in Est 1:6, "a floor (*riṣpah*) of malachite and alabaster."

Indeed, the description of the *ʾappiryon* of Solomon resembles the "court of the garden of the king's pavilion" described in Est 1:6. That pavilion was decorated with "white and violet curtains, fastened with linen and purple cords upon silver rods and alabaster pillars, with beds [*miṭṭot*] of gold and silver on a floor of malachite and alabaster, mother-of-pearl and colored stones." The royal pavilion stood in the garden and was called the king's *bitan*, "little house" or "kiosk" (1:5), and also *beyt mišteh hayyayin*, "the house of the drinking of wine" (7:8). According to Oppenheim (1965:

328ff.), the *bitan* was a structure known in Mesopotamia as *bitanu*, a small house or kiosk in the garden intended for the use of kings and their heirs. Garden pavilions are also pictured in Egypt. It is likely that the author of Canticles has in mind a structure of this sort. Just as the couches (*miṭṭot*) of Ahasuerus were set in his pavilion, so Solomon's couch (*miṭṭah*, v. 7) is set in his *ʾappiryon*, the latter word a metonym for the chamber it is set in. The canopied bower described in 3:9–11 is elsewhere called "the house of wine," a term similar to Ahasuerus' "house of drinking of wine." It is one of the "chambers" to which the "king" in Canticles brought his beloved (1:4).

(3:10bβ–11) *Girls of Jerusalem*: MT "from the girls of Jerusalem." But the girls of Jerusalem are an unlikely source of either stones or love for inlays. Read *bᵉnot* for *mbnwt*; the *mem* belongs to *ʾᵃbanim* or *hobnim*. In Zech 9:9, *bat ṣiyyon* is parallel to *bat yᵉrušalayim*, suggesting that *bᵉnot yᵉrušalayim* should be parallel with *bᵉnot ṣiyyon* here too, against the accents (Graetz).

go forth . . . behold: The girl addresses her companions here as in v. 5, and in fact the imperative implicit in *hinneh* in v. 7 is directed at them too. *Ṣᵉʾeynah* does not mean literally "to go forth"; it is an exclamation emphasizing the following verb, "behold." YṢʾ (imperative) indicates the immediate beginning of an action, just like *pwq ḥzy*, "go and see," a common expression in the Talmud (Ehrlich), or *ṣeʾ ulᵉmad*, "go and learn," in rabbinic Hebrew. Here the word pair *ṣᵉʾeynah urᵉʾeynah* is distributed between the two members of the parallelism.

LXX lacks "girls of Jerusalem" in v. 11a.

crown: The king's *ʿᵃṭarah* may be a crown or a wreath (Ginsburg argues for the latter). Here *ʿᵃṭarah* may refer both to a crown and to a wreath of the sort mentioned in the Egyptian love songs (nos. 19, 21E) and depicted in paintings of banquets. The Shulammite is speaking about this wreath as if it were a royal crown or a chaplet worthy of a king, and not just any king, but King Solomon himself, and not King Solomon on an ordinary feast day, but King Solomon on the very day of his wedding! My beloved and I—the Shulammite implies—are like king and queen on their wedding day, reclining in a splendid royal pavilion.

4:1–7

(Boy)

(1) How beautiful you are, my darling,
how beautiful!
Your eyes are doves
(seen) through your veil.
Your hair is like a flock of goats
streaming down Mount Gilead.

(2) Your teeth are like a flock of shorn sheep,
come up from the wash,
all of whom bear twins,
none of whom miscarries.
(3) Like a thread of scarlet are your lips,
and your mouth is lovely.
Like a slice of pomegranate is your cheek,
(seen) through your veil.
(4) Your neck is like the Tower of David,
built in courses.
A thousand shields are hung upon it,
all sorts of warriors' bucklers.
(5) Your two breasts are like two fawns,
twins of a gazelle,
which graze among the lilies.
(6) Before the day blows softly in,
and the shadows flee,
I'll make my way to the mountain of myrrh,
to the hill of frankincense.
(7) Wholly beautiful you are, my darling:
no blemish in you!

This unit takes as its starting point the declaration in 1:15, "How beautiful you are, my darling, how beautiful! Your eyes are doves," and develops that statement into a Praise Song whose opening and conclusion echo the simple declaration. (I will discuss the nature and function of the metaphors in the Praise Songs in chapter 7 and the concept of love in Canticles in chapter 8.) The lovers have previously praised each other several times in dialogue (see especially 1:9–17 and 2:1–3), but this is the first *waṣf*, a song in which one lover praises the other's body part by part. In 4:1–5 the boy describes the girl from her eyes to her breasts. TaMaKh, who was sensitive to the erotic drama of the Song, explained why the praise stops with the breasts: "After he had praised her part by part down to her breasts, he became as one afflicted by desire and was no longer able to continue in the details of her praise, but sought to unite with her."

It is difficult to say whether this unit ends with v. 6 or v. 7. Verses similar to 4:6 end units at 2:17 and 8:14, but since other Praise Songs end with generalizations in Canticles (5:16, 6:10, and 7:7) and in Egyptian love poetry as well (see pp. 52, 270), 4:7 may be taken as the ending of this Praise Song. Moreover, 4:7 forms an *inclusio* with v. 1 that brackets the unit. Finally, lovers' invitations in 2:10 and 7:12, as well as the closely related request for entry in 5:2b, begin without introductory praise. I therefore divide the unit after 4:6. The general declaration in 4:7 does, however, serve as a link between the praises in 4:1–6 and the invitation in vv. 8ff. and thus functions in both units.

(4:1) *your veil*: *Ṣammah* means "veil" (rather than "locks of hair," as Rashi interprets it), as Isa 47:2b shows: "remove [cf. the sense of GLH piel in Isa 22:8] your *ṣammah*, show your skirts, uncover your thigh." Maid Babylon, Isaiah says, will cease to be "soft and delicate." She must remove her veil, raise her skirts, and cross the river on foot like a peasant girl. The Shulammite's wearing a *ṣammah* implies that she too is no peasant, in spite of her stint working in the vineyard.

Your eyes are doves (seen) through your veil: The dove is known for its delicacy and softness. These qualities are part of the common denominator in the comparison, but only part of it. The words "through your veil" allude to two other characteristics of the dove, its bashfulness and its ability to "speak." In 2:14 the youth says "My dove in the clefts of the rock, in the covert of the cliff—let me see your form, let me hear your voice." The dove is bashful and hides in inaccessible places. So too the eyes of the Shulammite hide behind her veil, a quality that adds to their fascination. Furthermore, a dove calls aloud, "moans" (*hogah*), and coos (*homah*) (Ezek 7:16; Isa 38:14; 59:11; Nah 2:8; the last is from NHG, a by-form of HGH with the same meaning). Her eyes are like doves calling to the youth from their hiding place. They arouse in him longing and desire to reach her. The dove's voice is considered to be sad, but it is also sweet, as the comparison in 2:14 shows; and a sad voice, like sad eyes, may have an attractive pathos. Keel and Winter (1977) bring much evidence from Egypt and Western Asia for the motif of birds, especially doves, as news-bringers. A dove speaks to the girl in the Egyptian love song no. 14 too. The dove's qualities—gentleness, bashfulness, "speech" that touches the heart—combine to suggest the effect of the girl's eyes on the boy's heart.

through (*mibbaʿad*): i.e., seen from the outside; thus Ibn Ezra, who glosses *mibbipnim*, "from within."

like a flock of goats streaming down Mount Gilead: Flowing tresses of black hair may be said to resemble lines of black goats seen from afar as they wend their way down the mountainside. This image suggests the flow and movement of the maiden's hair.

(4:2) *Šekkulam—šakkulah*: a striking assonance.

all of whom bear twins, none of whom miscarries: V. 2b describes first of all the ewes rather than the girl's teeth. *Matʾimot* means "bear twins" and is the antithesis of *šakkulah*, "one who miscarries." This verse thus helps create an atmosphere of health and fecundity. Secondarily the verse can be understood as describing the girl's teeth, taking *matʾimot* as an intransitive hiphil, "match," "be identical," and understanding "none of whom miscarries" to imply that none of her teeth are missing.

(4:3) *Like a thread of scarlet*: Her lips are red like a thread of scarlet, an expensive material that epitomizes redness (Isa 1:18). The comparison does not intend to say that her lips are thin, if we may judge by the Egyptian ideal. Egyptian women painted their lips red to make them look thicker and more prominent.

and your mouth is lovely (*umidbareyk na'weh*): Except for the opening and closing generalizations in 4:1a and 7, all the other predications in this Praise Song are nominal and metaphorical. *Midbareyk na'weh* alone is an adjectival predication, and a rather pale one at that, in a series of vivid sensual metaphors. Furthermore, the poet, who elsewhere uses common words for parts of the body, here chooses a strange word for mouth, *midbar*, a hapax legomenon apparently meaning "speaking place" or the like. Both these peculiarities are explained when we recognize a double pun here. *Midbar* can be taken as "wilderness," and *na'weh* can be heard as *naweh*, "habitation," an area contrasted with *midbar*. In conjunction with *midbar*, *naweh* refers to an oasis; thus in Isa 27:10, "The fortified city is solitary, the *naweh* is deserted and abandoned like a *midbar*," and similarly in Joel 1:20, "For the channels of water have dried up and fire has consumed the oases of the desert" (*ne'ot hammidbar*; from the by-form *nawah*). Thus the youth is saying, in playful hyperbole: you are so lovely, so flawless, that whatever part of you might in comparison with the other parts be reckoned a wilderness, as somehow defective—even that "wilderness" is an oasis, fresh and refreshing. In 4:11 he says that her lips drip honey and that milk and honey are under her tongue. Thus her mouth, her "*midbar*," is indeed like an oasis, and we see that the phrase *umidbareyk na'weh* conceals a very clever metaphor.

Like a slice of pomegranate is your cheek (*raqqatek*) . . . : *Raqqah* appears only here and in Judg 4:21f. and 5:26, and its precise meaning is not clear there either. The comparison here is more understandable if we take *raqqah* as including the cheeks (thus TaMaKh, Ginsburg; similarly LXX *mēlon*), for most of the temple would be covered by hair. The color of a slice of pomegranate is "bright red mixed with a little white" (TaMaKh). But the resemblance is not in color alone. The expansion of the comparison, "through your veil," suggests that there is another feature relevant to the image, for the presence of the veil is irrelevant to color. In a slice of pomegranate the membranes separating the seeds form a webbing, which is suggested by the shadow the girl's veil casts on her cheek (thus M. Falk, 1982:84). The veil partially obscures her face and makes it all the more intriguing.

(4:4) *Your neck is like the Tower of David, built in courses*: A long neck was considered graceful in Egypt (cf. no. 31), and it must have been so in Israel too or the metaphor would be strident. But while length is a common denominator between neck and tower, it is not the main point of the simile. The extension of the simile places emphasis on another feature of the Tower of David: it is built in courses or rows of stones (*talpiyyot*, from LPY, "arrange in courses"; see Honeyman, 1949:51f.; similarly Delitzsch). The Shulammite's neck resembles a tower of this sort because she wears a necklace made up of several rows of beads. Such necklaces have been found in Mesopotamia and Cyprus (see Pope and Isserlin, 1958) and, above all, in Egypt, where many women and musicians pictured in banquet scenes wear them; see, for example, figs. 2, 3, 4, 5, 9.

A thousand shields are hung upon it: The strands of her necklace are like courses of stone, while the beads that make them up resemble shields hung on the tower (Ibn Ezra). Shields and armor were hung on city walls to ornament them; see Ezek 27:11b: "their shields which they hung (*šilṭeyhem tillu*) on your walls round about—these made your beauty complete." I Macc 4:57 speaks of gold wreaths and ornamental shields hung on the front of the temple.

Šeleṭ is translated variously in LXX in the seven passages in which the word appears: "quivers," "bracelets," "ornaments," "arms" (see Yadin, 1962:133f.). In Cant 4:4 LXX translates "darts" (*bolides*), which is clearly its meaning in II Sam 18:14 and in the Qumran Wars Scroll 6,2. In Ezek 27:11, on the other hand, it means "shields" or "armor" (cf. v. 10). *Šeleṭ* is probably a collective term for weaponry (Tur-Sinai, in Ben-Jehudah, *Thesaurus*; see Yadin, 1962:133f.).

(4:5) *Your two breasts are like two fawns, twins of a gazelle*: There is a certain outward resemblance between the image and the referent in this comparison insofar as her breasts are identical to each other, but the image's pictorial value is really trivial. More important, gazelles are graceful and sprightly. The gazelle embodies beauty and grace for the writer of Proverbs as well (Prov 5:19).

which graze among the lilies: This clause is not to be deleted as a later expansion (contrary to Pope et al.), even though it creates the only tristich in this Praise Song. The clause has several functions. (1) It stresses the delicacy of the fawns, inasmuch as they are pampered to the point of being pastured among lilies, not just on grass. (2) As TaMaKh observed: "[The lover] said 'who graze among the lilies,' for then they pick up the fragrance of the lilies, and he compared to this the scent of her breast." (3) The phrase "who graze among the lilies," said here of her breasts, gains special erotic significance when later on she compares her beloved's lips to lilies (5:13). (4) We are perhaps to imagine the girl with a wreath of lilies framing her breasts (John Hobbins, private communication). (5) The most important function of the clause is to create the delicate pastoral image itself: fawns grazing among lilies.

(4:6) *Before the day blows softly in . . .* : The girl's words of 2:17 are echoed in this verse, whose own echo will be heard later in 8:14. But the words of the boy here reverse the girl's request in 2:17, where she urged him to turn from her to flee upon the mountains of Bether. The youth declares that he will go *to* the mountain of myrrh and the hill of frankincense. These cannot be literal geographical references, because, as Delitzsch points out, these spices do not grow in Israel. Ibn Ezra perceived how the response reverses the girl's earlier request and recognized what these hills allude to: "'Your two breasts (are like twins of the gazelle, etc.),' which have a good odor, for they feed among the lilies. He said to her, 'You have told me that I should go to the mountains of Bether before the day blows, but I went rather to the mountain of myrrh.'" The "mountain of myrrh" and the "hill of frankincense" are the girl's breasts, for she is "perfumed with myrrh and frankincense" (3:6). There he will rest like a "bundle of myrrh" (1:13) in the hills of spices.

Wholly beautiful you are, my darling: no blemish in you!: 4:7b restates and explains 4:7a.

4:8–5:1

(Boy)

(8) ⟨Come⟩* from Lebanon, (my) bride,
  ⟨come⟩,* from Lebanon draw near.
Come forth from the peak of Amana,
  from the peak of Senir and Hermon,
from the dens of lions,
  from the ⟨lairs⟩* of leopards.
(9) You have captured my heart, my sister, my bride,
  you have captured my heart with one of your eyes,
    with a single strand of your necklace.
(10) Your caresses—how beautiful, my sister, my bride!
  Your caresses—how better than wine,
    the scent of your oils than all spices!
(11) Your lips, my bride, drip honeycomb,
  honey and milk are under your tongue,
    and the scent of your garments is like the scent of Lebanon.
(12) A garden locked is my sister, my bride,
  a ⟨garden⟩* locked, a spring sealed.
(13) Your watered fields are an orchard:
  pomegranates with luscious fruits,
    henna with spikenards,
(14) spikenard and saffron, cane and cinnamon,
  with frankincense trees of all kinds,
myrrh and aloes,
  with all the best spices.

(15) A garden spring,
a well of living water,
liquids from Lebanon.

(Girl)
(16) Awake, O north wind, and come, O south!
Blow on my garden that its spices may flow.
Let my beloved come into his garden,
and eat of its luscious fruit.

(Boy)
(5:1) I come into my garden, my sister, my bride,
I taste my myrrh with my spice,
I eat my nectar with my honey,
I drink my wine with my milk.

(Girls of Jerusalem?)
Eat (well), O friends,
drink yourselves drunk on caresses!

*4:8a *ʾ^{e}ti* (MT *ʾitti*); *ʾ^{e}ti* (MT *ʾitti*)
*8b *ḥorey-* (MT *har^{e}rey-*)
*12 *gan* (MT *gal*)

The youth invites his beloved to come away with him and praises her *dodim*, the erotic pleasures she gives him; she responds by offering him those very *dodim*. The unit progresses as follows. The boy invites his beloved to come to him from the mountains (4:8), describing the power and sweetness of her love (vv. 9–11) and the fragrance of her garments. He then praises her as both a fresh spring and a fragrant garden (vv. 12–15). In response she invites him into the "garden" he has described (v. 16), and he accepts gladly (5:1a). A third voice, probably that of the girls of Jerusalem, who are somehow present even in the lovers' privacy, urges them to give themselves over to the delights of lovemaking (5:1b). The dominant image in this unit is drinking and eating, which symbolize general enjoyment of sensuality, not only coitus.

Unlike the Praise Songs in 4:1–7, 6:3–10, and 7:2–8, which laud the girl part by part, this one celebrates her entire person. It is thus an Admiration Song, a type of Praise Song (see chapter 7).

The intertwining strands of word-echoes and word-plays in this unit are not merely ornamental devices. They unify its parts, clarify the meaning of the allusions, and interlock the words of the couple.

Paranomasia, puns, and repetitions found in this unit include the following:

l^{e}banon (4:8, 8, 11, 15)—(*raʾšey*) *l^{e}bonah* (4:14)
meroʾš (4:8, 8)—*raʾšey* (*b^{e}śamim*) (4:14)
ʾ^{a}rayot (4:8)—*ʾariti* (5:1)
ṭobu dodeyka miyyayin (4:10)—*šatiti yeyni* (5:1a)—*š^{e}tu w^{e}šikru dodim* (5:1b)
b^{e}śamim (4:10, 14)—*b^{e}śamayw* (4:16)—*b^{e}śami* (5:1a)
d^{e}baš w^{e}ḥalab (4:11)—*dibši . . . ḥ^{a}labi* (5:1)
maʿyan gannim (4:15)—*ganni* (4:16)—*ganno* (4:16)—*ganni* (5:1a)—*maʿyan ḥatum* (4:12)—*maʿyan gannim, b^{e}ʾer mayim ḥayyim* (4:15)—*š^{e}tu* (5:1b)
p^{e}ri m^{e}gadim (4:13)—*p^{e}ri m^{e}gadayw* (4:16)
kallah (4:8, 11)—*ʾ^{a}ḥoti kallah* (4:9, 10, 12; 5:1a) (*kallah* only in this unit in the Song; *ʾ^{a}ḥoti* elsewhere in the Song only in 5:2)

(4:8) *Come . . . come*: For MT *ʾitti*, "with me" (twice), point *ʾ^{e}ti*, "come"; LXX, Vulgate, and Peshitta understood the word this way. Here, as in 2:10–14, the youth invites his beloved to come *to* him (not with him) from her place of concealment. The youth's apparent presence in Lebanon, implied by MT "come," has puzzled some commentators. Budde (similarly Gordis and Würthwein) isolates the verse from its context and then says it makes no sense, claiming that it is a fragment inserted by a redactor who did not understand it either. Budde finds it surprising that the girl should be called *from* Lebanon without our being told that she had climbed up or that she lived there, and further that she should be called from the mountains without it being said where to. In fact, the geographical details are unimportant. Gerleman regards the mountains as a literary motif representing a dangerous and "heroic" place, in contrast to the Arcady described earlier, where lovers "feed among the lilies" with none to make them afraid. Gerleman is certainly correct in recognizing that the poet is not interested in real geography. The girl is not in Lebanon any more than she is sitting in the clefts of the rock in 2:14. The mountains of Lebanon, like the clefts of the rock, symbolize distance and inaccessibility and evoke a sense of loftiness and exoticism.

Although the youth is close enough to his beloved that she can hear his voice, at this moment he feels as though she were now in some far-off inaccessible mountains, which her "presence" makes into a place of beauty and enchantment. He gives them names that recall spices and sweet things, since she herself is "perfumed with myrrh and frankincense" (3:6). Her spices cling to whatever place, real or imaginary, she is in. By the end of this unit, the tension of inaccessibility that began it has been resolved in the successful union of the lovers, as the imagery has moved from mountains to garden.

The names of places and animals in this unit were chosen to call to mind the names of spices and sweet things: *Lᵉbanon*—*lᵉbonah* ("frankincense"), *ʾᵃrayot* ("lions")— *ʾariti* ("I taste"; see further on 5:1a), and perhaps *nᵉmerim* ("leopards")—*mor* ("myrrh") and *roʾš* ("peak")—*raʾšey* (*bᵉśa-mim*) ("best spices"). These exotic places and animals evoke an atmosphere of beauty and majesty—a wild setting in deliberate contrast to the gentle and idyllic landscape of the preceding Praise Song. The wild, threatening landscape is, as Gerleman says, a literary device to describe the experience of love "konkret und spannungsvoll." Gerleman draws a parallel to no. 4, in which a girl mentions far-off and threatening locales to represent a moment of uncertainty and threat. The girl of that song says that even were she banished to Syria, Nubia, the highlands, or the lowlands, she would not abandon her desire.

bride: This affectionate epithet does not show that the Song, or even this unit in itself, is a wedding song. The setting does not suggest a wedding, nor is there any hint of present marriage. "Bride," like "sister," is an expression of affection and intimacy, suggesting also a hope for the future.

tašuri: not "look" (ŠWR II in BDB), but rather, as the parallelism shows, "travel," "journey" (ŠWR I in BDB); thus LXX, Peshitta, Ginsburg, Pope. The youth is asking his beloved to come, not merely to look, from the mountaintop. If he wanted her to look at something, he would say at what. He invites her to come to him from the mountains, just as he came from the mountains to reach her in 2:8. Although the motif of mountains is meant literally in 2:8 and figuratively in 4:8, in both places it calls to mind the difficulties that must be overcome in attaining love.

⟨*lairs*⟩ *of leopards*: emending *harᵉrey* to *ḥorey* (NJPS) for the sake of tighter parallelism. Parallel terms are generally quite synonymous in this unit (*ḥor* is used in Nah 2:13 as a synonym of *maʿon*, "lions' den"). Both the graphic similarity of *ḥry* to *hrry* and the presence of mountain names in the immediate context could occasion this error.

(4:9) *You have captured my heart*: *Libbabtini* can be explained in a number of ways:

1. As derived from LBB "inflame" (cf. *labbat ʾeš* in Exod 3:2); thus: "you have inflamed my heart."
2. On the basis of LBB in mishnaic Hebrew, where it means "be aroused to fury" (e.g., Cant. Rab. iii 6), whence it may have come to mean "be aroused sexually," a semantic development paralleled in Greek *orgē*, *orgaō* and mishnaic ŠṬY (Waldman, 1970:215–17). Pope accepts this derivation and notes further the "sexual sense" of "heart" in Mesopota-

mian usage. Now certainly the arousal the boy speaks of here is sexual, but that does not show that this word means "sexually arouse" or (contrary to Pope) "[give sexual] potency." The youth nowhere hints at concern about his virility.

3. As a privative piel, "you have taken my heart" (Ibn Ezra, Delitzsch, Gordis).

The third seems most likely to be the primary sense. We may compare the Egyptian verses "she has captured my heart in her embrace" (no. 31) and "Indeed it is she who captures my heart" (no. 54).

LXX reads *ekardiōsas hēmas*, taking the object suffix as first plural. This reading (graphically very similar) is not impossible—compare the girl's use of the first plural in 1:3–4. But the singular "*my* sister" in 4:9 supports MT.

my sister: a term of endearment, as in the Egyptian love songs and the Mesopotamian Sacred Marriage songs (in the latter, however, it may also have its literal meaning). The basis of this expression is the closeness of the relationship between brother and sister. Elsewhere in the Bible and Apocrypha, "brother" and "sister" are used to denote close relationship without actual kinship, e.g., Job 30:29 (*ʾaḥ*//*reaʿ*) and Prov 7:4 (*ʾaḥot*//*modaʿ*); cf. Job 17:14, Tob 7:2, and Apoc Est 15:8.

my sister, my bride: This phrase, repeated five times, is the leitmotiv of 4:8–5:2. It asserts both current intimacy and future relationship.

with one of your eyes, with a single strand of your necklace: You don't need two eyes to capture my heart—one is enough; in fact, just one strand of your necklace can do this. The construction *ʾaḥad ʿanaq* is an Aramaism (Gordis). *ʿanaq* means "strand" (LXX, Ibn Ezra, Ginsburg) rather than "bead," judging from its meaning in mishnaic Hebrew (e.g., b. Erubin 54a, Yalqut Ps. §675; see further Jastrow, *Dictionary*), in which it also means "chain" (b. Bab. Bat. 75a). We may picture a multi-strand collar of the sort ubiquitous in Egypt and presupposed by the image in 4:4 (see figs. 1, 2, 3, 4, 5, 9).

A bead of precious stone is called "eye" (*inu*) in Akkadian (CAD). If this usage existed in Hebrew—and the application of the word "eye" to bead seems like a natural metaphorical transfer—then *ʾaḥad meʿeynayik* in our verse is a pun. The parallel phrase, "a single strand of your necklace," calls forth the second, more unusual, meaning of the word. *ʿanaq* too may be a pun: both "strand" of necklace and "neck" (Aramaic *ʿinqaʾ*; John Hobbins, private communication). Then we have a double pun: eye//neck::bead//strand of beads.

(4:10) *your caresses—how beautiful* . . . : an echo of the girl's words in 1:2–3.

your oils: LXX has "your garments," probably influenced by *śalmotayik* in v. 11b.

(4:11) *Your lips, my bride, drip honeycomb*: Note the striking assonance in *nopet tiṭṭopnah śiptotayik*. The metaphor describes two qualities: sweetness of kisses (1:2; 4:10), and sweetness of speech, whether in seduction (cf. Prov 5:3) or conversation (Prov 16:24). Sweetness is a metaphor for pleasant and thoughtful speech in no. 31 and App. A, no. vi.

honey and milk are under your tongue: "Under the tongue" is the place where speech originates (Ps 10:7; Job 20:12), so this phrase has the same ambiguity as "drip honeycomb."

(4:12) *a garden locked . . .* : Read *gan* for *gal* with LXX, Vulgate, and Peshitta. The meaning "fountain" for *gal* is not well established, and ab//ac couplets, where the word or phrase that opens the first stich begins the second as well, are frequent; see 1:15; 4:1, 8, 9, 10; 5:9; 6:1, 9; 7:1 (this type of couplet is characteristic of the present unit in particular). The girl is a "locked garden" to which the boy desires entry. The locked garden image both expresses the boy's desire for greater intimacy (as does the call in 4:8) and praises the girl's modesty and sexual exclusiveness. She is likewise a "sealed spring," a spring closed up so that its waters are not generally accessible (*ḥatum* is used of prevention of entry in Deut 32:34). "Spring" (*maᶜyan*) alludes to feminine sexuality, as in Prov 5:15ff. A woman's sexuality is a "spring," as she is a "garden"—images that suggest both sensuality and potential fertility. Prov 5:16 describes a woman who, having been betrayed, becomes the opposite of a "sealed spring." The writer asks, "Shall your springs [i.e., your wife's sexuality] spread out in the street, (like) puddles of water in the squares?" Prov 5:17 describes what Canticles calls a "sealed spring": "Let them [your springs] be for you alone, no one else with you."

(4:13) *Your watered fields are an orchard*: *Šᵉlaḥayik* is commonly explained as equivalent to *šᵉluḥah* (Isa 16:8)—"branches," "tendrils." But these nouns differ in form, and in any case branches or tendrils do not make an orchard. Rather, *šᵉlaḥim* are irrigation channels—*šlḥyn* (= *šᵉlaḥin*?) in mishnaic Hebrew (m. Moed Qaton 1:1; Tosephta, ibid.; b. Bab. Bat. 4:7); see Pope. In mishnaic Hebrew the area irrigated by the *šlḥyn* is called *byt šlḥyn*. Here *šᵉlaḥim* is a metonymy for that area, just as *naḥal* means the area irrigated by a wadi as well as the wadi proper (6:11). The field (*šᵉlaḥim*) that draws its sustenance from the "spring" (v. 12) is an orchard that, like that spring, is fresh and sweet. *Šᵉlaḥayik pardes* thus combines garden and water imagery. In this orchard grow luscious fruits and spices. It would appear that the girl is represented by images of both the spring and the orchard it waters; this duality is unmistakably present in v. 12.

The main point of the double metaphor is to convey the feelings that the girl stirs up in her lover. The praise of her *šᵉlaḥim* is not an anatomical description, as if the channels represented the vagina or womb (see Pope); for one thing, the plural "channels" would be inappropriate if the word were a euphemism for vagina. The youth is praising his beloved as a whole, not detailing her private parts.

The pause should be placed after *pardes*, against the accents. The Shulammite's *šᵉlaḥim* are an orchard not of pomegranates alone, but of a rich variety of fruits and spices. This stich-division accords with the structure of the following lines: "a with b," "c with d," etc.

(4:14) *spikenard and saffron . . .* : The profusion of exotic plant names suggests the intensity and fullness of the youth's feelings. For the identification of these plants, see Feliks, 1964:23–28. Of the nine types of spice mentioned in vv. 13–14, three grow in Israel, namely *habbośem* (balsam), *koper* (henna), and *karkom* (*Crocus sativus*). There is doubt about whether myrrh, cinnamon, and *qaneh* ("cane": *Cymbopogon martini* or *Andropogon nardus*) ever grew there. The remaining three, frankincense, aloes, and spikenard, had to be imported at high cost from great distances—from Arabia, India, Nepal, and China (Feliks, 1964:23–28). This can only be a fantasy garden of exotic and precious plants.

(4:15) *A garden spring*: *maʿyan gannim*—a fountain of the sort found in gardens, the *nomen rectum* representing the species (GKC §128m; cf. Cant 2:1). She is not an exposed public fountain, but an enclosed and very private one.

liquids from Lebanon: This phrase points back to v. 8 and with it brackets the praise. "Liquids [perhaps lit. "streams"] from Lebanon" elaborates on *mayim ḥayyim*, "fresh [lit., "living"] water." "Liquids from Lebanon" describes the quality of the water in the well rather than its source. Water cascading down Lebanon is clear and cool, that is, "living."

(4:16) *Awake, O north wind . . .* : The girl calls upon the winds to stir up the spices the youth has praised, to waft their fragrance to him and attract him to enter *his* garden. The Shulammite equates "my garden" with "his garden," just as the "vineyard" the boy calls his (8:12) is none other than the "vineyard" the girl calls hers (1:6). Her garden is his, for "I am my beloved's" (6:3a). Her invitation now "opens" the locked garden.

that its spices may flow: that their fragrance may waft to him on the breeze. For MT's "its spices" LXX and Peshitta have "my spices"; the latter is probably a haplography. The greater subtlety and indirectness of MT seem more in line with the way the Song usually treats sexual allusions.

its luscious fruit: or, "his luscious fruit."

(5:1a) *I come into my garden*: He accepts her invitation and enters the garden. The girl called herself "his garden"; he picks up the clue with alacrity and eagerly calls everything in the garden his own: "my garden," "my sister," "my myrrh," "my spice," "my nectar" (*yaʿar*), "my honey" (*dᵉbaš*), "my wine," "my milk": eight possessives in sixteen words. The verbs in 5:1a are probably to be taken as present tense, as indicated by the imperatives in 5:1b, which show that he has not yet finished eating and drinking (compare the tense of *dimmitik*, 1:9; *nasu*, 2:17, etc.). *Baʾti*, however, may mean "I have come." Verbs of eating and drinking can allude to sexual enjoyment; see Prov 5:15, 19.

I taste (*ʾariti*): or, "I pluck," used in the sense of "eat." Compare Ps 80:13–14: "Why have you breached its walls, so that all passers-by devour it (*wᵉʾaruha*), the forest boar chews it (*yᵉkarsᵉmennah*), and wild animals feed upon it (*yirʿennah*)?" (*ʾaruha* is the consequence of the breaching of the walls and parallels *yᵉkarsᵉmennah* and *yirʿennah* [Pope]; note in particular the parallelism between RʿH and ʾRH.) *ʾariti* plays on *ʾᵃrayot*, "lions" (4:8), and perhaps also on "honey" (5:1a), for the Arabic cognate *ʾary* ("honey") suggests that *ʾᵃri* in Hebrew may mean "honey" too. A play on *dᵉbaš* and *ʾᵃri* is the key to Samson's riddle, whose answer is, "What is sweeter than honey (*dᵉbaš*) and what is stronger than a lion (*ʾᵃri*)?" (Jud 14:18). So *ʾᵃri* may be taken three ways—"lion," "honey," and "eating" (Pope).

nectar: *Yaʿar* is honey from the comb. This unit uses three synonyms for honey—*dᵉbaš*, *yaʿar*, and *nopet*—and possibly hints at a fourth, *ʾᵃri*, in a pun. English translation cannot reflect this variety.

I drink my wine: *His* wine is her lovemaking, which is better than real wine (4:10). The response in 5:1b makes the meaning of this metaphor explicit by urging the lovers to drink themselves drunk on lovemaking (*dodim*). Compare "Your liquor is your lovemaking," meaning: the intoxicant you offer is not beer but sex (no. 4, see n. d).

(5:1b) *Eat well, O friends, drink yourselves drunk on caresses* [or *lovemaking (dodim)*]!: A third voice speaks up here. Gerleman attributes this sentence to the poet's voice, but since that voice does not intrude itself elsewhere, it is more likely that these words are spoken by the girls of Jerusalem, who are now urging the couple to enjoy love to the full. The girls of Jerusalem are similarly present during the exchange of affection in 2:1–6 and before the lovemaking implied in 2:7; see my remarks ad loc. Their words in 5:1b bring out the implications of the eating and drinking images. The lovers are to "eat" and "drink" love. "Get drunk on love" (lit., "drink and get drunk of love") means to give oneself over to sexual ecstasy, as in Prov 5:19: "Let her lovemaking [point *dodeyha*] slake you at all times, with her love be infatuated (?) always," and Prov 7:18, where the harlot says, "Come, let's slake ourselves on lovemaking [*nirweh dodim*] until morning, let's besport ourselves, in love" (*ʾᵒhabim*, which also refers specifically to sexual love).

5:2–6:3

(Girl)

(5:2) I slumbered, but my heart was alert.
Listen! My beloved is entreating:

(Boy)

"Open to me, my sister, my darling,
my dove, my perfect one,
for my head is drenched with dew,
my locks with the mist of the night."

(Girl)

(3) "I have slipped off my robe.
How can I put it on?
I have bathed my feet.
How can I get them soiled?"
(4) My beloved stretched his hand in through the hole,
and my insides moaned for him.
(5) I arose to open to my beloved,
and my hands dripped myrrh,
my fingers—liquid myrrh,
on the handles of the lock.
(6) I opened to my beloved,
but my beloved had turned away and gone.
⟨Because of him⟩* my soul went forth:
I sought him but did not find him,
I called him but he did not answer me.
(7) The watchmen who roam the city found me—
they beat me and bruised me,
took my shawl away from me—
those who watch the walls.
(8) I ask you to promise, girls of Jerusalem:
if you find my beloved
do not tell him
that I am sick with love.

(Girls of Jerusalem)

(9) Your beloved—how is he better than any other,
O most beautiful of women?
Your beloved—how is he better than any other
that you make us promise this?

(Girl)

(10) My beloved is bright and ruddy,
preeminent among a myriad.
(11) His head is finest gold,
his locks fronds of a palm,
black as a raven.

(12) His eyes are like doves
by water channels,
bathing in milk,
sitting by a brimming pool.
(13) His cheeks are like beds of spices,
towers of perfumes.
His lips are lilies—
they drip liquid myrrh.
(14) His arms are cylinders of gold,
inlaid with jasper.
His belly is an ivory bar,
adorned with lapis lazuli.
(15) His thighs are marble pillars,
set on pedestals of gold.
His form is like the Lebanon,
distinguished as the cedars.
(16) His palate is sweet drink;
he is wholly a delight.
This is my beloved, this is my darling,
O girls of Jerusalem!

(Girls of Jerusalem)
(6:1) Which way did your beloved go,
O most beautiful of women?
Which way did your beloved turn,
that we may seek him with you?

(Girl)
(2) My beloved has gone down to his garden,
to the beds of spices,
to graze in the gardens,
and to gather lilies.
(3) I am my beloved's and my beloved is mine:
he grazes among the lilies.

*5:6 *bidbaro* (MT *b^edabb^ero*)

The unity of 5:2–6:3, with its continuity of narrative and dialogue, is evident. In 5:2–8 the Shulammite tells the girls of Jerusalem about a nighttime visit by her lover and the events that followed. A dialogue between the Shulammite and the girls of Jerusalem ensues, a dialogue that includes a Praise Song (5:10–6:1) as an answer to their query (5:9). Finally the boy appears (6:2), and the girl exults (6:3). It is pointless to ascribe this unity to an editor (contrary to Murphy, 1981:117, who cites "widespread agreement among recent commentators"). It is hard to see what further signs of cohesiveness an interpreter could reasonably require before conceding the original literary unity of a composition.

In addition to its internal bonds, this unit has links to the preceding and following ones. While 5:2 clearly begins a new dramatic sequence, with the lovers separated again and the girl lying in bed one night, the similarity between the motifs of this unit and those of the preceding one shows that the placement of the units is not random. In the preceding unit the girl was called a "locked garden" (4:12). Here too the boy's entry to the desired place is prevented by a "lock," and here too the girl is willing "to open" to him (5:5–6; cf. 4:16). At the end of this unit, as in the preceding, the youth "goes down" to enjoy the fruits of love (6:2; cf. 5:1), and the girl opens her "garden" for him because "I am my beloved's and my beloved is mine" (6:3).

This unit ends at 6:3. The girl's declaration of mutual possession in 6:3, which brings the unit to a triumphant culmination and brings out the meaning of the boy's entry into his garden, is a natural caesura, and the dialogue that ensued from the story of the search comes to an end. Yet the disjunction between this unit and the next is not complete. The declaration in 6:3 also calls forth the boy's praise in the next unit, and his praise of her in 6:4–10 balances her praise of him in 5:10–16.

The Shulammite tells the girls of Jerusalem how she was sleeping restlessly (perhaps because she was yearning for her lover and thinking about him as she was wont to do—see 3:1) when suddenly she heard him asking to be let in. Although she had desired his coming and had even anticipated it (as is implied by 5:5), she hesitated at first to get up and let him in, giving unconvincing excuses for not doing so. When she finally rose to open the door, she found that she had lost her opportunity, for he had already disappeared. Now she had to go out and seek him. To wander the streets at night was a dangerous and strange deed. Perhaps her behavior made the watchmen suspect her of being a prostitute. And indeed her behavior does resemble that of the "strange woman" in Prov 7:5–21, who goes out "in the depths of the night" to hunt about in the "street" (*ḥuṣ*) and in the "squares" (*r^{e}ḥobot*) for a foolish lad passing in the "street" (*šuq*) near her house. In any case, it is clear that the Shulammite was breaching the walls of expected behavior and as a result suffered the mockery and brutality of the representatives of the social order, "those who watch the walls." The story thus dramatizes vividly—even violently—the tension between the girl's desires and society's suspicions. The watchmen, who roam the city and guard the walls, attacked her and stripped her. Now she is exposed and confused.

Through v. 7 she is telling this story. Then she begs the girls of Jerusalem not to tell her beloved of her love-sick, crazy behavior. Like the girl in "The Stroll" (no. 34), the Shulammite is embarrassed about the irrational behavior her love-sick heart has caused. In response, the girls of Jerusalem tease her: what is so special about this youth? She answers with a Praise Song (5:10–16), after which they are ready to help her in her search, and they ask where he went. She answers: "My beloved has gone down to his garden, to the beds of spices, to graze in the gardens, and to gather lilies" (6:2). Her reply is puzzling, because if she knows where her beloved is, whether in a literal or a figurative garden, why does she ask her friends to help her find him? The explanation, I believe, is that the audience, who must infer the events from the speaker's words, is to conclude from 6:2–3 that the girl has now found her beloved. The "garden" represents the girl herself and "grazing among the lilies" alludes to lovemaking. We thus learn of the success of the search only indirectly. Between the desperate search and the happy conclusion (the expression of mutual love, 6:3), the girl describes her lost lover. It is as if the girl's praise brings about his presence: he is absent, she describes him, and he is immediately at her side.

The section 5:2–8 parallels 3:1–6. The similarity of motifs and formulations is unmistakable: the search through the streets at night, the encounter with the watchmen, the reunion (this last being implied in 6:2–3 by the statement that the boy has entered his garden, followed by the declaration of mutual possession). The present unit draws on 2:8–17 as well. There the boy visits his beloved's house at night and speaks to her from outside. He requests that she come away (this resembles his entreaty in 5:2 in expressing the desire to unite with her), and he receives a gentle refusal (2:17; cf. 5:3). There are new elements in 5:2–6:3: the hostility of the watchmen, the dialogue with the girls of Jerusalem, the Shulammite's Praise Song, and her friends' offer of help. The poet thus combines and elaborates motifs present in earlier units, while adding new motifs that increase dramatic tension and give the lovers' experiences a social context.

(5:2) *I slumbered, but my heart was alert*: Since she was sleeping restlessly, her lover's whisper was enough to waken her; Qoh 2:23 speaks of a similar restless sleep: "even at night his [sc. the toiler's] heart does not lie down"; in other words, even when asleep his thoughts do not rest.

Listen!: See on 2:8.

entreating (*dopeq*): The meaning of *dapaq* in the Bible is not entirely clear. LXX, Peshitta, and Vulgate understand *dopeq* here as "knock," and this is the usual translation. Ibn Ezra, however, explains it as "importune," "bother" (*meṣiq*), and he is probably right. In Gen 33:13, *d^epaqum* means "urge them," "press them on," and the Arabic cognate means "to drive sheep." The root-meaning of DPQ is probably "to push" (*mitdapp^eqim* in Judg 19:22 means "pushed"). Here it means "urge," "entreat," or the like.

What she hears is not the knocking on the door (which might wake up the whole family!), but the words of entreaty her lover speaks.

Open to me: sc. the door. The emphasis placed on the word "open," which occurs three times in vv. 2–6, always without the direct object being specified, implies that she will open not just the door, but herself—physically and emotionally—to her lover.

for my head is drenched with dew, etc.: In Anacreon iii, 10, personified Love uses the same reasoning in begging admittance: "'Open!' he said. 'I am just a youth, do not fear. For I am drenched from wandering about in the moonlit night."' Compare also Propertius I, xvi, 23f., and Ovid, *Amores* ii, 19, 21. The youth's dew-drenched hair (5:2) suggests that he has come from afar at night, as in 2:8.

(5:3) *I have slipped off my robe . . .* : Her explanations are patently unpersuasive, as if she wished to get up but was hindered for reasons she could not explain.

(5:4) *My beloved stretched his hand in through (min) the hole*: *Šalaḥ yad* is a common phrase meaning "stretch out the hand." It is usually followed by *ʾel* or *bᵉ-*. It governs the preposition *m(in)* in Ps 144:7 and Ezek 10:7, but *m(in)* there means "from," not "through." *Min* here has the very same sense as in 2:9b, "in from outside," seen from the perspective of one who is inside (Delitzsch). *Min* approaches the semantic range of English "in," "into," only when used from this perspective. The "hole" is probably one of the "windows" and "lattices" mentioned in 2:9. Earlier he only *spoke* through the openings. Now he puts his hand through, perhaps to take hers, and she becomes extremely agitated.

and my insides moaned for him: Some fifty MSS and several editions read *ʿalay*, "my insides moaned within me"; cf. *tehᵉmi (napši) ʿalay*, Ps 42:6, 12, where, however, the phrase refers to emotional depression (*//tištoḥᵃḥi*). The Versions witness to *ʿalayw* in Cant 5:4. Either reading seems satisfactory.

Pope regards v. 4 as suggestive of "coital intromission": the male inserts (*šalaḥ*) his penis (*yad*, lit., "hand") into (*min*) the girl's vagina (*ḥor*). (One wonders how the poet could have said "he put his hand in through the hole" in such a way as to prevent that reading.) "Stretched his hand in through the hole" admittedly makes one think of intercourse, even though *min* is not the appropriate preposition to indicate insertion. Still, I do not think this double entendre fits in with the course of the narrative. If we explain v. 4 as a euphemistic (but unambiguous) reference to an "account of coition" (Exum, 1973: 50), the preceding and following verses lose their meaning. In vv. 2–3 the youth is standing outside his beloved's house, and in v. 5 she arises to open to him (after intercourse?). V. 6 makes it clear that he had not entered her house. Beyond that, interpreting these verses as a euphemistic description of coition produces a rather ugly picture of a male who lies with a female and immediately abandons her for no particular reason. We should certainly not read this passage as an elaborate gynecological conceit, in which each part of the door lock represents a specific part of the female genitals (an approach Eslinger, 1981:276, carries to an extreme). A reading of that sort detracts not only from the interest and tension of the narrative, but also from its erotic intensity.

There are indeed sexual allusions in 5:2–6:3, but they are delicate and indirect. The boy asks admittance when his girl is in bed, and she wants him to come in, but for unclear reasons she hesitates. The audience is invited to imagine that the couple *would* have had intercourse had the girl been quicker to open the door or the boy not fled so soon. But between his arrival (5:2) and his reappearance (6:2) they do not have intercourse. The boy's going down to his "garden" (6:2) is indeed an allusion to lovemaking, though not an unambiguous reference to coitus. In any case, whatever he will do in his garden he will do outside the framework of the dramatic action. The actions implied by "to graze in the gardens" and "to gather lilies" are formulated as infinitives of intention, meaning that he will do them later.

(5:5) *and my hands dripped myrrh . . .*: She had anointed herself with fragrant spices before going to bed, a sign that she had expected a visit from her lover and had prepared for it (Ehrlich, Gordis). The sexual implications of such preparations are evident in Prov 7:17, where the "strange woman" entices a boy by saying that she has perfumed her bed with myrrh, aloes, and cinnamon in anticipation of a night of love. Furthermore, there seems to be a particularly sensuous connotation to myrrh-filled hands. The claws of the bird from Punt (no. 9), who certainly represents the beloved youth, are similarly full of balm.

myrrh: here equivalent to oil of myrrh, mentioned in Est 2:12 (Ehrlich).

liquid myrrh (*mor ʿober*): a type of myrrh; *ʿober* is an adjective in v. 13 as well. The profusion of spices is evocative of sensual pleasures. The Egyptians too enjoyed profusion in spices and perfumes, lavishing on themselves great quantities at banquets, passing around vials to the guests, and placing cones of perfumes on their heads. One song (no. 42) calls a girl's perfumes "an inundating aroma that intoxicates those who are present." So it would not be unrealistic (and certainly not unappealing) for the Shulammite to claim that she had put on so much myrrh that it dripped from her hands onto the lock handles.

on the handles of the lock: adverbial to "my hands dripped myrrh."

(5:6) *turned* (*ḥamaq*): The root-meaning of ḤMQ is "turn"; thus *titḥammaqin* in Jer 31:21 = "turn yourself." *Ḥamaq ʿabar*: the asyndeton suggests quick succession; cf. 2:11. LXX lacks this verb.

Because of him my soul went forth: pointing *bidbaro* for MT *b*ᵉ*dabb*ᵉ*ro*, "when he spoke." The sequence of events indicates that it is her lover's disappearance that causes her longing, rather than his speech quoted three verses earlier. The phrase "(one's) soul went forth" is not used frequently enough to allow us to determine its precise meaning. In Gen 35:18 (cf. Ps 146:4, where the synonymous *ruaḥ* is used), the soul's "going forth" means "expire," "die." Here it might mean something like "I almost died," or "I fainted." Or it might mean that her soul went forth in longing after him, like the heart of the girl in "The Stroll" (no. 34), which goes forth and flees from her in agitation and longing. But the Shulammite, unlike the Egyptian, goes out to follow her soul and seek her lover.

(5:7) *my shawl* (*rᵉdidi*): The *rᵉdid* is a light garment. Isaiah includes the *rᵉdid* among the stylish clothes and ornaments that he condemns the girls of Jerusalem for traipsing about in (3:23), so he seems to regard it as ornamental rather than essential apparel. It is probably a light overgarment. LXX renders *theristron*, a summer overdress, the term that renders *ṣaᶜip*, "veil," in Gen 24:65. Targum Jerushalmi uses *rᵉdidaᵓ* to translate *ṣaᶜip*. So the *rᵉdid* appears to be little more than a veil or light overcloak, and we are to imagine the Shulammite running about the city hastily dressed and half-naked. The Egyptian girl of no. 34, also agitated by love and desire, says that her heart's flight has made her unable to dress herself properly.

(5:8) *I ask you to promise . . . do not tell him*: As far as I can tell, this verse has invariably been understood as a request by the Shulammite that the girls of Jerusalem inform her beloved that she is love-sick. Thus RSV: "I adjure you, O daughters of Jerusalem, if you find my beloved that you tell him that I am sick with love." This translation is based on the understanding of *mah taggidu lo* as a rhetorical question that the Shulammite herself immediately answers, a construction compared to Hos 9:14 (where, however, *mah* is very likely a relative pronoun, "what," "whatever"; thus Rashi, Meṣudat David). But the adjurations elsewhere in Canticles, which begin in precisely the same way as this one, are indisputably negative. In 2:7 and 3:5 the adjuration is introduced by *ᵓim . . . wᵉᵓim*. In 8:4 the same adjuration substitutes *mah . . . umah*. Clear examples of the negative use of *mah* are I Kgs 12:16 (// *loᵓ*; = *ᵓeyn* in II Sam 20:1) and Job 16:6 (// loᵓ). This usage is recognized by König, 1897:II, §§352β–δ, though not for this verse. (The negative use of *mah* originates in rhetorical questions eliciting a negative answer.) In our verse too *mah* is a substitute for negative *ᵓim*. The verse is a request that the girls *not* tell her beloved how she has behaved. She has acted in a distraught manner, running about the city at night half-dressed, and she is embarrassed over her behavior. Her concern is like that of the Egyptian girl who tells how her heart flees from her and makes her foolish and erratic. She says to her heart, "O my heart, don't make me foolish! Why do you act crazy?" She shows her embarrassment at her condition when she tells her heart, "Don't let people say about me: 'This woman has collapsed out of love'" (no. 34).

LXX adds "by the powers and the forces of the field" after "girls of Jerusalem," as in 2:7 and 8:4.

(5:9) *than any other*: lit., "than a beloved."

5:10–16. A Praise Song. Some of the imagery of this section is drawn from the arts: the head of gold, the arms like cylinders of gold, thighs like marble pillars on gold sockets, the belly like an ivory bar. Only the gold head is taken specifically from sculpture, so we cannot suppose that the boy is being described as if he were a statue (contrary to Gerleman).

(5:10) *bright*: *Ṣaḥ* means bright or shining, like the metals and stones mentioned further on (Pope). "Bright" (*ṣaḥ*) skin is compared to milk in Lam 4:7, but that does not show that *ṣaḥ* means "white" in the limited sense that word has in English. The concepts of shining and whiteness are closely related—compare Egyptian *ḥḏ*, which means both "white" and "shining" (like the sun). There is thus no incongruity between *ṣaḥ* and *ʾadom*, the two features of skin mentioned in this verse. A shining face was considered a sign of health (Ps 104:15), and a ruddy hue in the skin was thought to attest to health and youthfulness (I Sam 16:12; 17:42).

(5:11) *His head is finest gold*: *Ketem* and *paz* are names of two types of gold, joined in a bound structure for poetic hyperbole (Avishur, 1977:49). Beauty and ascribed value are the common denominators of the image and the referent. Pope points out that Nebuchadnezzar's statue had a head of gold (Dan 2:32). But even if the model for this item is an idol, no divinity is thereby ascribed to the youth, any more than the use of fauna imagery in praising the girl makes her out to be an animal.

fronds of a palm: According to Pope, Akkadian *taltallû* is used of the pollen of the date panicle (von Soden, however, glosses it more generally as "Pollen, Staubgefäss?" [HAS]). Pope notes further that Arabic *taltalat* is used of the envelope of the spadix of the date palm, and that *taltallim* is of the same pattern as three other words that designate plant shoots or branches: *zalzallim* (Isa 18:5), *salsillot* (Jer 6:9), and *sansinnim* (Cant 7:9). LXX and Vulgate too translate the word as referring to parts of the palm. The translation "fronds of a palm" assumes that the word was used metonymically of other parts of the date palm. In mishnaic Hebrew *taltallim* means "curls," but that usage is based on an interpretation of this verse and not evidence for the word's earlier meaning. In any case, "his locks are curls" is pleonastic, and nowhere else do the Praise Songs describe a part of the body with a synonym.

(5:12) *His eyes are like doves . . .* : Only "like doves" belongs to the simile proper. The rest of the verse is an expansion of the picture of the doves and does not apply directly to the eyes. The attempt to relate every part of the image to the eyes quickly runs aground. If the milk is the whites of his eyes, how can his eyes bathe in them? If "eyes" here—and only here—means pupils, which may be said to bathe in the whites of the eyes, what do the pupils have in common with doves, which are neither dark nor round? And if the entire image refers back to his eyes, are they sitting by the water channels (tear ducts?), *or* bathing in milk (the whites of the eyes?), *or* sitting by a pool or bowl (sockets?). Eyes cannot do all these things, even figuratively, but doves can do them—one after another. In other words, everything after "doves" describes doves, not eyes, and what is pictured is not a static scene but a series of actions that doves can do. The doves thus take on a life of their own.

The image of doves bathing in milk is a fantasy picture, and it is hard to see what actual event could underlie it. The image emphasizes whiteness and conveys a sense of luxury and delicacy, for milk was white, thick, and smooth. The contrast between the blackness of the boy's hair and the whiteness of his eyes is sharpened by the contrast between ravens (v. 11) and doves.

(5:13) *beds of spices*: Point as plural (thus Peshitta, Vulgate, LXX, and some MSS), because the subject is two cheeks.

towers of perfumes (*migd*^{e}*lot merqaḥim*): *Mgdlwt* is frequently repointed *m*^{e}*gadd*^{e}*lot*, "which grow" (transitive) (BHS, Pope, Gordis, and probably most modern commentators); thus LXX *phuousai*. But GDL piel is properly predicated not of the place where plants grow, but rather of the person who grows them or the water that makes them grow (Isa 44:14, Ezek 31:4), so *migd*^{e}*lot-*, "towers of," should be maintained. Gerleman's suggestion that the towers of spices are cones of perfumes of the sort Egyptians put on their heads at banquets (see figs. 1–4, 6, 9) is intriguing, but so far as we know the custom was strictly Egyptian and the cones were not called "towers." The image is hardly clarified by explaining *migdal* as "chest" or "box" (Ehrlich), a meaning it has in mishnaic Hebrew. *Migdal* means "tower" elsewhere in the Song, and that is its primary sense here. The comparison says that the scent of the youth's cheeks is as sweet as a tower *full* of spices. It is a hyperbolic and somewhat fantastic image, as many of the images in the Song are, but the towers of spices need not have been real any more than doves that bathe in milk.

(5:14) *cylinders of gold*: According to I Kgs 6:34, the *galil* is part of a door; the root-meaning ("to turn," "roll") suggests that it there refers to the hinge-bar.

His belly is an ivory bar: *Meʿayw* here obviously refers to the visible belly, as in Dan 2:32 (of a statue), and cf. *m*^{e}*ʿaʾ* translating *gaḥon* in the Targumim to Gen 3:14. *ʿešet*: the root is *ʿŠT*, the Aramaic equivalent of ḤŠB, used of fashioning works of art, rather than ʿŠŠ, "be smooth," a root whose existence in Hebrew is doubtful. *ʿešet* is the equivalent of Hebrew *ḥešeb*, "art work," which is used of a specific work of artistry, the belt of the ephod (Exod 28:27, 28; 29:5; etc.). In mishnaic Hebrew, *ᶜešet* is used specifically of a bar or polished block (e.g., b. Men. 28a, Cant. Rab. v 12; see Jastrow, *Dictionary*). The youth's flat and muscular stomach (or perhaps specifically his stomach muscles) resembles a bar of ivory.

adorned with lapis lazuli: *Meᶜullepet* = "covered"; cf. *wattitᶜallap* in Gen 38:14. Here it modifies "ivory" (*šen*, fem.), rather than "bar" (*ᶜešet*, masc.). "Inlaid with jasper" and "covered with lapis lazuli" extend the description of "cylinders of gold" and "an ivory bar" and do not refer directly to the youth's body.

(5:15) *His thighs are marble pillars, set on pedestals of gold*: Ben Sira (26:18) similarly compares "lovely legs" on a woman to "beams of gold on silver pedestals."

His form is like the Lebanon, distinguished as the cedars: luxuriant, fragrant, and tall; in other words, "preeminent among a myriad" (v. 10).

(5:16a) *His palate is sweet drink* (*mamtaqqim*): *Mamtaqqim* in Neh 8:10 refers to a drink, apparently sweet wine. This specific meaning, rather than the more general "sweets," matches better the praise the boy gives in 7:10, "your palate is like the best wine." The simile in 5:16a may praise either his kisses or his fine speech—or both (see on 4:11). This couplet (v. 16a) and the preceding one (v. 15b) sum up the praise of the parts of the youth's body with images implying preeminence and sweetness.

(5:16b) *This is my beloved, this is my darling, O girls of Jerusalem!*: This Praise Song too (see comment on 4:7) is capped off by an emphatic conclusion: This, precisely this, is my beloved, who is undoubtedly unrivaled among lovers and worthy of my love and desire. She speaks in triumphant satisfaction, as if her magnificent verbal creation has irrefutably answered the girls' skepticism. Now they can only agree to help her find him (6:1).

(6:2) *My beloved has gone down to his garden . . .*: This verse alludes to erotic pleasures yet to come; see on 5:1.

to graze in the gardens: The youth has gone down to "his garden" to feed in the "gardens." *Gannim* here does not indicate a plurality of gardens. Two likely explanations of the plural form are: (1) "To graze in the gardens" is an idiom that refers to lovemaking or one of the acts thereof—kissing, for example; (2) "gardens" is a plural of composition referring to the parts of a garden. The girl's body is both a garden and gardens. For other examples of plurals of composition, see GKC §124b.

(6:3) *I am my beloved's and my beloved is mine*: This statement appears in reverse order in 2:16. The second part of 6:3, "he grazes among the lilies," explains concretely (but allusively) how the lovers possess each other: they make love. This is the happy ending to the story that began in 5:2.

6:4–10

Boy

(4) You are as beautiful, my darling, as Tirzah,
as lovely as Jerusalem,
as awesome as the most eminent.
(5) Turn your eyes away from me,
for they make me tremble.
Your hair is like a flock of goats
streaming down Gilead.
(6) Your teeth are like a flock of ewes
come up from the wash,
all of whom bear twins,
none of whom miscarries.
(7) ⟨Like a thread of scarlet are your lips,
and your mouth is lovely.*⟩
Like a slice of pomegranate is your cheek,
(seen) through your veil.
(8) Threescore queens there are,
and fourscore concubines,
and maidens without number.
(9) (But) one alone is she—my dove, my perfect one—
one alone is she to her mother,
pure is she to her who bore her.
Girls beheld her and called her fortunate,
queens and concubines, and they praised her:
(10) "Look who's gazing down like the morning star,
beautiful as the moon,
pure as the sun,
as awesome as the most eminent!"

*6:7 First two stichs not in MT.

The girl's declaration in 6:3 of the love she and her lover share leads into the boy's response, a Praise Song balancing hers. The imagery here, however, is quite different, for the boy is not directly responding to her words of praise. Rather, he is expanding on the praise he gave her earlier (4:1–3), to which he adds the praise of queens and concubines, projecting his own impressions onto observers who are both neutral and noble, though hypothetical.

The first part of this Praise Song, 6:4–7, reiterates and expands the beginning of the earlier one, 4:1–3. Vv. 6:5b–7 are almost identical to 4:1b–

2 + 3b. The opening, 6:4–5a, is an expansion and development of 4:1a. Thus "How beautiful you are, my darling, how beautiful!" (4:1aα) becomes "You are as beautiful, my darling, as Tirzah, as lovely as Jerusalem, as awesome as the most eminent" (6:4), and the statement "Your eyes are doves (seen) through your veil" (4:1aβ) becomes "Turn your eyes away from me, for they make me tremble" (6:5a).

Because vv. 6:11–7:1 are quite obscure and much hinges on the interpretation of a crux in v. 12, it is not at all clear where this unit ends. I think it probable that vv. 11–12 are spoken by the girl (see below on v. 12), and that the boy's words end with the quotation of the women's praise in v. 10.

(6:4) *as Tirzah . . . as Jerusalem*: The point is not that she looks like these cities, but that the degree of her proud beauty equals theirs. Tirzah was probably half-legendary by the time the Song was composed, and probably little was known about it except that it was once the capital of the northern kingdom and thus offered an appropriate parallel to Jerusalem. The two capital cities are mentioned for their connotations of royalty, power, and height as well as their beauty. Another reason for the mention of Tirzah may have been the resemblance of its name to the verb RṢH, "want," "take pleasure in"; thus LXX *eudokia*, "pleasing one," Peshitta *ṣbynʾ*, "delight," and Vulgate *suavis et decora*, "pleasing and graceful." The Targum, followed by Rashi, derives *tirṣah* from RṢH in a midrashic explanation. Although "pleasing" is not the primary sense of the word here—for RṢH can mean "be pleasing" only in a passive formation—the interpretation of the word in this way in the Versions shows that a pun could easily be heard in the name Tirzah.

awesome: *ʾᵃyummah*, more lit., "terrible," "frightening." Great beauty may excite a man and agitate him, as the Shulammite's eyes do her lover (v. 5). The youth insists here and elsewhere that the Shulammite is not just a pretty girl, but a dignified, strong woman. Even if her brothers, the girls of Jerusalem, and the watchmen do not take her quite seriously, her lover sees her in images of majesty and stature (Lebanon, towers, palm trees, heavenly bodies)—images appropriate for the speaker of the proud and defiant words of 8:6–7.

As Pope points out, goddesses of love, such as Aphrodite, Ishtar, and Kali, are frequently also goddesses of war and are said to arouse terror. This combination is understandable because the excitement that love can arouse may in its intensity and confusion resemble the agitation of fear. We should not, however, exaggerate the degree of fear that *ʾᵃyummah* connotes. Goitein (1965) has noted the semantic shift undergone by several words in various languages from the sense of "causing fear, terrible," to "terrific, extraordinary, exquisite": e.g., English "terrific," French *terrible*, and Arabic *haʾil*. Such words need not, however, lose their original signification, and Hebrew *ʾayom* did not, even if it is used in a weakened sense here.

most eminent: *Nidgalot* appears only here and in v. 10. *Nidgol* (qal), of uncertain meaning, parallels *n^erann^enah*, "let us rejoice," in Ps 20:6. *Dagul*, a passive participle whose meaning may be expected to be close to that of the niphal participle, appears in Cant 5:10. Some derive *nidgalot* from *degel*, "banner." This interpretation probably underlies LXX's *tetagmenai* "ranked (phalanxes)"; similarly "camps with banners" (Ibn Ezra), "bannered hosts" (Ginsburg). Such a denominative from *degel* would, however, probably appear in the pual. The word is best explained as cognate to Akkadian *dagālu*, "to look," "see." This etymology allows a great many interpretations. Thus Gerleman: "fata morgana" (but this would not be an appropriate parallel to either the two cities or the heavenly bodies); Goitein (1965): "brilliant stars" (this provides a good parallel in v. 10 but not in v. 4); Peshitta: *gbyt*ʾ, "chosen, select thing" (a *seyamme*ʾ probably should be supplied, vocalizing then *gebyâtâ*ʾ, "select things"). The Peshitta's translation does not (contrary to Pope) presuppose *nibḥeret* in the Vorlage. The Peshitta translates *dagul* in 5:10 similarly: *gbe*ʾ, "choice," "select." (The Peshitta is very likely interpreting *nidgalot* according to the context of *dagul* in 5:10.) Using the derivation from DGL, "to look," Pope surmises that *nidgalot* are trophies of war, like Anat's necklace of severed heads and girdle of severed hands. But Anat's trophies are not called *nidgalot* or anything similar, and there is no reason whatsoever to relate the word to these items. In any case, such a comparison would be utterly incongruous with the tone and imagery of the Song. More suitable, though vague, is Gordis' "cynosures, great sights." The problem with this interpretation is that the other comparisons in the Praise Songs are more specific. But the specificity in this case may come from the context. *Nidgal* with the article can be a superlative: "the most conspicuous, most eminent" thing of its class. Similarly *dagul mer^ebabah* in 5:10 is elliptical for "preeminent among a myriad beloveds," the specification being provided by the preceding question, "Your beloved—how is he better than any other (beloved)?" (5:9).

(6:5) *they make me tremble* (*hirhibuni*): Syriac *r^eheb* means "to tremble"; ʾ*arheb* means "to frighten." A meaning such as "frighten" or "shake up" is indicated here.

(6:7) The couplet "Like a thread of scarlet are your lips, and your mouth is lovely," present in the parallel passage (4:3a), is missing here. It should be supplied after 6:6 in accordance with LXX, Peshitta, Symmachus and Aquila. Vv. 6:5b–7 are otherwise virtually identical to 4:1b–3.

(6:8–9a) *Threescore queens there are . . .* : The syntax of *šiššim hemmah m^elakot* is typically mishnaic; cf. ʾ*arba*ʿ*ah ra*ʾ*šey šanah hem* (m. Rosh Hashanah 1:1). The verse does not refer to any particular group of women, such as Solomon's wives and concubines. The youth is saying: There are numerous queens and noble ladies around, but my beloved is one of a kind. None of them can compare to her, and what's more, even *they* recognize her majesty.

(6:9a) *But one alone is she—my dove, my perfect one*: *Hiʾ* is the subject, not the copula, in the parallel clauses, and so here too.

one alone is she to her mother: "one" in the sense of uniquely precious; cf. *yaḥid* in Prov 4:3 and Gen 22:2.

pure: LXX, Peshitta, and Vulgate render "chosen," "select"; similarly Gordis, who takes *barah* from BWR, a by-form of BRR, "to choose." But *barah* from BWR, "choose," would not have a passive meaning, "chosen." *Barah* here means "pure," "clear" (an adjective from BRR), as in v. 10. The phrase "to her who bore her" is brought in for the sake of the parallelism and does not mean that the girl is pure *only* in her mother's eyes. The Shulammite is her lover's unblemished, pure white dove, her mother's darling. Speaking of the girl from her mother's point of view accentuates the girl's youth and innocence.

(6:9b) *called her fortunate . . . praised her*: The youth puts words of admiration in the women's mouths. The quoted praise is introduced by *way^{e}ʾ-ašš^{e}ruha . . . way^{e}hal^{e}luha*, as in Prov 31:28. These verbs are the only *waw*-conversives in the book, and in the context of the Song's late language they are definitely archaizing. They are probably an old phrase used for introducing quoted praise.

(6:10) "*Look who's gazing . . .*": lit., "Who is this gazing . . . ?" In this verse *mi zoʾt* is clearly a rhetorical question expressing surprise and admiration. The noble women are surprised to see the young commoner appear in stellar majesty. This verse is a concluding generalization typical of Praise Songs; cf. 4:7; 5:16aβb; 7:7; and see chapter 7.

gazing down: ŠQP in niphal and hiphil indicates looking down from above (Pope). Even in the eyes of lofty noble women the simple Shulammite is *ʾ^{a}yummah*, "awesome," as if looking down upon them from the heights. At the start of the song the Shulammite said that she was dark. Now these women, though accustomed to seeing the white and delicate skin of the nobility, testify that she is as splendid as the moon and as lustrous as the sun. She is not only as bright as these; she is lofty and impressive. The power of the comparison to the moon in this regard is better grasped if one has in mind the gigantic, refulgent moon one often sees in Israel.

Vv. 6:9–10 resemble the opening of "The Stroll" (no. 31) in asserting the girl's uniqueness and comparing her to celestial bodies.

6:11–7:7

(Girl)

(11) I've come down to the nut garden,
    to see the fruits of the valley—
  to see if the vine has blossomed,
    the pomegranates bloomed.
(12) I do not know myself—
    ⟨you've placed me in a chariot with a nobleman⟩!*

(Girls of Jerusalem?)

(7:1a) Come back, come back, O perfect one,
    come back, come back, that we may gaze at you!

(Boy)

(1b) Why would you gaze at the perfect one
    as if she were ⟨a camp-dancer⟩?!*

(2) How lovely are your feet in sandals,
    O noblewoman!
  The curves of your thighs are like jewelry,
    work of an artist's hands.
(3) Your navel is a rounded bowl—
    may it never lack mixed wine!
  Your belly is a heap of wheat,
    hedged about with lilies.
(4) Your two breasts are like two fawns,
    twins of a gazelle.
(5) Your neck is like an ivory tower.
    . . . (?)
  Your eyes are pools in Heshbon
    by the gate of Bath Rabbim.
  Your nose is like the tower of Lebanon,
    looking toward Damascus.
(6) Your head (sits) upon you like Carmel,
    and the thrums of your head are like purple:
      a king is captured by the locks!
(7) How beautiful you are, how pleasant,
    O love, ⟨delightful girl⟩!*

*6:12 *śamtani merkabat ʿim nadib* (MT *śamat*^{e}*ni*, *mark*^{e}*bot ʿammi nadib*)
*7:1b *kimḥolelet hammaḥ*^{a}*nim* (MT *kimḥolat hammaḥ*^{a}*nayim*)
*7 *bat ta*^{ca}*nugim* (MT *batta*^{ca}*nugim*)

The results of any attempt to divide 6:11–7:14 (and beyond) into units are inevitably uncertain. Any demarcation of units in 6:11–7:1 depends on one's understanding of three obscure verses, 6:11, 6:12, and 7:1. I suggest—hesitantly—that the movement of thought is as follows. The boy's Praise Song ends in 6:10, where he quotes the women's exclamation of admiration, inasmuch as the section that begins in V. 11 clearly does not continue the praise. 6:11 is said by the speaker of v. 12; what happens in the latter is the consequence of the former. In 7:1 a certain group (indicated by the first plural of *w^e neḥ^e zeh* and second plural of the response *mah teḥ^e zu*) calls the Shulammite to return to it. This demand implies that the Shulammite has already separated herself from that group (figuratively if not literally), whence we may conclude that the speaker of vv. 11 and 12, who went down to the nut garden, is the Shulammite. Her departure makes sense of the call to return (not "turn"; see below). Whatever the nut garden represents, in 7:1a the Shulammite is being called back from there. In the nut garden she was overwhelmed by the excitement of love (v. 12). This experience of the Shulammite sparks the curiosity of the girls of Jerusalem, whose attitude toward their companion's love is often skeptical, perhaps somewhat derisive. The boy's question—"Why would you gaze at the perfect one . . . ?"—implies an objection to something implied in the call to her in 7:1a. The girls have called her back to them so that they can have a look at her and see what is happening. The youth replies: Do not look at the "perfect one" (*haššulammit*; see below) as if she were a common dancing girl who frequents the camps and dances for the soldiers. She is a noblewoman, in looks and character if not in family. He goes on to describe her beauty, much as she had described *his* beauty to the girls of Jerusalem in response to their skeptical inquiry in 5:9–16. He uses imagery that suggests the qualities of wealth, plenitude, preciousness, nobility, and magnificence: an abundance of wheat, works of craftsmanship, a tower decorated with ivory, another tall tower, a pool of water apparently known for its limpidity, and costly purple cloth. As throughout the song, the youth asserts the true nobility of his beloved. She belongs to the aristocracy of lovers.

He describes parts of her body that clothing would cover: thighs, navel, belly, breasts. Since the boy's imagination, let alone his knowledge, would suffice for this description, we need not imagine a scene (such as Gordis, 1961:96, describes) where the Shulammite dances naked or in diaphanous veils before a group of spectators, who describe the parts of her body as she whirls around (Gordis, strangely, seems to think that this is a wedding scene [p. 68]).

(6:11) *I've come down to the nut garden . . .* : The Shulammite echoes her lover's call to go with him to the fields and see the blossoming of the land (2:10–14), as if now responding to his invitation.

fruits of the valley: the fruits (ʾ*ibbim* = Aramaic ʾ*inbin*) of the trees that grow in the valley of the wadi. "The vine" and "the pomegranates" specify the types of fruit.

LXX adds "there I will give you my breasts" (translating *ddym* as "breasts" as in 1:2,4, etc.), representing a phrase found in 7:13.

(6:12) *I do not know myself . . . nobleman*: Numerous interpretations (summarized by Pope) have been suggested for this crux. MT is untranslatable, and the various emendations that have been offered either involve radical changes in the text or produce readings that are not much more comprehensible than MT's. Gerleman suggests that *ʿmy ndyb* (which he takes as a proper name, like LXX's *Aminadab*) is a literary figure like Prince Mehi of "The Stroll" (no. 33), but this hypothesis attempts to explain one obscurity by another. All that these two characters have in common (if *ʿmy ndyb* really is a personal name) is that they ride in chariots.

I suggest emending 6:12b to *śamtani mirkebet* (or *merkabat*) *ʿim nadib*. The only consonantal change required is the elimination of the *yod* of *ʿmy*, a change supported by Peshitta *dʿmʾ dmṭyb*, which does not reflect a *yod* after *ʿm* (*ndyb* is translated *mṭybʾ* in 7:2 as well). *Mrkbt* is to be read without the *mater lectionis waw*. *Mrkbt* may be a bound form joined to a prepositional phrase, a construction attested with various prepositions (GKC §130a), though not, so far as I can ascertain, with *ʿim*. Alternatively, the *taw* may be the archaic feminine absolute ending (another archaizing nominal ending appears in 1:9, *susati*). The meaning of the phrase is the same in either case.

Now to the meaning of the verse as emended. Gordis recognized that the idiom *loʾ yadaʿ nepeš* means "to lose one's balance or normal composure," whether through great joy and excitement, as here, or through sorrow, as in Job 9:21. Paul (1978) found an equivalent in the Akkadian medical phrase *ramānšu la īde*, "he did not know himself," connoting a mental disturbance. I would point to the Egyptian phrase *smḫ ḏt*, lit., "to forget, be unaware of one's body." *Ḏt*, like *nepeš*, can be used as a reflexive pronoun. This phrase is used in no. 37 in a similar context, where the youth is describing his lovesickness: "my limbs have grown heavy, and I barely sense [lit., "have forgotten"] my own body" [*smḫ(.i) ḏt.i ḏs.i*], meaning: I am overwhelmed by love and have lost control of myself (see no. 37, n. b). The sentence "you've placed me in a chariot with a nobleman" I understand as an explanation of the girl's statement about her great agitation. She went down to the garden of love (6:11), where she was overwhelmed with excitement. It was as if he had placed her, a young commoner, in a chariot with a nobleman, for such is he to her. Just as the youth praises his beloved by calling her a noblewoman, a *bat nadib*, so she calls him a nobleman, a *nadib*. "The Flower Song" (no. 18) too speaks of lovers' feelings of exaltation in the garden. The girl says: "In it [sc. the garden] are *sʿ3m*-trees; before them one is exalted" (*sʿ3* passive: lit., "made great" or "made noble").

(7:1a) *Come back, come back*: ŠWB never means "to pivot," "to whirl" as in dance, so there is no basis for the common idea that the speaker here is a group watching the Shulammite dance and urging her on. Rather we must understand the call as spoken by some group that is calling her back from somewhere, apparently the nut garden. The speakers, in surprise or in skepticism, want to look her over.

O perfect one (*haššulammit*): I have been using "the Shulammite" as a convenient designation for the anonymous girl who speaks in the Song, but the article of *haššulammit* shows that it is not a personal name. Of the various interpretations offered, we should note the following:

1. *Haššulammit* is commonly thought to be a gentilic of the placename Shunem. LXX B apparently interprets the word this way, rendering *hē Soumaneitis*, which probably represents "Shunemite"; compare the LXX rendering of "Shunammite" in I Kgs 1:15, II Kgs 4:12: *hē Sōmanitis*. Nevertheless, Shunem is not called Shulem in the Bible, and Eusebius' identification of Shunem with the village Sulem near the Jezreel is a guess (see Rowley, 1938). In any case, the girl in the Song lives not in Shunem but in Jerusalem: she lives in a walled city (5:7), not a village, and her companions are called the girls of Jerusalem.
2. Goodspeed (1933) and Rowley (1938) explain *haššulammit* as the feminine equivalent of the name Solomon, as if "Solomon" were the title given a groom and "the Shulammite" the title given his bride (Rowley lists numerous commentators who explain it this way). But this hypothesis does not account for the definite article prefixed to *šulammit* (it is not prefixed to "Solomon") or for the form of the name. The feminine equivalent of *šᵉlomoh* is *šᵉlomit*, a name that appears in Lev 24:11 and I Chr 3:19.
3. Albright (1963:5) explains "the Shulammite" as a conflation of the name of the war goddess Shulmânîtu (Ishtar) with "Shunammite," that is, the Shunammite woman. But such a conflation of names is, so far as I know, unparalleled. In any case, the war goddess has no place in this song. Albright's hypothesis of conflation, we may note, implicitly recognizes that *haššulammit* is unlikely to be derived from either "Shulmânîtu" or "Shunammite."
4. Robert (1951) takes *šulammit* as a qal passive of the *qûtal* pattern meaning "la Pacifée" (cf. Pope). Similarly Aquila: *eirēneuousa*, "peaceable one"; thus Gerleman: "Friedfertiges," "Unschuldvolles."

The last explanation is, I believe, on the right track. However, since ŠLM is intransitive in the qal, we cannot expect it to appear in a qal passive form. It is better to derive *šūlammît* from a noun **šūlam* of the pattern *quttāl / qūtāl* (admittedly rare), whose meaning would be "perfection," and to take *šūlammît* (pointing *šūlāmit*?) as its "nisbe" form. The formation of adjectives (which in turn may function as nouns) by the addition of the gentilic *yod* is very common in mishnaic Hebrew. *Šulammit* then means "the perfect, unblemished one" (thus TaMaKh and the anonymous Bodleian MS, second explanation). This epithet is nearly synonymous with "the most beautiful of women" (1:8; 5:9; 6:1; the latter two verses too are said by the girls of Jerusalem) and *tammati*, "my perfect one" (5:2; 6:9). *Haššulammit* has basically the same meaning as the youth's declaration "Wholly beautiful you are, my darling: no blemish in you!" (4:7).

It seems that the epithet "perfect one" is used somewhat teasingly when said by the girls of Jerusalem, as "most beautiful of women" may be in 5:9, where too a skeptical note is heard. The Shulammite's defensiveness in 1:5 implies that her companions had some doubts about her "perfection," and calling her "most beautiful of women" (5:9) and "perfect one" (7:1) may be their jocular response to her assertion that she is lovely. The question in 7:1b—"Why would you [plural] gaze at the perfect one . . . ?"—is somewhat reproachful and suggests that the call in v. 1a was less than completely respectful. But when the boy for his part calls her the "perfect one" in v. 1b, he means it without reservation.

(7:1b) *Why would you gaze at the perfect one* . . . : a rhetorical question with *mah* implying a negative imperative; see König, 1897:II, §§352β–δ.

a camp-dancer: revocalizing *kim*[e]*ḥolelet hammaḥ*[a]*nim* (similarly Gerleman). *Maḥ*[a]*nim* (rather than the usual plural *maḥ*[a]*not*) appears in Num 13:19. The rarity of this form of the plural may have led the Massoretes to mistake it for the place name "Mahanayim," although "Mahanayim" does not elsewhere appear with the article, and neither that name nor "two camps" makes much sense here. LXX has *hē erchomenē hōs choroi parembolōn* ("who comes as bands of army camps"). Nor do the other Versions translate the words as dual.

The youth rebukes the girl's companions for looking upon her disdainfully as if she were a common dancer who roams the camps of the soldiers (or, possibly, the shepherds).

(7:2) *The curves of your thighs*: ḤMQ = "turn"; see on 5:6. *Ḥammuqey y*[e]*rekayik* is either "the place where your thigh turns" (an interpretation mentioned by Ibn Ezra) or the buttocks, which are curved.

like jewelry: *Ḥ*[a]*li* (Prov 25:12), variant *ḥelyah* (Hos 2:15), is a type of ornament, parallel to *nezem*, "nose ring," in both places. We do not know what *ḥ*[a]*la*ʾ*im* looked like.

(7:3a) *Your navel*: Haupt (1902a:239), Lys, Pope, et al. regard *šor* ("umbilicus," "navel") as a euphemism for vulva. It is hard to see any reason for this interpretation other than the assumption that the anatomical detailing of the Praise Song would not skip over the genitals. But the praise in this unit does not proceed in such a strict bottom-to-top order that this item must be below the belly, which is mentioned next. The eyes (7:5bα) are not lower than the item mentioned after them, the nose (v. 5bβ), nor is the head (v. 6aα) higher than they. There is no need to go to a secondary meaning of an Arabic word (*sirr*, "secret," whence "pudenda," "fornication") when the usual meaning of the Hebrew word is appropriate to the context. As to Pope's assertion that "navels are not notable for their capacity to store or dispense moisture," it is not the navel but the bowl that is supposed to do so. Eyes, for that matter, are not noted for bathing in milk (5:2).

Egyptian sculpture, as Gerleman points out, emphasizes the navel, often making it unusually wide or deep. The simile in this verse does not (contrary to Gerleman) show that the poet had Egyptian sculpture in mind, but only that the navel was considered pretty (as it is in the *Arabian Nights*), so that a comparison that emphasized its size would not be disagreeable.

a rounded bowl: The *ʾaggan* is a large, two-handled, ring-based bowl. Bowls have been discovered at Palmyra, Khirbet Semrin, and Petra with *ʾgn* inscribed on them (Honeyman, 1939:79; Milik, 1972:108; see Pope ad loc.). *Sahar* means "round," not "crescent-shaped," as the bowls themselves show. *Hassahar* is either a genitive of specification (cf. *yeyn haṭṭob*, 7:10), in which case the word is probably a technical term, or a noun of the *qattāl* pattern meaning a potter who works on a lathe, lit., a "turner" (Pope).

may it never lack mixed wine: This is said of the bowl, not of the girl's navel. This is not "which never lacks mixed wine." *ʾal* is rarely if ever used for the negative indicative. This clause is rather a wish whose purpose is to praise the bowl. The point is not that the bowl is always full, but that a bowl as lovely as this *deserves* never to lack wine.

Your belly is a heap of wheat: This simile does *not* mean that she had a potbelly. Contrary to a common notion, it is not true that "corpulency was deemed essential to an Eastern beauty" (Ginsburg). While fertility figurines were corpulent, that was not a general ideal of human beauty. A perusal of Mesopotamian and especially Egyptian art shows that women were almost always portrayed as slender. Egyptian women are often shown with a gently curved belly, but none are corpulent. The trait shared by the belly and a heap of wheat may be a gentle curve and a tawny hue (assuming that the Shulammite was exaggerating her blackness in her earlier complaint, 1:5–6).

hedged about with lilies: A thorn hedge around a pile of wheat would prevent its being scattered and would keep cattle away. For the precious heap to which the Shulammite's belly can be compared, only a hedge of lilies is appropriate.

(7:4) *Your two breasts . . . gazelle*: = 4:5a.

(7:5a) *Your neck is like an ivory tower*: This stich is awkwardly abrupt as it stands. A stich has probably been lost after v. 5a. Every other simile in the itemized Praise Songs (4:1–5; 6:4–10; 7:2–7) is extended by further description, by parallels restating the point, or by exclamations.

The maiden's neck is compared to a tower in 4:4 as well. The image of an ivory tower suggests a long neck, a quality praised in no. 31 too. Like the ivory palace at Samaria (I Kgs 22:39), the "ivory tower" envisaged here would be decorated with ivory, not made entirely of it. The image of such a tower may have been suggested by a necklace made of pieces of ivory, just as the tower bedecked with shields in 4:4 is evoked by strands of a necklace.

(7:5b) *Your eyes are pools in Heshbon*: Ruins of a large reservoir dating from the eighth century B.C.E. remain in Heshbon, 80 km. east of Jerusalem. Heshbon was noted for its fertile fields and vineyards (Isa 16:8–9). The comparison of eyes with pools puns on *ʿayin* = "eye" and "spring." The plural form of *ʿayin* is elsewhere *ʿeynot* when the meaning is "spring," but such slight grammatical violations are common in puns. LXX has *hōs* before *limnai*, probably reflecting a *kaph* as in the other images in this passage.

by the gate of Bath Rabbim: Bath Rabbim was presumably the name of the gate near the pools in Heshbon. But we may wonder whether this phrase adds something besides geographical precision. Perhaps the gate of Bath Rabbim was mentioned because of the meaning of its name, which is nearly synonymous with *bat nadib*—lit., "nobleman's daughter"—in 7:2 (*rabbim* means "important people," "grandees," or the like; see Job 32:9 [//"elders"]; Jer 39:13; 41:1). As a pun, *bat rabbim* is a vocative, "O noble girl" (again like *bat nadib*), and "gate" is not a bound form.

Your nose is like the tower of Lebanon: or, "a tower of the Lebanon." One physical quality common to her nose and the tower is straightness (TaMaKh). The name Lebanon itself is suggestive of fragrance and plays on *lᵉbonah*, "frankincense."[4] If the boy's cheeks are "towers of perfumes" (5:13), the girl's nose can be a "tower of frankincense." And her nose is indeed fragrant (7:9). Height and pride are further qualities conveyed by this image. The Lebanon is a tall and proud range; a tower on it must hold itself high above all others.

(7:6) *Your head (sits) upon you like Carmel*: Your head sits (lit., "is") upon you as tall and proud as Mount Carmel. Tall stature was considered beautiful; see 7:8. "Carmel" sounds like *karmil*, a sort of red-purple cloth (mentioned in II Chr 2:6, 13; 3:14, alongside *ʾargaman*). *Karmil* is a synonym, perhaps a late one, for *šani*, "scarlet (see Bilik, 1979). This stich too is a Janus pun: *karmel* is Mount Carmel, a placename like those mentioned in v. 5, and *karmel* suggests *karmil*, a purple cloth like *ʾargaman*, to which her hair is compared in the continuation of the verse (Bilik, 1979:226).

and the thrums of your head are like purple: *Dallah* means "thrums,"

4. That the association is not far-fetched is shown by the way frankincense came to be called *libanon* in Greek, the same word used for Lebanon.

the threads that hang down in a weaver's loom (Isa 38:12). The root of *dallah* is DLL, "hang down." The hairstyle suggested by the metaphor is well attested in Egyptian paintings. Egyptian women typically wore their hair in long cascading curls; see figs. 1–4, 6, 7, 9. Hair styled like this can certainly be said to "stream down" (4:1; 6:5). The Shulammite's tresses hang down her head, which is "on her" like lofty Mount Carmel, just as they "stream down" Mount Gilead (4:1; 6:5). The cloth of which her "thrums" are made is the expensive *ʾargaman*, purple cloth, for the sheen of deep-black hair resembles dark blue or purple.

a king is captured by the locks!: She had made him a "king," and then captivated him by her tresses. Similarly the boy in no. 3 is captured by his beloved's hair like a bird in a trap, and the boy in no. 43 is caught by his girl's hair like an ox by a lasso. The youth in Canticles, being a "king," is trapped, most appropriately, by purple, the expensive royal cloth.

locks (*rᵉhaṭim*): *Rᵉhaṭim* refers to conduits or water troughs in Gen 30:38, 41, and Exod 2:16. The form *rᵉhiṭim*, which appears (with a first plural suffix) in the *qere* in 1:17 (the *qere* is certainly the correct form; no such root as RḤṬ, the *ketiv*, is known) is from the same root as *rᵉhaṭim* and means "rafters" or "beams." Both "conduits" and "beams" can easily be derived from RHṬ "run" (a borrowing from Aramaic). LXX's *paradromais* is based on a similar understanding of the word. In the present context *rᵉhaṭim* refers to long, flowing tresses (Delitzsch). There may be a pun in the Hebrew similar to the pun on "locks" in English, for *rᵉhaṭim*, meaning "beams," "runners" (or the like), could be used of the bars in a trap as well as of long cylindrical curls.

(7:7) *O love*: "Love" is a vocative addressed to the girl, thus LXX (*agapē*), Vulgate (*charissima*), and Peshitta *rḥimtaʾ*. Compare the Egyptian usage, no. 11, n. e.

delightful girl: lit., "daughter of delights"; thus Aquila *thugatēr truphōn* and Peshitta *brt pwnqʾ*, which renderings evidence the reading *bt tʿnwgym* for MT *btʿnwgym*. Compare *bᵉney taʿᵃnugayik*, "the sons in whom you delight," Mic 1:16.

7:8–14

(Boy)

(8) Thus your stature: it resembles a palm,
and your breasts are like clusters.
(9) I said (to myself), I shall climb the palm
and lay hold of its branches.
Let your breasts be like clusters on a vine,
the scent of your nose like apricots,
(10aα) and your palate like the best wine—

(Girl)

(10aβ) flowing smoothly to my beloved,
(10b) dripping on ⟨scarlet⟩* lips.
(11) I am my beloved's and his passion is for me.

(12) Come, my beloved, let's go to the field.
We'll pass the night in the countryside;
(13) we'll go early to the vineyards.
We'll see if the vine has blossomed,
the bud opened,
the pomegranates bloomed.
There I will give you my love.
(14) The mandragoras give off fragrance,
and at our doors are all sorts of luscious fruits,
(fruits) both new and old:
my ⟨caresses⟩*, which I've saved for you.

*7:10b *šanim* (MT *y^ešenim*)
*14 *doday* (MT *dodi*)

This unit is not disjunct from the preceding one, for the boy's detailed praise of his beloved in 7:2–7 implies an intention to enjoy her charms (vv. 8–10aα). Still, the major division falls between v. 7, which concludes the Praise Song with a summarizing exclamation, and v. 8, which begins a dialogue whose imagery is unrelated to that of the preceding Praise Song, having instead its most significant precursors in 2:10–13, 6:11, and to a lesser degree 5:10–14.

The youth expresses his desire to embrace his beloved and to enjoy her love (7:8–10aα), and she immediately consents and invites him to go with her to the countryside (10aβ–14). The formulation of her invitation closely resembles his invitation in 2:10–13 and the statement in 6:11 about the nut garden.

This unit is an Admiration Dialogue, like 1:9–17 and 2:1–3. It is thoroughly erotic, not in its sexual intimations alone—although the couple's desire to enjoy sexual pleasures is obvious enough—but in the totality of the pleasures that the lovers derive from nature and love. All the senses take part in the experience of love in the midst of nature. (On the theme of love in the garden, or countryside, in Egyptian love poetry and the Song, see chapter 7.) The girl's developing sexuality is adumbrated by images of blossoming trees and ripening fruits. The external world in the spring of the year is in harmony with the internal world of the lovers in the spring of their lives.

Vv. 7:8–10aα: The girl is as tall and stately as a palm (Ben Sirah applies this image to Wisdom in 24:13–14). As she called him a cedar, he calls her a palm. Like the earlier motifs of the "dove in the clefts of the rock" (2:14) and the call to come from Lebanon (4:8), the palm tree image conveys a certain feeling of inaccessibility. Her breasts are clusters of sweet dates, but, being the fruit of the tall palm, cannot be easily reached. But the youth has resolved ("I said") to climb his "palm tree," to reach her "clusters," to embrace her, and to enjoy the fruits of love.

Changing the image, he then hopes (*na*ʾ, v. 9) that her breasts will be his to enjoy like grape clusters, that the "fragrance of her nose" will be like apricots, and that her palate will be like sweet wine—all easily accessible—so that he may "eat" and "drink" love (cf. 5:1). Here the motif of eating and drinking clearly alludes to various aspects of lovemaking, including kissing breasts, smelling the nose, and kissing the open mouth.

(7:9) *its branches*: *Sansinnim* part of the palm. Akkadian *sinsinnu/sissinnu* is the date panicle; it is also a type of jewelry. The *sansinnim* represent either the maiden's arms or her hair. The latter is more likely, since in 5:11 the boy's locks are compared to *taltallim*, which are probably palm fronds.

the scent of your nose (ʾ*appek*): ʾ*ap* means "nose," not "face" (Gordis) or "vagina" or "clitoris" (Pope; is this the meaning of ʾ*ap* in v. 5?). On the scent of the nose and the custom of nose kissing, see above on 1:2.

(7:10aα) *and your palate like the best wine*: *Yeyn haṭṭob* is probably a superlative; see GKC §133h and cf. Isa 22:24. It is also possible that *ṭob* is a specific type of wine, like *yayin hareqaḥ* (8:2). Earlier the youth praised the sweetness of his girl's mouth (4:11), and she said that his caresses, which in context meant mouth kisses, are sweeter than wine (1:2).

(7:10aβ) *flowing smoothly to my beloved*: The girl speaks (only she could say *dodi*). She impatiently interrupts her lover's praise and completes his sentence, showing that she reciprocates his desire and is eager to fulfill his wishes. His desire and hers are in such harmony that they can be uttered in a single sentence.

Holek = "flowing"; see Qoh 1:7 and compare Prov 23:31, in which *yithallek* refers specifically to the flow of wine.

Lᵉmeyšarim = *bᵉmeyšarim*, "smoothly" (Prov 23:31).

dripping on scarlet lips: DBB in mishnaic Hebrew, like its by-form DBʾ, means flow or drip (= Aramaic DWB, cognate to Hebrew ZWB), meanings appropriate to this context. Peshitta and Aquila translate "my lips and my teeth," reflecting *śpty wšny*. This reading is not suitable either, since the girl is speaking here, and the "wine" of her palate will drip not on *her* lips and teeth, but on her lover's. Rather emend to *śiptey šanim*, a change assuming only a single dittography (Schoville, 1969:99). Lips are compared to a thread of scarlet in 4:3. The plural form *šanim*, "scarlet," appears in Prov 31:21 and Isa 1:18.

(7:11) *I am my beloved's and his passion is for me*: In Gen 3:16, the sentence *w^{e}ʾel ʾišek t^{e}šuqatek*, "and your desire will be for your husband," is explained in the continuation, "and he will rule over you." This sentence implies that the object of desire "rules over" or controls the one who desires (only thus can Gen 3:16a be understood as a curse). The Shulammite's statement, "and his passion is for me," implies approximately: I hold sway over him; that is to say: he belongs to me. In this way 7:11b complements 7:11a, "I am my beloved's," and the verse as a whole rephrases the formula of mutual possession (2:16; 6:3).

(7:12) *We'll pass the night in the countryside*: *K^{e}parim* may be taken two ways: villages in the countryside and henna bushes (4:13). Thus the stich is another Janus pun, the first sense looking back to "field," the second ahead to "vineyards."

(7:13) *we'll go early to the vineyards . . .* : The henna, pomegranates, and luscious fruits (*m^{e}gadim*) all grow in the garden mentioned in 4:13–15, which is called *pardes*, "orchard" (as the Bodleian commentary points out). The *pardes* in 4:13–15 is the girl herself. When the fruits have blossomed, she is ripe for love.

the bud opened (*pittaḥ hass^{e}madar*): *Pittaḥ* (piel) is intransitive in Isa 48:8 as well.

Vv. 7:12–13a play on 1:13–14:

7:12–13a	1:13–14
l^{e}kah dodi neṣeʾ [1] *haśśadeh*	*ṣ^{e}ror hammor dodi li*
[2] *nalinah* [3] *bakk^{e}parim*	*beyn* [1] *šaday* [2] *yalin*
naškimah [4] *lakk^{e}ramim*	*ʾeškol* [3] *hakkoper dodi li*
	[4] *b^{e}karmey ʿeyn gedi*

Šin and *śin* can interchange in word-plays. (This striking form of word-play is noted by Exum, 1973:73f.)

(7:14) *The mandragoras give off fragrance*: The preceding verse resonates in this one: *šam ʾetten ʾet doday lak—hadduda'im nat^{e}nu reaḥ*. "There" is emphatic: there, where the *dudaʾim* (an aphrodisiac) give forth their fragrance, she will give her beloved the *dodim* she has stored up for him. The chiastic linkage of this sentence to the preceding one emphasizes the congruence between the processes of nature and the events of love.

and at our doors: lit., "at our openings," including perhaps the windows or other small openings in the walls. "Our openings" is hardly an allusion to the girl's vagina (contrary to Wittekindt). Such a reference would not fit the plural of *p^{e}taḥeynu* or the first plural of the suffix. "Our" may refer to her family or, more probably, to the young lovers. This verse continues to describe the countryside—"there"—where the mandragoras give off their fragrance. "Our doors" are in "our house"—their booth in the field (1:16–17).

Again the girl praises the attractions of their "house," to which she invites her lover to come with her for the night (implied by *nalinah* in v. 12 and *naŠkimah* in v. 13). There he will find "luscious fruits" of all varieties.

both new and old: "Old" fruits are not necessarily last year's fruits, but may be fruits that grow on the trees earlier. The phrase is a merism meaning "fruits of all kinds"; cf. "plants aplenty from yesterday and today, and fruits of all kinds for delight" (no. 30) (Gerleman).

my caresses, which I've saved for you: pointing *doday*, for MT, "(fruits) both new and old, my beloved [*dodi*], I have stored up for you" (Schoville, 1969:101). The Bodleian MS explains *dodi* to mean "my virginity." While this interpretation is correct in recognizing that *dwdy* (rather than "luscious fruits") is the object of "stored up," *dod* means "love" only in the plural and so *dwdy* requires repointing. The sentence "My caresses [*doday*; more precisely, "sexual love"] I've saved for you," both elaborates her promise, "there I will give you my love (*doday*)," and explains just what "luscious fruits" he will find near at hand when he goes to the field with her. The vine has blossomed, the bud opened, the pomegranates bloomed. The fruits of love are ripe for eating.

8:1–5a

(Girl)

(1) If only you were like a brother to me,
  one who nursed at my mother's breasts!
 When I met you in the street I would kiss you,
  and no one would mock me.
(2) I would take and lead you to my mother's house,
  ⟨to the room of her who bore me⟩.*
 I would give you spiced wine to drink,
  the juice of my pomegranate.

(3) His left hand is under my head,
  and his right hand embraces me.
(4) I ask you to promise, girls of Jerusalem:
  do not disturb, do not bestir love,
   before it wishes.

(Girls of Jerusalem)

(5a) Look who's coming up from the wilderness,
  leaning on her beloved!

*8:2 *w^{eʾ}el ḥeder yolad^{e}ti* (MT *t^{e}lamm^{e}deni*)

The scene has changed. The lovers are now lying in each other's arms, perhaps in the bower to which the Shulammite invited her lover in the preceding unit. The setting is like that of 1:9–17, 2:1–7, and probably 3:7–11. Now, however, in spite of the special delights of love in the countryside, the Shulammite wishes that their relationship were publicly recognized so that she could kiss her beloved openly, as she could a brother, and bring him home. Like the Egyptian girl in "The Stroll" (no. 36), the Shulammite wishes for public acceptance of her right to love and to be united with the one she has chosen.

V. 8:3 suggests that she and her lover are going to make love. As in 3:5–6, the adjuration to the girls of Jerusalem in 8:4 not to disturb love brings with it a reaction of surprise and admiration (v. 5a is presumably spoken by them, since they are addressed in the adjuration immediately following). V. 5b may be the Shulammite's words on the day after their tryst, when she—and not the girls of Jerusalem—"disturbs" love by waking her lover up (*ʿorartika*) from sleep. The statement "Under the apricot tree I woke you" indicates the passage of time between v. 5a and v. 5b and suggests what happened "between the lines."

(8:1) *If only you were like a brother to me*: *k*^{e}*ʾaḥ li*, "like a brother to me," and not *k*^{e}*ʾaḥi*, "like my brother." She is not wishing for a sibling relationship with her lover. She mentions the brother only as an example of a person she could kiss openly and bring home. This verse shows that the couple is not betrothed, let alone married.

who nursed at my mother's breasts: This phrase is brought in for the sake of parallelism and obviously modifies "brother." At the same time it intimates that the Shulammite would like her lover to suck her breasts. The Egyptian girl in no. 1 says: "Then take my breasts, that their gift may flow forth to you."

(8:2) *I would take and lead you to my mother's house*: If he were like a brother to her, she would be able to bring him home openly. She identifies her home as "my mother's house," as in 3:4.

t^{e}*lamm*^{e}*deni*: lit., "you will teach me." This word is obscure and does not constitute a complete stich. LXX reads, "and to the room of her that conceived me"—*w*^{e}*ʾel ḥeder horati* (*tēs sullabousēs me*). Peshitta too has the stich. This plus may be an expansion based on 3:4; cf. the expansions at 1:3; 3:1; etc. In any case, the parallels in 3:4, 6:9, and 8:5 strongly support restoring the phrase here. MT's *tlmdny* may contain the remnants of *yldty*.

ʾašq^{e}*ka* (v. 2) and *ʾeššaq*^{e}*ka* (v. 1) form the same play on words implicit in the pun in *yiššaqeni* in 1:2, q.v.

spiced wine—the juice of my pomegranate: The possessive pronoun of "my pomegranate" shows that she is using "pomegranate" figuratively, probably to mean "breast." "Spiced wine" probably alludes to kisses (cf.

1:2; 5:16a; 7:10a). *Yayin* and *hareqaḥ* are in apposition; cf. *yayin tarᶜelah* (Ps 60:5).

In 8:2–5a the component phrases of 2:6–7 and 3:4–6 are brought together to compose a single sequence; see "Associative Sequences" in chapter 4.

(8:5a) *Look who's coming up from the wilderness*: See my remarks on 3:6.

leaning (*mitrappeqet*): or, "reclining"; used only here. In mishnaic Hebrew its meaning (which is probably based on an interpretation of this verse) is "be joined (to)," whence "be loved by" (Gen. Rab. §45, 5). It is not clear whether she is leaning on him while walking or pressed up against him while lying down, but the second sense fits better with v. 3. Ibn Ezra explains *mitrappeqet* on the basis of an Arabic cognate to mean *mitḥabberet*, "be joined to" (i.e., while lying down; see his interpretation in the second section of his commentary on this passage).

8:5b–7

(Girl)

(5b) Under the apricot tree I woke you—
there your mother conceived you,
there she conceived you, she who bore you.
(6) Place me as a seal upon your heart,
as a seal upon your arm,
for love is as strong as death,
jealousy as hard as Sheol.
Its darts are darts of fire—
lightning (itself)!
(7) Mighty waters cannot extinguish love,
nor rivers wash it away.
Should one offer all his estate for love,
it would be utterly scorned.

Although 8:5b–14 is composed of discrete parts that lack clear continuity from one to the next and are best treated as several units, these verses together form the Song's finale, making general declarations about the power and value of love and presenting the brothers' new attitude.

It is not clear what relation 8:5b has to its context, whether looking ahead or looking back. I include it in this unit rather than having it close the preceding one because after the exclamation by the girls of Jerusalem (v. 5a), an isolated remark by the Shulammite to the boy seems awkward, whereas this remark may be an appropriate prelude to her demands for everlasting faithfulness: we have made love; now our bond is eternal.

Vv. 8:6–7 are the highpoint of the poem, its moment of greatest generality, where it draws a conclusion from the particular experience it has been portraying. Only here does the poet draw an explicit lesson or make an abstract pronouncement. The Shulammite has discovered in herself the inexorable power of love and can now speak of it without seeming extravagant.

The Shulammite uses powerful, even violent, images to express her determination to attain her desire and implicitly to warn off anyone who might try to hinder her. The teasing of her companions cannot affect her, nor will her brothers any longer hold her under their control. She has already gone forth from her home to open spaces—literally and figuratively—to blossom with the land, even as her own "vineyard" has blossomed. She knows love, and knows that no one can stand up to the fierce power it bestows on its possessors.

(8:5b) *Under the apricot tree I woke you*: *ʿorer* here means simply to wake one from sleep. There is no sign that it refers to sexual stimulation or to sexual intercourse (contrary to Exum, 1973:51, Pope, et al.). The "sexual context" in which ʿWR is used elsewhere in the Song does not (contrary to Exum, 1973:58) prove that ʿWR refers to sexual stimulation or coitus, for a great number of things, including waking up in the morning, can happen in a "sexual context." It is not the word *ʿorartika* that has sexual implications, but the motif of waking up in the countryside, which intimates that the couple has passed the night together. The audience is left to imagine for itself what went on.

there your mother conceived you: *Ḥibbel* means both "give birth" and (as here) "get pregnant" (thus also in mishnaic Hebrew, Jewish Aramaic, etc.; see HAL); compare the sequence *ḥibbel-harah-yalad* in Ps 7:15. The girl says that the place where she woke her beloved is the very place where his mother conceived him (M. Falk, 1982:130).

she who bore you: It is not necessary to point *yoladtᵉka* for MT *yᵉladatka*, although LXX translates this word as a participle. MT has a finite verb serving as a noun; thus "she-bore-you" = "she who bore you"; see Grossberg, 1980:488. *Yᵉladatᵉka* is not to be understood as a verbal clause, "(there . . .) she gave birth to you," because it is most unlikely that his mother gave birth to him in the field, and if it were so it would be irrelevant. The girl is saying that the act in which his mother conceived him took place under the apricot tree, where she and her beloved find themselves now. Jerome, though interpreting *ḥabbel* as "destroy," understood the verse as referring to coitus (rather than to giving birth): "ibi corrupta est mater tua, ibi violata est genitrix tua" ("there your mother was corrupted; there she who bore you was violated"). Ibn Ezra caught the girl's point, paraphrasing her words thus:

"It seems to me that your mother could only have conceived (*har^etah*) you and gotten pregnant (*yiḥ^emah*) with you under the apple tree,[5] which is why your scent is like the apple among the trees of the woods"—just as she said to him earlier, when she wished and desired to sit in his shade and to have his left hand under her head.

The story of Jacob and the sheep (Gen 30:31–43) shows the ancient and widespread idea that the setting of coitus affects the offspring.

(8:6) *as a seal upon your heart . . . your arm*: To be as a seal on the heart and arm implies belonging and special intimacy; see Jer 22:24; Hag 2:23. This motif appears in "Seven Wishes" (no. 21C): "If only I were her little seal ring, the keeper of her finger!" See also nos. 20B and 54. The seal was like a signature and as such would be kept on one's person continually. A seal could be worn on a cord around the neck so that it rested on the chest (Gen 38:18, 25) or kept on one's hand as a ring (Jer 22:24; Sir 49:11). *Z^eroᶜa* may refer to the entire arm, including the finger, where seals were usually worn, or the image may be of a seal worn higher up on the arm (the usual meaning of *z^eroᶜa*) as an amulet. *Śimeni kaḥotam* does not mean "stamp me as a seal"; that would require the verb *ḥatom*, and in any case *ḥotam* always refers to the signet, not to the impression it makes. "Upon your heart . . . upon your arm" expresses the Shulammite's hope to be bound to her lover in all his thoughts and actions.

for love is as strong as death: "strong" in the sense of demanding, ineluctable. This clause motivates the preceding demand that her lover bind her to him as tightly and permanently as a seal. To do anything less would be to defy love's power, which is no less than death's irresistible force. The Shulammite speaks of "love," not of "my love," for love's power is universal.

jealousy is as hard as Sheol: Jealousy is as possessive as the netherworld. *Qin'ah* does not mean "passion," contrary to most modern translators and commentators (e.g., Ginsburg, Pope, Gordis), but rather "jealousy" (LXX, Vulgate, Peshitta). In fact, nowhere does QN' mean sexual desire or simply a powerful emotion. QN' always refers to the anger or suspicion that a jealous person feels toward that which causes the jealousy. That cause is a third party that either violates the proprietary rights of the one party or impinges on the relationship between one party (a lover, an owner, etc.) and a second party (that which is loved, that which is owned). Yahweh, for example, is jealous for his name (which is his possession) when foreign gods receive the honor due it alone. Yahweh is jealous of anything that receives the love and fear that he alone should receive from his beloved possession Israel. QN' is also used to indicate the feelings of a person who, though not one of the two principal parties to the relationship, chooses to share the jealousy of the first party.

5. He presumably understood *tappuaḥ* this way.

Thus, for example, Elijah felt the jealousy of Yahweh, meaning that he shared the jealousy that God felt (I Kgs 19:10). Another type of *qinʾah* is *envy*, in which it is an outside party who feels the *qinʾah*; that is, a third party desires to possess something that belongs to someone else. Thus QNʾ everywhere involves the existence of an outside party who interferes in the relationship. *Qinʾah*, as Delitzsch (on this verse) says, is "the jealousy of love asserting its possession and right of property; the reaction of love against any diminution of its possession, against any reserve in its response, the 'self-vindication of angry love.'"

Who, then, is the third party that might arouse the Shulammite's jealousy? Her jealousy is not directed at other girls. Suspicion of that sort is not suggested anywhere in the Song, not even when the Shulammite mentions the love that other girls must feel for her beloved. She is always confident in her lover and in the security of their love. The interfering and threatening party presupposed by her warning must be society conceived generally, including any outside party who might try to interfere, as have her brothers and the watchmen. The Shulammite declares that love is so powerful that the jealousy it sparks is as ineluctable as the insatiable appetite of Sheol. A similar note of steely determination is heard in the violent images the Egyptian girl in no. 4 uses in declaring her refusal to abandon her desire.

Vv. 8:6b–7a: two distichs on the fire of love.

Its darts are darts of fire: The exact meaning of *rešep* is uncertain. The phrase *rišpey qešet* (Ps 76:4) suggests that *rešep* is a sort of arrow, perhaps a flaming arrow. The Canaanite god Reshep was known by the epithets *ršp ḥṣ* (in an inscription from Cyprus) and *bʿl ḥṣ ršp*, "Reshep possessor of arrows" (UT 1001.1.3); see Fulco, 1976. Reshep is portrayed in Egyptian iconography holding weapons and often flanked by a fertility goddess and the ithyphallic god Min (see Pope). *Rᵉšapim* may be used of lightning bolts (Ps 78:48 // *barad*, "hail").

lightning (itself): in apposition to "love" rather than "darts" (plural). *Šalhebetyah* may be either one word with an affixed *-yah* (thus in the Ben Asher text), which affix may have intensive force, or two words, with a *mappiq* in the *heh* (thus Ben Naphtali), meaning, lit., "flame of Yah." The earlier reading is probably *šlhbtyh*. LXX's "its flames" shows that *šalhebetyah* was written as a single word in its Vorlage, as do Vulgate's *atque flammarum* and Peshitta's *šlhbytʾ*, "flame." The Ben Asher writing *šlhbtyh* suggests that the affix was not recognized as an independent element in the meaning of the word. It is likely that the Ben Naphtali writing arose as a scribal midrash. The other possibility, that an original *šlhbt yh*, which, though fitting in well with the allegorical interpretation, had its theological potential removed by reading the consonants as a single noun, is less likely.

The same problem arises for *maʾpelyah* (Jer 2:31) and *merḥabyah* (Ps

118:5), where it is, however, clear that the affix has no particular theological significance, whether or not it is derived from the divine name. Even if *-yah* does derive from the divine name, it may be just a vivid term for lightning, like "the fire of Yahweh" (Num 11:1; I Kgs 18:38, etc.; see BDB, p. 77b, §2). We certainly should not try to hang too much theological weight on this very uncertain reference to God.

(8:7) *Should one offer . . .* : Love is precious beyond any price and cannot be bought.

it would be utterly scorned: The antecedent of *lo* is "wealth" not "one" ("man"), for the verse emphasizes the value of love rather than the disgrace of the man who would try to buy it.

8:8–10

(Brothers)

(8) We have a sister, a little one,
who has no breasts.
What shall we do for our sister
when she is spoken for?
(9) Is she a wall?
We'll build on it a silver turret.
Is she a door?
We'll panel it with a cedar board.

(Girl)

(10) I am a wall,
but my breasts are like towers!
So now I've become in ⟨your⟩ eyes*
one who finds* good will.

*8:10b *b^{e}ʿeyneykem* (MT *b^{e}ʿeynayw*); *moṣʾet* (MT *k^{e}moṣʾet*)

It is probably the brothers, mentioned in 1:6, who are speaking in this difficult unit, offering reconciliation in place of their earlier rebuke. Gordis suggests that the speakers are a group of suitors. The existence of other suitors is not, however, hinted at elsewhere in Canticles (or, for that matter, in the Egyptian songs, where there are never several rivals suing for a girl's affections). Furthermore, suitors would not act as a single group in giving gifts, but each one would offer his own. Nor is the speaker the Shulammite's lover, who is unlikely to refer to his beloved as "*our* sister" and who certainly would not say that she has no breasts. It is unlikely, though not impossible, that the girls of Jerusalem speak here (thus Exum, 1973:75f.), for the responsibility of caring for the girl's needs at marriage would fall upon the brothers; compare the role of Dinah's brothers, Gen 34:6–18, and of Rebecca's brother, Gen 24:50–51, 55, and consider too the fraternal authority the Shulammite's brothers wielded earlier (1:6). Also, inasmuch as the concluding units of the Song correspond in various other ways to its beginning (see on 8:11–12) it is probable that "our sister" is said by the group that the Shulammite calls "my mother's sons" in 1:6.

The brothers promise something; it is not clear just what. Most commentators understand the wall as a metaphor for chastity. There is disagreement as to whether the door, since it can bar entry, represents chastity or, since it can allow entry, stands for sexual accessibility. Those who see "door" as representing basically the same concept as "wall" (e.g., Gordis, Ringgren, Tur-Sinai) understand both statements as promises to adorn the sister. Those who interpret "door" as representing accessibility (e.g., Pope) regard the second statement as a threat to buttress the defenses about her. All seem to agree that the speakers are delivering a straight-faced lecture on chastity.

The significance of "door" does not matter too much for the interpretation of the passage, since the girl asserts that she is a wall. If, however, the door *is* symbolic, it probably represents chastity, since the word used is *delet*, the door proper, whose function is to bar entry, rather than *petaḥ*, the doorway, which allows it.

The meaning of the verse rests more on the significance of the wall. The main difficulty with the common interpretation of "wall" is that if the wall represents chastity, the audience might very well be skeptical about the strict accuracy of the claim, since they know that the lovers have spent the night together (implied in 1:13–14 and 7:12–13—at the least) and have indulged in the pleasures of lovemaking (e.g., 5:1). The Shulammite's lover did declare that she is a locked garden (4:12), but she straightway invited him in (4:16). Although our song never unambiguously indicates that the lovers have had sexual intercourse, it certainly does arouse such a suspicion. Chastity is not the issue, and certainly not the great virtue, in this poem. The question of chastity may simply be irrelevant to the verse.

The note of playful banter in this exchange has escaped notice of the commentators, though it is rightly stressed by Segal (1962:480f.). While the brothers take her seriously enough to consent to provide for her when she is spoken for, they tease her: she's still just a kid—she doesn't even have breasts yet. But they'll do right by her, even if she *is* as flat as a wall or door. They will lavish upon her the most appropriate ornaments: a silver turret for a wall, a cedar panel for a door. She retorts that she is indeed like a wall, but one with towers—namely her mature breasts (this is a variation of Segal's interpretation, ibid.). She chooses to call herself a wall so that she can retort that she has towers. Her brothers may be teasing her, but they have still consented in principle to her marriage. She is grateful for their consent and promise, and in v. 10 expresses pleasure at their assent to her marriage.

(8:8) *We have a sister, a little one* (*ʾaḥot lanu qᵉṭannah*): *Qᵉṭannah* is not an adjective modifying *ʾaḥot*, but a noun in apposition to it. *Qᵉṭannah* refers not to her size but to her supposed sexual immaturity, as in mishnaic Hebrew, in which *qᵉṭannah* means a minor (less than 12 years old).

when she is spoken for: sc. in marriage; see I Sam 25:39.

(8:9) *Is she . . . Is she*: Or, "*If . . . if*"—*ʾim . . . (wᵉ)ʾim* may denote distinction without opposition, like *sive . . . sive* (e.g., Gen 31:50; Qoh 11:3; see GKC §150h). I translate *ʾim* as an interrogative (which it often serves to mark) because I understand the main point of the brothers' words to be not conditionality but *promise*: whatever she may be, we will take care of her.

a silver turret: *Ṭirot* in Ezek 46:23 denotes structures on top of a wall, but it is not clear just what they are. Whatever they may be, to make them out of silver rather than stone would add splendor to this wall.

We'll panel it with a cedar board: This phrase too implies ornamentation rather than fortification. For a door to be given a cedar panel would be an unusual expenditure. Cedar was used for paneling in David's palace and Solomon's temple. Jeremiah regards Jehoiakim's use of cedar paneling in his palace as the epitome of profligate luxury (Jer 22:14–15). A cheaper wood or even stones would be a more suitable material for merely blocking up a door, if such were the intent. *Naṣur* is to be derived from ṢWR/ṢRR, "to bind," "fasten." It does not mean "besiege" or "encompass," because one would not do either (even figuratively) with an inflexible board.

(8:10) *my breasts are like towers*: a strong assertion of sexual maturity.

So now I've become in your eyes one who finds good will: a crux. MT's "in his eyes like one who finds good will [*šalom*]" makes little sense. Since the girl is here addressing a group, and since there is no antecedent for the third singular suffix of "his eyes," we should probably read *bʿynykm mwṣʾt* for MT *bʿynyw kmwṣʾt*, an emendation that presupposes only minor consonantal changes: the addition of *waw* before the *kaph* and the subsequent haplography of *mem*. *Šalom* here means "friendship," "friendly attitude," as in the expression *ʾiš šᵉlomi*, in which *šalom* means "amity," "partnership," "Gemeinschaft," hence "friendship" (whether genuine or ostensible); see Eisenbeis, 1969:156f. Similarly, "to speak *šalom*" means to speak in a friendly manner (Ps 28:3; 35:20; Jer 9:7). The meaning "friendly attitude," "favor," is seen most clearly in Jer 16:5, where God's *šalom* refers to his attitude toward Israel, alongside his *ḥesed* and his *raḥᵃmim*. The Shulammite says to her brothers: since you now assent to my marriage, I know that I am finally enjoying your favor, in place of your earlier unkind treatment of me. *ʾaz*, "so," "then," indicates logical rather than temporal consecution (BDB, p. 23a, §2).

8:11–12

(Boy)

(11) Solomon had a vineyard in Baal Hamon.
He gave the vineyard to keepers;
each would bring in for his fruit
a thousand pieces of silver.
(12) But *my* vineyard is before me.
You can have the thousand, Solomon,
but two hundred (go) to those who keep its fruit.

This short unit recalls motifs and phrases from the girl's statement in 1:6: vineyards, the tending (NṬR) of vineyards, and the phrase *karmi šelli*, "my vineyard." Here the motif of tending vineyards appears immediately after the brothers' reconciliation with the Shulammite; in 1:6 it appears right after she speaks of the mistreatment she received from them.

The parable of the vineyard reinforces what was said in 8:7—that love is valuable beyond compare. The boy says that even the vineyard of Solomon, rich and fertile as it may be, is as nothing compared to his own vineyard, which is his beloved herself.

At the start of the Song we learned that the girl was prevented from tending her vineyard. Now the problem is resolved, and the "vineyard" is "before" the youth; in other words, he is the one who will have it and care for it from now on. In contrast to Solomon, *he* will not turn his vineyard over to others for keeping.

The boy is speaking here, not the girl (contrary to Ibn Ezra, Delitzsch, and Exum, 1973:76). It would not make sense for the girl to declare that she prefers her own body to Solomon's vineyard or to say that her body is "before" her. Furthermore, the speaker's possession of a "vineyard" is parallel to Solomon's possession of a vineyard, and if "vineyard" represents a female, only the boy can be said to possess a "vineyard" in the same way that Solomon does.

(8:11) *Solomon had a vineyard* (*kerem hayah lišlomoh*): This phrase may use a standard opening for a parable; compare the opening of the parable of the vineyard in Isa 5:1: *kerem hayah liydidi*, "My beloved had a vineyard."

Baal Hamon: It may be that Solomon did own a vineyard in a place called Baal Hamon (Judith 8:3 mentions a Belamon), but the historical existence of the place and the vineyard is irrelevant to the point of the parable. The name Baal Hamon was chosen, perhaps simply invented, because of its meaning: "the possessor of wealth."

This vineyard is first of all a literal (if fictive) vineyard mentioned for the sake of contrast with the figurative vineyard belonging to the youth. But Solomon's vineyard has a secondary meaning as well. Since the boy's vineyard undoubtedly refers to the girl he loves (or perhaps more abstractly to her sexuality), the audience will naturally suspect that Solomon's vineyard too is a trope for his women, especially since "the thousand" recalls the thousand wives of Solomon. In that case, *baʿal hamon* will also mean "husband of a multitude" of wives.

He gave the vineyard to keepers: This sentence does not contribute to the description of the wealth. Its importance lies rather in sharpening the contrast between the king and the youth. Solomon turned his vineyard over to the care of keepers, whereas the youth keeps *his* "vineyard" with him and cares for it himself. Marcia Falk points to another layer of meaning implicit in the contrast between the way Solomon and the youth possess their vineyards:

> Woman as sexual other may be treated as a beloved (the speaker's relationship to his "own" vineyard) or as a sexual object (Solomon's vineyard is a harem which must be kept under constant guard). Using the motif of regality as foil, the poem advocates the one-to-one I-Thou relationship and rejects the debasement of sexuality inherent in treating others as sexual objects or property. (1982:133)

each would bring in for his fruit a thousand pieces of silver: *Yabiʾ* = "earn," "procure"; cf. Lam 5:9; Ps 90:12. Each keeper would market the fruit he tended and get a thousand pieces of silver for it, of which he would keep two hundred. A vineyard that earned a thousand silver shekels was a very rich one (Isa 7:23). Solomon's vineyard had several subplots of that value.

(8:12) *But* my *vineyard*: Inasmuch as "my beloved is mine and I am his," the girl's "vineyard" is likewise the "vineyard" of her beloved; cf. "my garden" (1:6, said by the girl), which is also "his garden" (4:16).

before me: i.e., near at hand; thus: in my care, in the center of my attention, as in Prov 4:3; Isa 53:2; and Gen 17:18. "Before me" is the opposite of *loʾ naṭarti*, "I could not keep" (1:6).

but two hundred go to those who keep its fruit: The specification of the keepers' wages seems superfluous, so we should consider whether the phrase does more than just describe the business arrangements. This sentence makes the point that others besides Solomon will partake of the fruit of his vineyard, whereas the youth's vineyard is his alone to enjoy, a locked garden to which only he can gain entry. If the vineyard of Solomon alludes to his harem (a thousand wives) as seems likely, this sentence makes fun of the great king, who possessed so many women that he could not keep their "fruit" to himself.

its fruit: that is, the fruit of Solomon's vineyard.

8:13–14

(Boy)

(13) O you who dwell in gardens—
⟨my⟩ companions* attend—
let me hear your voice!

(Girl)

(14) Bolt away, my beloved, and be as a gazelle
or as a young roe
on the mountains of spices.

*8:13 *ḥ^{a}beray* (MT *ḥ^{a}berim*)

The ending of the Song is extremely difficult, not so much because the sentences are opaque as because they make a peculiar ending for a love song or even for a love song collection. One is tempted to agree with Ehrlich that "an dieser Stelle ist der Text hoffnunglos verderbt." Perhaps the end of the song, which would be exposed on a rolled-up scroll, was lost.

And yet the poet may intend to leave the reader *in medias res*, where the Song began, for love is an ongoing experience, and marriage not the end of the story. In Lys's words:

> Quelle que soit la réponse que l'on donne au problème de la structure du Cant., on ne peut ignorer le fait que, même si ce n'est qu'une anthologie, dans la vision du rédacteur final (à moins de le prendre pour un imbécile) le Cant. ne finit pas: l'amour authentique est toujours quête l'un de l'autre, il est tension constante vers l'unité de celui qui est le chéri par excellence et de la compagne qui est l'unique.[6]

(8:13) *O you who dwell in gardens*: On the plural of *gannim*, see above on 6:2. Either *gannim* is a plural of composition, or *hayyošebet bagganim* is an epithet, "garden-dweller" (Gerleman). The import of the phrase is not clear in either case, but perhaps it simply means that she goes often to the fields, vineyards, and gardens.

My companions [masc.] *attend*: dividing with Vulgate after *maqšibim*, against the accents, to provide a better stichometric balance: *ḥ^{a}beray maqšibim // l^{e}qolek hašmi^{c}ini* rather than *ḥ^{a}berim maqšibim l^{e}qolek // hašmi^{c}ini*. The minor emendation *ḥ^{a}beray*, "my companions" (Graetz), for MT *ḥ^{a}berim*,

6. "Whatever answer one may give to the problem of Canticles' structure, one cannot be unaware of the fact that even if it is only an anthology, in the vision of the final redactor (unless he be taken for a simpleton), Canticles does not end: true love is always a quest of one person for another; it is constant straining toward the unity of the one who is preeminently the beloved with the companion who is the unique one."

"companions" (dittography), makes better sense, and "companions" alone is rather vague. On *lamed* introducing a direct object, see König, 1897: II, §289a.

let me hear your voice: The youth wants the maiden's love made known to his companions. Similar hopes are revealed in nos. 32, 36, and 54.

(8:14) *Bolt away, my beloved . . .*: This verse uses phrases from 2:9, 17, and 4:6. *Berah* is a problem. It does not mean simply "hurry," "make haste" (Ginsburg, Gordis, and many others). BRḤ always indicates a hasty movement *away from* something. It always implies leaving, even when the place from which one is fleeing is not specified. Nor does the verse mean "flee *with me*" (Schonfield, Delitzsch), for that would certainly require "with me" to be explicit. Since BRḤ, when used of people or animals, always means movement away from something, what is the Shulammite asking her lover to flee *from*? Two possibilities present themselves: that she is telling him to go *away from* her and depart over the mountains, or that she is urging him to leave his friends and come *to* her. The latter interpretation is preferable, for her call, "flee ["bolt away"] my beloved," comes close upon his statement, "⟨my⟩ companions attend," making it fairly clear what it is that he should go away from. Since "the mountains of spices" are nearly synonymous with "the mountain of myrrh [and] the hill of frankincense" to which the boy earlier said he would go (4:6), and which seem to represent the perfumed breasts of the girl whose beauties he described in 4:1–5, her entreaty here that he be like a gazelle on the mountains of spices is best understood as an appeal that he leave his listening companions and come to her by himself to spend the night between her breasts (cf. 1:13).

The verb *baroaḥ* is used of a bolt (*b^eriaḥ*) passing through its sockets in Exod 36:33. Whether *baroaḥ* in that sense can be connected directly with the root-meaning of BRḤ ("be fleet"?) or is rather a denominative from *b^eriaḥ*, a sexual double entendre may easily be heard here (Haupt, 1902a:233; Pope), for young gazelles or deers are a byword for lust and sexual potency (see Pope on 2:7). This may even be a triple entendre, since BRḤ is used of bolting a lock: the young lover should bolt the gate of the locked garden that is his beloved (4:12), for he alone may enter and enjoy the mountains of spices there.

PART TWO

The Literary Treatment of Love

CHAPTER 3

Language, Dating, and Historical Context

The Egyptian Love Songs

Dating

The manuscripts of the Egyptian love songs date from the 19th dynasty (ca. 1305–1200 B.C.E.) and the early part of the 20th (1200–ca. 1150 B.C.E.):

I. P. Harris 500: early 19th dynasty, dated paleographically by Erman (1927:244) to the time of Sethos I
II. Cairo Love Songs: 19th or 20th dynasty
III. P. Turin 1966: early 20th dynasty
IV. P. Chester Beatty I: 20th dynasty (group C inscribed during the reign of Ramses V, and groups A and B somewhat later)
V. Miscellaneous (nos. 49–54): Ramesside

While it is possible that the songs were composed earlier and transmitted either orally or in writing before being inscribed in the extant manuscripts, it is most likely that their composition too dates from the Ramesside period.

The main evidence for composition date is linguistic. The love songs are in literary Late Egyptian, a non-spoken language taught as a "second language" in the scribal schools. Non-literary LE developed from the spoken language of the late Middle Kingdom and emerged as a written language under Akhenaton. Its verbal system combines elements from Middle Egyptian (regarded as the classical literary language), forms and usages from non-literary LE, and forms found only in the LE literary dialect (on which see Groll, 1975–76).

P. Harris 500 is the earliest of the love song documents, written in the early 19th dynasty (about 1290 B.C.E.). The question is, how much earlier were the songs composed? Hermann (1959:138–44) may be right in dating them to the late 18th dynasty, although most of his arguments are not very persuasive, especially those that would push the date of some of the songs back to the 15th or early 14th centuries. The connections he finds between certain motifs in the songs and motifs in 18th dynasty art are tenuous, and certainly not specific enough to require a dating as early as Amenophis III–Akhenaton (the time he generally prefers) for any of the songs or to exclude a 19th dynasty dating.[1] Any of these motifs could appear in poetry after they had ceased to be popular in mortuary art. Among the motifs that Hermann mentions, only one, the image of a person trapping birds with a spring-trap (no. 3), might help set the 18th dynasty as the earliest likely date. The antiquity of the songs of P. Harris 500 relative to the other love songs is clear. Of the major texts, the language of its songs is unmistakably the closest to ME. Furthermore, without presupposing that literary development follows a straight line from simple to complex, it still seems likely that the short and simple songs of this papyrus belong to an earlier stage of the genre's development than the complex Cairo Love Songs and "The Stroll" and "Three Wishes" in Chester Beatty I, with their key-word patterns and multistanza songs. The songs of P. Harris 500, then, are probably the oldest of the love songs, coming from the late 18th or early 19th dynasty.

1. Hermann regards the following as 18th dynasty motifs: (1) The *mater lactans* motif in no. 1 (in 18th dynasty tombs the king is occasionally portrayed as an adult nursing at his nursemaid's breast); (2) bird trapping with spring-traps rather than nets in no. 3 (a motif favored in 18th dynasty tombs but missing in those of the 19th dynasty); (3) a team of horses as an image of speed in no. 2 (after the 18th dynasty horses were restricted to monumental art and so, Hermann says, lost their "intimate character"); (4) the mention of banishment to four directions in no. 4 (the old concept of four directions received new vitality as a result of the events of the 18th dynasty); (5) the voyage to Memphis in no. 5 (supposedly most suitable in the late 18th dynasty, when Memphis became the seat of Horemhab); (6) the comparison between the girl and "the Mistress of the Two Lands" in no. 8 (he thinks such a comparison most likely to appear in the reigns of Tey, Nefertiti, and Anchesenamun, when the queens displayed their marital affection in public monuments); (7) the girl as bird trapper in nos. 9–12 (bird trapping is frequently shown in 18th dynasty tombs but is rare in the 19th dynasty); (8) the land of Punt and its perfume in no. 9 (motifs most likely to appear in the wake of Hatshepsut's expedition [We should note, however, that Egyptians sent expeditions to Punt as early as the Old Kingdom; see Kitchen, 1971:191f., Herzog, 1968:10f.]); (9) the swallow motif—he prefers "swallow" to "dove"—in no. 14 (the swallow, he argues in 1955:120f., is closely connected with the temple at Deir el-Bahari, which was especially important from the time of Hatshepsut to that of Amenophis III); (10) the hand-in-hand motif in no. 14 (shown in art just before and during the Amarna period); (11) flowers (the Egyptian predilection for flowers was supposedly especially strong during the Amarna period).

We do not yet have the criteria for relative dating among the other groups. Hermann's relative dating[2] is based on a radically different understanding of the structure and composition of the love song groups from the one I argue for in chapter 4, and it requires presuppositions about the cultural atmosphere of the Ramesside period that I find dubious. I doubt that the erotic innuendos in "Three Wishes" (nos. 38–40) and in nos. 41–42 are more characteristic of the "later" Ramesside period than of the earlier. P. Turin 55001, the pornographic papyrus upon which Hermann bases his judgment of the Ramesside spirit, makes no use of innuendo, and it is in any case only one document and so an inadequate basis for conclusions about the character of the 20th dynasty as a whole.

At present, then, we can only set a general date for the love songs: they were written down in the Ramesside period and probably composed then or only slightly earlier.

Historical-Cultural Setting

The place of love poetry in the broad historical and cultural setting of Egypt is not clearly defined. It is of doubtful value to go back several hundred years to the Old and Middle Kingdoms (as Hermann does) to look for the early cultural conditions prerequisite to the emergence of love poetry. Only when we come to the Amarna period, which is to say, no more than sixty years before the inscription of the first of the extant love poems, does the historical-cultural background seem to illuminate the nature of this genre.

The heresy of Akhenaton (1367–50), which demanded exclusive worship of the Aton (the sun disk), led to the flowering of the well-known Amarna revolution in art, one of whose striking characteristics was the naturalism and openness with which it portrayed the royal family on public monuments. In the reign of the preceding ruler, Amenophis III, affection between king and queen was already frequently displayed on official monuments. Akhenaton made portrayal of royal intimacies a hallmark of official art. He is shown eating with his family, playing with his daughters, embracing them and his wife, holding her hand, holds her on his lap while she puts a necklace on him, and even kissing her while riding in a chariot. As Hermann points out (1959:62), this open display of intimacy began as part of Akhenaton's ideological program, for he sought to show that the Aton's influence extended to personal emotions. Thus most of these scenes show the arms of the sun disk reaching down to the royal family. By the end of the Amarna period, the de-

2. Oldest: P. Harris 500 and the Cairo Love Songs; middle: Turin 1966; latest: Beatty I (Hermann, 1959:137–56).

piction of intimate emotion had become independent of its original ideological function, and such scenes appear without the sun rays. This type of scene continues in the art of Akhenaton's successors, even though they repudiated his religious program. Objects from the tomb of Tutankhamon show tender scenes of the young royal couple alone at private moments, as when they stand together in a garden bower or when the queen rubs oil on her husband's shoulder while gazing into his eyes. In this way, depiction of varied emotions, in particular love between man and woman, was introduced into art as a matter of public policy, and it was not a long step from rendering affectionate intimacies in art to representing them in poetry.

Amarna art idealized the present moment rather than eternity. It strove to show things as people see them. With little modification Aldred's remarks on the graphic art of Amarna can be applied to the verbal art of Ramesside love poetry:

> The imposing of new subjects demanding a treatment not prescribed by tradition was a further stimulus towards a freer and fresher vision. . . . This is the real revolutionary character of Amarna art, that it substitutes a visual representation of things as they appear for the former intellectual symbolising of things as they were known to exist. It is not only in original observation, in psychological differentiation, in naturalistic representation, that the Amarna artist makes a departure—the Egyptian had often in details betrayed these as aberrations—it is in a new space concept that he makes his most important contribution. . . . the emphasis is now upon a unity of the whole, in place of the former assemblage of parts. (1961:26f.)

The influence of the Amarna revolution on art persisted after the collapse of the religious heresy, though the extremes of artistic unorthodoxy were purged. The fluid, naturalistic qualities of Amarna art are still recognizable to some extent in the tomb paintings of the 19th and 20th dynasties (see Wilson, 1951:261). Some of the qualities of Amarna art are among the salient features of Ramesside literature, including prayers,[3] stories, and love poems. The latter in particular inherited qualities that characterize Amarna art: the naturalism, the fluidity of expression, the interest in varieties of emotions, and the fascination with the particularity of the moment.

3. Many hymns and prayers from this period are intimate expressions of feelings of love, gratitude, and reverence for the gods. Such expressions are not lacking in prayers of other times, but they are the earmark of personal hymns and prayers from the Ramesside period. An example:

> Let your hearts be happy, you who live on my street.
> Rejoice, my neighbors!
> Behold my lord—it is he who made me.
> Thus my heart longs for him.
> Thoth, you will be my champion.
> I shall not fear the (evil) eye.

(From P. Anastasi III; see Fecht, 1965:53.)

The 18th–20th dynasties were a time of cosmopolitanism and active international trade. In the graphic art of this time, sensual pleasures are prominent motifs. The ancient motif of the pleasure trip in a papyrus boat is frequently portrayed, with its erotic implications now made explicit (Hermann, 1959:163).[4] Frescos and ostraca from Deir el-Medineh show dancing girls (one of them identified as a courtesan by the tattoo of the goddess Bes on her thigh) and women on beds (a motif represented earlier as well). Some bed scenes are childbirth scenes, but one shows a woman with a festive hairdo sitting on a bed and holding a wineskin. Undressed women are often shown in bed on ostraca and, in the 20th dynasty, in clay models (Hermann, 1959:161–63). Some are representations of mother and child and lack sexual implications, but they do show a pleasure in the female form.

The extreme example of blatant sexuality in Ramesside art is P. Turin 55001, a bawdy, comic papyrus showing unkempt, ithyphallic men copulating with women in different positions as the women urge them on (Omlin, 1973).

In narrative literature of this period too, sexuality is a subject of major interest.[5] While these narratives may have had Old or Middle Kingdom antecedents (many of the mythological motifs are undoubtedly earlier), in the form in which we have them, these texts belong to the New Kingdom.

Sexual (including homosexual) motifs are important in the episodic tale "Horus and Seth," where they are treated for their mythological significance with little attention to portrayal of emotion. The emotions of sexuality receive deeper and more nuanced literary scrutiny in other tales.

One complex and powerful tale, "Two Brothers," tells of a series of conflicts between Bata, a virtuous young man who after several metamorphoses becomes king of Egypt, and two lustful, murderous, treacherous women, one the wife of Bata's brother, Anubis, the other Bata's own wife (who is to be understood as a metamorphosis of the first woman). The story is a vehement rejection of sexuality and femininity. The first woman in the tale, Bata's sister-in-law, who is "like a mother" to him (a motif emphasized by repetition), tries to seduce him and, when she fails, slanders him to his brother. Bata must flee Anubis' rage until, with a lake between him and his brother, he convinces Anubis of his innocence and declares that the misunderstanding is the work of "a filthy vagina." Bata then cuts off his penis to repudiate his own sexuality. He flees abroad to live alone in a forest, with his heart lodged in a pine tree, until the gods make for him a wife, the most beautiful of women. One day

4. Note in particular the fragment of a stone cup (which may, however, be later than the New Kingdom) showing a goose-shaped boat with two naked women holding geese, a goose-headed staff, and blossoms, next to a naked, ithyphallic man holding blossoms with one hand and touching the genitals of one of the women with the other (Bissing, 1907:144; Cairo cat. no. 18,682).

5. Translated in Lichtheim, 1976:197–230.

a lock of her hair floats to the palace and its scent entrances Pharaoh, who has her brought to him and gives her high rank. She then begins scheming to destroy Bata, pursuing him out of an unexplained, obsessive hatred. She murders him in various ways, but each time he returns in a new form until he becomes two persea trees. When the woman has the trees chopped down, a splinter flies into her mouth and impregnates her. The son born of this brutal—and sexless—copulation turns out to be none other than Bata himself, who in due course reigns as king and brings the woman to judgment, having survived the lustful hatred of his sister-in-law / wife / mother.

The tale of "Truth and Falsehood" too puts sexuality in an ugly light. Personified Truth is blinded by his brother, Falsehood. As Truth lies desolate in a thicket, a lady (who is also probably a personification, but of what it is not known) comes upon him and lusts after him and has him brought to her house for her sexual pleasure. This received, she degrades him to doorkeeper. She does not tell the son born of this union who his father is until the son confronts her many years later. The son goes on to avenge his father in court.

Far more tender is the love of princess for prince in "The Doomed Prince." A young Egyptian prince, traveling incognito in Syria, wins the heart of a princess. Her father has arranged a jumping contest with her as prize. The prince alone can leap up to her window, and she falls in love with him at once. Her father tries to renege on the promise, but the princess says she cannot live without this youth, the king relents, and they are married. As the story proceeds, the princess does her best to protect her young husband from the three fates to which he is doomed.

In Ramesside art and literature, then, sex is viewed in several radically different ways: with crude hilarity in the pornographic papyrus; with loathing in "Two Brothers" and (less intensely) "Truth and Falsehood"; and with tender appreciation in "The Doomed Prince" and, above all, in the love poetry. Love poetry was born in an artistic environment of keen interest in the literary exploration of the forms and implications of human sexuality.

The Song of Songs

Dating

The Song of Songs is difficult to date. It lacks allusions to historical events and has no apparent rhetorical goals that might point to a specific historical or political context.

The attempts to date the Song to the time of Solomon, its putative author, are not persuasive. While Solomon is, to be sure, mentioned in the Song, that does not mean that the Song or any part of it must have been written in his time. Since Solomon never ceased to be famous for his wealth and the number of his wives as well as for his literary abilities, various late compositions were ascribed to him. In any case, outside the title he is mentioned only for the sake of comparison, as a foil with which the lovers in the Song can be contrasted (as I argue in the commentary to 3:7–11 and 8:11). If we do not take the mention of his wedding day in 3:11 literally—and I argue that it is not to be so taken—then the references to Solomon do not help us even to date the background of the *events* of the Song, let alone to determine the time of its composition. Even if we do take 3:11 literally, as a call to the girls of Jerusalem to come out and see the actual wedding procession of Solomon, the verse still provides no evidence as to the date of the Song's composition, for poets in all times could write about the famous king's wedding, and furthermore snatches of song from his time could be incorporated into later compositions.

It has been suggested that the Song displays an atmosphere of luxury and wealth that would fit best the period of Solomonic prosperity.[6] However, the young people themselves do not live in special luxury, and most of the valuable items referred to in the Song are mentioned only for the sake of comparison and not as the property of the lovers. The author was certainly familiar with luxury goods and objects of art, but we can hardly suppose that only in the time of Solomon were poets able to describe such things.

We cannot conclude from the mention of Tirzah (6:4) that the Song must have been written during the period in which that city served as the capital of the northern kingdom (from the time of Jeroboam son of Nebat to 870 B.C.E., when Omri moved the capital to Samaria), as if Tirzah could appear parallel to Jerusalem only while it was capital of the north.[7] Even when Tirzah ceased being capital of the north, it was not forgotten. In later times people would have known about it at least from the same sources as we do. The mention of Tirzah in parallel with Jerusalem does, on the other hand, show that the Song, or at least that particular unit (6:1–10), was not written during the United Monarchy, when Tirzah had not yet become the northern counterpart of Jerusalem.

Linguistic criteria are all we can go on in determining the general period of the Song's composition. The language of the Song resembles mishnaic Hebrew in many ways. Among the characteristically mishnaic words and constructions in the Song are: *pardes* (4:13); *ṭannep* (5:3); *ʾomman* (7:2; for the earlier *ḥaraš*); SWG (7:3; for ŚKK); *kotel* (2:9; for *qir*); *ʾaḥuzey ḥereb* (3:8; with the passive participle in an active sense, as often in Aramaic, instead of *ʾoḥazey ḥereb*);[8] *mezeg* (7:3; for *mesek* or *mimsak*); *meseb* (1:12; for *miškab* or *miṭṭah*); *qewuṣṣot* (5:2, 11; for *maḥlapot*). Certain syntactical usages

6. E.g., Delitzsch, 1885:11; Segal, 1962:481–83.

7. Thus Gordis, 1961:23 (with regard to 6:4–7).

8. The use of the passive participle to indicate the state of the actor after the completion of the act is rare in the Bible but very frequent in mishnaic Hebrew, as it is in Aramaic; see Hurvitz, 1972:119.

strongly resemble those of mishnaic Hebrew: *karmi šelli* (1:6; 8:12; for *karmi ʾ^a^ni*) and *miṭṭato šellišlomoh* (3:7; for *miṭṭat š^e^lomoh* or *hammiṭṭah ʾ^a^šer lišlomoh*); *beyn habbanim* (2:3; for *babbanim*); *kimʿaṭ še(ʿabarti mehem) ʿad še(mmaṣaʾti)* (3:4; for *kimʿaṭ (ʿabarti mehem) waʾemṣaʾ*). (See further Bendavid, 1967:74–76.) The *waw*-conversive, which is absent from mishnaic Hebrew, occurs in only one verse of the Song (6:9, twice).

The most prominent mishnaic characteristic in Canticles is the exclusive use of the particle *še-* for *ʾ^a^šer*, which appears only in the title, a later addition in an antique style. The particle *še-* (*ša-*) does appear in preexilic strata of biblical literature, including the ancient Song of Deborah (Judg 5:7, twice). But outside of Canticles, Qohelet (which is also in the transition between biblical and mishnaic Hebrew), and some indisputably postexilic passages, it is extremely rare, relative to the thousands of times *ʾ^a^šer* occurs. *Še-* appears 6 times in definitely preexilic passages,[9] 17 times in ten psalms of uncertain date,[10] and 3 times in Jonah, which is almost certainly postexilic.[11] Evidence that this particle is merely a northernism is insufficient, consisting only of the rare use of it (alongside *ʾ^a^šer*) by Deborah, Gideon, and the king of Aram. *ʾ^a^šer* is used as late as Ben Sirah and the Qumran writings, both of which try to imitate the classical language, but it disappears entirely in mishnaic Hebrew. Not the appearance of *še-*, but its exclusive use, indicates the lateness of the language of the Song. Further mishnaic constructions in the Song include *qorot batteynu* (1:17; with the *nomen rectum* in the plural, for classical *qorot beytenu*); *šiššim hemmah* (6:8; for *yeš šiššim*, "there are sixty"); *ʾet šeʾa-h^a^bah napši* (3:1; for *ʾ^a^hub napši*). All these usages are rare or absent in the classical language but are characteristic of mishnaic Hebrew. Again, it is the frequency—rather than the mere presence—of mishnaic elements in this small scroll that brings its language closer than that of any other book in the Bible to mishnaic Hebrew.

At the same time, the language of the Song maintains some specifically classical usages, such as: the words *ʾanah*, *šammah*, *hemmah*; the cohortative *nagilah*, *niśm^e^ḥah*, *nazkirah*, etc. (this form appears in the Judean Desert scrolls as well, but it is an archaism there); the infinitive of emphasis (e.g., *boz yabuzu*, 8:7); the second and third feminine plural imperfect form (such as *ṣ^e^ʾeynah ur^e^ʾeynah*, 3:11, and *tiṭṭopnah*, 4:11); and the appearance (though infrequent) of the *waw*-conversive (e.g., *way^e^ʾašš^e^ruha*, *way^e^hal^e^-luha*, 6:9, where it may be formulaic).

Hence the language of the Song is not classical biblical Hebrew. What

9. Gen 6:3; Judg 5:7 (twice); 6:17; 7:12; 8:26; II Kgs 6:11.

10. Pss 122:3, 4; 123:2; 124:1, 2, 6; 129:6, 7; 133:2, 3; 135:2, 8, 10; 136:23; 144:15; 146:3, 5. Ps 137:8–9 is postexilic.

11. Jon 1:7,12; 4:10. For further linguistic indices of Jonah's lateness relative to most of the biblical literature, see Bendavid, 1967:60f.

dialect, then, is it? There is no reason to identify it as a northern dialect[12] (which, in any case, is not known to us). The content does not suggest a northern provenience. The incidental mention of northern place names (Lebanon, Hermon, Damascus, etc.) no more proves a northern provenience than the reference to Heshbon in Transjordan proves an eastern one. The events of the Song take place in Jerusalem. The heroine lives in a walled city, and since she converses with the girls of Jerusalem, it is fair to conclude that Jerusalem is her home. And it would be more natural for a Judean than for a northerner to choose Jerusalem as the setting for the poem.

The Aramaic usages are more likely a sign of lateness than of northern origin. While specific Aramaisms cannot usually be identified with certainty, the relative frequency of likely Aramaisms is an argument for postexilic dating. According to Wagner's reckoning (1966: 145), borrowings from Aramaic (or from other languages by way of Aramaic) are by far more frequent in Canticles, Qohelet and Esther than in the other books of the Bible. The words in Canticles that Wagner lists as likely Aramaisms include *ʾomman*, *ʾᵉgoz*, *bᵉrotim*, *ginnah*, *ṭannep*, *kotel*, *mezeg*, *naṭor* (in the sense of "keep"), *sugah*, *sᵉmadar*, *sansinnim*, *sᵉtayw*, *pardes*, *qappeṣ*, *rᵉhaṭim*, *šallamah*, *šalhebet*.

While many linguistic features that appear to us today as distinctively mishnaic most likely were present in one or more of the spoken, non-literary dialects of the First Commonwealth, it is hardly justifiable to date the Song to that period on the grounds of supposed linguistic similarities between it and one of the otherwise unknown dialects. It is in any case unlikely that this book alone would preserve such a high concentration of features of the presumed spoken dialect.

The explanation for the linguistic character of the Song involving fewest unsupported assumptions is that it was composed in the period of transition between classical biblical Hebrew and mishnaic Hebrew. Its language certainly is not earlier than the Second Temple period.

As for the *terminus ad quem*, the existence of a fragment of the Song at Qumran shows that the Song was written and had attained a degree of sanctity before the first century C.E. Allowing time for the Song to undergo religious reinterpretation, we are left with the fourth to second centuries B.C.E. as the likely period of composition. Ben Sirah's reference to Solomon's "song" (47: 15, 17) shows only that Ben Sirah was familiar with I Kgs 5: 12 and does not help set a *terminus* any farther back.

If the content of the Song pointed clearly to an early (preexilic) date of composition, we could assume that the Song had undergone linguistic revision prior to receiving its present form (we would in fact be obliged to make

12. As does, for example, S. R. Driver (1913:449).

that assumption). But nothing in the Song requires such an assumption. Nor does the Song show signs of deliberate linguistic revision of the sort exhibited by the Isaiah-A scroll from Qumran, which includes numerous linguistic and orthographic modifications meant to facilitate pedagogy and private reading (see Kutscher, 1974: pt. I). The text of the Song does not make extensive use of *plene* spelling or of double *matres lectionis* (e.g., *kyʾ* for *ky*, *bwʾ* for *bw*) as does the Isaiah scroll. Furthermore, the exclusive use of *še-* in the body of the Song is not evidence for linguistic "modernization" of this sort, for readers in the Second Temple period would have found no difficulty with *ʾašer*. In general, most of the classical usages replaced in the Hebrew language by the later usages found in the Song (such as *karmi ʾani* for emphatic possession, replaced by *karmi šelli*, *ʾahub napši* instead of the later paraphrasis *ʾet šeʾahabah napši*, and *yeš šiššim* instead of mishnaic *šiššim hemmah*) would have been quite comprehensible to a reader in the Second Temple period, so that there would have been no need to update the language of the Song in these details.

On the other hand, the Song may well have had a prehistory of centuries during which love songs were composed and transmitted, constantly mutating until they attained the form we know, in which form they were then written down. Transmission of this sort probably would "update" the language continually. But whereas *revision* seeks to make an old text more comprehensible while maintaining its content essentially unchanged, dynamic, free transmission (known in the study of folk poetry as *Zersingen*; see chapter 4) is not constrained by fidelity to an original text, but rather continually produces new poems out of old ones. If this was the way the Song was transmitted, it is pointless to speak of the Song as "really" being much older than its linguistic garb. Its present linguistic garb is all we have, and we have no way of reconstructing an earlier stage in its history (as we might do for a text that is more time-bound). *This* song is, to judge from its linguistic characteristics, postexilic and probably Hellenistic, and we have no way of even speculating reasonably about the earlier forms from which it supposedly evolved.

Historical-Cultural Setting

We cannot fix the Song in a particular intellectual and historical setting. First of all, the dating suggested above, which relies on linguistic criteria alone, is not certain. Yet even if we do narrow our scope to a postexilic dating for the Song, there are still several historical periods and social settings into which it could fit comfortably, and we cannot say which was the setting for its composition. The absence of recognizable Greek influence on the poem (except for one or two loanwords), for example, does not exclude a Hellenistic date, for there is no reason to expect Greek influence in literature of this sort, especially during the early Hellenistic period. Nor does the Song seem to grow out of any specific artistic or historical environment. The events it describes are not of a particular time. Its tranquil atmosphere could be taken to exclude times of exile, harsh persecution, or general impoverishment, but on the other hand this atmosphere could in fact be an *answer* to such conditions.[13] Its attitudes, in particular its attitudes toward relationships between the sexes, seem characteristic of no particular period. On the contrary, these attitudes are quite unlike the attitudes expressed elsewhere in the surviving literature, but that may be because nothing else quite like the Song was preserved. Thus there is at present no basis for asserting that the Song reflects this or that specific historical-cultural setting, even if we can make a reasonable estimate of its approximate date.

Channels of Literary Transmission

There is a gap of perhaps a thousand years between the Egyptian love songs and the Song of Songs, but the gap is not so great as to preclude the influence of the former on the latter. Egyptian love poetry could have made its entrance into Palestine at almost any time from the 13th century B.C.E. on (or the 15th century, if the genre began that early). Channels for literary transmission existed at many times, if not continuously, throughout the centuries. The unmistakable ties between Proverbs and Egyptian wisdom literature—many sayings in Proverbs are nearly identical with teachings of Egyptian works—show beyond reasonable doubt that some, perhaps much, literary transmission occurred.[14]

The most opportune time for the importation of the Egyptian love songs was during the 18th–20th dynasties, the period of Egyptian imperial rule in Syro-Palestine (the early 15th century through the late 12th century B.C.E.).[15] Egypt controlled Palestine through a network of officials, many of whom were Egyptians trained in the scribal schools, where literary arts were cultivated alongside the professional skills needed by scribes. The scribes in these centers are one likely means of literary transmission. There were many Egyptians in garrison towns and administrative centers.[16] In addition, sons of vas-

13. Ezek 33:31–33 shows that even in the tormented decade between the first and second waves of exile, Jews in Babylonia liked to gather to hear erotic songs.

14. For a survey of research on Egyptian influence on Israel, see Williams, 1975:231ff. The following discussion of paths of influence includes several of his observations (250–52).

15. See Weinstein, 1981:22f.

16. Weinstein (ibid., pp. 18–22) musters the archaeological and epigraphic evidence for an "impressive Egyptian presence" in Palestine in the 13th and early 12th centuries B.C.E.

sals in Palestine were often raised and educated in the Egyptian court, where they undoubtedly learned Egyptian and probably acquired a taste for the style and art of their prestigious and powerful neighbor.

The first artistic love songs sung in Palestine may well have been sung in Egyptian. Professional singers could have brought Egyptian love poetry to Palestine.[17] In the "Report of Wenamun," written at the beginning of the 11th century B.C.E., when Egyptian political control had sharply declined if not entirely disappeared, we hear of an Egyptian songstress serving in the court of the prince of Byblos. The reason for her presence could only be the desire to hear Egyptian music. This same prince regards Egypt as the homeland of the crafts and wisdom and believes that this knowledge has *already* gone forth from there, meaning that Egypt has already played out its role in the history of culture:

> Indeed, Amun founded all the lands. He founded them after having first founded the land of Egypt from which you have come. Thus craftsmanship came from it in order to reach the place where I am! Thus learning came from it in order to reach the place where I am! (Lichtheim, 1976:227)

Even at a time of Egyptian decline, the Canaanite prince sees Egypt as the fountainhead of the arts.

The Megiddo ivories (1350–1150) include a hieroglyphic dedicatory inscription by a female votary, Kerker, "the singer of Ptah-South-of-His-Wall" (KRI V,5,256,8ff.) We need not suppose that she and the singer in "Wenamun" alone sang songs of Egypt in the land of Canaan.

The Empire was a period of extensive political and mercantile contacts between Egypt and Palestine, contacts that provided ample opportunity for literary influence. Furthermore, this is the only period from which Egyptian love songs have survived. Yet influence during a later period is also a possibility. The love song genre may have continued in use in Egypt after this, though there is no evidence for such a continuity.[18] Literary influence was possible, indeed probable, at least for some types of literature, during the reign of Solomon (ca. 960–922, the period of the 22nd dynasty in Egypt), for Solomon had both literary interests and Egyptian connections. The time of Hezekiah too (the turn of the seventh century B.C.E.) was also an opportune time for Egyptian influence (Williams, 1975:252). Still, the Ramesside period was the time when love poetry flourished and is therefore a more likely time for its importation and influence than a later time when (judging from the

17. Thus Helck, 1971:609.

18. Some tomb inscriptions from the Late Period and the Ptolemaic period (e.g., App. A, nos. v, vi) use the form of the Praise Song to laud dead women, but this practice is probably due to continuity within the tradition of tomb inscriptions; see App. A, no. i, for an earlier example.

time-range of extant texts) artistic interest in love poetry was greatly diminished if alive at all.

The path from Ramesside Egyptian love poetry to Canticles was a long one. Perhaps as much as a thousand years separate the Israelite love poem from its Egyptian counterparts. The love song genre certainly underwent many changes between its presumed Egyptian origins and the time when it reached Palestine, took root in Hebrew literature, grew in native forms, and blossomed as the Song of Songs. Nevertheless, many significant similarities in form and content remain. We see a good parallel to this tenacity of traditions within a genre in the history of the sonnet in Europe. The sonnet maintained its identity from the 13th to the 19th centuries while developing new forms and being incorporated into different national traditions throughout Europe.

CHAPTER 4

The Composition of the Sources and the Songs

How long is a love song? Is Canticles a single song, or a collection of short ones, as most commentators nowadays believe? Is an Egyptian love song only as long as the text between the pause-marks (the units that I have numbered from 1 to 54), or can one song encompass several such units? Hermann, in his influential study of Egyptian love poetry, *Altägyptische Liebesdichtung* (1959), regards these units as independent songs, some of which are assembled in loose collections, others arranged in "cycles." (Songs in cycles are linked together by formal devices, such as repetition of an opening sentence or a type of word play, although with respect to content they have few or no interconnections.) This view has, as far as I can tell, gone unchallenged and has been used to support the theory that Canticles is itself a collection of songs.

There are other possibilities. Canticles may be a single poem, and among the Egyptian songs some, if not all, of the groups[1] of units may form complex, unified songs. In such cases each unit is a stanza, not a song.

Our interpretation of the love songs is clearly dependent on our understanding of the way the units are demarcated and interconnected. If we treat what is really an anthology of independent poems as if it were a single, unified poem, we create artificial connections among originally unrelated units. To do so is to create a "found poem," not to interpret an ancient one. If, on the other hand, we treat what are actually stanzas or literary units of a single poem as if they were discrete poems, we do the poem an injustice, closing our

1. For an explanation of the terms "group" and "unit" with respect to the Egyptian songs, see p. 6.

eyes to the meaning of the whole and failing to consider how the story develops, how the characters affect each other, and how their personalities are portrayed in the poem in its entirety. We slight the depth of its artistry.

In considering the question of literary composition, we should distinguish literary unity from unity of authorship, for a single author can write separate poems, while, conversely, the work of many hands may result in a literary unity. Literary unity means that the text is to be read as a whole; its parts shape one another's meaning, together forming a whole with a meaning of its own. The question of literary unity is the crucial one for interpretation, for it determines the way we read the work. An argument for literary unity often, however, depends in part on arguments for unity of authorship, such as homogeneity of style and repeated associative patterns. The assumption of this argument is that if one poet rather than several wrote the various parts of the text it is more likely to be a unified work of literature. Later on in this chapter, under "Multiple Authorship: *Zersingen*," I will discuss some ways literary unity can be created.

The decision on literary unity must grow out of interpretation. In the commentary on the Song I pointed out some signs of continuity and cross-reference among the units. In the commentary to the Egyptian poems I have already argued that many groups are far too highly organized to be regarded as mere collections or even as cycles. In this chapter I survey the documents, considering the interrelationship of their parts.

We can argue for the unity of a text by pointing to cohesiveness in plot, theme, character, and ideas, as well as to formal patterns. It is more difficult to prove *disunity*. Poems naturally share many traits with others in their genre, so that even a random compilation of songs of a single genre will have some appearance of unity. To argue that a group lacks unity, we can only point to the absence of discovered formal structures encompassing the units and to discontinuity and incompatibility of scene, event, and character. But the possibility always remains that another interpreter will find a unifying principle that persuasively encompasses and explains the ostensibly disparate components.

The Egyptian Love Songs

Survey

Let us begin by taking an overview of the format of the sources of the Egyptian love songs:

I. P. Harris 500, containing three groups of individual love songs (nos. 1–8, 9–16, 17–19), a mortuary song ("Antef"), two short (and now fragmentary) love songs (nos. 19A–19B), and two stories ("The Doomed Prince" and "The Capture of Joppa").

II. A large vase, now broken, on which were written the Cairo Love Songs (nos. 20A–20G, nos. 21A–21G). A vase was a cheap, readily available writing surface. The text was originally written on the complete vase, not on ostraca.

III. P. Turin 1966, containing one group of love poems with three units (nos. 28–30), followed by a short business note. I cannot ascertain what else, if anything, was originally on the papyrus.

IV. P. Chester Beatty I, containing three groups of love songs (nos. 31–37, 38–40, 41–47), a long mythological tale ("Horus and Seth"), two hymns to the king, and short business notes). Some of these texts may have been copied to exhibit the scribal art of advanced students (Erman, 1925: 19f., 24f.); others may have been commissioned by a literate person with literary interests. And, since papyrus was expensive, a papyrus with free space would be used for business notes.

V. Miscellaneous texts: no. 48–54 and untranslated fragments on ostraca. These miscellaneous texts are presumably all independent, short poems, copied as school exercises. However, the similarity of some motifs and the frequency of some words occurring on different ostraca suggest the possibility that some of the fragmentary texts were copied from a larger poetic work.

The three papyri and the Cairo vase present us with the problem of composition: what are the relationships of form and content among the units in the text?

SOURCE I: P. HARRIS 500

Group A (nos. 1–8) I judge to be an anthology of eight independent songs. In the songs of this group, a variety of characters speak in unrelated circumstances:[2] the girl in no. 1 is in bed with her lover, the boy in no. 5 is sailing to Memphis, the boy in no. 7 stands in disappointment outside the house of the girl he desires, and the girl in no. 8 eagerly sails to meet her lover in Heliopolis.

Group B (nos. 9–16) too is an anthology of eight songs with no single narrative or structural principle and no repetition of key-words or formal patterns to connect the eight units. Different personalities appear in different

2. Suys (1934: 448–58) did attempt to weave these units together with the next group to form one long story. But the story Suys constructs requires leaps of the imagination from song to song far greater than any audience could reasonably be expected to complete.

songs. The suspicious and jealous girl speaking in no. 15 is not the same person as the confident optimist of the preceding units of this group (see especially the end of no. 12: "I have obtained forever and ever what Amon has granted me"). The first two or three units, however (nos. 9 and 10 and probably no. 11), are related to one another thematically through the use of bird trapping as a symbol of falling in love (no. 11 speaks of one bird leaving the flock and landing in a garden, which is associated with "net" by a pun). These songs may have been inscribed together because of their common theme, but they do not seem to form a sequence. There is no thematic connection between the first three units of this group and the last five.

Finally, the heading given this group, "Entertainment Song," is not evidence for internal unity, see p. 16.

Group C (nos. 17–19), "The Flower Song," is a single song of three stanzas, each beginning with a word-play on a kind of flower or blossom. Each flower the speaker sees as she strolls through the garden gives rise to a thought about love. These word-plays are not mere decorative openings, but are rather introductions connected integrally to the content of the stanza. In no. 17 the girl says: because our hearts are in balance (*mḫ3*, "balance," plays on "*mḫmḫ*-flowers"), I'll do for you what my heart wills. In no. 18 she begins with a word-play on "exalted" (*sʿ3*—*sʿ3m*) and goes on to express her feelings of exaltation: "I am your favorite sister." In no. 19 the *ṯ3yt*-flower makes her think about how she "took" (*ṯ3y*) his wreaths and took care of him when he came back intoxicated (from a banquet). Clearly, then, we see here a poem shaped around a central idea and formed in accordance with a conscious schema.

Nos. 19A and 19B are two short (now fragmentary) songs with headings written in red.

The scribe of P. Harris 500 carefully marked off different groups by headings in red ink, probably so demarcating them because he was copying them from different manuscripts. He did not distinguish groups that are composed of several songs (groups A and B) from groups that are single songs composed of stanzas (group C) or even from short songs of one stanza each (nos. 19A–19B and the "Antef Song").[3] Nevertheless, internal considerations justify the distinction among the three kinds of groupings, and this distinction is important to interpretation.

SOURCE II: THE CAIRO LOVE SONGS

Group A (nos. 20A–20G), "The Crossing," is a cohesive song of seven stanzas. Its unity is manifest in its narrative sequence, consistency of char-

3. The internal divisions of the "Antef Song" (App. A, no. ii) are not marked off by pause-marks (the bent arm), but the ending is labeled *m3wt* ("refrain"?) in red.

acter portrayal, repetition of key motifs, and echoing of the girl's words in the boy's (see no. 20E, n. b, and the literary comment on "The Crossing"). This poem has a symmetrical structure, with the crossing of the river as its pivot point. Part one (stanzas 1–3) deals with the girl's thoughts and her longing for union; part two (stanza 4) with the boy's experiences in the water; and part three (stanzas 5–7) with the boy's thoughts and his delight in being united with the girl:

Part One. The girl's thoughts
- 1. Her constant contemplation of her lover
- 2. Her delight in his love:
  - A. The present relation
  - B. The future relation
- 3. Her desire to show him her beauty in the water

Part Two. The boy's experience
- 4. The crossing:
  - A. Before and during the crossing
  - B. After the crossing

Part Three. The boy's thoughts
- 5. Her presence
- 6. Her embrace
- 7. The culmination:
  - A. Her kiss
  - B. Preparation of the bed

Further subdivisions are possible but not so clear-cut as those in stanzas 2, 4, and 7.

Group B (nos. 21A–21G), "Seven Wishes," is a carefully structured song portraying a single character (see comment after no. 21G). Each stanza (except, possibly, the last, which has a lacuna at its start) begins with the wish-particle *ḥnr n.i* and continues with an extended simile by which the youth expresses his desire for the constant presence of his beloved. The structure of "Seven Wishes" is as follows:

Part One. The wish that he be close to her
- 1. Like her Nubian maid
- 2. Like her laundryman
- 3. Like her seal-ring
- 4. Like her mirror

Part Two. The wish that she be close to him
- 5. That she be connected to him as flowers to a wreath
- 6. That she come to him
- 7. That she be given to him by the god (?)

V. L. Davis (1980:113) has suggested that the two sets of seven stanzas in the Cairo Love Songs form a single poem, the characters being complementary, like rain and sunshine or inundation and dry land. The fourteen stanzas thus compose a true *cycle*, with the longings of the youth of "Seven Wishes" fulfilled repeatedly, as the reader goes from the end of the text back to its beginning. I agree that the characters are complementary, but only in the sense that the artist is portraying two kinds of lover, active and passive. The structure of these poems, on the other hand, is not circular. There is no formal continuity from the first poem to the second, and nothing at the end of the second poem directs us back to the beginning of the first. Furthermore, the characters of the second song cannot be identified with those of the first. The boy in "The Crossing" achieves his desire through his own efforts. The boy in "Seven Wishes" neither possesses his beloved nor makes an effort to get her. She does not even seem aware of his existence, and he does nothing to make her so. Both lovers in "The Crossing," on the contrary, assume the mutuality of their love.[4]

SOURCE III: P. TURIN 1966

"The Orchard Song" (nos. 28–30) is a single song whose three stanzas form a thematic unit organized climactically, the personae (all trees) showing a progressively higher degree of generosity toward the lovers.

1. The first tree boasts of his beauty and threatens to expose the couple if they do not give him the attention he deserves.
2. The second tree boasts of his willingness to serve the girl and threatens to expose the couple if they do not give him the attention he deserves.
3. The third tree is praised by the poet; she then speaks to offer shelter and secrecy to the lovers without demanding anything in return.

SOURCE IV: P. CHESTER BEATTY I

Group A (nos. 31–37), "The Stroll," is a complex but cohesive song whose unity is manifest first of all in the numbering of the stanzas and in the evident word-plays upon the names of the numerals. All stanzas except the first are numbered, and all, including the first, begin and end with words that play on the sound of the stanza number. Furthermore, connections among the stanzas are not merely associative or formal, contrary to Hermann (1959:149), who regards this song as a "cycle" of songs in which we can expect to find "keinen logischen Gedankengang und damit auch keine Gedankengruppierung und -steigerung." Actually the song presents two consistent characters and speaks about a single event in their lives. The song is further unified by a single view of the nature of adolescent love. In the commentary on "The Stroll," I discuss

4. To Davis' criticism that my evaluation of the two characters as incompatible "implies an arbitrariness in the arrangement for which there is no evidence" (1980:113), I must reply that this incompatibility is itself evidence that there was no particular reason for inscribing one song before the other.

the underlying plot, the numerous cross-allusions among the stanzas, and the development of the characters. The plural "sayings" of the poem's heading probably refers to the seven stanzas and does not prove that the group is a collection.

The structure of this song follows the outlines of its plot:

Part One. The stroll and falling in love:

I. A boy sees a girl and falls in love with her.

II. A girl sees a boy and falls in love with him.

Part Two. The frustration of the attempt to meet:

III. The boy starts to go to her but never makes it there.

IV. The girl's heart tries to go to the boy, but she restrains it.

Part Three. Retrospect and a prayer:

V. The boy tells how he saw the girl and prays to see her again.

VI. The girl tells how she saw the youth and prays that her mother will enable her to see him again.

Part Four. The unfortunate outcome:

VII. The boy becomes love-sick and longs to see the girl again, but in vain.

Group B (nos. 38–40), "Three Wishes," is a single song with three identically structured stanzas, each consisting of the following elements:

1. A wish: "If only you would come (to your sister swiftly) . . ."
2. An extended simile emphasizing the desired speed: "like a . . ."
3. A concluding generalization

There is a progression in the intensity of the images, from the royal messenger of the first stanza, to the speedy royal horse of the second, to the panic-driven gazelle chased by the hunter of the third.

Group C (nos. 41–47), "Nakhtsobek Songs," is a loose anthology of seven songs. The title identifies the collection as a "beautiful saying" (*ṯs*) in the singular, in spite of the diversity of its contents (but see p. 16). Nos. 41 and 42, however, form a thematic unit describing the festivities and sexual pleasures awaiting the youth at the house of the "sister." In fact, they are so close in choice of motifs and speaker's perspective that they probably constitute a single song. Nos. 43–45 are separate short poems. Nos. 46 and 47 are separate poems with a theme in common, the complaint of the excluded lover.

Unity and Diversity

Each of the eight extant song groups (excluding the songs of the miscellaneous ostraca) thus can be classified either as an anthology of independent songs or as a single, complex song.

The anthologies are P. Harris 500, groups A and B, and P. Beatty I, group C. There is virtually no organizing principle in the disposition of the songs in any of these groups. Even thematic grouping is of minor importance, occurring only in nos. 9–11 and nos. 46–47 (nos. 41–42 are probably a single song). Observe that the collector or editor of P. Harris 500, group A, did not consider it necessary either to collocate the two songs with the theme of sailing to a rendezvous (nos. 5 and 8), or to place the two "dawn songs" (nos. 1 and 4) next to each other.

The complex songs are P. Harris 500, group C ("The Flower Song"); the Cairo Love Songs, groups A ("The Crossing") and B ("Seven Wishes"); P. Turin 1966 ("The Orchard"); and P. Beatty I, groups A ("The Stroll") and B ("Three Wishes"). These songs evidence their organization in one or more of the following ways:

1. The stanzas may have the same structure, as in "Seven Wishes" and "Three Wishes."
2. The stanzas may all begin with the same formal device but otherwise not have the same structure throughout, as in "The Orchard" and "The Flower Song." In "The Stroll" the opening device is used also at the end of each stanza and thus brackets it.
3. The stanzas may proceed generally in a narrative sequence, as in "The Crossing" and "The Stroll."
4. The stanzas may progress to a climax without significant temporal sequence, as in "The Orchard" and "Three Wishes." If "Seven Wishes" does in fact conclude with a prayer and a vow to a god (the last stanza is very fragmentary), then it too ends climactically, though it is difficult to see a progression in the earlier stanzas.
5. The song as a whole may have a symmetrically or hierarchically ordered pattern, as in "The Crossing," "Seven Wishes," and "The Stroll."

Most of these songs use more than one of these structuring devices. "The Stroll" uses several.

The formal patterns formed by repetitions of words and phrases and by word-play are not merely ornamental, nor are they editorial devices for splicing separate songs into a cycle. They are usually integral to the content of the songs. In the case of the Wish Songs (a form defined in chapter 7), the formal pattern is inextricable from the content. The pattern *is* the wish, formulated with different images in each stanza. In "The Stroll," "The Orchard," and "The Flower Song," the bond between formal pattern and content is, to be sure, less tight, but in these poems too the formal devices help convey the content. In "The Stroll" the framework of puns on the stanza numbers provides a chronology that helps organize the events of the song. In addition to its formal function, this framework contributes to the depiction of the personae and helps evoke their peculiar situation, showing them speaking each the same way as the other, yet without hearing each other. This formal congruity between the utterances of the lovers in itself suggests how similar the lovers are, and their similarity is a major source of the song's irony. In "The Orchard" the quoting phrases that start off each stanza not only tell us that different trees are speaking, but also introduce the voice of the poet, who in the third stanza pronounces an "objective" evaluation of the little sycamore. In "The Flower Song" the puns on flower names, though only loosely related to the rest of the girl's words, set and maintain the scene: a girl walking in a garden with her lover.

The formal devices also guide the audience in associating the stanzas. The formal patterning first marks off the units, then controls the perspective of the audience, directing its focus to certain personae or settings. The audience can, for example, be expected to recognize the girl who puns on *ṯ3yt*-flowers in no. 19 as the same one who earlier made puns on *mḫmḫ*-flowers in no. 17 and *sꜥ3m*-flowers in no. 18. In this way the poet leads us to interpret the third stanza and the first two stanzas as expressions of the same personality. In "The Orchard" the introduction of three trees in similar fashion implies that the three trees are in the same setting. In "The Stroll" the punning framework that brackets each stanza helps show that the speakers of the stanzas are a single couple. The audience, hearing each stanza introduced in the same way, will probably assume (insofar as that assumption is nowhere contradicted) that the same two personae are speaking in all the stanzas. The numbers emphasized by this framework and reinforced by puns serve further to provide a seven-day chronology that helps integrate the parts of the poem. An audience would certainly identify the boy who says, "Seven whole days I have not seen my sister" (no. 37) with the one who said, "these five days she has been gone from me" (no. 35) two stanzas earlier. In general, a formal pattern repeated in different units, even when limited in scope, encourages the audience to regard units as parallel components of a whole and so to expect and look for additional parallels and less conspicuous interconnections.

The Song of Songs

Is the Song of Songs a song or a collection of songs? Scholars have often assumed that if they did not see a design or structural principle in the book, the book was by default a collection. But, contrariwise, because the book has come to us as a unity, without titles or other indicators separating songs as we have in the Psalter or the Egyptian love song anthologies, the burden of proof lies primarily on those who wish to assert *disunity*. Yet the arguments that have been mustered for the book's disunity are very weak. There are six main arguments.

1. The Song is said to depict a variety of life-settings. Gordis says that since some songs are connected with wedding ceremonies and others not, "The only justifiable conclusion is that the Song of Songs, like the Psalter, is an anthology" (1961:17f.). In fact, however, only 3:11 and 8:8 even allude to weddings, and the units they belong to need not have been sung in that setting at all. Unmarried lovers, after all, might naturally refer to marriage at least occasionally.

2. The Song contains a variety of geographical references. Places in various parts of Syro-Palestine and Transjordan in particular are mentioned, but this in no way proves a variety of proveniences for the units of the Song (as Jastrow, 1921:145f., Gordis, 1961:25, and White, 1978:33, think). Was 7:5bβ written in Lebanon and 7:5bα in Transjordan? By the same argument we might say that the book of Jonah was written partly in Nineveh, partly in Jaffa, and partly at sea.

3. The Song is said to display varied linguistic characteristics. Gordis (1961:24) and White (1978:33) argue that there is a mixture of linguistic traits in the Song indicating diverse dates of composition for its parts. In fact, however, the language of the Song has traits of both biblical Hebrew and mishnaic Hebrew (see chapter 3), not because its units originated in different periods, but because it comes from a transitional stage in the development of the language. The Song's language may indeed be a mixture, but what is significant is that the same sort of mixture is characteristic of all parts of the book, a fact that weighs toward literary unity more than toward disunity.

4. The Song contains doublets (Jastrow, 1921:129–38, Fohrer, 1970:303). But the mere presence of doublets does not show multiple sources. Doublets are an argument for composite authorship only when the doublets differ in style, as they frequently do in the Pentateuch. In the case of the doublets in Canticles, in particular in the Praise Songs (4:1b–2, 3b//6:5b–7), not only is the same style in evidence, but nearly the same words recur. Doublets of this sort are well known from the Ugaritic texts and Homer and do not indicate multiple authorship.

5. The Song is said to present a variety of personae. Fohrer, in arguing against the dramatic theory (1970:302), claims that there are at least two male protagonists, a king and a shepherd, and two females, a country girl and a city dweller. But Fohrer then seems to obviate his own distinction between king and shepherd by applying the theory of "travesties," or disguises, to these figures (see "Excursus: 'The Travesties'"), which means that "king" and "shepherd" are only disguises, not separate personae. Certainly the boy is not literally a king. Nor does the distinction between two female protago-

nists hold, for a family in the city could very well hold vineyards and flocks outside the city walls (in the *migraš*). Marcia Falk, in a similar vein, says that there are different speakers addressing different audiences in the Song (1982: 69, 73–79). There are, to be sure, a variety of characters in the Song, but it is no sign of disunity that sometimes a female lover speaks, sometimes a male, and at other times a group of females, for there is no hint that different female lovers speak in different units or that different male lovers are addressed in different units, and so on.

6. Analogies with love poetry from other cultures are thought to show that ancient Near Eastern love poetry consisted of short poems that were often collected in anthologies. The assumption that Egyptian love poetry presents only loose collections has been used to argue that it is *a priori* likely that Canticles too is an anthology.[5] In fact, however, Egyptian love poetry does not provide a good analogy to Canticles in this regard.

First of all, no group of Egyptian love poems is organized quite like Canticles. In the anthological collections (P. Harris 500, groups A and B; P. Chester Beatty I, group C), the units are manifestly independent and autonomous songs, with only occasional thematic ties between adjacent units. Certainly these collections show nothing like the uniformity of style and frequency of repetitions that characterize Canticles. Nor do these collections evidence any attempt to join the songs by means of key-words or motifs—a hypothesis advanced by some commentators in order to explain the homogeneous style and the high frequency of repetitions in the Song.[6] These three Egyptian collections show what an anthology of love songs looks like, and it does not look like Canticles.

On the other hand, the six *complex* songs ("The Flower Song," "The Crossing," "Seven Wishes," "The Orchard," "The Stroll," and "Three Wishes") show a far higher degree of structural organization and formal design than does Canticles. Some of them develop a narrative line, some are ordered in climactic progression, and some display throughout a clear and uniform formal pattern that leaves no doubt as to where each stanza begins and that at the same time marks the stanzas as components of a larger unity. Certainly Canticles is not so clearly segmented and schematically patterned as any of these songs.

Neither are the Mesopotamian Sacred Marriage songs (Kramer, 1969; see

5. This argument has been made by Rudolph (1962:99), Würthwein (1969:26), and Murphy (1977:487); Murphy, however, presented a different view in 1979, arguing now for the unity of the song.

6. Rudolph (1962:100), Jastrow (1921:127f.), and others. Landsberger (1954) regards this as the principle whereby numerous epigrammatic songs (apparently scores of them, though he does not give a number), were strung together to compose the Song.

chapter 5) a satisfactory analogue to Canticles from the standpoint of style. The various texts relating to the courtship and marriage of the divine couple are mostly unitary compositions with little in common among them beyond the essential themes and characters of the ritual they served. Each text seems to deal with a single scene or dialogue (usually a dialogue between the lovers). The extremely repetitious character of these texts and the tight narrative sequences leave no doubt that the individual texts are unities. Canticles shows greater variety of setting, theme, and language than any one of these texts but greater homogeneity than the Sacred Marriage poetry taken as a whole.

The usual argument made for the Song's disunity comes from commentators who see no comprehensive structure and leave the burden of proof to those who assert the Song's unity. But if the burden of proof were shifted, how could one prove *disunity*? That is to say, how can one prove that the book is a loose anthology that has undergone at most a superficial editing? The following criteria could be used in such an argument:

1. Lack of systematic structure or sequential development, when this lack is conjoined with consistent variations in style.
2. Protagonists who cannot be identified with one another as one person. The boy in the "The Crossing," for example, who achieves his desire, is different from the boy in "Seven Wishes," who only yearns for his beloved. (The two poems can be separated on this basis even though they are probably by the same author.)
3. Contradictions in facts or events. A boy sailing to Memphis (no. 5) and a girl sailing to Heliopolis (no. 8), for example, will not meet each other in the same song.
4. Doublets that differ in style, especially when there are a number of doublets that, when separated, can be grouped into internally consistent series. (This criterion was significant in the separation of the Pentateuchal sources because the duplicated stories there are cast in distinctly different styles.)
5. Two or more blocks of material in sequence, each with its distinctive content and form, and with no cross-references among the blocks (e.g., groups A and B of P. Harris 500).

To be strong, an argument would require a conjunction of the above criteria. But, in fact, I doubt very much that any one of these criteria could be effectively applied to Canticles.

I do not grant the validity of the assumption that the lack of a comprehensive design proves a book to be an anthology. If there are other unifying factors, a poet can create a single, cohesive poem without organizing its parts in sequential, hierarchical, or symmetrical designs. But in the case of Canticles, can the converse argument be made, that this book *does* show a design sufficiently extensive and detailed to prove that it is a literary unity and should be interpreted as such? Since I do not think any such design has yet been demonstrated, I will not rely on an argument from design in asserting the book's unity.[7] On the other hand, I see no need to refute the various proposals for a comprehensive design that have appeared. None of these theories has won many adherents. My main argument against previous structural arguments lies in my exegesis (offered in Part One), which, I believe, accounts for the disposition of the Song's contents more adequately than other approaches do. I will, however, look briefly at two types of designs that have been suggested, the sequential and the schematic.

Let us first consider the argument for a sequential pattern. Some commentators have argued for an underlying narrative presupposing a sequence of events, even when the poem does not proceed chronologically. Various commentators in the 18th and 19th centuries, most of them advocating the theory that the Song is a drama,[8] attempted to discover narrative continuity or a single sequence of events running through all parts of the book: thus, among others, Jacobi (1771), Ewald (1826), Ginsburg (1970), Renan (1884), Delitzsch (1885), S. R. Driver (1913:438–47), and Harper (1907).[9] But the proposed plots require reconstruction of elaborate dramatic settings and complex sequences of events far beyond anything implied by the text, and the theory has not been accepted by the major commentators beyond the early years of this century.[10]

7. There seems to be a general appropriateness in the placement of the opening and closing units of the Song (see "Narrative Frame" below), but this framework is too loose to constitute an argument from design. I include this framework as one unifying factor among many, not as an independent argument for literary unity, such as an intricate comprehensive design would provide.

8. Although theories of narrative continuity have often been bound up with the theory that the Song is a drama whose parts were recited by different actors or singers in some sort of theatrical setting, this connection is unnecessary. Narrative continuity would not prove that the Song is a script for a drama, nor could the lack of such continuity prove that the Song was not presented by different players speaking or acting out the parts. Theatrical-type presentation of that sort would undoubtedly allow the audience to discern changes of scene and continuities of plot that are lost to the reader, but the use of theatrical presentation cannot be proved from the Song itself. For the "dramatic theory" see further "Drama" in chapter 6.

9. See S. R. Driver, 1913:437–47, and Jastrow, 1921:91–115, for surveys of the main representatives of the "dramatic theory." Driver basically supports the theory; Jastrow argues against it at length.

10. S. R. Driver (1913:437f.) identifies two views on the composition of the presumed drama. According to the "traditional view," as expounded, for example, by Delitzsch (1885), there are *two* main characters, Solomon and a Shulammite maiden whom he loves. The poet describes how this beautiful maiden "is taken away from her rustic home by the king and raised to

Next we turn to the argument for schematic design. Prominent nowadays is the attempt to use formal criteria to uncover a schema embracing all parts of the book and thereby to reveal the hand of a single poet creating a single poem. The most thoroughgoing and influential of these attempts is that of J. C. Exum (1973).[11] Since her study excels in its attention to stylistic detail even while being weakened by the flaws typical of literary formalism, it deserves special attention.

Exum finds six "poems" (themselves parts of the larger poem) organized in the following schema (p. 77):

I. 1:2–2:6, containing (a) 1:2–11 and (b) 1:12–2:6, the latter being a transitional element
II. 2:7–3:5
III. 3:6–5:1, containing (a′) 4:10–5:1, which also serves as a transitional element
IV. 5:2–6:3
V. 6:4–8:3, containing (b′) 7:7–8:3
VI. 8:4–14

The "poems" are further divided into "strophes."

Exum's detailed analysis reveals many interconnections among the various parts of the book. She points out not only recurrences of motifs but

the summit of honour and felicity by being made his bride at Jerusalem" (Driver, ibid.). The dialogue consists largely of expressions of mutual love and admiration by these two characters. According to the "modern" view, propounded by Jacobi (1771), developed by Ewald (1826), and accepted by Driver, there are *three* main characters—Solomon, the Shulammite, and her shepherd lover. "A beautiful Shulammite maiden, surprised by the king and his train on a royal progress in the north (6:11–12), has been brought to the palace at Jerusalem (1:4 etc.), where the king hopes to win her affections, and to induce her to exchange her rustic home for the honour and enjoyments which a court life could afford. She has, however, already pledged her heart to a young shepherd; and the admiration and blandishments which the king lavishes upon her are powerless to make her forget him. In the end she is permitted to return to her mountain home, where at the close of the poem, the lovers appear hand in hand (8:5), and express, in warm and glowing words, the superiority of genuine, spontaneous affection over that which may be purchased by wealth or rank (8:6–7)" (S. R. Driver, 1913:437f.). This is only a summary of the plot. The expositions of the Song as drama went into great detail about the course of events and emotions implied by it.

11. For other suggested structures see the survey in Pope, 44–47. Two recent studies using similar methods but less carefully are Webster (1982) and Shea (1980). Both draw parallels on the scantiest similarities, as when Shea connects 1:8–11 with 8:11 because both mention silver in their concluding lines (p. 384), or when Webster connects 4:16–5:1 with 6:2–3 as complementary parts of a "ring construction" on the grounds that both passages have the "garden motif" and "the mood of fulfillment" (p. 79). These schemas too require unnatural unit divisions and ignore conspicuous parallels that cut across and disturb the structures they outline.

recurrences of clusters and series of motifs, all of which contribute to the homogeneous texture of the poem. She also notes many of the Song's internal parallels and cross-allusions. Yet although her analysis is useful, I do not think that these interconnections form a comprehensive design. There are three main flaws in her schema.

First, the units that Exum designates "poems" are different sorts of subdivisions, and likewise the various "strophes" are a mixed bag. Her poems I, II, III, V, and VI are not units in the same way that IV is a unit, that is to say, a segment with internal cohesiveness and continuity of thought. In II there is no special contentual link between 3:1–5 and 2:7–17. V. 3:1 clearly begins a new narrative sequence. Within III 4:1 marks a much sharper division than does either 4:7 or 4:10, which are also supposed to start strophes. It is arbitrary to designate 3:6–11 a "strophe" when this set of verses is no less independent than the units designated "poems." Poem V contains very diverse material: 8:1–3 is certainly not part of the same unit as the Praise Song in 6:4–10, by any unit division that attends to content. Likewise VI lacks unity. There is no special connection between 8:6ff. and the preceding context. In other words, Exum often lumps passages together as "strophes" of the same poem although they are no less distinct from one another than the "poems" that are supposed to be the major building blocks of the Song. The validity of the "poem"-"strophe" hierarchy is crucial to Exum's outline because she wants to show patterns of connections among entire "poems" and not only among various passages. Without this hierarchy, which surely no auditor could be expected to discern, the parts of the book do not form a design of the sort Exum proposes.

Second, the boundaries chosen to mark the "poems" are not always drawn in the places most appropriate to the content. Thus 2:6 and 2:7 actually belong to the same unit, as we see in 8:3–4, where the same combination of sentences occurs (she is forcing her argument in starting the next unit with 8:4). The mention of the lovers' embrace naturally leads into the adjuration not to disturb love. Likewise 3:6 is linked to 3:5, as the combination in 8:4–5 shows, for "Who is this coming up from the desert?" (as she renders the sentence) is a rhetorical question, an exclamation evoked by the adjuration (see commentary on 3:6).

Third, there are parallels that connect sections not linked according to the suggested schema: 8:14 (VI) with 2:17 (II) and 4:6 (III); 8:4 (VI) with 3:5 (II) and 2:7 (II); 8:2a (V) with 3:4b (II); 5:16 (IV) with 2:4 (I); 5:8 (IV) with 2:5b (I); 4:5b–6 (III) with 2:16b–17 (II); see the list below under "Repetends." These parallels cut directly across Exum's suggested structure.

Now in reality an audience hears the words of a song sequentially and although the listeners will segment the sequence as required by the content and by formal indicators, they could not possibly divide Canticles according to the suggested outline and then, keeping in mind that precise segmentation and hierarchy, proceed to make just the connections Exum points out, ignoring the other parallels. When all the data are registered, the Song presents not a neat schema of interconnections, nor an overall schematic design, but a tangle of parallels, cross-references, and echoes. If surface structure is to be significant for interpretation, it must be more accessible than the meaning it is supposed to support, for the purpose of a schema is to help the audience in the task of interpretation. If the schema is itself too tangled, it cannot do this.

Literary Unity

With neither a structural argument to prove unity, nor yet a variety of linguistic and literary arguments to prove disunity, let us look at factors that do at least give a fair degree of homogeneity and cohesiveness to the book, and then ask how these qualities bear on the weightier question of literary unity. The four most important unifying factors are: (1) a network of repetends, (2) associative sequences, (3) consistency of character portrayal, and (4) a (loose) narrative framework.[12]

Repetends

Numerous phrases and sentences recur in the same or somewhat varied form in different parts of the book. These repetitions are quite conspicuous and have been well noted in the commentaries. They are not actually "refrains," as they are commonly called. Properly speaking a refrain recurs at fixed inter-

12. The following arguments incorporate many of the observations of R. E. Murphy (1979), who affirms the poem's unity on the basis of the high frequency of repetitions, including "refrains," themes, and simple repetitions of words and phrases. He observes that "one would not expect to find this inner thread of unity (significant repetitions) in poems that are widely presumed to have been written over many years by different hands. What if one should urge that the unity was achieved by an editor who locked together several poems by means of these repetitions? Perhaps an adequate reply is that the original poet would have been as expert at this kind of thing as the (later) editor would have been" (p. 436).

A statistical analysis of the Song's linguistic characteristics in comparison with those of texts of other genres might tend to show that the Song's style is more uniform than we would expect in a compilation of poems belonging to a single genre of comparable thematic scope. Such a study would, however, be hampered, if not precluded, by our lack of an external reference point within Hebrew literature. Not knowing what the style of the love song genre was like in Israel, we cannot determine if the Song's style has characteristics that distinguish it from the genre as a whole.

vals in a fixed form, or at most with only minor variations. The repetitions in the Song are mostly *repetends*:[13] phrases, verses, or short passages that recur, sometimes in different forms, at varying intervals. Repetends have less weight than refrains in marking unit boundaries and determining a poem's formal structure.[14] Some repetends in the Song occur within what some commentators consider single units, but most are in different units according to any unit division that has been suggested; that is, they occur in different *songs* if the book is an anthology. In the following listing, repetends occurring within a single unit (according to the segmentation I propose) appear in the same column, since I do not bring them forward as *additional* evidence for the Song's overall unity. Note further that a sentence may contain more than one repetend, linking it with several passages. In such a case we have more than one connecting thread, and so the sentence appears twice in the list.

One passage can recall another even without arousing conscious association, just as repetitions of themes and motifs in music can impress themselves on the audience and create a sense of continuity and cohesiveness without the listeners' being aware that this is happening.

Since repetends may vary slightly each time they recur, it is sometimes uncertain whether the resemblance between two sentences or phrases is so strong that the later occurrence must recall the earlier. When the verbal resemblance is virtually complete (as it is, for example, in the case of the adjuration to the girls of Jerusalem), further comment is unnecessary. When I claim that a repetend is present in passages where the verbal resemblance is not virtually complete, I will point out the similarities in theme, motif, and context that join forces with the verbal repetitions to connect the passages in question. The parallels between phrases that are nearly synonymous but do not use the same words or roots should be sufficiently clear from the column alignment.

There are many more repeated words and phrases in the Song than are listed among the repetends below. Even single words and short phrases, if they are unusual or foregrounded in some way, can point back to earlier sections of the song: for example, "shepherding" (1:7, 8; 2:16; 4:5; 6:2, 3; RʿH is foregrounded by word-play and by cross-allusion to other images of eating); *ʿoper* (2:9, 17; 4:5; 7:4; 8:14—only in Canticles); *s^{e}madar* (2:13, 15; 7:13—only in Canticles); *dodim* (1:2, 4; 4:10; 5:1; 7:13); *ḥolat ʾah^{a}bah* (2:5; 5:8—only in Canticles); *raʿyah* (1:9, 15; 2:2, 10, 13; 4:1, 7; 5:2;

13. This useful term is defined in the *Princeton Encyclopedia of Literature*, 1974:699.

14. "Repetend" is a more specific term than "repetition," which could be used of sequential repetition such as "Come from Lebanon, my bride, come, from Lebanon draw near" (4:8, emended). Sequential repetitions do not connect different units of the poem and so do not bear on the question of its unity.

6:4; elsewhere only Judg 11:37 *ketiv*); *nerd* (1:12; 4:13, 14—only in Canticles); *koper*, "henna" (1:14; 4:13—only in Canticles); *hayyapah bannašim* (1:8; 5:9; 6:1); *yonati tammati* (5:2; 6:9—only in Canticles); "Let me hear your voice" (2:14//8:13). Some of the locutions, especially the two-word phrases, could perhaps be regarded as repetends; in any case they certainly contribute to the uniformity of poetic texture. Still, because such repetitions are more likely to be due to generic style or the demands of content than to individual style, as evidence for unity they are less compelling than the longer phrases, word clusters, and sentences.

(1) 8:14 (Girl)	4:6b (Boy)	2:17b (Girl)
Bolt away, my beloved,		Turn, my beloved,
and be as a gazelle,		and be as a gazelle,
or as a young roe		or as a young roe
	I'll make my way	
on the mountains of spices.	to the mountain of myrrh,	on the mountains of Bether
	to the hill of frankincense.	
		2:9a (Girl)
		My beloved is like a gazelle or a young roe.

The association between 4:6b and 2:17b is strengthened by the clause that precedes them both, *ʿad šeyyapuaḥ hayyom w^{e}nasu haṣṣ^{e}lalim*. V. 8:14 resembles 2:17b verbally, while *harey b^{e}śamim* (8:14) parallels *har hammor—gibʿat hall^{e}bonah* (4:6).

(2) 8:11–12 (Boy)	1:6b (Girl)
Solomon had a vineyard in Baal Hamon. He gave the vineyard to keepers; . . . But *my* vineyard is before me.	My mother's sons were mean to me, made me keeper of the vineyards. *My* vineyard I could not keep.

The resemblance here is reinforced by the underlying theme, the tending of vineyards as symbolic of sexuality.

(3) 8:5aα (Girls of Jerusalem)	3:6aα (Girls of Jerusalem)
Look who's coming up from the wilderness!	Look who's coming up from the wilderness!

(4) 8:4	5:8a	3:5	2:7
(Girl)	(Girl)	(Girl)	(Girl)
I ask you	I ask you	I ask you	I ask you
to promise,	to promise,	to promise,	to promise,
girls of	girls of	girls of	girls of
Jerusalem:	Jerusalem:	Jerusalem,	Jerusalem,
		by the gaz-	by the gaz-
		elles or	elles or
		the hinds	the hinds
		of the wild:	of the wild:
do not dis-	do not . . .	do not dis-	do not dis-
turb, do not		turb, do not	turb, do not
bestir love,		bestir love,	bestir love,
before it		before it	before it
wishes.		wishes.	wishes.

(5) 8:3 (Girl)	2:6 (Girl)
His left hand is under my	His left hand is under my
head, and his right hand head,	head, and his right hand
embraces me.	embraces me.

(6) 8:2a (Girl)	3:4b (Girl)
I would take and lead you	I seized him—now I won't
	let him go, till I've brought him
to my mother's house . . .	to my mother's house,
	to the room of her who
	conceived me.

We should probably read *w*^{e}*ʾel ḥeder yolad*^{e}*ti (or horati)* in 8:2a as well, see commentary. Compare (19).

(7) 7:13aβ, 14aα	6:11b	2:12aα, 13a
(Boy)	(Girl?)	(Boy)
We'll see (RʾH)	to see (RʾH)	The blossoms have
if the vine has	if the vine has	appeared (RʾH) in
blossomed,	blossomed,	the land . . .
the bud opened,		
the pomegranates	the pomegranates	the vine is in bud,
bloomed.	bloomed.	
There I will give		
you my love.		
The mandragoras		
give off		giving off
fragrance.		fragrance.

The proximity of 7:13f. to 6:11 and the verbal resemblances between them allow them to work as repetends. Vv. 7:13f. and 2:12f. are both preceded by an invitation to come away to the countryside.

(8) 7:11 (Girl)	6:3a (Girl)	2:16 (Girl)
I am my beloved's	I am my beloved's	My beloved is mine
and his passion	and my beloved is	and I am his:
is for me.	mine:	
	he grazes among	he grazes among
	the lilies.	the lilies.

"His passion is for me" (7:11) is a near paraphrase of "my beloved is mine" (6:3); see commentary. Vv. 6:3b//2:16b are part of another sequence as well; see (14).

(9) 7:7 (Boy)	1:16a (Girl)
How beautiful you are,	How beautiful you are, my
how pleasant (*naʿamt*),	beloved, indeed delightful
	(*naʿim*)!
O love, delightful girl!	

Both passages are in units with the "Praise of the Beloved" theme; see chapter 7.

(10) 4:1a (Boy)	1:15 (Boy)
How beautiful you are,	How beautiful you are,
my darling, how beauti-	my darling, how beauti-
ful! Your eyes	ful! Your eyes
are doves	are doves.
seen through your veil.	

V. 4:1a recalls 1:16a as well. Both 4:1a and 1:15 are in units with the "Praise of the Beloved" theme.

(11) 7:5a (Boy)	4:4aα (Boy)
Your neck is like an	Your neck is like the Tower
ivory tower.	of David.

The praise series in 4:1–5 has been split, with 4:1b–3 recurring (with the omission, probably accidental, of one sentence, 4:3a) in 6:5b–7 (see [13]), and 4:4–5 incorporated in different form in 7:4–5a (see [11–12]).

(12) 7:4 (Boy)	4:5a (Boy)
Your two breasts are like	Your two breasts are like
two fawns, twins	two fawns, twins
of a gazelle.	of a gazelle.

(13) 6:5b–7 (Boy) Your hair is like a flock of goats streaming down Gilead. Your teeth are like a flock of ewes come up from the wash, all of whom bear twins, none of whom miscarries.	4:1b–3 (Boy) Your hair is like a flock of goats streaming down Mount Gilead. Your teeth are like a flock of shorn sheep, come up from the wash, all of whom bear twins, none of whom miscarries . . .
Like a slice of pomegran- ate is your cheek, seen through your veil.	Like a slice of pomegran- ate is your cheek, seen through your veil.

This passage is best regarded as a single repetend because its constituent phrases do not appear in other combinations elsewhere. "Like a thread . . ." (4:3a) is probably to be supplied in the parallel unit as well (see commentary).

(14) 6:3b (Girl) grazes among the lilies.	4:5b (Boy) graze among the lilies.	2:16b (Girl) grazes among the lilies.

I include this phrase among the repetends in spite of its brevity because it is preceded by the declaration of mutual possession in both 6:3a and 2:16a.

(15) 5:13b (Girl) His lips are lilies —they drip liquid myrrh.	4:11a–bα (Boy) Your lips, my bride, drip honeycomb.
(16) 5:8bβ (Girl) . . . I am sick with love.	2:5b (Girl) . . . I am sick with love.
(17) 4:10b (Boy) Your caresses—how better than wine, the scent of your oils than all spices!	1:2b–3a (Girl) for your caresses are better than wine! As for scent, your oils are good: "Oil of Turaq" is your name.
(18) 4:6a (Boy) Before the day blows softly in, and the shadows flee . . .	2:17 (Girl) Before the day blows softly in, and the shadows flee . . .

See (1).

(19) 2:4a (Girl) He brought me to the house of wine.	1:4bα (Girl) The king has brought me to his chambers.

Vv. 2:4a and 1:4bα refer to the same event; see commentary. They are reminiscent of (6), having in common with it the elements *hebi*ʾ and *beyt*// *ḥeder*. "The house of wine" and the king's "chambers" refer to the same structure.

Associative Sequences

Associative sequences are groups of words, sentences, or motifs (they may be repetends as well) that recur in the same order even though that order does not seem required by narrative sequence or logical continuity.

Some simple associative sequences are the following: "How beautiful you are, my darling" in 4:1aα and 1:15abα, followed by "Your eyes are doves" in 4:1aβ and 1:15bβ; "who/which graze(s) among the lilies" in 2:16b and 4:5b, followed by "Before the day blows softly in, and the shadows flee" in 2:17 and 4:6.

Four components of 1:13–14 are repeated in the same order in 7:12–13a, but the parallels involve puns and word plays: *šaday*, *yalin*, *koper*, *karmey-* (1:13–14) and *śadeh*, *nalinah*, *k*ᵉ*parim*, *k*ᵉ*ramim* (7:12–13a, see commentary).

Complex associative sequences appear when independent motifs or sentences are combined to form a single passage in the order they appeared in earlier. For example, the youth's nocturnal visit in 2:8–17 is followed by the girl's nocturnal search in 3:1–5. Here these events are not part of the same narrative, although there is a certain associative connection between the two units, for a boy's visit to a girl at night may bring to mind a girl's search for a boy at night. In 5:2–6:3 these motifs are joined into a continuous narrative, connected in the same order as before.

An associative sequence may involve elaboration and distribution of the components. This occurs in 2:3 and 5:10–16. Exum (1973:60) has observed the intricate connections between the passages. (a) Both 2:3a, "Like an apricot tree among trees of the thicket, so is my beloved among boys," and 5:10, "My beloved is bright and ruddy, preeminent among a myriad," declare the superiority of the beloved youth to all others. V. 2:3a could in fact answer the question of 5:9, "Your beloved—how is he better than any other, O most beautiful among women . . . ?" (b) In both places the Shulammite uses an analogy to trees to make her point. According to 2:3a her lover is like the apricot, the sweetest of trees, and according to 5:15b he is like the cedar, the most majestic. (c) Mention of the apricot tree gives rise to a remark about the youth's sweetness in 2:3b. In 5:15b the mention of the cedar likewise—but less expectedly—leads into praise of his sweetness. Vv. 5:16aα and 2:3b use the same three roots in chiastic order: *ḥimmad*ᵉ*ti*, *matoq*, *ḥikki* in 2:3b and *ḥikko*, *mamtaqqim*, and *maḥ*ᵃ*maddim* in 5:16aα. The motifs of 2:3

are thus incorporated into the Praise Song in 5:10–16 in the same sequence: (1) specialness of the beloved + (2) tree image + (3) sweetness and delightfulness, expressed by ḤMD, MTQ, and ḤK.

A more complex associative sequence appears in 8:2–5, which closely parallels both 3:4b–6a and 2:6–7, using components of both in the same order as in the earlier passages.

	(e) (3:4b) I seized him—now I won't let him go till I've brought him to my mother's house, to the room of her who conceived me.	(e) (8:2) I would take and lead you to my mother's house, ⟨to the room of her who bore me⟩.[15]
(a) (2:6) His left hand is under my head, and his right hand embraces me.		(a) (8:3) His left hand is under my head, and his right hand embraces me.
(b) (2:7) I ask you to promise, girls of Jerusalem,	(b) (3:5) I ask you to promise, girls of Jerusalem,	(b) (8:4) I ask you to promise, girls of Jerusalem:
(c) by the gazelles or the hinds of wild:	(c) by the gazelles or the hinds of the wild:	
(d) do not disturb, do not bestir love, before it wishes.	(d) do not disturb, do not bestir love, before it wishes.	(d) do not disturb, do not bestir love, before it wishes.
	(f) (3:6a) Look who's coming up from the wilderness . . .	(f) (8:5a) Look who's coming up from the wilderness . . .

Six components, to which I have assigned letters by order of appearance, recur and recombine. Although they are not free-floating formulas—for (c) and (d) make no sense unless preceded by (a)—there is flexibility in the choice of formulas used in a given passage. The components that *are* used recur in the same order. The passage 3:4b–6a leaves out component (a) but adds two new ones, (e) and (f), while 8:2–5 uses these two new components as well as (a), though omitting (c). While not claiming that this pattern shows a deliberate structuring principle or that it forms a design significant for inter-

15. For the emendation, see commentary.

pretation, I think that it shows a tendency for certain ideas or motifs to cluster together and reappear in a certain order. The bearing of this tendency on the question of literary unity will be considered later.

Character Portrayal

The Song is notably consistent in its character portrayal: the same two personalities speak throughout. This consistency is, I think, generally recognized, if only tacitly. Few commentators describe more than two lovers in the Song, and even those who look upon it as an anthology rarely attempt to differentiate among lovers portrayed in various songs.[16]

It is difficult to separate character portrayal from style, phraseology, and imagery in Canticles because the personae are known only from their speech, so that consistency in these features may in itself give the appearance of consistency of character. Still, even apart from the qualities of their language, the personae appear as coherent personalities. (This the proponents of the "dramatic theory" recognized, but we do not need to follow them in assuming an ongoing narrative continuity in order to recognize consistency in character portrayal.) From the start the girl is forthright and open about her love and desires. Her lover, though the lines of his personality are less clearly developed, shares these qualities. While she does have some concern for public opinion (1:7; 8:1), her love is powerful enough to overcome this concern, and she publicly declares her love throughout the song (e.g., 2:5–7; 3:3; 3:10bβ–11; 5:10–16; 8:3–4). When she does show hesitation (5:2ff.), she quickly rebounds and goes out in search of her lover, her desire prevailing over her fears. The lovers' affection and loyalty to each other is never in doubt and never doubted. They praise each other in the same way throughout, call to each other in the same way, express the same desires, and, as I will show in chapter 8, see each other and the world in the same way.

Narrative Frame

The Song has the same setting throughout: the springtime. Although (as Goitein, 1967:284f., points out) other seasons, such as the autumn harvest,

16. As noted above, Fohrer (1970:302) speaks of at least two male and two female protagonists. Some commentators divided the male's lines between Solomon and the shepherd. The first to do so was Ibn Ezra. Later commentators, mostly advocates of the "dramatic theory" who were attempting to reveal a consistent plot-line extending throughout the book, developed this idea in various ways: e.g., Jacobi (1771: see Ginsburg, 1970:87f.), Ewald (1826), Delitzsch (1885), Ginsburg (1970), and S. R. Driver (1913:437–46). This distinction is forced and has not

are suitable backgrounds for songs of love (and are so used in Arabic love poetry), only one season is implied in Canticles. Furthermore, the theme of leaving the city and going to the countryside pervades the Song from beginning to end.

As further evidence for unity, we may add that the Song alludes to events in the girl's life in a way that suggests a certain development in her relations with her brothers. Although this movement does not proceed step by step, it does have its start near the beginning of the book and its culmination near the end. In 1:5–6, after the Shulammite has set down the basic fact of the Song—her love and desire for her kingly beloved—she expresses her vexation at the limitations her brothers placed upon her, making her tend to family duties rather than letting her go out and develop as a woman (tend her own "vineyard"). But even now it seems that things are going to change, for she immediately determines that she will go to find her beloved (1:7).

Furthermore, the material at the end of the Song (at least 8:6–12; vv. 13–14 are puzzling) is appropriate only to the poem's conclusion. As we near the end of the poem, the Shulammite declares the irresistible power of love: her brothers, though still doubting her maturity, agree in principle to give her in marriage and to adorn her generously (8:8–9). By then she has left no doubt as to the power of her love. Her brothers are only giving the family imprimatur. Then her lover declares the incomparable value of love. The statements of love's power and value are most appropriate to the end of the song, for they derive their force and credibility from the experiences of the speakers. At the start of the poem, they would sound grandiose, even somewhat hollow. Now they are a satisfying and convincing statement of truths the poem has demonstrated.

The Unity of the Song

We have looked at four factors that give the Song a fair degree of cohesiveness. How do these factors bear on the problem of the Song's composition?

Those who regard the book as a collection of separate love songs do not regard the unifying factors (to the extent that they grant their existence at all) as evidence for unity of authorship, but rather take them mostly as characteristics of the genre, stock elements that would give any random collection of Hebrew love songs an appearance of unity.[17] We may grant that homogeneity

---

been followed by the major commentators of this century. In any case, the earlier scholars were tracing the same two male characters throughout the book. The distinction between the two personae was supposed to show its dramatic unity, not to prove its disunity.

17. Thus Budde (1898:xvii), Rudolph (1962:99), M. Falk (1982:65), et al. Segal (1962:489) says that the "general uniformity of background, of atmosphere, of mental and moral out-

of this sort, if not of this degree, may indeed be characteristic of certain very narrow genres, such as the Individual Lament in Psalms or New Kingdom solar hymns. If Canticles were not a song but a selection of songs from an extremely uniform body of poems—far more uniform than the Egyptian love poetry—we would still be justified in interpreting its meaning as a whole. We could look for its overall meaning, describe the concept of love shared by the songs of the collection, and ascertain the stereotypical characteristics of the lovers. We would also be justified in looking for loose lines of development in narrative or character, since the presence of the narrative frame suggests that the compiler (if it is indeed to a compiler that the book owes its present form) did give some thought to the general shape of the collection and thus had an idea of what the resulting work would show. But exegesis that went beyond the constituent units would be essentially an examination of the characteristics of the genre.

Some scholars explain the Song's homogeneity entirely or in part by positing a more active editor, a redactor who not only gathered love songs but also composed the repetends or created them by repeating verses and phrases originally found in only one song.[18] What are the implications of this type of editorship for interpretation?

---

look and of language which prevails in all parts of the Song shows that the authors shared one environment and lived in the same age which, as we have seen, was the age of Solomon. Perhaps they formed some sort of a school of popular love poetry the work of which survived in the poems of our Song and in the stray stanzas and fragments scattered in its various parts."

Douglas Young (1967) has argued forcefully against Parry and Lord's theory of the formulaic nature of oral composition, according to which an oral poet draws extensively upon traditional formulas in composing his own work, insisting that repeated phrases and sentences in a single author (whether oral or literate) are usually a matter of an author's repeating a phrase or sentence he himself has composed. Young quotes R. F. Christian's insight on *War and Peace* as applicable to ancient poetry as well. Christian finds in Tolstoy an "insistent use of identical words to express identical content. . . . Tolstoy repeats the same words because he wants to repeat the same idea, which can only be repeated exactly by using again the form in which they originally occurred" (ibid., p. 319). Watters (1976) too rejects the widespread assumption that repeated formulas (he deals specifically with word-pairs) in a single work are usually derived from a traditional stock of formulas rather than from the author's own creativity.

Pope calls attention to the use in Ugaritic literature of "refrains" or "distant repetitions" similar to the repetends in Canticles and asserts their importance for the question of Canticles' literary integrity (1977:50), but he does not say what their implications are for this question. Repetitions and parallel passages in Ugaritic literature in fact usually occur within a single myth cycle (though it is not clear to what degree these are unitary compositions). Of the 48 parallel passages that G. D. Young lists in his study of Ugaritic prosody (1950:129), only 3 are distributed between different myth cycles: 1 Aqht 59–60//51:IV:13–15; ʿAnat pl. IX:III:23–25//2 Aqht VI:48–51; and 67:IV:14–20//2 Aqht VI:4–8.

18. Landsberger sees the book as composed of numerous epigrammatic songs joined by a redactor using "juxtaposition of key words" as his organizing principle (1954:205); similarly Segal (1962:477). Loretz (1971) makes the most thoroughgoing effort to reveal the work of the

Consider what it means in practical terms to transfer a repetend—the adjuration, for example (2:7; 3:5; 5:8; 8:4)—from its presumed original place to other songs.[19] A redactor copying—either from another text or from memory—the song of which 2:7 was a part, comes across this verse and decides to keep it in mind for use elsewhere, perhaps to fill a lack felt in another song, perhaps to create a new cohesiveness in the older material. Doing this with several repetends (although perhaps not with all those I listed), this redactor deliberately weaves new—and very conspicuous—threads into the fabric of the individual songs, threads that extend beyond the originally separate songs and create a network interlacing them in many ways. Without an idea of the collection as a whole, a redactor working in this way would not bother to change the original form of the parts, and therefore the interpreter is quite justified in looking for that overarching idea. We may still feel that the project did not arrive at the cohesiveness that we would expect to see in a unified work,[20] but we should certainly be ready to interpret the new unity thus created. This new unity owes its particular character and overall meaning to the specific choice of material, to the way the repetends were added, and to the placement of the units that form the narrative frame. This is indeed the work of an "editor bent upon connecting the songs," as Jastrow (1921:180) no less bent upon disconnecting them, put it. The resulting collage is a new poem with a meaning quite apart from that of the original components, and the redactor is its author.[21]

In fact, however, there is no reason to posit an editor to explain the Song's cohesiveness and stylistic homogeneity. The most likely explanation of these qualities is that the Song is a single poem composed, originally at least, by a single poet. The poet may have used earlier materials, and later singers and scribes may have made changes of their own, but the result is a unified text.

The repetends in the Song produce a degree of homogeneity that—judging from the Egyptian love poetry and even from the Sacred Marriage songs with their common subject—is not characteristic of ancient Near Eastern love songs. Even if we were to gather Egyptian love songs on the basis of thematic similarity, we could not come up with a collection with as many repetends as Canticles has or with such consistency of character portrayal. Certainly none

---

redactor, attributing to his hand most of the major repetitions, while also attributing a number of words and verses to later interpreters and glossers (see especially pp. 61f.).

19. Jastrow (1921:180), for example, explains the recurrence of the adjuration in this way.

20. Thus Segal (1962:447) denies the unity of the work while asserting that "the collector of these precious gems of ancient Hebrew folk poetry made a brave effort to arrange his varied material in a methodical fashion," without, however, succeeding in this attempt.

21. An example of collage composition from a later period is the practice in Jewish liturgical poetry of composing prayers largely or entirely of biblical quotations with brief connecting phrases. The meanings of the verses in their new settings are often radically different from in their original ones.

of the existing anthological groups show such homogeneity. Not even Group B of P. Harris 500 (nos. 9–16), with its thematic clustering of three songs (nos. 9–11), has so many repetends. Significant repetition of phrases and motifs is to be found only within single songs, in particular "Seven Wishes," "Three Wishes," and "The Stroll." Yet not even these clearly unitary songs show a network of repetends as extensive and complex as that of Canticles. And indeed they do not *have* to do so, for they gain cohesiveness from schematic designs or narrative sequences. Likewise, very few phrases and sentences recur from one Sacred Marriage text to another. The associative sequences too are less likely to be generic conventions than idiosyncratic patterns of thought. The intricate parallels between 2:3 and 5:10–15 outlined above are unlikely to have occurred accidentally, whether or not the author was conscious of their existence. In particular, the punning sequence in 1:13–14 and 7:12–13a points to the workings of an individual mind. While the poet of the Song was free to choose which elements would appear, the elements that do appear tend to maintain a specific order.

Nor is consistency of character portrayal likely to be a characteristic of the genre rather than of an individual poet. Again, judging from Egyptian love poetry, different love songs may be expected to portray different lovers. In the Egyptian poems we find considerable nuancing of character and an interest in portraying diverse personality types. Compare, for example, the hesitant girl who speaks in "The Stroll," the confident but passive girl in "The Crossing," the anxious girl who works herself into a jealous pout in no. 15, and the demanding young lady of no. 1. Or contrast the bold youth of "The Crossing" with the passive yearner of "Seven Wishes." This last case is significant because although these two songs are found in the same text and probably have one author, they portray sharply differing characters, showing that a single poet could conceive of different types of lovers. Likewise, the Sacred Marriage texts, taken as a whole, do not present highly uniform characters.[22] While the main personae remain the same—namely Dumuzi and Inanna or their representatives—they are sometimes portrayed quite differently and even incompatibly in different texts. Thus in one text Inanna chooses Dumuzi enthusiastically and without reservation, while in another she first rejects him in favor of the farmer, consenting to his suit only after lengthy persuasion, promises of gifts, and angry arguments (Kramer, 1969:67–72). Both the Egyptian love songs and the Mesopotamian Sacred Marriage Songs, then, show that even within a specific literary tradition, songs that deal with love and sex cannot be assumed to be so uniform in character portrayal and themes

22. There are extant six poems with five different and often mutually contradictory versions of the romance, and five compositions relating to the marriage, which present unclear, often mutually inconsistent, pictures of the rites (Kramer, 1969:67, 78–80).

that a collection from various texts will accidently create consistent personae.

The narrative frame too, though it is not sufficiently complex and extensive to prove unity by itself, tends to support arguments for literary unity. If the frame were a secondary editorial addition, it would probably have been spliced onto the book at the very beginning and end, rather than being integrated, as it is in Canticles, into the girl's words a few verses into the opening passage and a few verses before the end. It is true that the plot is not developed throughout the body of the Song, being only lightly suggested by the boy's stealth during his nighttime visits and the girl's urging that he flee before morning. But there are good literary reasons why the narrative line is submerged throughout the body of the poem. If the poet were to pursue the development of the girl's relations with her brothers in greater detail, our attention would focus on problems external to the romantic relationship. To make us concentrate on the lovers' private world, the poet keeps the girl's conflict with her brothers well in the background, strictly subordinating the framework-plot to the portrayal of the lovers' relationship.

Multiple Authorship: Zersingen

We are, I believe, justified in interpreting the Song as a unity. A unified work may, however, have many creators. Pickens' conclusions about the creation and transmission of the songs of the 12th century troubadour Jaufré Rudel might well apply, *mutatis mutandis*, to Canticles. Pickens, seeking to explain variations in wording and strophic sequence among the manuscripts, writes:

> Jaufré's courtly lyric is not . . . authoritative in the same sense as Scripture and learned tracts which must be transmitted free from error and interpreted and "perfected" only in glosses kept distinct and separate from the principal text. Rather, his function as "author" is that of a prime creator and generator whose work is freed to be re-created and regenerated. Doubtless, the author himself participated in the regeneration of his own songs, but, doubtless also, other re-creators, scribes, performers, patrons, undertook to perfect received texts consciously and within the intention of the troubadour. Transmitters also became, therefore, authors in their own right. (1978:36)

This process, known in studies of Germanic folk song as *Zersingen*,[23] can occur in both oral and written transmission. The case of Jaufré is particularly interesting because we know that his lyric had a single original author, and yet we find considerable variations in the order, wording, and selection of the

23. Terms such as *Umsingen* or *Zurechtsingen* may better convey the positive adaptive power of the process, a process that lies somewhere on the continuum between individual errors of hearing and conscious artistic variation and that shows the vitality of transmission; see Bausinger, 1980:268f.

strophes in the extant manuscripts, which date to 100–250 years after the author flourished. The variations among even the earliest surviving manuscripts show that in the eyes of the troubadour's immediate successors, variants differing with respect to order and wording could yet be recognized as a single song and attributed to a single author. Many variants might be the author's own work. Each version is an artistic unity (though none is tightly structured), and had one version alone survived it might well be thought an exact copy of a holograph. Since we have only one manuscript tradition for Canticles (the variants in the Versions are very minor), we cannot know if the Song underwent *Zersingen* before it became Scripture. It may be a fair copy of an author's (or compiler's) holograph, or it may be a moment in the fluid stream of transmission frozen in manuscript form. The looseness of its sequential order, however, suggests to me that Canticles is the type of text that would allow for flexibility in its oral and written transmission. Limitless possible permutations of authorship, compilation, transmission, and copying could have produced the version of the Song we have, but the poem would be none the less a unity. The result is the same and can be interpreted in the same way.[24]

Zersingen differs from an editing process of the sort considered earlier. Editorial compilation moves from independent songs toward literary unity (without necessarily attaining it) as several songs are combined and manipulated, to a greater or lesser degree, by a redactor. If the redactor has not reworked the wording too extensively, enough of the individual characteristics of the original songs may be preserved to allow us to identify the constituents of the collection. Literary creation of the sort Pickens hypothesizes for Jaufré, on the other hand, moves from one literary unity to another, as a single author produces a poem that undergoes subsequent permutations. The transmission process might loosen up a structure that was originally more highly organized

24. The process of *Zersingen*, which very likely lies behind the (proto-) MT, can be seen continuing beyond the MT in the Septuagint (as suggested to me by John Hobbins, private communication). LXX-Canticles is a highly literal translation, almost Aquilan in character. Its pluses, then, are undoubtedly evidence of differences in the underlying Hebrew text rather than expansions by the translator. (The LXX minuses, however, seem to represent scribal errors rather than expansions in MT.) The pluses in LXX usually represent elaborations of the sort a singer might make in performing the song from memory, elaborations such as the addition of phrases familiar from elsewhere in the Song. These pluses may also be phrases added by scribes, who also play a part in the *Zersingen* process. As Talmon (1977) has shown, in the formation of the Hebrew Bible there was no absolute distinction among authors, redactors, and copyists, and copyists would often contribute their own modifications in accordance with long-established techniques of Hebrew style and composition. Examples of expansions in LXX: "my dove" added to "my darling, my beautiful" in 2:10 and 13; "on the mountains of Bethel" in 2:9; and "There I will give you my breasts [for *ddy*]" in 6:11; see further 3:1, 5:8, and 8:2. The Peshitta, also a literal translation, has an expansion of this sort at 7:4, adding "who feed among the lilies"; cf. 4:5. (The LXX and Peshitta pluses at 8:2 and 6:2, however, probably represent an earlier text than MT, for the phrases in question were, I believe, inadvertently omitted.)

by, for example, adding passages that disturb the schema. It might, on the other hand, increase the cohesiveness of a song that was originally even less clearly structured by, for example, adding a framework narrative. This process will not, however, dissolve a unified work into a collection of independent constituents, for the later participants in this process are themselves aiming at a literary unity, albeit one slightly different from the original. Their motive, too, is literary creation:

> The same positive principle that moves an author to attempt to perfect his own work must also have impelled transmitters to new creative acts—reordering strophes, fracturing and compressing strophes, composing new formal elements, changing language. (Pickens, 1978:34)

The nature of Canticles does not seem to me to allow reconstruction of its redaction history. Redaction history is possible only when we have an external reference point, such as earlier versions of the text or tradition, or internal reference points, such as generally consistent patterns formed by narrative sequences, chronologies, formal designs, or constellations of ideology—in other words, patterns whose *violation* might be best explained by hypotheses of editorial intervention. We lack such reference points in Canticles. But regardless of how it got into its current form, it is now a unity without discernible stratification.

Constituent Units and the Structure of the Song

To affirm the unity of the Song while denying that it is structured according to a narrative or schematic design, as I have done, is not to assert that the poem is indivisible. Literary units are discernible, even if not always well demarcated. The scene may switch, the dialogue or episode may come to an end, or the subject may change. In the absence of a comprehensive schema, ascertaining the constituent units becomes integral to exegesis, not preparatory to it, since each division must be explained separately. There is no single criterion that will determine all unit divisions, and the criteria we do have are not always decisive.

We follow the flow of dialogue until we sense a break, then prepare to hear about a new subject. An author who wants us to pause or change direction has to give us signals *at that point*. Such signals include change of scene, change of theme (although a unit may contain more than one theme), a prominent inclusio to give a sense of wrapping things up, a generalization that sums up a preceding section, a prominent repetend, which functions like a refrain in breaking the flow of thought and capping off a passage, and an intimation of the culmination of desire, which discreetly closes the scene. Since we lack the aural and visual signals that would have helped the ancient audience segment the song, unit demarcation is often uncertain. But the overall continuity of the song reduces the importance of the unit division in most places. Where the separation of units is more important for understanding the text, the boundary between them can usually be expected to stand out more clearly: there is little danger of a reader or auditor's failing to sense the change of scene at 2:8 or 5:2, for example.

There are different gradations of caesuras, which cannot be adequately indicated by an outline. At 1:5 the girl turns from her lover to the girls of Jerusalem and speaks of her personal situation; certainly something new begins here. Yet there is also continuity, for the maidens are mentioned in the preceding section (1:2–4), where the Shulammite seems to include them in the first-person plural ("We will be glad and rejoice in you . . . ," v. 4b), while in v. 7 she turns back to her lover, who is also addressed in vv. 2–4. So 1:5–6 stands out from vv. 2–4 and 7–8 even while belonging to the same dialogue. Once we recognize both the distinctiveness of 1:2–8 and its general internal continuity, it is not important for exegesis whether we call vv. 2–4, 5–6, and 7–8 three different units or different subsections of the same unit. Where it is essential for the audience to understand a break in continuity, as it is at 5:2, the author usually signals the break quite clearly (5:1 pulls together the motifs of the preceding unit, while 5:2 moves to a different scene on another night). There are, however, places such as 6:11–12 where the obscurity of the text makes the division uncertain even where it may be significant.

I claim no more for the unit division I propose in the commentary than that it is a convenient way of arranging the book for purposes of discussion. It attempts to point out the natural pauses in the flow of thought without subdividing segments whose internal bonds are greater than their connections to other segments of the poem. The Song is like a meandering river. It flows continuously yet twists and turns at irregular intervals. Sometimes sharp bends mark off short sections of flow; sometimes the river flows straight for a longer stretch before turning. The unit division I propose is only an attempt to point out the main bends.

I find no overall schema or continuous development in the poem, beyond the loose narrative framework provided by 1:5–6 and 8:6–12. Within this framework the course of events does not move in the straight line of narrative progression, but rather twists and wanders affectionately through different parts of one territory. This movement is well described by Cook:

> From beginning to end the lovers go from seeking each other to finding each other. But this action does not move in a straight line from separation to union: it leaps, in impulsions of voiced desire, from anticipated joy to actualized joy, and back again. Any speech may discover itself anywhere on the circle of seeking and finding. (1968:133)

The basic love story repeats itself, for lovers—and not only those in our song—must seek each other continually, time after time, as long as their love exists; one "finding" is never the end of the story. Near the end of the Song, the cycle of seeking and finding pauses for the declarations of love's power and value and for the brothers' consent, but the poem does not end there. Two rather enigmatic verses (8:13–14) set us back to a point earlier in the cycle, as the boy again asks to hear his beloved's voice, and she again tells him to flee. The poet breaks off, not with the stasis of familial acceptance, but with an image of movement, the gazelle on the mountains. The conclusion of the Song is not the end of this love story, but only a pause in its movement. Love of the sort shown in Canticles must be ever dynamic.

Canticles is a love song of a new sort. It is longer than any of the Egyptian songs but less tightly organized in its surface structure. In a study of theme and structure in the French novel, E. H. Falk concluded that in novels where story and plot receive less emphasis, the generic coherence of themes becomes more important in creating the unity of the thematic fabric (1967: 178). This is true of Canticles, where to compensate for the looseness of structure, the poem achieves unity through coherence of thematic and verbal texture. The Song takes a single romance and turns it around and around like a gem, displaying all its facets. The reader finally sees the gem as a whole, and the order in which the facets were shown does not much matter.

CHAPTER 5

What the Love Songs Were Used For: Function and Social Setting

Form Criticism and Life Setting

An enigma: a secular song of sexual love in the canon of sacred scripture. To solve this enigma scholars often assign the poem a function seemingly more appropriate to religious literature, and then use that presumed function as a guide to interpretation. I think, however, that the love songs, Egyptian and Israelite, originally had only this connection with religion: the banquets at which they were sung were commonly held during the leisure time afforded by religious holidays.[1]

To ask about the love songs' extrinsic functions[2]—what they were originally meant to be used for[3]—is to inquire into their life-setting (*Sitz im*

1. The question of whether the Song is a drama is distinct from the question of its secularity and largely separate from the question of its original setting. If it is a drama, it could have been either a religious or a secular one, and it could have been presented in any one of a variety of settings. Drama is a way of presenting a story or situation to the audience. I will therefore discuss this question in chapter 6.

2. Their intrinsic purpose is, of course, to express their meanings and to influence their readers in accordance with the literary and (possibly) didactic or rhetorical goals of their author.

3. That is, meant by the author. I follow Hirsch (1967) in regarding authorial meaning as (at least in principle) recoverable and as the primary object of interpretation. Any later uses a text might be put to, such as synagogal reading, are to be deemed part of its *significance*. Hirsch draws the distinction between meaning and significance thus: "*Meaning* is that which is represented by a text; it is what the author meant by his use of a particular sign sequence; it is what the signs represent. *Significance*, on the other hand, names a relationship between that meaning and a

Leben), the recurrent situation or social occasion for which songs such as these were created. This is one of the principal questions that form criticism seeks to answer, but one not always best answered by form-critical methods. Form criticism has sought to isolate units within Canticles that were once independent songs and to determine from their content the type of situation for which such texts were composed.

There has been no comprehensive form-critical study of the Egyptian love songs. Hermann (1959:124–36) discusses three types (*Gattungen*) of love songs, the Description Song (*Beschreibungslied* or *waṣf*), the Alba (*Tagelied*), and the Paraclausithyron (*Türklage*). He hesitates to assign a specific life-setting to the Description Song, suggesting only that the occasion of a festival could inspire a youth to sing the praises of his beloved (p. 125). The Alba would have been called forth by the need for unmarried lovers to part in the morning (p. 130), and the Paraclausithyron by a lover's being refused admittance to his beloved's house (p. 133).

Several commentaries and studies of Canticles, on the other hand, apply form-critical observations, first dividing it into a number of short songs, then grouping these into literary types (*Gattungen*), and then undertaking to ascertain the life-settings in which these *Gattungen* originated. The most valuable form-critical studies of Canticles are Horst (1935) and Murphy (1981). In all such studies, the life-setting commonly suggested for most of the units of Canticles is the celebration of weddings. Thus Horst, who does not attempt to determine the life-setting of most of the types he defines, locates the "Description Song" in a nuptial setting. Würthwein (1969) finds the wedding to be the life-setting for at least 24 of the 29 songs and fragments into which he divides the book. For example, he supposes 1:2–4 to be a wedding song expressing the bride's desire for her husband to bring her home, and 4:1–7 he explains as praise lavished on the bride at her wedding (see ad loc.). Murphy's form-critical survey is far more cautious in determining the life-settings of the 30 songs he marks out in Canticles, observing that most are "love poems which can be uttered in the innumerable settings which are associated with the relationship of lovers" (1981:103).

Even if we suppose that Canticles and all the Egyptian song-groups were composed of originally independent songs, I doubt that we are justified in distributing either the various Egyptian love songs or the units of the Song of Songs among different life-settings, and in any case we cannot read the life-settings for which the songs were written *directly* out of the fictional settings depicted within the love songs. The fictional setting of the *wechsel* of the me-

---

person, or a conception, or a situation, or indeed anything imaginable" (1967:8). Meaning (by this definition) is stable, while significance, the "meaning-to" someone, constantly changes. Similarly a text with a single primary, intended function may take on many and diverse secondary functions, including some even the author could not have imagined.

dieval *Minnesang*, for example, was often an exchange of affectionate messages delivered by a messenger, but we should not assume that such songs actually were delivered by messenger. The *wechsel* was rather one of many types of song composed for the amusement of the well-to-do classes and the court. Cant 5:2–6:3 is set in the streets of Jerusalem, but that does not make it a "street song." It is no less gratuitous to assume that because 1:12–14 refers to banqueting, it is a "table song" (Krinetzki, 1964), or that 8:8–10 was sung at a marriage celebration, where the girl "justifies her conduct against the programmatic supervision of her brothers" (Murphy, 1981:123). The scene shown in a song is not necessarily the life-setting for which it was composed.

Therefore, instead of proceeding from a consideration of the "form" of the individual songs or of their constituent units (though this may be justified for some literary genres), I will ask about the function of the love song genre as a whole in Egypt and in Israel, considering which of the settings available in these cultures is the context most suitable for the creation of such songs. I will approach the question of life-setting by narrowing the range of possibilities: that is, by excluding situations for which songs about love might well be written but for which the love songs at hand were not. (This negative approach is useful because it can be far more misleading to interpret a text in accordance with an irrelevant social context than to interpret it without regard to social context.) Most of the situations I will exclude have actually been proposed by various scholars as life-settings for the love songs, but in certain cases I will be trying to anticipate theories about the Egyptian songs that might be raised by analogy with theories about the Song of Songs.

Courting Songs

Canticles is not a courting song. R. Shimon ben Gamaliel (late first century C.E.), recalling the celebrations of the 15th of Ab and the Day of Atonement, told how the girls of Jerusalem would go out to dance in the vineyards and urge the young men to choose wives:

> And what did [the maidens] say? "Young man, lift up your eyes and see what you would choose for yourself. Do not consider good looks; consider rather family, (as it is said): "Charm is deceitful and beauty a vanity, etc." It is also said: "Give her of the fruit of her hands and let her works praise her" (Prov 31:30–31). Likewise it says: "Go forth, daughters of Zion, and see King Solomon, in the crown that his mother put on him on the day of his wedding, and on the day of the gladness of his heart" (Cant 3:11). "On the day of his wedding"—this is the giving of the law; "and on the day of the gladness of his heart"—this is the building of the Temple, may it be rebuilt speedily in our days! Amen! (M. Taanit 4:8)

While this mishna has the girls quoting Canticles in their invitation to potential mates, we cannot conclude that the Song, any more than Prov 31:10–31—or the allegorical interpretation of Cant 3:11—originated in that setting. R. Shimon quotes the Song, along with Prov 31, in the way typical for quoting proof texts (*w^eken hu^ʾ ʾomer*), because he considers these scriptural verses appropriate to the occasion. Similarly, the injunctions about the vanity of beauty and the importance of family connections do not seem authentic in the mouths of girls dancing in the vineyards. Rather, they belong to R. Shimon's idealized notion of what was said on such occasions.

Canticles of course includes passages that, taken in isolation, could be used by one lover in courting another (e.g., 2:10b–14; 4:8–15; 7:12–14). But the poem as a whole, including as it does the words of both lovers, with the boy's words of admiration and persuasion sometimes incorporated into the girl's narration (2:10b–14), would not have been written for courting.

The Song is certainly not a stenographic record of songs sung by the young people in the streets and vineyards. Its artistry and control of language far surpass what we could reasonably expect adolescents to produce for their flirtations.

Wedding Songs

Because of the widely held opinion that Canticles consists of or includes wedding songs, we might consider whether the Egyptian love songs were meant to be sung at weddings. The Egyptians do not, in fact, seem to have had any special wedding ceremonies or marriage celebrations of sacral character. Mention of wedding festivities of any sort is very rare. In the Ptolemaic story of Setne Khamwas (Setne I), a woman says that on the day of her marriage, her husband, who was the king's son and her brother, "made holiday with me, and he entertained all Pharaoh's household" (Lichtheim, 1980:128). The marriage of Ramses II to the Hittite princess may have been accompanied by public festivities (KRI III, 251), but these festivities may not have been specifically wedding feasts. Nuptial celebrations in Egypt were (to the extent the scanty evidence allows us to surmise) not religious solemnities, but simply parties in honor of a happy occasion.[4] Since we do not know just what marriage festivities were like in ancient Egypt, we cannot say whether such songs could have been sung for them. In any case, love songs do not seem to be

4. The formation of a marriage in Egypt was essentially a familial-social act devoid of religious character. Marriage consisted of the (ideally) permanent cohabitation of a man and a woman in a shared household, and sometimes (at least in later periods) was accompanied by a marriage contract. The contract was separate from the act of matrimony and could be written some time later. For a comprehensive study of Egyptian marriage, see Allam, 1981:116f.

intended to serve the specific needs of a wedding more than those of any other festivity. They never speak of the couple as presently married; on the contrary, they often tell of the obstacles still on the way to the fulfillment of love (nos. 4, 20D, 32, 36, etc.). The lovers sometimes must come from afar to get together (nos. 5, 8). While at times they express the hope that they will spend their lives together (nos. 14, 18, 20B), it is generally clear that they are not yet married. None of the songs express the hopes for the couple's future that would be appropriate in wedding festivities.

Nor is Canticles a wedding song. To be sure, it may well have been sung at weddings as part of the general entertainment, along with timbrel playing, dances, and songs of all sorts, for the general theme of love would certainly be suitable to the wedding atmosphere. But little in the Song connects it directly with weddings and marriage, and—more important for interpretation—the couple that speak in it are not a bride and groom.

The lovers in Canticles are not married or getting married as yet. The Shulammite is still under her brothers' control (1:6), or at least they would have it so. The lovers' behavior in general is not that of newlyweds. No bridegroom would have to sneak up to his beloved's house at night, peeking in the windows, and asking to be let in. Neither (one hopes) would a new bride have to leave her bed at night to chase about the city looking for her husband. Nor would the lovers behave in this fashion if they were formally betrothed and her family recognized the youth as her future husband. No betrothed woman—let alone a new bride—would have to wish that her beloved were like a brother to her so that she could kiss him openly and bring him home to mother (8:1f.). In 8:8 her betrothal is spoken of as an event in the future: "when she is spoken for." The lovers go off to the countryside to make love, not to a bed of matrimony. Nor would the Song be an appropriate "autobiography" for a bride: it is not recited from the vantage point of a bride at her wedding looking back at things she did in the past, many of of which she would in any case be hesitant to relate to assembled wedding guests. Even if the Song was sung at weddings—and there is no evidence that it was—it was quite obviously not sung *about* the wedding or about the couple getting married. It would therefore be a mistake to impose a wedding interpretation on the Song.

Only two brief passages, 3:7–11 and 8:8–9, speak of marriage explicitly. Cant 3:7–11 describes Solomon's bed and refers to the crown his mother made for his wedding day. While this passage *may* have been a wedding song before its inclusion in Canticles, in context it is part of the couple's playful and fantastic description of their garden bower as if it were the royal bed (see commentary). However this passage is to be interpreted, its presence does not make Canticles into a song that is about marriage or that was written specifically for weddings. In Cant 8:8–9 the Shulammite's brothers promise to give her ornaments when, sometime in the future, she is spoken for in marriage. Cant 3:4 and 8:2 also seem to allude to marriage, but again as a hoped-for event in the indefinite future.

Various parts of the Song (e.g., 2:1–7) may have been sung at weddings—as they are today. The Praise Songs, too, could have been sung at weddings, just as *waṣf*s were sung at the Syrian weddings observed by Wetzstein.[5] We should, however, observe that the *waṣf*s among the Egyptian love songs (nos. 31, 54, and the first part of no. 3) are in no way set in the context of weddings, and the *waṣf* spoken by Ludingira about his mother (see n. 23 below, and chapter 7) is certainly not related to marriage. The Arabic *waṣf*s themselves are sung on various occasions, not just at weddings, nor are the numerous *waṣf*s in the *Arabian Nights* set in weddings (see Rudolph, 1962: 103f., with references). There is therefore no reason to assume that the *waṣf*s in Canticles must be wedding songs. Furthermore, the Sacred Marriage Songs, which *are* meant for a wedding ritual, contain no *waṣf*s. In any case, in Canticles the Praise Songs are integrated into a dialogue between two lovers whom we know from the rest of the song, and these lovers are clearly not celebrating their wedding. Cant 5:10–16 is particularly well integrated into the narrative, being the Shulammite's response to a question asked by the girls of Jerusalem.

Canticles' life-setting is not a wedding celebration. The lovers are unmarried, and the essential hopes of a new marriage—fertility, health, prosperity—are not touched upon. I cannot help agreeing with Gerleman's explanation of many scholars insistence on putting the Song's celebration of sex comfortably between the covers of the marriage bed:

> Die Forderung, dass es sich bei jeder Erwähnung sinnlich erotischer Szenen um Hochzeit und Ehe handeln müsst lässt sich nur als das Hineinlesen einer kirchlichen Eheethik in das Hohelied verstehen und führt wieder aufs neue zu willkürlichen Textinterpretationen. (1965:207)[6]

5. Wetzstein first described 19th century Syrian weddings and compared the songs sung at them to Canticles in "Die syrische Dreschtafel," 1873 (see also his appendix to Delitzsch's commentary, 1885). His observations led Budde to see in Canticles "the text book of a Palestinian-Israelite wedding" (1898:xix). A. Harper argued persuasively against Budde's approach at length (1907:74–93), showing that the wedding-week theory cannot explain the present form, personae, events, or general character of the Song, and further that the Song is quite unlike the wedding songs that Wetzstein described. Recent commentators, most of whom see the Song as a collection of short songs, generally explain only some of these units as wedding songs. Rudolph, for example, says that only 1:2–4; 1:9–17; 4:8; 4:9–11; 4:12–5:1; 7:1–6; and 8:5–7 reflect the nuptial setting (1962:103). Gordis says that "it is clear that some of the lyrics in the Song of Songs are not connected with wedding ceremonies or with married love at all" (1961:17), but he does not say which these are.

6. "The insistence that every mention of sensuous erotic scenes must deal with wedding and marriage can only be understood as the reading of an ecclesiastical marriage ethic into the Song

Love Magic

Perhaps the idea that Canticles is love magic is unlikely to arise, but Davis has argued that the Cairo Love Songs constitute a sort of magic charm whose utterance was supposed to guarantee an unbroken "cycle of love" (1980:113). Yet love songs are fundamentally different from magical spells. Here is an example of love magic:

> Hail to thee, O Reᶜ-Ḥarakhte, Father of the Gods!
> Hail to you, O ye Seven Ḥatḥors
> Who are adorned with strings of red thread!
> Hail to you, ye Gods lords of heaven and earth!
> Come make so-and-so (fem.) born of so-and-so come after me,
> Like an ox after grass,
> Like a servant after her children,
> Like a drover after his herd!
> If you do not make her come after me,
> Then I will set fire to Busiris and burn up Osiris.
>
> (Smither, 1941:131)

If the love songs are in any way love spells, they are very subtle ones, which Egyptian magic never is elsewhere. Magic spells exhibit their magical character plainly, making demands on the gods or on unspecified supernatural forces and enforcing them with threats, entreaties, and strange potions.[7] To add force to the demands, they are often repeated many times (preferably seven) in different ways. Although this repetition may accidentally produce a parallelism that gives the spell a lyrical quality, as in the spell quoted above, literary artistry is essentially irrelevant to the working of magic. The most fundamental difference is that in our love songs the speaker never tries to

---

of Songs and leads again and again to arbitrary interpretations of the text." An example in hand is Budde's defense of his wedding-song interpretation: "Es handelt sich also nicht um Liebeslieder schlechthin, etwa gar um die Zeugnisse einer unkeuschen Dichterliebe, sondern um Gelegenheitsgedichte im engsten Sinne des Wortes, und zwar solche auf die vollkommen gesetzliche Liebe eines Gatten und seiner Gattin. . . . Damit ist der Stoff allerdings, wie es die dramatische Auffassung will, vollkommen moralisch; denn die Ehe ist die Grundlage aller Gesellschaftsmoral" (1989:xix f.). ("We are thus not dealing with love songs as such, and certainly not with evidence for the unchaste love of a poet, but with *occasional* poems in the narrowest sense of the word, and, in fact, such as deal with the completely lawful love of a husband and his wife. . . . Thus the material is indeed completely moral, as the dramatic interpretation would have it; for marriage is the basis of all social morality.") I do not think it is necessary to set the Song in a wedding ceremony in order to recognize its morality, which is founded on the values of loyalty and devotion.

7. E.g., the London-Leyden Demotic papyrus, 15,1–21 (Griffith and Thompson, 1904: 105f. = Brier, 1980:288).

force love, either by natural or supernatural means. Not even wishes, such as we have in "Three Wishes," and "Seven Wishes" try to manipulate reality in the way magic does.

Religious Poetry

One vast and notable area of public and personal activity that it is *not* Canticles' or the Egyptian love poems' purpose to serve is religion, the manifold manifestations of belief about the divine and the expressions of reverence toward the gods. The love songs do not attempt to show anything about the gods or their relations with mankind.

THE EGYPTIAN LOVE SONGS

Granted that the distinction between the religious and the secular was less sharp in the ancient world than it is today (Davis, 1980: 112), the Egyptian love songs are still well on the secular side of the border. There are a few references to gods and cultic activities, but these are incidental and of minor importance. The songs make no attempt to impart beliefs about the gods, to commune with them through private prayer, or to adore them and influence their will through cultic worship.

The lovers are not gods, nor do they represent gods. Although the girl in "The Stroll" has divine qualities in her lover's eyes (no. 31), she is not a goddess but a shy young girl (hardly Hathor-like) living at home with her mother. The girl in no. 20C calls her lover "my god," but this is just a hyperbolic expression of esteem. We hear his thoughts soon after and can see that he is quite mortal.

It has not yet been suggested, so far as I know, that the lovers in the Egyptian love songs are divinities, but Davis has argued briefly that although the lovers are human, they take on the *guises* of gods in a way that is to be compared to "serious transformations" of the sort so important in Egyptian religion (1980: 112). Thus in addition to the fictions that White describes (1978: 112),[8] there is a "divine fiction" in which the lovers are "transformed" into gods: the "brother" is Re, the "sister" Hathor, or, in the Cairo Love Songs, the boy is Nefertem and the girl Sothis (Davis, 1980: 112).

Now while it is true that many mortuary spells are meant to allow the dead to turn into gods—"any god that a man might wish"—the lovers in the

8. These are the three "travesties" or disguises that Hermann argues are important in Egyptian love poetry: the "'Ritter'-Travestie," the "'Diener'-Travestie," and the "'Hirten'-Travestie" (1959: 111–24), on which see my remarks in "Excursus: The 'Travesties'."

love songs are not even pretending to be gods. On the contrary, if the girl personified Hathor ("The Golden One") or were taking on her guise, it would make no sense for her to pray to that goddess (as she does in no. 36), or to declare that the goddess has destined her for the boy she loves (no. 32). Gods can take on human form in Egyptian belief, and humans can become gods, so if the lovers were in any way divine there would be no reason for the poets or scribes to hide it. Moreover, divinity can be easily indicated in Egyptian by the use of the god determinative, which is used freely in connection with anything associated with divinity. Inasmuch as girls are female and boys male, there will inevitably be similarities between them and female and male deities. But the love songs themselves do not draw any "extended analogy between divine and human affairs" (contrary to Davis, 1980:112).

None of the love songs are prayers or hymns to Hathor.[9] We know that people prayed to Hathor in her temple for success in love. She "hears the requests of all maidens who weep" (Naville, 1913: pl. 9a). The love songs contain some *references* to prayers (nos. 21F, 35), in one place (no. 36) a line of prayer is quoted ("O Golden One, put that in her [sc. my mother's] heart!"); and in another (no. 21F) a boy expresses a wish that he wants his god to fulfill ("May he grant me my lady every day!"). But such prayers are mentioned or quoted in a manner incidental to the portrayal of the lovers and their situations. The lovers' thoughts may include prayers, but the songs themselves are not prayers.

Schröder (1951) pointed to various motifs he felt were derived from myth or cult and argued that the love songs are secularized sacral lyrics, whose formerly sacred character bears on their present meaning. Now, even if we were to accept all the connections he claims between love song motifs and mythology, we would not have to conclude that the songs were originally sacred, but only that they incorporated some reworked sacral motifs. But in fact the connections he asserts are extremely tenuous. For example, with the help of a northeast Siberian legend and a saying from the Pyramid Texts, he explains the girl's offer of her breast to her lover (no. 1) as derived from the mortuary motif of the goddess nursing the king. Or when the girl in no. 18 says, "I am your first sister" (he translates *tpy* "first" (in time); it literally means "foremost" here), we are to think of Isis, the "first sister" of the mythical primordial time. The comparison between a girl and a garden in no. 18 he associ-

9. Contrary to Bleeker, 1973b:85: "Weil Hathor die Göttin der Liebe war, wandten die verliebten Leute sich gern an sie mit der Bitte, dass sie ihr Liebesverlangen erfüllen möge. Das ist die Tendenz der schönen Liebeslieder, die der Hathor gewidmet sind." ("Because Hathor was the goddess of love, people in love readily turned to her with the prayer that she fulfill their longing for love. This is the intention of the lovely love songs, which were dedicated to Hathor.") Although Hathor was the goddess of love and had many songstresses in her service, neither the love song texts nor any external evidence suggests that the love songs were dedicated to her.

ates with hymns to the Nile, for the Nile fertilizes the fields. The particular sacral motifs that Schröder argues for are doubtful at best. There are indeed a number of "sacral motifs" in the songs,[10] but that does not show a sacral origin for the genre, any more than bird-trapping motifs show that the songs originated among bird-trappers.

Again, allusions to deities are undoubtedly present in "The Crossing" (see Derchain, 1975, and above, no. 20C, n. a, no. 20D, n. c, and no. 20G, n. e): the lotus, the primeval flood Nun, and the goddess Menqet are all Egyptian divinities. But the lovers are not gods, nor are their experiences religiously typological. Nor do these allusions give us a clue to the life-setting of the songs in which they appear.

The Egyptians felt divinity's presence everywhere. They were, as Herodotus saw, the most religious of peoples (II.37.1). It is then all the more striking that in the love songs the gods stay well in the background. Hermann does not exaggerate in observing:

> Es muss auffallen, dass die Gottheit niemals als übergeordnete Macht gekennzeichnet wird, der sich der Mensch gerade auch in seiner Liebe unterstellte. Vielmehr werden die einbezogenen Götter dem Leben in den Liedern untergeordnet gezeigt. Das persönliche Erlebnis ist das zunächst Gegebene, wovon ausgegangen wird, und dem sich die göttliche Macht anzubequemen hat. (1959:84)[11]

THE SONG OF SONGS

The understanding of the Song that has dominated traditional Jewish (and Christian) interpretation is that it is a divinely inspired work whose function is to teach about God's relationship with Israel (or in Christian interpretation, Christ's relationship with the Church). Such interpreters generally explained the Song as allegory, using a variety of midrashic expository techniques.[12]

10. In no. 31 the girl is compared to Sothis. In no. 20C the girl calls her lover "my god, my lotus" (= Nefertem). In no. 47 the boy addresses the door of a girl's house as if it were the divine door to the afterlife. "The Orchard" (nos. 28–30) mentions giving offerings to the trees, as if they were divinities. The sycamore-goddess motif may underlie the picture of the gracious sycamore in no. 30. See the comments on these songs.

11. "It is surprising that divinity is never characterized as a superior power to whom man subjects himself even in his love. Rather the gods who are referred to are shown in the songs as subordinated to life. The personal experience is the primary given, from which everything proceeds, and to which the divine power must accommodate itself."

12. The sources for early Jewish allegorical interpretation are the Targum, three midrashic compilations (*Canticles Rabba*, *Aggadat Shir Hashirim*, *Midrash Shir Hashirim*), a number of remarks in the Talmud and early homiletical midrashim, and a fragment from an unknown midrash; see Urbach, 1971:247. Origen is a valuable source for reconstructing Tannaitic exposition of the Song; see ibid. Schneekloth (1977:295–331) classifies the methods the Targum uses in its paraphrastic exposition thus: allegory (i.e., interpreting words as tropes), different pointing of Hebrew words, same root with different meaning, similar sound, change of consonant, transposition of consonants, *gematria*, *notarikon*, and extension of the meaning of a word.

Midrashic interpretation sees in the Song mystical allegories (describing the quest of the individual soul for God and revealing mysteries of God's appearance in the Chariot),[13] historical allegories (telling of the relationship between God and the community of Israel), and eschatological allegories (giving reassurance of the coming of the Messiah). Since the allegorical interpretations usually (but not always)[14] identify the male lover with God and the female with Israel, we can say in summary that the allegorical approach understands the Song as representing the love between God and Israel (or the individual Israelite). The premedieval expositors do not, however, try to give an overall meaning to the book. They usually treat verses, and sometimes words, in isolation, using the wording of the Song to formulate and reinforce diverse ideas or to exemplify various events and teachings.[15]

As modern commentators generally recognize, the Song was not written as an allegory of the love between Israel and God. Equality is the essence of the relationship between the young lovers in the Song, and this can hardly have been intended as a model for God's relation to Israel (or to an individual soul). Patriarchal marriage, where the man initiates the relationship and provides for a woman, from whom he can then demand fidelity, is a more appropriate metaphor for the relationship between God and Israel and is so used by the prophets, most notably Hosea and Ezekiel. But premarital courtship of equals such as we see in the Song, where the only bond is mutual attraction and equivalent need, and where full consummation depends on social acceptance by individuals outside the relationship, is a poor correlative of the relationship between God the master and Israel his possession. The equality of the lovers and the quality of their love, rather than the Song's earthy sensuality, are what makes their union an inappropriate analogy for the bond between God and Israel.

The prophets use marriage as a metaphor to emphasize the heinousness of Israel's apostasy and to explain how reconciliation is yet possible (e.g., Hos 2–3; Isa 5:1–7; Ezek 16, 23). In the Song, on the other hand, there is no infidelity or reconciliation. In any case, when the prophets use the marriage metaphor, they make it quite clear who the partners are and what the parable

13. *Shiur Komah*, a fragmentary text that represents a second century C.E. tradition, interprets 5:11–16 as a description of the mystical body of God (Scholem, 1960:36–42; Lieberman, 1960:118–26).

14. Cant. Rab. (ii 31), for example, takes "your [fem.] appearance" (*mar'ayik, mar'eyk*) in 2:14 as referring to God's appearance at Sinai. In the Targum, the male lover is identified with Israel in 2:2, and in a few verses where the female is speaking, the words are attributed to God (2:10–12; 7:14). The words spoken by the youth in 7:10 are put into the mouths of Daniel and his companions. On the whole, however, the allegorical identification of the male with God and the female with Israel is carried through consistently (Schneekloth, 1977:310–17).

15. The Targum (early Islamic period) seems to be the first attempt to read the Song as a historical sequence.

means. Thus in Hos 2 the speaker is not an unidentified lover, but God himself, who addresses his unfaithful beloved in the feminine singular and also in the masculine plural (2:20). In 3:1 God tells Hosea to love an adulterous woman "just as God loves the Israelites, though they turn to other gods and love fruit clusters." In Isa 5:1–7 the lover (*dod*) and his beloved (who is spoken of under the figure of a vineyard) are not identified at first, but at the end of the song Isaiah says: "for the vineyard of the Lord of hosts is the House of Israel and the people of Judah are the planting in which he delights" (5:7a). The lover and the beloved are explicitly identified as God and Jerusalem in Ezek 16. In Ezek 23 God identifies the two women he loves as Samaria and Jerusalem (23:4), even though when the husband is clearly God, as in this chapter, there is never really any doubt about the identity of the beloved "woman" or "women."

In general, parables and allegories do not hide their identity. Their purpose is to give insight into a truth that might otherwise be difficult to accept or comprehend, so they must invite interpretation. Why then would the Song hide its allegorical function if it had one? The far greater part of midrashic exegesis found nothing under the literal "covering" that would have to be hidden. While one ancient tradition of mystical interpretation saw truly esoteric mysteries in the Song, the dominant historical and eschatological interpretations found none. It was the literal sense that almost all premodern exegetes felt had to be concealed. The midrashic interpretation of Canticles differs from that of other books not in the nature of its exposition, but in its denial of the significance of the literal meaning.

The midrashic interpreters (in this case almost all premodern interpreters) considered the literal meaning to be unworthy of inspired scripture, an unseemly covering hiding a treasure. As Shemariah ben Elijah of Crete (1275–1355) put it:

> If [the words of the Song] had their literal meaning, there would be nothing in the world so thoroughly profane as they, and there would have been nothing more damaging to Israel than the day the Song of Songs was given to them, for its literal meaning stirs up desire, above all sexual desire, than which nothing is more blameworthy. (quoted in Leiman, 1976:201)

Allegorical exegesis, thinking to reveal the treasure that lay under the cover of literal meaning, in effect covered the literal meaning under layers of allegory. These layers, though beautiful and valuable in themselves, lie outside the scope of this book.

The difficulty with the allegorical approach is that it is too easy to apply. By way of *reductio ad absurdum*, we could just as easily interpret the *Egyptian* love songs as allegories of God's love for Israel. We could say that in Egyptian song no. 4 Israel declares that her loyalty to Yahweh will persist even if she is exiled to the four corners of the earth, while in no. 8 she waits for the Shekinah to appear at the Temple, where booths (for the Feast of Tabernacles?) are set up. Conversely, we could interpret Canticles as a *pagan* religious allegory, with the girl representing, say, Isis (or Ishtar), who must search for her brother Osiris (or Tammuz), who is lost in the netherworld (5:2–7). Or we might say in general that Canticles celebrates the love and sacred marriage of a goddess and a god. The latter form of religious interpretation, which will be discussed in the next section, has in fact been attempted and vigorously defended.

Love Songs and the Sacred Marriage

None of the Egyptian love songs are suited to a role in a Sacred Marriage liturgy, which, as the Mesopotamian Sacred Marriage songs show, can be expected to emphasize strongly the connection between the divine sexual union and the fertility of the land. In fact, we have no clear evidence for a Sacred Marriage ritual in Egypt. Fairman has claimed that Hathor's visit to Horus at Edfu, a festival described at length in Ptolemaic texts, was a Sacred Marriage (1954:196ff.). But, as Bleeker has shown, it is doubtful whether a true *hieros gamos* took place on that occasion (1973a:95–101).

Fertility was, of course, a major concern in Egyptian cult, and one song with a possible tangential connection to a fertility cult is no. 8, where the lovers meet in a booth or pavilion in a garden near the temple at Heliopolis. The garden is called a *dd*, which may mean "love garden." But although the lovers are meeting in a cultic setting, one *possibly* associated with fertility, the poem itself is not concerned with fertility and shows no signs of playing a role in the cult. It is simply *about* lovers who meet at a festival.

It is curious that although no one (so far as I know) has argued that love songs are a liturgy for a divine marriage ritual in Egypt, where such a ritual would be a legitimate expression of mythology, many scholars have argued that similar love songs served just that purpose in Israel, where such a ritual would be totally incompatible with the attitudes toward religious activity reflected in the other religious literature that has survived from that culture.

Neuschotz de Jassy (1914) interpreted Canticles as a litany describing the resurrection of Osiris (called Solomon) from the land of the dead (Jerusalem). Happily, this theory found no following. Erbt (1906) was the first to argue that the Song describes the love between the fertility god Tammuz and the goddess of love, Ishtar. This hypothesis first received serious attention following Meek's vigorous advocacy (1922, 1924a, 1924b). Wittekindt (1925) and Schmökel (1956) wrote commentaries interpreting the Song as a liturgy for a Sacred Marriage, Schmökel thoroughly rearranging the verses to produce an orderly three-scene liturgical drama.

According to the Tammuz-Ishtar myth, when Tammuz descended to the netherworld and Ishtar went to seek him, all the earth withered and died. When she found him and brought him back to the land of the living, the earth too revived. These events were presented yearly in ritual dramas. The drama and celebrations of this cult included, according to one hypothesis, a Sacred Marriage in which king and priestess represented the god and goddess in sexual acts that were supposed to restore fertility to the sun-scorched earth. Using methods reminiscent of allegorical interpretation, Meek hunted for words and images in the Song that could be explained as allusions to mythical events or ritual acts. Thus *dodi* ("my beloved") is said to refer to the god Dod or Dadu, supposedly the Palestinian counterpart of Tammuz; myrrh, to which the lovers are compared, was used as incense in the festival of Adonis-Tammuz; raisin cakes, mentioned in 2:5, are connected with the Ishtar cult (cf. Jer 7:18; 44:19); gazelles and hinds are symbols of Astarte; and so on (Meek, 1922).

Schmidt (1926) and Rowley (1952:220–32) have, I believe, shown how tenuous the suggested connections are. At most, as Rowley says, the Song contains isolated linguistic and literary remnants from the Tammuz-Ishtar cult, these having entirely lost their religious meaning. But in fact not even remnants are clearly evidenced.

Kramer (1969) offered a modified version of Meeks' theory. He sought to explain the Song as a liturgy for the Sacred Marriage between the *king* and the goddess Astarte (= Ishtar-Inanna). Kramer found parallels to the Song of Songs in the joyous Sumerian songs from the Sacred Marriage ritual rather than in the Akkadian Tammuz dirges. The Sacred Marriage was enacted—not necessarily annually—in Mesopotamia for some two thousand years.[16] Six songs, representing five versions of the love story of the Sumerian shepherd-king Dumuzi (= Tammuz) and his sister Inanna (Ishtar), have been discovered, as well as five texts that describe the marriage and wedding night.[17] The texts, which date from the Neo-Sumerian period (ca.2000 B.C.E.), describe in detail the lovers' desire for each other and praise their sexual attractions. Although the meaning of these compositions and the details of the ceremonies are still obscure in many ways, it appears that the king (the incarnation of Dumuzi and the representative of the land) ritually married the goddess (represented by a priestess) and had intercourse with her. This ritual was intended to ensure abundance and fertility for the land. In the following passage, as the king is led to his divine bride, the poet prays that she will bless the king and his reign with good fortune:

16. Thus Kramer, 1969:49. But Renger (RA:II, 258) says that there is no evidence for the continuation of the ritual after the first dynasty of Isin, 1794 B.C.E.

17. Jacobsen says that while the texts dealing with Dumuzi's wedding are ritual in nature, those telling of his courtship are "lightweight stuff," popular ditties whose only apparent purpose was entertainment (1976:27, 32).

May the lord whom you have called to your heart,
The king, your beloved husband, enjoy long days at your holy lap, the sweet. . . .
Under his reign may there be plants, may there be grain,
At the river may there be overflow,
In the field may there be rich grain. . . .
May the holy queen of vegetation pile high the grain in heaps and mounds. . . .

(Kramer, 1969:83)

Following are three excerpts from Sacred Marriage songs that are reminiscent of the Song of Songs. In the first the goddess complains about the lack of vegetation. Her lover, King Shulgi, invites her to go with him to the fields:

My sister, I would go with you to my field,
My fair sister, I would go with you to my field,
I would go with you to my large field,
I would go with you to my small field,
To my 'early' grain irrigated with its 'early' water,
To my 'late' grain irrigated with its 'late' water,
Do you [fructify?] its grain,
Do you [fructify?] its sheaves.

(Kramer, 1969:100)

In another composition, Inanna exults in her fertility:

He has brought me into it, he has brought me into it,
My brother has brought me into the garden.
Dumuzi has brought me into the garden,
I strolled [?] with him among the standing trees.
I stood with him by its lying trees,
By an apple tree I kneeled as is proper.
Before my brother coming in song,
Before the lord Dumuzi who came toward me. . . .
I poured out plants from my womb,
I placed plants before him, I poured out plants before him,
I placed grain before him, I poured out grain before him.

(Kramer, 1969:101)

In the following passage Kubatum, a votary of Inanna, tries to arouse the passion of King Shulgi:

My god, sweet is the drink of the wine-maid
Like her drink sweet is her vulva, sweet is her drink,
Like her lips sweet is her vulva, sweet is her drink,
Sweet is her mixed drink, her drink.

(Kramer, 1969:94)

Similarities between Sacred Marriage songs and the Song of Songs can be seen in some of the ways they express love and desire, the nature motifs, the invitation to the garden, the praise of the beloved's sweetness, and the brother-sister address. Still, it is very unlikely that the Song is a reworked Sacred Marriage liturgy in the same tradition. First of all, if Renger is right in saying that the Sacred Marriage was a localized ritual, part of the coronation ceremonies of certain kings of the Ur III and Isin dynasties, and that it had no continuation in later times (RA II, 257f.), it is hard to see how the ceremony could have been incorporated into Syro-Palestinian practices.

Beyond this, significant differences exist between the Sacred Marriage texts and the Song of Songs, differences so profound as to undermine any theory that the Song was a liturgy of the same sort or was even derived from one. Most significantly, the Song never alludes to a myth or ritual, while the Sacred Marriage texts consistently do so. The Song makes no attempt to effect universal fertility and well-being, as does the Sacred Marriage. The Song never speaks of the invigoration of nature in terms of resurrection from death (as do the Tammuz litanies), nor does it present it as an event in doubt whose realization requires divine intervention. When the land in the Song blossoms, it does so in a natural and expected process. Canticles, like the Egyptian love songs and unlike the Sacred Marriage liturgies, is not interested in woman's fertility. Even when describing the land's blossoming, the Song emphasizes not fecundity but beauty. Sexuality in the Song is a human desire and a bond between two individuals, not the source of universal plenitude.

Furthermore, the gentle eroticism of the Song is far removed from the detailed and explicit sexuality of the Mesopotamian liturgies. Sexual explicitness is important in those liturgies, for the sex act is considered a means to national well-being. The sexuality in the Song, on the other hand, has no goal outside the romantic relationship between the two lovers. Such resemblances as there are between the Song and the Sacred Marriage songs can be explained in two ways. First, since both speak of sexual love, a general human experience, some similarities in formulation and motif are inevitable. How can divine sexuality, after all, be spoken of other than in terms of human sexuality? Second, it is possible that miscellaneous expressions and motifs used in Mesopotamian literature—oral or written—found their way to Canaan, where they were taken into secular love poetry.

Finally, we nowhere hear of a Sacred Marriage rite in Israel, though ritual copulation between a king and a priestess of Astarte would hardly have escaped the prophets' notice. The Tammuz mourning rites, whose existence in Israel is evidenced explicitly in Ezek 8:14, may have been the vehicle for the transfer of some motifs, although the Song shows no traces of lamentation. But if that did happen, these influences left no clear impressions on the Song and certainly did not affect its basic character.

Mortuary Songs: Love and Death

Although festivities associated with the mortuary cult were an important part of Egyptian culture, the Egyptian love songs are not mortuary songs. Egyptians had mortuary festivals the way other people have weddings. One major festival, the Lovely Festival of the Valley, included a procession to the Theban necropolis, where participants lived it up in the company, as it were, of their dead relatives (Schott, 1952). The entertainment at such feasts may well have included love songs, for, as the tomb murals show, these festivities were not essentially different from those enjoyed on other occasions. As the visitors wanted their dead relatives to enjoy the pleasures they had known in this life, amusements of all sorts, love songs among them, would have been in order. But nothing links the love songs with a specifically mortuary setting. Mortuary texts speak at length of death and the life beyond; love poetry scarcely alludes to either. If love songs were sung at mortuary festivals, they were just part of the general entertainment.

The above denial was prompted by Pope's theory that Canticles' original setting was in orgiastic feasts of the sort that (he argues) took place in mortuary cults throughout the Near East and Mediterranean world (1977:210–29). Pope amasses evidence for the existence of funerary banquets of various sorts in various places without showing how performances of the Song functioned in them. Funerary meals undoubtedly did take place in Israel, but no evidence suggests that sexual activity was commonly part of them. The prophets, who are hardly hesitant to condemn other kinds of illicit sex, especially in a cultic setting, condemn various mourning practices, in particular self-laceration and donations to the dead, without mentioning sacral coitus.

Nothing in the Song connects it with death or the afterlife. The subject of 8:6 is love; death is mentioned only incidentally, by way of comparison, along with unquenchable fire. And the atmosphere of the Song is certainly not orgiastic. The sexual acts alluded to are not group acts. Nor does the Song hold up fertility or love as an answer to death.

Love Poetry as Entertainment

The love songs were, I believe, entertainment. When people gather in their leisure time and seek diversion, many forms of entertainment are appropriate. Songs of love have always been popular on such occasions.

THE EGYPTIAN LOVE SONGS

Among the Egyptian love songs, the headings to three groups state their purpose clearly: *sḫmḫ ib*, "entertainment" or "diversion" (literally, "making the heart forget").[18] The scribes claim no more for the songs than that they are good entertainment. Being "entertainment songs," love songs were probably sung at banquets of the sort depicted with great frequency in tomb murals (see figs. 1–3, 6, 9). Banquet scenes are more vivacious and detailed in 18th dynasty tombs than in those of the Ramesside period, when "worldly" motifs in general recede in tomb art, but the basic features appear both before and after the 18th dynasty. These are scenes of life's "best parts," the parts the dead person had hoped to repeat through eternity. Typically the tomb owner and his wife sit before food and drink, often served by their children (figs. 2, 6). Guests, sometimes quite a few, sit before the host, often designated by name and relationship to the deceased. Frequently dancers and singers entertain the participants (figs. 1, 2, 9). Servants offer wreaths, food, drink, and ointments, urging the guests to "spend a good day" and to drink—to excess.

Although no love songs are recorded in the tomb murals, motifs seen also in the love songs do appear. Like three of the love song groups, the banquets in many murals are labeled *sḫmḫ ib*, "entertainment," "diversion." Some of the people depicted urge the other participants to amuse themselves, to divert their heart (*sḫmḫ.k ib.k*), meaning that they should do all the things shown in the scenes: sitting with friends and relatives, putting on aromatic ointments, eating, drinking, and listening to music. Other motifs appearing in both the love songs and the tomb murals are the north wind, drinking to intoxication, anointing oneself with perfumes and oils, dressing in fine linen, offering flowers and wreaths, resting in gardens—and love. The tomb owner is usually depicted sitting next to his wife, called "the beloved of his heart," an expression common in love songs as well.

Another indication of the connection between the love songs and the banquets of the tomb murals is the arrangement of P. Harris 500. Between groups B and C the copyist inserted a harper's song. This song, the "Antef Song" (App. A, no. ii), urges merrymaking of the very sort shown in the ban-

18. P. Harris 500, group B (nos. 9–16) and group C (nos. 17–19); P. Beatty I, group A (nos. 31–37). The heading of the last ascribes the song to the "Great Entertainer."

quet scenes. It is a slightly expanded version of a song found in the tomb of Paatenemheb from the time of Akhenaton, where it accompanies a picture of the tomb owner sitting with his wife and daughters and receiving ritual offerings. This song, sung by an orchestral quartet, first bewails the uncertainty of mortuary rites and then advises self-forgetfulness and the enjoyment of such pleasant things as perfumes and fine linens. Many songs in banquet murals urge similar delights, including the pleasures of song:

> Put songs of singing girls before you.
> Cast aside all evil,
> and think of joy.[19]

The absence of love songs from the texts inscribed in the tomb murals does not prove that they were not sung at banquets of the sort depicted. The banquet murals themselves had two major functions in the mortuary cult, neither of which the love songs could fulfill. First, the murals, including the words quoted in them, were thought to provide the dead with food, drink, entertainment, and companionship in the afterlife, through the power of representational magic. Second, the murals were meant to teach tomb visitors the efficacy of the mortuary cult by showing the dead man continuing to enjoy life's pleasures. Some songs that appear in murals fulfill these functions by urging the owner to enjoy himself, thereby indicating that he is still capable of doing so: for example, "A pleasant day! Spend a good morning!" (Amenemhet, TT 82; Davies and Gardiner, 1915: pl. XV). Others praise his present happiness: "Fortunate are these years, which the god commanded you to spend, while you enjoy his lovingkindness and health, etc." (Kenamun, TT 93; Davies, 1930: pl. IX). Other songs have explicitly mortuary significance: for example, "You call to heaven, and your voice is answered. Atum answers you . . ." (Neferrenpet, TT 178; Lichtheim, 1945:205; see further Fox, 1982).

Love songs did not serve the purposes of the tomb murals, since they speak of unmarried, sometimes frustrated, love. None shows—as do the murals—the serene pleasures of a paterfamilias enjoying the company of his wife and family throughout eternity. At the banquets that were the model for the tomb murals, on the other hand, love songs would be quite suitable.

If this hypothesis of the Egyptian love songs' life-setting is accepted, we may inquire whether the entertainment scenes give any information about the occasions on which banqueting took place and love songs were sung. One difficulty is that the banquet scenes—which must be clearly distinguished

19. Neferhotep (TT 50); Müller, 1899: pl. I. See further Lichtheim, 1945, and Wente, 1962.

from the actual banquets they are modeled on—are a tangle of mortuary and earthly motifs. (This tangle served the murals' main purpose, which was to transfer the joys the deceased knew on earth to eternal life by binding together this life and the next.) Some murals associate a banquet with a particular occasion by labels, broader pictorial context, or the words of the participants. These occasions are the following:

1. Special events in the life of the deceased, such as when Rekhmire returned from greeting Amenhotep II upon his accession (fig. 2; TT 100; Davies, 1943: pls. LXIII–LXVII).

2. Funerals. Funerals would culminate in a meal shared, as it were, by mourners and the (newly revived) dead. This meal may have been in reality a simple funerary offering, but ideally, at least, the dead person's first meal was a banquet (e.g., Amenemhet, TT 82; Davies and Gardiner, 1915: pl. XV).[20] We should observe that the funerary banquet is pictured as a pleasant, quiet meal, by no means an orgy (even the drunkenness is sedate), and that the songs quoted in the scene are gentle wishes for eternal happiness.

3. Festivals. Many banquet scenes are associated with festivals such as New Year's Day (e.g., Puyemre, TT 39; Davies, 1922–23: pls. LXIII–LXIV), the Festival of Djesru (TT 247; Schott, 1952: source 118), the Lovely Festival of the Valley (TT 129 and TT 56; ibid., sources 116, 117).[21]

4. "Every day." Some scenes contain a phrase signifying daily recurrence of the entertainment, as when a harper says to Puyemre, "Enjoy yourself [in these 1000] years, while your days are (spent) in happiness, [your hours] in delight, your months as one great in favor and love for the length of eternity" (TT 39; Davies, 1922–23: pl. XLII). This does not mean that parties took place every day in the tombs, but rather that the dead man's ongoing needs were to be lavishly provided for (so it was hoped) by offerings contracted for with mortuary priests, by donations from occasional visitors, and by the pictures themselves.

Since special events like a king's accession were rare and one could not have a lavish banquet every day in this life, and since one's funeral banquet was beyond this life, it stands to reason that the occasions for most banquets of the sort depicted in the murals were festival days, of which there were a great many in ancient Egypt. In joyous, even boisterous, public celebrations,

20. The scene reproduced in Davies and Gardiner, 1915:pl. XV, forms a continuation of the funerary ceremonies beginning on the south wall (pls. X–XIII) and extending onto the north wall (pl. XVII). Significantly, the offering on the north wall (pl. XIV) is paralleled by the offering on the south wall (pl. X), but on the north wall it is elaborated into a full banquet. This suggests that the full banquet scene is an idealized interpretation of a simple funerary offering. Nevertheless, a funeral would theoretically culminate in a banquet.

21. Schott, 1952, described the latter festival in detail and showed that it culminated in a procession to the tombs, where the participants joined their dead relatives in a banquet in which intoxication became a means of uniting living and dead.

crowds filled the streets and the grounds of the sanctuary to take part in procession, see religious drama, sing, dance, and get drunk.[22] Details of public festivities come mainly from the Ptolemaic texts of Edfu, but the joyous character of religious celebrations was certainly not a late development. "Festivals of Egypt" was long a byword for joy and gaiety. The annals of Thutmoses III compare the victory celebrations of the army to the festivals of Egypt: "The army of His Majesty was drunk and anointed with spices all the days, as happens in the festivals of Egypt" (Urk. IV, 688).

In the circumstances offered by the festival days, young lovers could meet, go off alone, and celebrate privately (nos. 8, 30). In private homes, the well-to-do would hold banquets where they would eat, drink, enjoy themselves, and be entertained by dance, instrumental music, and song, including—we may reasonably assume—love songs. In this way, love songs could have acquired a secondary, peripheral connection to the religious life of the people. This hypothesized connection did not, however, influence the way love songs were written.

THE SONG OF SONGS

Canticles too was probably entertainment, a song to be enjoyed on any occasion—including religious holidays—when song, dance, or other ordinary diversions were in order. The Egyptian parallels suggest that the Song too was *sḫmḫ-ib*—"diversion of the heart"—and nothing in the poem indicates otherwise.

To call the Song "entertainment" is not to trivialize it. Great music has been composed and great literature written to serve no social or religious function other than entertaining audiences. It is possible to entertain people by arousing finely nuanced and complex emotions, engaging their intellects, conveying new insights, and promulgating significant ideas. Still, we should not exaggerate the gravity of the Song's aims. It is full of fun, erotic allusions, sensual word-paintings of the lovers and their worlds, and heart-warming sentiments. It diverts the mind from everyday cares by inviting the audience to share the fresh, sensuous world of the young lovers and their erotic adventures. Such secular love songs existed in Egypt and probably in Mesopotamia as well, although none of the latter are extant.[23]

22. See Drioton, 1957b, and compare the Hymn to the Nile, P. Sallier II, 14,2–9 (transl. Lichtheim, 1973:204f.) and the Hathor hymn in Drioton, 1957b:141.

23. Evidence for the existence of secular love songs from Mesopotamia include the incipits of KAR 158, many of which seem to have belonged to Akkadian love lyrics (Held, 1961:5). Two extant texts from Mesopotamia are related to secular love poetry: "The Message of Ludingira to His Mother," a Sumerian literary text (Cooper, 1971), and an Old Babylonian dialogue, "A Faithful Lover" (Held, 1961).

In the Sumerian text, a man called Ludingira sends a messenger to his mother, giving him

Ezek 33:31–32 gives us some information about how love songs were used among the Israelites. God warns Ezekiel that the people will not take his rhetoric seriously, because it is so interesting that it has become entertaining:

(31) My people will come to you as to a public gathering (*kimbo*ʾ *ʿam*) and sit before you. They will listen to your words but not do them. For they have a taste for erotica (*ʿagabim*).[24] . . . [25] (32) As far as they're concerned you're just a (singer of) erotic songs,[26] who sings nicely and plays well. So they'll hear your words—but *do* them they will not!

---

five "signs" to enable him to recognize her. Four of these signs are passages consisting of metaphors similar to those in the Praise Songs in Canticles (see chapter 7). The main difference, of course, is that the description in "Ludingira" depicts the speaker's mother, not his lover. Still, the description has certain erotic overtones. It may be that the mother is really Inanna in motherly guise, but as it stands the text is secular and is not a song about sexual love (Freudian implications aside). Nevertheless, the poet may be drawing techniques from a tradition of love songs.

The Old Babylonian text (Held, 1961, 1962) is a complex dialogue about love. A young lady has lost her lover to a slanderous rival. She prays that her rival will come to shame and determines to win back the man's affections. He haughtily rebuffs her, telling her he no longer loves her and does not want her—indeed, "Your love means no more to me than trouble and vexation" (1961:9). But somehow she persuades him and he deigns to return to her: "My one and only, your features are not unlovely" (ibid.). Held, stressing the secularity of the composition, assigns it to the category of love lyrics. It seems to me closer in kind to "The Dialogue of Pessimism" or "The Babylonian Theodicy," which discuss philosophical questions in urbane and sometimes witty dialogue. The Old Babylonian dialogue in question speaks of the value and constancy of love with the same acrid humor with which "The Dialogue of Pessimism" debates the value of human activity. It would be stretching the category of love songs too far to include "Ludingira" in it; nevertheless, the text does show that human love was a subject of literary interest in Mesopotamia as well as in Egypt and Israel.

A fragmentary Old Babylonian text from Kish, studied by Dr. Joan Westenholz ("A Forgotten Love Song") appears to be part of a love song. It is unclear whether it is a monologue or dialogue and whether the setting is secular or religious. What is clear is its sexual nature. In col. i, the better preserved of the two columns, the woman coaxes her lover to have intercourse with her. Her blandishments include: . . . your caresses are sweet / growing luxuriantly is your fruit / . . . O by the crown of our head, the rings of our ears /, the mountains of our shoulders, and the charms of our chest / the bracelet with date spadix charms of our wrists / the belt of our waist / reach forth with your left hand and honor our vulva / play with our breasts. . . ." Observe that the woman speaks of herself in the first plural, a practice found elsewhere in amatory contexts (Westenholz refers to Gilgamesh VI, 69 and the Sumerian Sacred Marriage texts). It is likely that certain first plurals in the Song of Songs, such as in 2:15, should likewise be understood as the girl's words (see commentary). I thank Dr. Westenholz for allowing me to see and quote from a prepublication copy of her study.

24. It is unnecessary to emend *ʿagabim* to *kezabim*, in spite of LXX *pseudos*. For *ʿagabim bepiyhem* compare *ki ṣayid bepiyw*, "for he had a taste for game," Gen 25:28. In Ezek 33:31, *ki ʿagabim bepiyhem* explains why the people will come and sit before Ezekiel and listen to his words.

25. The rest of the verse is corrupt, but it does not bear on the issue at hand.

26. *Kešir ʿagabim*, elliptical for *kešar šir ʿagabim*.

ᶜᵃgabim refers to matters of lust or words that stir up lust. BDB appropriately renders "love songs," although ᶜGB always denotes sexual desire, and the implication of lust should not be obscured. Ezekiel may be using a deliberately acerbic term to describe the people's interest, yet the songs he has in mind would not have to be much more erotically explicit than Canticles to warrant this designation (see Shemariah ben Elijah's remark on the Song's literal meaning, above, p. 238). Even in exile people gathered to hear erotic songs for diversion and amusement.

Isaiah, at the start of his "Song of the Vineyard" (5:1–7), takes on the guise of a minnesinger (as Rudolph, 1962:105, aptly puts it) to get his audience's attention. *Širat dodi lᵉkarmo*, as Isaiah labels his song, means "my beloved's song about his vineyard." The audience is to think that Isaiah is singing about a beloved woman—a "vineyard" (cf. Cant 1:6, 14; 8:12)—but he quickly turns the song into a reproach and throws it in their faces (vv. 3–7).[27]

These two passages show us that entertainers sang love songs to amuse audiences during the time of the First Commonwealth. A remark of Rabbi Akiva's gives us information about the use of Canticles itself in the century after the destruction of the Second Temple: "Whoever warbles the Song of Songs at banqueting houses (*battey hammišta'ot*), treating it like an ordinary song (*ka'ᵃḥad hazzᵉmarim*: lit., "as one of the songs"), has no portion in the World to Come" (Tos. San. 12:10). In the second century C.E., when the allegorical interpretation was largely taken for granted,[28] some people were still singing it as entertainment at banquets.

What bothers Rabbi Akiva is not (contrary to Pope) that people were using the Song in a sacral setting,[29] but that they were using it in a way he

27. Note that the love song Isaiah is supposed to be singing creates a speaking persona distinct from the singer. I argue in chapter 6 that the speakers in most, if not all, love songs are personae.

28. The canonicity of the Song was not seriously in dispute in the middle of the second century C.E. In the discussions about the canonicity of Qohelet and the Song of Songs in M. Yadayim 3:5, the issue is whether the status of the Song as inspired scripture *had been* in dispute at a council session at Jamnia that took place sometime between 75 and 117 C.E. (Leiman, 1976:123). Rabbi Akiva insists that no one ever disputed the Song's sanctity. The Song's interpretation as sacred scripture had begun well before Jamnia. Its presence in the Qumran library shows that the religious interpretation was accepted by some groups in the first century C.E. at the latest (the dating of the manuscript is uncertain).

29. There is no evidence whatsoever for Pope's contention (1977:221) that *beyt mišt ᵉya'* in Dan 5:10, *beyt mišteh hayyayin* in Est 7:8, *beyt hayyayin* in Cant 2:4, and *batey hammišta'ot* in Tos. San. 12:10 refer to places for "sacral feasting and drinking." *Beyt hammišta'ot*, as well as the other terms listed above, can indicate any place where banquets are held. These may include banquets where, among other things, one could praise the gods (Dan 5:4). Such practices would not make the banquet essentially sacral and would not mean that the banquet hall was a cult place. In the case of Est 7:8, we know that the occasion was definitely not a sacral celebration—Esther

considered improper. While he considered the Song most holy, others treated it as "an ordinary song." But extraordinary as its artistry is, Canticles is indeed an "ordinary song" in the sense in which Rabbi Akiva used this term.

Excursus: The Sacralization of the Song of Songs

How then did a song of this sort become holy scripture? We do not know. While the ascription to Solomon would facilitate acceptance, since it attributed the book to an ancient and inspired author, that attribution would not in itself lead to canonization, for other books and songs ascribed to him were not accepted. Besides, in the discussion in M. Yad. 3:5, none of the Tannaim mention Solomonic authorship to justify canonization. Certainly allegorization was necessary prior to canonization, but what impelled the rabbis to allegorize it to start with? Here was a dangerous choice for allegorization, for the Song's eroticism could never be entirely obscured, and the identification of the lover with God suggests some audacious, uncharacteristic anthropomorphisms.[30] In any case, one does not simply come upon a song and interpret it by midrash. Midrashic exposition is applicable only to a text that is considered authoritative and inspired. The Song must have been regarded as in some way part of the national religious literature *before* it was read allegorically.

Advocates of the cultic interpretation argue that the sacred aura the Song had in its presumed pagan use would have clung to it and led to its appropriation to Jewish religious literature. Meek says that Canticles "got into the Canon because it was an ancient book, a religious book, and one that had always been religious" (1924b:52f.; similarly Kramer, 1969:90). But a pagan religious origin would hardly make the book *more* acceptable. Meek, in fact, considered the Song's presumed cultic background as the reason some rabbis hesitated to accept it (1922:3), but there is no hint that this is what

simply invited the king and Haman to dinner. Haman was caught prostrate at Esther's couch not because he was intoxicated from sacral drinking (contrary to Pope), but because he was pleading for mercy. This banquet was not a celebration of Purim or a precursor to it, so that speculations that Purim originated in a Persian "feast of the dead" (Pope, 1977:221) are irrelevant to the identification of the "house of wine." Rabbi Akiva does not suggest that illicit cultic activities were going on in the banquets he knew about, and certainly such things would not have escaped his ire. Likewise, the term *beyt mišteh* in Rabbi Akiva's remark cannot be restricted to wedding banquets (contrary to Würthwein, 1969:32), although it may include them.

30. The dangers of allegorizing the Song are shown by early attempts to obviate such interpretations. For example, in order to neutralize the anthropomorphism suggested by an allegorical interpretation of 1:2, R. Yohanan ben Zakkai stated that the lover referred to in "Let him kiss me with kisses of his mouth" is not God but an angel (Cant. Rab. i 13; see Urbach, 1971:255). The Targum similarly reads the description of the lover in 5:10ff. as praise of the Torah. The mystical midrash *Shiur Komah* shows that despite such precautions allegorical interpretation could quickly lead to extreme anthropomorphism.

bothered them. Pagan religious usages could undoubtedly be incorporated into Yahwism, but only after their original meaning had been suppressed and forgotten. So while a pagan background might not prevent canonization, it would hardly be the reason for it. In any case, there are no traces of a revision replacing pagan characteristics with Yahwistic ones, and as Rowley points out, "an intelligent reviser would have taken care that the Yahwism whose interests the book was to serve would be unequivocally displayed in it, and not left to the reader to supply" (1952:223).

Nor does the theory that Canticles was a wedding song explain its canonization. First of all, the Song exalts not marriage but the sexual love that may lead to marriage, and the Tannaim never glorified sexual pleasure as sacred in itself. Second, if an original nuptial setting was the key factor in the Song's canonization, we would expect to find this legitimizing factor reflected in the early discussions and comments on the Song, and in particular the arguments on behalf of its canonicity. Unlike the cultic theory, which says that the original use was suppressed before canonization, the wedding song theory presumes an original use that continued to be legitimate and would not have needed to be obscured by the early interpreters. But the early references to the Song in no way point to an original use at weddings.

Of the various speculations offered to explain the Song's canonization, Bentzen's (1953) seems to me closest to the mark. He suggests that the sacralization of the Song grew out of an incidental connection between it and religious festivals, particularly those in the spring festival season, whence its later association with Passover. I agree that such an incidental context would be likely to call forth learned midrashic reinterpretation to justify the Song's presence among the religious usages of the festival season. There is, however, no evidence that the Song was associated with Passover until well after its canonization. The earliest allegorical interpretations do not refer specifically to Passover.[31]

To explain how the Song came to be regarded as part of the sacred literature of Israel, it may be enough to postulate that the Song, though not intrinsically religious, was sung as part of the entertainment and merrymaking at feasts and celebrations, which would naturally take place for the most part on holidays in the religious calendar.

Festivals in ancient Israel and Judea were not days of prayer, sacrifice, and ritual alone. From various evidence, early and late, we know that they were joyous, even raucous, festivities in which the people ate, drank, and

31. Canticles is now the first of the Five Scrolls because it is read on Passover, but this arrangement is a secondary development. According to B. Babba Batra 14b–15a, in the older arrangement the three Solomonic books were grouped together (Proverbs, Qohelet, Song of Songs), and so the order in the printed editions is not evidence for an early liturgical use of the Song on Passover.

made merry both in the sanctuary area ("before the Lord") and in private homes ("in your gates"). Behaviour could even become licentious (Amos 2:8, and cf. Eli's assumption in I Sam 1:14). During the time of the judges, on the "festival of the Lord at Shiloh," girls would go out "year by year" to the fields to dance near the vineyards (Judg 21:19–23). Some thousand years later, during the Second Temple period, on the 15th of Ab (probably the beginning of the grape harvest) and—most surprisingly—on the Day of Atonement, girls would dress up,[32] dance in the vineyards, and flirt with the eligible young men (M. Taanit 4:8). Thus on even the most sacred of festivals, fun, flirtation, dance, and talk of love were at home in the popular celebrations. The feasts at which R. Akiva saw people singing the Song may have taken place on festival days, although he did not consider them a sufficiently sacred context.

When (according to this hypothesis) the Song had worked its way into the people's religious life and had thus acquired a certain aura of sanctity, the religious leadership legitimized that association by means of allegorical interpretation. (In a similar process the tassles that decorated the garments of the nobility throughout the ancient Near East were interpreted by the priestly writer [Num 15:37–41] as a device to remind Israelites of God's commandments and as a sign that all Israel had priestly and noble status [cf. Milgrom, 1981]).[33] Once the Song was accepted as sacred scripture, as it was a few generations before Akiva, its use outside an unambiguously sacred setting, such as the synagogue, seemed to violate the Song's sanctity and so was anathematized. Even if many of the banquets to which Akiva refers took place on holy days, he objected to the performance of Canticles at them, for he regarded it as the holiest of the writings:[34] "For all the writings are holy, but the Song of Songs is the holiest of the holy" (M. Yad. 3:5).

32. According to R. Shimon's idealized memory, the girls dressed in borrowed white garments so as not to embarrass those who lacked finery. But this detail seems part of the moralizing thrust of the passage; see "Courting Songs" above.

33. There is an interesting parallel to this process in Chinese literature. The anthology called "The Classic of Song," whose editing was traditionally ascribed to Confucius, includes simple folk songs. Confucius required study of these songs as models of self-expression and correct thought. Later Chinese scholars could not understand why he attributed such importance to these simple songs and therefore interpreted them allegorically: a lover's longing for his beloved, for example, was the king's love for his people. (Liu, 1966:216).

34. That is, of the Hagiographa and Prophets. Palestinian midrashic traditions read (less probably) "for all the songs are holy" instead of "for all the writings are holy" (Lieberman, 1937–39:II, 9).

CHAPTER 6

Who Is Speaking and How? Voice and Mode of Presentation

In this chapter I seek to sharpen our analytical focus by zeroing in on the most significant formal features of character presentation: the overall dramatic character of the poems; the forms of discourse; and the special uses of grammatical person when the personae speak of and to themselves, of and to their lovers.

Dramatic Character

AUTHOR AND PERSONAE

The speakers in the Egyptian love songs and the Song of Songs are, as a rule, *personae*, created characters through whom the poets speak but who are not to be identified with them. While I have seen no explicit discussion of this issue in the scholarly literature, my impression is that commentators tend to assume that the words spoken in the Egyptian love songs and the Song of Songs are direct expressions of their authors' emotions and experiences. This issue is important for interpretation, for if the speakers are personae we must ask not only what the lovers are like, but also how the poets view them and present them to us.

The literary quality of these poems in itself tends to distinguish the speakers from the authors, particularly in the case of Canticles. It is highly unlikely that lovestruck young people such as those who appear in these poems could have produced lyrics of such artistic power and sophistication. This poetry seems rather to be the work of mature and practiced artists.[1]

1. P. Anastasi III, 3,7–8 (LEM, 23/10) mentions a "school" for songstresses.

In many of the songs there are other, less impressionistic, signs that the speakers are dramatic creations. Among the Egyptian songs, two, "The Crossing" and "The Stroll," have two speakers, both of whom speak their thoughts, with neither speaker being quoted by the other. Clearly both characters have been created and are controlled by an author who is not to be identified with either. "The Stroll" is attributed to a woman called "The Great Entertainer" (according to the most likely interpretation of the title, see commentary). This poet (and/or singer) is certainly not to be identified with the love-sick girl who speaks in alternate stanzas. The poet is the girl's creator. In "The Orchard" the speakers are trees, obviously personae. Often the speaker is the sort of person who is unlikely to be composing poetry, such as the young bird-trapper, who is speaking on the day she captures a lover (no. 10). It is likewise doubtful that the poet of no. 1 really is a girl recording somehow the words she used in scolding her lover for hastening to leave her bed. The poet is rather presenting a libidinous young lady to the audience to give it the empathetic and voyeuristic pleasure of seeing her at a very private moment.

Many poems include no clear clues to the author-persona distinction, but drawing that distinction enriches the reading. Thus in no. 15 a girl sits at home and fumes as she waits for her lover. If she is herself the author relating her immediate experience, the poem is only a rather mean expression of jealousy, whereas if she is a persona, we can join the poet in looking at the young lover with humor.

In some songs, to be sure, the distance between speaker and poet is not perceptible. Thus when a male tells how he is "trapped" by love (nos. 3, 43), or declares how beautiful his beloved is and how he longs to kiss her in public (no. 54), there appears to be no reason why the speaker could not be the poet giving utterance to his own immediate experience in his own voice. But rather than posit a radical bifurcation in the genre between expressive lyric,[2] spoken in the authorial voice, and dramatic lyric, spoken by a persona, I will take a cue from those songs in which the speakers are clearly personae and assume this to be the rule generally. Even if the author-persona distinction is not important for all the songs, it is a useful starting assumption, for it leads us to

2. My understanding of dramatic monologue is based largely on Rader (1976), who carefully differentiates among forms of first-person poems. In "expressive lyric" [which our love songs are not] ". . . the poet speaks in his own person out of the stimulus of a real situation, seeking an expressive catharsis the shape of which he does not foresee but discovers, finding as he goes words adequate to his inner sense of his outward circumstances" (p. 150). In dramatic monologue, by contrast, "the poet simulates the activity of a person imagined as virtually real whom we understand as we would an 'other' natural person, inferring from outward act and expression to inward purpose. In both dramatic lyric and dramatic monologue our pleasure is compounded of our participation in the dramatic actor's act and our appreciation of the simulative activity of the chameleon poet" (ibid.).

ask first if and then how the author's viewpoint differs from the persona's and what the relationship is between these two viewpoints.

There may be, however, a few times when we do hear the poet's voice,[3] speaking to the lovers or commenting on them from a vantage point outside and above the reality of the poem. This authorial voice is possibly heard in the introduction to no. 9 and the closing verse of no. 36, though both these cases are doubtful and can be interpreted otherwise (as I argue in no. 9, n. a, and no. 36, n. i).

More significant is the authorial voice in "The Orchard." In each stanza of this song, the poet introduces the words of the trees with a quoting phrase (e.g., "The fig-sycamore moves his mouth, and his foliage comes to speak" in no. 29). In the third stanza (no. 30) this voice becomes dominant, as the quoting phrase is expanded into a Praise Song extolling the generous little sycamore. The authorial voice in this poem provides an "objective" judge, speaking from an external, privileged vantage-point, who can declare authoritatively which tree is the most praiseworthy. The intervention of the authorial voice is significant elsewhere only in nos. 41–42 (probably a single song). An unidentified speaker gives advice to an unidentified "you" (masc.), who could be taken as any male in the audience or as a youth whose existence within the song is implied by the address itself. The speaker instructs him on how to gain his desire of a female who is very likely a courtesan (see comment on no. 42). An external voice is needed to give authoritative advice on how to accomplish this.

The Song of Songs creates its world entirely through the words of *dramatis personae*. We encounter this world without preparation, thrown *in medias res*, guided by the speakers' words alone. Various people speak in the Song (girl, boy, girls of Jerusalem, brothers). We could identify one of them as the author only by fragmenting the Song into short ditties in which only one person speaks, and then assuming an editor who wove poems written by males into poems written by females, thereby creating a new text profoundly unlike the presumed original lyrics in spirit and structure. Such an editor—whom we could well call author—would in effect have turned the various lyric writers into one boy and one girl who love each other, thereby making the presumed original poets into personae.

Almost all the verses of the Song are too well integrated into the speech of the characters to allow us to attribute them to an external authorial voice. Even when we cannot say for certain which character is speaking in a given verse, it is usually clear that the speaker is one of the characters taking part in the action and not the author.

3. That is, the implied author; see n. 6 below and Booth, 1961:71–76.

A few verses have been interpreted as interjections in the author's voice. Cant 5:1b ("Eat well, O friends, drink yourselves drunk on caresses") is possibly an authorial interjection (thus Gerleman, 1965; Würthwein, 1969). But more likely, these are the words of the girls of Jerusalem urging the couple to enjoy their lovemaking. Two other passages that *could* be assigned to an authorial voice are 3:7–11 (the description of Solomon's couch) and the enigmatic 2:15 ("Catch us foxes . . ."). But there is no particular reason to assume in either passage the sudden intrusion of an external speaker; besides, such an assumption makes these passages no less enigmatic. The words are best ascribed to the Shulammite, who in 2:15 seems to be teasing her beloved and in 3:7–11 describing their bower (see commentary).

The Song of Songs and most Egyptian love songs thus have a dramatic quality, at least in the limited sense in which Robert Browning understood his monologues to be dramatic: "These [idyls] of mine are called 'Dramatic' because the story is told by some actor in it, not by the poet himself."[4] Since the Egyptian love songs, and probably the Song of Songs, were meant to be sung by singers of the kind depicted in countless Egyptian paintings, stelae, and statuettes, they are furthermore dramatic in the fundamental Aristotelian understanding of drama as *mimesis*: the singers represent personae before an audience.

DRAMA

It is possible that beyond this the poems were fully dramatic, with mimesis of actions as well as words. Imitation would probably be in the form of mimetic dance, such as was undoubtedly known in Egypt. One song (which is not a love song) that we know was presented in this fully dramatic way is "The Song of the Four Winds." A tomb painting at Beni Hasan shows a small orchestral chorus singing this song while dancing girls represent the characters (Drioton, 1957a). Mimetic dance played a role in the mortuary cult and in temple rituals from the Old Kingdom to the end of the Ptolemaic period, and perhaps beyond (ibid., and Lexová, 1935:30–32 and passim). Some pictures of dances other than the "Four Winds" strongly suggest that the dancers are acting out stories (Lexová, 1935:30–32). Mimetic accompaniment would have facilitated understanding of the love songs, but since actions do not play an important role in most of them, it would not have been essential.

Canticles too could have been acted out. Influential interpreters in the 19th and early 20th centuries (in particular Renan [1884], Ewald [1826], Delitzsch [1885], and S. R. Driver [1913]) explained the Song as a drama.

4. Quoted by Honan (1961:122), who paraphrases Browning's definition more precisely: "pertaining to that which is told by one whose presence is indicated by the poet but who is not the poet himself."

(They had in mind a drama of the Greco-Roman type, in which various actors represented the roles in a play that told a story.) But most commentators in this century have felt that the story-lines the earlier interpreters claimed to find are just not implied by the text; there is certainly no sequence of events running through the Song and forming a plot of the sort predominant in Western drama. It is nevertheless possible that the song was sung by different singers representing the various characters, a technique that at least would have identified the speaker of every verse for the immediate audience. Still, a solo singer could, though not as easily, convey the rapid switches of speaker. Another hypothesis that is reasonable but lacks evidence is that the Song was meant to be accompanied by mimetic action. Some of the events, in particular the boy's nighttime visits and the girl's two searches in the city (2:8–14; 3:1–5; 5:2–6:3), could be vividly represented in dance. But these events, it should be noted, are incorporated into narrative passages spoken by the Shulammite (apparently to the girls of Jerusalem), so that mimetic accompaniment, though useful, would not be essential.

Both the advocates of the dramatic theory and its opponents have argued the issue on the basis of an unnecessarily restrictive view of drama. Thus Rudolph is convinced that the Song cannot possibly be a drama because

> ein Drama muss einen Fortschritt und muss ein Ziel haben, und in einem Liebesdrama, wie es das HL wäre, könnte dieses Ziel nur sein, dass nach allerlei Zwischenfällen, volkstümlich gesprochen, Er und Sie sich kriegen. Im HL kriegen sie sich einerseits viel zu früh. (1962:97)[5]

The notion that a drama must develop in a straight line toward a single goal is a Western one, and is probably not applicable even to all Western drama. It is not true of the Egyptian drama of the Victory of Horus (Fairman, 1974), in which Horus defeats Seth three times: his killing him in act one does not prevent him from killing him again in acts two and three. A drama may present a single truth several ways rather than showing a single course of events progressing logically.

Thus we cannot deduce from evidence internal to the love song texts that they were commonly accompanied by mimetic actions or that, in the ones involving more than one character, different singers or actors took the roles of different personae. And while external evidence shows that full dramatic presentation was a possibility inasmuch as it was a known art form, this alone does not decide the issue. This is as much as we can say with confidence: that

5. "A drama must have a progression and a goal, and in a love drama, as the Song of Songs is imagined to be, this goal could only be that after various hitches, to put it colloquially, he and she catch each other. In the Song of Songs they catch each other much too early"—i.e., no later than the end of chap. 4, whereas in chap. 7 and the beginning of chap. 8 (according to Rudolph's understanding), the physical consummation of their love lies still in the future.

insofar as the poems create their worlds through personae, they may be said to use a dramatic mode of presentation.[6]

THE LITERARY FUNCTION OF DRAMATIC PRESENTATION

We experience the world of a dramatic poem (even when it is dramatic only in the limited sense described above) by means of the words of the characters in it, rather than by means of an authorial voice that comes from a point of view above and outside the world of the characters. Whatever we know of character, scene, or event we learn through the words of the personae, just as all our knowledge about what occurs in a play is derived from observation of the characters' words and actions. Informed in this way, our understanding of the characters' motives and personalities may be superior to their own understanding, for we stand and observe with the author. In a dramatic poem, a privileged vantage-point often allows the audience to experience a sense of collusion with the implied author, to feel that they are being let in on a secret, even to enjoy a certain voyeuristic pleasure.

Dramatic presentation of this sort shows characters objectively, insofar as it gives just the "facts," showing only what the characters say, with no overt commentary or evaluation. We are to discover for ourselves what this love and these lovers are like, just as in real life we discover what people are like by observing their words and actions. The feeling that we have made such discoveries for ourselves, and that we have done so by the same methods we employ in life, makes our perceptions all the more convincing. The author's absence is, however, a carefully wrought illusion. The author is present behind the scenes, communicating to us attitudes about the personae by shaping their words, determining their responses, and setting many of the norms by which we are to understand and evaluate the characters.[7]

6. Thus I follow Cannon in regarding Canticles as a dramatic poem in the way that Browning's monologues are dramatic; that is, the action of the poem is brought out by the agency of speakers who are introduced and characterized by what they say. I also agree with his idea that Canticles was designed to be recited or sung on festive occasions, though not meant for stage presentation (1913:9–15). Murphy (1979:442) says that although the Song is not drama proper (that is to say, is not meant for presentation as a stage play), it does have dramatic character in that there is movement from one love experience to the next. I agree with this characterization, but (like Cannon) I am using "dramatic" to refer to the mode of presentation rather than to the quality of its literary effect or to the relation between the parts of the dialogue.

7. Ewen defines the implied author as "a construction in the mind of the reader who realises the work in reading. While reading a story, the reader extracts and constructs its unity, and can discern a subtle artistic will imbuing the work with it. . . . Whenever a reader manages to give (or discover) a consistent meaning to a certain work, it should be attributed to the 'implied author' " (1974:ix).

The implied author is not necessarily to be identified with a single, real-life individual. A text (such as Canticles) may come into being by a long process involving many singers and

Forms of Discourse

In order to understand better the purposes of the various poems and the ways the lovers in them are characterized, it is useful to categorize speech in these poems as interior monologue, exterior monologue, double monologue, and dialogue. Discourse in the Egyptian love songs falls into the first three categories only.

INTERIOR MONOLOGUE (SOLILOQUY)

Most Egyptian love songs are interior monologues, in which the speaker addresses her heart,[8] or no one in particular, rather than speaking to someone in the world of the poem. Nor does the speaker in an interior monologue directly address the actual audience as, for example, in a Shakespearean epilogue. The words are to be understood as thoughts.

Interior monologue makes us, the external audience, privy to the speakers' deepest thoughts and feelings, showing what the personae are really like behind the mask of public behavior that people put on when speaking to others. We, the audience, are allowed to know that the girl who walked decorously down the street at her mother's side, who obeyed her command not to see the boy, and who is now sitting quietly in her house, is really in a ferment of love and desire (no. 34). We alone can know that the girl watching her boyfriend build an altar is fascinated by his exposed nakedness (no. 45). We alone know that the boy lying in bed and seemingly afflicted by illness is really trying a stratagem to get a girl to visit him (no. 6). And we alone know something not even the speaker in this poem shows awareness of, that he is indeed "sick"—love-sick. In these interior monologues the poet grants us the conspiratorial pleasure of observing unseen a young lover's sex-swept thoughts.

To determine whether a monologue is interior, we ask whether there is a listener implicit within the song. If not, the discourse is interior. The answer is usually clear. In the Egyptian songs, the use of the third person with reference to a beloved is a fairly good indicator of interior speech, for although the third person could be used to address another individual (as it is in Canticles), this does not seem to occur in the Egyptian love poems. Nowhere does a poem use the third person in speaking to or about the beloved when that person is clearly imagined as listening. One problematic case is the last part of "The Crossing" (nos. 20E–20G(A)), in which the boy speaks of his beloved in the third person as he embraces her:

---

scribes, and yet present "a single implied author, a homogeneous philosophical and artistic consciousness" (ibid.).

8. In the extant poems, only females address their hearts explicitly. Yet it is possible that boys' interior monologues are to be understood as addressed to their hearts.

My sister has come . . .
my arms are opened to embrace her.

(No. 20E)

Although he is with the girl, I think it is his thoughts that we are hearing. These stanzas are a natural continuation of the interior speech of the fourth stanza, in which the audience alone hears his thoughts as he crosses the river. In any case, he does not expect to elicit a reaction in the final three stanzas and is not asking her to do anything. In no. 45, too, the beloved is present, yet the girl's words seem to be her unspoken thoughts, as she describes to herself what she sees. In no. 14 the girl speaks as she is lying in bed with her beloved, but her words, ostensibly addressed to the dove, are apparently thoughts:

Stop it, bird!
You're teasing me.
I found my brother in his bedroom,
and my heart was exceedingly joyful.

All songs in which the speakers are males are apparently interior monologues. To be sure, if it was customary (and there is no evidence that it was) to praise a girl to her face in the third person, some of the boys' songs might be understood as spoken to their lovers (e.g., nos. 3 and 54). But since the boys do not direct their words to girls in the second person in these songs or say anything that calls for a response, and since there are no songs in which the third person is used while the other lover definitely is listening, we can safely interpret all songs formulated in the third person as interior monologues.

The use of the second person does not rule out a stanza's being interior speech. A girl can address her lover in the second person even in his absence; thus:

O my hero, my brother,
come, look upon me!

(No. 20C)

Her lover is across the river, and we can hardly imagine her attempting to shout to him across the Nile. In nos. 20A, 32, 36, 38, and 39, the second person is used alongside the third although the beloved is absent. In no. 20C, 34, and 40, the girl uses only the second person, while the boy's absence is implied. Such cases are apostrophes and should be understood as interior speech. Likewise, non-human objects, such as a bird (no. 14), a door (no. 47), the night (no. 20E), or a god (no. 36), can be addressed in interior speech, for one may speak to these in thought or when alone.

Some interior monologues represent the flow of consciousness by showing not a static moment of thought, but rather the movement of the speaker's thought, spoken as it takes shape. In no. 15 the speaker's words reveal her thought as it develops. Sitting at home waiting for her beloved to come, she begins to suspect that he is betraying her. By the end of the poem, she has convinced herself of this and is trying to persuade herself that she does not even care:

Well, what is it to me
that another's nasty heart
makes me into a stranger!

The fourth stanza of "The Crossing" (no. 20D) is also dynamic, moving from the boy's fears as he stands on one side of the river, through the crossing, where he faces his fears and overcomes them, to his exultation as he embraces his beloved (no. 20E). "The Stroll" taken as a whole also depicts developing attitudes, from the excitements and hopes of love at first sight to the sighs and despair of unfulfilled desires. The development of thought is not revealed in a straight line, however, for the fourth and fifth stanzas (nos. 34, 35) contain flashbacks to the original encounter. Song no. 8 too traces movement in thought, as the girl sails into the canal, meets her beloved, and walks with him into the garden.

The introspective nature of the interior monologue, together with the omniscient point of view it affords the audience, makes it a highly suitable vehicle for the sort of psychological observation that seems to have so interested the Egyptian poets in their explorations of the feelings and thoughts occasioned by love.

Interior monologues found in the Egyptian songs may be broken down as follows: spoken by a girl—nos. 2, 8(A)–(B), 11, 12, 14, 15, 20A–20C, 32, 34, 36, 38–40, 44, 45; spoken by a boy—nos. 3, 5, 6, 7, 20D–20G(A), 31, 33, 35, 37, 43, 46, 47, 51, 52, 53, 54.

EXTERIOR MONOLOGUE

In exterior monologue the speaker addresses another person, who is understood as present and listening; one persona addresses another. In the Egyptian love songs, the speaker of an exterior monologue is always a girl and the listener always the male lover, with the insignificant exception of no. 20G(B)–(C), where the boy gives orders to a servant, and the more problematic exception of "The Orchard," where it is sometimes unclear who is speaking to whom.

In an exterior monologue we hear one side of a dialogue. Yet what we hear is often sufficient to let us feel that we are overhearing an intimate conversation between lovers:

> This hour flows forth for me forever—
> it began when I lay with you.
> In sorrow and in joy,
> you have exalted my heart.
> Do not [leave] me

(No. 17)

> Then take my breasts,
> that their gift may flow forth to you . . .

(No. 1)

The exterior monologue creates an implicit listener, a silent partner in the conversation whose personality and attitudes can sometimes be read out of the words of the speaker. Thus in no. 1 we see reflected in the girl's words a young man exhausted after a night of lovemaking, perhaps also worried about getting caught where he should not be, trying to make his excuses and get away. Usually, however, the silent listener only advances the characterization of the speaker, and the listener's personality is not developed on its own.

Only rarely do both interior and exterior monologues appear within a single short song or a single stanza of a complex song. Song no. 8 begins in interior monologue as the girl sails to a rendezvous with her lover (sections (A)–(B), then when they meet ((C)–(E)) it turns into an exterior monologue. The last stanza of "The Crossing" (no. 20G) moves from interior monologue, in which the boy thinks how intoxicating it is to kiss his beloved, to exterior speech, as he commands a servant to prepare the bed.

The speech in "The Orchard" is difficult to classify. For the most part the trees speak to an indefinite audience, but in no. 28(F) the tree seems to address the boy. Perhaps the trees' "speech" is really the rustling of their leaves in the wind and is in that sense audible to those near it. In no. 28(G) the girl seems to be speaking to the boy in exterior monologue, but this is very uncertain.

Exterior monologues are found in the following Egyptian songs: spoken by a girl—nos. 1, 4, 8(C)–(E), 9, 10, 13(?), 16, 17–19, 50, 54; spoken by a boy (to servant)—nos. 20G(B)–(C); spoken by trees—nos. 28, 29, 30(C)–(E).

DOUBLE MONOLOGUE

So far in this chapter we have been considering the form of presentation of individual units, which may be either short songs or stanzas of longer songs.

In two of the longer songs, "The Crossing" and "The Stroll," stanzas spoken by a boy are joined to stanzas spoken by a girl to create a new form, the double monologue. Speech in the double monologue is always interior (with the minor exception of no. 20G(B)–(C), where the boy apparently addresses a servant). In "The Crossing" the boy's words (nos. 20D–20G) are simply put after the girl's (nos. 20A–20C). In "The Stroll" the boy and girl speak in alternate stanzas.[9]

Neither "The Crossing" nor "The Stroll" includes *dialogue*, because the lovers do not converse with each other. In "The Crossing" the girl addresses her lover in the second person only when he is on the other side of the river, and what we hear are her wishes, which her lover fulfills on his own initiative. For his part, he does not address her, even while embracing her. There is certainly no two-way communication. In "The Stroll" the interwoven monologues are also clearly interior. The lovers are isolated at separate homes as they speak of their experiences, and neither is aware of the thoughts of the other.

There is a progression in technical sophistication from the simple monologue to the double monologue in which one lover's words are conjoined to the other's ("The Crossing"), and then to the double monologue in which the speakers alternate ("The Stroll"). In the last, the interplay between the two voices is more complex and subtle, and the time-line does not proceed in chronological sequence. The audience must not merely look first at one persona and then at the other, but must alternate between two speakers, reconstructing events and personalities from hints and allusions interspersed in the two monologues. It seems likely, then, that songs like "The Crossing," which develop in a direct and simple sequence, preceded and prepared the way for more complex structures, such as that of "The Stroll." I would not, however, try to fix the relative dates of the particular songs on the basis of this hypothesis.

DIALOGUE

True love dialogue, logically the next step in the developmental sequence, is not used in the extant Egyptian poems. The extant corpus is large enough to justify the hypothesis that dialogue was not among the forms of Egyptian love poetry. The contemporaneous narrative literature makes extensive use of dialogue, so the technical resource was available to the love poets. Mixed male and female choruses, judging from the tomb paintings, were infrequent, but the double monologues show that both sexes could speak in a single

9. A close analogue to the alternating double monologue is the *wechsel*, common among the early poets of the medieval German *Minnesang*. In the *wechsel* loosely connected strophes are spoken alternately by the man and woman in an echoing exchange in which the lovers do not address each other directly, but speak in monologue or address a messenger (Sayce, 1967:xiv).

song. It seems fair to conclude that the Egyptian love poets did not use dialogue because they did not need it. They did not choose to portray interaction that requires dialogue (see further "Communication Between Lovers" in chapter 8).

In sharp contrast, the Song of Songs makes extensive use of dialogue. None of the speech is interior: the speakers never address their hearts or an indefinite audience, but rather speak to each other and respond to each other. In some passages, to be sure, it is difficult to identify the listener, but for the most part it is clear that some listener is intended and it is generally obvious who this is.

Most of the words are spoken by one lover to the other. In one brief bit of dialogue, the Shulammite's brothers seem to be the speakers (8:8–9; see commentary). The Shulammite directs much of what she says to the girls of Jerusalem (2:5–7; 3:7–11 [see v. 11]; 5:2–8, 10–16; 6:2; 8:3–4; and probably 2:8–17 and 3:15).[10] Once it seems to be the boy who is addressing them (7:1b; see commentary). Occasionally it is they who speak, usually in response to the Shulammite (3:6[?]; 5:1b[?]; 5:9; 6:1; 7:1a[?]). Their presence makes interior monologue unnecessary. The poet chooses to show us how lovers behave—with each other and with others—thereby revealing their thoughts entirely through their dialogue.

Unlike the lovers in the Egyptian songs, the lovers in Canticles communicate with each other: they speak to each other, hear each other's words, and respond to them. Some of the lovers' dialogue is quoted within narrative sections spoken to the girls of Jerusalem (2:10b–15[?]; 5:2b–3). Some dialogue includes passages that are spoken by one of the lovers and are so long that they give the impression of being monologues, as when the Shulammite alone speaks in 3:1–5, 5:2–8, and 5:10–16. But these passages are part of dialogues with the girls of Jerusalem, as is shown by the Shulammite's address to them (3:5; 5:8) and by their responses (3:6; 5:9; see commentary).

Other relatively long passages spoken by one person begin or end as dialogues. Cant 1:1–8, in which the Shulammite praises the boy's lovemaking and explains her situation to the girls of Jerusalem, concludes with her question to him and his response. Cant 7:1b–10a (praise of the Shulammite) is apparently a response to 7:1a ("Come back, come back, O perfect one") and leads into dialogue at 7:10b. The Praise Song in 4:8–15 too develops into an exchange of words (4:16–5:1a). On the other hand, 3:7–11 (the description of the royal bed), 4:1–7 (a Praise Song), and 6:4–10 (a Praise Song) do not elicit immediate responses.

10. Cant 2:8–17 includes a quoting phrase, "My beloved spoke and said to me" (2:10), which suggests that the Shulammite is telling these events *to* someone. The adjuration to the girls of Jerusalem in 3:5 suggests that the events of 3:1–5 are told to them. Furthermore, 5:2–7, which is parallel to these two passages together, is explicitly narrated to the girls of Jerusalem; see 5:8.

Nevertheless the Song taken as a whole is dialogue—people are always talking with other people, who often respond in a way that shows that they were listening and were affected by what they heard. The function of dialogue in characterizing the interaction between the lovers will be discussed under "Communication Between Lovers" in chapter 8.

GRAMMATICAL PERSON

Some of the uses of grammatical person in the love songs are unexpected and worthy of attention, for they throw light on the behavior of the characters and the poets' views of love. As was noted above, males and females in the Egyptian love songs differ in the ways they use grammatical person. The second person is used by boys to address servants, gods, non-humans (door, night), and by girls to address gods, non-humans, and their lovers, both in their presence (in exterior and interior speech) and in their absence (interior speech). The third person is used by boys to refer to girls (in interior speech), in their absence and in their presence, and by girls to refer to boys in their absence (in interior speech).

Thus, while girls often speak to boys in the second person, in thought and in overt speech, boys never address girls in the second person, even in thought.[11] I am not aware of a similar avoidance of the second person anywhere else in Egyptian literature. Even kings and gods could be addressed in the second person. There are enough Egyptian love songs extant to make it likely that this usage is a genuine convention of the genre and not merely an accident of discovery. Chosen deliberately or not, this convention seems to reveal assumptions about the ways males and females differ in love. I therefore consider its significance in chapter 8 in the context of the poets' ideas about the relations between the sexes.

In the Song, unlike the Egyptian love poems, both sexes use the second person freely. A different peculiarity, however, is to be noted in the forms of address in the Song: the use of indirect (third person) address alongside direct (second person) address. The exchange of praise that began in the second person in 1:15, "How beautiful you are, my darling . . . ," continues in 2:2 in the third person: "Like a lily among brambles, so is my darling among girls." "Like an apricot tree among trees of the thicket, so is my beloved among boys: I delight to sit in his shade, and his fruit is sweet to my palate" (2:2–3).

11. The male who speaks in the fragmentary song no. 51 *quotes* what he says to his beloved: "I spend the day imploring [my lady]: . . . 'Don't do (that) to me.'" Within the framework of the poem, however, he is not addressing her. In no. 14 the girl quotes what she and her lover say to each other. Since the males' words in both cases are quotations, neither of these songs is an exception to the rule that males do not speak to their lovers in the Egyptian love songs. It is possible, though in my opinion doubtful, that no. 28(G) is spoken by the boy to the girl.

There is no doubt that the lovers are speaking *to* each other in 2:2–3 and hearing each other, although they use the third person. Likewise in 4:16 it is clear that the girl's invitation, "Let my beloved come into his garden," is spoken to the boy, for he responds immediately and directly (5:1). Similarly his statement "But one alone is she—my dove, my perfect one" (6:9) is only formally third person; in intent it is address, spoken to the Shulammite as is the rest of 6:4–11. The third-person declaration, "I am my beloved's and his passion is for me" (7:11), is likewise incorporated in a second-person exchange.

In light of this usage there is no reason to be surprised by similar enallage elsewhere—or to emend it away, as does, for example, BHK in 1:2. Cant 1:2aα, "Oh that he'd kiss me with the kisses of his mouth," is spoken *to* the boy no less than is 1:2aβ, "for your caresses are better than wine." Similarly the words of 1:4, "Take me with you, let us hasten! The king has brought me to his chambers [i.e., *you* have brought me to your chambers]. We will be glad and rejoice in you . . . ," and those of 1:12, "While the king is on his couch . . . ," all are spoken to the boy. Indirect address is used because of its slight alteration of tone. In Hebrew (and Aramaic) the third person is often used as a respectful way of addressing superiors, especially kings (e.g., Gen 27:31; Ezra 5:17; 9:6–15 passim; Est 1:19; 3:8–9; II Sam 14 passim, especially vv. 11, 13, 17, where the second and third persons are used with the same referent in a single sentence). Through its indirectness third-person address conveys a tone of respect and awe. It is a verbal gesture that resembles the physical gesture of averting one's eyes instead of staring boldly at the king's face. Something of that tone of courtesy and awe is suggested when the lovers address each other in the third person in Canticles. It is a tone similar to that implied by the epithets of respect the lovers use of each other: "king," "prince," and "noblewoman." The slight distancing suggested by indirect address is balanced by the directness and intimacy of the direct address with which it is closely linked. The lovers in Canticles are at once respectful and intimate.

CHAPTER 7

What the Love Songs Speak About: The Major Themes

A theme, as I will use the term, is a prominent event, image, or verbal pattern that maintains its identity even as it is reworked and endowed with new meanings in new poems.[1]

The thematic resources of a literary genre are both flexible and persistent—as Richmond (1964) has shown so clearly for Western love poetry[2]

1. This admittedly (and unavoidably) loose working definition has the virtue of not requiring us to distinguish between content and form—a distinction that is sometimes useful but often uncertain or impossible. Formal features are significant for the definition of some themes. The Wishes theme, for example, has a distinctive structure (see below), but it also has a clearly definable content—a wish to be near the beloved—without which the structure could hardly be described. In other cases, however, such as the Love Trap theme, there is no characteristic structural pattern. See Levin, 1968, for a discussion of the scope and purpose of "thematology" and a survey of the ways in which "theme" (or *Stoff*) has been used. The term is not susceptible of tight definition but is nevertheless found useful by many literary scholars.

2. An example of the history of a theme in Western poetry will help to clarify the concept and to show how traditional thematic material can be used by different poets (traced by Richmond, 1964:251ff.). The image of the fleeing hind, representing the beloved, begins with Horace as a minor trope describing the unnecessary timidity of Chloë (Odes, I, xxiii). Petrarch (CXC) elaborates the figure into an ornate allegory heavy with medieval heraldic emblems as well as with Christian and neoplatonic allusions. Wyatt's "Who so list to hount" maintains many of the details of Petrarch's figure but strips the theme of its allegorical significance and ornate imagery, intensifying its impact by colloquial, unmannered, personal expression. This classical theme is exploited variously by other poets, who build on the earlier uses to develop further insights and new forms of expression. Finally, the 17th century poet John Hall in "The Call" synthesizes the tradition by taking it in his "rhetorical stride" (as Richmond puts it) and condensing the theme

—and they are of great importance in the individual creative act. Poets use old themes in shaping new content. Thus themes are significant clues to the literary critic who wishes to illuminate the poet's attitudes, feelings, and intentions.

A single theme can be treated in radically different ways in literature as in music, where a certain melody or harmonic structure can undergo limitless variations in tempo, rhythm, volume, instrumentation, and so on, producing profoundly different effects while remaining recognizably the same theme.

A theme may extend over an entire poem, or it may be restricted to a stanza or a section thereof, with the result that a song or a poetic unit can have more than one theme. Song no. 3, for example, combines the themes of Praise of the Beloved and the Love Trap. A poem that presents Love in a Garden may also offer Description of Love or Praise of the Beloved. The scope and shape of a theme may vary widely as it is used and reused.

Themes are not indivisible. Many themes I list could be subdivided into more limited ones, and if more songs were extant it might prove useful to do so. I would hesitate, however, to pursue a detailed taxonomy, for an atomistic approach probably would do little more than produce long lists of "topoi" or motifs such as characterize some exercises in "*Motivforschung*."

Theme is an important factor in determining literary type (*Gattung*), though not the only one. The Wishes theme, for example, is the salient characteristic of a type we may call the "Wish Song," and songs or units whose dominant theme is Praise of the Beloved can be designated "Praise Songs." Having few examples of love poetry from ancient Egypt and only one from Israel, we can neither define all the themes clearly nor trace the historical development of themes with confidence. Some topics, images, and settings in the love poems might prove to be themes if more poems were extant. For example, in no. 4 the girl's defiant refusal to quit her lover might be a distinct theme. But as we have no other poems with this topic, I have included the song among the exemplars of the Description of Love.

Many and diverse sources besides the Egyptian love songs may have influenced the Israelite love poets, either indirectly, as Hebrew literature in general grew out of a broader cultural milieu, or directly, as the love song poets themselves drew on foreign models. Scholars looking for parallels have most often turned to Mesopotamian Sacred Marriage poetry and have argued that there are extensive and significant thematic connections between the two (see chapter 5). In fact, however, texts associated with the Sacred Marriage rites use a very different stock of themes, of which the most important are: suitors (farmer and shepherd) who vie for a wife by describing the gifts they can offer

into a brief phrase: "like a young roe" (ibid., p. 258). The theme that Petrarch developed so elaborately would hardly be recognizable in this simple image if we did not know the place of this theme in the ongoing dialectic among European love poets. The thematic tradition imbues the brief simile with a broad halo of associations that it would not have in an artistic vacuum.

her (Kramer, 1969:68–72); the fertility of the goddess (ibid., p. 81); ritual preparations for marriage (ibid., pp. 80–82); prayers to the bride (Inanna) for blessings, such as long life and royal power, fertility of the land and of the womb (ibid., pp. 83, 99f.); the goddess's gift of abundance and fertility (ibid., pp. 101f.); the goddess's praise of her vulva (ibid., pp. 94, 98); mating of animals (ibid., p. 103); Dumuzi's death and resurrection (ibid., pp. 104–6, 107–33, passim). These themes have parallels neither in the Egyptian love songs nor in the Song of Songs. The only important theme shared by Canticles and the Sacred Marriage Songs is Love in the Garden (see further below).

Whether themes in the Song that have Egyptian parallels are rightly seen as continuations of the Egyptian themes, as I tend to think, or are rather independent developments, cannot be determined with any certainty. But even where creation is independent, parallel themes can serve as analogues that highlight the particular character and meaning of the poems in which they appear. Here then are the most prominent themes and the use the love poets made of them.

Praise of the Beloved

"Praise of the Beloved" refers to a series of statements lauding and describing the beloved boy or girl with anything from simple adjectives to extended metaphors. Poems or literary units in which Praise of the Beloved is dominant constitute a literary type known as the Praise Song.

THE EGYPTIAN LOVE SONGS

This theme is dominant in only two Egyptian love songs—nos. 31 and 54. When we turn to Canticles, it will be useful to distinguish different forms of Praise Songs. The only form represented in the Egyptian love poems, however, is the Description Song (the *waṣf*), in which the beloved's body is praised part by part:

> Long of neck, white of breast,
> her hair true lapis lazuli.
> Her arms surpass gold,
> her fingers are like lotuses.

(No. 31)

Songs that are not primarily praise of a lover may use the Description form for humor and surprise. In the first stanza of "The Orchard" (no. 28), the tree includes in its self-praise comparisons between its parts and those of the girl: "My pits resemble her teeth, my fruit resembles her breasts." Such comparisons are a parodic reversal of the Praise Song, in which a girl's parts are praised by being compared to plants. Another humorous twist in this song is the use of the form of the Praise of the Beloved in self-praise. In the third stanza (no. 30), a little sycamore is the subject of a Praise Song. This time, however, the praise is spoken by the poet. This theme is modified playfully in song no. 3 too, where it leads into the Love Trap theme:

> [The mouth of] my sister is a lotus,
> her breasts are mandragoras,
> [her] arms are [branches] . . .

Halfway through we learn that the girl is being described as a verdant marsh in which a bird trap lies hidden: "her head is the trap of 'love-wood.'"

Systematic praise of women also appears outside the love song genre. Among the examples quoted in Appendix A, no. i (praise of Nefertari, 19th dynasty), no. v (a 22nd dynasty memorial inscription), and no. vi (a Ptolemaic inscription) laud women in a way reminiscent of the Praise of the Beloved theme. The Mutirdis inscription (no. v) in particular is similar to the earlier Praise Songs. Compare "most beautiful of women: a lass whose like has never been seen" (no. v) with "One alone is my sister, having no peer: more gracious than all other women" (no. 31). Compare further the itemized praise of hair, teeth, and breasts with the itemized praise of the girl's features in no. 31. Such similarities may be fortuitous, but it may be that usages familiar from Praise Songs were incorporated into memorial inscriptions.

The Praise of the Beloved typically concludes with a generalization summarizing the beauty of the girl (or, in the case of no. 30, of the tree)[3] and telling of her effect on the speaker (no. 54) or on all who see her (nos. 30, 31). In no. 3 the boy describes his beloved's effect on him by identifying himself as the bird caught in the trap.

In the Egyptian songs praise tends to be literal and graphic: "Long of neck, white of breast" (no. 31); "Her necklace is of flowers" (no. 54), and so on. The metaphorical comparisons that do appear for the most part use fairly obvious tropes to enhance physical description (e.g., "her hair is true lapis lazuli" in no. 31), or to assert value and beauty (e.g., "Her arms surpass gold," ibid.), gold and lapis lazuli being Egyptian clichés for beauty and preciousness. In one unusually bold image, "Behold her, like Sothis rising at the beginning of a good year" (no. 31), the poet immediately uses literal descriptives to explicate and control the implications of the metaphor: "shining, precious, white of skin." Only one other image in this song allows much scope to the audience's imagination: "her fingers are like lotuses." In none of the

3. The Praise Song in the first part of no. 30 concludes: "She attracts those not beneath her, for her shadow cools the air."

Praise Songs is there an attempt to make the images of a song work together to create an atmosphere or a cohesive background picture. Song no. 3, however, does coordinate metaphors in a playful way in describing the girl as a bird trap.

Hermann (1955) argued that the erotic Description Song developed from the cultic Description Hymn, which identified the parts of the body of the dead king (and later of ordinary mortals) with those of divinities: for example, "Your head is that of the Horus of the morning sun. Your visage is that of *Mḫnty-irty*, your eyes and ears are the twin children of Atum," and so on (Pyr. §§148ff.). In fact, however, the erotic Description Songs have nothing in common with the cultic Description Hymns besides the listing of parts of the body. Nowhere in the love songs are the parts of the girl's or boy's body identified with gods or anything belonging to gods. Furthermore, the predications in the cultic hymns are not meant to praise the dead man's body but rather to bestow upon it the protective power of divinity.

THE SONG OF SONGS

Praise of the Beloved is the most important theme in Canticles, both in simple quantity and in the decisive role it plays in conveying the poem's meaning. The following passages are Praise Songs:[4]: 1:9–16a (both lovers speak), 2:1–3 (both lovers), 4:1–7 (the boy speaks), 4:9–15 (boy), 5:10–16 (girl), 6:4–10 (boy), and 7:2–10a (boy).

In Canticles the theme of Praise of the Beloved takes three forms:

1. The *waṣf* or "Description Song"[5] (*Beschreibungslied*), which is composed mainly of simple, item-by-item praise of parts of the beloved's body or other qualities (4:1–7; 5:10–16; 6:4–10; 7:2–10a)
2. The Admiration Song (*Bewunderungslied*), in which one lover speaks and in which most of the declarations and metaphors apply to the beloved's beauty as a whole and its effect on the onlooker (4:9–15)
3. Admiration Dialogue, in which statements of praise and admiration are spoken by both lovers (1:9–16a; 2:1–3)[6]

4. I use the conventional term "Praise Song" to designate these passages, although properly speaking the exemplars of this theme in Canticles are sections within a larger song.

5. I again use the widely accepted term. While it is appropriate insofar as these units have the *appearance* of being descriptive, description is not their *purpose*, as I try to show in the following pages.

6. Horst (1961:176–78, 180–82) draws a distinction between *Bewunderungslied* and *Beschreibungslied*, assigning the Admiration Dialogues to the former. Since I divide the Song into different units from those he suggests, I assign different verses to the two categories. Murphy too (1973:418–21) distinguishes between the Description Song and the Admiration Song (in which category he includes the Admiration Dialogues), while doubting the complete discreteness of the two categories. The distinction is useful only if one keeps in mind that the dichotomy is not absolute and that the types can merge.

In Canticles, as in Egyptian song no. 3, Praise of the Beloved may be the theme of one poetic component set within a larger unit with a different main theme. Thus the *waṣf* in 5:10–16 is not an independent unit, but rather serves as an answer to the girls of Jerusalem, who have asked the Shulammite what is so special about her lover. This exchange is itself part of a longer unit, 5:2–6:3, whose theme is the Search for the Beloved. Even when a Praise Song has a degree of independence that justifies our reckoning it a separate section, it may still be linked to its immediate context. The Praise Song in 4:1–7 culminates naturally in the invitation to come away (4:8–9), which invitation is then supported by another Praise Song in 4:10–15, the latter in effect explaining the intensity of the girl's effect on the boy. The Praise Song in 7:2–10a seems to be spoken in response to a challenge implicit in 7:1a, but that verse is obscure (see commentary). The praise in 7:2–10a flows into the Shulammite's acceptance of the boy's love and her invitation to him to come away (7:10aβ–14).

Praise Songs in Canticles consist mostly of metaphors predicated of parts of the beloved's body or of the beloved person as a whole. As in the Egyptian songs, the *waṣfs* usually begin and end with a categorical declaration of the beloved's beauty or effect on the speaker and others (4:1a and 7; 5:10 and 15b–16; 6:4 and 10). Three of the four *waṣfs* (4:1–7; 5:10–16; 6:4–10) proceed more or less from the top of the body downward, while the other (7:2–10a) proceeds generally upward.

Certainly the outstanding characteristic of the Praise Songs is the profusion of metaphors praising the beloved's body and its parts. Such metaphors are rare outside the Praise Songs, appearing elsewhere in Canticles only in 1:3 and, in a somewhat different form, in 2:9. It is therefore important to examine the nature of these metaphors.

Imagery: The Problem and Some Proposals

The imagery of the Praise Songs in Canticles, particularly the Description Songs, has presented a perennial problem to interpreters. These passages seem to describe the lovers, but their imagery is unexpected, sometimes even disconcerting. Interpreters, assuming that the purpose of the imagery is physical description, have often tried to maximize the quantity of sensory data that could be transferred from the vehicles of the metaphors to their referents.[7] The smell of goats in her hair? A nose as long as a tower? A shining gold head

7. The *vehicle* is the element of a metaphor, usually a physical image, that elucidates the "given" element, the *referent*. It does not, strictly speaking, "carry" the meaning of the metaphor, but rather carries the *tenor*, the quality of the vehicle to be applied to the referent. The tenor is a component of the metaphor; it is not its meaning. "Tenor" has often been used inconsistently, sometimes to designate the subject spoken about, the "given" or "literal" term of the metaphor (which I will call the "referent"), sometimes to designate the quality conveyed by the vehicle.

on a boy—or is it red? Or white? Such a literalistic approach is obviously foreign to the spirit of the poem. Not only does the imagery convey little in the way of specific sensory information; it often actually frustrates transference of prominent physical attributes from image to referent. Take for example, the statement "Your nose is like the tower of Lebanon" (7:5). If the image is taken as *descriptive* of the length of the girl's nose,[8] then it is hyperbolic to the point of being grotesque. If the purpose is merely to describe its straightness, the simile says little and says it obscurely. The girls of Jerusalem could not be expected to identify the lost lover on the basis of the Shulammite's answer to their question (5:9–16)—and indeed the "description" she gives is not supposed to enable them to do so, for they do not ask *what* he looks like but, rather, what is so special about him. Besides, much of the imagery gives us information that does not even ostensibly describe the lovers, such as the specification of the places where the doves sit and bathe (5:12), the type of jewels that decorate the ivory bar (5:14b), and the name of the mountain from which the flock of goats streams down (4:1b; 6:5b). There is too much in the Praise Songs that is extraneous to depiction or that even works against it for that to be their purpose.

Gerleman (1965:68–72) took an original approach to the metaphors in the Praise Songs, claiming that the imagery of the *waṣf*s, as well as such literal descriptions as "bright and ruddy" (5:10), are indeed depictive, but that their models are not people but rather works of Egyptian art. The colors "white" (thus he understands *ṣaḥ*) and "ruddy" (5:10), for example, are not those of the youth but of statues and bronzes such as we find in Egypt. The comparison of hands to gold pivots in 5:14, he says, recalls the practice of overlaying the limbs of corpses with gold foil, a practice that—Gerleman

8. Some commentators have interpreted the image this way. For example, Pope presents as alternatives the explanations that the poet has "pressed his enthusiasm for salient features a bit far" or that the passage describes a "superhuman" (i.e., a goddess), in which case "the dismay about her towering or mountainous nose disappears as the perspective and proportions fall into focus" (1977:627). According to Rudolph, "Der Vergleich der Nase mit dem Libanonturm wirkt allzu grotesk, wenn man sich diesen als ein Bauwerk oben auf dem Libanon denkt; viel näher liegt ein Felsgebilde oder ein Gebirgsvorsprung, der 'Libanonturm' hiess . . ."(1977:173). ("The comparison of the nose to the tower of Lebanon makes far too grotesque an impression if one visualizes this as an edifice on the top of the Lebanon; it is more likely a rock formation or a mountain protrusion called the 'tower of Lebanon.'") This gratuitous assumption does not help matters much, for a rock formation or mountain projection seems hardly more appropriate—as straightforward description—than a tower. Segal sees this and other images as grotesque, but ascribes a literary function to the grotesquery: "Only as playful banter can be rationally explained the grotesque description by the lover to the damsel of her neck as 'like the tower of David built for an armoury,' of her nose 'as the tower of Lebanon which looketh toward Damascus,' and of her head like mount Carmel (iv 4, vii 5.6) and similar comical comparisons of her other limbs" (1962:480). Playful banter does have a place in the Song, but not here. Long series of *insults* would not be playful but merely offensive.

hypothesizes—may have had a parallel in the plastic arts. The eyes of the girl are compared to doves because the oval eyes in Egyptian paintings resemble (in Gerleman's opinion) doves. The description of legs as columns of alabaster set in pedestals of gold (5:15) is, he claims, clearly derived from sculpture.

Now it is true that the poet draws some images from the plastic arts (especially in 5:10–16) and even mentions the "work of an artist's hands" in 7:2. Yet even in 5:10–16 most of the images are taken from the natural world. The poet of Canticles draws upon many and diverse areas of life for images—as did the Egyptian poets. The poet of no. 31, for example, compares the girl's hair to lapis lazuli, her arms to gold, and her fingers to lotuses. And since the Egyptian love poets themselves did not take their imagery from Egyptian art, it is most unlikely that the poet of Canticles would have turned to it as a prime source of imagery. Moreover, the images in Canticles that Gerleman supposes to have been taken from Egyptian art nowhere appear in Egyptian love poetry. Eyes, for example, are never compared to doves or breasts to fawns. As for Cant 5:10–16, the images do in part suggest sculpture, but the details do not allow us to determine whether it is specifically *Egyptian* sculpture the author is drawing upon. When the poet clearly uses imagery from the plastic arts, foreign influence is indeed likely, since these arts were not well developed in Israel, and it was certainly possible for a learned Israelite to be familiar with Egyptian or Mesopotamian art, or both. But such art at most contributed to the reservoir of images at the poet's disposal and cannot be the key to understanding how the images are used. In any case, what is to be gained by looking to Egyptian art for the connection between eyes and doves? If artists indeed made eyes look like doves, a poet could just as easily have thought of the eye-dove comparison independently.

Yet even if we do not accept Gerleman's explanation of the Praise Song imagery, we can use Egyptian art to clarify the meaning of some of the metaphors in the Song because they seem to reflect an ideal of feminine beauty that resembles the Egyptian ideal. Societies, or at least their upper classes, often borrow tastes in fashion and beauty from foreign cultures that they consider more prestigious. Thus, for example, upper-class Jews of the second and first centuries B.C.E. drew upon Hellenistic physical ideals, and Russians in the 18th and 19th centuries looked to France in all matters of fashion and taste. We cannot, of course, say that Egypt was the sole source of influence in the formation of the ideal of beauty expressed in the Song, but it seems to have been one source.

The Nature of the Song's Imagery

Soulen (1967) made an important contribution to the interpretation of the metaphors in the Praise Songs by arguing that the *waṣf*s are not intended as pictorial representations. The metaphors are not "representational" but "presentational"; that is to say, they are not intended to describe the girl's physical features by visual comparisons, but rather to arouse "emotions consonant with those experienced by the suitor as he beholds the fullness of his beloved's attributes" (p. 189):

It should be obvious that comparisons of the female body to jewels (7:1), bowls of wine (7:2a), heaps of wheat (7:2b), and so on, are not intended to aid a mental image of the maiden's appearance or merely to draw parallels to her qualities; they, and others like them, seek to overwhelm and delight the hearer, just as the suitor is overwhelmed and delighted in her presence. (p. 190)

In T. S. Eliot's terminology, the images are "objective correlatives."

I certainly agree that the poet is not aiming at a physical depiction. For simple depiction, images closer in appearance to the object represented could have been chosen. As it is, the description provided by the Praise Songs hardly gives us a picture of either lover.

Nevertheless I think that Soulen slights the representational qualities of the metaphors. First of all, the imagery of the *waṣf*s takes the *form* of an itemized physical description, with one-to-one correspondences between the images and parts of the body (your eyes are like *X*, your cheeks are like *Y*, etc.), as if the poet were seeking to be analytical and precise. The poet does not merely heap up lovely images (or images of lovely things) to overwhelm us with imagined sense-impressions, but rather seeks a particular image for each part of the body and organizes these images in an itemized list. The one-to-one correspondences between images and parts of the body make us feel that some quality peculiar to each part, and not just a general feeling of affection, calls forth these images.

Second, the images have some sensory, objective feature[9] in common with their referents, such as the length of the neck, suggested by the tower, or the whiteness of the teeth, indicated by the washed sheep. Images are selected to match the specific item of which they are predicated. Thus the scarlet thread is an image of lips, not of the belly, and the flock of goats streaming down a mountainside is said to be like the girl's hair, not her eyes. It is two gazelles, and not one or three, to which her breasts are compared.

Conversely, the teeth, white and matched, are compared to shorn sheep, not to the (probably black) goats streaming down Gilead, although goats have more or less the same affective overtones as sheep. Moreover, the metaphors in the *waṣf*s are formulated as comparisons[10] rather than as statements of atti-

9. "Objective" in the sense that this feature's presence in image and referent could be easily verified by an outside observer: e.g., blackness, evenness, height. "Subjective" in this context means that the congruity between image and referent resides in the speaker's attitude toward both; such qualities are gentleness, nobility, and preciousness.

10. There is widespread agreement among modern literary theorists that the classical grammatical distinction between simile and metaphor is not in itself significant with regard to poetic effect. Simile and nominal predication are two ways of formulating a metaphor; see, e.g., No-

tude: "Your hair is like a flock of goats," rather than "Your hair is to me like a flock of goats."[11] In the Description Songs the speaker connects the referent and image directly, rather than explicitly making personal perceptions mediate between them.

In spite of the ostensibly descriptive qualities of the Praise Songs, we cannot fully explain the meaning of a metaphor merely by pointing out the sensory resemblance between an image and its referent. What an objectively shared trait does is to bridge the terms of the metaphor and allow the reader to think of the referent in terms of the image. In descriptive metaphor, where the sensory link is prominent and extensive, the linkage serves to communicate a sharper picture of the referent. But that is not the case with these metaphors, where the primary role of the sensory common denominator is to make the metaphor *possible*. As Ricoeur (1976:51) argues, metaphor does not consist in clothing an idea in an image, but rather in reducing the shock engendered by two incompatible ideas, so that "it is in the reduction of this gap or difference that resemblance plays a role." Thus shorn ewes are a pleasant and effective image for teeth because of their evenness and whiteness, whereas a comparison such as "your teeth are like gazelles" lacks a bridge between the terms to allow the transfer of affective qualities. But a metaphor depends for its meaning—its full contextual meaning with its new and unparaphrasable connotations—not only on the extent of the common ground but also on the "metaphoric distance" between image and referent: that is, the degree of unexpectedness or incongruity between the juxtaposed elements and the magnitude of the dissonance or surprise it produces.[12] Greater metaphoric distance produces psychological arousal, a necessary component of aesthetic pleasure.[13] On the other hand, distance to the point of incompatibility of image and referent—for example, "Your teeth are like leafy boughs"—makes a metaphor ineffective if not absurd.[14]

In explicating these metaphors we should point out the sensory links between image and referent, not as if doing so would pin down the metaphors'

wottny, 1962:50f., and Wheelwright, 1962:71. The force of "Your eyes are doves" (4:1), for example, is not noticeably different from that of "his eyes are like doves" (5:12). Most metaphors in Canticles use the *kaph* of comparison, but others lacking it do appear, apparently at random. By "comparison" I mean a metaphor where the image is explicitly predicated of the subject, whether or not *kaph* is used. A metaphorical epithet like "my dove" is not a comparison.

11. This type of comparison appears in an Admiration Song, 1:13–14.

12. Martindale, 1975:23–30, 119–29. Ricoeur (1975:78) calls this "semantic impertinence": "the mutual unsuitability of the terms when interpreted literally."

13. In a computer-aided study of a large sample of French poetry (ca. 1800 to ca. 1940) and English poetry (ca. 1700 to ca. 1840), Martindale (1975:chap. 8 and passim) found a clear and measurable progression in both series toward greater metaphoric distance and more frequent juxtaposition of incongruous words.

14. Unless its purpose is to convey grotesqueness, humor, or disturbance, or deliberately to grate or shock.

meanings, but with the purpose of showing what enables these images to function in metaphors. We can examine the extent of the representational force of a particular metaphor also to ascertain which qualities of the image are *not* relevant to this specific comparison, so as to avoid the distortions in the force of the metaphor that would arise if we were to transfer inappropriate traits from image to referent. The relevant similarities between the belly and a heap of wheat, for example, do not include the size of the heap, nor is the movement of the sheep meaningful in the connection between the sheep and the girl's teeth. It is often difficult to determine just what does belong to the sensory nexus. In principle we should beware of attributing to the image qualities not in harmony with the ideal of beauty suggested elsewhere in the Song or with the general atmosphere that the imagery creates. There is no objective way of applying this principle; only the reader's aesthetic sensitivity can decide the pertinence of this or that association.

The poet chooses images in such a way as to make us feel their sensory—even erotic—substantiality and not only their affective congruity with their referents. We are to see, smell, taste, and feel the things spoken of, and not merely to enjoy the pleasant connotations of the imagery in its totality. At the same time, a tension is created: the sensory common denominator attracts image to referent, while a metaphoric distance is adamantly maintained by a certain incongruity between the terms.[15] The existence of this tension is evidenced by the commentators' frequent discomfort. The tension should not be slighted by an exclusive focus on either the representational force of the metaphors or their undoubted presentational function. This tension, I will argue in chapter 8, is in fact essential to the creation of a profoundly new vision of love.

MESOPOTAMIAN PARALLELS

Although the Praise Songs in Canticles are far bolder in their use of metaphors than are the Egyptian Praise Songs, the Praise Songs in both clearly resemble each other in structure and content. There are, on the other hand, no strong correspondences to them in extant Mesopotamian or Syrian literature, in which goddesses are praised, but not human lovers. Nor does the sort of itemized "description" characteristic of the *waṣf*s have good parallels in Mesopotamia or Syro-Palestine. The closest Mesopotamian parallel to Canticles' Praise Songs is "The Message of Ludingira to His Mother" (Cooper, 1971), a Sumerian literary text. A man called Ludingira sends a message to his mother and gives the messenger five "signs" to enable him to recognize

15. This is to be distinguished from the tension that Ricoeur (1976:50) identifies as the source of all metaphorical meaning, namely the tension between two *interpretations* of the utterance—the literal interpretation and the metaphorical interpretation, the latter created by the self-destruction of the former.

her. Four of these "signs" are passages consisting of rhapsodic metaphors strikingly similar to those in the Praise Songs in Canticles. For example:

My mother is brilliant in the heavens, a doe in the mountains,
A morning star abroad at noon,
Precious carnelian, a topaz from Marhashi,
A prize for the king's daughter, full of charm,
A *nir*-stone seal, an ornament like the sun,
A bracelet of tin, a ring of *antasura*,
A shining piece of gold and silver,
. . .
An alabaster statuette set on a lapis pedestal,
A living rod of ivory, whose limbs are filled with charm.

(Cooper, 1971:160)

The hyperbolic, rhapsodic "description" in this text resembles Canticles in the quality of the metaphors more than the Egyptian Praise Songs do. On the other hand, the praise in "Ludingira" is general, not itemized part by part. In its generality it resembles the Admiration Song in Cant 4:12–15 more than the other Praise Songs, but the images are completely different. The main difference between "Ludingira" and Canticles is, of course, that the former describes the speaker's mother, the latter the speaker's beloved. "Ludingira" is not a love song, but it is quite possible that this poem borrows forms and images from a lost Mesopotamian love song tradition.

Description of Love

The Description of Love is an introspective report on the emotions of love and the feelings associated with it. Whereas in the Praise of the Beloved the speaker describes the beauties of the lover, in the Description of Love the speaker—usually the girl—describes her feelings, telling of her beloved's effect on her. The Description of Love, unlike Praise of the Beloved, is not identifiable with a distinctive literary form.

THE EGYPTIAN LOVE SONGS

In the Egyptian love songs, where this theme is prominent, it appears mostly in interior monologue and is thus not a way of complimenting the beloved. It is rather a type of self-revelation. The lover seeks to express the intensity and the pervasive effects of the emotions of love. She may simply declare that love's influence is powerful and incessant—for example: "[I dwell on] your love through day and night . . . " (no. 20A); this is interior monologue. More frequently she seeks imagery that expresses the nuances and intensity of her emotions, attempting to communicate subjective feelings by objective images, usually images of harmonious pairs and mixtures. These images express thorough blending and mixing, as well as a sense of sweetness and pleasantness. For example:

> Your love [i.e., my love for you] is mixed in my body,
> like . . . ,
> [like honey] mixed with water,
> like mandragoras in which gum is mixed.
>
> (No. 2)

> It [your love] is like a mandragora
> in a man's hand.
> It is like dates
> he mixes in beer.
>
> (No. 20B)

Love fulfilled is the highest joy. Several songs describe the ecstasy of a lover's embrace: "Seeing you has brightened my eyes," says a girl to her lover (no. 17). A boy hugs his beloved and says: "My heart is as happy in its place as a fish within its pond" (no. 20E). His girl's embrace and kiss are intoxicating (nos. 20F, 20G (A)). The moment of lovemaking flows forth forever like a fountain (no. 17).

The girl speaking in no. 4 describes the intoxicating pleasure of lovemaking by declaring her determination never to stop. Here the girl seems to be speaking aloud to her lover, letting him know the power of her feelings. Nothing short of being physically beaten away to the far reaches of the earth could remove her from the delights her beloved has to offer.

Some Descriptions of Love tell of the sickness love causes when the beloved is absent. Descriptions of love-sickness use imagery similar to that used in descriptions of love's pleasures and have the same introspective quality. Love, in the absence of the beloved, causes illness. The lover becomes paralyzed, a symptom meant literally and described in detail in no. 37. One's body becomes heavy and out of control (no. 37). Normal pleasures are nullified and tastes confused:

> When I behold sweet cakes,
> [they seem like] salt.
> Pomegranate wine, once sweet in my mouth—
> it is now like the gall of birds.
>
> (No. 12)

In the agitation of desire, one's heart may "flee" the body and go forth to seek the beloved, making normal activities impossible and causing one to behave irrationally, to be like one who has "collapsed out of love" (no. 34). In no. 16 a girl describes the distraction to which love has driven her, though not depicting it quite as an illness. No. 15 shows the workings of jealousy. Lovesickness is treated humorously in no. 6, where the youth decides to feign illness as a ruse to get his beloved to come to him.

Many of the mixtures used to describe the feelings of love are identifiable as medicines (see no. 2, n. b; no. 20B, n. a; no. 20F, n. d), for love is strong medicine. It brings about vitality, well-being, and wholeness. Love's fulfillment by the presence of the beloved is the only medicine effective for a lover: "The scent of your nose alone is what revives my heart," says the love-sick girl in no. 12, and the bed-ridden youth in no. 37 states that no medicines, but only the announcement of his beloved's visit, can revive him, for "She is more powerful for me than the Compendium" (of medicine). The presence of the beloved also nourishes and invigorates the healthy:

> To hear your voice is pomegranate wine to me:
> I draw life from hearing it.
> Could I see you with every glance,
> it would be better for me
> than to eat or to drink.
>
> (No. 18)

> Your form revives hearts . . .
> . . . your voice,
> which makes my body strong.
>
> (No. 20A)

The girl in no. 13 calls her beloved her "health and life," for without him she is like "one who lies in her grave."

Although the Description of Love usually seeks to characterize the feelings of a single individual, one image encapsulates the love relationship: "My heart is in balance with yours" (no. 17, cf. no. 11, no. 20A), meaning that their desires are the same.

THE SONG OF SONGS

The introspective description of love, so prominent in Egyptian poems, can scarcely be said to exist as a theme in Canticles. Only a few isolated sentences *directly* describe the speaker's feelings: "and his fruit is sweet to my palate" (2:3b); "for I am sick with love!" (2:5b); "You have captured my heart, my sister, my bride, you have captured my heart" (4:9); "Because of him my soul went forth" (5:6b); "Turn your eyes away from me, for they make me tremble" (6:5a); "I do not know myself" (6:12a; see commentary). Most of these statements simply reinforce praise of the beloved. The declaration beginning "for love is as strong as death" (8:6–7) is a generalization on the nature of love and not primarily a description of the particular emotion of the speaker, although the statement is, to be sure, to be understood as based on her own experience. Some verses tell of the pleasure of love in a more "objective" fashion, without explicitly attributing the feelings to the speaker—for example: "for your caresses are better than wine" (1:2b). These too describe love but lack the introspective quality characteristic of the Egyptian songs that build on the Description of Love theme. The lovers in the Song reveal the nature of their emotions not by speaking of them directly, but by narrating experiences, by inviting each other away, and, above all, by praising each other. The scarcity of introspective descriptions of love in the Song is not accidental: it reflects a view of love different from the one dominant in the Egyptian songs. I discuss these views in chapter 8.

Wishes

The Wish theme, which has a distinctive form and constitutes a literary type—the "Wish Song"—is marked in the Egyptian poems by a wish introduced by the particle *ḥnr*, "if only." This theme appears in rudimentary form in no. 7, "If only I were appointed doorkeeper. . . ," where the wish does not open the poem and is not thematically dominant. A wish becomes dominant in two Wish Songs, "Seven Wishes" and "Three Wishes." In both songs each stanza begins with the wish-particle, expresses a desire for the proximity of the beloved, and continues with an extended image that emphasizes the urgency of the wish or shows the nature of the contact desired. Most of each stanza expands and develops the image.

The Egyptian Wish Songs are vehicles for poetic virtuosity. The poets seem interested in unusual and arresting images for their own sake, such as the proud royal horse racing without pause, the panicked gazelle dashing over the desert, the little servant girl watching her naked mistress, the lowly laundryman deriving secret pleasure from his mistress's clothing, and the mirror that gazes at the girl as she looks into it. While the striking imagery serves to characterize the speakers, the images turn out to be more memorable than the personalities of the lovers whose fantasies create them.

Like the Egyptian Wish Songs, Cant 8:1–5 opens with a wish-phrase (*mi yitten*, "if only") introducing a wish concerning the beloved, and then, like "Seven Wishes," pictures what would happen if the wish were fulfilled. The following two passages correspond in structure and development:

Cant 8:1–2
(a) If only you were like a brother to me, one who nursed at my mother's breasts!
(b) When I met you in the street I would kiss you, and no one would mock me. I would take and lead you to my mother's house ⟨to the room of her who bore me⟩. I would give you spiced wine to drink, the juice of my pomegranate.

No. 21B
(a) If only I were the laundryman of my sister's linen garment even for one month!

(b) I would be strengthened by grasping [the clothes] that touch her body. . . . [Oh I would be in] joy and delight, my body vigorous!

The little Wish Song in Canticles differs from the Egyptian Wish Songs in two important ways. First, the Shulammite is not wishing for her lover's presence—that is already secure (8:3–4)—but rather for social recognition of their relationship. Perhaps for that reason her wish lacks the anxiety and passivity heard in the wishes in the Egyptian songs. Second, whereas in the Egyptian songs intriguing and provocative images are developed at length, often detaching themselves from the desired reality and becoming the center of interest, in Cant 8:1–2 the image that encapsulates the wished-for state is not elaborated; rather, the immediate continuation (8:1b–2) applies literally to the lover as well as to a brother. Thus the brother comparison does not control the development of the Shulammite's wish in the way that the laundryman image, for example, dominates the development of the stanza it introduces.

The Paraclausithyron

In the Paraclausithyron, which takes its name from a theme important in classical poetry (on which see Copley, 1956), a youth stands outside a girl's house complaining of his exclusion and longing to be let in.

This is the dominant theme in three of the Egyptian songs—nos. 7, 46, and 47. The Egyptian theme, like many exemplars of its classical counterpart, is a vehicle for a humorous view of lovers' anger. In no. 7 we hear the thoughts of a boy standing outside the house of a girl who is apparently unaware of his existence. He wishes he were her doorkeeper, whom she is now chastising for negligence—then, at least, he'd have her attention! In no. 47 the youth addresses the door (in a take-off on the Book of the Dead, spell 125) and offers to give sacrifices to its parts if it will let him in. Then, perhaps despairing of help from the door, he promises the richest rewards to the carpenter lad if he will make a straw door that cannot exclude him. Song no. 46 seems to be no more than a complaint, though it just possibly contains a risqué pun, if Gardiner's interpretation of *wḥ*ᶜ as "release" (i.e., "orgasm") is correct (but see no. 46, n. b).

In the Egyptian Paraclausithyra, the excluded lover does not address the girl, as he frequently does in classical poetry. He pouts, pines, and makes futile wishes, all in thought (the speech to the door is a form of interior monologue). The lover in classical poems, by contrast, is generally more aggressive and boisterous (frequently from drink) as he rages aloud at the woman who excluded him and pleads for admittance.

In Cant 2:10–14 and 5:2b, the boy stands outside his beloved's house at night and speaks to her, in the first passage inviting her to come away with him, in the second entreating her to let him in. Since in Cant 2:8–17 and 5:2–6:3 the boy's location outside the door or wall is essential in setting the scene, we are justified in seeing the Paraclausithyron as one of the themes in these passages, in spite of the brevity of the speeches themselves.

In the Egyptian Paraclausithyra the door that excludes the lover embodies the girl's will: she is at best angry at him, at worst indifferent (see no. 7). In Canticles, on the contrary, the girl's affection is secure. The door or wall in Canticles separates lovers who desire to get together.

The boy's attitudes in the Egyptian Paraclausithyra—plaintive resentment and passive sexual fantasizing—bear no resemblance to the boy's proud, joyous invitations in Canticles. Nor are the boy's exclusion and his petulance an object of humor in Canticles as they are in the Egyptian songs.

Love in the Garden

The hallmark of this theme is the *setting* of lovemaking: a garden, orchard, or field—it is not usually clear which. I use "garden" in a broad sense to include any verdant, fruitful, natural setting (as in the "garden of Eden"). The garden provides privacy and fresh, natural beauties that appropriately frame the lovemaking and are congruent with the lovers' state of mind.

THE EGYPTIAN LOVE SONGS

Song no. 8 begins during the girl's boat trip to Heliopolis, moving then to a garden near the temple, where her rendezvous with her lover takes place. This garden presumably has cultic significance and may be a fertility garden. Cult and concern for fertility, however, stay well in the background. In the foreground is the lovers' experience.

A garden is the setting for a rendezvous in "The Orchard." The occasion is apparently a festival day. Many young people are participating in the celebrations, "festival booths" are set up under the trees, and servants bring food, drink, and flowers, all suggesting a special occasion rather than a private rendezvous. But here too the religious nature of the occasion stays very much in the background, as do the lovers themselves. In this song the garden is the center of attention, as we are shown the thoughts and claims of the trees.

Booths or huts are the sites of garden trysts in some songs. In no. 8 the lovers go together to the *imw* ("booths" or "tents"), which are located near the canal. These may be the same as the "Houses of ———" (P. Harris 500, 3, 5?, 9, 10—the reading and exact sense are obscure; see note in App. C, ad loc.). The "Houses of ———" are in the *dd*, which may mean "love garden" (see n. m). In "The Orchard" (no. 30), the third tree says to the lovers: "Under me are a festival booth and a hut" (or possibly just "a festival booth"). Later this tree describes the scene beneath its boughs:

> Her friend is at her right,
> as she gets him intoxicated
> and does whatever he says.
> The beer hut [*ᶜt ḥnḳt*] is disarrayed from drink.

The "beer hut" is apparently a shelter under the tree where the lovers drink beer and get intoxicated. The first stanza of this song (no. 28) mentions merrymaking "in a hut of reeds, in a guarded place."

Love in the Garden is the main theme in the "Flower Song," becoming especially prominent in no. 18, where the garden becomes a metaphor for the girl:

> I am yours like the field
> planted with flowers
> and with all sorts of fragrant plants.

The flowers in the extended metaphor may allude to her perfumes. This garden is also

> A lovely place for strolling about,
> with your hand upon mine!

While a girl may be compared to a garden, the garden never seems to be an independent symbol for a girl or for feminine sexuality in the Egyptian love songs.

THE SONG OF SONGS

In Canticles too the lovers meet in "gardens": enclosed gardens, cultivated fields, vineyards, orchards, and naturally growing garden spots. For the purposes of the theme, these places have much the same function.[16] In its basic form, this theme depicts the couple exchanging words of affection as they embrace in their garden bower. The garden may in addition be emblematic of the girl herself.

The setting for love is sometimes a garden (or open field) in which the couple has a bower or booth. The bower is first introduced somewhat enigmatically in 1:4b, "The king has brought me to his chambers." These "chambers" are described in 1:16b–17, where the girl praises the loveliness of the verdant bed, the rafters, and the beams of the bower. She mentions the bower again in 2:4, describing it as a royal kiosk (*beyt yayin*) for feasting. The bower becomes the subject of 3:7–11, which (as I argue in the commentary) is really an indirect description of it in terms of a royal canopied bed. The garden with its bower is not merely the place where the lovers happen to be; it is the site of their lovemaking, and the lovers' feelings radiate onto it.

The references to garden booths in the Egyptian songs show that the motif of lovemaking and feasting in booths in fields and under trees was traditional in the love song genre. The "house of wine" in 2:4 is, I suggest, much the same as the "beer hut" in Egyptian song no. 30. I would not, however, transfer the specific circumstances mentioned in the Egyptian songs to Canticles, especially since even within the Egyptian songs the motif of booths for lovemaking is not limited to a specific occasion.

In 2:10–14 and 7:12–14 the theme of Love in the Garden develops out of an invitation to come away. In these passages the setting seems to be the open countryside (*śadeh*) rather than an enclosed garden.

Gerleman (1965:124) has pointed out that 2:10–14 (like 7:12–14) has a remarkably modern tone. The phenomena of nature are not described here for any external purpose such as illustrative comparison (as in wisdom literature), but belong rather to a lyrical, emotionally heightened reflection on nature for its own sake, such as we find nowhere else in the Hebrew Bible or in ancient Egyptian love poetry. The closest approach to this view of nature in the Egyptian songs is the "Flower Song," in particular the second stanza (no. 18), where the girl describes the garden in which she is strolling with her lover.

16. Observe that in 4:12–13 the Shulammite is compared to both a *pardes* ("orchard" or "park") and a *gan* ("garden"), while in 8:12 she is referred to as a *kerem* ("vineyard"), and further that the flowering of the *śadeh*, "field," in 7:13 is described in terms very similar to those used of the blooming of the *ginnat* ᵓ*ᵉgoz*, the "nut garden," in 6:11. M. Falk (1982:101) observes that *kerem* has different meanings in different passages. In 1:14 *kerem* seems to be a place where various types of vegetation grow, rather than specifically a vineyard, since Ein Gedi is an oasis and henna does not grow on vines.

No. 21E too, though difficult and fragmentary, seems to delight in a description of flora for its own sake.

A description of the fruits of the field is a prominent feature in these passages—for example, 7:12–14:

> We'll see if the vine has blossomed,
> the bud opened,
> the pomegranates bloomed.
> There I will give you my love.

(7:13aβ–b)

In 6:11–12 the girl (it seems) comes down to the nut garden to see if the vines and trees are in blossom. The passage is very obscure, but the descent to the nut garden seems to symbolize lovemaking, for the speaker falls into an ecstatic confusion.

The "garden" (or "vineyard") is sometimes a figure for the maiden, as in 4:12–5:1:

> A garden locked is my sister, my bride,
> a ⟨garden⟩ locked, a spring sealed.

(4:12)

In Cant 4:12–15 the youth speaks at length of his beloved as a garden, thereby making its sweetness hers. She then picks up this image and uses it in her invitation to him to enter the garden he has just described (she calls it both "my garden" and "his garden") and to enjoy its fruits (4:16). It is not clear whether the garden represents the girl, her sexuality, or specifically her vagina (so Pope, 1977, understands it). Its meaning seems to vary. While "a garden locked is my sister, my bride" (4:12) seems to equate the garden with the girl as a whole, the girl's invitation to her lover, "Let my beloved come into his garden" (4:16), indicates that the garden is something that can be "entered," namely her vagina or her sexuality more abstractly conceived. In any case, the garden is not a fixed symbol in the sense that a reference to a garden would in itself call to mind a girl or her sexuality. Rather the symbolism is created through the explicit identification of girl with garden (4:12) as the Shulammite presses the implications of her lover's metaphor: if I am indeed a garden, let my beloved enter his garden and enjoy the fruits he has described.

Again in 6:2 the garden seems to refer to the girl:

> My beloved has gone down to his garden,
> to the beds of spices,
> to graze in the gardens,
> and to gather lilies.

We might take "Love in the (literal) Garden" and "Love in the (symbolic) Garden" as two distinct themes, but the similar descriptions of the fruits and spices in both types of garden link the two and allows the sensual connotations of girl and garden to interpenetrate.

MESOPOTAMIAN SACRED MARRIAGE SONGS

Love in the Garden is one theme prominent in both Canticles and the Sumerian Sacred Marriage songs. In the latter it is one of the most important themes, for the garden and field are the setting of the divine lovers' sexual congress and the land's fecundity is its desired outcome. For example:

> He has brought me into it, he has brought me into it.
> My brother has brought me into the garden.
> Dumuzi has brought me into the garden,
> I strolled [?] with him among the standing trees.
> I stood with him by its lying trees,
> By an apple tree I kneeled as is proper.
>
> Before my brother coming in song,
> Before the lord Dumuzi who came toward me,
> Who from the . . . of the tamarisk, came toward me,
> Who from the . . . of the date clusters, came toward me,
> I poured out plants from my womb,
> I placed plants before him, I poured out plants before him.
> I placed grain before him, I poured out grain before him.
>
> (Kramer, 1969:101)

The absence of any explicit concern with fertility distinguishes both the Egyptian love songs and the Song of Songs from the Sacred Marriage songs. This absence is striking in view of the natural and expected connection between garden and fertility. Even in no. 8, where the scene of the rendezvous is probably a garden in the temple area, there is no mention of fertility or reproduction. The avoidance of explicit association between garden and fertility helps define the goals of the genre in Egypt and Israel, for although it might have been religiously motivated in Israel, that could not be the case in Egypt, where fertility and gardens had an important place in cult. The love poets in Israel and Egypt were concerned with observing and depicting the premarital experience of love, not love within marriage, in which the bond between the partners is in large part defined by social and familial concerns rather than by individual emotions, and in which reproduction rather than satisfaction of the individual's desires is of primary importance. Even when the Egyptian and Israelite love poems allude to marriage—which is not often—they do not mention fertility and offspring. In their focus on premarital romantic love, both the Egyptian love songs and the Song of Songs are far closer to Western poetic tradition than to the Mesopotamian Sacred Marriage songs.

The Nobility of Lovers

Love makes lovers noble, even royal, and even greater than royalty! This is the meaning of all the references to kings, nobles, and royal chambers in Canticles.

The youth calls the Shulammite "noble" (*bat nadib*, 7:2). She calls him "king" and speaks of their leafy bed and bower as if it were the king's couch and chambers (1:4a,12; 3:7–11). Her lover is, *as it were*, King Solomon. (The "as it were" is very much a part of the girl's attitude; she is identifying her lover with "King Solomon" only for the purposes of the extravagant conceit.)

The youth goes even farther. In 8:11–12 he says that he is *richer* than Solomon. His own "vineyard" is far more precious than Solomon's proverbially rich vineyard in Baal Hamon (a name that means "possessor of wealth"), and it belongs to him alone. In a similar vein he says that his beloved is not *merely* a queen or noblewoman. They are many; *she* is incomparable: even queens and concubines stand in awe of her (6:8–10).

The Nobility of Lovers is not developed thematically in any of the Egyptian songs, but the theme is latent in epithets that express that idea: "my prince" (or "nobleman": *rmṯ* ꜥ3, no. 13), "prince [or nobleman] of my heart" (no. 17), and "Mistress of the Two Lands" (i.e., queen; no. 8). Nobility is hinted at in no. 7, where the girl's house is called a *bẖn*, a term reserved for castles and major mansions.

The Alba

The Alba, like the following themes, appears in only one of the literatures. In the Alba (the name is taken from a theme popular among the troubadours), a girl, awakened after a night of love, complains of the disturbance of her bliss and the separation that daybreak brings.

Two Egyptian songs, no. 1 and no. 14, use this theme. In no. 1 a young lady teases her lover for being too quick to leave her in the morning. Is he more interested in food and clothing than in the delights of love? Can't *she* offer him all the covering and "nourishment" he needs? The girl in no. 14 rebukes the dove whose call announces the dawn. In both songs the true subject is not the pain of parting (contrary to Hermann, 1959:130f.), but rather the nighttime pleasures of love. In no. 1 the complaint provides the setting for an unusually explicit demand for love's sensual pleasures. In no. 14 the dove's call, "Day has dawned—when are you going home?," leads the girl to a recollection of the preceding night and to thoughts of the permanence of her love. The dove reminds the girl that she must leave the bed of her beloved, to which she replies that they have resolved to spend their lives together and never to part.

Against the background of this theme, we can better understand the declaration of the youth in "The Crossing" as he embraces his beloved—"O night, you are mine forever, since my lady came to me" (no. 20E)—and the boy's reference to "my night" in no. 46, meaning the night of love that should have been his. Night belongs to lovers and the Alba extols its joys (*nfrw*) by bemoaning its termination.

There is no Alba in Canticles, but dawn's intrusion on lovemaking seems to be implied by 2:17:

> Before the day blows softly in,
> and the shadows flee,
> turn, my beloved, and be as a gazelle,
> or a young roe,
> on the mountains of Bether.

The Shulammite is not complaining of morning's advent, but her tone of urgency suggests that a night of joy is about to be disturbed by dawn (see commentary).

The Love Trap

The "trap" in the Love Trap theme is the girl,[17] whose charms attract and ensnare the young man like a bird. This is the dominant theme in nos. 3, 9, and 10, and is probably implicit in no. 11. A variant of the theme is the trope in no. 43, where the girl catches the boy by a noose, binds him, and brands him, as if he were a young bull. It is always the girl who does the trapping, although at the end of no. 10 the girl too is trapped—by love itself.

Nos. 3, 9, 10, and 43 use this theme as a sort of riddle. In no. 3 Praise of the Beloved leads into the Love Trap theme in a surprising way. For the first five stichs, the audience thinks that it is hearing a Praise Song. The sixth stich too is in the usual praise form—"her head is the trap of 'love-wood'"—but it

17. To be precise, the trap in no. 3 is the girl's *head*. but this slight variation does not affect the meaning of the theme.

is unusual praise. Only now do we discover that the main theme of the song is really the Love Trap, and that the Praise of the Beloved has only been used to lead our expectations in a certain direction so as to trap us, as it were, in the surprise ending. In no. 9 a girl tells how the first bird of the flock, who is anointed with myrhh, lands and takes her bait. No. 10 presents a paradox: how can the girl have caught a bird without having set her snare? No. 43 too suggests a riddle: if the girl is so skilled at casting the lasso, why doesn't she catch cattle? No. 11 uses the motif of the goose alighting in the garden to represent a boy falling in love. Trapping is not mentioned explicitly, but it is suggested by the trapping motif of the two preceding poems, in which birds also alight, and by the pun on *šnw*, meaning "garden," "hair," and "net."

The Love Trap is not developed thematically in the Song of Songs, but it appears as a motif in 7:6aβb:

> the thrums of your head are like purple:
> a king is captured by the locks!

The "king"—that is, the lover—is caught or "imprisoned" (*ʾasur*) by the girl's hair, which hangs down, perhaps in long, straight tresses that resemble the bars of a cage.

Traveling to a Rendezvous

In no. 5 and the first part of no. 8 (sections (A) and (B)), lovers speak their thoughts as they sail down the Nile to a rendezvous. The journey itself is the organizing principle of their thoughts, as the speakers describe what they see around them. In no. 8 the lovers will meet at a festival at the temple, and we may surmise that a festival is the occasion for the meeting in no. 5 too, for in the latter the youth is sailing to Ankh-Towy, a major cult center, and he imagines Ptah's pleasure in his city, a thought that would be especially appropriate to a festival time, since the celebrations were believed to delight the god to whom they were dedicated.

Traveling to a Rendezvous is not used as a theme in Canticles. The youth's journey over the hills to his beloved is mentioned in 2:8–9a, but the allusion is too incidental and brief to be reckoned a theme, and the journey is not used as an occasion for expressing the traveler's thoughts.

Seeking the Beloved

"Seeking the Beloved" means that one lover (in Canticles always the girl) goes out looking for the other. This theme is important in Canticles because the search is paradigmatic of the process of love, in which a lover must be willing to take the initiative and actively seek the loved one.

Cant 1:7–8 is a bit of humorous banter that refers to a search rather than reporting on one. Where will you be at noon? the Shulammite asks her lover. Do you want me to go about from man to man like a loose woman looking for you? He replies teasingly, in a mock pout: If you don't know where I "graze" and "cause to lie down" (playing on the words *tirᶜeh* and *tarbiṣ*; see commentary), then go ahead, wander among the shepherds' huts. The Shulammite's concern shows that for a girl to roam about searching for her lover would be considered, at the least, improper. Yet later on she does go forth on quests that will demand far more audacity than the one she wishes to avoid here.

"Seek" and "find": these words appear and reappear in 3:1–6 and 5:2–6:3. In both passages the Shulammite leaves her bed—on which she had "sought" her beloved night after night—to seek him through the city streets. In 5:2–6:3 the city watchmen "find" her before she finds him, and they beat her. Clearly "those who watch the walls" consider her behavior aberrant, perhaps taking her for a prostitute. But it was her hesitation to "open to" her beloved (5:3) that made the search necessary. Now the willingness to defy social expectations and to brave dangers gains her her desire.

This theme has no clear parallels in the Egyptian songs, in which the girl often sits at home waiting and wishing for her lover to appear. The theme's message, however, has a counterpart in "The Stroll," whose poignancy lies in the lovers' *failure* to go to each other. The author is implicitly affirming the importance of going forth boldly to seek one's beloved, an affirmation implied also in "The Crossing." This is the message of much romantic literature, in which the intensity of love's fulfillment is proportionate to the difficulties undergone to achieve it, and in which success in love may require the violation of social norms.

The Invitation to Come Away

One lover calls the other to come away. The Invitation to Come Away is the converse of Seeking the Beloved.

In Cant 2:10–14 the boy invites his beloved to come with him to the fields, describing the land's blossoming in spring. In 7:12–14 she invites him to come away with her to the field, picturing the blossoming of nature in words that echo his earlier invitation.

In 4:8 he invites her to come away from her mountainlike remoteness. To persuade her, he delares the intensity of her effect on him (4:9) and then describes that intensity by comparing her beauties to a fragrant garden (4:10–15). She accepts his invitation by inviting him into her garden (4:16).

The lovers in the Egyptian love songs do not invite each other to come away. The girl in no. 20C does call her beloved to come to her, but she is probably to be understood as *thinking* a wish.

Excursus: The "Travesties"

In discussing the thematics of Egyptian love poetry, Hermann (1959:111–24) arranged the motifs of the love songs into three schemata, which, following Jolles (1932), he called "travesties": that is, changes of costume, disguises. These disguises provide ways to escape from one's social situation by imaginatively moving either upward to the aristocratic world (the "Knight Travesty"), or downward to a lower rung of society (the "Servant Travesty," corresponding to Jolles's "Shepherd Travesty"), or laterally to the periphery of society (the "Shepherd Travesty,"[18] in place of Jolles's "Rogue Travesty," the change being due to the different significance of the bucolic for ancient Egypt). Hermann classified motifs in the Egyptian songs according to which "world" they belong to and found the three "travesties" present in at least rudimentary form in the Egyptian songs. Thus, for example, he classifies both a reference to the beloved woman as "my lady" (no. 51) and the wish that the beloved come as quickly as a royal messenger (no. 38) as "Knight Travesties." The wish to be the girl's maidservant (no. 21A) belongs, he says, to the "Servant Travesty," as does (less explicably) the wish to be her seal ring. Virtually any mention of flowers, trees, animals, and so on is classified with the "Shepherd Travesty."

Other scholars built on Hermann's theory. Davis (1980:112) added a "divine fiction," which she finds, for example, in no. 20C, where the girl calls her lover "my god." White (1978:146–48) applied Hermann's categories to Canticles and pointed to motifs that, he felt, belong to a "Royal Fiction" (e.g., 1:4; 1:12–14; 3:6–11; 7:6) and a "Shepherd Fiction" (1:5–6, 7–8; 2:7, and all other images "from the rustic *Hirtenwelt*"). The Egyptian "Servant Fiction," he says, is not present in Canticles but does have a counterpart in the girl's wish that her lover be like a brother to her (8:1) and be bound to her as a seal (8:6). Gerleman's commentary (1965) uses Hermann's categories throughout in classifying the motifs of Canticles. Murphy too affirms the application of Hermann's categories to Canticles in his form-critical survey (1981:102). Clearly Hermann's theory has been highly influential in the study of both the Egyptian love songs and the Song of Songs.

Hermann was, in fact, misapplying Jolles's theory. Jolles's categories are a way of describing entire works and cannot properly be applied to isolated motifs and certainly not to epithets. A "travesty" is a type of fantasy, a dis-

18. Hermann uses "Hirten" to include all pastoral figures, which in the case of the Egyptian songs means fowlers, gardeners, and fellahin.

guise that an author, and also a reader, may put on in order to escape temporarily from their usual place in society without abandoning their "selves" through ecstasy or possession. Such a disguise allows an abandonment of one's ordinary situation by identification with a character outside one's usual station in society. It is not the characters, but the author and reader, who put on "disguises" by identifying with the fictional characters. This schema is at best awkwardly applicable to the songs we are studying. For Canticles or a section thereof to be a "royal disguise" (equivalent to Jolles's "Knight Travesty"), the characters would have to *be* royalty, not just pretending to be royalty or merely using terms associated with royalty. (If the lover really were supposed to be King Solomon, the Song would indeed be a "royal disguise," but I do not think that is the case.) Since the youth is a shepherd, the element of lateral escape that Hermann associates with the "shepherd disguise" may operate in the Song—assuming that the intended audience was urban or landed gentry. The lovers in the Egyptian songs, on the other hand, seem to be in the same social class as the audience (if I am right in identifying the intended audience with groups of the sort portrayed in the banqueting murals), and so no disguise is involved. Still, the songs that stress a bucolic setting may fulfill the function attributed to the "shepherd disguise" (in Hermann's sense) by encouraging the audience to imagine itself in the fields and gardens. The "Servant Travesty" is not present. The wish to be a servant to the beloved (no. 21A) or her laundryman (no. 21B) is in a sense a "servant disguise" *for the boy who makes the wish*, although he is not pretending to be these servants but wishing he were in their place. Secondarily the audience can identify with his wish and imagine "escaping downward" into the role of servants. But it is stretching Jolles's schema to apply it to such disguises at one remove.

In a limited sense, there is a "royal disguise" in Canticles, namely in 1:4, 12 and 3:7–11, where the girl speaks of her lover as if he were a king. This disguise is not an attempt on the characters' part to escape their social situation, but a way of expressing their emotional exaltation, their joy in their current state.

Jolles was inquiring into the ways in which literature makes possible the "transformation" (*Verwandlung*) of the reader. He said that if one observed how people dressed for a costume ball, one would be able to group most disguises into three categories (namely the "travesties"). If we extend his inquiry to the love songs, we must add another disguise to his triad: that of young lovers. Lovers, like rogues, free themselves from the strictures of society by escaping it laterally. They depart by going to the fields and vineyards and by defying social expectations (see in particular no. 4 and Cant 5:6–8). But unlike rogues, lovers escape society not for the pleasure of defiance, or even for the sake of liberation in itself, but in order to define themselves as a new unit within society. The lovers' escape is thus temporary and ultimately affirmative.

The audience can identify with the young lovers and escape with them. Much of the pleasure these songs offer comes from the fantasy "disguise" they let us wear: the doubly desirable costume of young person and lover. The love songs give the audience the combined delights of vicarious escape and erotic fantasy.

CHAPTER 8

Love and Lovers in the Love Songs

Three things there are too wondrous for me,
four I cannot fathom:
the way of the eagle in the sky,
the way of a snake on a rock,
the way of a ship in the heart of the sea—
and the way of a man with a maid.

(Prov 30:18–19)

The way of a man and a maid is a wonder and a mystery, and poets in all ages have delighted in exploring it. What is this peculiar, unseen force that draws the sexes together? How does it feel? How does it affect those in its power? The poets of ancient Egypt and Israel approached the mystery in many ways, not to solve it, but to heighten the wonder. How did they see this wonder? What ideas underlie their portrayal of love and lovers?

Speaking About Love

The Egyptian love songs and the Song of Songs are first of all poems about lovers. The poets reveal their views of love not by speaking about love in the abstract, but by portraying people in love, making lovers' words reveal lovers' thoughts, feelings, and deeds. The poets invite us to observe lovers, to smile at them, to empathize with them, to sympathize with them, to recall in their adolescent pains our own, to share their desires, to enjoy in fantasy their pleasures. The poets show us young lovers flush with desire and awash in waves of new and overwhelming emotions. We watch lovers sailing down the Nile to a rendezvous, walking hand in hand through gardens, lying together in garden bowers. We come upon them sitting at home aching for the one they love, standing outside the loved one's door and pouting, swimming across rivers, running frantically through the streets at night, kissing, fondling, hugging, and snuggling face to face and face to breast, and—no less erotically—telling each other's praises in sensuous similes.

The poets do not scrutinize love with a philosopher's eye, attempting to ascertain its essence or cosmic function. In all our poems, only a few verses at the end of Canticles speak about love in generalities, and even these grow out of the experiences of the lovers in the poem.

These loves are not symbols. They do not, for example, represent the union of divine male and female principles, a union supposed to bless the land with fertility and plenitude. Nor do they represent historical or religious experiences, such as the love between God and Israel. The loves in these poems transcend the experience of the personae only in the sense that poetry speaks of the general through the specific and insofar as other lovers may know the like. Rather than presenting a grand, symbolic, typical, archetypal, abstract, or universal love, the love poets seek to capture and convey nuances of ordinary human emotion and desire.

Our poets speak of specifics: specific lovers, specific feelings and urges, specific events and experiences. But *we* may generalize, looking for the poets' underlying ideas and assumptions about lovers and love. In this chapter I will look into these tender, humorous, and delicately lubricious portraits to gain a more deliberate and analytical understanding of the ideas, assumptions, and attitudes that went into the making of these poems.

The Song of Songs views young love with an unabashed earnestness. This is not a grim seriousness—for the Song does not lack fun—but rather an earnestness that respects the young lovers' ardor as the highest knowledge of love. The poets of the Egyptian love songs are usually more detached, looking on the lovers they portray with pleasure, but sometimes with a smiling condescension as well, for the poets see more than their personae can. In the "Stroll" in particular, the poet looks at the lovers from above. She, the "Great Entertainer," sees into the hearts of both her characters, and her perspective comprehends things that neither of the lovers is aware of. The poet of the Song, on the other hand, is a "listener" along with us, so that there is almost no point where we can separate the poet's attitude from that of the lovers. The poet of the Song almost never suggests that there is a greater or deeper knowledge of love than the personae reveal.[1] *They* are the source of knowledge

1. The poet may, however, be smiling at the Shulammite in 5:9, where it seems that the maidens are not so taken with the youth as she thought (1:2–4).

about love: no patronizing or parental wisdom here. The lovers alone teach us about love, and when they do (as when the Shulammite declares that love is as strong as death), the reader takes their words with unreserved seriousness.

The concept of love we find in most love songs is more likely an ideal of love than a reality. We probably do not learn from these songs what people in love commonly did and felt in ancient Egypt or Israel, any more than we discover what love truly is today by listening to popular songs or even by reading contemporary love poetry. In all such cases we learn how particular writers have perceived love and defined its potentialities, but their view of love need not conform to the picture of social realities we get from other sources. Attitudes expressed in song need not be the ones the audience would hold in all aspects of everyday life. A poet may choose to reject the common attitudes of society, to push them into the background, or simply to ignore them.

As for the audience, people can accept in fantasy attitudes they would find intolerable in their own lives. A middle-aged Egyptian banquet guest might have fun hearing about a young lady waking up at dawn in her lover's bed—he might even picture that lover as remarkably like himself (with a bit more hair)—and yet be furious if he found his own daughter trysting with a lover.

I make this rather obvious point because there is a tendency to draw inferences too quickly and uncritically about a society's mores from literary works that may not be, and probably do not intend to be, accurate reportage, and a converse tendency to impose a society's public attitudes on the interpretation of its poetry. In other words, we should not assume that the Egyptians or the Israelites were libertine because they sang about unmarried sex, nor need we assume (as did Ginsburg and Delitzsch in the last century) that the Shulammite would only have behaved in accordance with the rules of propriety and chastity that the patriarchal attitudes and stern laws of ancient Israel would seem to require of a nice Jewish girl.[2]

While the love songs may be assumed to reflect some attitudes present in their social context, the external evidence we have from their respective cultures is insufficient to allow us to generalize from the songs to the common attitudes of ancient Egypt and Israel. Therefore my conclusions are intended to explain the ideas of the poets whose works have reached us, rather than to ascertain the prevailing Israelite or Egyptian concepts of love. Indeed, it may not even be the poets' own working attitudes or ideas that the poems reveal, but only their fantasies or their fancies, or even more specifically the fancies

2. A case in point: in arguing against Rudolph (1962), who says that the mountains mentioned in 4:8 symbolize the unpleasantnesses and dangers of life, Würthwein (1960), commenting on Cant 4:8, says: "Aber war ein jüdisches Mädchen, im Elternhaus streng gehütet, diesen ausgesetzt?" ("But would a Jewish maiden, who was strictly guarded in her parents' home, be exposed to these things?")

and the fantasies shared and enjoyed by their audiences. The love songs are a world unto themselves, and their connections with social realities may be too tenuous, complex, and shifting to be described meaningfully on the basis of the sparse evidence that has reached us.

Speaking About Sex

I would like to emphasize at the outset the place of eroticism in these songs: everywhere. Sexual desire pervades the songs, and sexual pleasure is happily widespread in them. But their eroticism is not concentrated where commentators most often seek it: in specific allusions to genitalia and coitus. Such allusions are not as frequent as some modern exegesis suggests. For example, the phrase "mountains of Bether" in Cant 2:17 has been interpreted as an allusion to the vulva (*beter* being translated "cleft"). The "channels"[3] in Cant 4:13 have been identified with the Shulammite's vagina, and "hand" in 5:4 has been interpreted as a euphemism for penis. Other words have been taken not as euphemisms, but as explicit designations of genitalia. Thus Pope explains both the "hole" in 5:4 and *šorrek* in 7:3 (usually translated "navel") as vagina. He also explains *ʾap* in 7:9 (which usually denotes "nose") as vagina or clitoris and interprets the verse as praising the scent of the young lady's vaginal secretions. I have generally rejected such interpretations in my comments on these verses, yet in other places I do find allusions to genitals and sexual intercourse.

In the search for sexual innuendoes, I must admit to frequent uncertainty about my own conclusions. I am far from confident, for example, that I am not overinterpreting the sexual implications of Cant 4:6 (where I take "mountain of myrrh—hill of frankincense" as alluding to the Shulammite's breasts, to which the boy determines to go before dawn). On the other hand, I am not entirely certain that similar implications are not present in 2:17 (which I take as the girl's urging her lover to go *from* her to the mountains of Bether before dawn). Nor am I confident that I am right in interpreting the "cave" in no. 40—but not the "hole" in Cant 5:4 or the *šᵉlaḥim* (literally, "channels") in 4:13—as referring to the vagina.

Readers, like young lovers, have a problem of knowing how far to go; but if we sometimes go too far, that is part of the fun, and we can even blame the poets for leading us astray. Love poets tease us with sexual double entendre. Sexual innuendoes, not to mention explicit sexual references, start us looking for more of the same until we begin seeing them everywhere. There are no hard and fast rules in this game—and a game it is, especially in the playful Egyptian songs. But not everything goes, for going too far carries with it its own dangers. It can disturb the integrity of the broader context by creat-

3. *Šᵉlaḥim*, which I take as a synecdoche for "irrigated field," see commentary.

ing irrelevancies and can, ironically, restrict the scope of a poem's eroticism by drawing too much attention to anatomical details at the expense of other erotic sensations and sexuality in a broader, more subtle sense.

Interpreting too many things as penises and vaginas imposes upon the poems a genital focus that is foreign to the Egyptian love songs and certainly to the Song of Songs.[4] The painstaking scholarly search for genitalia in effect slights the breadth and variety of the lovers' sexual interests and pleasures. There is no need, for example, to interpret *ʾap* in Cant 7:9 as "vulva" or "clitoris" (meanings it has nowhere else in Hebrew or, for that matter, in Ugaritic). *ʾap* means "nose." The boy in Canticles finds his girl's nose sexy—it smells good. This *is* an erotic allusion—to nose kissing, a form of intimacy that we should not overlook by making the verse refer to something more familiar to the practices of our own culture.

Likewise, the efforts to show that *šorrek* can mean "your vulva" in Cant 7:3 seem to me misdirected. The youth finds the girl's navel lovely. Many of us might find that fascination peculiar, but it was one apparently shared by Egyptian sculptors, who emphasized the navel in various ways, by the tellers of the *Arabian Nights*, who delighted in the size and roundness of girls' navels, and even by Ian Fleming, whose erotic references are not particularly subtle.

Similarly, to interpret Cant 5:2–6 as a description, however veiled, of coitus (thus Wittekindt, 1925, and Pope, 1977), contradicts the point of the passage—that the girl's hesitation to open the door to her lover leads to his sudden departure and to her dangerous search for him—and blurs the meaning of the specific experience described (see my comments ad loc.).

Many things happen in love besides sexual intercourse, and we obscure the particularity of these experiences if we reduce them all to veils that conceal sexual intercourse or to symbols that "really" represent coitus. We can recognize that the lush eroticism of these songs is pervasive without seeing channels as vaginas, hands as penises, noses as clitorises, or (heaven help us) a door latch as a "vaginal vestibule and bulbs, along with the bulbospongiosus muscle" (Eslinger, 1981:276).

In exploring the concepts of love expressed in the love songs, we are at every step exploring their view of sexuality, and we find that their eroticism extends to the entire body. Eyes, hair, noses, fingers, navels, bellies, palates—everything about one's lover is charged with erotic energy. Sexual desire ignites, fuels, powers their love, so that emotion and libido can scarcely be distinguished.

The songs' eroticism extends even beyond the body. Sexual urges and pleasures suffuse each lover's being and control the way the two behave to-

4. Such a focus is characteristic of the Mesopotamian Sacred Marriage songs (see the songs quoted in chapter 5), but that is because their purpose is to enhance universal fertility, and the locus of fertility is the genitals.

ward each other. The lovers each want to smell the other's fragrance, to taste the sweetness of the other's mouth, to hear the other's voice, to embrace, to kiss, and to caress. Thus their intercourse—both physical and verbal—is always sexual. Beyond this, sexual love even governs the way they *see*—each other and the world. Eros is everywhere. Of this, more later.

Lovers and Others

Lovers at times find family and others in their immediate vicinity interfering nuisances, but they also look to others for recognition of the legitimacy of their love and for confirmation that they have found true love.

The Egyptian love songs show very little of the society surrounding the lovers, and the glimpses we do get are always through the lovers' eyes. None of these other persons speak in the Egyptian songs as personae, though the mother is quoted in no. 32 and what a girl fears people *will* say is quoted in no. 34.

In the Egyptian love songs, we see occasional signs of the world in opposition to the romance (no. 4) and of the limitations placed on a girl's freedom of movement (no. 32). A mother's watchful eye makes its presence felt, though lightly, in a "Love Trap" song (no. 10), where a girl wonders what excuse she can give her mother for not having completed her accustomed task of bird trapping. In "The Stroll" (no. 32), the girl's mother has forbidden her to see the boy she loves. She accepts this, though reluctantly:

> Mother is good in commanding me thus:
> "Avoid seeing him!"
> Yet my heart is vexed when he comes to mind . . .

Lovers are not oblivious to public opinion. The girl in "The Stroll" is worried about how her love-wrought craziness may make her seem to others (no. 34). To be able to love openly would heighten the lovers' joy. This same girl says (in thought) to the boy she loves:

> Come to me that I may see your beauty!
> May father and mother be glad!
> May all people rejoice in you together,
> rejoice in you, my brother!
>
> (No. 32)

We see a lover's concern for public recognition also in no. 36 and in no. 54:

> I kiss her before everyone,
> that they may see my love.

Lovers feel that they have the best beloved of all and are convinced that other people are similarly affected by the beloved's charms. The girl in "The Crossing" says that her lover's form revives "hearts"—all hearts, and not hers alone (no. 20A). The girl in "The Stroll" says

> Love of him captures the heart
> of all who stride upon the way
>
> (No. 36)

—such as she. The boy similarly believes that his beloved affects others the way she affects him:

> She makes the heads of all the men
> turn about when seeing her.
>
> (No. 31)

Even other males in love, he feels, are struck by *his* beloved's beauty:

> No sooner had she come than the "lovers" bowed down
> because of the greatness of her love.[5]
>
> (No. 35)

The Song of Songs too shows various persons affecting the lovers. The Shulammite feels that people in general, the indefinite "they," are likely to scorn her if she displays her affection publicly at present. She wishes that her bonds to her lover were recognized no less than a sister's bonds to her brother:

> If only you were like a brother to me,
> one who nursed at my mother's breasts!
> When I met you in the street I would kiss you,
> and no one would mock me.
> I would take and lead you to my mother's house . . .
>
> (8:1–2a)

The brothers had set obstacles in the Shulammite's way (1:6). Their opposition creates a tension between the girl and her immediate society, a tension that enables her to form and express her own will (she would otherwise be just a young girl given in marriage), and also enables the lovers to define themselves as a distinct unit within society.

We get no sense that the current public attitude is inevitable. Except for the watchmen, the outsiders are not basically hostile. The brothers, at first

5. I interpret "her love" to mean the love they feel for her or, less likely, her lovemaking or caresses (no. 35, n. d).

hostile, finally (if my interpretation of 8:8–10 is correct) consent to her marriage. The mother is not said to have either hindered or helped the lovers, but again the Shulammite's wish that her beloved be to her as a brother whom she could bring to her mother's house (8:1–2) implies that she cannot do so at present. Still, she does intend to bring him home to mother (3:4), so she sees her mother as potentially favorable and expects her to accept him.

The most severe public rebuff was the attack by the "watchmen who roam the city" (5:7). No explanation is given. Perhaps they think she is a prostitute (see commentary). Her answer to this brutality is to ignore it, neither explaining it nor complaining about it, but continuing resolutely on her quest.

Of all persons besides the couple, the girls of Jerusalem, who seem to be the Shulammite's constant companions, play the most significant role, speaking to her and listening. They seem to be speaking in 3:6; 5:1b; 5:9; 6:1; 7:1; and 8:5 (only 5:9 and 6:1 can be ascribed to them with certainty; see the commentary for my reasons for assigning the other verses to them as well). It seems to be they who exclaim, in admiration and surprise, "Look who's coming up from the wilderness!" (3:6aα). Theirs is probably the voice encouraging the lovers to enjoy love (5:1b). They also challenge the Shulammite to show how her lover is so special (5:9), and in response to her praise of him they offer to join in her search (6:1; but are they simply offering to help, or are they at the same time teasing her a bit: where in the world *has* your lover gone now?). If they are speaking in 7:1a—"Come back, come back, O perfect one, come back, come back, that we may gaze at you!"—their tone is bantering and skeptical there too, for the boy rebukes them for staring at the "perfect one" as if she were just a camp-dancer (a word whose meaning is uncertain; see commentary). The tone of their words, to the extent that it can be ascertained from the few sentences they speak, is somewhat skeptical and jocular, but still friendly.

We are to imagine the girls of Jerusalem listening throughout the poem. Near its start the Shulammite explains to them why she is swarthy (1:5–6). She is on the defensive, as if expecting them to look down on her, but she is certainly not hostile toward them. She asks them to prepare her sickbed with fruit clusters and apricots (2:5). This is probably a rhetorical imperative: she is not trying to get them to do something, but rather letting them know the power of her feelings. She also asks them three times not to disturb lovemaking (2:7; 3:5; 8:4), indicating that she is about to make love. This request too shows that she does not see them as inimical. She asks their help in 5:8 also, where she urges them not to tell her lover how crazy she has been acting. It is to them that she reports her searches for her lover in 3:1–6 (they are addressed in v. 5) and 5:2–6:3. During the second search they listen as she praises her beloved to prove his preeminence (5:10–16). They also seem to be listening to the description of the royal couch (3:7–11), for they are addressed by name in 3:10b–11. As I interpret this passage, the Shulammite is boasting to them about the majesty of her lover's bower, trying to get them to see things the way she does. So the girls of Jerusalem seem to be present throughout the poem, even at times of intimacy between the lovers (e.g., 2:7; 5:1). What is their role?

Their presence allows us to see the interaction between the Shulammite and her peers. More important than what the girls of Jerusalem say is the fact that they are there to be spoken to. We see the Shulammite's desire to communicate her experience to the other girls. She is eager to have them appreciate her lover's excellence, to recognize his noble qualities, to be aware of the power of his effect on her. She may also be boasting (gloating?) a bit when she declares that *all* the maidens love him (1:2–4), for she alone has him. It seems important to her to let them know the intensity of her emotion. The most amazing thing is happening to her—love. Her love is unique, she believes, and her beloved is the most excellent of young men. The other girls, she feels, must recognize and grant this too (see especially 4:10–16).

THE GIRLS OF JERUSALEM AND THE "LOVERS"

The identity of the girls of Jerusalem is far from certain, for they do not say enough to give a clear picture of themselves. We must grant the possibility that they are a dramatic convention whose purpose entirely escapes us. It is likewise unclear who the (male) "lovers" in "The Stroll" (nos. 31, 33, 35) are. Nevertheless we may consider the possibility that the (male) "lovers" are to the boy in that poem what the girls of Jerusalem are to the Shulammite in Canticles. That is to say, the girls of Jerusalem and the "lovers" seem to be other persons whose opinions are important to the lovers.

The Egyptian boy in "The Stroll" says that the "lovers" bowed down because of the greatness of their love for his beloved or, possibly, because of the greatness of her lovemaking (that is, what he believes other youths imagine the girl's caresses to be like; see nos. 35, n. d). By either interpretation, his attitude is like the Shulammite's, who says:

As for scent, your oils are good:
"Oil of Turaq" is your name.
That's why maidens love you.
. . . .
We will be glad and rejoice in you;
we will praise your caresses [*dodim*].
More than smooth wine do they love you.

(1:3–4)

She is convinced that the maidens (*ᶜᵃlamot*), who may be identical with the girls of Jerusalem or may be a more inclusive group, love this boy as she does. She believes that they join in praise of his *dodim*, his caresses or lovemaking. Now, since her lover does not give the impression of being a Lothario, we may wonder how she thinks the other girls can know about the pleasure of his caresses. Most likely she is projecting her feelings onto her peers, so certain is she of the "objective" excellence of his love. "We will praise your caresses" shows the same expansive inclusion of others in one's feelings that the Egyptian boy in no. 31 reveals when he says,

> Fortunate is whoever embraces her—
> he is like the foremost of lovers,

and that his beloved reveals when she says,

> Love of him captures the heart
> of all who stride upon the way.
>
> (No. 36)

The Shulammite's lover too believes that others must recognize his girl's preeminence, although he projects his awe onto queens and concubines rather than onto other young men (6:9–10). Lovers, especially adolescent ones, can be quite opinionated and easily mistaken in their assessment of other people's feelings. Remembering the Shulammite's claim that all the girls love her beloved (1:3–4), the audience might well smile at hearing the Jerusalem girls' query: "Your beloved—how is he better than any other" (5:9a). The other maidens are not so ready to grant the preeminence of *her* beloved or to "praise his caresses" after all.

By bringing in the "lovers" and the girls of Jerusalem, the poets reveal something lovers themselves might not realize: however entranced they are with each other, young lovers occasionally cast a sideways glance at their peers, anxious for confirmation of their choice of beloved, wishing others to be aware of the wondrous new experience they are going through, and desiring recognition and acceptance of their love.

Lover and Lover: Love as Mutual Relationship

Not all loves are mutual relationships. The boy who wishes for a certain girl in seven ways but does nothing to get her (nos. 21A–21G), and the boys who stand moping and fantasizing outside girls' doors (nos. 7, 46, 47), are not in a love relationship. But most songs do imply two lovers who know and love and affect each other.

Although all but two of the Egyptian love songs have only one of the lovers speaking, we are generally able to infer from the words of the speaker some things about the other's character and behavior, in the same way that we can deduce the nature of a telephone conversation when listening to one side of it. In Canticles both lovers speak, giving us a more complete picture of their relationship. In analyzing the love relationships portrayed in these poems, I will examine three factors in the lovers' interaction: sex roles (in what ways do males and females act differently in love?); sexual relations (just what *are* they doing, and what does it mean to them?); and communication (what do they have to say to each other, and how do they say it?).

SEX ROLES AND DISTINCTIONS

Somewhere within the context of society's norms and presuppositions, young lovers must work out their own sexual identities and their distinctions with respect to each other. What attitudes toward sexual differences do the poets reflect, and how do they see the sexes behaving in love?

The Egyptian love songs do not show a single conception or strict stereotype of the ways the sexes behave. From one song to another, the behavior of the sexes differs. There are boys who pine passively for the girls they love (nos. 6, 7, 21A–21G, 31, 33, 35, 37, 46, 47), and there are more active lovers who take the initiative and go after the girls they desire (as in no. 5 and "The Crossing"). Some of the girls are assertive and take the initiative (as in nos. 1, 14, and 44), while others wait for their lovers to do so (such as the girls in "The Stroll," "Three Wishes," and no. 15).

In some songs neither sex seems more active in taking the initiative or more assertive than the other. In "The Flower Song," for example, the girl is secure in her lover's company in the garden after they have made love and speaks of the life they will share (no. 17). The tone of no. 8 is similar. This song begins with the girl's telling how she sails to Heliopolis to meet her lover in the "Love Garden," while he sails there to join her. They meet at the entrance to the canal and walk together into the garden. The picture of the lovers traveling independently to join each other epitomizes equality in love.

In many songs, however, the girls are the more intent on love and the more sexually assertive, and on balance this seems characteristic of the genre. Except for the hero of "The Crossing," no boy shows quite the fiery resolve of the love-intoxicated girl of no. 4, who defies the world to separate her from her lover; the insatiable girl of no. 1, who will not let her lover out of bed; the passionate, serious young lady of no. 14, who goes out at night (so it is implied) to find her lover and crawls into bed with him; or the girl who gets fed up with waiting for her lover and goes out to meet him (no. 44). Even the girl in "Three Wishes," who is awaiting her lover's arrival, takes on an air of aggressiveness through the ferocity of the images she uses to express the speed with which he must hurry to her "cave." The fantasies of the boy in the similarly structured "Seven Wishes" are, in contrast, static.

In poems with the Love Trap theme, which compare falling in love to being trapped or lassoed (chapter 7), the girl is always the trap or trapper. In no. 10 the girl both traps and is trapped, but it is not her lover but love itself that traps her. The boy caught like a bird in a trap (nos. 3, 9, 10) is the epitome of bewildered helplessness (Grapow, 1924:91f.; and cf. Prov 7:23; Qoh 9:12). The boy is similarly helpless in no. 43, where the girl catches him as if with a lasso. The treatment of this theme, then, asserts the female's power in love.

On the other hand, the Love Trap theme does not embrace a "femme fatale" stereotype. The femme fatale is prominent in Egyptian narratives (see the summaries of "Two Brothers" and "Truth and Falsehood" in chapter 3; compare also the murderous succubus Tabubu of "Setne I" in Lichtheim, 1980:133–36). But love poetry does not use the Love Trap theme in this fashion. The point of this theme is never generalized to suggest that "that's the way girls are," and its consistently light-hearted, gentle treatment avoids any hint of the *danger* implied by the femme fatale stereotype. The Egyptians used the Love Trap theme to assert the female's active role in creating the love bond (contrary to a "retreating female" stereotype), yet they did not push this theme (or any other) to an extreme.

The boys are awed by the powerful effect their girls have on them, but they do not try to affect them in return. They see themselves as "captured," their hearts as "taken." They are more acted upon than acting of their own initiative. The boys make no demands of the girls and express no hopes or wishes directly to them. They watch love rather than make it happen. They lie in bed sick with love, waiting for the cure to come to them rather than pursuing it on their own (nos. 6, 37). They stand before girls' doors and brood or devise fantasic plans (nos. 7, 46, 47), rather than urging her to let them in (as does the boy in Canticles) or kicking up a ruckus and demanding entry (as do the males in many classical Paraclausithyra). The boys in the Egyptian Paraclausithyra just pout.

Males also appear less assertive because they never speak to their lovers in the second person, even in thought, even during an embrace (nos. 20D–20G). For all the diversity in their personalities, the males in the Egyptian love songs are alike in never saying "you" of their lovers, but only "she" and "her" (see "Grammatical Person" in chapter 6). I think this practice reflects an assumption about the way the sexes behave in love. We may surmise what kind of mental picture would produce a convention like this.

Speaking to someone in the second person is more intimate and direct than speaking about someone in the third person or even speaking indirectly to someone in the third person. The Egyptian love poems do not show the boys addressing girls, and the result is that the boys seem more remote. This is not to say that the boys in all the Egyptian songs *would not* or *could not* speak to girls in the second person, but rather that when the poets pictured young lovers doing whatever young lovers do, they envisaged girls speaking directly to boys but not boys speaking directly to girls. This view did not, however, lead to the creation of male and female stereotypes, for even within each sex the poets portray a variety of personalities, different people who pursue their desires with differing degrees of assertiveness and boldness.

There are signs in the Egyptian love songs of demands and expectations *outside* the love relationship that restrict a girl's freedom and mobility more than a boy's. Thus the girl in no. 4 feels that people are putting pressure on her to abandon her desire, something no male complains of. And although the girl comes to the boy in some songs (nos. 8, 14), this might not be the expected course of events, for the girl in no. 44 implies that her lover *should* have taken the initiative: "While you yet argued with your heart . . . ," she chides, "it was I who came to you." Moreover, while the boy in "The Stroll" at least attempts to reach the girl (no. 33), for her part she finds it necessary to wait and to hope that her mother will go to the boy's house and take her along (no. 36). Yet even within a society in which females are expected to exhibit greater passivity and tolerate greater limits on their freedom, they may act with equal freedom and even greater assertiveness within the one-to-one love relationship.

As in Egyptian love poetry, neither lover in Canticles is a sexual stereotype. There is only one kind of erotic love. Boy and girl love and desire each other in the same way and with the same intensity. Many stereotypes of sexual differences prominent in other love poetries are absent from the Song. It includes no stock types, such as a pleading or aggressive man and an unyielding or coy mistress who must be coaxed into compliance; nor, conversely, a sexually rapacious woman and a malleable man; nor a strong and masterful man and a tender and submissive woman; nor a gallant and self-sacrificing man and a chaste and *spirituelle* woman, who is but a device for the male's spiritual education.

In the Song, the behavior of the sexes in love is fundamentally similar. Each lover invites the other to come away; each goes out at night to find the other; each knows moments of hesitation; each desires sexual fulfillment. The two lovers say similar things to each other, express the same desires and delights, and praise each other in the same ways. Most important, neither feels an asymmetry in the quality or intensity of their emotions, a feeling that would be revealed if, for example, one lover tried to wheedle the reluctant other into love or worried about the steadfastness of the other's affections.

This egalitarian view of love is no deliberate rejection of preordained sex roles, nor are the girl's assertiveness and her equality with her lover a social statement, for she does not imply: although I am a female I will not wait at home but will go out and pursue my love; although I am a female I will seek to satisfy my sexual desires; although I am a female I will brave the night; although I am a female I will not demur at telling my lover how I feel. Such "althoughs" would have to be implied if the girl's forthright assertion of her sexuality were meant as a rejection of a sex role or a socially imposed stereotype. When the Shulammite bridles at the restrictions placed upon her and insists on her right to love, it is not because of any feeling that females should not be thus restricted, but rather because of her conviction that she is sexually mature, whatever anyone else may think (8:10).

Thus the portrayal of the sexes is not forced into the mold of sexual stereotypes. Nor do the lovers represent sexual *archetypes*. There is no effort to bring out the essentially female in the Shulammite or the essentially male in the youth. Krinetzki's Jungian analysis of the two lovers does not ring true (1970:408f.). He says that the lovers represent sexual archetypes, the Great Male Principle ("das Grosse Männliche") and the Great Female Principle ("das Grosse Weibliche"):

> Jeder der beiden Partner wird auf Grund der Projektion der eigenen *Animus*- oder *Anima*-Vorstellungen auf den andern zu einer Art Konkretisierung eines Teils des gegengeschlechtlichen Archetypus und damit zu einem Zugang zur "grossen Welt", in die die archetypischen Bilder gleichfalls hineinprojiziert werden. (1970:416)[6]

Each is to the other an archetypal "prince" or "princess" (ibid.).

Now this is just what we do *not* see in Canticles. The lovers are two individuals, not type-figures, and they do not have archetypically male or female traits. They differ anatomically, of course, and the girl is spoken of in images implying softness more often than the boy is.[7] Nevertheless she is not "rounder" ("das Grosse Rund"), more receiving, more passive, more "vessel-like" than he. And she certainly does not have the terrifying traits of the Jungian female archetype, the "Fearsome Mother" ("die Furchtbare Mutter") who rips up her children (as Krinetzki, 1970:411, thinks), even if the lovestruck young man does find her awesome and her eyes do unnerve him. The lovers see each other in similar ways. The eyes of both are like doves (4:1; 5:12). Both are tall and proud like trees (5:15; 7:8). Parts of both are rounded and crafted like works of art (5:14, 15a; 7:2b, 3a). If she is as lofty

6. "By virtue of the projection of each [lover's] *animus* or *anima* idea onto the other, each of the two partners becomes a sort of concretization of a part of the opposite sexual archetype and thereby a means of access to the 'great world,' into which the archetypal images are projected likewise."

7. Still, some of the images used of the boy also suggest softness, such as lilies (5:13) and doves in milk (5:12), while some of the images used of the girl are definitely "hard," in particular the towers (4:4; 7:5a, 5b).

as towers or as exalted as the morning star in her lover's eyes, he is as lofty and majestic as the Lebanon in hers. The imagery is not distributed in a way that would separate the sexes into two fundamentally different types.

Nor does the Song mention or even allude to the most essential of sexual differentia, which is not the external genitalia but the womb. That women alone can bear children is a fact of limitless social, economic, and personal consequence. But this quintessentially female ability, vital for the race and crucial to individual well-being and happiness, is passed over in silence in Canticles as in the Egyptian love songs. The lovers do not even *muse* about the children they will have together. In the carefully circumscribed horizon of these love poems, anatomy is not destiny.

Yet it is evident that the sexes are not equally free as far as society is concerned. The boy's freedom of movement seems greater: he appears (we never learn from where) and disappears at will. The girl is subject to restrictions that her brothers place upon her. But these imposed restrictions are an external obstacle, not an inequality within the love relationship. While social realities do impinge upon the world of the poem, *within their one-to-one relationship* the lovers act with equal freedom and express their love in the same ways.

That is not to say that the lovers' personalities are identical. A difference between the lovers is felt first of all because the poet focuses primarily on the girl, thereby delineating her character much more clearly. She speaks more than the boy does, so her feelings are emphasized by the quantity of the utterance alone, and she says things that he presumably could say but does not (e.g., 8:6–7). The Song is *her* song, and there is no scene from which she is absent. The poem opens with her expression of desire and her complaint, immediately giving us a bit of her personal history. The boy first speaks in 1:8, in response to her question. All events are narrated from her point of view, though not always in her voice, whereas from the boy's angle of vision we know little besides how he sees her. Thus in 2:8 we are with her as her lover approaches, not with him as he bounds over the hills. In 3:1–5 we follow her as she gets out of bed and seeks him. In 5:2–6:3 too we start in the house with her and then follow her into the streets. We know only what she hears and sees, and we make discoveries as she does. The boy is not always "on stage," but she is.

The girl's personality is more fully defined than the boy's also because she is shown in a broader range of social interactions. She talks with the girls of Jerusalem and with her brothers as well as with her lover, while he speaks only with *her* (except for one sentence, 7:1b, in which he seems to address the girls of Jerusalem). She is given a fuller social context—brothers, mother, house, companions. Of him we know only that he is a shepherd and has companions (1:7; 8:13). The Song could be characterized as "a girl and her lover" more precisely than as "two lovers." This asymmetry in the depiction of the characters does not arise from a different view of the sexes, but from a literary choice. The poet puts the girl in center stage and develops the action around her, in this way creating a center to give coherence to a rather rambling series of speeches and events.

The girl appears generally to be the more resolute and zealous in pursuing the fulfillment of their mutual love. They both brave danger. But while he bounds over the mountains at night to visit her—an act whose danger (which in reality might be great) is not mentioned—her risks receive emphasis, as she twice faces the explicit danger of searching for her lover through the city at night, acting in an aberrant way that may give the impression that she is a prostitute (a possibility she may have been aware of, for in 1:7 she seems to show a concern that just such a suspicion might arise if she were to wander about among the shepherds looking for her beloved). It is she who must defy family ire; he does not seem to have such problems. Above all, it is she who makes the proud declaration of love's hard, burning power (8:6–7). Whatever he feels, she is the one we hear proclaiming the power of love, so that we know firsthand that *she* feels love's fire. Thus she appears the tougher, more determined, more vehement lover. She needs these qualities because she is the one who must break through family restrictions and societal expectations and shrug off companions' teasing. In this way the limitations that society places on girls do affect the Shulammite, not by making her a female "type," but by hardening her, forcing her to pursue her goals more obstinately.

SEXUAL RELATIONS

Various kinds of sexual pleasures, including coitus, are mentioned or hinted at in the love songs, though just where these allusions are is a matter of inevitable uncertainty. Let us consider more prosaically and less delicately than the songs themselves do just what sexual intercourse means to the lovers' relationships.

Some Egyptian love songs allude more or less openly to sexual intercourse. The girl in no. 1, who chides her lover for wanting to leave her bed and urges him to stay with her under the sheet, has, we may reasonably assume, just had intercourse and will do it again if she has her way. The girl in no. 4 says quite clearly that she has not yet had enough sex (*dd*, cognate to *dodim* and determined by the phallus sign, means sexual lovemaking, probably specifically coitus). Another girl (no. 14) scolds a dove for announcing the day. She has just spent the night in bed with her lover. The boy in "The Crossing" embraces his girl ("I'll embrace her: her arms are opened"), smells her fragrance ("Her scent is that of the *ibr*-balm"), kisses her deeply ("I'll kiss her, her lips are parted"), then tells a servant to prepare her bed: "Put fine linen between her legs, while spreading her bed with royal linen" (no. 20G).

We picture her there wrapped in a sheet, waiting. The poet gives clear direction to our imagination while leaving the details to our fancy.

The Egyptian love songs are deeply erotic without dwelling on the details of sexual activity. The sex act is never *described*, even euphemistically. It is only alluded to as something that happened in the past or will yet happen. The poets never[8] make a direct appeal to salaciousness by spreading out the details of intercourse to titillate the audience, although the Egyptians were quite capable of doing this, as the pictures in a contemporaneous pornographic papyrus show (Omlin, 1973).

Poems treat sexual intercourse with restraint and indirection, but rarely with embarrassment, coyness, or apology. Only one poem, "The Orchard," is coy about sex, demonstratively calling attention to the fact that it is hiding something. The first two trees in "The Orchard" threaten to reveal what they have seen (no. 28), while the third tree, under which the lovers have spent two days concealed in a bower, promises not to tell, meaning that we can very well guess. The most forthright mention of coitus comes in the most earnest of the Egyptian poems, "The Flower Song" (no. 17). The girl, walking hand in hand with her lover in the garden, tells him how her joy began "when I lay with you."

The partners in these sexual relationships (as in the love songs in general) seem to be unmarried. In no. 1, where the girl is trying to keep her lover from leaving her bed, his haste to leave suggests that he has a reason to be off that is more pressing than just getting to work on time. The girl in no. 4, who speaks of the lovemaking of her "little wolf cub" declares, "I will not listen to their advice to abandon the one I desire." We may surmise that the people who are giving her this advice are not trying to break up a marriage. The girl who is awakened by the dove in no. 14 does not live with her lover, for she says, "I found my brother in his bedroom," indicating that she came to his place the preceding night. She and her lover resolve to spend their lives together, a pledge most appropriate to lovers still unmarried. In "The Crossing" the boy's struggle to get to his beloved would not be necessary in the more secure sexual union of marriage.

Marriage is only infrequently alluded to. One young lady tells her lover that she wants to be

> the mistress of your house,[9]
> while your arm rests on my arm,
> for my love has surrounded you.
>
> (No. 13)

8. Or hardly ever. Nos. 41–42 come close to this through a number of allusions to anatomy and sex acts, but the details are obscure. No. 1 is a bit salacious too, but there is an openness and freshness about the girl's demands that keep the appeal of the song from being primarily voyeuristic.

9. A common idiom designating a wife.

Another hopes that the boy she loves will send a message to her mother, and that her whole family will rejoice on receiving it. The message would presumably be a request for the girl in marriage (no. 32). The girl in "The Crossing" (no. 20B) plans to live with her beloved, taking care of him until death, and perhaps beyond:[10]

We will be together
even when there come to pass
the days of peace of old age.
I will be with you every day,
setting [food before you
like a maidservant] before her master.

Lovers sometimes tell each other that they will possess each other for ever. Such declarations seem to imply an intention to get married:

I have obtained forever and ever
what Amon has granted me.

(No. 12)

I will never be far away.
My hand will be with your hand,
as I stroll about,
I with you,
in every pleasant place.

(No. 14)

How lovely is my hour with you!
This hour flows forth for me forever—
it began when I lay with you.
In sorrow and in joy,
you have exalted my heart.
Do not [leave] me.

(No. 17)

Sexual intercourse for this last girl is not a culmination but a beginning, a source of lasting pleasure, a fountain from which joy will flow forth throughout their lives. Intercourse is not restricted to marriage, but it is on the path to it. This attitude toward sexuality is not necessarily present in all the Egyptian love songs (nos. 41–42 may refer to orgiastic pleasure in a brothel). But mostly the lovers seem to be fully committed to each other, and sex is not casual.

10. "The days of peace of old age" probably refers to life after death; see no. 20B, n. f.

The intensity of the Egyptian lovers makes us feel that they are intent on a lifetime together, even when this is not said explicitly. Yet marriage is never the focal point of the songs. The lovers concentrate on their immediate experience, which, when it is a happy one, they expect to continue throughout their lives.

Like most of the Egyptian songs, Canticles treats sexual relations as a natural part of the love experience, though not as its goal or culmination. The lovers in Canticles make love in many ways. They caress each other with words of affection, kiss deeply, smell each other's fragrance, lie snuggled in each other's embrace. They "eat" and "drink" love—imbibe it, fill themselves with it, get drunk on it. All the senses partake. The Song does not, however, describe coitus. It alludes to it, sometimes quite transparently, but always as something that will occur outside the scene. Allusions (unlike euphemisms, which are one-to-one substitutions) always maintain some ambiguity.

Still, the poet of Canticles gives us adequate reason to suppose that sexual intercourse is part of the lovers' relationship. The youth spends the night nestled between his beloved's breasts in their garden bower (1:13f.). This scene does not continue through the night, so the audience can only imagine what the couple is likely to do in such circumstances. Later the Shulammite invites her beloved to spend the night in the countryside, to wake up and go early in the morning to the vineyards. "There I will give you my love [*doday*]" (7:13). This is close to an explicit declaration that she will have intercourse with him, for *dodim* means sexual lovemaking and can certainly include coitus. Still, some (though not too much) uncertainty remains even here, since *dodim* apparently can refer to other types of lovemaking as well (see the comment on 1:2). Three times when the couple lie embracing, the Shulammite asks the girls of Jerusalem not to disturb love (2:7; 8:4; cf. 5:8), a request that hints rather openly that the couple is about to make love,[11] though again the specific acts are veiled. The boy comes into his garden, which is at the same time the girl's garden, "to graze in the gardens and to gather lilies" (6:2), acts that, as comparison with 4:16–5:1 shows, allude to physical lovemaking, probably to sexual intercourse. Vv. 4:16–5:1 virtually define coming into one's garden to eat myrrh, spices, and honey and to drink wine and milk (5:1a) as sating oneself on sex, *dodim* (5:1b). There are other phrases that suggest lovemaking of such intensity and intimacy that intercourse is the likely outcome; see, for example, 4:6—"Before the day blows softly in, and the shadows flee, I'll make my way to the mountain of myrrh, to the hill of frankincense" (see commentary); similarly 7:8–10.

Within Canticles sexual intercourse does not consummate marriage.[12]

11. This is so even according to understandings of the verse other than the one I accept; see commentary.

12. The lovers in Canticles *are* unmarried; see the discussion on pp. 231f. Even if the Song

Rather, marriage will consummate sex: the lovers are already enjoying sexual pleasures, but they want public acceptance of their union in marriage as well. Their concern for marriage, though not a major topic in the poem, is implied by the affectionate epithet "my bride" (4:8–12), for such the boy wishes her to be, by the girl's wish to take her beloved to her mother's house and display their love publicly (3:4; 8:2), and by her dialogue with her brothers in which they consent in principle to her marriage ("when she is spoken for" in 8:8 is the only reference to her actual betrothal or wedding). In 3:7–11 they are fantasizing that their garden bower is their marriage bed. Marriage is also indirectly implied by the Shulammite's demand that her lover place her as a seal upon his heart and arm (8:6), meaning that he is to keep her with him always.

This song is surely not about mere dalliance. The lovers are intensely serious about their love and fully committed to each other. Canticles is a song about a love that—as the lovers see it—will inevitably lead to marriage and continue throughout their lives, for nothing but death can match its power. But the lovers are so intent upon the present moment that they do not think of anything beyond the wedding, and they give little thought even to that. This nearly exclusive focus on the immediate experience gives their love, for all its seriousness, an adolescent quality—as indeed it should, for they are adolescents, blossoming with the land and scarcely aware of anything beyond the springtime of their lives.

While the Song does not assume that marriage is the prerequisite for sexual relations, it does not seem to be deliberately defying strictures on premarital sex. Rather, it accepts sexuality with a naturalness matching its delicacy. The Shulammite exudes her sexual love (*ʾetten ʾet doday lak*, 7:13) as naturally and unselfconsciously as the mandragoras give off their scent (*hadduda'im natᵉnu reaḥ*, 7:14). The lovers show no embarrassment, make no apology, express no defiance. They do not relish sex as a forbidden fruit, just as they do not eschew it as a sin. Moreover, the avoidance of description of coitus, even euphemistic description, is not done in a naughty, teasing fashion. The poet does not conceal something and then point to what is concealed (as happens in "The Orchard"). The fade-out comes unobtrusively with the lovers lying in each other's embrace.

While a society with strong religious and social strictures on unmarried sexual activity[13] might well produce a "naughty" literature that toys with

---

were a collection of love ditties, a view I argue against in chapter 4, the only passage that even *seems* to describe marriage as a present fact is 3:7–11, and that is not where the sex is.

13. It is difficult to gauge just how strong these strictures were in First and Second Temple times among the population as a whole, but we may be sure that premarital intercourse was anathematized by religious teachers (Ben Sirah is certainly vehement about it; see 42:9–13) and worried about by parents (Ben Sirah, 42:9, says that a daughter is a "sleep-disturbing worry"). Sexual intercourse between a man and a woman who is neither married nor betrothed to someone else

forbidden fruit, it is surprising to find such a society producing a poem that accepts premarital sexuality so naturally that it does not even try to draw attention to its own liberality. But of vast areas of Israelite life, society, and attitudes we know nothing, for the overwhelming majority of the documents we have were preserved because they served religious and ideological purposes of various groups within that society. (In the case of Canticles, it was not the book itself but an interpretation of it that served religious purposes.)

Furthermore, rather than social realities or even widespread principles, works of literature may show poetic fantasies. To a certain extent our song does this by offering a "lover disguise" (see Excursus in chapter 7). By allowing the audience to identify with two determined young lovers as they follow their desire, this "disguise" enables the "lateral" escape from society that comes from ignoring some of the proprieties society usually demands. In other words, it would not be nearly so much fun to hear about a young lady who behaved just as her brothers felt she should.

The Song does assume a sexual ethic, but the sexual virtue cherished is not chastity. It is fidelity: unquestioned devotion to one's lover, a devotion that can make one risk the anger of family, the teasing of peers, the violence of society's guardians, and the dangers of the night to reach and unite with one's lover. It is a love that binds lovers together as closely and constantly as a seal upon the heart and arm and that makes one as vehemently possessive as the grave, which gets what it wants and holds it forever.

The virtue of sexual exclusiveness in such a love is not a virtue of the individuals involved so much as a quality innate to the relationship. The Shulammite is a locked garden, which only her beloved can enter, where he can enjoy the fragrance of its spices and the sweetness of its new fruits.

COMMUNICATION BETWEEN LOVERS

For all their similarities, Canticles and the Egyptian love poetry show one remarkable difference: Canticles shows lovers interacting in speech. In the Egyptian songs such interaction is usually absent; when present it is only implicit and always well in the background.

All the Egyptian love songs are monologues, most of them dramatic monologues spoken by one of the lovers (see chapter 6).[14] Lovers tell how

---

is not explicitly forbidden in the Bible. In the earliest stratum of biblical law it is, however, viewed as a violation of the property rights of the girl's father, inasmuch as it reduced the bride-price she could bring in.

14. The following observations would probably be valid as generalizations even if some poems with dialogue did exist. Since there is no dialogue in any of the extant texts, which seem to be a random sampling, the chances are that even if love dialogue was used in love poems, it was very rare.

their beloved affects them, but we do not hear the words that have that effect. The Egyptian poets chose the monologue form because they were primarily interested in showing the experience of *individuals* in love. Significantly, the two Egyptian songs that do portray both lovers are double monologues, in which both lovers speak, but not to each other, neither exchanging words nor affecting each other by speech. The double monologues are series of vignettes, with only one lover in each vignette.

Contemporaneous Egyptian narrative fiction, in contrast, uses dialogue extensively. I would conclude that the Egyptian love poets did not choose to write dialogue; their purposes of exploring and depicting emotions did not require it. When they do have both lovers speaking in a single song, it is only to enhance the vividness of the portrayal of each individual's emotions, to show how the "balancing of hearts" intensifies love's power within each lover (in the case of "The Crossing"), or to sharpen the irony of self-imposed isolation (in "The Stroll"). They create a variety of personalities and study each one in isolation, painting a picture of love as a state of emotion. Love fulfilled is a state of pleasant harmony within an individual, a state brought about by the presence of the beloved and by sexual contact rather than by verbal interaction.

The rarity of direct requests and direct compliments likewise indicates the poems' limited view of love. In only a few very brief passages do girls ask something of their lovers when they are present.[15] (Demands *in absentia* are really wishes.) Boys do not make any requests of girls; as noted above, boys do not speak *to* their lovers at all. Indeed, in the Egyptian songs nothing a lover says seems to have any effect on his or her beloved. We never get the impression that a boy does something in response to what we hear his girl say to him. Compliments are even rarer. Although a beloved is praised in the third person in various songs, the closest thing to a compliment spoken *directly* to a lover is: "For are you not health and life itself?" in no. 13.[16] Often girls speak of the effect their lovers have on them, for example: "To hear your voice is pomegranate wine to me: I draw life from hearing it" (no. 18). But they do not say, "You're beautiful," or the like, in so many words.

In contrast, the Song of Songs is true dialogue throughout. Even in passages that have the appearance of monologue because one of the personae

15. The girl in no. 1 urges her beloved to stay in bed with her. The girl in no. 9 says to hers, "Let us release it together" (meaning the worm in the trap, so as to let the bird go). The girl in no. 17 concludes, "Do not leave me." In no. 28(G) it is not clear who is speaking to whom, but the girl (or possibly the poet) seems to be urging the boy to join in flattering the tree. The second stich of no. 19 might be translated "take your wreaths." No. 50 *may* include an imperative, see n. a ad loc.

16. The praises in no. iii (App. A) are spoken directly to a male, but that text is probably a royal encomium and not a love song. The Praise Songs spoken by males, nos. 31 and 54, are soliloquies.

speaks alone for a relatively long time, there is always a listener inside the poem. It is usually clear that the lovers are speaking and listening to each other (see chapter 6). Furthermore, they *influence* each other through speech: they respond to what they hear. What each says and does depends in large part on what the other says. This is a notable broadening of poetic potentials in comparison with the Egyptian songs.

Often one lover responds directly to a request or hint given by the other. For example, in 1:7 the Shulammite asks:

> Tell me, my soul's beloved:
> where do you graze,
> where do you rest (your flocks) at noon?

and in 1:8 he replies:

> If you don't know,
> most beautiful of women,
> go on out in the tracks of the flock,
> and graze your kids
> by the shepherds' camps.

In 4:12–14 he describes her as a garden of spices:

> A garden locked is my sister, my bride . . .
> spikenard and saffron, cane and cinnamon,
> with frankincense trees of all kinds,
> myrrh and aloes,
> with all the best spices.

She picks up the hint and invites him in:

> Awake, O north wind, and come, O south!
> Blow on my garden that its spices may flow.
> Let my beloved come into his garden,
> and eat of its luscious fruit.
>
> (4:16)

And he accepts:

> I come into my garden, my sister, my bride,
> I taste my myrrh with my spice . . .
>
> (5:1)

Such feedback in communication is so frequent that its significance is easily overlooked. But its absence in the Egyptian love songs shows that its presence in the Song of Songs should not be taken for granted.

The poet further brings out the interaction of the lovers and establishes the reciprocity of their communication by the use of *echoing*, in which the words of one lover are patterned on the other's and thus recall them. Distance between a statement and its echo suggests that the lovers remember each other's words and find in them the most suitable vehicle for expressing their own feelings. An example of a distant echo is 7:12, where the Shulammite calls her lover to come away:

> *l^{e}kah dodi neṣeʾ haśśadeh*
> Come, my beloved, let's go to the field.

Here she is echoing his earlier invitation (2:13; compare 2:10):

> *qumi lak raʿyati yapati ul^{e}ki lak*
> Arise, my darling, my beautiful, and come away.

In that passage he described the blossoming of the countryside thus:

> *hannişşanim nirʾu baʾareṣ*
> *hatt^{e}ʾenah ḥan^{e}ṭah paggeyhah,*
> *w^{e}hagg^{e}panim s^{e}madar nat^{e}nu reaḥ*
> The blossoms have appeared in the land . . . .
> The fig tree sweetens its young fruit,
> and the vine is in bud, giving off fragrance.
>
> (2:12aα, 13a)

When she invites him away, she describes the land in nearly the same words, urging him to come with her:

> *nirʾeh ʾim par^{e}ḥah haggepen,*
> *pittaḥ hass^{e}madar,*
> *heneṣu harimmonim*
> We'll see if the vine has blossomed,
> the bud opened,
> the pomegranates bloomed.
>
> (7:13a$\beta\gamma$)

Elsewhere he says to her:

nopet tiṭṭopnah śiptotayik kallah
Your lips, my bride, drip honeycomb,

(4:11abα)

and she praises him for the same sweetness:

śiptotayw šošannim
noṭᵉpot mor ᶜober
His lips are lilies—
they drip liquid myrrh.

(5:13b)

She says:

ki ṭobim dodeyka miyyayin
lᵉreaḥ šᵉmaneyka ṭobim
for your caresses are better than wine!
As for scent, your oils are good

(1:2b–3a)

and he says:

mah ṭobu dodayik miyyayin
wᵉreaḥ šᵉmanayik mikkol bᵉśammim
Your caresses—how better than wine,
the scent of your oils than all spices!

(4:10b)

In 4:6b the youth responds in similar language to the maiden's request in 2:17b, and 8:14 recalls both passages.

Often the echo comes close upon the words that call it forth—for example, in 1:15–16, where the boy says:

hinnak yapah raᶜyati hinnak yapah
ᶜeynayik yonim
How beautiful you are, my darling,
how beautiful!
Your eyes are doves,

and without pause the girl takes up his words, returns the compliment, and intensifies it:

hinn^{e}*ka yapeh dodi*
ʾap naʿim
How beautiful you are, my beloved, indeed delightful!

Later on (7:7) her lover closely echoes her words in another compliment:

mah yapit umah naʿamt
ʾah^{a}*bah ba⟨t⟩ taʿ*^{a}*nugim*
How beautiful you are, how pleasant,
O love, delightful girl!

Their words intertwine closely in the rapid exchange in 2:1–3a. The girl begins:

ʾ^{a}*ni ḥ*^{a}*baṣṣelet haššaron,*
šošannat haʿ^{a}*maqim*
I'm just a crocus of Sharon,
a valley-lily.

Self praise would be pointless here; rather, this is a modest self-appraisal: I'm just one among myriads. The point of this mild self-depreciation can only be to fish for praise and reassurance. To this her lover immediately responds by turning her own words to use in praising her preeminence:

k^{e}*šošannah beyn haḥoḥim*
ken raʿyati beyn habbanot
Like a lily among brambles,
so is my darling among girls.

She in turn patterns her praise of him on *his* words, likewise declaring him one of a kind:

k^{e}*tappuaḥ baʿ*^{a}*ṣey hayyaʿar*
ken dodi beyn habbanim
Like an apricot tree among trees of the thicket,
so is my beloved among boys.

Their words are even more closely interlocked in 7:10. The boy says, continuing his Praise Song:

> *w^{e}ḥikkek k^{e}yeyn haṭṭob*
> and your palate [is] like the best wine . . .

The girl completes his sentence by turning the compliment into an offer of the sweetness of her mouth:

> *holek l^{e}dodi l^{e}meyšarim*
> *dobeb śiptey ⟨šanim⟩*
> flowing smoothly to my beloved,
> dripping on scarlet lips.

Such echoing suggests the lovers' involvement in each other. In particular the rapidity of the exchanges where the words of the two lovers are closely intertwined makes us feel that the lovers are highly sensitive to each other, that the words of one quickly impress themselves on the heart and mind of the other. The alacrity of their response gives their expressions of love and desire an exhilaration and urgency rarely heard in the Egyptian love songs, where even assertive lovers tend to be more contemplative and passive.[17] The rapid movement of the dialogue in Canticles is appropriate to the impatient ardor of the Shulammite, who runs through the dark streets seeking her lover, and to the energetic eagerness of her lover, who leaps gazelle-like over the mountains as he hastens to reach her and invite her away.

The characters thus affect each other through what they say as well as through what they are and what they do. The echoing of lovers' words in "The Crossing" and "The Stroll" too shows the harmony of their feelings. But since these words are unspoken thoughts, it is not a harmony *created* through words. The echoes are not responses.

An Egyptian poet had a girl say, "My heart is in balance with yours" (no. 17), meaning that her desires are the same as her lover's. The author of the Song shows the balancing of lovers' hearts through the balancing of their words, so that the form of their expression embodies the truth of the declaration of mutual possession: "My beloved is mine and I am his" (2:16).

What the lovers say to each other is quite simple: You're beautiful, I love you, I want you, let's go. Unlike their Egyptian counterparts, they often make requests and urge each other to do things, and they most certainly exchange

17. A notable exception is no. 20D, where the boy crosses the river. The movement of that stanza is maintained by the rapid succession of action verbs and by the pace of the action itself, which takes the youth across the river in the course of the stanza. The urgency of the girl's sexual demands in no. 1 gives that song too an especially rapid pace.

praise. Each says essentially the same things as the other, often in nearly identical words. Although their rich and elegant speech is a poet's idealization of adolescent love, their talk conforms to the easily observable reality of young lovers' hypnotic absorption in each other.

The communication of these lovers is more than transmission of thoughts. It is *communion*, intimate and reciprocal influence through language. The words of each lover penetrate the other's thought and speech. Love in Canticles is thus the interinanimation of two souls, as John Donne defined love's essence. In fact, Donne's love poetry in many ways parallels the view of love implicit in Canticles:

> If any, so by love refin'd
>   that he soules language understood
> And by good love were growen all minde,
>   Within convenient distance stood,
> He (though he knew not which soule spake,
>   Because both meant, both spake the same)
> Might thence a new concoction take
>   And part farre purer then he came.
>
> ("The Extasie")

And indeed, the meshing and echoing of the lovers' words in Canticles does produce a "new concoction," one not reducible to the sum of each lover's statements.

Lover and Self

LOVE AS EMOTION

Lovers are absorbed in each other. They are also absorbed in the *experience* of love, and the poets reveal this experience. The love poets treat the varieties of lovers' emotions as worthy of artistic exploration. These feelings and drives, which might so easily be dismissed as ephemeral or even silly, and which society tries, sensibly, to harness to "greater" goals—marriage, reproduction, social continuity, family alliances, national welfare—are here observed, even cherished, for their own sake. In these songs young love is powerful and precious independently of any extrinsic goals it might serve. This intense and affectionate attention is in itself a statement of basic values: individual emotions are important.

The love poets show young love as a great force that creates a moral order of its own, for love demands—and engenders—total commitment. Obedience to its demands overrides other considerations. One stakes all for it and shares in its power, or hesitates to obey its dictates and so feels the pangs of hopeless desire. This idea of love is common to the Egyptian love poems and the Song of Songs.

Love's power can give a lover strength and determination, even vehemence, creating a singlemindedness that can—and should—make a lover courageous and even reckless. The power of love is epitomized by the deed of the youth in "The Crossing," who plunges into the flood-swollen river and swims past a crocodile to get to his beloved, finding the threats of flood and beast evaporating before the power love grants lovers. The youth (and the poet behind him) is exalting dedication to love above considerations of expediency and safety. The youth obeyed love's demand and so received its power.

As "The Stroll" shows, love's demands can be denied, but with unfortunate consequences. A boy and a girl sit in their respective homes longing for each other and waiting for something to happen that would bring them together. But nothing does, and by the end of the song they are still apart. The boy lies helplessly in bed, love's power having produced paralysis instead of strength. The poet conveys the message that lovers should obey their hearts by showing two lovers who, though they feel and think alike and are thoroughly infatuated with each other, fail to unite and communicate their love because they resist the impulses of their hearts.

The effects of love's power are shown as diverse and paradoxical. Love is the dominant force in a lover's life, giving illness or health, weakness or power, pain or pleasure. It is mainly the presence or absence of the beloved, or the expectation of that presence, that determines what effects love will work. In fulfillment love gives a delight that only a concatenation of sweet images can even start to convey. In the absence of the beloved, love's power agitates and disturbs, confusing tastes and nullifying normal pleasures. The Egyptian poets describe this effect in images of physical illness, enervation, deadening of senses, and paralysis, these ailments being curable only by the restorative power of the loved one's presence, the source of life and health. The imagery of the Egyptian songs thus implies a general state of being: love fulfilled is harmony, wholeness, health, life.

Sexual desire fuels love's power. Its demands can make a young lady rather ferocious. When the boy in song no. 1 tries to leave his beloved's bed—undoubtedly the prudent thing to do, if day is near—he catches a rebuke: are you hungry? need clothes? she chides him. Come back here, crawl under the sheets, caress my thighs, suck my breasts. What more do you need? Love is enough, is everything.

Similarly the girl in no. 4, drunk on love, is not ready to call it quits:

My heart is not yet done with your lovemaking,
my little wolf cub!
Your liquor is your lovemaking.

They—all those people out there—can beat her off to the highlands or the lowlands, to Syria or Nubia, with sticks and rods and palm-staves and whatever else they please, but

I will not listen to their advice
to abandon the one I desire.

The violence of the imagery she uses—a beating with five kinds of staves—mirrors the vehemence of her resolve not to be moved by the demands of society. What is more, that vehemence is meant to impress her lover too, for when such a girl says, "My heart is not yet done with your lovemaking," and then expresses with such fervor her determination not to abandon it, he would be well advised not to try to make off in the morning like the youth in no. 1.

No less fierce is the power of love in Canticles; the lovers are no less vehement. The Shulammite refuses to neglect her own "vineyard" any more, whatever her brothers say, and she immediately asks her lover where she can find him. She does not ask him just to visit her some time. She wants to know exactly where he spends the noon hours so that *she* can go find *him*. She will do that even if it means wandering around the shepherds' camps at risk to her reputation (1:5–8).

The Shulammite shows recklessness equal to that of the youth who crosses the Nile when, impelled by desire, she twice goes out at night to look for her lover in the city streets. The beating she gets the second time does not faze her; she does not even pause to complain, for she is regardless of anything but finding her beloved. He too is reckless, though not quite so much as she. He twice sneaks up to her house at night, once inviting her away, once asking to be let in. Now the Shulammite is not living alone; she is living in her mother's house together with, or at least near, some irritable brothers. So the boy too is taking chances.

Love's power receives its quintessential expression in the Shulammite's declaration, "for love is as strong as death, jealousy as hard as Sheol" (8:6). Death's power is absolute and inexorable; yet love's power is no less. The love in an adolescent's heart is so easily shrugged off. A girl wants to marry a shepherd boy—how ordinary. But the Song (and surely the poet's own thoughts are heard distinctly in this climactic declaration) asserts that no other power in human experience is comparable to this emotion.

The love songs, particularly the Egyptian songs, try to convey not only the power of love, but also the varieties and textures of emotions that love may engender, a task demanding no little poetic virtuosity. I will recapitulate a few of these emotions to emphasize the considerable variety of feelings and attitudes exhibited in the Egyptian love songs: courage and pride ("The Crossing"); self-denigrating fantasies ("Seven Wishes" and song no. 7, the latter in a humorous tone); a bewildered sense of pleasant entrapment (nos. 3, 10, 43); anger at being ignored (no. 46—contrast the boy in nos. 21A–21D, who would not mind being ignored); angry frustration together with fantastic hopes for success (no. 47); defiance of the world (no. 4); paralysis and confusion of tastes (nos. 6, 12, 37); exaltation and pride (no. 8, 17, 18); sexual exhilaration and emotional intoxication (nos. 4, 20F, 20G); suspicion and jealousy (no. 15); excited confusion (no. 16, 34); sharp, almost wild craving for the beloved (nos. 2, 38–40); and, above all, pleasure in the beloved's presence and deep, confident joy in mutual love (nos. 8, 9, 11, 13, 14, 17–19, 20D–20G, and more).

Canticles naturally shows a narrower range of emotions than the numerous Egyptian love songs do, though the emotions of the lovers are more varied in it than in any single Egyptian song. Mainly the lovers feel joy in the beloved's presence and confidence in the mutuality of their love. The tenor of their emotions is usually steady and upbeat, though it is not always serene. Love can shake up and awe a lover (6:4, 5, 10). It can cause unremitting desire (3:1). It can bring about love-sickness, a wild yearning that may lead to irrational behavior (5:8), even in the beloved's presence. The symptoms of the two types of love-sickness are similar, though the causes are different: when the youth, intent on lovemaking, brings his beloved to the house of wine, she cannot bear up under the weight of desire and asks her friends to make her bed, "for I am sick with love" (2:4, 5). Desire floods her body and causes physical lassitude (a symptom already diagnosed by the Egyptian love poets), but in this case it is not accompanied by pain, for its cure is near at hand.

The Egyptian lovers are fascinated by love, amazed at its power and its sensations. In attempting to show how love feels, the Egyptian poems characteristically use introspective reports on the speaker's emotions—the Description of Love (see chapter 7). We get the impression of lovers taking their own emotional pulses and revealing what love does to them. The Ramesside love poets, like their contemporaries in religious poetry[18] and narrative fiction,[19] are feeling their strength in the analysis and depiction of nuances of emotion.

18. A type of prayer expressing personal piety, often quite poignantly, develops in this period; see Fecht, 1965.

19. The prime example of this is the long and bitter tale of love, sex, and sexual hatred, "Two Brothers." "The Doomed Prince" shows a more tender love relationship. The sexual exploitation of personified Truth by a female is the subject of another tale of this period, "Truth and Falsehood"; see chapter 3 for summaries.

The Egyptian poems with the Description of Love theme are analytic. The speakers typically seek to grasp and convey moods with images that evoke a sense of harmonious interpenetration. For example,

> Your love is mixed in my body, . . .
> [like honey] mixed with water,
> like mandragoras in which gum is mixed.
>
> (No. 2)

This harmony, we should note, is not between the speaker and her lover but between the speaker and her emotions. It is love itself that so thoroughly and sweetly infuses the lover's body. The speaker concentrates more on her own emotions than on her beloved. The young lover loves love.

Canticles spends far less time than the Egyptian songs do on analytic descriptions of love's feelings. In only a few verses do the lovers look inward and describe what they feel (2:3b; 4:9; 6:5a; 6:12a; see chapter 7), and even these few sentences are meant more to praise the other lover than to explore an inner state. The poet makes no attempt to add precision to the description of emotion by heaping up similes. Amassing of similes is used instead when the lovers praise each other.

In fact, the Egyptian Descriptions of Love often convey a sense of urgency, as lovers dwell upon their own emotions, approaching their feelings from many angles and trying to grasp them in various ways, as if to pin them down. It seems important to the lovers (and to the poets behind them) to communicate just what is going on inside. In contrast, the urgency of the lovers in Canticles is to tell what they see in each other.

Here then is a significant difference between the Song of Songs and the Egyptian love songs: the inward orientation characteristic of the Egyptian lovers contrasts with the basically outward orientation of their counterparts in Canticles. The Egyptian poets, fascinated by what goes on inside a lover's heart, have the lovers try to tell us what this is. The poet of the Song, on the other hand, has the lovers concentrate on each other rather than on their emotions. Of course they do convey their feelings quite effectively, but they do so mainly by speaking of realities external to their emotional states. They *display* their emotions rather than reporting on them, for it is the relationship that arises from the emotions of love, more than the emotions themselves, that concerns the poet of the Song.

LOVE AS VISION

As well as reaching into feelings and relationships, love affects perception: lovers *see* things differently from the way others do.

One Egyptian love poem (no. 5) shows this happening. A youth is sailing to Memphis to meet his beloved:

> I'm headed for Ankh-Towy.
> I'll say to Ptah, the Lord of Truth:
> "Give me my sister tonight!"

He looks about him and sees divinity in the beauties of nature:

> The river—it is wine,
> its reeds are Ptah,
> the leaves of its lotus-buds are Sekhmet,
> its lotus-buds are Yadit,
> its lotus-blossoms are Nefertem.

His beloved's beauty too becomes a divine force that illumines the whole world: "The earth has grown light through her beauty."[20] Egyptians saw divinity in all phenomena of nature, so the boy's perceptions are by no means bizarre or incomprehensible, but neither should they be taken for granted. He is not reciting a religious disquisition or a hymn. His description of nature follows immediately upon his statement that he is going to meet his beloved, so that his vision of the world seems to flow directly from his thoughts of her. As he concentrates his thoughts on his beloved, a spiritual vision of strong and mysterious power grows within him, and the flora of the river glows with divinity in his eyes. Finally, the boy takes a god's-eye view and sees Memphis as "a jar of mandragoras set before the Gracious One," that is Ptah. The mandragora, so frequently mentioned in the love songs, has erotic connotations (see no. 2, n. a). The boy, contemplating his beloved, takes sensual delight in the world and feels that his god does too.

Lovers' vision is at the very heart of the Song's concern: the lovers' descriptions of the world about them show how they see each other, and their descriptions of each other show how they see the world.

The lovers in the Song focus intensely on each other. They give little thought to society, none to the future except for the wedding itself, and none to difficulties other than immediate obstacles that sometimes keep them apart. Their thoughts and conversations concentrate almost entirely on what they see and feel right now. Love is not blind, but young lovers do have tunnel vision. They see nothing but each other and care little about anything but the immediate experience. This narrowness of vision gives their romance an adolescent quality—what an outside observer might call infatuation.

20. It is not certain that the antecedent of "her beauty" is the beloved girl, but see no. 5, n. j.

The lovers project their feelings onto the world they see about them. When they look at the blossoming countryside, they sense in nature the same lush, erotic efflorescence that they feel within themselves. The sensuousness of nature becomes a correlative of the sensuousness of love. In particular the girl's experience of sexuality has its counterpart in nature, for the Song is first of all the song of her sexual blossoming. The lovers describe the blossoming of the land in spring (2:10–13; 7:13–14), but at the same time they sense in it the blossoming of the girl. She herself is a vineyard (1:6; 8:12), which, now that it is being tended, is blossoming, or, perhaps, now that it is blossoming, is being tended. She is a garden with sweet fruits and fragrant spices, an orchard with pomegranates and choice fruits (4:12–16). She will let him drink the juice of her pomegranate (8:2b), which is surely her breast, now ripe.

She will give him her vernal love in the field among the blossoming fruits and spices, in the countryside. "*There* I will give you my love," she says (7:13). *There*—the garden or field—is the place suitable for the giving of sexual love (*dodim*), for the flowering of youthful love is as one of the inevitable events of the universal flowering in the spring.

As the Egyptian youth saw the world infused with his beloved's beauty (no. 5), so the youth in Canticles senses the world blossoming with his girl's loveliness.[21] Eroticism is diffused throughout the body—and projected onto the world beyond.

The lovers' description of the countryside in spring is so sensual because they see—and smell, and hear, and taste—their beloved in the world about them. They also see, smell, hear, and taste the world in their beloved.

The nature of lovers' perception is revealed above all in the Praise Songs in Canticles (4:1–7; 4:9–15; 5:10–16; 6:4–10; and 7:2–10a). The imagery of the Praise Songs is impressive and intriguing, yet at the same time difficult and foreign, perhaps the most foreign aspect of the Song for the modern reader. Nor is there anything quite like it elsewhere in ancient Near Eastern poetry. Yet it is this imagery above all that reveals to us the poet's view of a lover's perception.

Praise of the Beloved in Canticles has clear parallels in the Egyptian love poems, yet significant differences exist. The theme is not nearly so prominent in the Egyptian poetry as in Canticles. Furthermore, the Egyptian Praise Songs tend to use metaphor in a restrained, limited fashion, mainly to reinforce literal description.

21. ". . . and my imagination drawing strength from contact with my sensuality, my sensuality expanding through all the realm of my imagination, my desire no longer had any bounds. The girl whom I invariably saw dappled with the shadows of their leaves was to me herself a plant of local growth, merely of a higher species than the rest, and one whose structure would enable me to get closer than through them to the intimate savour of the country" (Proust, *Remembrance of Things Past*, I, 171).

In Canticles, on the other hand, literal description is rare, and the metaphors offer little information about how the lovers look, often seeming actually to interfere with the formation of a mental picture of them. Many images are startling:

> Your nose is like the tower of Lebanon,
> looking toward Damascus.
>
> (7:5b)

> Your navel is a rounded bowl—
> may it never lack mixed wine!
>
> (7:3a)

> His belly is an ivory bar,
> adorned with lapis lazuli.
>
> (5:14b)

The poet, as I argued earlier (pp. 274ff.) maintains a "metaphoric distance"—an unexpectedness or incongruity—between image and referent, yet bridges that distance by making us see each part of the body in terms of the image in two ways: (1) through the poetic form, which in the *waṣf*s consists mostly of predications with one-to-one correspondences between images and parts of the body, and (2) through a choice of images that share with the referent a sensory, "objective" quality, such as the whiteness of sheep and teeth, or the height and straightness of nose and tower.

The poet's strategy is thus to point us to each part of the lovers' bodies as if describing it, then to set before our eyes images that cannot comfortably be assimilated to their referents. This dislocation of expectations directs our attention to the images themselves rather than to the parts of the body. The images, not quickly serving the task that seems to have been laid upon them, become independent of their referents and memorable in themselves. In other words, what do you remember more vividly after having read the Song—a boy and a girl who look a certain way, or black goats filing down a distant mountainside, perky young gazelle twins, heaps of wheat hedged by lilies, and so on? For me it is the imagery itself that makes the sharpest, most enduring impression, and I think that this is the author's intention.

As the poem proceeds, the images, given an importance independent of their referents, combine to form a cohesive picture of a self-contained world: a peaceful, fruitful world, resplendent with the blessings of nature and the beauties of human art. That world blossoms in a perpetual spring. Doves hide shyly, sit near water channels, and bathe in milk. Spices give forth their fragrance. Springs flow with clear water. Fruits and wines offer their sweetness. Mounds of wheat are surrounded by lilies. Ewes, white and clean, bear twins and never miscarry. Goats stream gently down the mountainside. Proud and ornate towers stand tall above the landscape. Nor are there lacking silver and gold, precious stones, and objects of art: a rich and blessed world.

This world provides a harmonious backdrop to the expressions of love. Far more important, it also reveals the author's idea of the way a lover views the world. It is a psychological reality that the poet discloses. The dramatic mode of presentation helps show subjectivity, for the lovers, not the poet, say these things. The point is not the beloved's beauty (which, strictly speaking, the *poet* never asserts), but rather what a lover perceives in and through this beauty. The imagery of the praise thus shows us not how the lovers *look*, but how they *see*. Lovers look at each other and, through the prism of physical form, see an ever-present Arcady. Further, since that world comes into being and is unified only through the lovers' perception of each other, the imagery reveals a *new* world—one *created* by love.

Lovers see each other as unique. In the Praise Songs they say: my lover is like no other lover, my love is like no other love, my world is fresh and new and charged with a strange loveliness. Literal physical descriptions or standard, easily grasped tropes would not convey this freshness of vision, whereas the peculiar, surprising images in which the lovers in Canticles speak of each other do so. The poet puts bold, unexpected images into a traditional pattern, creating metaphors that stretch our imaginations by maintaining a distance between what is spoken of and what is said about it. In this way we can join in the excitement of discovery as the lovers discover a new world in each other.

The eroticism of the Praise Songs in Canticles thus transcends physical beauty. The imagery is inadequate as physical description because the lovers are not seeing physical features so much as looking *through* them to materializations of their own emotion.

The Song sees no male or female principle in sexual love. There is only one type of sexuality, an indivisible eros, and this pervades the universe projected by the lovers' imagery. The sexual egalitarianism of the Song thus reflects a metaphysics of love rather than a social reality or even a social ideal.

For the Egyptian poets, love was primarily a way of feeling, well represented by images of harmony and pleasantness. It was a feeling inspired by a lover but remaining within the confines of the individual soul. Thus it was that monologue could fully convey its quality. Love in Canticles, on the other hand, is not only feeling: it is also a confluence of souls, best expressed by tightly interlocking dialogue; and it is a mode of perception, best communicated through the imagery of praise. This presention of discourse and use of imagery thus reinforce each other in conveying a concept of love: love is a communion in which lovers look at each other with an intensely concentrated vision that broadens to elicit a world of its own. For Canticles, love is a way of seeing—and creating—a world, a private, idyllic universe.

The idea of love implicit in the Song is much like one John Donne expresses explicitly and analytically in his songs and sonnets. In Donne's view, lovers possess a world within each other. In "The Sun Rising" he says:

> Ask for those Kings whom thou saw'st yesterday,
> And thou shalt hear: 'All here in one bed lay'.
> She is all States, and all Princes, I,
> Nothing else is:
> Princes do but play us; compar'd to this,
> All honour's mimic, all wealth alchemy.

In similar fashion, in the world of the lovers' vision in the Song, the young shepherd is a king, the vineyard keeper a noblewoman, and their bower under the trees a royal chamber, for love gives them wealth beyond that of Solomon's vineyards or a rich man's house (8:7, 11–12). In Donne's words:

> For love, all love of other sights controules,
> And makes one little roome, an every where.
> . . . .
> Let us possesse one world, each hath one, and is one.
> ("The Good Morrow")

And further: "So we shall be one, and one another's All" ("Lovers Infiniteness").

Or, in the words of Genesis:

> *w^ehayu l^ebaśar ʾeḥad*
> and they shall become one flesh.

Illustrations

Appendices

Bibliography

Indexes

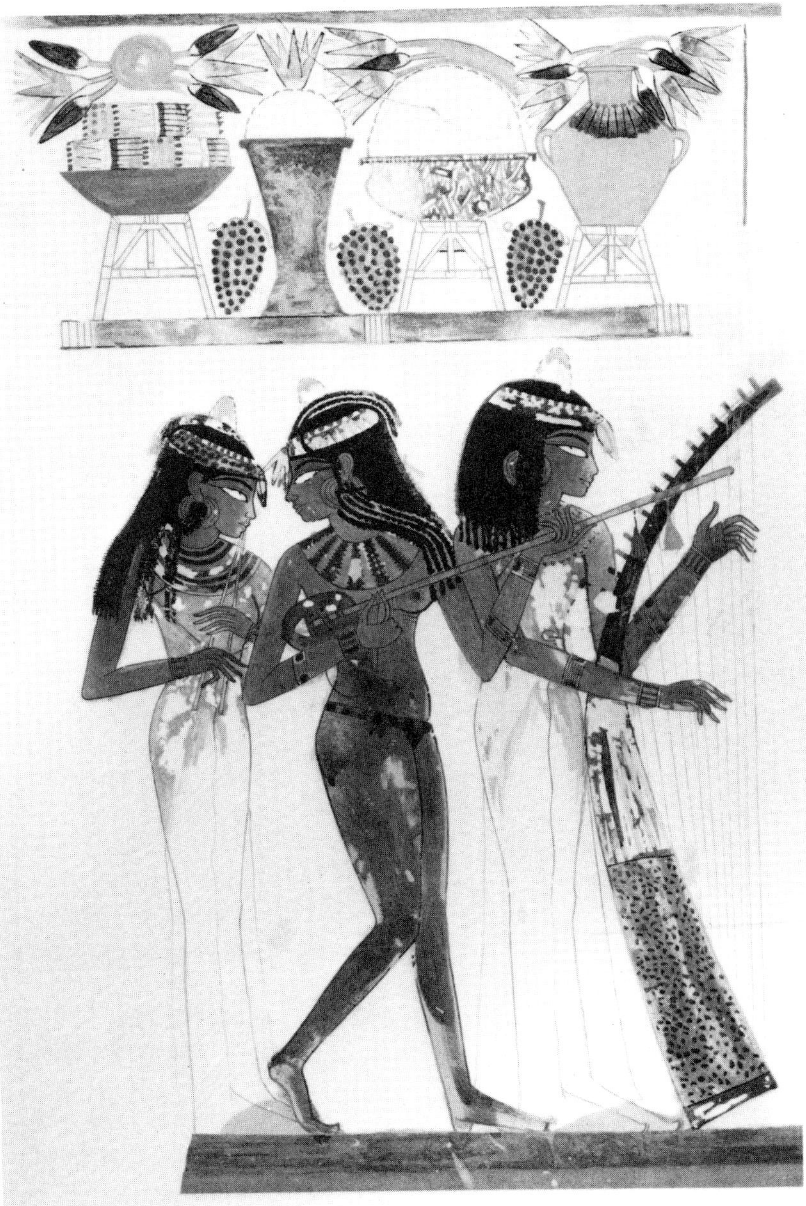

Figure 1. Musicians at Banquet, from the Tomb of Nakht (TT 52); mid-15th century B.C.E. The Metropolitan Museum of Art (15.5.19).

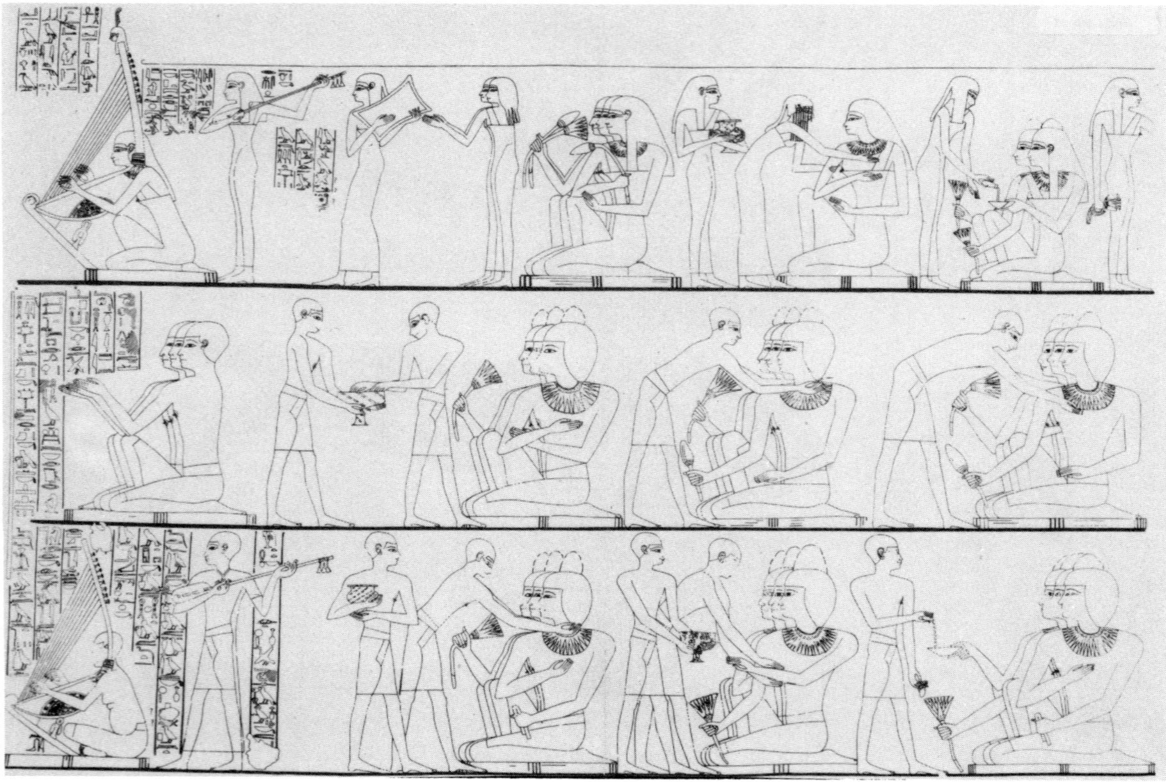

Figure 2. From a Banquet Scene in the Tomb of Rekhmire (TT 100); 15th century B.C.E.

Figure 3. Women at Banquet, Holding Mandragoras, from the Tomb of Nakht (TT 52); mid-15th century B.C.E. Detail from photograph by Egyptian Expedition, The Metropolitan Museum of Art.

Figure 4. Woman at her Toilet, with Maidservant (Tomb of Djeserkarasonb (TT 38); 15th century B.C.E. From *Egypt*, Paintings from Tombs and Temples, UNESCO World Art Series, © UNESCO 1954. Reproduced by permission of UNESCO.

Figure 5. Portrait of Queen Nefertari; mid-13th century B.C.E. From *Nofretari: A Documentation of Her Tomb and Its Decoration.* First published by Akademische Druck- u. Verlagsanstalt, Graz, 1971.

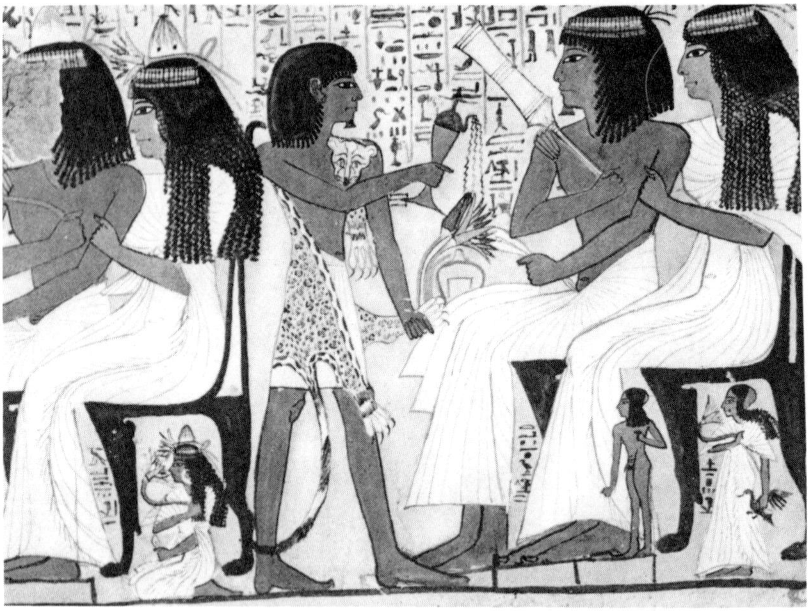

Figure 6. Offering Scene from the Tomb of Sennedjem (TT 1); 13th century B.C.E.

Figure 7. Acrobatic Dancer (Turin ostracon).

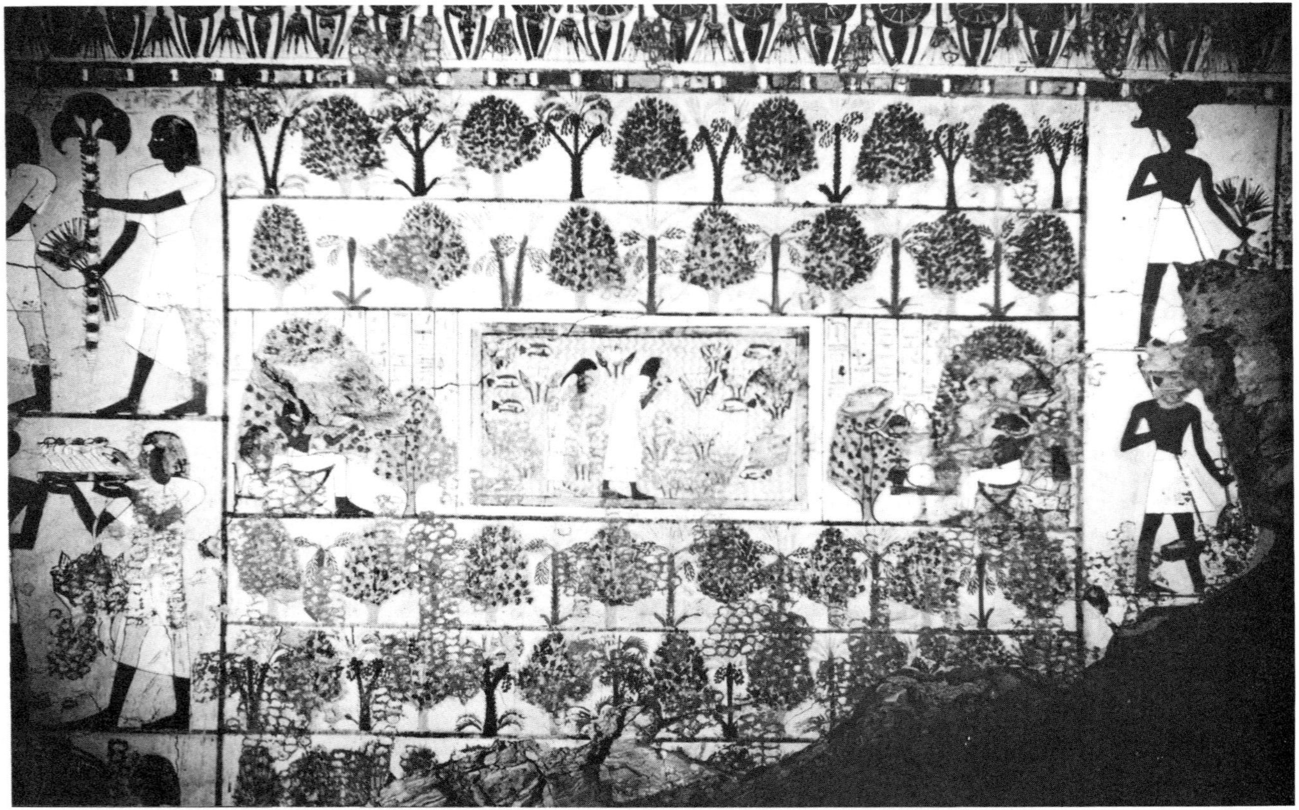

Figure 8. Garden, with Sycamore Goddess, from the Tomb of Sebekhhotep (TT 63); ca. 1419–1386 B.C.E. Courtesy of the Oriental Institute, University of Chicago.

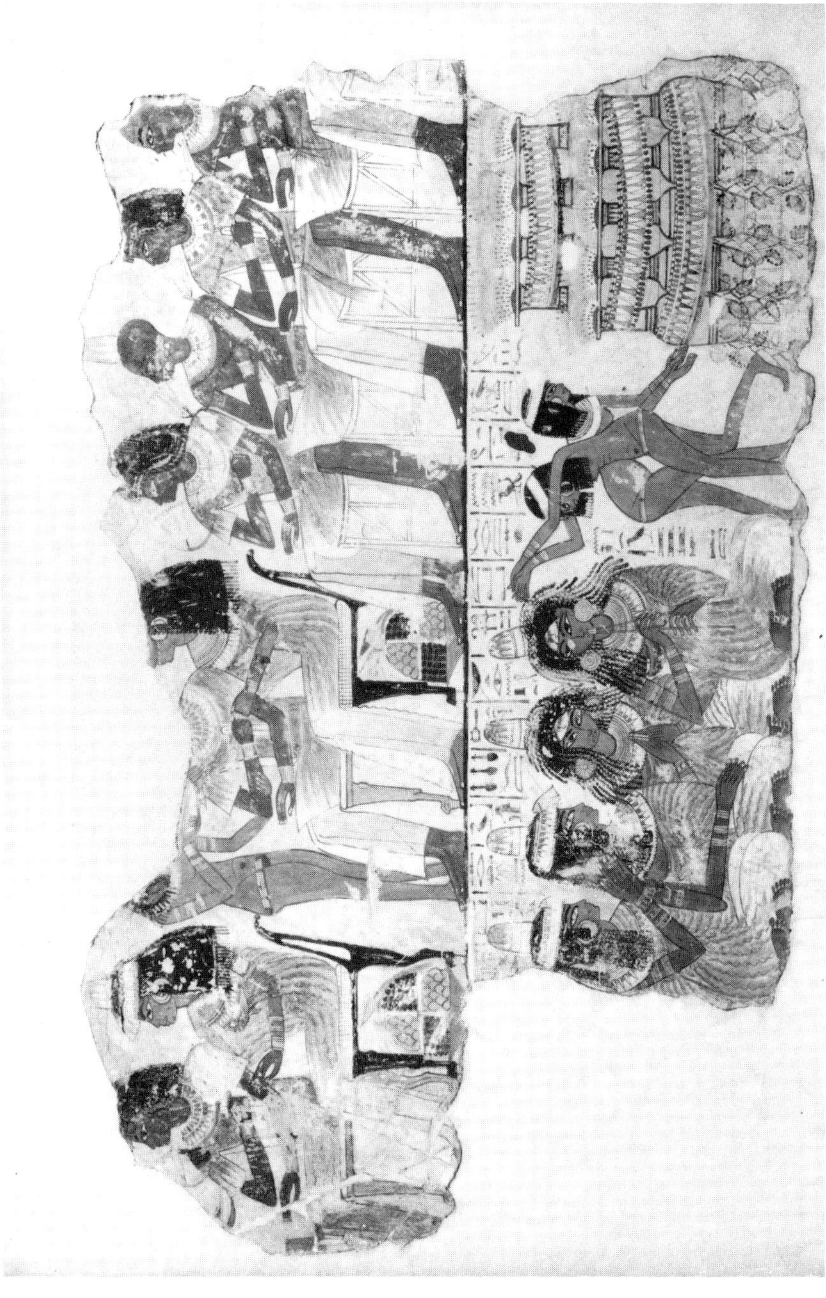

Figure 9. Musicians with Dancers, from an Unknown Tomb. Courtesy of the Trustees of the British Museum.

Figure 10. Musicians at Banquet, Tomb of Rekhmire (TT 100); 15th century B.C.E. Courtesy of the Oriental Institute, University of Chicago.

APPENDIX A

Related Texts

i. Inscription in Praise of Queen Nefertari

(RT 14, 1893: text LI): 19th dynasty

(A) The princess greatly praised,
  mistress of charm,
sweet in love,
  [ruler of] Upper and Lower Egypt,
(B) [skilled] of hands with sistra,
  contenting her father Amon,
greatly loved when (wearing) the headband,
  singer beautiful of face,
lovely in the (royal) plumes,
  greatest of the harem of the palace ladies,
(C) in whose utterance one takes pleasure.
  All that she says is done for her—
every good thing she desires.
  All her words give pleasure to (all) faces.
One lives from hearing her voice. . .

Accompanying a picture of the queen celebrating the Lovely Festival of the Valley. For a portrait of Queen Nefertari (the wife of Ramses II), see fig. 5.

ii. The Antef Song

(P. Harris 500, 6,2–7,3): late 18th dynasty

The song that is from the tomb of King Antef the departed, which is
  in front of the harper:

(A) Flourishing is this noble.
Good is the fate.[a]
Good is the injury.
(B) A generation passes on, another remains,
since the time of the ancestors.
The gods who came into being long ago
rest in their sepulchres.
(C) Revivified nobles as well
are buried in their sepulchres.
(But) those who built tombs—they have no (burial) places.[b]
Look what has become of them!
(D) Now I have heard the words of Imhotep and Djedef-Hor
that are so often quoted as their sayings.[c]
Look at *their* (burial) places!
Their walls have crumbled—
they have no (burial) places,
like those who never were.
(E) No one there is who returns from there
to tell their condition,
to tell their needs,
and thus to heal our hearts,
ere we hasten to the place they have gone.
(F) Be hale,
while your heart (seeks the) self-forgetfulness
that performs the *s3ḫ*-rites upon you.[d]
(G) Follow your heart while you live:
put myrrh on your head,
dress in fine linen,
anoint yourself with true wonders from the god's property.[e]
(H) Increase your pleasures greatly,
let ⟨not⟩ your heart be weary,
follow your heart and your pleasure,
conduct your affairs on earth,
let not your heart be sad.
(I) That day of lamentation shall come upon you—
and the Weary of Heart[f] heeds not their wailing:
their weeping cannot save a man from the Netherworld.
Refrain(?):[g]
(J) Spend a pleasant day!
Weary not of it!
None there is who can send his wealth with him.[h]
None there is who goes who can return again.[i]

a. "Fate" refers to death; see Morenz, 1960: 19f.

b. Apparently the poet is referring to *other* people who built tombs, besides the gods (kings) and "revivified nobles" (*sꜥḥw*).

c. Two wise-men of the Old Kingdom. Djedef-Hor advised: "Make excellent your house of the necropolis; furnish well your place in the West. . . . The house of death is for life." No words of Imhotep remain, but he was a noted tomb architect and known for the wisdom of his writings (see P. Chester Beatty IV, 3,5), so he too may have advised mortuary preparation.

d. These are the rites that make a dead person into an *3ḫ*, an effective, fully functioning being.

e. Excellent oil received as reverted offerings from the temple, considered to be the gift of the god.

f. Osiris, the god of the Netherworld.

g. *M3wt*, apparently a musical direction. Perhaps from *m33*, "be new," and thus: "refrain." This section is lacking in Leyden K.6.

h. Lit., "There is no one who can make a man's property go with him."

i. The above translation uses readings from both P. Harris 500 and Leyden K.6. For philological notes see Fox, 1977.

The "Antef Song" casts doubt on the efficacy of the mortuary cult: tombs—ordinary tombs at least—do not last, and we cannot know the condition of the dead. Therefore, it advises, seek pleasure and self-forgetfulness in this life. Let these perform, as it were, the mortuary rites for you and make you into an Akh, an "effective spirit," on earth. Enjoy the pleasures of this life, for they are all you have. No one—not even the mortuary priests—can enable you to take your goods with you. The poet's pessimism may have been sparked by the depredation of tomb inscriptions and murals by the Atenists.

As Maspero (1883:40) pointed out, the presence of this song in the midst of love songs is in line with Herodotus' report of Egyptian banquets, where a servant would pass around a small mummy and say to the guests, "Observe this, then drink and have a good time, for such you will be after death!" (II, 78).

iii. O. Hermitage 1125

(Matthiew, 1930:25–27; de Walle, 1952:108): 19th or 20th dynasty.

(A) Your[a] love is the love of a bird;
    Your form is the form of a (royal) youth.
Your scent is the scent of the. . . .
    Your skin is like the mandragora.
Your lifetime is the wheat,
    powerful in nourishing life.

(B) The ———[b] of your . . .
[praise(?)] Pre[c] daily.
Your eyes shine. . . .[d]
Your arms are bent in worship.
[Your] mouth [is open] to exalt Re in his rising.
Your fortune . . . in the ———[e] of the god,
with engraving (an inscription) to the Lord of Hermopolis.
The scribe Amon-nakhtu son of Ipui made this.

a. Masc.: a male is being addressed.

b. *Bnk*: Matthiew (1930) mentions the suggestions "fruit" and "gift" (from Semitic BRK).

c. Pre: a New Kingdom name for the sun god Re.

d. *Brḳ*: a semiticism; it appears also in Anastasi IV, 1b,5.

e. *Hty* + wood det. (M 3), an unknown word.

Although this song uses a form resembling the Praise Song (chapter 7), it is probably a hymn praising a royal figure. This person is described as resembling a *sfy*, "youth," here determined by the child crowned with a uraeus (a symbol of royalty and divinity) and the sign for divinity (A 41). "Form" too has the determinative for divinity. The object of praise is not necessarily a young king (as Matthiew, 1930, thinks), for it is not said that the person himself is young, but rather that his form is like a youth's, a compliment more appropriately given an adult. The second part of the poem praises the man's piety, and this compliment too is more to be expected in a royal hymn than in a love song.

iv. O. Gardiner 339 Recto

(HO I, 43,1): Ramesside.

(1) I (masc.) found (my) sister in her . . . (2) little . . . which is under . . . (3) [revel]ers(?),[a] while taking blossoms . . . (4)his (divine) face. Beer is sweet. I (fem.) will . . . (5) in my (fem.) body, like reeds upon[b] the wind . . . (6) many [man]dragoras in my (fem.) hand. He scorns(?)[c] a bowl(?)[d] . . . (7) May you hear the voice of the fishermen and fowlers, in the choicest of. . . . (8) They act weak while awake[e] . . . (9) We empty[f] upon the entry-house of the temple [of the god] . . . (10) all (plants) ———[g] ———. She takes birds in the wood. Noble . . . (11) before him while skipping, skipping, while dancing . . .[h]

a. Nose (D 20) + man, woman, and plural dets. at the start of line 3—a combination that suggests a populace rejoicing.

b. *Ḥr-ʿwy*, lit., "upon the hands": i.e., "under the control of."

c. *Bḥnr* (= *bḥl*), a rare word appearing also in Harris 500, 2,11 (see no. 6, n. d), where it means something like "sport," "mock."

d. The bowl-det. (W 22) is lacking.

e. Meaning that they are staggering drunk?

f. "Empty" has no direct object; perhaps stative: "we have been emptied"? One thinks of the paintings of inebriated guests vomiting at banquets.

g. *Mnrw* (= *mlw*?), or: *m-di* ("with") *nrw* (= *lw*?); meaning unknown.

h. *Wb3*: probably a mistaken hieratic writing of *w3r*; cf. the writing in l. 10.

Though identified by Černý and Gardiner (HO I) as a love song or several love songs, this ostracon scarcely seems to be made up of connected sentences. It may be a writing exercise composed of miscellaneous phrases, many of which resemble usages frequent in the love songs, for which reason I include it here. If the text as a whole has a meaning, I would guess that it has to do with a religious celebration, with the couple enjoying fruits, beer, feasting, and dancing in the vicinity of the temple. Only the first line is definitely spoken by a male. From the fourth line on, a female speaks. *Ḏd* ("say") appears in a broken context at the end of line 2, so perhaps a boy is quoting a girl from that point on.

v. Memorial Inscription for Mutirdis

(Louvre C 100): 22nd dynasty

(A) Sweet, sweet of love,
the priestess of Hathor, Mutirdis.
Sweet, sweet of love,
says King Menkheperre.
Sweet, say men.
Mistress of love, say women.

(B) A princess is she,
sweet of love,
most beautiful of women:
a lass whose like has never been seen.

(C) Blacker her hair than the black of night,
than grapes[a] of the riverbank.
[Whiter] her teeth
than bits of plaster,[b]
than ———[c] in a *ḥn*-plant.
Her breasts are set firm on her bosom.

a. *Irr* = *i3rrt*, see Wb. I, 32,12.

b. *Ḳ3w*(?): "powder," "grains"; exact meaning uncertain. *Ḳḥ*: "plaster(?)", see Wb. V, 67, 1; cf. RAD 64/5, 66/4, 9, and see discussion in Harris, 1961:90, 205f.

c. *Ḫb*: "hacking up"? Obscure.

vi. Inscription from the Tomb of Petosiris, written above the portrait of his wife Renpet-nefret

(Lefebvre, 1923–24: I, 101 and II, 35): Ptolemaic

(A) His wife, his beloved:
    mistress of grace,
sweet in love,
    expert with (her) mouth,
sweet in speech,
    excellent in counsel in her writings.
Whatever passes over her lips
    surpasses the work of truth.

(B) An excellent wife,
    great of praise in her city,
who stretches forth (her) hand to everyone,
    who speaks good things,
        and repeats what is loved.

(C) Who does what everyone loves,
    upon whose lips no bad thing passes,
greatly beloved by all:
    Renpet-nefret.

This Ptolemaic memorial inscription is in effect a love song to a wife, an Egyptian "Woman of Valor." It uses formulations similar to those in the Praise Songs; compare especially no. 31.

APPENDIX B

Concordance of Egyptian Words

Abbreviations
B = P. Chester Beatty I
C = Cairo Love Songs
H = P. Harris 500
T = P. Turin 1966
Other texts are designated by number. Songs designated by lowercase roman numbers are in App. A. This concordance does not contain the most common verbs and particles. The index on pp. 439ff. lists the Egyptian words that are discussed in the book.

3	emphatic particle	C 6
3t	moment	C 25; T 2,7
3b	to brand	B 17,3
3bi	to desire, desire	H 2,5; C 2; 3; B c2,2; 16,12
3bḫ	to mix	H 1,6,7
3bd	month	C 19; T 1,4
3pd	bird	H 4,3,10; 5,2,6; no. iii,1; no. iv,10
3ḫ	good, useful	H 1,5; 7,10f.; B c4,10; no. vi (twice)
3ḫ	spirit	B 17,9
3ḫ3ḫ	verdant	T 2,2
3s	to hurry; fast	H 1,8; 5,10; B c2,9; g1,1,1; g2,1
3tp	to load	H 4,9; T 2,3
i3w	praise	B c3,5; no. iii,6
i3w	old	C 6
i3mt	charm	no. i,2
i3dt	Yadit (goddess) (or Yarit)	H 2,8
iʿi	to wash	C 20
iw	island	no. 52,2
iwt	walking	B c1,5
iw3	ox	B 17,9,10,11
iwn (var. inw)	color, skin	C 19 (*ini inw*); T 2,4?,4; B c1,2; 17,5; no. iii,2f.

Iwn-rʿ	Heliopolis H 3,8
iwnr (iwl)	noose B 17,2,2
iwḥ	drenched C 18
iwty-ib	senseless B c2,2
ibr	an oil from a tree (laudanum?) C 16
ibḥ	tooth T 1,1; no. v,4
Ipwy	PN no. iii,9
ipwt, ipwty	see *wpwt, wpwty*
ifd	to flee B c2,9; c3,4
ifd	linen cloth H 1,4
imy-r	chief T 2,6 (*imy-r šnw*); B 17,13 (*imy-r niwt*)
imy-ḫt	following B c2,9
imw	booth, tent H 3,3; T 2,7
imt	form C 2; no. vi
Imn	Amon H 5,2; B 17,4; no. i,3
Imn-nḫt	PN no. iii,9
ini	to bring C 18f.; T 1,15; 2,5; B g2,3; 16,12; 17,3
inw	color, see *iwn*
inw	for *inty*, q.v.
inm	skin no. iii,[2]f.
inty	to hold back B g1,7
iri n ḥ3t	to overtake B g1,8
irt	eye H 5,9; 7,4,5; B c1,2; c3,1; c5,1; 17,3; no. iii,5
iry	keeper H 2,12f.; C 18; 21; B 17,8
iryw	friends and relations T 1,6; B c4,4
irw	cattle? B 17,2
irp	wine H 2,7; B 16,10; T 1,3
irr	grapes no. v,3
iḥw	horses' stable B g1,2,6
iḫ	what? H 5,6,11
is	tomb H 5,5
Isy	Isy (place) C 22
isw, isy	reeds H 2,6,7; C 9; 23; T 1,9; B 17,11; no. 54,3; no. iv,5
isbr	whip B g1,7
isḳ	to hinder no. 51,2
iḳr	precious; exceedingly B c1,2; c2,7; c4,1; no. vi
it	father B c2,3; no. i,3
it	barley, wheat no. iii,3
Ity	a canal H 3,3,7
it(r)w	river H 2,7; C 11; B c2,6; g2,4; 17,5
iṯ3	to take, steal; see also *ṯ3i, iṯi* no. 51,3; no. 54,6
iṯi	to take H 4,8,9; B c1,4,6; c2,l,6; c4,l
idb	riverbank no. v,3
idn	ear B 17,7?
idn	to represent? govern? no. 49,1
idg	kerchief C 20

y3	Oh!	no. 54,6
yḥ	Ah!	B c3,7
ᶜ	piece, garment	C 19
ᶜ	arm, hand	B g2,4; no. 53,4; no. iii,6
ᶜt	limb	C 11; 17,17
ᶜt	room, hut, etc.	T 1,2 (*ᶜt nt ẖt*), 13 (same); 2,13 (*ᶜt ḥnḳt*)
ᶜt	canal?	H 7,8
ᶜ3	great; greatness	H 5,4; 7,5; C 12; B c1,1; c3,7,8; no. vi
ᶜ3	door	H 2,12 (*ᶜ3wy*); B c3,10; 17,8
ᶜwn	rod	H 2,4
ᶜb	offerings, feast	C [26]
ᶜpr	to provide, equip	B 16,10; T 2,9
ᶜm3	to know, perceive	B c4,5; no. 54,5
ᶜn	again	T 1,6
ᶜn	lovely	B c1,2; T 2,2; no. i,4
ᶜnḫ	to live; life	H 5,5; 7,10; 8,3; no. i,6
ᶜnḫ wḏ3 snb	may he live, prosper, and be healthy!	H 3,1; no. 53,7
ᶜnḫ t3wy	Ankh-Towy (place)	H 2,7
ᶜnty	claw	H 4,5
ᶜntyw	myrrh	H 4,4,6
ᶜrr	stones	no. 49,3
ᶜḥ	palace	no. i,4
ᶜḥ3w	lifetime	C 22; B 17,1; no. iii,3
ᶜḥ3wty	hero, man, warrior	H 1,9?; C [10]
ᶜḥᶜ	to stand, stop, remain	H 3,7; 5,1; C 12; 13; T 1,5; B c3,2,10; 17,6
ᶜš3	many	H 4,10
ᶜḳ	to enter	H 2,10; 3,1,6; 5,11; C [4]; B c4,3,9; c5,1; g2,2
ᶜḳ3	precise; right before	C 13
ᶜḳᶜḳ	to enter	B c4,7
ᶜd	part of door	B 17,10
ᶜḏ	fat	C 3
ᶜḏ3	to deceive; deceit	H 2,10; 5,11; T 1,7
ᶜḏᶜḏ	to rejoice	C 14; T 2,[8]
ᶜḏd	lad, youth	T 2,7
w3i	to be far	H 1,9; 4,11; 5,7; C 25; B g2,1; no. 53,[3]
w3t	way, road	H 5,6,9; B c2,5,7; c4,1,8; g1,4; g2,4?
w3ḥ	to place, offer	H 2,9; 5,3; C 10; T 1,13; B 17,5; no. 52,4
w3ḥ	to endure (used in oath)	T 1,15; B 17,4
w3ḏw3ḏ	a green plant; to become green	C 22; 24; 24
wᶜ	one, unique (excluding indef. article)	C 19; B c1,1,8; c2,4
wᶜi	to be alone; alone	H 4,5,11; 5,2,10; C 3; B c4,2; 16,11
wᶜwy	worm	H 2,1; 4,4,7
wᶜb	to bathe	C 9
wb3	?	no. iv,11
wbḫ	to shine, make shine	H 7,4; B c1,2,3

wpwt	message	B g1,2
wpwty (ipwty)	messenger	H 5,10; B c4,9f.; g1,1; no. 51,6
wpt-r	opening, mouth (of canal)	H 3,3
wn	to open	H 2,12; C 16; B c3,10; c5,1; 17,8,8,12
wnt-ḥr	mirror	C 22
wnwt	hour, time	H 7,5,6; C 1
wnf	joy; joyful	H 7,6; C 14
wnm	to eat; food	H 1,3; 7,11; B g1,6; no. 49,4
wnm	right side	T 2,12
wnm	fatling, short-horned cattle	B 17,10
wnrḫ	hall?	B 16,11
wnḫ	clothes; to clothe	H 6,1; B c3,1
wnš	wolf, jackal	H 2,2; no. 49,1
wnḏww	kinds	T 1,9; 2,10
wr	to be great	B c3,7; c4,8 (*wr swnw*),10; no. vi; no. i,2,3,4
wrryt	chariot	B g1,3
wrḥ	to anoint	H 4,4,6; B c3,1
wrš	to spend time	H 2,3; B 17,5; no. 51,1; no. 52,5
wḥꜥ	to return home	B 17,7
wḥꜥ	to loosen	H [6,1]
wḥꜥ	fishermen and fowlers	no. iv,7
wḥm	to repeat	T 1,6; no. vi
wḫꜣ	folly	B c3,2
wḫꜣ	to seek	H 1,2; 5,6,12; 7,4; C 27
wḫꜣ	to be dark, befogged	B 17,8
wsr	powerful	C 11; no. 53,5
wsḫ	to be wide	B 17,6
wsḫt	hall	B 16,11
wstnw	message	T 2,5
wsṯn	to stride freely	B c2,6,7; g1,6
wšbt	answer	C 26
wgꜣ	?	H 1,12?
wdn	heavy	B c4,7
wḏ	fish	C 10 (*wḏ dšr*); 14
wḏ	to command, ordain	B c2,3; c3,6; g2,5
wḏꜣ	amulet; well-being	B c5,1
wḏi	to send, move	T 1,11; 2,1,9; B 17,1
wḏꜥ	to judge, diagnose	B c4,8
bꜣw	strength	B 17,9
bꜣḳ	moringa oil, tree	C 20; T 1,3; no. 49,3
bꜣk	servant	T 1,12
biꜣt	character	B c4,1
bit	honey	C 3
bit	bee	T 2,2
bꜥy	palm-staves	H 2,4
bꜥḥ	to overflow	H 1,5; B 17,1

bw nb	everyone	no. 54,5; no. vi (twice)
bbt	a plant	C 23
bnty	nipples	no. v,4
bnr	sweet	H 5,1; B c1,3; no. v,1 (four times), 2,2; no. vi
bnr	dates	H 5,[1]; C 5; no. i,2
bnr (bl)	outside	H 5,9; B c5,1
bnš	part of door	B 17,10
bnk	?	no. iii,4
brḳ	to shine	no. iii,5
bht (bhꜣ)	fan	H 3,11
bhn	overgarment	B c3,1
bḥnr (bḥl)	sport, object of mockery	H 2,11; no. iv,6
bḫn	residence	H 2,11
bsbs	a plant	C 23; T 2,5
bss	to flow	H 7,6
bkrṯ	bird?	H 2,1
bdš	loose	B c1,5
pt	sky	H 1,9; B 16,12
pꜣ	past-tense aux. vb.	no. v,3
pꜣ (pwy)	to fly, soar	H 4,9
Pꜣ-Rʿ	Pre	H 3,2,5; no. iii,5
pꜣt	meadow	C 24
pꜣḳt	fine linen	C 17; B 17,13
pwy	see *pꜣ*, fly	
Pwnt	Punt (land)	H 4,3,5; C 15
pfs	to cook; to ripen	C 23
pnʿ	to turn over	no. 50,1
pnʿyt	threshold	B 17,10
pnw	mouse	C 12
pr	house	H 2,12; 3,6,9,10; 5,3; B c1,9; c2,5; c3,10; g1,4; 16,9,10; 17,6,7,12; T 1,9; no. iv,9
pri	to go out, etc.	H 2,12; 4,11; 5,10; C 10; 15; 23; B c1,7; c3,9; c4,5,9; c5,2; T 1,10; no. iii,7
pr-r	utterance	no. i,4
prḫ	blossom	C 8; 23; [23]; T 1,5,8
pḥ	to reach	C 8; B c3,2
pḥwy	buttocks	B c1,5
pḫꜣ	trap	H 1,12; 2,1; 4,3,6,9
pẖr	go about, encompass	H 5,3; C 26
pẖrw	turnings	B c2,8
pẖrt	medicine	B c4,8,10
pš	to open	C 14; 15
pgꜣ	battlefield	H 1,8
ptr	to see (not including "behold!")	H 2,10; 3,5f.,12; 5,1; 7,10,10; C [10]; 11; T 1,6,7,10; B c1,7; g2,3,3
Ptḥ	Ptah	H 2,[6],7

f3i	to take, set out H 3,4
f3it	gift B 17,1
fnd	nose H 5,2; C 4
fd	cast-off, rag C [20]
fdwt	four B c2,9; g2,4
m-di	with, etc. H 5,7; C 24 (= *mḏr* B 17,3)
m33	to see H 1,8; 4,2; 7,5; C 13; 21; 21; 24; 25; T 2,8,14; B c1,6; c2,1,3,4; c3,7; c4,6; no. v,3
m3ʿ, m3ʿt	true; truth H 2,7; T 1,10; B c1,4; no. vi
m3ʿ	temple H 5,12
m3ḥ	wreath H 7,11; C 22; 24
m3st	sandbank C 12
mi	come! H 8,8; C 10; T 2,6,11
misy	a plant C 15
mitt	the like B c4,1; 16,11; no. v,3
mw	water H 1,7; C 10; 12; T 1,14; no. 51,5
mwt	mother H 4,8; B c1,9,9; c2,3,4; c3,10; c4,3
Mwtirdis	PN no. v,1
mfkt	malachite T 2,3
mn	to remain T 1,2
mny	necklace B 17,3
(m) mnt	daily C 22; 24; 25; no. iii,5
mnt	dove H 5,6
mnty	thighs H 1,[2]; B c1,5; 17,3
Mn-nfr	Memphis H 2,9
mnfi	thus B c2,1
mnrw? nrw?	? no. iv,10
mnḫ	appropriate, powerful, etc. C 10
mnḫt	garments C 4
Mnḫprrʿ	PN (king) no. v,1
mnḳ	to bring to an end, to complete B 16,11; 17,1
Mnḳt	Menqet (goddess) C 16
mnḏ (mndt)	breast H 1,5,11; T 1,1
mr	to bind, weave into; narrow? B c1,5; C 23
mr	riverbank C 12
mr	desert B g2,1
mr	canal H 3,3,7
mr	be ill; illness H 2,10,11
mri	to love H 4,7; B c3,4; no. vi (twice—pass. pple.)
mry/mryt	beloved H 4,1,2; C 13; T 1,7,13,15; 2,6; no. vi (twice)
mrt(i)	lovemaking H 2,2
mryw	lovers (phallus-det.) B c1,7; c2,5f.; c3,8
mrwt	love (noun) H 1,6,9; 2,1; 4,2,7,9,11; 5,1,4,10,12; 7,5; 8,6?; C 1; 3; 11; 13; 21; B c2,1,10; c3,8; c4,1,10; g2,5; no. 51,3; no. 52,5; no. 54,1,5; no. iii,1,1,2,2; no. v,1,1,2,2; no. vi; no. 1,2,3
mryt	type of wood H 1,12f.

mrw	bundle	H 2,6
mrbb	a plant	C 23
mrsw	a wine	no. 53,5
mhȝ	?	H 5,9f.
mḥ	(in ordinal numbers)	B c1,8; c2,4,9; c3,4,10
mḥ	to fill	H 3,13; 4,5; T 1,14
mḥ	to catch, trap	H 4,7
Mḥy	Mehi (PN)	B c2,5,7; in cartouche: no. 52,4; no. 53,7
mḥyt	north wind	H 7,8f.; C 7
Mḥw	Lower Egypt	no. i,[2]
mḫȝ	to balance, resemble	H 4,11; 7,3; C 3
mḫmḫ	type of flower (purslane?)	H 7,3
mẖnmt	current?	H 2,5
ms	child	B 17,2?,11,13?
ms	to bring	B 16,9,11; 17,2?
msbb	to disturb?	H 4,10?
msḥn (=*msnḥ*?)	to turn	B c1,6
mss	waterfowl	H 8,10
mss	tunic	C 9; B c3,1; 17,4
msdt	upper legs	H 1,2
msḏr	ear	H 5,9
mšȝ	pond	C 14
mkt	(proper) place (of heart)	C 14; B c2,10; c3,1
mkḥȝ	back of head	H 6,1
mtnw	?	H 1,12
mdw, mdt	to speak; word	H 5,6; B c1,3; c5,2; T 2,1,15; no. vi
nt	water, water surface; (see also *nwyt*)	C 13
niwt	city	B 17,13; no. vi
nʿ	to be lenient	H 2,2
nw	hunter	B g2,2
nw	to look	C 22; no. 54,6
nw	moment, time	H 6,2; C 22; B c4,3; 17,12
nw (nwn)	flood waters	C 11
nwyt	flood	C 12
nb, nb(t)	master, mistress	H 2,7 (*nb mȝʿt*); 4,1 (*nb(t) tȝwy*); 5,3 (*nb(t) pr*); C 6; B c3,5 (*nbt pt*); g1,1,6; 16,10 (*nbt pr*); no. i,2,4,4; no. iii,8; no. v,2; no. vi
nb	the Golden One (Hathor)	B c2,3; c3,5; c4,3; g2,5; 17,1; no. 52,3
nbw	gold	B c1,4; no. 52,3
nbd	locks, braids; to plait	H 5,12; 6,2; C [9]
npy (= npry)	seed, berry	T 1,1
nfy	that	no. 50,4
nfy	to blow	B 16,
nfr, nfrw	beautiful; beauty	H 2,9; 4,1,6,6,11; 5,3,8,8; 7,5,9; 8,8; C 9; 22; 26; T 1,9; 2,2,11; B c1,1,2,5,9; c2,3,4,5; c4,6; 17,7,8,13; no. 52,3; no. i,4; no. v,2; no. vi.
nfr-ḥr	beautiful of face, gracious	H 2,9 (Ptah); B c1,1

nfry	a garment	C 20
Nfrtm	Nefertem (god)	H 2,8
nmʿ	to clothe a bed, sleep, lie down	C 17; B 17,12; no. 51,4
nny	weary; weariness	H 8,9
nny	part of tree	T 2,5
nhꜣ	sycamore	T 1,11 (*nhꜣ db*),15 (*nhꜣ šry*); no. 48
nhw (nhꜣ)	lack	C 16
nhm	to shout, rejoice	H 8,2; B c2,4,4; c4,2
nḥt	prayer, wish	H 5,4; 7,4
nḥb	to yoke, harness	B g1,2,3
nḥbt	neck	B c1,3,6
nḥm (= nḥb)	lotus-bud	H 1,11; 2,8; T 1,8
(n)ḥḥ	eternity	H 5,3; 7,6; C 15
Nḥsy	Nubian	C 18
nḫb	lowlands, fresh land	H 2,4
Nḫt-sbk	Nakhtsobek (PN)	B 16,9
nẖʿ	?	C 17
nsw	king	B g1,1,5; no. v,1 (*nsw bit*), 2
nš	hairdo	H 6,1
nšmt	green feldspar	T 2,4
nḳw (= nḳʿw)	ripe, notched figs of sycamore	T 2,3
nṯr, nṯrt	god, goddess	C 4; 7; 25; B c3,9; c4,5; no. 49,4; no. iii,8
nḏm	sweet, pleasant; pleasure	H 5,2,7; 7,8,8; C 8; B 16,9; no. 50,4; no. 53,3; no. iv,4; no. vi
r	door, opening, mouth (of canal), mouth, sayings	H 2,12; 3,3,7; 5,2; T 1,11; 2,1,1; B c1,1; 17,6; no. 51,8; no. iii,6; no. vi
rʿ	day	C 6
Rʿ	Re	no. iii,7
rwiꜣ (rit)	side	C 11
rwr, rwrwt	cave, den	B g2,4; 16,9; no. 49,2
rwḏ	to flourish, be strong	C 2; 13; 19; 24; B c5,2
rpt	plants	T 2,10
rpʿt	noblewoman	no. i,2
rmi	weep	B c4,4
rmn	shoulder	H 2,6
rmṯ	person, people	H 7,5 (*rmṯ ʿꜣ*); B c2,4,10; c3,3; c4,4
rn	name	B c2,8; c3,9; c4,9
rnpi	to become young, vigorous	C 20; B c5,1
rnpt	year	B c1,2
rnpyt	plants; see *rpt*	
rnnt	fortune	no. iii,7
rrmt	a plant	H 1,7,11; 2,9; C 5; 18; 19; 23; no. iii,3; no. iv,[6]
rhn	to wade	C 12
rḫ	to know	H 2,11; 4,8; B c1,9; c2,2,6,7; c4,3,5; g1,6,7,8; 17,2
rḫty	laundryman	C 19
rs	to wake	C 1; no. iv,8

rš, ršwt	joyous; joy	H 5,[5]; 7,9; C 20; 22; B c1,6f.; c2,3; c4,4
ršrš	to rejoice	T 2,8
rdwy	feet	H 5,10; 7,12; C 13; 18; B c2,7; g1,6; g2,2; 17,5
h3i	to go down	C 8; 10; 12; 27; B c3,4; 16,12
h3y	Oh!	B c2,3; c4,3
h3w	vicinity	B c3,10
h3b	to send	H 5,10; B c2,2
h3n	if only!	B c4,3
hn	laden	H 3,13
hnt	?	H 1,12
hrw	day	H 4,9; 8,11; C 1; 6; 21; T 1,9,10,14; 2,7,11,11,12; B c3,9,9; c5,2
hrw	to ease, to please (and intrans.)	B c4,8; no. i,4,5
hty	?	no. iii,8
ḥ3	behind, outside	B c1,7; no. 49,1
ḥ3t	channel of water	H 7,[8]
ḥ3t, ḥ3ty	foremost, first	T 1,5; B c1,2
ḥ3t-ʿ	beginning	H 4,1; 7,3; B c1,1; 16,9
ḥ3w	excess	H 5,7; B c1,3
ḥ3p-ẖt	discreet	T 2,14
ḥ3ḳ	booty	T 1,13
ḥʿwt	body, limbs	C 2; 4,4; 17; 19; 20; 20; 27; 27; B c4,7; c5,1; g2,2,2; no. 50,2,5; no. 54,2; no. iv,5
ḥʿ, ḥʿʿ	to rejoice	B c3,7
ḥʿb	dance	B 16,10
ḥwt	house, stanza	B c1,8; c2,4,9; c3,4,10; 17,13
Ḥwt-ḥr	Hathor	B c3,5; no. v,1
ḥwnt	girl	no. v,2
ḥb	festival	C 25; B c4,5
ḥb	hut	T 2,7
ḥbs	clothing	H 1,4
ḥp	to hurry	T 2,9
ḥpt	to embrace	H 1,1; 1,5; C 15; B c1,6,7; c2,2; c5,2
ḥfnw	100,000	H 1,6
ḥm	majesty	B c3,5
ḥm	servant	T 1,12; 2,8; no. v,1 (*ḥmt nṯr*)
ḥmt	woman	no. v,2,2; no. vi
ḥm3	salt	H 5,1
ḥmww	carpenter	B 17,11
ḥms	to sit	T 2,12; B c2,5; c3,3
ḥn	to hurry, run	C [26]; B c4,4; T 2,6
ḥn	a plant	no. v,4
ḥnt	marsh	H 1,10
ḥnw	to command	B c1,9
ḥnw	bundle?	C 23
ḥnw	?	H 4,[10]

ḥnwt	lady	C 15; 25; T 1,12; B c3,6,6; no. 51,2; 52,1
ḥnwt	service	C 22
ḥnr (ḥl)	if only!	H 2,12; C 18; 19; 21; 21; 22; 24; B g1,1,5; g2,1
ḥnḳt	beer	C 5; 16; T 2,10,13 (*ʿt ḥnḳt*); B 17,5
ḥnkt	bedroom	H 5,7; 7,12; C 16f.; B 17,5
ḥnty	crocodile	C 12
ḥr	to prepare	H 3,2
ḥr	face	H 3,12; 5,8,11; C 13; no. 50,3; no. iv,4 (divine); no. i,4,5
ḥry-ib	middle	H 2,12; B c1,5
ḥr-ʿwy	on the hands of	no. iv,5
ḥryt	fear	H 2,13; B g2,2
ḥrr	blossoms	H 7,7f.; C [23]; 24; no. 54,2; no. iv,3
ḥḥ	eternity	H 5,3; 7,6
ḥs	to sing; song	H 4,1; 7,3; B 16,10; no. i,3
ḥst	praise	no. i,2; no. vi
ḥsy	water-spell	C 13
ḥsꜣ	dough	H 1,7
ḥḳꜣ	ruler	H [3,1?] (a canal); T 2,8
ḥḳr	to be hungry	H 1,4
ḥknw	praise	B c3,5f.
ḥgꜣ	snare	B 16,12
ḥty	bed	B 17,12
ḥty	?	H 1,10
ḥtp, ḥtpt	to rest; resting place	C 6; B g1,3; g2,3
ḥtpw	offerings	no. 49,4
ḥtr	horse	B c2,5
ḥḏ	to hurt	H 5,8,11
ḥḏt	white garment	C 17
ḥḏ-tꜣ	dawn	H 2,9; 5,6; C 1; B 16,11
ḥḏꜣy	to sail?	no. 52,2
ḥḏn	to vex	B c2,1
ḥḏnḏn	anger	H 2,13
ḫt	things, content	H 1,6; 5,3; no. i,5
ḫꜣ	thousand	B g1,5
ḫꜣ n tꜣ	type of land	H 7,7
ḫꜣw	plants	H 7,8
ḫꜣin	see *ḫn*	
ḫꜣyt	illness	B c1,8; c4,7,8
ḫꜣʿ	to abandon, stop, throw	H 2,3,5; B c2,1; 17,2,2; T 1,5; no. 51,2; no. 52,3
ḫꜣwt	altar	B 17,5
ḫꜣb	to bend	no. iii,6
ḫꜣp	to bound	B g2,1
Ḫꜣrw	placename, in Syro-Palestine	H 2,3
ḫy	how!	C 16
ḫyḫy	to blow, flutter	B 16,12

ḫʿi	to rise	B c1,2
ḫʿw	utensils	T 2,9
ḫʿb	dance	B 16,10
ḫʿm	to approach	C 27
ḫw	to set aside	B 16,10
ḫb	?	no. v,4
ḫbyt	rod	H 2,4
ḫpp	to make strange?	H 5,12
ḫm	to be ignorant; not to know	B c2,7
ḫm	to plan	B c2,4
ḫmw	dust	B g2,3
ḫmt	three	B c2,4; c3,9
Ḫmnw	Hermopolis	no. iii,8
ḫn (ḫꜣiniw)	folly, madness	B c3,3
ḫnw	utterance	B c1,3
ḫnw	to alight	H 4,4,10
ḫnm	scent, fragrance	H 5,2; B 16,12; no. iii,2,2
ḫnm	to give pleasure	C 18
ḫnms	friend	T 1,7; 2,12; B g2,5
ḫnmt	red jasper	T 2,3
ḫnr	harem	no. i,4
ḫnr	hoarse	no. 53,6
ḫnty	crocodile	C 12
ḫntš	to be joyful	C 16; 18; B c3,7; c4,2
ḫnd	to stride	B c1,5; c4,1
ḫr	(particle)	C 15; B c2,3; 16,11,11
ḫr	say	B c3,2; no. v,1,2,2
ḫr	necropolis	B 16,9
ḫrt	concern, desire	H 5,10; B g1,2
ḫrʿ	gate?	B 16,10
ḫrw	voice, sound	H 2,13; 4,5,7; 5,6; 7,10; C 2; B c1,8; g1,7; no. 53, 6; no. i,6 no. iv,7
ḫrp	to lead no. 51,4	
ḫḫ	to storm?	B 16,12
ḫsbd	lapis lazuli	B c1,4
ḫsbd	"lapis-lazuli" plant	C 23
ḫt	wood, tree	T 1,2 (*ʿt nt ḫt*),13; 2,4; no. iv,10
ḫti	inscribe	no. iii,8
Ḫtꜣ	Hatti	C 23
ḫtm	seal ring	C [4]; 21; B 17,3; no. 54,3
ḫtḫt	to turn back	H 3,8
ḫd	to sail downstream	H 2,5,13; no. 52,[1]
ẖt	belly, body	H 1,3,6; 5,4; 7,9; C 26; T 1,14; 2,14
ẖbyt	rod	H 2,4
ẖn	to approach	H 7,5
ẖnini	channel?	B 17,5

ḫry-ḥb	lector priest	B c4,8
ḫrdw	child	H 2,13; 7,12
s	man	H 1,3; C 5
st	woman	B c3,3; no. vi
st	place	H 5,8; 7,9; C 27; T 1,9; B c2,7; g1,3
sꜣt	daughter	T 2,6; no. v,2
sꜣi	to be satisfied	H 7,9
sꜣw	to look after, keep	C 17; T 1,9; no. 50,2
sꜣḥw	neighbors	H 2,10; B c1,8f.
siswt	six	B c3,10
sʿꜣ	to make great	H 7,7
sʿꜣm	a tree	H 7,7
sʿb	to adorn	C 16
sʿnḫ	to revive, nourish	H 5,2; C 1; B c4,9,10; no. iii,4
swꜣ	to pass by	B c3,10; c4,6
swꜣš (sšwꜣ)	to praise, honor	C 26; B c3,5; no. iii,7
swnw	physician	H 2,11; B c4,8
swnwn	to flatter, entice	T 1,10; no. 51,1
swri	to drink	H 7,11; T 1,13,15; 2,9
swhy	to boast	B c2,8
swtwt	to walk about	H 5,7; 7,9; T 2,14
sb	to go	T 1,4
sbꜣ	door	H 5,8f.
sbꜣ	star	C 22
sbꜣyt	lesson, punishment	T 1,7
sbḥ	to cry out	H 4,7
sbḳ	fortunate	C 22
sp	deed	H 1,1
sp, n-sp	time; together, etc.	H 4,5; 7,10; 8,7; B g2,4
spi	to remain	T 2,13
spt	lip	C 16; B c1,3; no. vi (twice)
spr	to arrive	H 1,1; B g1,4; g2,4
spr	to supplicate, supplication	B c3,6,9
Spdt	Sothis	B c1,1
sf	yesterday	B c3,9; c4,6; T 2,11
sfy	youth	B c4,1; no. 53,8?; no. iii,2 (with uraeus)
sfḫ	seven	B c4,6,6; c5,2
sfḫ	to release	H 4,5,8
sfṯ (sft)	to slaughter	B 17,9,10
smꜣʿ	to pray, offer	C 26; B c3,8
smi	to call	B c3,6
smy	plants	H 1,10?
smn	to be firm	B c3,4
smḫ	to forget, ignore	B c4,7
sn, sn-nw	two; second	B c1,1,8; T 1,6; 2,12
sn	brother	H 3,6; 4,2; 5,7,9,10; C 10; T 1,2; 2,13; B c1,8; c2,3,4; c3,3,10; c4,1,2,4,6; 17,5,12

snt	sister	H 1,8,11; 2,7,11,12; 4,1; 7,7; C 11; 14; 19; 22; 27; T 1,2; 2,14; B c1,1; c3,9; c4,6,⟨10⟩; g1,1,4,8; g2,1,1,5; 16,9,11; 17,2,6; no. 54,1
sni	to surpass	no. vi
snw	siblings	B c3,10
snw	trees	T 2,6
snb	health; to be healthy	H 5,5,5; 8,3; B c5,1
snf	next year	T 1,5
snn	to pass by	B c2,6,8; c4,2; 17,7
snn	to kiss	C 16; B c4,4; g2,4; no. 54,4
snsn	to be together	C 6
snṯr	incense	C 4
srw	type of goose	B 17,10
srpt	leaves of the lotus blossom	H 2,7f.
srf	rest	B g1,4
srsr?	switches	H 2,5
srd	to plant	H 7,7
sḥ	counsel	no. vi
sḥwr	marshes	H 2,3
sḥn	to command; commander (captain)	H 2,6
sḥr	to expel	C 28; B c5,2
sḥtp	to please	no. i,3
sḫt	field	H 4,7
sḫ3	to think of, remember	H 1,3; 3,4f.; 5,12; B c2,1,10; c3,2,4
sḫ3s	see *sḫs*	
sḫwy	gall, bile	H 5,2
sḫmḫ-ib	entertainment	H 4,1; 7,3; B c1,1 (fem. = entertainer)
Sḫmt	Sekhmet	H 2,7
sḫr	advice	H 2,5
sḫs	to hurry	H 1,8?; 5,12
sḫsḫ	to hurry	H 3,4
sḫtḫt	to hold back, restrain	H 4,8
sẖ3	oar-strokes?	H 2,6
sẖkr	adornment	C 17
ssm	horse	H 1,8; B g1,3,5; no. 51,3
sš	to spread out	T 2,14
sš	scribe, book	B 16,9; no. iii,9
sš	to pass by	no. vi (twice)
sšw	to empty	no. iv,9
sšw3	see *sw3š*	
sšm	to lead	C 16
sšn	lotus	C 7; B c1,4; T 1,8; no. 54,4
sššn?	lotus-blossoms	H 2,8
sšd	headband	no. i,3
sḳ3	to exalt, raise	B c3,5; 16,10
sḳ3ḳ3?	?	H 4,3
sḳbb	cool	T 2,5; no. 52,[2]

sk	to wipe	C 20
sgb	cry	H 4,5f.
sgnn	unguent	T 1,8
stꜣḥ	to confuse	B c1,8
sty	scent	H 4,4f.; 7,8; C 15; B 16,12
stp	to choose, choice	B c4,1; g1,5; 17,11; no. iv,7
stf n bit	bees' honey (honeycomb?)	T 2,2
stnw = *sṯnw*?	choicest?	B 17,5
sṯf (= *sft*)	to slaughter	B 16,10
sṯnw	to distinguish	B 17,5?
sdsd?	see *srsr*	
sḏꜣ-ḥr	amusement	H 1,2; T 1,14; 2,11
sḏm	hear	H 2,5,13; 4,5; 5,9; 7,10,10; B c3,6; g1,2,7; no. i,6; no. iv,7
sḏm	servant	T 2,9
sḏm	eye-paint; to paint (eyes)	H 7,4; B c3,1
sḏr	to lie down, sleep	H 2,9; 7,6; 7,12; C 1
šꜣ	plants, foliage	T 1,11
šꜣ	meadow	H 4,2; 8,7; T 1,4; 2,7
šꜣy	fate	B 17,9
šꜣm (šm)	to reel	B g2,2
šꜥyt	cake	H 5,1
šw	dry	C 23
šw	shade	T 2,5,12
šwty	plumes	no. i,4
šwb	persea	H 3,13
šb	to mix	H 1,7
šbyw	an aromatic plant	no. 54,2
šbb	variety	T 2,10
šbd	staff	H 2,3; T 1,8
špsy	noble	H [4,1]; T 1,12; no. iv,10
šm	to go	H 1,3,4,7,9; 4,8; B c4,9 *(šm-ii)*
Šmꜥ	Upper Egypt	no. i,2
šms	to follow	T 2,13
šnw	hair	H 2,[1]; 3,13; B c1,4; 17,2; no. v,3
šnw	trap, net	H 4,8
šnw	garden	H 4,10
šnw	trees	H 3,9,10
šry	little	C [4]; 21; T 1,15; no. 54,3; no. iv,2
šrit	maid	B 17,13,13
šrgḥ	?	B 16,11
šs	linen	C 19
šs nsw	royal linen	C 9; 17
šsp	bright	B c1,2
šsp	to take	H 1,5; 3,10f.
št = *šd*	to remove	H 2,3
šd	waterskin	T 1,14

šd	to dig	H 7,8
šdḥ	pomegranate(?) wine	H 5,1; 7,10; T 1,3
šdšd	?	H 5,9
ḳ3i	to be high	B c1,3; 17,6
ḳ3w	grains; chips?	H 4,3?; no. v,5
ḳ3yt	high ground, arable land	H 2,4
ḳ3bt, ḳbyt	breast, nipple	H 5,3?; B c1,4; no. v,4
ḳ3rt	bolt, latch	B 17,8,10,11
ḳi	form; entire	C 24; B 16,10; T 1,1; no. iii,1,2
ḳʿḥ	shoulders, back	B 17,4
ḳb, ḳbb	cool	H 7,8; B c3,3; no. 54,6
ḳbyt	breast (see *ḳ3bt*)	
ḳf3w	bolt (read *kr3t*?)	H 2,12
ḳm3	to create	H 4,2
ḳmi	gum-resin	H 1,7; 3,13f.; 4,5; T 1,3
ḳmḥ (ḳm3ḥ)	leaves? branches?	T 2,2
ḳn	to complete	H 6,2
ḳni	powerful	no. iii,4
ḳni	to embrace, bosom	H 3,12; 7,4; 8,11; C 14; B 16,11; 17,4
ḳnw	many	B c3,3; T 2,11; no. iv,6
ḳnb	to subjugate, fetter	B 17,3
ḳnḳn	to eat?	no. 49,2
ḳnḳn	blows	H 2,3
ḳnd	to be angry	H 2,12,13
ḳri	see *ḳ3rt*	
ḳḥ	chips of stone?	no. v,4
ḳsn	bone	no. 54,3
ḳdi	circle	H 4,10
k3	so, then	H 2,10 (three times); C 13; B c4,4; c5,1,2
k3	to say	H 4,8; B c2,8
k3	soul	C 26; T 1,15; no. 53,5
k3 ḏd	in other words	H 5,11; C 18
k3t	work	no. vi
k3w	unripe fruit of sycamore	T 2,3
k3p	to hide; hiding	C 18; T 1,11
K3š	Nubia	H 2,4
ky, ktt	other	H 5,11,12; B 16,11
kpwy	a group—the "trapped ones"?	B c2,9
(m) kf3	at all	B c3,1
km	black	no. v,3,3
km	to complete	C 16
Kmt	Egypt	H 4,4
krṯ?	part of trap	H 2,1
ksks	to dance, skip	no. iv,11,11
ktt	little girl	T 2,6
kṯ (k3ṯ3)	safflower	C 23

g3	horse, stallion H 1,[8]; B g1,5f.
g3y	jar H 2,9; C [18]; no. iv,6?
g3b	arm H 1,11; 5,3,⟨3⟩; C 14; 15; B c1,4
g3b	see *gbi*
g3bt	leaves T 2,3
g3ḥ	weary B g2,2
g3s	sorrow H 7,6
g3g3 (gg)	to gaze H 5,11
gb	goose H 2,1; 4,7,9
gbi (g3b)	to be weak; damage no. 50,4
gm	to find H 5,2,7,11; C 12; 17; T 1,14; B c2,5; c3,10; 16,9; 17,4, 12,12; no. iv,1
gmḥ	to look B c1,2f.; c4,2,6
gmgm	to rub, caress H 1,2; 7,12
gnw	oriole B 17,10
gnn	to be weak no. iv,8
gr	to be silent, cease H 3,4; 5,10; T 1,6; B 17,6
gr	also no. i,3
gry	bird H 4,9
grḥ	night H 2,7; 5,4; C 1; 14; 26; B c4,6; 16,11; 17,7,8; no. v,3
grg	equipment T 2,10
grg	to prepare, set H 4,2,6,9; no. v,4
gḥs	gazelle B g2,1
gs	half, side H 5,12; B c3,10; no. 53,3
t	bread C 5; T 2,10; no. 49,4
t3	land, earth H 2,3,4; 5,6; C 13; 22; B c1,5; 16,11
t3ḥ	to disturb H 4,10
tir	see *ṯrt*
tišps	an oil from a tree C 9; 18
tw	this B c3,3
twt	lovely B c1,5
tbs	heel no. 52,3
tp, tpy	head, foremost, first H 1,12; 4,4; 5,8; 7,7; C 9; B c1,7; c2,9; g1,6,7
tf3, tfy	that C 11; B c1,7
tfi	to jump out, depart B c2,10; c4,5
tnw	where H 1,1?
tnw	whenever, etc. H 4,8; C 2; 21; B c3,2,4
tnw? (rnw?)	? B 17,3
tr	season C 11; T 1,2
tr (= ṯrt)	willow C 24
thm	to knock B 17,8
thr	foreign troops B g1,8
tḫ	beer H 2,2; no. 52,2; no. 53,1; no. iv,4
tḫ	to be drunk H 7,12; T 1,3; 2,9,13,13; B 17,1
tḫb	to immerse C 9; T 1,3

tḫḫw	?	H 1,10 (read *tḫtḫ*)
tḫtḫ	disorder; to confuse	H 1,[10]; B 16,10; T 2,13
tši	to be absent, separated	C 25
tkn	see *ṯkn*	
ṯꜣi	to take, steal; see also *iṯꜣ*, *iṯi*	H 3,10; 7,11; C 19; 21; B c1,8; c2,10; 16,9?; no. iv,3,10
ṯꜣy	(scroll) box?	B 16,9
ṯꜣy	a plant	H 7,11
ṯꜣy	cub, young animal	H 2,2
ṯꜣy	male	B c1,6; no. v,2
ṯꜣw	wind	C 8?; B 16,12; T 2,5; no. 48; no. 51,3; no. 53,4; no. iv,5
ṯꜣw	to blow	B 16,9; no. 53,4
ṯꜣrt	fortress	no. 53,7
ṯwiꜣ, *ṯwy*?	?	H 8,12
ṯb	cage	H 4,3
ṯm	to be ashamed (for *rmi*?)	B c4,4
ṯnw	see *tnw*	
ṯr	door?	B 17,8,9,11
ṯr	fortress; see *ṯꜣrt*	
ṯḥw	joy	B c4,2
ṯḥn	to approach, meet, touch	H 5,5; C 19
ṯḥn	faience	T 2,4
ṯḥḥ, *ṯḥḥwt*	to rejoice; rejoicing	C 20; B g1,4
ṯs	utterance	B 16,9
ṯs	to bind, attach	no. v,[4]
ṯsi	to raise	H 7,6; B c4,9
ṯsm	hound	B g2,2
ṯkn	to approach	C 17
di	gift	B c3,9
diw	five	B c3,4,9
dwꜣ	morning	H 8,2; C 21; T 2,12,12
dwꜣ	to praise	B c3,4
dwn	to stretch forth	no. vi
db	see *ṯb*	
dbw	figs	T 1,11
dpy	crocodile	C 12
dmi	to mix	C 5
dmḏ	mixture	C 15
dmḏt	compendium	B c4,10
dni	to block up	B 17,7
dni	to allot	B c2,9
drf	scroll, writing	B 16,9; no. vi
dšr	red	C 10; T 2,3
dgꜣ	see *idg*	
dgꜣ	to plant	T 2,1
dgꜣ	fruit	T 2,11

dt	type of plant	H 1,9
dd	lovemaking, copulation	H 2,2; no. 49,1
dd	garden	H 3,12
ḏt	eternity	H 5,3
ḏt	body, self	B c4,7
ḏ3i	to extend, carry over?	B c1,5
ḏ3is	a plant	B 17,⟨12⟩
ḏ3ḏ3	entry-building	no. iv,9
ḏyḏy (*ḏtḏt*?)	to tease, bother	H 5,6
ḏwt	badness	C 27; B c5,2; no. vi
ḏb^{c}	finger	C 4; 10; 21; B c1,4
ḏrt	hand	H 5,7,7; 7,8,9,9; C 5; 19; T 2,1,5; no. 54,4; no. iv,6; no. vi
ḏry	stout	B 17,10
ḏrww	loins	B 17,6
ḏsr	type of oil	T 1,9
ḏsr	ale	B 16,10
(r) ḏd mdw	matters? "things"?	T 2,15
ḏXḏ	?	T 2,1
(*12*)	twelve	T 1,4

APPENDIX C

Hieroglyphic Transcription

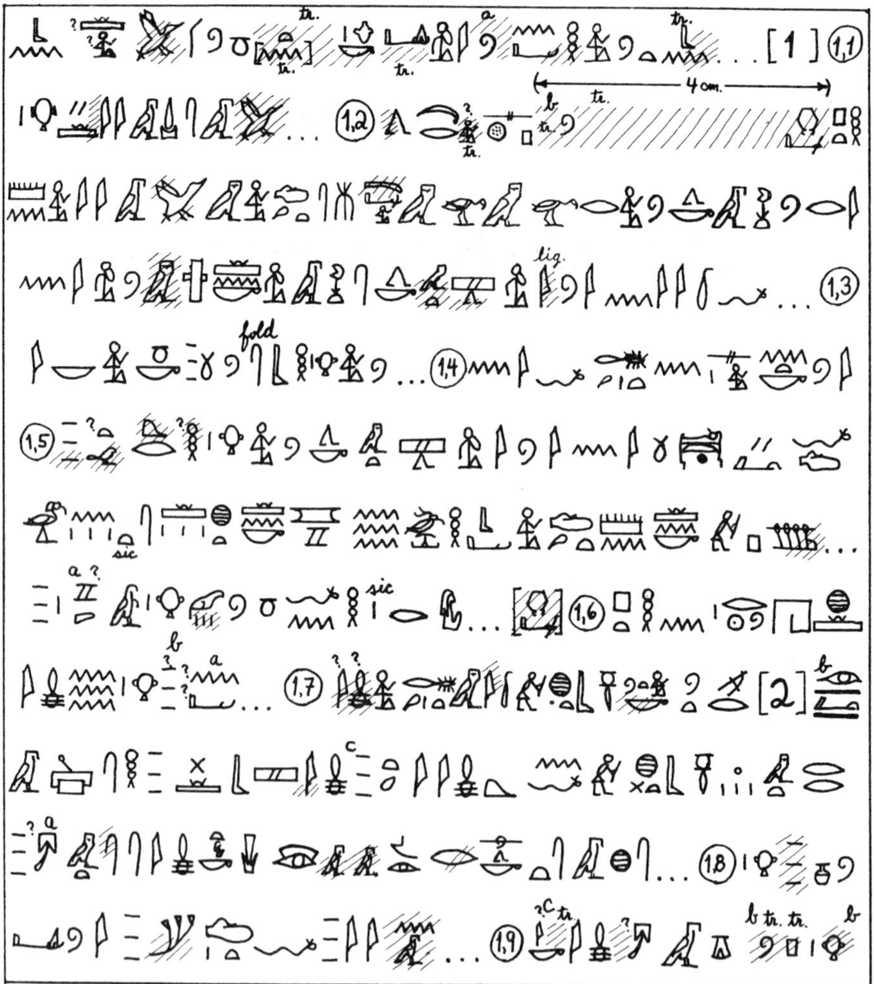

1-1 Column 1: 14 cm. width remains. Approx. 1/4 of each line is lost.
a ḵ required by context, but lacuna is too narrow. b Possibly (Müller). 1,6a Müller: b Inserted above line. 1,7a Possibly (Müller), but cf. 5,9,12, etc. b c sic, for . 1,8a b-b Thus Müller.
c = ? (Müller).

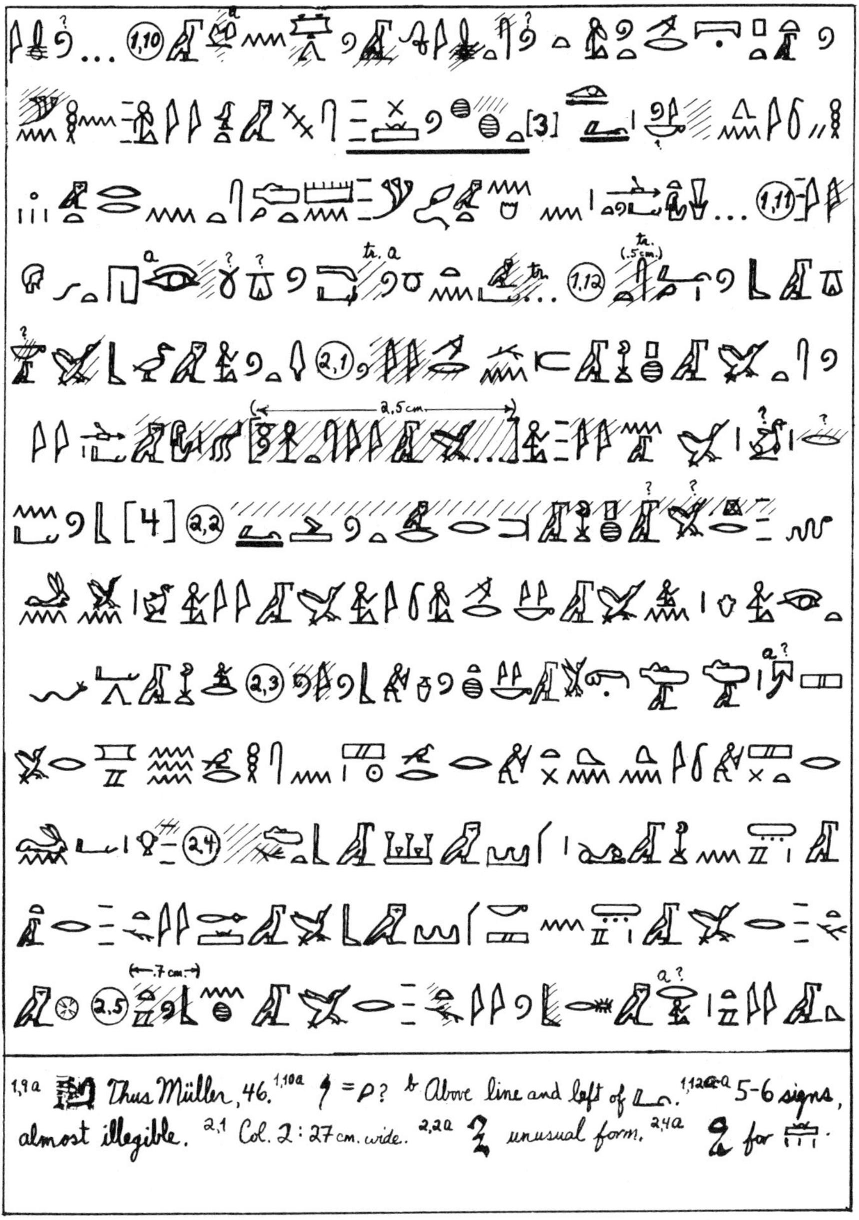

1,9a Thus Müller, 46. 1,10a = p? b Above line and left of . 1,12a 5-6 signs, almost illegible. 2,1 Col. 2: 27 cm. wide. 2,2a unusual form. 2,4a for .

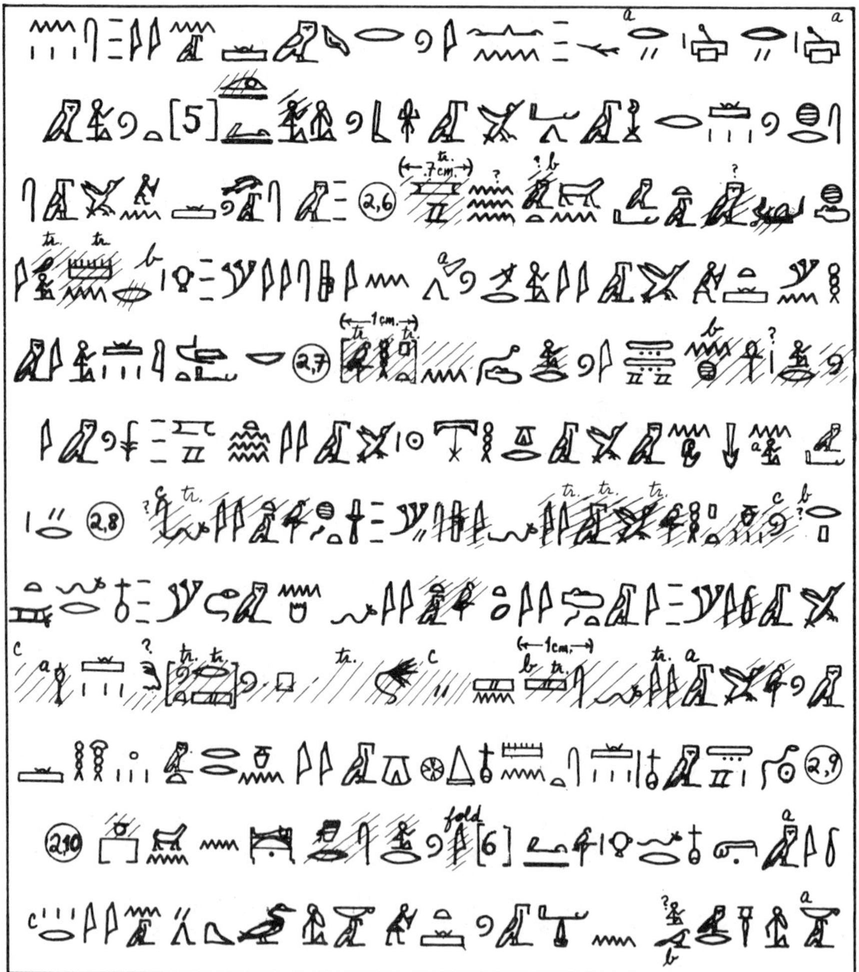

2,5a-a Or: [hieroglyph], or: [hieroglyph]. b Müller: [hieroglyph]. 2,6a False determinatives; for [hieroglyph]. b-b Badly damaged. 2,7a Blurred. b [hieroglyph] cf: [hieroglyph] at end of 2,12. c-c Faint and damaged. 2,8a-a Damaged and unclear; very uncertain. b There are traces of two [hieroglyph], as in Wb. III, 487, 9. c-c Bottom of line lost; 5.5 cm. 2,9a [hieroglyph]. 2,10a [hieroglyph] erased. b [hieroglyph] erased. c ||| blurred; emend [hieroglyph] to [hieroglyph].

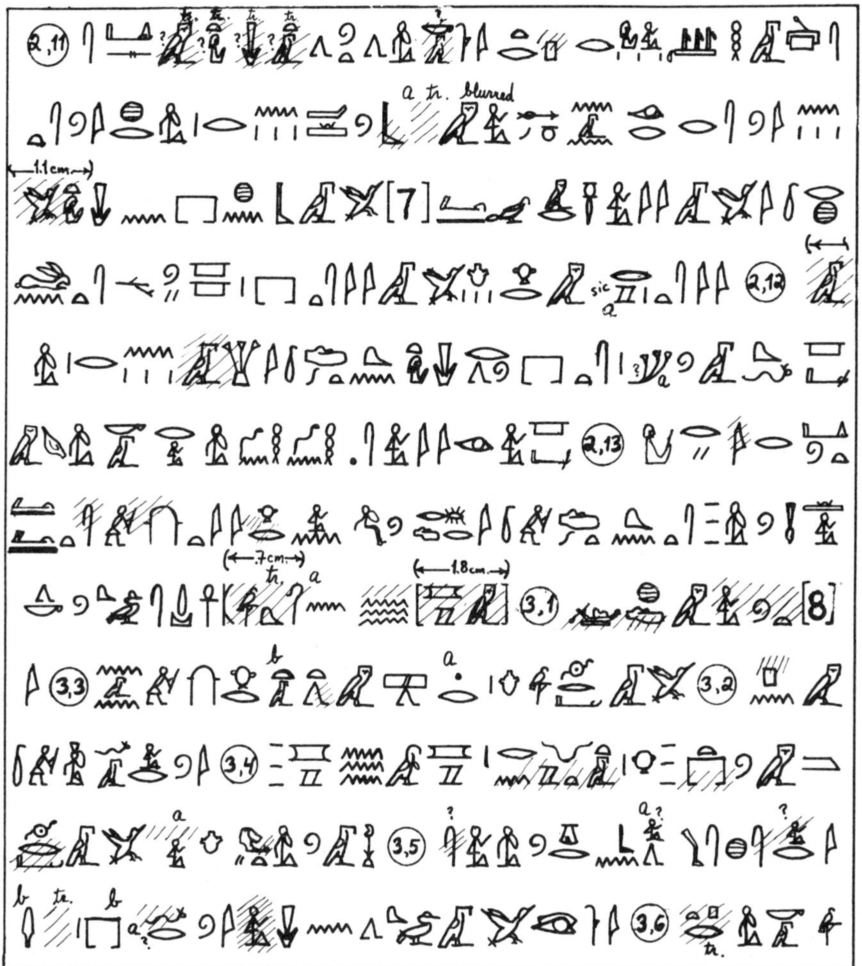

2,11a Erased ? 2,12a for . 2,12b Col. 3: 8 cm. wide.
a Beginning of cartouche apparently not written. 3,2a For .
b Müller: ; unlikely. 3,4a Or: 3,5a Or: ; just barely possible on left. 3,6a Faded. b-b Very unclear. Possibly to be restored according to ll. 9 and 10, q.v. Müller: ?1 ? ? 1.

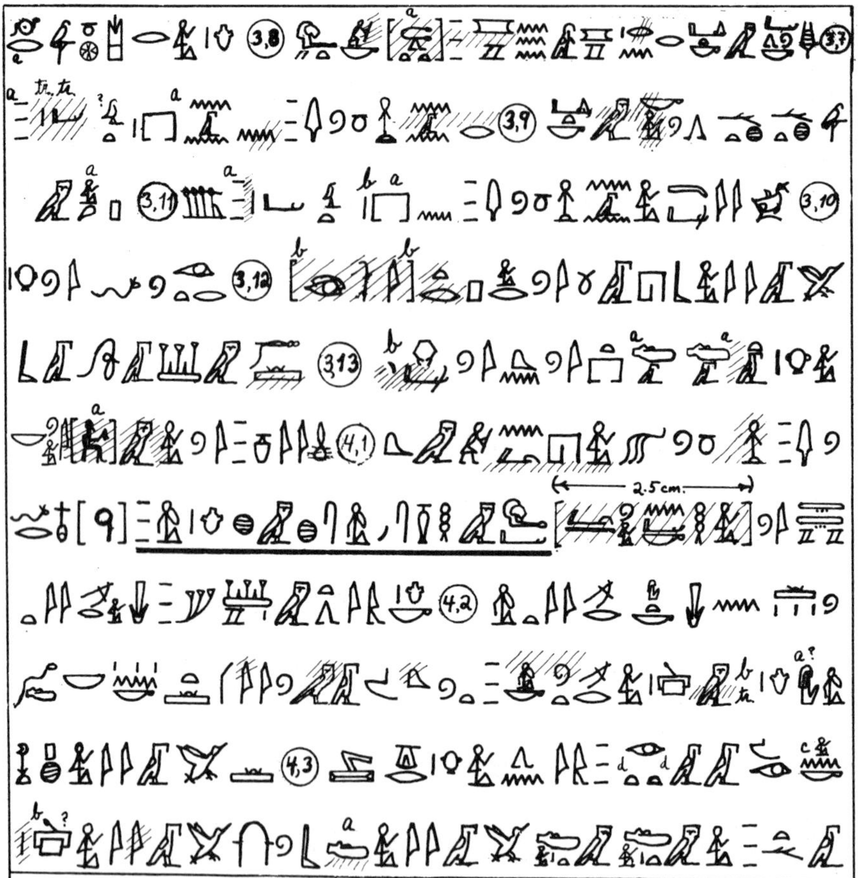

3,7a Thus Müller. 3,8a [hieroglyph]; [hieroglyph] may be fused. 3,9a-a Unclear; see l. 10. 3,10a-a Müller: [hieroglyph], with | and [hieroglyph] fused. But the presence of [hieroglyph] is uncertain in all three occurrences (ll. 6, 9, 10). b Probably a blurred vertical stroke: [hieroglyph] 3,11a Or: [hieroglyph]; blurred. b-b Left blank (1.1 cm.)? Vague traces. 3,12a-a Or: [hieroglyph] (Müller), but cf. 2,2. b A trace [hieroglyph]; does not conform well with [hieroglyph] or [hieroglyph]. Col. 4: 21.5 cm. wide. 4,1a Existing traces allow this reading. 4,2a Dot too high for normal [hieroglyph]. b Obscure mark ([hieroglyph]). Emend to [hieroglyph]. c Blurred: [hieroglyph] d-d Or: [hieroglyph]. 4,3a For [hieroglyph], though t with faded tick may in fact be the correct reading.

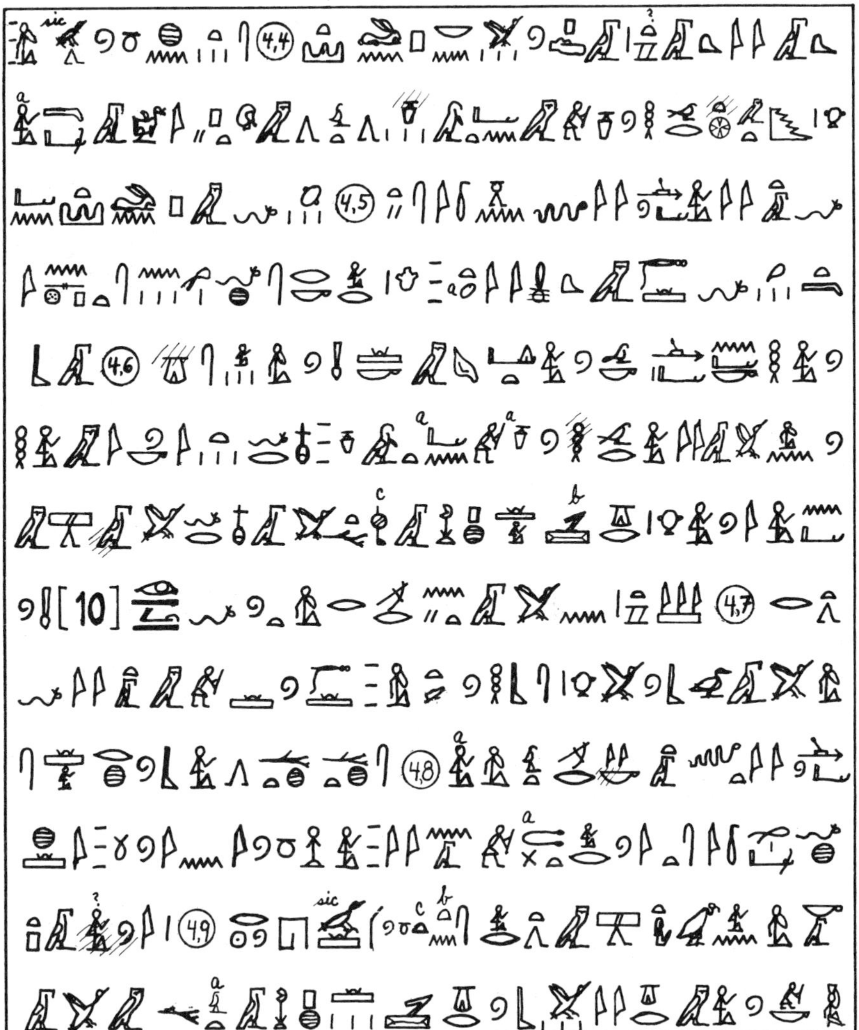

4,3b [sign]; doubtful.
4,4a Delete. 4,5a For ∘. 4,6a-a Blurred. b Unusual form: [sign]; thus 4,9. c [sign] Not in Müller, Hierat. Pal. II. 4,7a Blurred. 4,8a Tick lacking. b [sign]
c [sign] : resembles 9. 4,9a [sign]; [sign] (Müller) expected but not written here.

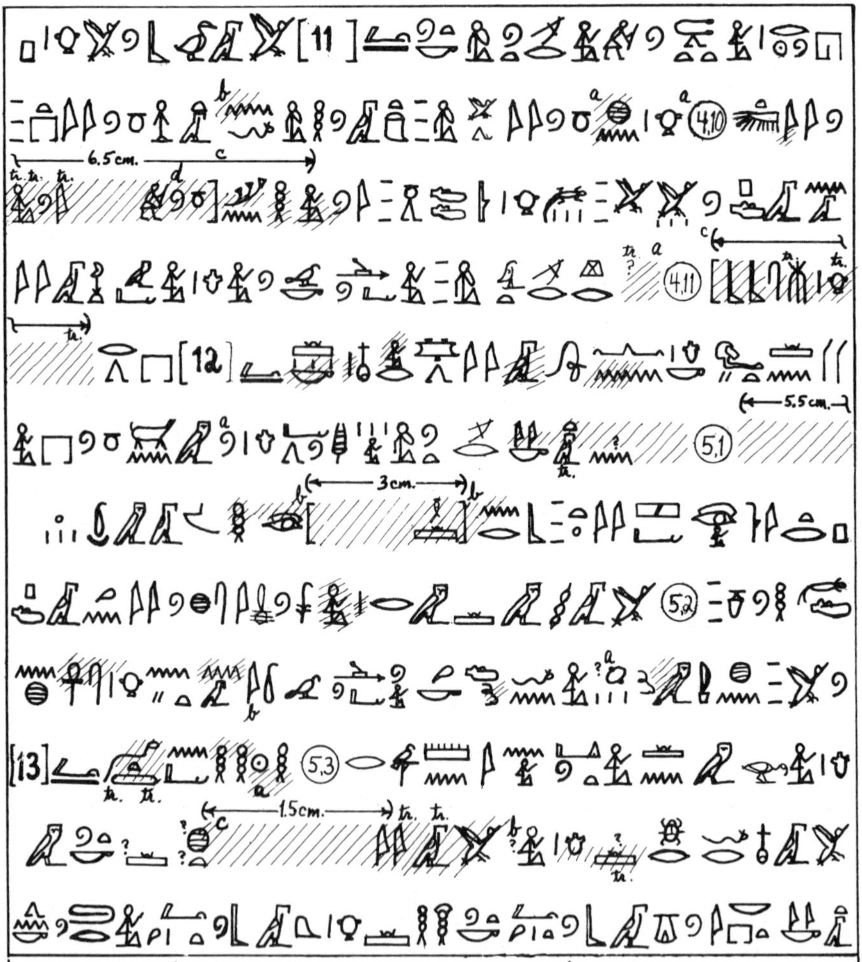

4,10a-a Faded. b Fold. c-c Traces remain over lacuna. d visible above lacuna; perhaps . 4,11a Müller: . Doubtful. Col. 5: 22.5 cm. wide.
5,1a Emend to . b-b Possible restoration: [ ]. 5,2a Damaged and distorted, but reading fairly certain. b . 5,3a Traces of writing below line. b The expected seems to be missing (the traces following are required for p3).
c Müller, p. 23, n. 7 suggests restoring sꜥnḫt.k ; is quite uncertain.

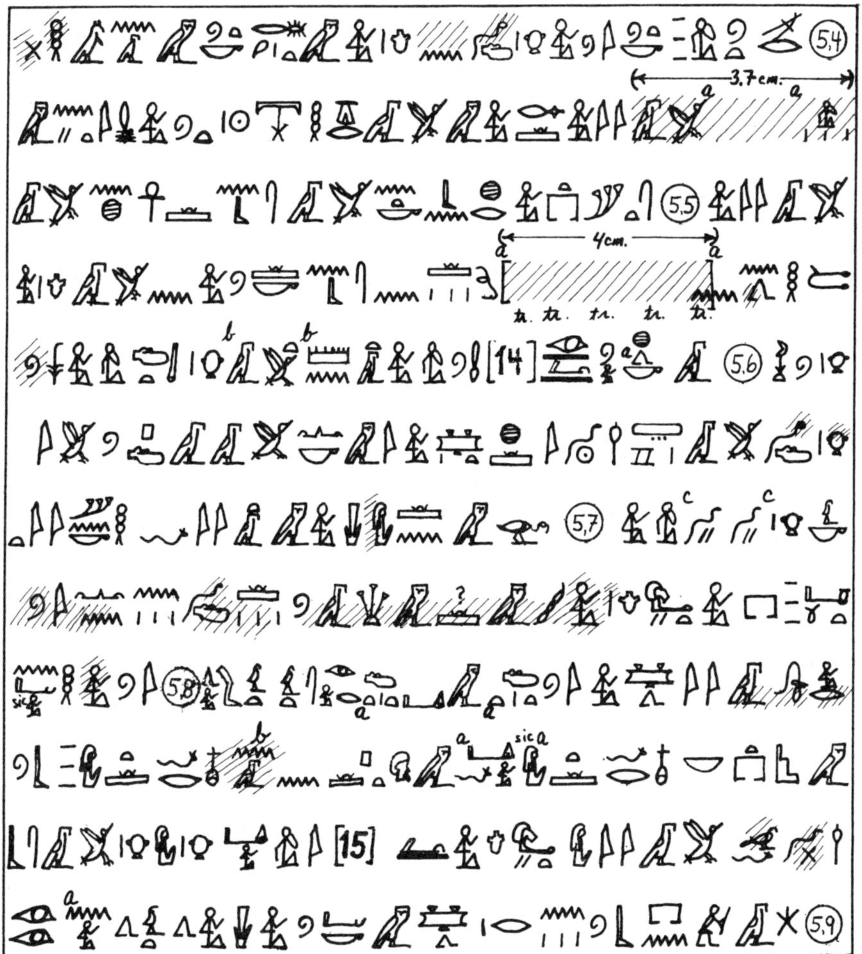

5,4a-a Perhaps restore: cf. 2,7. 5,5a-a Here, possible. 5,6a (Connected.) Perhaps over. b-b ; omit. c-c Perhaps. 5,7a,a ; less likely. 5,8a-a For. The was written under the influence of the following nfrwt. b Traces of one group. 5,9a merged with.

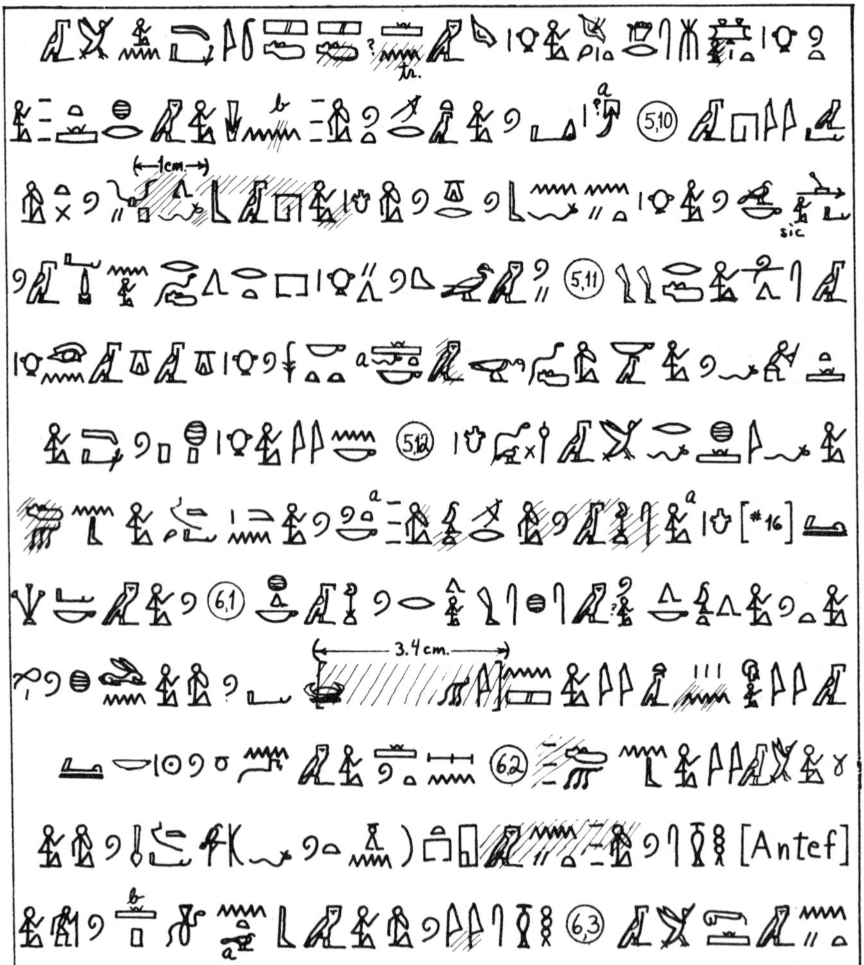

5,10a (Müller); just possible; cf. determ. of wnš, 2,2. b A very long mm broken in middle. 5,11a Müller reads (without), but is clear, though superfluous (dittography). 5,12a-a 4 cm. damaged. Col. 6: 18.2 cm. wide. 6,3a By association with bin? Emend to . b ; compare □ in 6,12 and 8,7.

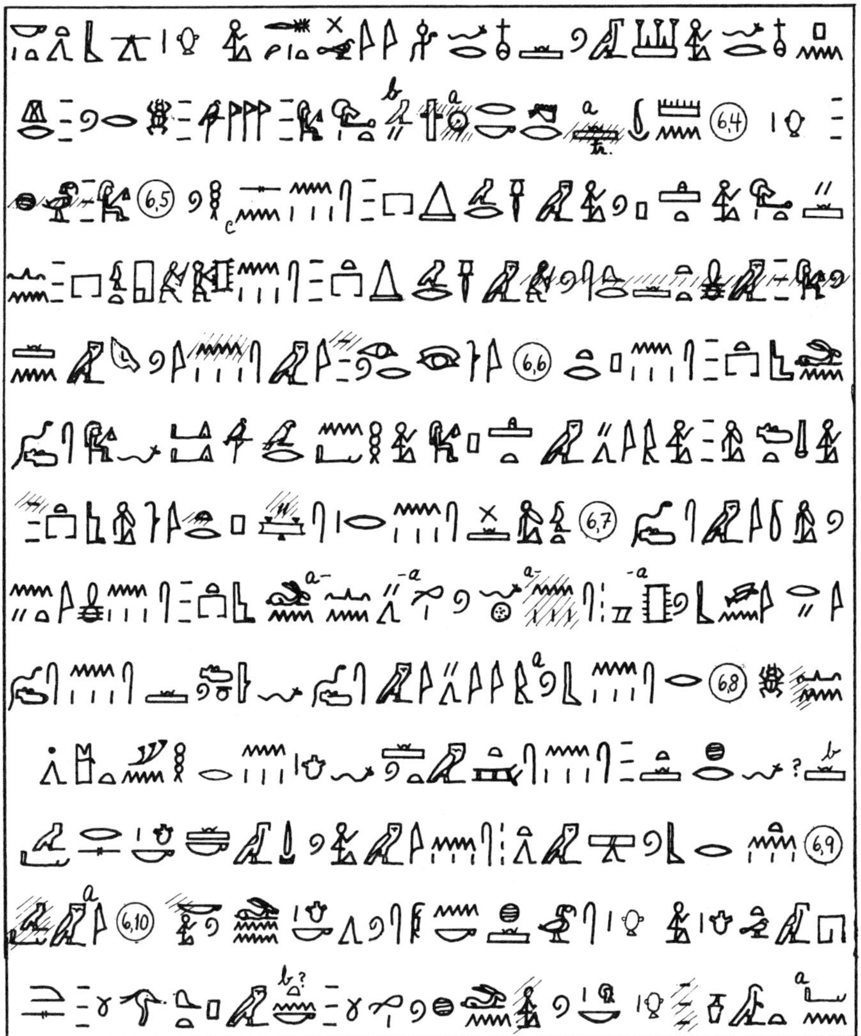

6,4 a,a Damaged. b c Emend to .
6,7 a-a Partially blurred and effaced. 6,8 a Leyden K., 6 .
b Blurred. Perhaps written over . 6,10 a-a Faded. 6,10 b

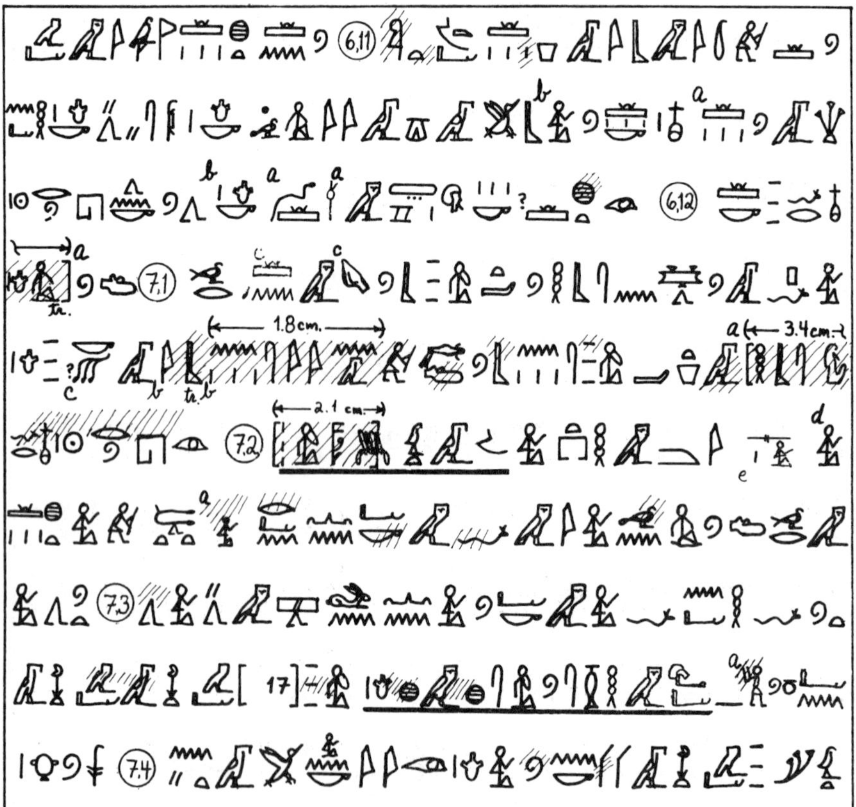

6,11a Leyden K.6 adds . b Leyden K.6 adds . 6,12a-a Leyden K.6 reads (ḥḏt). b Leyden K.6 adds . c-c Unclear; curve on left—perhaps tracing of pen from . Col. 7: 19.5 cm. width. 7,1a-a Müller's restoration. b also possible. c unusual form of . d ib not in Leyden K.6. e perhaps present and very short. In any case, to be restored; Leyden K.6: . 7,2a is expected, but there is scarcely enough room in the lacuna for ; still, the text is to be emended to . 7,3a Arms not clear. Line poss. remains of (Müller); more likely a space filler.

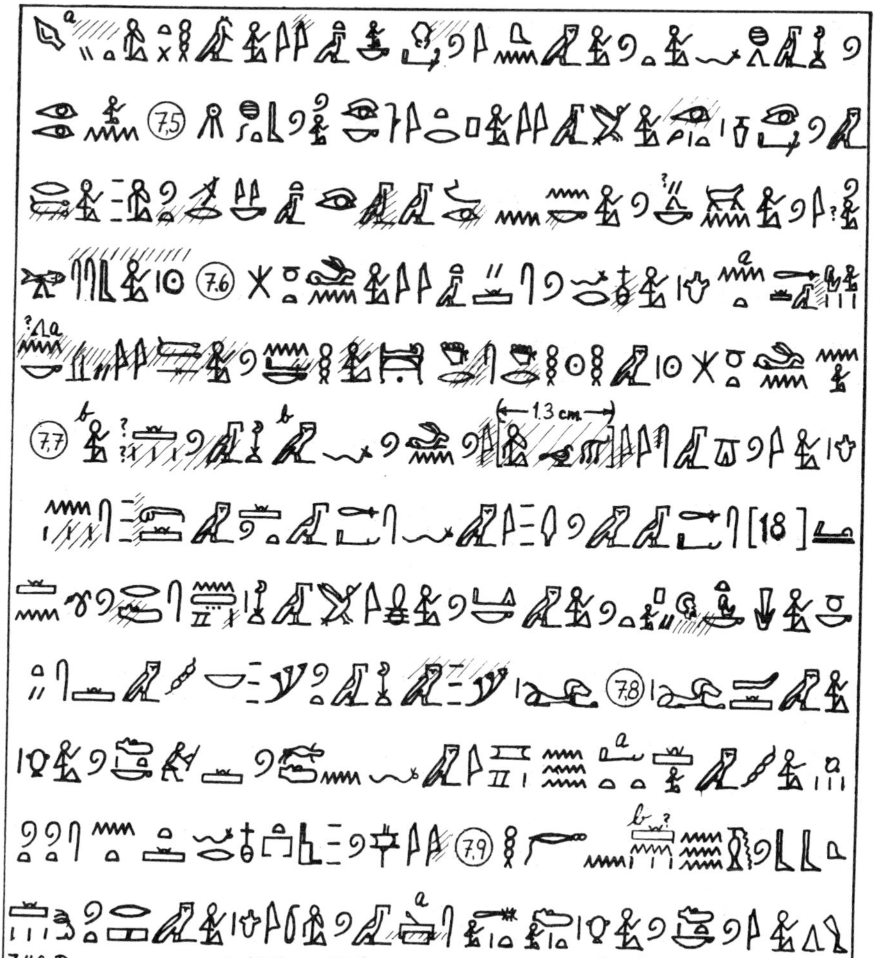

7,4a Remains suggest , cf. 7,3, but not syntactical. ?

7,5a ; for , cf. 7,9. Müller: . Possible. 7,6a Thus Müller. Legs uncertain.

b-b : uncertain. possible. 7,8a Perhaps (for).

7,8 b is required by context, but and ||| not usual forms.

7,9a Müller: .

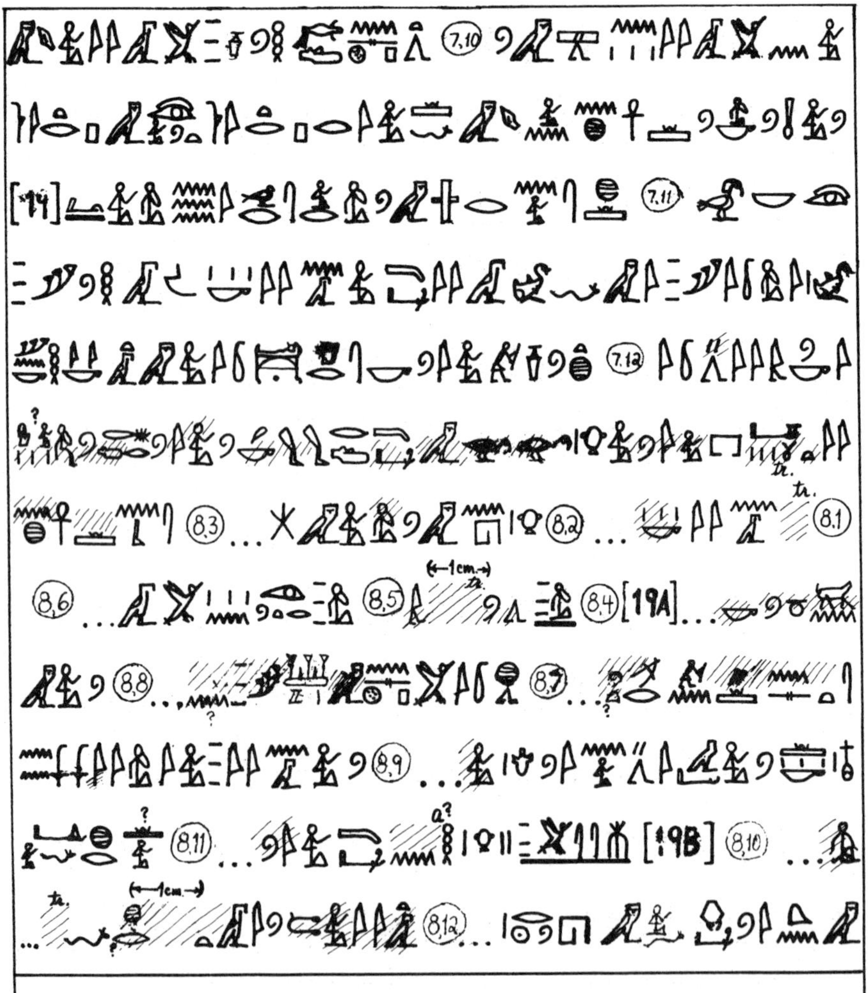

Col. 8 mostly lost. Remains: l. 1: 1.5cm.; ll. 2-6: 3cm.; l. 7: 5cm; ll. 8-12: 5.5cm. 8,10a ? ? ( ).

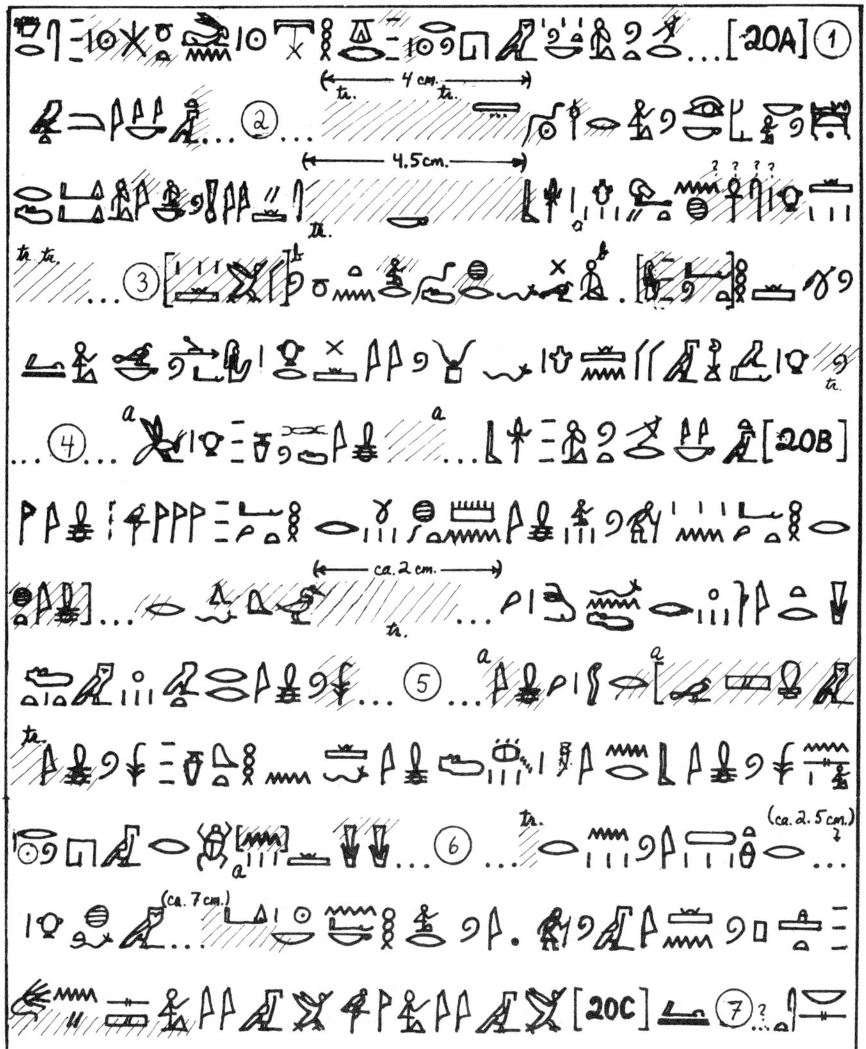

2a [glyph] Not [glyph]; see ll. 12, 14 et al. b-b Fragment, pl. 75. 3a-a Fragment, pl. 75. 4a-a Fragment, pl. 75. 6a [glyph] Posener: [glyph].

* Deir el Medineh 1266 + O. Cairo cat. 25218: Posener, HIFAO xviii, pl. 79a. The lengths of the lacunae are often indeterminable.

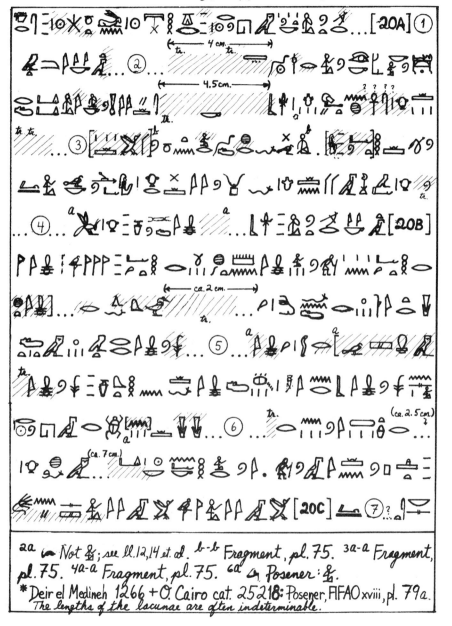

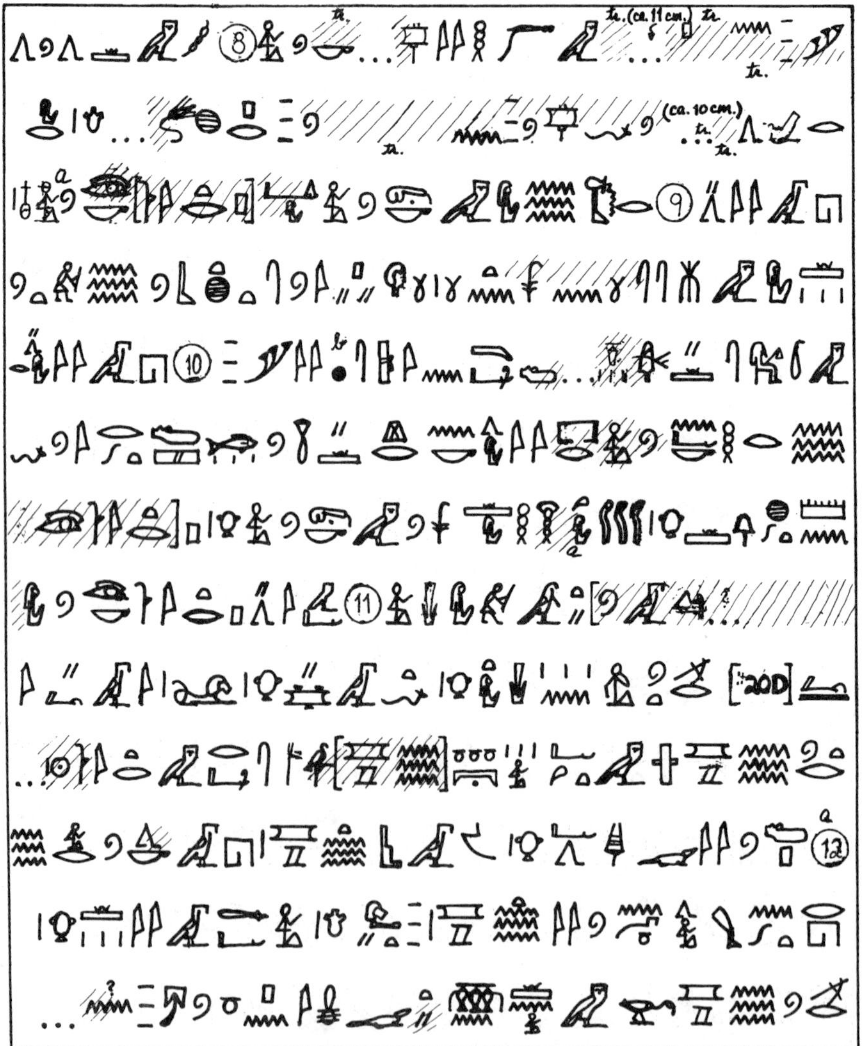

9a b Blurred, for //. 10a Like . Tick lost. 12a Ll. 12-20 seem to be complete except for internal lacunae.

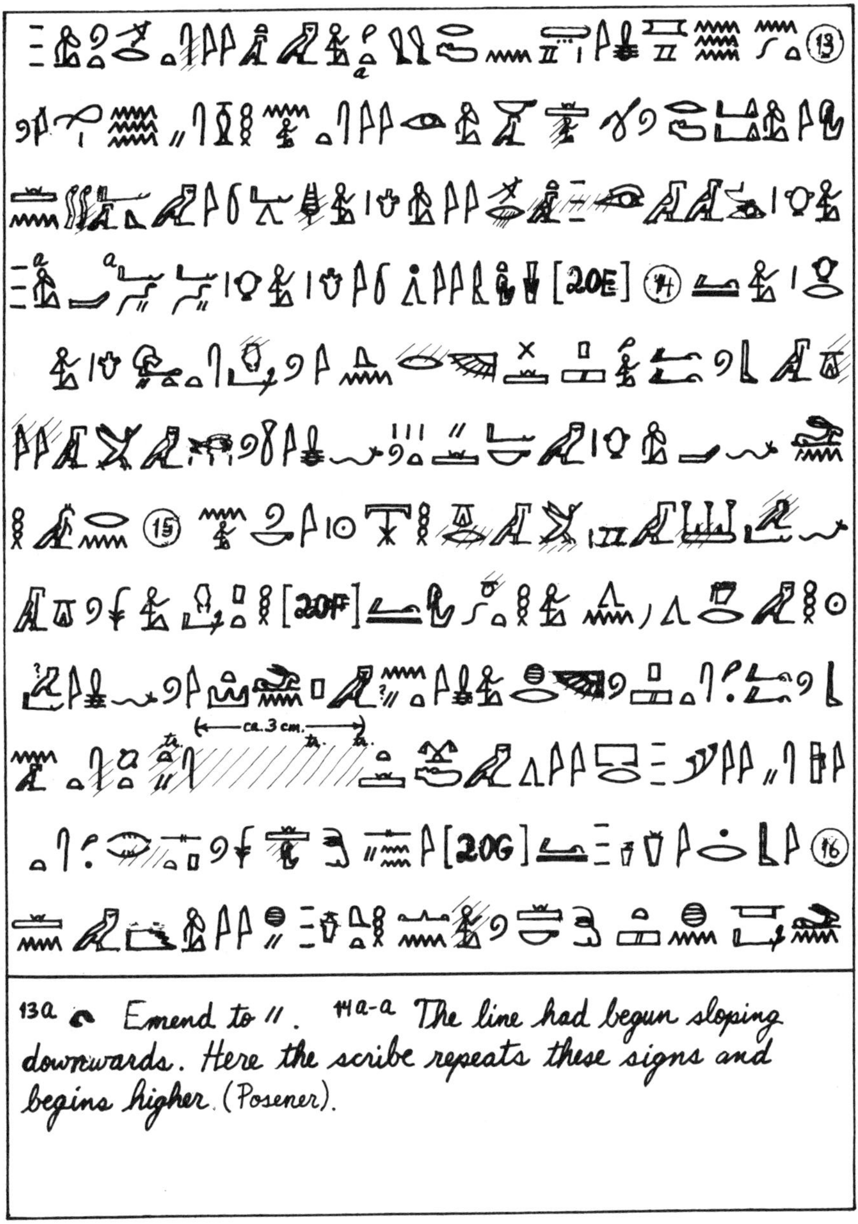

13a Emend to //. 14a-a The line had begun sloping downwards. Here the scribe repeats these signs and begins higher. (Posener).

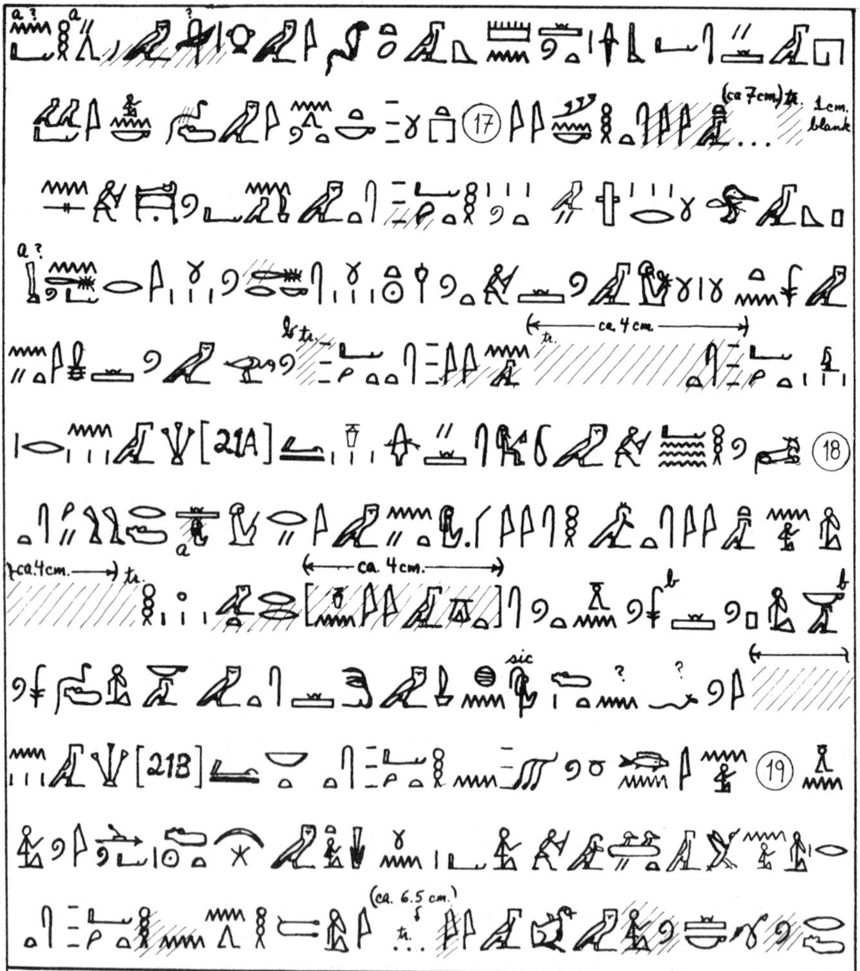

16a-a Posener's alternative ( ) doubtful from facsimile. 17a b erased? 18a Or . b-b = (), cf. in Hymn to the Nile, § xiv, c, e.

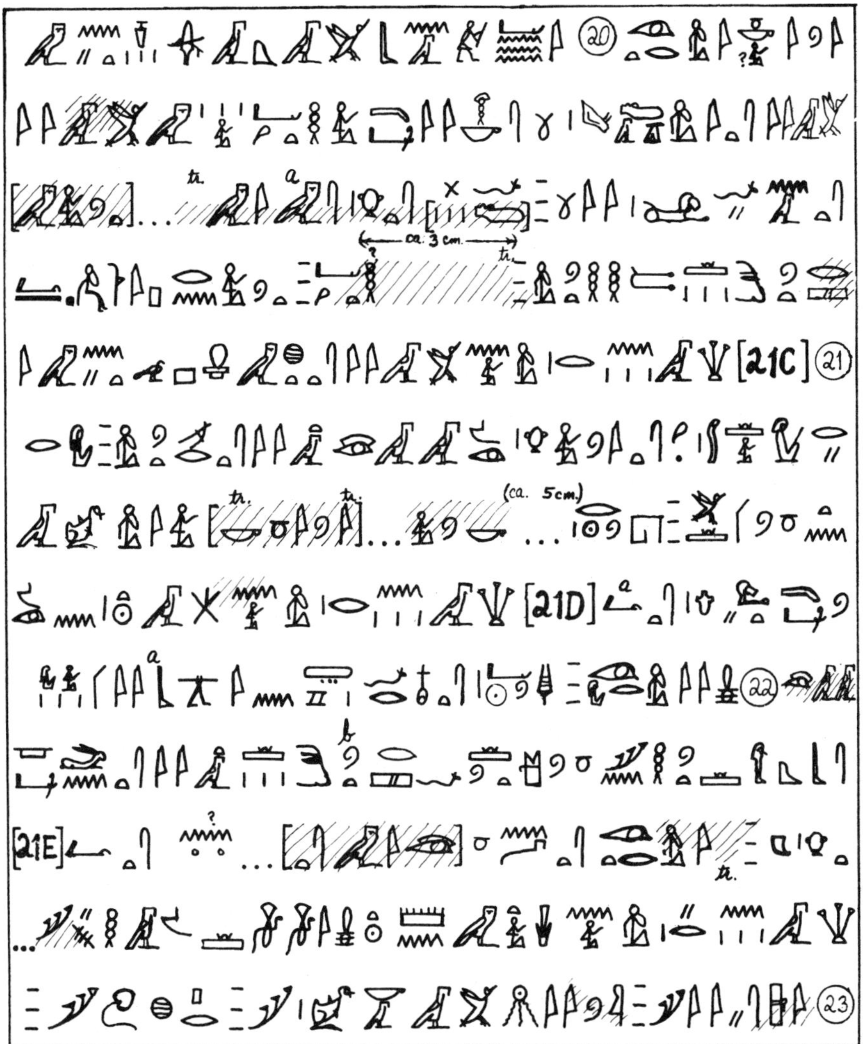

20a [sign] ([sign]?) added. 21a Henceforth, [sign] not in red. 22a [sign] Possibly = [sign]. b [sign]

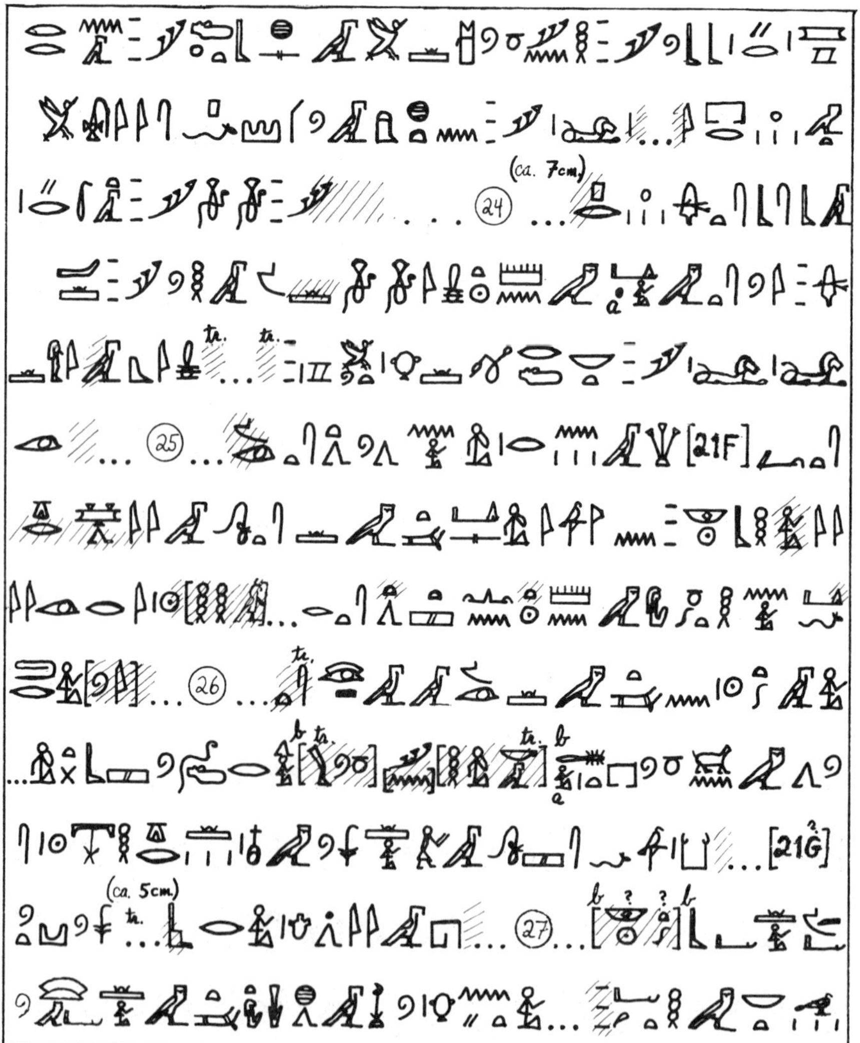

[24]a Posener: . Emend to . [26]a Or: . b-b Posener's restoration.

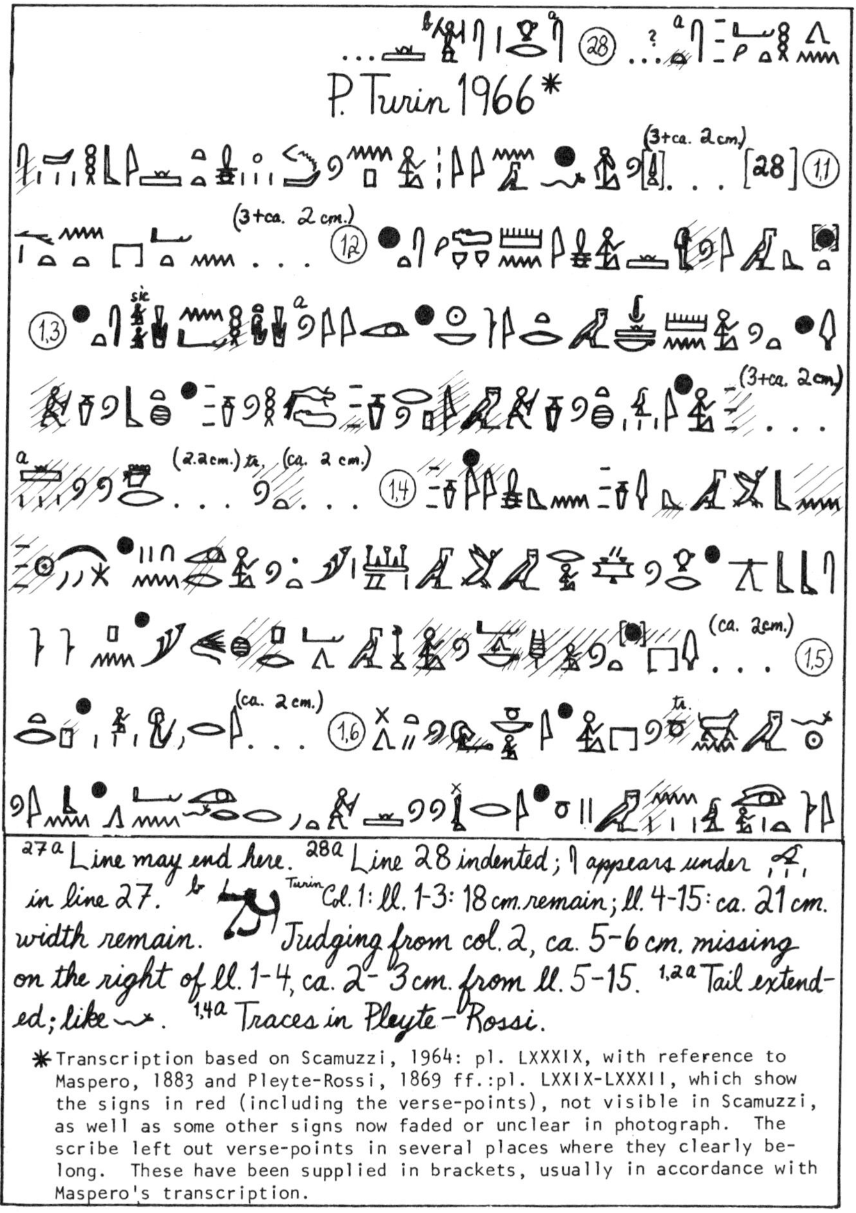

[27a] *Line may end here.* [28a] *Line 28 indented; appears under , in line 27.* [b] [Turin] *Col. 1: ll. 1-3: 18 cm. remain; ll. 4-15: ca. 21 cm. width remain. Judging from col. 2, ca. 5-6 cm. missing on the right of ll. 1-4, ca. 2-3 cm. from ll. 5-15.* [1,2a] *Tail extended; like .* [1,4a] *Traces in Pleyte-Rossi.*

* Transcription based on Scamuzzi, 1964: pl. LXXXIX, with reference to Maspero, 1883 and Pleyte-Rossi, 1869 ff.:pl. LXXIX-LXXXII, which show the signs in red (including the verse-points), not visible in Scamuzzi, as well as some other signs now faded or unclear in photograph. The scribe left out verse-points in several places where they clearly belong. These have been supplied in brackets, usually in accordance with Maspero's transcription.

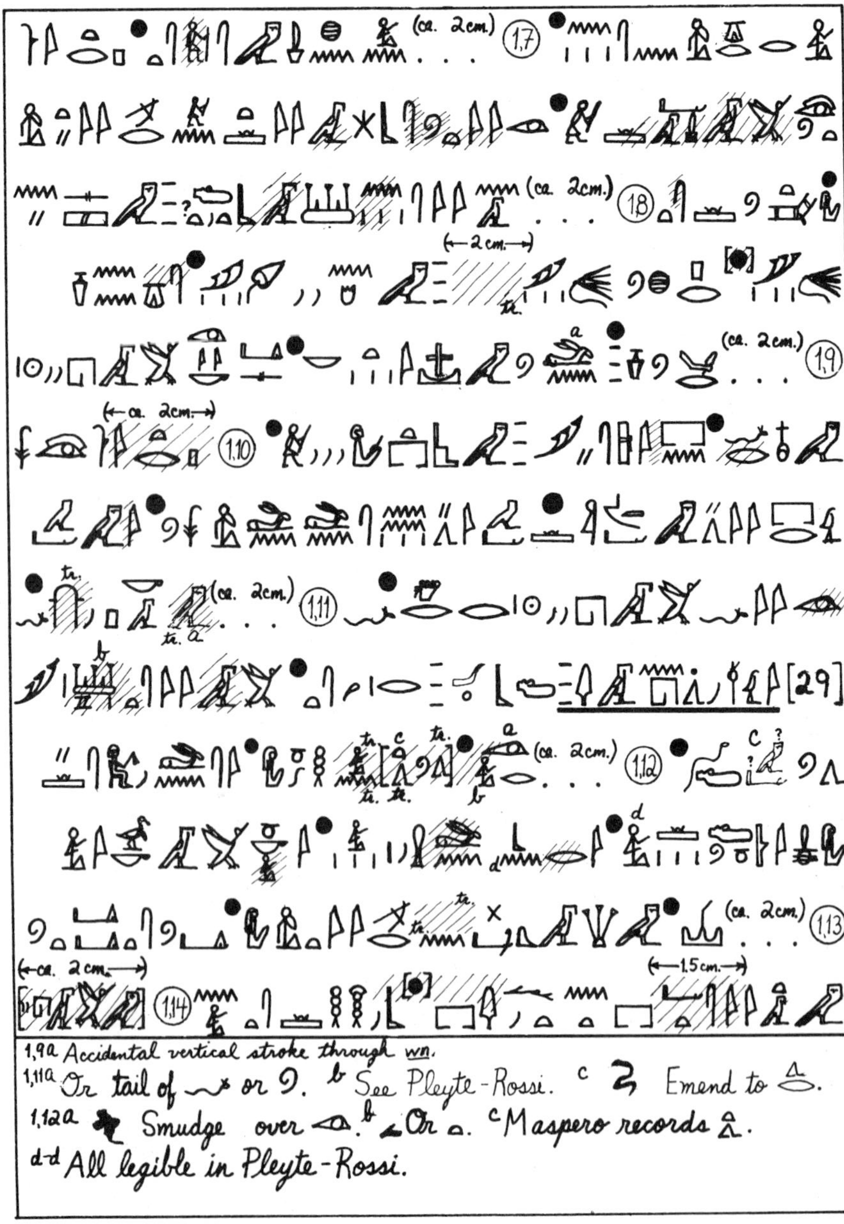

1,9a Accidental vertical stroke through *wn*.

1,11a Or tail of [hieroglyph] or [hieroglyph]. b See Pleyte-Rossi. c [hieroglyph] Emend to [hieroglyph].

1,12a [hieroglyph] Smudge over [hieroglyph]. b [hieroglyph] Or [hieroglyph]. c Maspero records [hieroglyph].

d-d All legible in Pleyte-Rossi.

1,15a-a In Maspero. Col. 2: 24 cm. remain; nearly complete on left. 2,1a Thus Maspero records; not entirely in accord with traces. b Tail of ? Most similar to tail of in 1,11 and 2,8. 2,2a Perhaps read . b Traces in Maspero's copy. c Maspero records ; not visible in facsimile. d-d obscure. 2,3a for . b-b, b-b Clearer in Pleyte-Rossi. 2,4a for ? b Haplography of

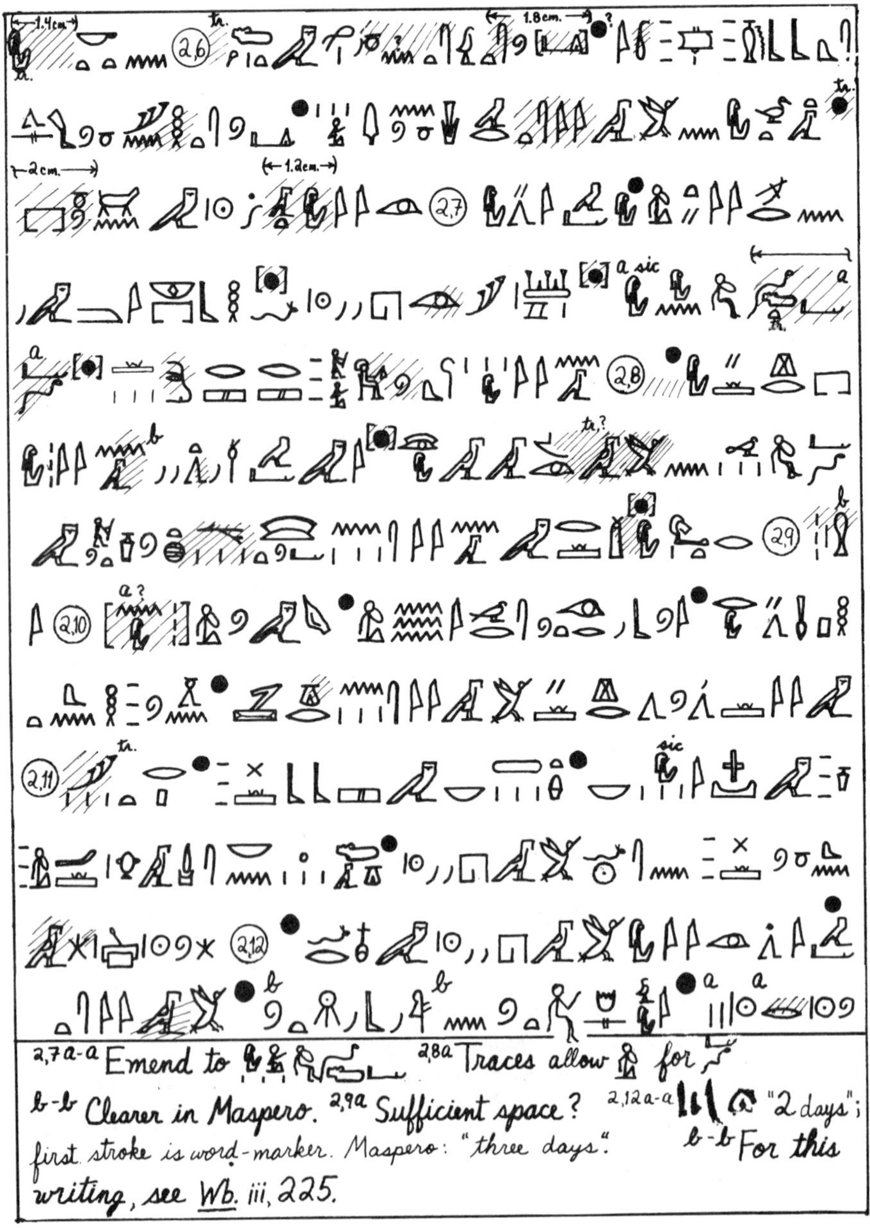

2,7a-a Emend to 2,8a Traces allow for
b-b Clearer in Maspero. 2,9a Sufficient space? 2,12a-a "2 days"; first stroke is word-marker. Maspero: "three days." b-b For this writing, see Wb. iii, 225.

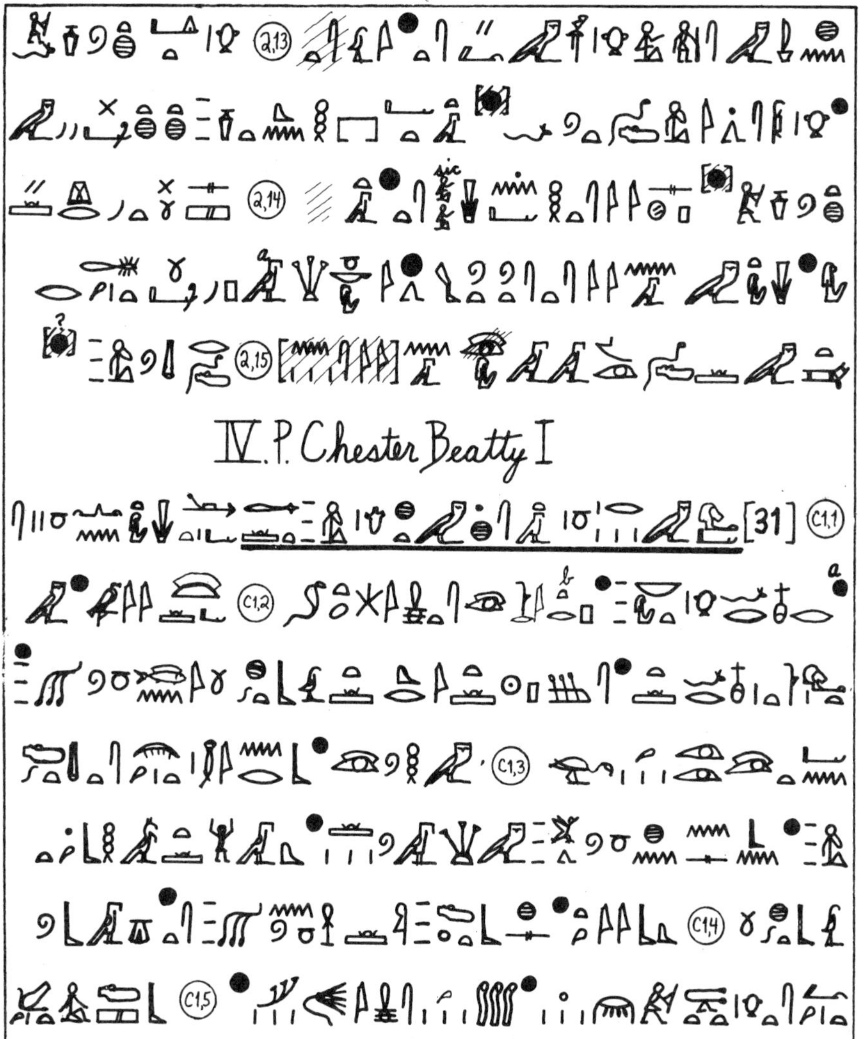

2,14a for .

Beatty I: c1: 2.5cm. wide. c1,1a Dots, as well as pause signs [ ] and stanza numeration, in red throughout. b ligature for ; thus in 1,7; 2,5; 5,1; g2.3.

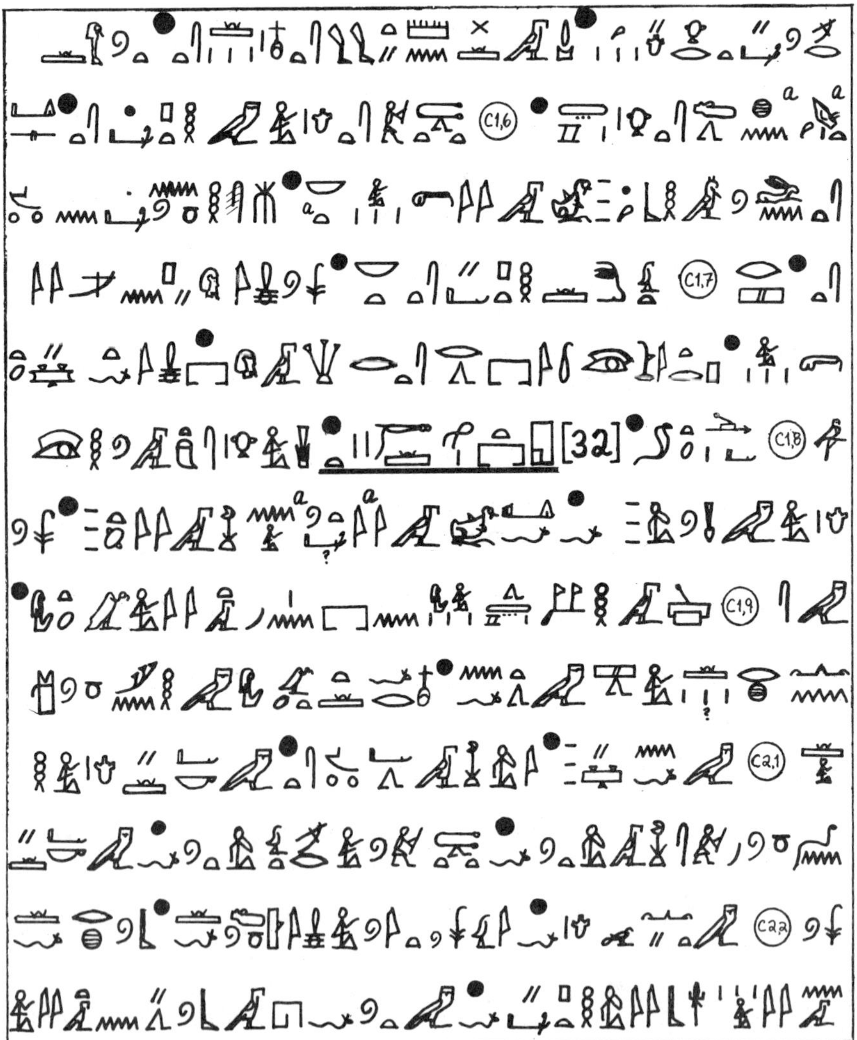

C1,5 a-a Emend to (Gardiner) or , which it closely resembles, cf. g1,1. C1,6a consistently for . C1,8a-a The stick in the hand may be merged with preceding reed. c2: 26 cm. wide.

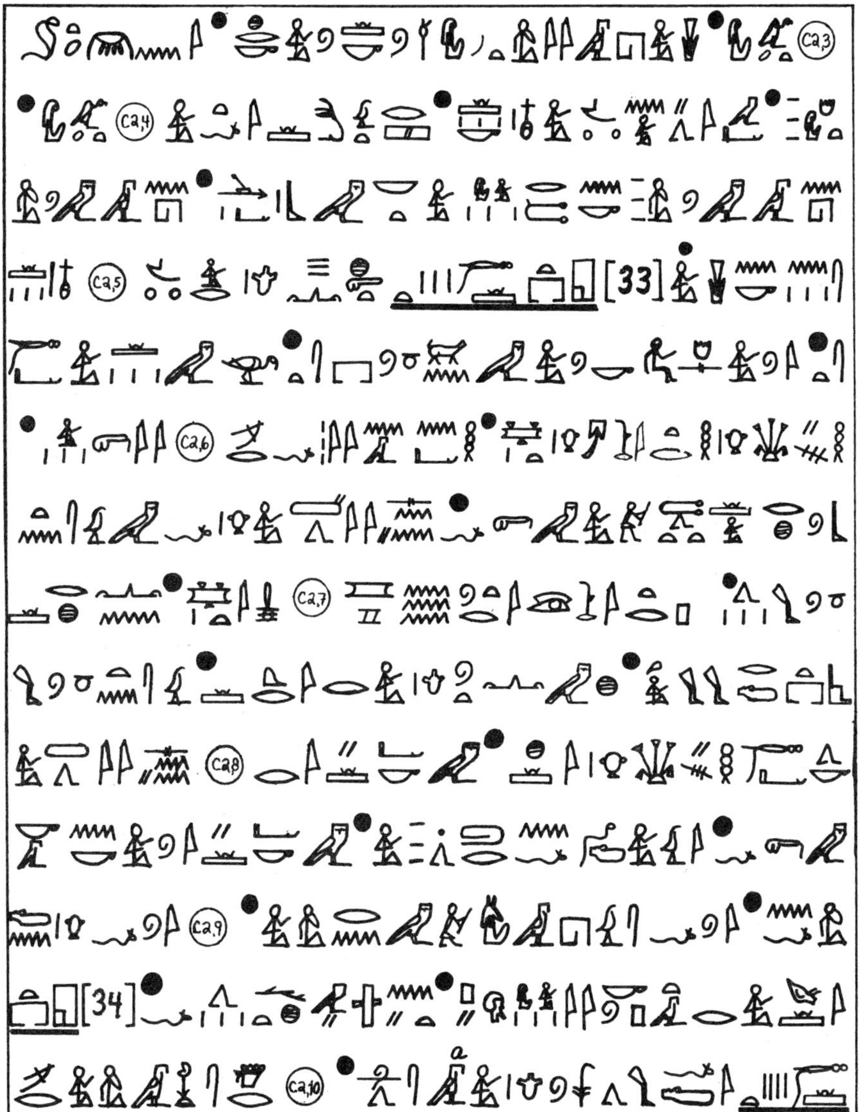

c2,9a in 3s (see also g1,1; 2,1) has an unusual form, close to and not used for elsewhere in this text.

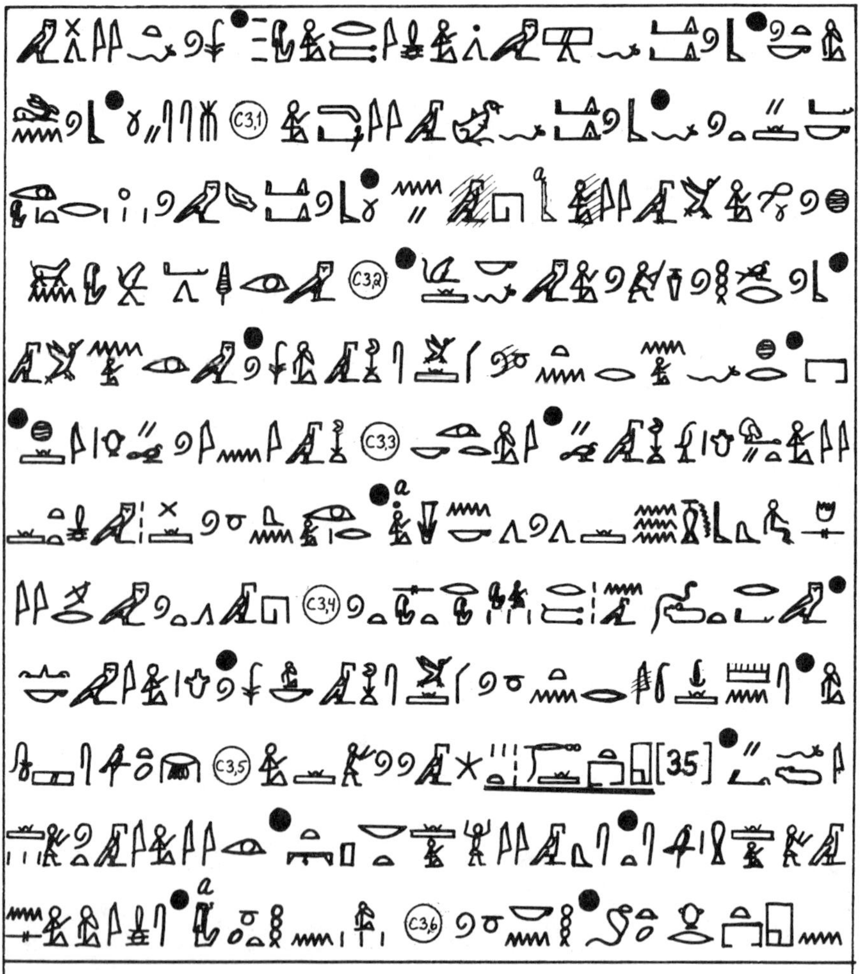

C3: 28.5cm. wide. C3,1a Gardiner adds . C3,3a Gardiner reads and emends to , but has a clear tick elsewhere in this text.

C3,6a  Unusual sign, not in Möller, <u>Hierat. Pal.</u>

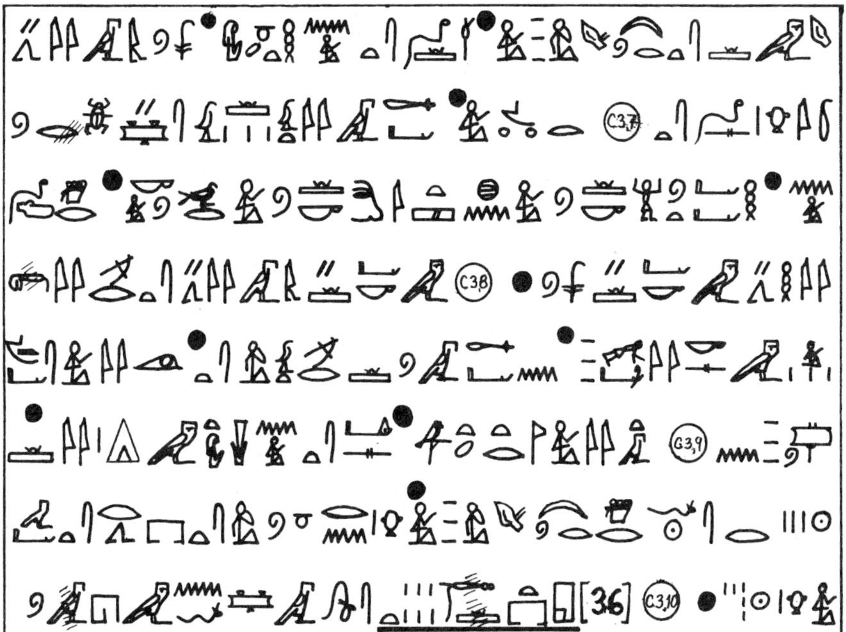

c4: 28.5 cm. wide. L.4: additional 2 cm. at right.

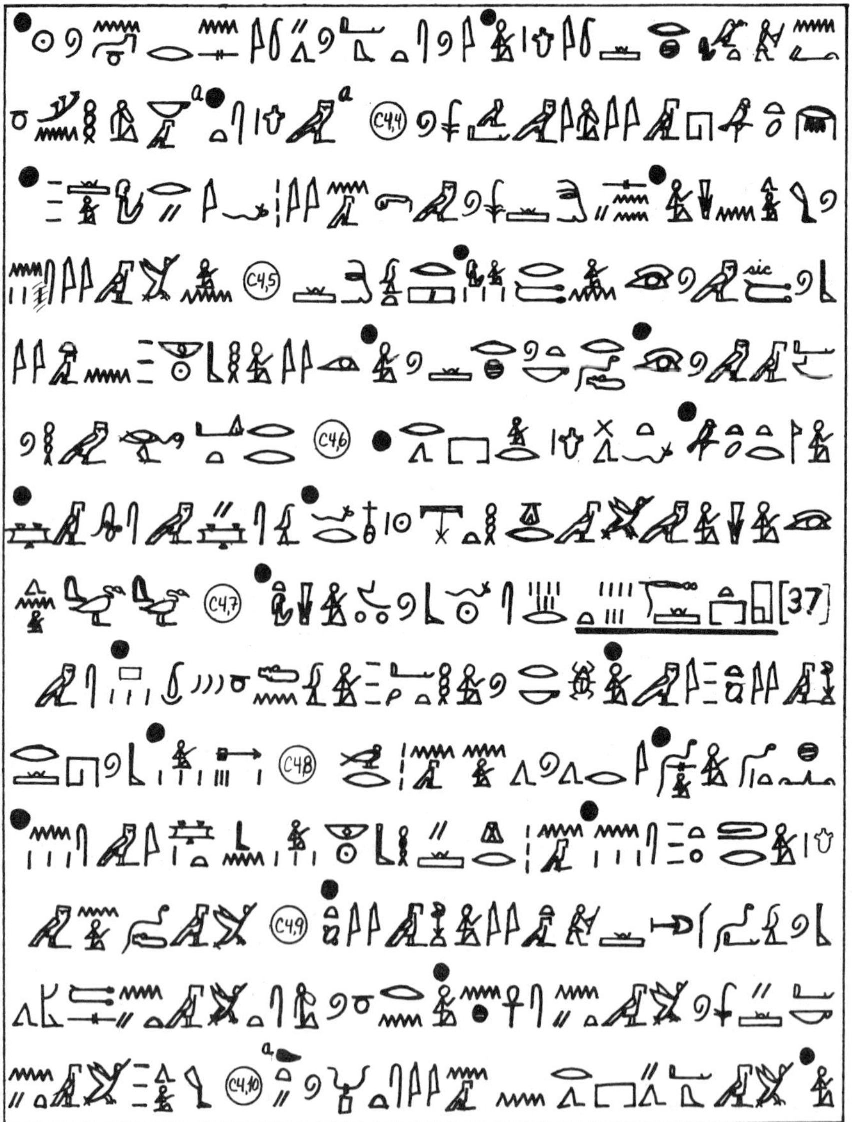

C4,4a-a Later addition; right of column. C4,9a A red blot.

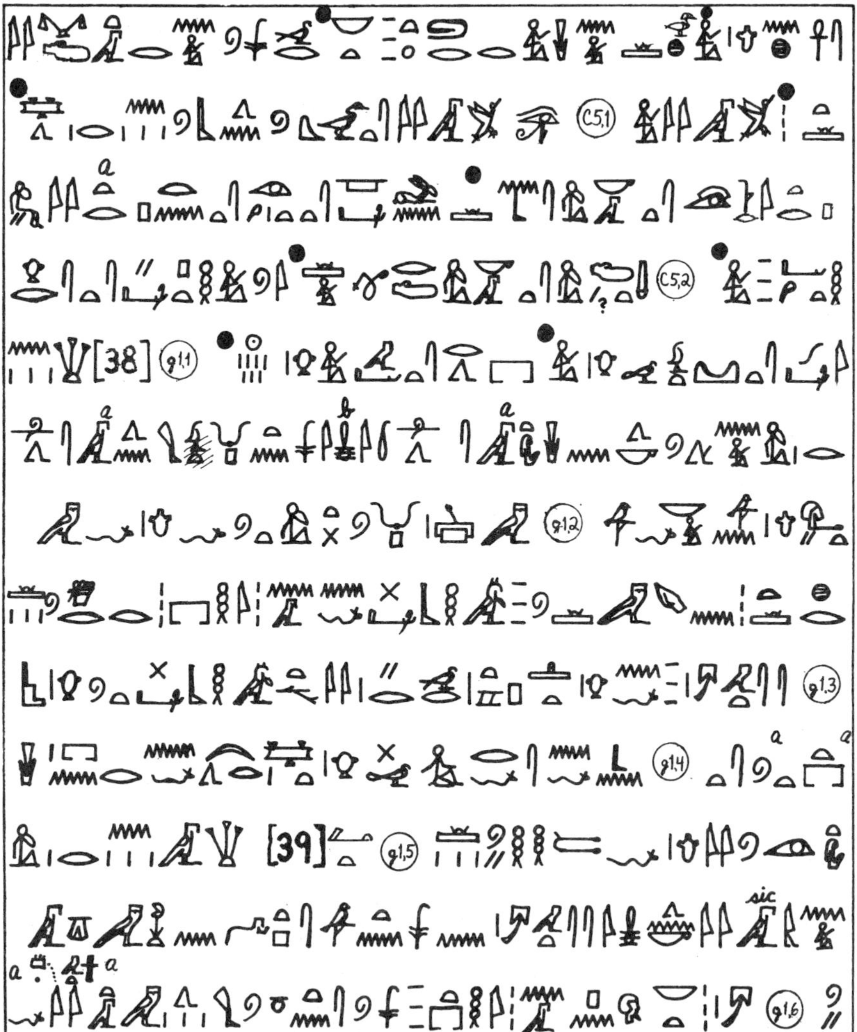

c5: L1: 31cm. wide. L2: 23cm. c5,1a [glyph], the ligature for [glyph], by confusion with ptr (Gardiner). Omit. g1: 20-21 cm. wide. g1,1a,a See c2,9n.a. b [glyph] crossed by a red stroke. g1,3a-a [glyph], ligature. g1,6a-a A later addition in red. Place after t3y·f.

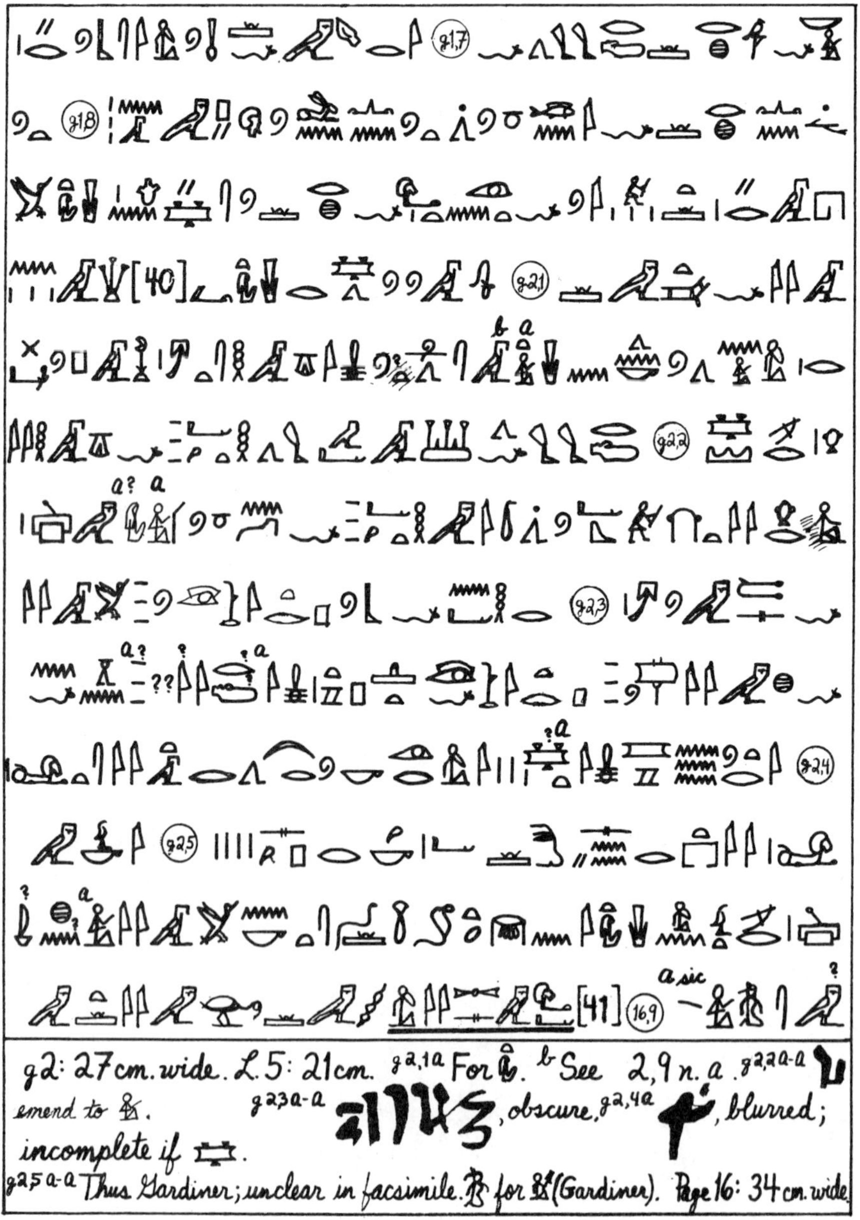

g2: 27 cm. wide. L. 5: 21 cm. g2,1a For [hieroglyph]. b See 2,9 n. a. g2,2a-a [hieroglyph] emend to [hieroglyph]. g2,3a-a [hieratic], obscure. g2,4a [hieratic], blurred; incomplete if [hieroglyph].

g2,5a-a Thus Gardiner; unclear in facsimile. [hieroglyph] for [hieroglyph] (Gardiner). Page 16: 34 cm. wide.

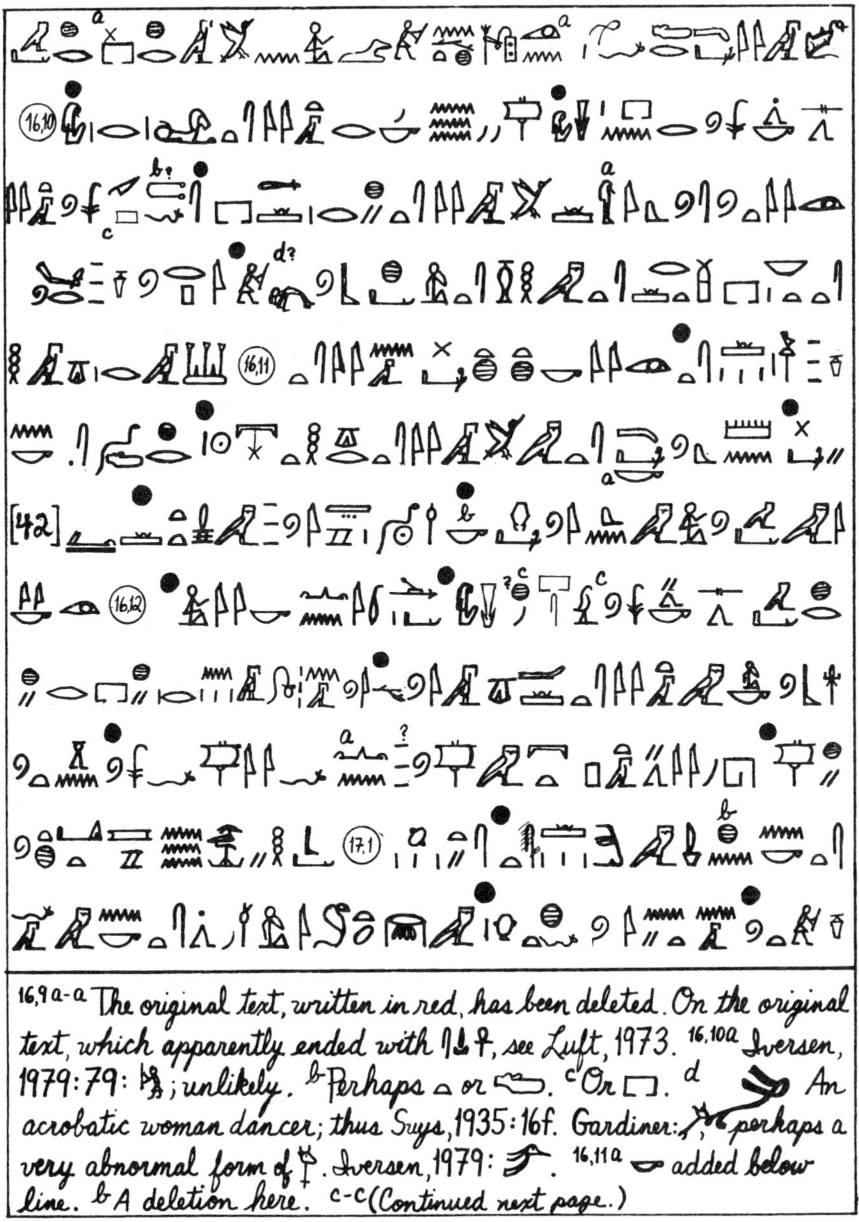

16,9 a-a The original text, written in red, has been deleted. On the original text, which apparently ended with , see Luft, 1973. 16,10a Iversen, 1979:79: ; unlikely. b Perhaps or . c Or . d An acrobatic woman dancer; thus Suys, 1935:16f. Gardiner: , perhaps a very abnormal form of . Iversen, 1979: . 16,11a added below line. b A deletion here. c-c (Continued next page.)

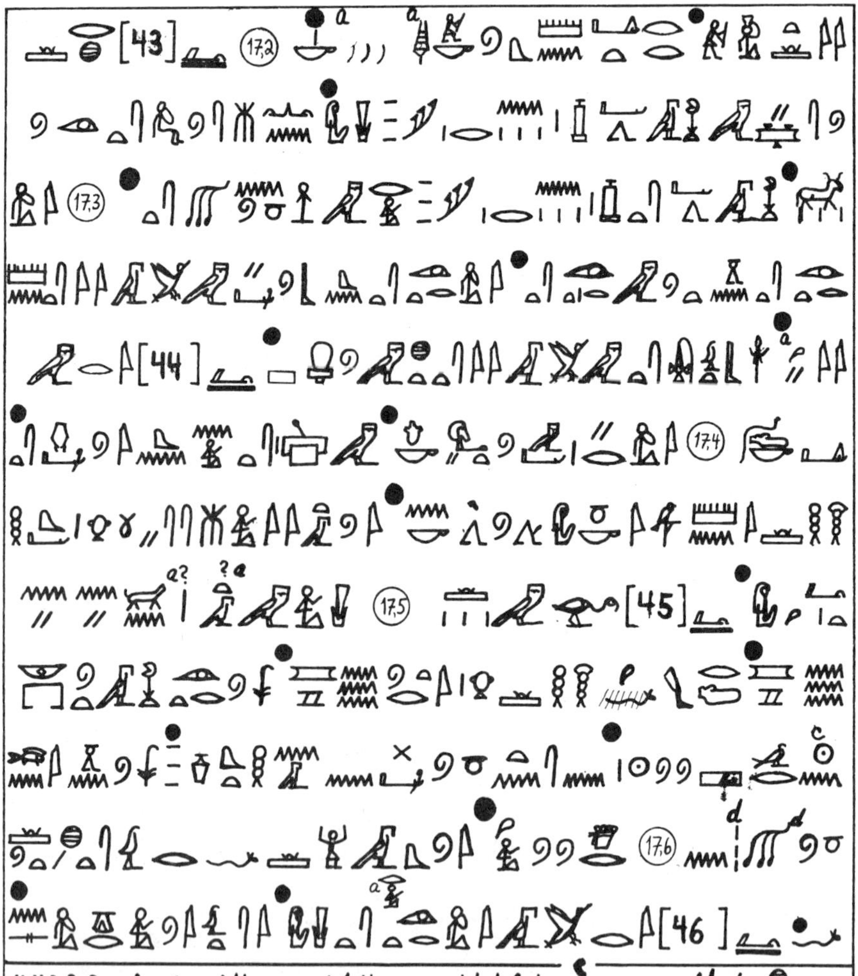

16,11 c-c Carelessly written over deletion. ▭ added later. presumably for .

16,12a Over a deleted ? b Over ı. Page 17: 27.5 cm. wide. L.5: 29 cm.

17,1a-a For : ( ) 17,3a cf. mnty in c1,5. or lost through haplography with similar-looking ? Read .

17,5a-a . c Gardiner: . d-d Malformed group: .

17,6a Added later.

17,7a {Bottom sign undoubtedly (Iversen), not (Gardiner). Phallus always written by this scribe, e.g., 11,4 & 12. 17,9a (ligature). 17,12a close to . Perhaps a distorted or .
17,12b Gardiner: .

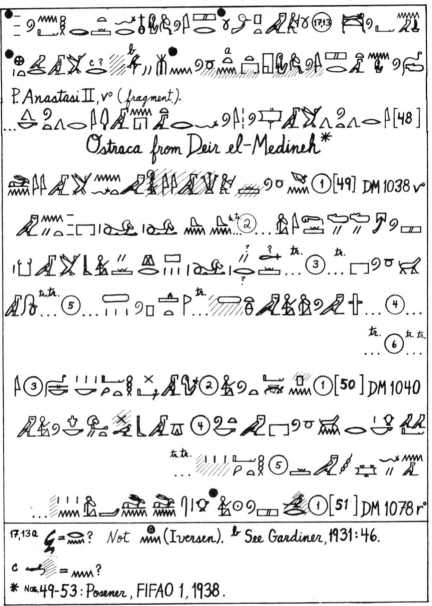

P. Chester Beatty I, 17,12–17,13 [No. 47]; P. Anastasi II v° [No. 48]; DM 1038 v° [No. 49]; DM 1040 [No. 50]; DM 1078 r° [No. 51]

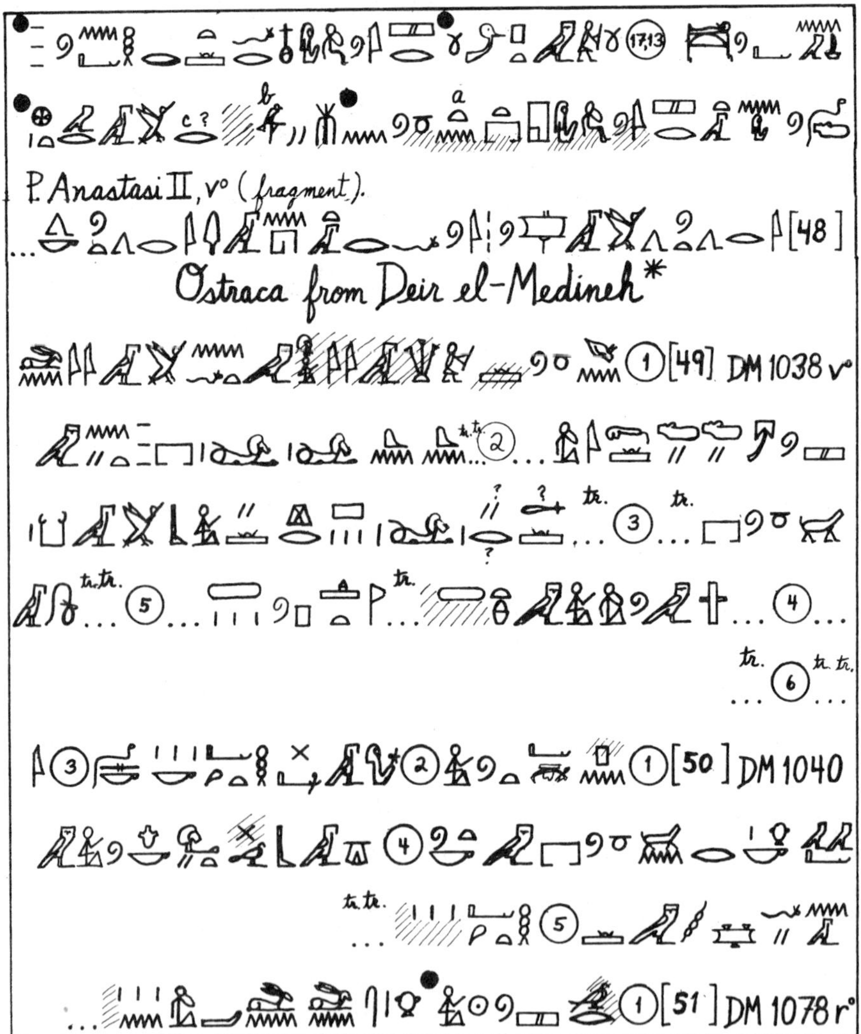

17,13a = ? Not (Iversen). b See Gardiner, 1931:46.

c = ?

* Nos. 49-53: Posener, FIFAO 1, 1938.

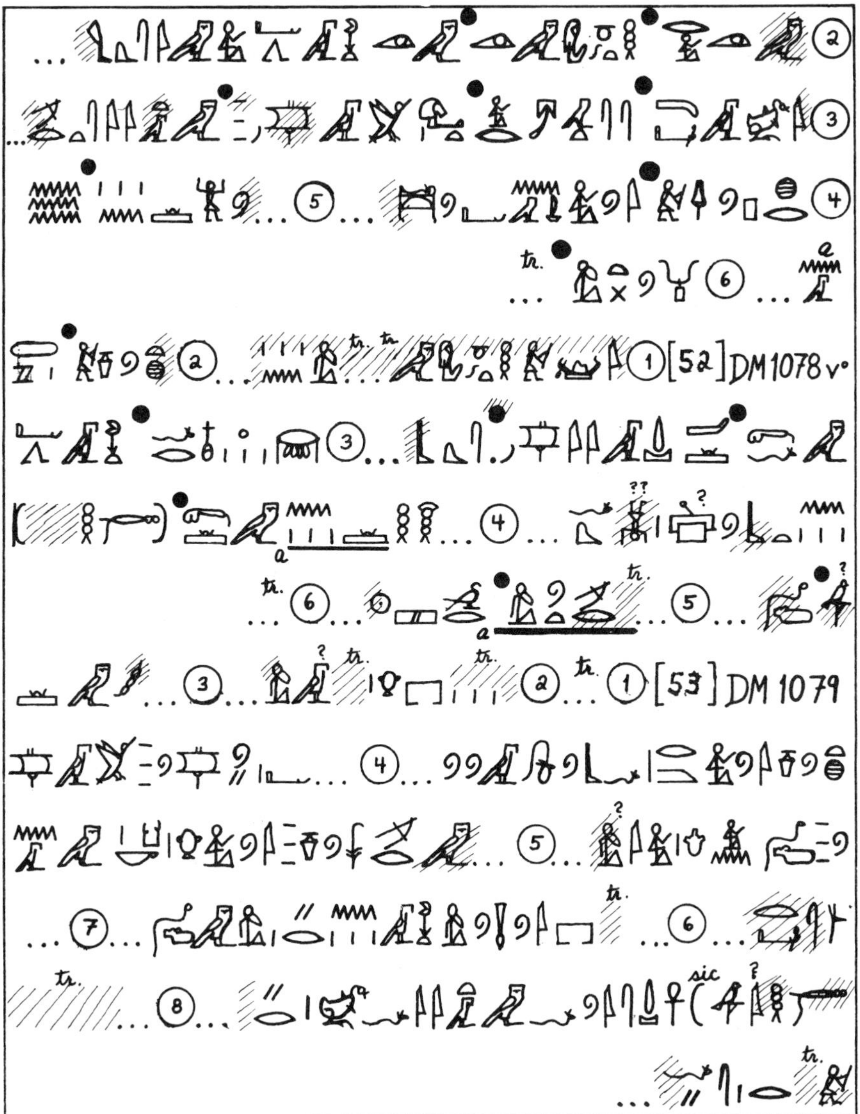

1078 r°, 5a Perhaps [hieroglyph]. 1078 v°, 4/5 a Corrections in red.

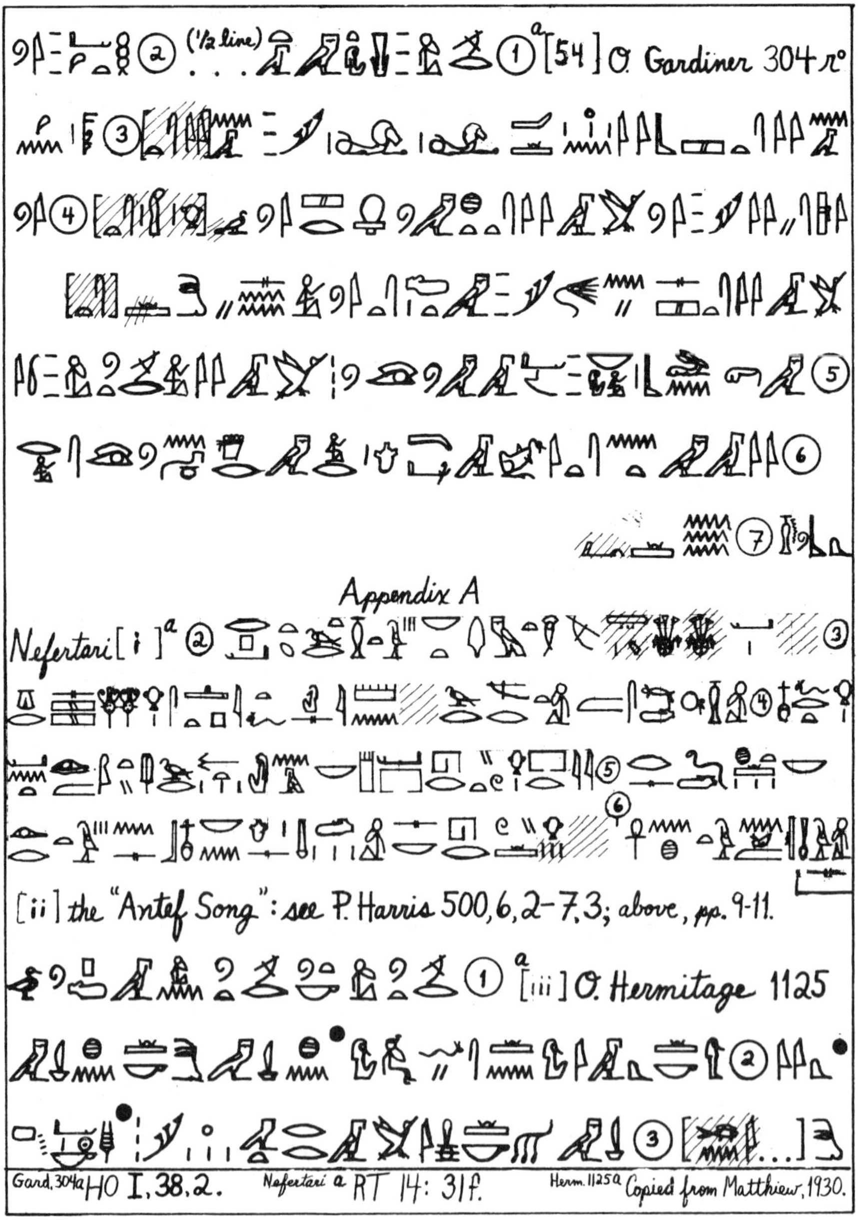
[54] O. Gardiner 304 r°
(½ line)
Appendix A
Nefertari [i]
[ii] the "Antef Song": see P. Harris 500, 6, 2–7, 3; above, pp. 9-11.
[iii] O. Hermitage 1125
Gard. 304a HO I, 38, 2.
Nefertari a RT 14: 31f.
Herm. 1125a Copied from Matthiew, 1930.

O. Hermitage 1125, 4–9 [No. iii]; O. Gardiner 339 r° [No. iv]

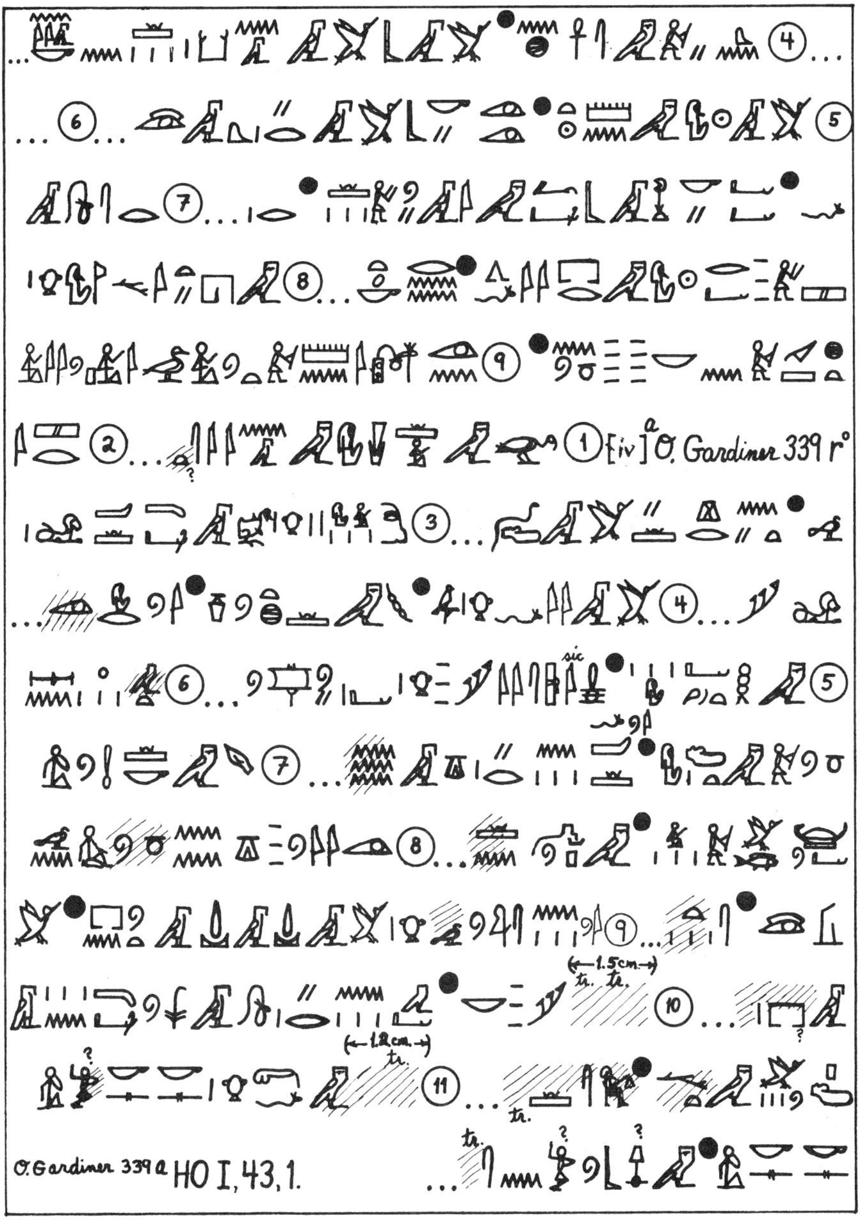

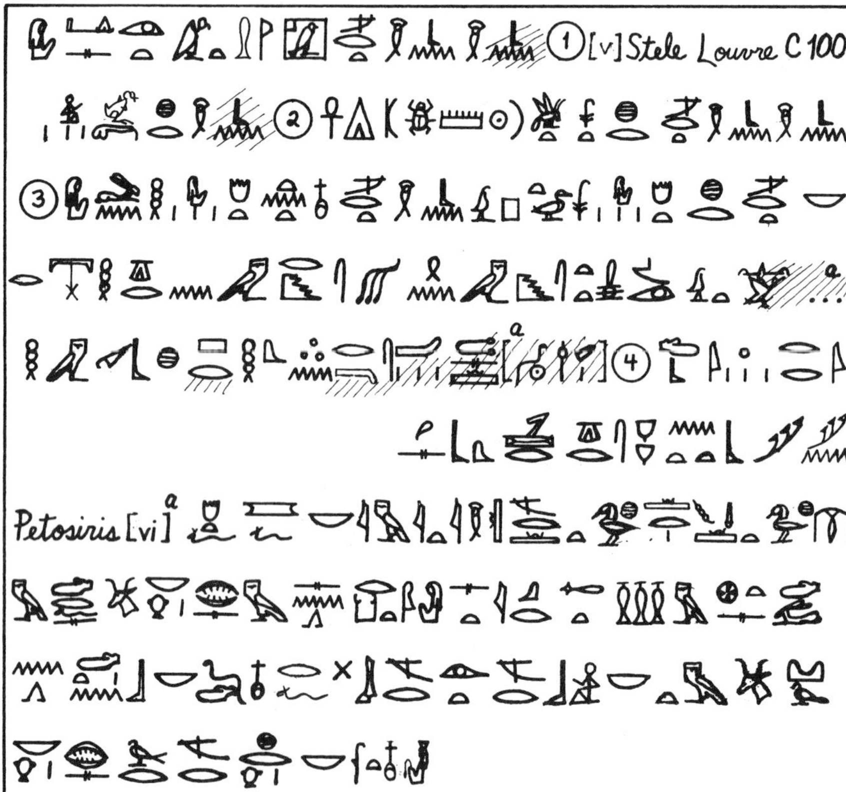

Louvre C100, 3a One-two groups missing. 4a Two-three groups missing.
Petosiris a Lefebvre, 1924: I, 101, II, 35.

Bibliography

ALBRIGHT, William F.

1963 "Archaic Survivals in the Text of Canticles." In *Hebrew and Semitic Studies Presented to G. R. Driver*, edited by D. Winton Thomas and W. D. McHardy. Oxford: Clarendon, 1–7.

ALDRED, Cyril.

1961 *New Kingdom Art in Ancient Egypt*. 2nd ed. London: Tiranti.

ALLAM, S.

1981 "Quelques aspects du mariage dans l'Égypte ancienne." JEA 67:116–35.

ALLEN, Thomas G.

1974 *The Book of the Dead; or, Going Forth by Day*. Chicago: Oriental Institute.

ALTENMÜLLER, Brigitte K.

1975 *Synkretismus in den Sargtexten* (Göttinger Orientforschungen, IV, 7). Wiesbaden: Harrassowitz.

AQNIN: Yosef ben Yehudah ben Ya'aqov Aqnin

1964 *Commentary to Canticles*. Edited by A. S. Halkin. Jerusalem: Meqitzey Nirdamim.

Aruch Completum by Nathan ben Yehiel.

1878–92 Revised by Alexander Kohut (8 vols. in 4). Reprint (Hebrew). Jerusalem: Makor, 1969–70.

AVISHUR, Yischak.

1977 *The Construct State of Synonyms in Biblical Rhetoric* (Hebrew). Jerusalem: Kiryat Sepher.

BAILLET, M.; MILIK, J. T., VAUX, R. de.

1962 *Les Petites Grottes de Qumrân* (Discoveries in the Judaean Desert of Jordan, III). Oxford: Clarendon, 1962.

BARR, James.

1961 *The Semantics of Biblical Language*. London: Oxford University Press.

BAUMGARTNER, Walter: see Koehler-Baumgartner.

BAUSINGER, Hermann.

1980 *Formen der "Volkspoesie"*. 2nd ed. Berlin: Erich Schmidt.

BENDAVID, Abba.

1967 *Biblical Hebrew and Mishnaic Hebrew* (Hebrew), vol. I. Tel Aviv: Devir.

BENTZEN, Aage.

1953 "Remarks on the Canonisation of the Song of Solomon." In *Studia Orientalia Ioanni Pedersen*. Copenhagen: Munksgaard, 41–47.

BEN-YEHUDAH, Eliezer.

1960 *A Complete Dictionary of Ancient and Modern Hebrew* (Hebrew). 8 vols. Reprint. New York: Thomas Yoseloff.

BIGGS, Robert D.

1967 *Šà.zi.ga: Ancient Mesopotamian Potency Incantations*. Locust Valley, N.Y.: J. J. Augustin.

BISSING, Friedrich W. von.

1904–7 *Steingefässe: Catalogue général des antiquités égyptiennes du Musée du Caire*. 2 vols. Vienna: A. Holzhausen.

BISSING, Friedrich W. von, and BLOK, H. P.

1926 "Eine Weihung an die sieben Hathoren." ZÄS 61:83–93.

BLACKMAN, Aylward M.

1915 *The Rock Tombs of Meir, Part III: The Tomb-Chapel of Ukh-Ḥotp son of Ukh-Ḥotp and Mersi (B, No. 4)* (24th Memoir of the Archaeological Survey of Egypt, edited by F. Ll. Griffith). London: Wm. Clowes & Sons.

1933 "Review of A. H. Gardiner, Pap. Chester Beatty I." JEA 19:200–204.

1938 "The Use of the Egyptian Word *ḥt* 'house' in the Sense of 'Stanza.'" *Orientalia* 7:64–67.

BLANK, S.: see Ginsburg.

BLEEKER, C. J.

1973a *Hathor and Thoth*. Leiden: E. J. Brill.

1973b "Der religiöse Gehalt einiger Hathor-Lieder." ZÄS 99:82–88.

Bodleian MS Oppenheim 625 (anon.): see Mathews, 1896.

BOOTH, Wayne C.

1961 *The Rhetoric of Fiction*. Chicago: University of Chicago Press.

1979 "Metaphor as Rhetoric: The Problem of Evaluation." In *On Metaphor*, edited by Sheldon Sacks, pp. 47–70. Chicago: University of Chicago Press.

BRENNER, Athalya.

1983 "Aromatics and Perfumes in the Song of Songs." JSOT 25:75–81.

BRIER, Bob.

1980 *Ancient Egyptian Magic*. New York: William Morrow.

BRUNNER-TRAUT, Emma.

1978 "Altägyptische Literatur." In *Altorientalische Literaturen*, edited by Wolfgang Röllig, pp. 25–99. Wiesbaden: Athenaion.

BUDDE, Karl F. R.

1898 "Das Hohelied." In *Die Fünf Megillot*, edited by Karl Budde et al. (KAT 17). Tübingen: J. C. B. Mohr.

BUDGE, E. A. Wallis.
1923 *Facsimiles of Egyptian Hieratic Papyri in the British Museum*. 2nd ser. London: British Museum.
BUZY, Denis.
1940 "La Composition littéraire du Cantique des Cantiques." RB 49: 169–194.
CAMINOS, Ricardo A.
1954 *Late-Egyptian Miscellanies*. London: Oxford University Press.
1956 *Literary Fragments in the Hieratic Script*. Oxford: Griffith Institute.
1964 "The Nitocris Adoption Stela." JEA 50: 71–101.
1977 *A Tale of Woe*. Oxford: Griffith Institute.
CANNON, William W.
1913 *The Song of Songs*. Cambridge: Cambridge University Press.
CARROLL, W. D.
1923–24 "Bittîr and Its Archaeological Remains." AASOR 5: 77–103.
ČERNÝ, Jaroslav.
1939 *Late Ramesside Letters*. Brussels: La Fondation Égyptologique Reine Élisabeth.
1976 *Coptic Etymological Dictionary*. Cambridge: Cambridge University Press.
ČERNÝ, Jaroslav, and GARDINER, Alan H.
1957 *Hieratic Ostraca I*. Oxford: Griffith Institute.
ČERNÝ, Jaroslav, and GROLL, Sarah Israelit.
1978 *A Late Egyptian Grammar*. 2nd ed. (Studia Pohl; Series Maior, 4). Rome: Pontifical Biblical Institute.
CHASSINAT, Émile Gaston.
1897–1934 *Le Temple d'Edfou*. MIFAO 3–14.
COHEN, Gerson D.
1966 *The Song of Songs and the Jewish Religious Mentality* (The Samuel Friedland Lectures). New York: Jewish Theological Seminary.
COOK, Albert S.
1968 *The Root of the Thing*. Bloomington: Indiana University Press.
COOPER, Jerrold S.
1971 "New Cuneiform Parallels to the Song of Songs." JBL 90: 157–162.
1972–75 "Heilige Hochzeit." In *Reallexikon der Assyriologie* IV: 259–269.
COPLEY, F. O.
1956 *Exclusus Amator: A Study in Latin Love Poetry* (American Philological Monographs, XVII). Madison, Wisc.
DAHOOD, Mitchell.
1966 *Psalms* (Anchor Bible, nos. 16, 17, 17a). Garden City, N.Y.: Doubleday.
DARBY, William J.; GHALIOUNGUI, Paul; and GRIVETTI, Louis.
1977 *Food, the Gift of Osiris*. London: Academic Press.
DARESSY, Georges.
1901 *Catalogue général des antiquités égyptiennes du Musée du Caire*. Cairo: IFAO.
DAVIES, Nina M., and GARDINER, Alan H.
1915 *The Tomb of Amenemhet* (TT 82). London: EEF.

DAVIES, Norman de G.
1922–23 *The Tomb of Puyemrê at Thebes* (TT 39). New York: Metropolitan Museum of Art Egyptian Expedition.
1930 *The Tomb of Ḳen-Amun at Thebes* (TT 93). New York: Metropolitan Museum of Art Egyptian Expedition.
1943 *The Tomb of Rekh-mi-Reᶜ at Thebes* (TT 100). New York: Plantin.
DAVIS, Virginia L.
1980 "Remarks on Michael V. Fox's 'The Cairo Love Songs.'" JAOS 100: 111–14.
DEINES, Hildegard von, and GRAPOW, Hermann.
1959 *Wörterbuch der ägyptischen Drogennamen*. Berlin: Akademie Verlag.
DELITZSCH, Franz.
1885 *Commentary on the Song of Songs and Ecclesiastes*. Translated by M. G. Easton. Reprint. Grand Rapids, Mich.: William B. Eerdmans, (German ed. 1875).
DERCHAIN, Philippe.
1975 "Le Lotus, la mandragore et le perséa." CdE 50:65–86.
DRIOTON, Étienne.
1957a "La Chanson des Quatres Vents." In *Pages d'Égyptologie*, pp. 363–72. Cairo: Éditions de la Revue du Caire.
1957b "Les fêtes égyptiennes." In *Pages d'Égyptologie*. Cairo: Éditions de la Revue du Caire, 133–158.
1961 "Review of Hermann, *Altägyptische Liebesdichtung*." *Revue d'Egypt* 13:138–142.
DRIVER, Godfrey R.
1950 "Hebrew Notes on 'Song of Songs' and 'Lamentations.'" In Festschrift A. Bertholet, edited by Walter Baumgartner, pp. 134–146. Tübingen: J.C.B. Mohr.
DRIVER, Samuel R.
1913 *An Introduction to the Literature of the Old Testament*. Reprint. Cleveland: Meridian, 1957.
EBERS (Papyrus): see Wreszinski, 1913.
EDGERTON, William, and WILSON, John A.
1936 *Historical Records of Ramses III. The Texts in Medinet Habu*, vols. 1–2 (SAOC, 12). Chicago: University of Chicago Press.
EHRLICH, Arnold B.
1914 *Randglossen zur hebräischen Bibel*. Reprint. Hildesheim: Georg Olms, 1968.
EISENBEIS, Walter.
1969 *Die Wurzel ŠLM im Alten Testament* (BZAW, 113). Berlin: de Gruyter.
ERBT, Wilhelm.
1906 *Die Hebräer*. Leipzig: J. C. Hinrichs.
ERICHSEN, Wolja.
1954 *Demotisches Glossar*. Copenhagen: Munksgaard.
ERMAN, Adolf.
1901 "Bruchstück eines Liebesliedes." ZÄS 39:147.

1925 "Die ägyptischen Schülerhandschriften." *Abh. der Preuss. Akad. der Wiss.: Phil.-hist. Kl.*, 1–32.

1927 *The Ancient Egyptians*. Translated by A. M. Blackman. New York: Harper & Row, 1966.

1933 *Neuägyptische Grammatik*. 2nd ed. Reprint. Hildesheim: Georg Olms, 1968.

ERMAN, Adolf, and GRAPOW, Hermann.

1926–50 *Wörterbuch der ägyptischen Sprache*. 6 vols. Leipzig: J. C. Hinrichs.

ESLINGER, Lyle.

1981 "The Case of an Immodest Lady Wrestler in Deuteronomy XXV 11–12." VT 31:269–281.

EWALD, Heinrich G. A.

1826 *Das Hohelied Salomo's*. Göttingen: R. Deuerlich.

EWEN, Yosef.

1974 "Writer, Narrator, and Implied Author" (Hebrew), *Hasifrut* 18–19:137–63 (English abstract vii–ix).

EXUM, J. Cheryl.

1973 "A Literary and Structural Analysis of the Song of Songs." ZAW 85: 47–79.

FAIRMAN, H. W.

1954 "Worship and Festivals in an Egyptian Temple." BJRL 34:165–203.

1974 *The Triumph of Horus*. London: B. T. Batsford.

FALK, Eugene H.

1967 *Types of Thematic Structure*. Chicago: University of Chicago Press.

FALK, Marcia.

1982 *Love Lyrics from the Bible*. Sheffield: Almond.

FAULKNER, Raymond O.

1936 "The Bremner-Rhind Papyrus I." JEA 22:121–40.

1962 *A Concise Dictionary of Middle Egyptian*. Oxford: Griffith Institute.

1972 See Simpson, 1972.

FECHT, Gerhard.

1963 "Die Wiedergewinnung der altägyptischen Verskunst." MDAIK 19: 54–70.

1965 *Literarische Zeugnisse zur "Persönlichen Frömmigkeit" in Ägypten*. Heidelberg: Carl Winter.

FEDERN, Walter.

1966 ". . . As does a potter's wheel." ZÄS 93:55–56.

FELDMAN, Leon, ed.

1970 *Commentary on the Song of Songs* by R. Abraham b. Isaac ha-Levi TaMaKH. Assen: Van Gorcum.

FELIKS, Jehuda.

1964 *The Song of Songs: Nature, Epic, and Allegory* (Hebrew). Jerusalem: Hahevra Leheqer Hamiqra Beyisrael.

FOHRER, Georg.

1970 *Introduction to the Old Testament*. London: Society for Promoting Christian Knowledge.

FOSTER, John L.

1977 *Thought Couplets and Clause Sequences in a Literary Text*. Toronto: Society for the Study of Egyptian Antiquities.

FOX, Michael V.

1977 "A Study of Antef." *Orientalia* 46:393–423.

1980 "The Cairo Love Songs." JAOS 100:101–9.

1981 " 'Love' in the Love Songs." JEA 67:181–82.

1982 "The 'Entertainment Song' Genre in Egyptian Literature." *Scripta Hierosolymitana* 28:268–316.

1983 "Scholia to Canticles (i 4b,ii 4,i 4a,iv 3,v 8,v 12)," VT 33, 199–206.

FULCO, William J.

1976 *The Canaanite God Rešep* (AOS, 8). New Haven: American Oriental Society.

GARDINER, Alan H.

1905 "Hymns to Amon from a Leiden Papyrus." ZÄS 42:12–42.

1911 *Egyptian Hieratic Texts*. Leipzig: J. C. Hinrichs.

1931 *The Library of A. Chester Beatty: The Chester Beatty Papyri, No. I*. London: Oxford University Press.

1932 *Late-Egyptian Stories*. Brussels: La Fondation Égyptologique Reine Élisabeth.

1935 *Hieratic Papyri in the British Museum*. Series III: Chester Beatty Gift. London: British Museum.

1937 *Late-Egyptian Miscellanies*. Brussels: La Fondation Égyptologique Reine Élisabeth.

1938 "The Egyptian for 'In Other Words', 'In Short.'" JEA 24:243–44.

1941–52 *The Wilbour Papyrus*. London: Oxford University Press.

1947 *Ancient Egyptian Onomastica*. 3 vols. Reprint. London: Oxford University Press, 1968.

1948a "The First Two Pages of the Wörterbuch." JEA 34:12–18.

1948b *Ramesside Administrative Documents*. London: Oxford University Press.

1969 *Egyptian Grammar*. 3rd ed. London: Oxford University Press.

GARDINER, Alan H., and DAVIES, Nina M.

1915 *The Tomb of Amenemhet* (TT 82). London: EEF.

GASTER, Theodor H.

1961 "Canticles i. 4." ET 72:195.

GAUTHIER, H.

1925–31 *Dictionnaire des noms géographiques contenus dans les textes hiéroglyphiques*. Cairo: IFAO.

1931 *Les Fêtes du dieu Min*. Cairo: IFAO.

GEBHARDT, Carl.

1931 *Das Lied der Lieder übertragen mit Einführung und Kommentar*. Berlin: Philo.

GELLER, Stephen A.

1979 *Parallelism in Early Biblical Poetry* (Harvard Semitic Monograph, 20). Missoula, Mont.: Scholars Press.

GERLEMAN, Gillis.
1965 *Ruth, Das Hohelied* (BKAT, XVIII, 2–3). Neukirchen-Vluyn: Neukirchener Verlag.
GESENIUS, Friedrich H. W., and KAUTZSCH, E.
1910 *Hebrew Grammar*. 2nd English ed. Reprint. Oxford: Clarendon, 1966.
GINSBURG, Christian D.
1857 *The Song of Songs and Coheleth*. Reprint. New York: KTAV, 1970.
GIVEON, Raphael.
1974 *Footsteps of the Pharaohs in Canaan* (Hebrew). Tel Aviv: Hamador Liydiᶜat Haʾaretz Batnuah Haqibutzit.
GOITEIN, S. D.
1965 "*Ayumma Kannidgalot* (Song of Songs VI. 10)." JSS 10:220–221.
1967 "The Song of Songs, a New Approach" (Hebrew). In *ᶜIyyunim Bamiqraʾ*, 283–317. Tel Aviv: Yavneh.
GOODSPEED, E. J.
1933 "The Shulammite." AJSL 50:102–4.
GORDIS, Robert.
1961 *The Song of Songs*. New York: Jewish Theological Seminary of America.
GORDON, Cyrus.
1965 *Ugaritic Textbook* (Analecta Orientalia, 38). Rome: Pontifical Biblical Institute.
1978 "New Directions." BASP 15:59–66.
GRAETZ, Heinrich.
1885 *Schir Ha-Schirim oder das Salomonische Hohelied*. Breslau: W. Jacobsohn.
GRANQVIST, Hilma.
1931, 1935 *Marriage Conditions in a Palestinian Village*. 2 vols. (Commentationes humanarum litterarum, vol. 3 no. 8 and vol. 6 no. 8.). Helsinki: Finska vetenskaps-societeten.
GRAPOW, Hermann.
1924 *Die bildlichen Ausdrücke des Aegyptischen*. Leipzig: J. C. Hinrichs'sche Buchhandlung.
GRDSELOFF, Bernhard.
1938 "Zum Volgelfang." ZÄS 74:52–55.
GREEN, Lynda.
1983 "Egyptian Words for Dancers and Dancing." *The Ancient World* 6: 29–38.
GREENFIELD, Jonas C.
1964 "Ugaritic *mdl* and Its Cognates." *Biblica* 45:527–34.
GRIFFITH, F. Ll.
1898 *Hieratic Papyri from Kahun and Gurob*. London: Bernard Quaritch.
GRIFFITH, F. Ll., and THOMPSON, Herbert.
1904 *The Leyden Papyrus*. Reprint: New York: Dover, 1974.
GRIMAL, Pierre, ed.
1965 *Histoire mondiale de la femme*. Paris: Nouvelle Librairie de France.

GROLL, Sarah Israelit.
1975–76 "The Literary and the Non-literary Verbal Systems in Late Egyptian." *Orientalia Lovaniensia Periodica* 6–7:237–46.
GROSSBERG, Daniel.
1980 "Noun/Verb Parallelism: Syntactic or Asyntactic." JBL 99:481–88.
GUNN, Battiscombe.
1955 "The Decree of Amonrasonther for Neskhons." JEA 41:83–95.
HARAN, Menachem.
1972 "The Graded Numerical Sequence and the Phenomenon of 'Automatism' in Biblical Poetry." Supp. VT 22:238–67.
HARPER, Andrew.
1907 *The Song of Solomon* (Cambridge Bible). Cambridge: Cambridge University Press.
HARRIS, John R.
1961 *Lexicographical Studies in Ancient Egyptian Minerals*. Berlin: Akademie Verlag.
HAUPT, Paul.
1902a "The Book of Canticles." AJSL 18:193–245.
1902b "The Book of Canticles." AJSL 19:1–21.
HELCK, Wolfgang.
1971 *Die Beziehungen Ägyptens zu Vorderasien im 3. und 2. Jahrtausend v. Chr*. 2nd ed. Wiesbaden: Harrassowitz.
HELCK, Wolfgang, and OTTO, Eberhard.
1975– *Lexikon der Ägyptologie*. Wiesbaden: Harrassowitz.
HELD, Moshe.
1961 "A Faithful Lover in Old Babylonian Dialogue." JCS 15:1–26.
1962 "A Faithful Lover in Old Babylonian Dialogue: Addenda and Corrigenda." JCS 16:37–39.
HERMANN, Alfred.
1955 "Beiträge zur Erklärung der ägyptischen Liebesdichtung." In *Ägyptologische Studien*, edited by O. Firchow (Deutsche Akad. d. Wiss. zu Berlin, Inst. für Orientforschung, 29). Berlin: Akademie Verlag.
1959 *Altägyptische Liebesdichtung*. Wiesbaden: Harrassowitz.
HERODOTUS.
1960 *Histories*. Translated by A. D. Godley. Loeb Classical Library. Cambridge, Mass.: Harvard University Press.
HERRMANN, Wolfram.
1963 "Gedanken zur Geschichte des altorientalischen Beschreibungsliedes." ZAW 75:176–97.
HERZOG, Rolf.
1968 *Punt* (Abh. Deutschen Arch. Inst. Kairo, Ägyptologische Reihe, 6). Glückstadt: J. J. Augustin.
HIRSCH, E. D., Jr.
1967 *Validity in Interpretation*. New Haven: Yale.
HODGES, Carleton T.
1971 "Is Elohim Dead?" *Anthropological Linguistics* 13:311–319.

HOLLADAY, William L.
1958 *The Root Šûbh in the Old Testament.* Leiden: E. J. Brill.
HONAN, Park.
1961 *Browning's Characters.* New Haven: Yale University Press.
HONEYMAN, A. M.
1949 "Two Contributions to Canaanite Toponomy." JTS 50:50–52.
HORNUNG, Erik.
1963 *Das Amduat* (Äg. Abh., 7). Wiesbaden: Harrassowitz.
HORST, Friedrich.
1935 "Die Formen des althebräischen Liebesliedes." In Festschrift E. Littmann. Reprinted in *Gottes Recht*, pp. 176–87. Munich: Chr. Kaiser, 1961.
HURVITZ, Avi.
1972 *The Transition Period in Biblical Hebrew* (Hebrew). Jerusalem: Bialik Institute.
ISSERLIN, B. S. J.
1958 "Song of Songs IV, 4: An Archaeological Note." PEQ 90:59–61.
IVERSEN, E.
1979 "The Chester Beatty Papyrus, No. 1, Recto XVI, 9–XVII, 13." JEA 65:78–88.
JACOBSEN, Thorkild.
1976 *The Treasures of Darkness.* New Haven: Yale University Press.
JAMES, Thomas G. H., ed.
1961 *Hieratic Texts from Egyptian Stelae, Part I.* 2nd ed. London: British Museum.
1962 *The Ḥekanakhte Papers and Other Early Middle Kingdom Documents* (Egyptian Expedition, 19). New York: Metropolitan Museum of Art.
JANSSEN, J. J.
1969 "New Letters from the Time of Ramses II." OMRO 41:31–47.
1975 *Commodity Prices from the Ramessid Period.* Leiden: E. J. Brill.
JASTROW, Morris.
1921 *The Song of Songs.* Philadelphia: J. B. Lippincott.
JÉQUIER, G.
1922 "Matériaux pour servir à l'établissement d'un dictionnaire d'archéologie égyptienne." BIFAO 19:1–249.
JOLLES, André.
1932 "Die literarischen Travestien." *Blätter Deutsche Philosophie* 6:281–94.
KEEL, Othmar, and WINTER, Urs.
1977 *Vögel als Boten.* Orbis Biblicus et Orientalis, 14. Freiburg: Universitätsverlag.
KEES, Hermann.
1938 "Die Lebensgrundsätze eines Amonspriesters der 22. Dynastie." ZÄS 74:73–87.
KEIMER, Ludwig.
1924 *Die Gartenpflanzen im alten Aegypten.* Reprint. Hildesheim: Georg Olms, 1967.
1951 "La baie qui fait aimer, Mandragora officinarum L." BIE 32:351.

KIMELMAN, Reuven.

1980 "Rabbi Yohanan and Origen on the Song of Songs: A Third Century Jewish-Christian Disputation." HTR 73:567–595.

KITCHEN, Kenneth A.

1971 "Punt and How to Get There." *Orientalia* 40:184–208.

1972– *Ramesside Inscriptions*. Oxford: B. H. Blackwell.

KOEHLER, L., and BAUMGARTNER, W.

1967 *Hebräisches und aramäisches Lexikon zum Alten Testament*. 3rd ed. Edited by W. Baumgartner. Leiden: E. J. Brill.

KÖNIG, Eduard.

1897 *Lehrgebäude der hebräischen Sprache*. Vol. II, 2. Leipzig: J. C. Hinrichs.

KOROSTOVTSEV, M.

1973 *Grammaire du Néo-Égyptien*. Moscow: Naouka.

KRAMER, Samuel N.

1969 *The Sacred Marriage Rite*. Bloomington: Indiana University Press.

KRAUSS, Samuel.

1936a "Die Rechtslage im biblischen Hohenliede." MGWJ 80:330–339.

1936b "Der richtige Sinn von 'Schrecken in der Nacht', HL III 8." In *Occident and Orient* (Moses Gaster 80th anniversary volume). Edited by B. Schindler and A. Marmorstein, pp. 323–30. London: Taylor's Foreign Press.

KRINETZKI, Leo.

1964 *Das Hohe Lied*. Düsseldorf: Patmos.

1970 "Die erotische Psychologie des Hohen Liedes." TQ 150:404–416.

1981 *Kommentar zum Hohenlied* (Beiträge zur biblischen Exegese und Theologie, 16). Frankfurt am Main: Peter D. Lang.

KUENTZ, M. C.

1923 "Les textes du tombeau no. 38 à Thèbes." BIFAO 21:119–130.

KUTSCHER, Eduard Yechezkel.

1974 *The Language and Linguistic Background of the Isaiah Scroll (I Q Isa*[a]*)* (Studies on the Texts of the Desert of Judah, VI). Leiden: E. J. Brill.

LANDSBERGER, Franz.

1954 "Poetic Units within the Song of Songs." JBL 73:203–216.

LANDY, Francis.

1979 "The Song of Songs and the Garden of Eden." JBL 98:513–528.

1980 "Beauty and the Enigma." JSOT 17:55–106.

1983 Paradoxes of Paradise. Sheffield: Almond.

LANGE, H. O.

1927 *Der magische Papyrus Harris*. Copenhagen: A. F. Host.

LEFEBVRE, Gustave.

1923–24 *Le Tombeau de Petosiris*. 2 vols. Cairo: IFAO.

LEIMAN, Sid Z.

1976 *The Canonization of Hebrew Scripture: The Talmudic and Midrashic Evidence* (Transactions of the Connecticut Academy of Arts and Sciences, 47). Hamden, Conn.: Archon Books.

LEMAIRE, André.

1975 "Zamir dans la tablette de Gezer et le Cantique des Cantiques." VT 25:15–26.

LESKO, Leonard H., ed.
1982 *A Dictionary of Late Egyptian*. Vol. 1. Berkeley, Cal.: B. C. Scribe Publications.
LEVIN, Harry.
1968 "Thematics and Criticism." *The Disciplines of Criticism: Essays in Literary Theory, Interpretation, and History*. In P. Demetz et al., pp. 125–145. New Haven: Yale University Press.
LEVY, Yishayahu.
1907 *The Book of The Song of Songs* (Hebrew). Warsaw: N. Strovolsky.
LEXOVA, Irena.
1935 *Ancient Egyptian Dances*. Prague: Oriental Institute.
LHOTE, André.
1954 *Les Chefs-d'oeuvre de la peinture égyptienne*. Paris: Hachette.
LICHTHEIM, Miriam.
1945 "The Songs of the Harpers." JNES 4:178–212 + pls. XVI–XIX.
1972 "Have the Principles of Ancient Egyptian Metrics Been Discovered?" JARCE 9:103–10.
1973–80 *Ancient Egyptian Literature*. 3 vols. (vol. 1: 1973; vol. 2: 1976; vol. 3: 1980) Berkeley: University of California Press.
LIEBERMAN, Saul.
1937–39 *Tosefet Rishonim*. 4 vols. Jerusalem: Bamberger & Wahrmann.
1942 *Greek in Jewish Palestine*. New York: Jewish Theological Seminary.
1960 *Mishnath Shir ha-Shirim* in Scholem, 118–126.
LIU Wu-chi.
1966 *An Introduction to Chinese Literature*. Bloomington: Indiana University Press.
LORETZ, Oswald.
1971 *Das althebräische Liebeslied* (Alter Orient und Altes Testament, 14, 1). Neukirchen-Vluyn: Butzon and Bercker Kevelaer.
LORTON, David.
1968 "The Expression *šms-ib*." JARCE 7:41–54.
LUCAS, Alfred A.
1962 *Ancient Egyptian Materials and Industries*. 4th ed., revised by J. R. Harris. London: Edward Arnold.
LUFT, Ulrich.
1973 "Zur Einleitung der Liebesgedichte auf Papyrus Chester Beatty I ro. XVI 9 ff." ZÄS 99:108–116.
LUZZATTO, Samuel D. (SHaDaL).
1855 *Commentary to the Book of Isaiah* (Hebrew). Reprint. Tel Aviv: Devir, 1970.
LYS, Daniel.
1968 *Le Plus Beau Chant de la création* (Lectio Divina, 51). Paris: Cerf.
MANNICHE, Lise.
1977 "Some Aspects of Ancient Egyptian Sexual Life." AcOr 38:11–23.
MARTINDALE, Colin.
1975 *Romantic Progression: The Psychology of Literary History*. New York: Hemisphere.

MASPERO, M. G.

1883 "Les Chants d'Amour du Papyrus de Turin et du Papyrus Harris no. 500." *Journal Asiatique*, ser. 8, 1:5–47.

MATHEWS, H. J.

1896 "A Commentary to the Song of Songs" (Hebrew) (Bodleian MS Oppenheim 625). In *Festschrift zum 80. Geburtstage M. Steinschneiders*, Hebrew section, pp. 164–85. Leipzig: Harrassowitz.

MATTHIEW, M.

1930 "The Ostracon No. 1125 in the Hermitage Museum." *Publication of the Egyptological Society of the State University of Leningrad* 5:25–27.

MEEK, Theophile.

1922 "Canticles and the Tammuz Cult." AJSL 39:1–14.

1924a "Babylonian Parallels to the Song of Songs." JBL 43:245–52.

1924b "The Song of Songs and the Fertility Cult." In *A Symposium on the Song of Songs*, edited by W. H. Schoff, pp. 48–79. Philadelphia: Commercial Museum.

MEISSNER, B.

1934 "Der Kuss im alten Orient." SPAW, 28:913–30.

MILGROM, Jacob.

1981 *The Tassel and the Tallith.* The Fourth Annual Rabbi Louis Feinberg Memorial Lecture, University of Cincinnati.

MILIK, Jøzef T.

1972 *Dédicaces faites par des dieux (Palmyre, Hatra, Tyr) et des thiases sémitiques à l'époque romaine* (Bibl. arch. et hist., 92). Paris: Paul Geuthner.

MOLDENKE, Harold N.

1952 *Plants of the Bible.* Waltham, Mass.: Chronica Botanica.

MONTET, Pierre.

1957 *Géographie de l'Égypte ancienne.* Paris: Imprimerie nationale.

MORENZ, Siegfried.

1960 *Untersuchungen zur Rolle des Schicksals in der Ägyptischen Religion* (Abh. der Sächsischen Akad. der Wiss. zu Leipzig: Phil.-Hist. Kl., 52/1). Berlin: Akademie Verlag.

MÜLLER, W. Max.

1899 *Die Liebespoesie der alten Ägypter.* Leipzig: J. C. Hinrichs.

MURNANE, William.

1978 "Review of *Love Songs of the New Kingdom*, translated by John L. Foster." JNES 37:363–365.

MURPHY, Roland E.

1973 "Form-Critical Studies in the Song of Songs." Int 27:413–22.

1977 "Towards a Commentary on the Song of Songs." CBQ 39:482–496.

1979 "The Unity of the Song of Songs." VT 29:436–43.

1981 *Wisdom Literature* (The Forms of the Old Testament Literature, 13). Grand Rapids, Mich.: Wm. B. Eerdmans.

NAVILLE, Édouard.

1886 *Das Ägyptische Todtenbuch der XVIII. bis XX. Dynastie.* Berlin: A. Asher.

1913 *The XIth Dynasty Temple at Deir el-Baḥari* (EEF Memoirs, vol. 32). London: EEF.

NEUSCHOTZ de Jassy, Oswald.
1914 *Le Cantique des Cantiques et le mythe d'Osiris-Hetep*. Paris: Reinwald.
NORTON, David L., and KILLE, Mary F.
1971 *Philosophies of Love*. San Francisco: Chandler.
NOWOTTNY, Winfred.
1962 *The Language Poets Use*. London: Athlone.
OMLIN, Joseph A.
1973 *Der Papyrus 55001 und seine satirisch-erotischen Zeichnungen und Inschriften*. Turin: Fratelli Pozzo.
OPPENHEIM, A. Leo.
1965 "On Royal Gardens in Mesopotamia." JNES 24:328–33.
PAUL, Shalom.
1978 "An Unrecognized Medical Idiom in Canticles 6, 12 and Job 9, 21." *Biblica* 59:545–547.
PEET, Thomas.
1914 *The Cemeteries of Abydos*. London: EEF.
1930 *The Great Tomb Robberies of the Twentieth Egyptian Dynasty*. Oxford: Clarendon.
PERLES, Felix.
1922 *Analekten zur Textkritik des Alten Testaments (NF)*. Leipzig: Gustav Engel.
PESHIṬTA.
1979 *The Old Testament in Syriac—The Song of Songs* (The Peshiṭta Institute of Leiden, part II, fasc. 5). Leiden: E. J. Brill.
PESTMAN, P. W.
1961 *Marriage and Matrimonial Property in Ancient Egypt* (Papyrologica Lugduno-Batava, ix). Leiden: E. J. Brill.
PICKENS, Rupert T.
1978 *The Songs of Jaufré Rudel*. Toronto: Pontifical Institute of Mediaeval Studies.
PLEYTE, Willem, and ROSSI, F.
1869–76 *Papyrus de Turin*. Leiden: E. J. Brill.
PLINY (the Younger).
1938 *Natural History*. Translated by H. Rackham. Loeb Classical Library. Cambridge, Mass.: Harvard University Press.
POPE, Marvin.
1977 *The Song of Songs* (Anchor Bible, no. 7c). Garden City, N.Y.: Doubleday.
POSENER, Georges.
1938 *Catalogue des ostraca hiératiques littéraires de Deir el Médineh*, vol. 1. FIFAO 1.
1972 Idem., vol. 2. FIFAO 18.
1977–80 Idem., vol. 3, part iii. FIFAO 20.
PROUST, Marcel.
1981 *Remembrance of Things Past*. Translated by C. K. Scott Moncrieff and T. Kilmartin. New York: Random House.
QIMRON, Elisha.
1976 "A Grammar of the Hebrew Language of the Dead Sea Scrolls" (Hebrew). Ph.D. dissertation, Hebrew University, Jerusalem.

QUAEGEBEUR, Jan.

1975 *Le Dieu Égyptien Shai dans la religion et l'onomastique*. Leuven: Leuven University Press.

RABIN, Chaim.

1973 "The Song of Songs and Tamil Poetry." *Studies in Religion* 3:205–219.

1975 "The Indian Connections of the Song of Songs" (Hebrew). In *B. Kurzweil Memorial Volume*, pp. 264–74. Jerusalem: Schoken.

RADER, Ralph W.

1976 "The Dramatic Monologue and Related Lyric Forms." *Critical Inquiry* 3:131–151.

RANKE, Herman.

1935 *Die ägyptischen Personennamen*. Glückstadt: J. J. Augustin.

REISSNER, George A.

1918 "The Tomb of Hepzefa, Nomarch of Siûṭ." JEA 5:79–98.

RENAN, Ernest.

1884 *Le Cantique des Cantiques*. Paris: Michel Lévy Frères.

RENGER, J.

1972– "Heilige Hochzeit." In RA II:251–59.

RICHMOND, Hugh M.

1964 *The School of Love*. Princeton: Princeton University Press.

RICOEUR, Paul.

1975 "Biblical Hermeneutics." *Semeia* 4:29–148.

1976 *Interpretation Theory*. Fort Worth: Texas Christian University Press.

RINGGREN, Helmer.

1962 *Das Hohe Lied* (Das Alte Testament Deutsch, 16). Göttingen: Vandenhoeck & Ruprecht.

ROBERT, André.

1945 "La Description de L'Époux et de l'épouse dans Cnt. V, 11–15 et VIII, 2–6." In *Mélanges É. Podechard*, pp. 211–223 Lyons: Facultés catholiques.

1951 *Cantique des Cantiques* (La Sainte Bible). Paris: Cerf.

ROBERT, André; TOURNAY, Robert; and FEUILLET, A.

1963 *Le Cantique des Cantiques: traduction et commentaire*. Paris: J. Gabalda.

ROWLEY, H. H.

1938 "The Meaning of 'The Shulammite.'" AJSL 56:84–91.

1952 "The Interpretation of the Song of Songs." In *The Servant of the Lord and Other Essays on the Old Testament*, pp. 189–234. London: Lutterworth.

RUDOLPH, Wilhelm.

1962 *Das Hohe Lied* (KAT, XXVII, 1–3). Gütersloh: Gerd Mohn.

RUNDGREN, Frithiof.

1962 "(*ʾappiryon*) 'Tragsessel, Sänfte.'" ZAW 74:70–72.

SACKS, Sheldon, ed.

1979 *On Metaphor*. Chicago: University of Chicago Press.

SAYCE, Olive.

1967 *Poets of the Minnesang*. Oxford: Clarendon.

SCAMUZZI, Ernesto.

1964 *Egyptian Art in the Egyptian Museum of Turin*. Turin: Fratelli Pozzo.

SCHÄFER, Hermann.
1918–19 "Ägyptischer Vogelfang." *Amtliche Berichte aus den Preuszischen Kunstsammlungen* 40:163–84.
1974 *Principles of Egyptian Art*. Translated by John Baines. Oxford: Clarendon.
SCHMIDT, Nathaniel.
1926 "Is Canticles an Adonis Litany?" JAOS 46:154–164.
SCHMÖKEL, Harmut.
1956 *Heilige Hochzeit und Hoheslied* (*Abh. für d. Kunde des Morgenlandes* xxxii,1). Wiesbaden: Deutsche Morgenländische Gesellschaft.
SCHNEEKLOTH, Larry G.
1977 *The Targum of the Song of Songs: A Study in Rabbinic Biblical Interpretation*. Ph.D. dissertation, University of Wisconsin-Madison.
SCHOLEM, Gershom G.
1960 *Jewish Gnosticism, Merkabah Mysticism, and Talmudic Tradition*. New York: Jewish Theological Seminary.
SCHONFIELD, Hugh J.
1960 *The Song of Songs*. London: Elek Books.
SCHOTT, Siegfried.
1950 *Altägyptische Liebeslieder*. Zurich: Artemis.
1952 *Das schöne Fest vom Wüstentale* (Akad. d. Wiss. und d. Lit. Mainz, Abh. d. Geistes- u. Sozialwiss. Kl., ll). Wiesbaden: F. Steiner.
SCHOVILLE, Keith N.
1969 "The Impact of the Ras Shamra Texts on the Study of the Song of Songs." Ph.D. dissertation, University of Wisconsin-Madison.
SCHRÖDER, Franz R.
1951 "Sakrale Grundlagen der altägyptischen Lyrik." *Deutsche Vierteljahrsschrift für Literaturwissenschaft und Geistesgeschichte* 25:273–293.
SCHULMAN, Alan R.
1964 *Military Rank, Title and Organization in the Egyptian New Kingdom* (MÄS, 6). Berlin: B. Hessling.
SEGAL, Morris (Moshe) Hirsch.
1936 *Grammar of Mishnaic Hebrew* (Hebrew). Tel Aviv: Devir.
1960 *Introduction to the Bible* (Hebrew). Jerusalem: Kiryat Sepher.
1962 "The Song of Songs." VT 12:470–90.
SHEA, William H.
1980 "The Chiastic Structure of the Song of Songs." ZAW 92:378–396.
SIMPSON, W. K.; FAULKNER, R. O.; and WENTE, E. F., Jr., ed.
1972 *The Literature of Ancient Egypt*. New Haven: Yale University Press.
SMITHER, Paul.
1941 "A Ramesside Love Charm." JEA 27:131–132.
1948 "Prince Meḥy of the Love Songs." JEA 34:116.
SODEN, Wolfram von.
1950 "Ein Zwiegespräch Hammurabis mit einer Frau." *Zeitschrift für Assyriologie* 49:151–94.
1959– *Akkadisches Handwörterbuch*. Wiesbaden: Harrassowitz.
SOULEN, Richard N.
1967 "The *Waṣf*s of the Song of Songs and Hermeneutic." JBL 86:183–90.

SOUVAGE, Jacques.

1965 *An Introduction to the Study of the Novel*. Ghent: E. Story-Scientia.

SPIEGELBERG, Wilhelm.

1897 "Eine neue Sammlung von Liebesliedern." In *Festschrift Georg Ebers: Aegyptiaca*, pp. 117–21. Leipzig: Engelmann.

1917 "Die Bedeutung von *nfr-ḥr*." ZÄS 53:115.

1930 "Das Herz als zweites Wesen des Menschen." ZÄS 66:35–37.

STRICKER, B. H.

1937 "Une orthographie méconnue." *Alte Orient* 15:21–25.

SUYS, Émile.

1934 "Le genre dramatique dans l'Égypte ancienne." *Revue des Questions Scientifiques* 105:437–63.

1935 *La Sagesse d'Ani*. Rome: Pontifical Biblical Institute.

TALMON, Shemaryahu.

1977 "The Textual Study of the Bible—A New Outlook" (Hebrew), *Shnaton* 2:116–63.

TaMaKh. See Feldman.

TRIBLE, Phyllis.

1978 *God and the Rhetoric of Sexuality*. Philadelphia: Fortress.

TSEVAT, Matitiahu.

1965 "*Yhwh Ṣebaᵓot*." HUCA 36:49–58.

TUR SINAI, Naphtali.

1962– *The Literal Meaning of Scripture* (Hebrew: *Pešuṭo Šel Miqraᵓ*). Jerusalem: Kiryat Sepher.

TYLOR, Joseph J., and GRIFFITH, F. Ll.

1895 *Wall Drawings and Monuments of El Kab: The Tomb of Paḥeri*. London: EEF.

URBACH, Ephraim E.

1960–61 "Rabbinic Exegesis and Origen's Commentary on the Song of Songs and Jewish-Christian Polemics" (Hebrew), *Tarbiz* 30:148–70.

1971 "The Homiletical Interpretations of the Sages and the Expositions of Origen on Canticles and the Jewish-Christian Disputation." In *Studies in Aggadah and Folk Literature*, edited by J. Heinemann and D. Noy, pp. 247–275 (*Scripta Hierosolymitana* 22).

VARILLE, Alexandre.

1935 "Trois nouveaux chants de harpistes." BIFAO 35:153ff. + pls. I–III.

VOGELSANG, Friedrich.

1913 *Kommentar zu den Klagen des Bauern*. Leipzig: J. C. Hinrichs.

WAGNER, Max.

1966 *Die Lexikalischen und grammatikalischen Aramaismen im alttestamentlichen Hebräisch* (BZAW, 96). Berlin: Alfred Töpelmann.

WALDMAN, Nahum.

1970 "A note on Canticles 4:9." JBL 89:215–217.

WALLE, B. van de.

1952 (Ostraca Hermitage no. 1125). BO 9:108.

WATERMAN, Leroy.

1948 *The Song of Songs*. Ann Arbor: University of Michigan Press.

WATTERS, William R.
1976 *Formula Criticism and the Poetry of the Old Testament* (BZAW, 138). Berlin: de Gruyter.
WEBSTER, Edwin C.
1982 "Pattern in the Song of Songs." JSOT 22:73–93.
WEINSTEIN, James M.
1981 "The Egyptian Empire in Palestine: A Reassessment." BASOR 241: 1–28.
WENDEL, Carl.
1914 *Scholia in Theocritum Vetera*. Leipzig: B. G. Teubner.
WENTE, Edward F., Jr.
1962 "The Egyptian 'Make-Merry' Songs Reconsidered." JNES 21:118–127 + pl. XVII.
1967 *Late Ramesside Letters* (SAOC, 33). Chicago: University of Chicago Press.
1972 See Simpson, 1972.
WESTENDORF, Wolfhart.
1965– *Koptisches Handwörterbuch*. Heidelberg: C. Winter.
1967 "Bemerkungen zur 'Kammer der Wiedergeburt' im Tutanchamungrab." ZÄS 94:139–50.
1974 "Papyrus Berlin 10456." In *Festschrift zum 150jähren Bestehen des Berliner Ägyptischen Museums* (Mitt. äg. Samm., 8). Berlin: Akademie Verlag.
WESTENDORF, Wolfhart, and DEINES, Hildegard von.
1961 *Wörterbuch der medizinischen Texte* (Grundriss der Medizin der alten Ägypter, 7). 2 vols. Berlin: Akademie Verlag.
WETZSTEIN, J. G.
1873 "Die syrische Dreschtafel." *Zeitschrift für Ethnologie* 5:270–302.
WHALLEY, George.
1953 *Poetic Process*. London: Routledge and K. Paul.
WHEELWRIGHT, Philip.
1962 *Metaphor and Reality*. Bloomington: Indiana University Press.
1968 *The Burning Fountain*. Bloomington: Indiana University Press.
WHITE, John B.
1978 *A Study of the Language of Love in the Song of Songs and Ancient Egyptian Poetry* (SBL Dissertation Series, no. 38). Missoula, Montana: Scholars Press.
WILLIAMS, Ronald J.
1975 " 'A People Come Out of Egypt.' " VT 28:231–252.
WILSON, John A.
1956 *The Culture of Ancient Egypt*. Chicago: University of Chicago Press.
WITTEKINDT, Wilhelm.
1925 *Das Hohelied und seine Beziehungen zum Ištarkult*. Hanover: H. Lafaire.
WRESZINSKI, Walter.
1909–13 *Die Medizin der alten Ägypter*. Leipzig: J. C. Hinrichs.
1913 *Der Papyrus Ebers*. Leipzig: J. C. Hinrichs.
1914 *Atlas zur altägyptischen Kulturgeschichte*. Leipzig: J. C. Hinrichs.

WÜRTHWEIN, Ernst.
1969 *Die Fünf Megilloth: Ruth, das Hohelied, Esther* (HAT, 18). Tübingen: J. C. B. Mohr.
YADIN, Yigael, ed.
1962 *The Scroll of the War of the Sons of Light Against the Sons of Darkness*. Translated by Batya and Chaim Rabin. Oxford: Oxford University Press.
YOUNG, Douglas.
1967 "Never Blotted a Line?—Formula and Premeditation in Homer and Hesiod." *Arion* 6:279–324.
YOUNG, G. Douglas.
1950 "Ugaritic Prosody." JNES 9:124–33.
ŽABA, Z.
1956 *Les Maximes de Ptahhotep*. Prague: Czechoslovak Academy of Sciences.
ŽABKAR, Louis V.
1968 *A Study of the Ba Concept in Ancient Egyptian Texts* (SAOC, 34). Chicago: Oriental Institute.

Index of Subjects

Index of Authors

Index of Foreign Words

Greek

Hebrew

(alphabetized consonantally by the form in which they appear)

Latin

Ugaritic

Index of Scriptural and Rabbinic Texts

Apocrypha and New Testament

Rabbinic and Qumran Texts

Index of Egyptian Texts

Egyptian Love Songs

Other Egyptian Texts